slightly warped top TL middle 10-16 pages

THE FOUR FORGES

The Elven Ways: Book One

THE FOUR FORGES

The Elven Ways: Book One

Jenna Rhodes

DAW BOOKS, INC.
DONALD A. WOLLHEIM, FOUNDER
375 Hudson Street, New York, NY 10014
ELIZABETH R. WOLLHEIM
SHEILA E. GILBERT
PUBLISHERS
http://www.dawbooks.com

Jacket art by Jody A. Lee.

DAW Book Collectors No. 1363.

DAW Books are distributed by Penguin Group (USA) Inc.

Book designed by Elizabeth M. Glover.

First Printing, May 2006
1 2 3 4 5 6 7 8 9

DAW TRADEMARK REGISTERED
U.S. PAT. OFF AND FOREIGN COUNTRIES
—MARCA REGISTRADA
HECHO EN U.S.A.

PRINTED IN THE U.S.A.

Dedicated to:

My friends and family,
and especially to my encouraging family of Sheila and Betsy, Debra,
Peter, Marsha, and Anne at DAW Books, and Paula, too!

Also to Michael and Lori, my very first audience.

Foreword One: On Histories

Under the Eyes of the Seven Gods and
By the hand of Carandol, of House Caranth,
Holder of Ferstanthe, Archivist

HISTORY CHANGES AS eyes age and souls pass. This is irrefutable. Histories can be struck to paper by hands that inscribe bigotry with every writing stroke and, if written honestly, can be burned to ashes later, so it is with some hesitation that I even attempt this. And who would read it? Should I tell all that we Vaelinars know as we know our own skin? Does a history then become a weapon in another's hand, to strike like the most potent of venoms? Yet, although we are still first and second generation, the third generation to come will be privy to most of us, as we are an exceedingly long-lived race. Even the Gods here bow before us, and there is none who can hold us accountable except ourselves, and that alone bodes ill. It is a universe out of balance, and the Gods will not long allow that. Kerith is theirs, not ours, although we have claimed it.

We were born on the whirlwind, brought in with the storm. Those on Kerith before us say that we came with the Hammer of War. Three blows did it strike their earth and when the lightning and rain and clouds of ash cleared, the Vaelinars stepped forth from the destruction. I do not know if any of the eyes of Kerith saw it to record the event. I was there. Even I cannot say exactly what happened.

Let me state at the first setting of ink to paper here that over the years I will add to our history, but I will not rewrite what I have written. There will be no revising. Correcting, perhaps, but my original words will stay as set even as wrong or disillusioned as they might have been, as seen in later years. It is the only way our life can be assessed.

We stepped out of storm and devastation, and with that singular catastrophe we lost our former lives, our memories, our heritage, our Gods, our entire world. We knew only the moment, remembered only that last, second blow that obliterated our past. Stunned and thrown into confusion, our people and animals wheeled and screamed and desperately sought an anchor in the chaos, the ground blackened under us, timber thrown for leagues about us, plucked out of the earth and shorn and charred and dropped down in piles. The mud steamed. When we reached for help, it was to those around us whose faces we knew no more than we knew our own names. We had been rent asunder. Horses lay in harness, torn in two, their shaking hulks lost to an awful death. I saw a beast or two which had been turned inside out before falling to the ground with a keening squeal of passing. Most of us were fortunate to have come through whole of limb, if not mind. The dogs howled mournfully voicing the despair and fear that overwhelmed all of us.

Those reading this who may not be Vaelinar might ask how we knew we were Lost. We knew almost instantly because when we reached for the Gods and the elements by which we rule our lives and powers, They were gone. We have seven Gods, the Three Great, and the Four of Elements . . . Vae, Goddess of Light; Nar, God of War; and Daran, God of Dark. Fair Lina who rules Water, Aymar of Wind and Air, Dhuriel of Fire, and Banh of Earth in their aspects of male and female, dark and light, had intertwined with every Vaelinar soul, and could be reached no longer. We touched other Gods, other elementals, other Demons. They quailed or bridled at our touch, they as foreign to us as we to them. Searching for our Gods, we then knew that we had been blasted from our earth to another, and thus did a number of us grow mad and die of the desperation of being Godless. Even Their names would have been taken from us, but for the pamphlet of a novice priest who came with us, and whose shaking fingers opened brittle pages to find names for the aching emptiness welling inside us.

We were a war troop. That much was obvious to any who looked on us. We gathered our survivors and made camp. After burials, those alive read our shields and armor and weapons, even the riggings on our horses, gleaning our names and House lineage from whatever we could. To this day, I have no doubt that some of our names taken then might actually have been the name of a much beloved and depended-upon war steed, engraved upon his halter strap, but then—who among us cannot say that some of us deserve to be named after a horse's ass?

Many of us had brought our younger siblings or older children with us, to assist and squire as they might, or to carry messages. We brought horses and our hunting dogs and falcons. Others fought side by side with their loved ones because our race has both male and female warriors, and still others had cooks and farriers and camp followers in wagons close behind. Not one of us knew for sure what had happened save that, according to a sparsely worded soldier's journal, we had been riding hard to a great and final meet in the war between our queen and the despot called Pyradeen. The Hammer of War which struck us, and the storm which issued forth, caught up soldiers from both sides in its fury. That, too, became clear over days as natural animosities seemed to spring forth anew despite the fact that our queen and the lands for which we had fought no longer existed for us, nor did the tyranny of Pyradeen.

Knowing only that a massive weapon or magic was to have been called to use to end a centuries' old struggle, we had ridden hard to this final meeting. Then we had been struck. Ridden too late, caught in its backlash? Ambushed by other magics to prevent our arrival? No one can say. This and no more we pieced together from the old soldier's journal of few words and fewer emotions. Most of what we gleaned came from between the lines he wrote. Some went mad and killed themselves, others threw themselves upon those wearing the uniform of the enemy and died in battle.

Others grew determined to live so that we might make our way back, fulfilling our oath to country and queen, and return to family not remembered, yet their loss mourned. We have found other thinking beings on this vastness known as Kerith and have apprenticed many of them to our service. We will lift them, willing or no, by their bootstraps and collars, into an Age they can barely imagine. We will establish our abilities in this new place, exert our control over the elements once again, anchoring our Houses and Strongholds in foreign soil, planting our superiority as deep as any root into this ground. These new Gods can hear us, and we will bend them as we never bent our old Gods, for they are inferior and malleable to us. Through them, we will reach what is rightfully ours again. They fear us, as indeed they should. Some of us will cajole them. Others will hunt them down till they have what they wish.

So begins the forging of our Elven Ways. We will master this earth as we had our old one, searching for the path back.

Foreword Two: A Smoking Tale

THERE ARE MANY TALES TOLD in the smoking dens of the Dwellers and other fair folk of Kerith, passed through the years by retelling and embellishing. This is one such tale, and ought to be heeded, for it is a mainstay of a teller's pack of stories.

From a haze of herb-scented blue smoke will come the speaker's voice, in the tradition of toback shop-told stories, interrupted only by the occasional deep draft upon a pipe or the tamping and relighting of its bowl.

"In the beginning came the Dwellers."

This should not surprise the listener, as the storyteller is generally a Dweller, sturdy if shorter than many of the world's other races, with a thick shock of hair, weather-marked eyes, and calloused hands.

"We Dwellers are the shepherds of the earth and its children, all which grow and graze upon it. The Gods blessed us with a love of our lives here, and we are a fortunate people. To balance that fortune and love, the Bolgers were born from the dark. Where we build, they destroy. They are not a people as we are, only a near-people, and one might pity them if it were not for their vile natures."

Smoke will fill the room then, as the listener contemplates, within the pause that has been given for such contemplation, the balancing of the world with good and bad, light and dark.

The storyteller will inhale and accent his next words with a smoke cloud or clever ring. "Kernans came after, a taller people with ambitious souls. If we were the roots, they were the treetops, but they aspired to be mountain peaks. They built great cities, with gates, and armies, and levied taxes to keep their households furnished. It is said that from them sprang the Magi, when magic existed on Kerith. We know the Kernans love to talk to the Gods and in those days, the Gods talked back and even lay with them. Thus came the Mageborn, few but powerful.

"From the Kernans, the Magi bred the tall and arrogant Galdarkans to guard the Magi and their fortresses of magical power. When the Magis destroyed themselves fighting to see who was greatest, it was said the Gods turned against them and stripped all magic away. Not a Mageborn survived. The Kernans were left bowed in humility and guilt for their past as the Galdarkans who survived took over the Empire. They did not hold it long, and there was strife on Kerith. Eventually, all fell."

The Dweller will pause, waiting patiently for the inevitable question, "What of the Raymy?" If asked, he will answer, if not asked, he will ask the question of himself, with a wreath or two of smoke to accent it.

"What of the Raymy? The Raymy are not a people, as we reckon it. They do not birth young, they do not have compassion, and they cannot be reasoned with. Their existence cannot be fathomed and all we can do is be thankful they were driven back across the great ocean and pray they never return. To this end, the Magi were true, and with the defeat of the great enemy, and only then, did the Magi fall to arguing among themselves and earned the wrath of the Gods.

"As for the Ravers, who can say what they are but a curse upon the living ground, wraiths of the Raymy left behind. Perhaps they are haunts of the Magi, twisted and corrupted and cut off from mortal Kerith. Smarter minds than ours have often contemplated this, with no answers."

At this point, the toback is usually bolstered with new leaf and tamped and relit carefully while the listener considers his or her own past and how the dread Raymy effected it.

"We had peace for a while, uneasy and slow. The Galdarkans scattered away to the eastern lands, feuding clan lords loyal to Magi of old, fighting one another but leaving us alone. Our farmers and traders rebuilt the free cities, a light but strong spiderweb that wove us all together, and we began to prosper again.

"Then the Gods struck Kerith with a great, resounding blow, the Hammer of the End Days themselves, and when the ground stopped shaking and smoking, the Vaelinars stepped out. If we can call the Bolgers a near-people, then I suppose we must call the Vaelinars a greater-people. High elves from our oldest wish-tales, closest to the Gods without actually being one or a Demon, some say, far nearer to the Gods than the Mageborn ever hoped to be. They came because they were God-ridden, but they do not accept that, and until they do, their lives here on Kerith will remain restless and fraught with anger and difficulty. Some of us they enslaved, others of us they taught and nurtured. They fought against us and have fought for us. Such are they, both light and dark in one people, and strangers amongst us. Yet here they are, and so are counted within our tales as a people of Kerith."

A last, fragrant cloud of smoke will be exhaled. A moment will pass in case any wish to add or correct the tale, but politeness dictates that it should stand as the teller has related it.

"So be it," the tale speaker will end.

It is only the ending of one tale, and the beginning of others, or of much argument as to the wisdom of the tale itself, a wheel of life forever churning.

Part I

Chapter One

703 After Empire, Stocking Month by Dweller Calendar

THE LEADEN SKY WEIGHED DOWN on them, as their horses carefully picked out a trail up a treacherous mountain scape with necks and backs bowed against the incline and the cold wind shivering down about them as their hooves sent pebbles and shale clattering downslope. Sevryn pulled his greatcoat close, fanning the high collar around his neck to no avail, for nothing could keep out the bitter wind for long. Red and orange leaves lay flattened to the ground, the thinning tree stands little more than stark branches as they climbed upward. A somber song ran through his head from the last tavern they'd slept in, days ago, about the pursuit of a Vaelinar father after his kidnapped daughter, and the tragedy which ensued, and it fit the mood of the day. The sturdy folk of Kerith and its western city provinces would be salting away meat, preserving the last of their fresh goods, stocking away stores for the bitter winter to come, not far behind the heels of these storm clouds. It would rain again soon, it had to; he could feel the humidity building and the only question in his mind was whether the skies would open up with water, hail, or snow. It felt cold enough for snow but too damp. What did he know of things like that, really, he who preferred bad weather under a stout roof? What he knew of snow he'd learned on trails like this, following after his resolute vagabond teacher.

Riding ahead of him, Gilgarran wore a hooded cloak against the climate, fastened sturdily in front with a series of cloak pins, each a small golden masterpiece of craftsmanship, holding the cloak tightly shut even in the face of the ever increasing wind. Lacings kept the hood secure as well, and although Sevryn had once laughed at the garment, he realized now that his own greatcoat and leather hat served him more poorly, and left his legs bare to the cold and what had been, for days, a frigid, driving rain. It would take him a month to dry out and he doubted that the weather would hold more than another candlemark or two before the sky opened up again.

City-born, he still did not like being out in the open, although he had gotten used to it over his years spent with Gilgarran on one trail or another, in pursuit of goals that often seemed obscure. He did not complain. What lay behind him, in city sewers and middens and back alleys, had always been far worse, and he bore the scars to remind him. However, a midmorning fire and warming brew would be welcome as the weather closed in about them, Stocking month indeed, before the snows and harsher times descended. "How much farther up the mountain lives this friend of yours?"

Gilgarran reined to a halt, and turned his horse toward Sevryn. "I am not sure."

Their gazes met. "He is a friend," Sevryn said, his voice rising slightly, almost making a question of it.

Gilgarran dropped his gloved hands to the withers of his mount. "Actually, he is more of an acquaintance than a friend. If that."

"Which explains why the directions to his abode have been a bit obscure."

"Indeed." Gilgarran's mount twitched slightly as if betraying a nervousness under his equine skin that his rider's neutral expression refused to convey. Gilgarran had the agelessness of all Vaelinars, along with the high cheekbones, the slightly pointed ears, the eyes of brilliant gemlike colors, his of green and blue-green, a nice counterpoint to his amber hair. He wore an ear stud of a two-carat aquamarine as if to accent his eyes further. "Does that concern you?"

Sevryn's dapple-gray gelding stamped the ground, telegraphing further what neither man allowed to ripple through their eyes or slightly smiling mouths. Sevryn stretched his legs in the stirrups and resettled as Gilgarran teased at his loyalty. "I would ask, does it concern you?"

"It does."

"Then it worries me, for what concerns you can devastate me." Sevryn grinned then, wryly, one corner of his mouth lifting as it had the habit of doing.

Gilgarran turned his face, glancing up the rough mountain scape, its peak hidden by the lowering cloud banks of blue and ever darkening grays. "This," he said slowly, "is why I found and began to train you."

Sevryn felt his crooked grin fade. Nearly twenty years under Gilgarran's tutelage and he no longer asked why he'd been taken in and trained, grateful only that this one Vaelinar did not look down upon him or question his half-blood lineage or wish him dead. His hand tightened imperceptibly on the reins, and he shifted his weight slightly, taking stock of the various weapons in holsters and sleeves placed discreetly about his body.

Gilgarran gestured with his gloved hand toward the broken peaks. "Up there, if I am right, we will enter into a supposed alliance or, if I am wrong, we'll make a formidable enemy. I shall know where we are going, but you have to mark it, too."

Few words, but enough to quicken his pulse. No more questions now.

Gilgarran worked alone, save for him, and there would be no rescue to follow, and if there were recriminations to be had by their actions, the two of them alone would bear them. He knew this and had agreed to it long ago. The astiri, the way, would be but a single thread among all those that were natural in the elemental weaving of the world, and ought to shine through to him like a newly minted copper bit tossed in a clear pool of rainwater for a midsummer's wish.

Sevryn took a shallow breath to steady himself, then opened his senses as Gilgarran had been teaching him these past decades, and let the essence of the elements about them fill him. The moment came with awe. He would never grow used to it, the rushing wealth of sensory information filling him. He felt the tiny creatures huddled underground against the storm in their crooks, caves, and boles of the world. The trees below hugging the stony mountain in the thinning air and water, their roots going deep even while their gnarled branches waited for whatever sun might strike them. He knew the birds in their nests and holds, wings tucked in sleep. He could feel the seeds which would stir to life in the spring, and he could hear and taste the river that ran through the roots of these peaks, underground, through cave and cavern and deep into the broken rock of the earth, before it tumbled free onto the greening valleys and became a true river. All this and more, he felt in an instant.

He also felt the moment that was coming upon them and what it could mean, as well as where it would happen. The prescience danced upon the raw nerves of his body. There were moments when everything in life could change, and one of them approached.

Sevryn opened his eyes, reflecting only the gray of the stormy sky overhead, and nodded to Gilgarran. He had the astiri firmly in his mind now and knew the path leading around and above to the man-made holdings they sought. Moreover, he tasted the soot of the stronghold's forges in the air, heard the pound of hammer and tong, and knew the bite of hot iron being cooled in troughs of water drawn from the mountain's underground streams. He could feel the flesh huddled, tired and sore, in the work camps riddling the caverns above, enslaved and miserable.

Formidable enemy, indeed. The forge which lay above them, hidden among the twisting crags and buttes, was not the simple ironworks of the Kernans on the eastern plains, devoted to basic breastplates and short swords for the ever quibbling Bolger tribes or the independent Galdarkans. No. The enclave he felt moved in full production, amassing weapons and armor, in direct violation of the Accords. No wonder the secrecy.

"It is not a good place we ride to," Gilgarran acknowledged, meeting his stare. "Once up there, stay with me, but be quiet. Say as little as possible, do as little as possible."

"Attract no attention."

Gilgarran nodded. "I will not be shielding you otherwise."

"All right."

Gilgarran lifted his reins. His horse shook his head. "Anything to tell me?"

Surprise shivered through him like the fingers of the wind swirling about them. His teacher had told him once never to prophesy for him. Never had he offered or been asked before. His Kernan blood, Gilgarran said, tainted the Vaelinar in him, and his talents were likely to be muddied through no fault of his own. Because of it and his eyes, no one had ever offered to teach him, not even those Vaelinars who had recognized their blood in him, although Gilgarran had been pleasantly surprised at his abilities. Still, his mentor had made that request of him at the beginning and had never gone back on it. It was said the Vaelinars recognized their own by the eyes even more than the ears, the longevity, the agility, and the slenderness of build. It was also said that Talent passed with Vaelinar eyes, but he had proved that axiom wrong. Gilgarran said Sevryn was the only one he'd ever run across who manifested Talent though his eyes were perfectly ordinary, making him even more valuable to Gilgarran's intrigues. There was an advantage to being discounted in the scheme of things.

Sevryn began to shake his head quickly to Gilgarran's question, then the words tumbled out in spite of that. "Be careful."

It happened like that. A darkness filled with sudden lightning, a flash of thought or word. He snapped his mouth shut, teeth biting off his words.

Gilgarran smiled thinly. "That," he responded, "goes without saying." He turned his horse about and began to pick his way uphill again, following the hidden trail their elven senses had marked.

"Wait," Sevryn called, but the howling wind tore the sound from him and swallowed it down, and if Gilgarran heard him at all, he gave no sign of it. He gathered himself to follow, and do what he had been trained for.

Chapter Two

Earlier That Day

FYRVAE STOOD IN THE DARKNESS, back bowed, head down instinctively, knowing where the cavern roof dipped low, his body protesting as he moved, rising from sleep, and braiding his hair back from his face, fingers gaining nimbleness as he worked. The stone crouched about him like the skeleton of another body he knew intimately, cradling and caging him as one might a lover. He listened. The inner mountain no longer beat like a drum, bass vibrato resounding in the bones of the earth and inside his bones, and that meant the thunder and rain outside had ceased. Too soon! Too soon! His jaw clenched upon the lamentation yet he could not quell his dismay. The river nearby swelled and tumbled downward in its rock-cut path through the underground, but not powerfully enough. Not deep enough, swift enough, for his needs, even when unleashed by the Vaelinar who drove it here, who had coaxed it into the caverns of this mountain, away from its natural bed, and kept it tamed for the master who owned them both.

The woman at his feet stirred as if roused by his thoughts of her, and put her hand out, touched his ankle. "Fyrvae?" She spoke softly so as not to disturb the closed silence of the caves. The fragile tone of her voice belied the strength and hold she had on this one river, the strength and hold she had on his soul.

His anger softened, and he bent over, running calloused fingers through her tangled hair. "Lindala. Pray for more rain. Pray for more than your river can hold."

"It did stop, then."

"Hours ago, I imagine."

"Help me light a small fire. It's so cold."

He could feel her shiver under his hand, and it hurt him to answer. "No. We need every scrap of kindling. It's all we've got. I can't steal any more from the forge fires. They're keeping track."

"I know, I know." She sighed. "I can feel the rain. It's close, but . . . it's almost as if it's watching. Waiting for something."

He could feel it, too. His kinship lay with the earth and the fires deep inside it, but he could feel the pressure of the storm waiting to break. They needed it. They had no hope without it; indeed, had little hope with it. Flood might do what they alone could not. He stroked Lindala's face, tracing her fine bones with his rough fingertips, brushing his thumb across her chapped lips. Such a beautiful mouth. He longed to see her smiling again, in full sunlight, the glow of happiness lighting her face.

"I'll be back soon. Try to keep each other warm."

"Where—"

"I've got to make sure the forge is hot enough. Buyers are coming. They've put aside the veil on the mountain. They're at the talus now, working their way up." No one found their way to the forge unless Quendius allowed them, and he'd felt their steady progress at the edge of his thoughts. "Quendius will want a blade finished to show the quality, and I want the forge ready. It's another workday for me. Do you understand?"

"Yes, I . . . I understand." Lindala repressed another shiver, and grasped his hand with both of hers, her strength grown frail over the past seasons, the natural slenderness of her hands now gaunt, and he swallowed tightly as he felt her bones just under the skin in his hold. They both gave food up for the third, but they didn't think about her, couldn't, lest Quendius or another sense her. Lindala hid her with all the meager strength of her waning talents, and even that might not be enough much longer.

Rain! Let the storms come again! He clasped her, and brought the fire up in his body, heating himself from the inside out, and knelt beside her, taking her in his arms, warming her. He couldn't sustain the effort long, but she stopped shivering, her face buried in the hollow of his neck. Little enough to do, and yet never enough. "We are truly the Suldarran, the Lost," he murmured to her softly. "But I will do everything in my power never to lose you. Believe in me."

She made a wordless sound in answer, holding him tightly. After a long moment, he began to draw her arms from about his neck, and she whispered to the curve of his ear, "I am with child again."

He stiffened. She felt it in him, could not help but feel it, and a dampness trickled between their pressed together cheeks. He cursed at himself for bringing tears from her. She tried to draw back from him, but he did not allow her. "It is a joy," he said to her, finally, his voice and words muffled against her skin. "We are blessed twice over with what many Vaelinars can only hope for. Can you carry it?"

"How can I not? It is as much a part of me as I am part of it."

"You're so thin . . ." he stroked her forearm. The birth of the other had nearly done her in, and he did not see how Lindala could do this again.

Fyrvae drew back reluctantly and stood, bowed, under the low ceiling. Lindala curled up, murmuring, and he could hear the prayer in her softly chanted words. All Vaelinars were lost in this world, and some more than others, he thought. No one would look for him or those of his family, for his blood no longer existed, and if his slavery were known, the Vaelinars would simply say to him, "An ironic punishment."

She had left her people, her lineage anchored securely in the House of Vayernol, to follow him, and he had promised her a life worth living, only to bring her to this. Yet she had done it of her own free will, and for love of him. Their child . . . children . . . had not made such a choice. He leaned down, and tucked the soft rags of her tunic and skirt about her. His father Briban had destroyed his family by attempting to raise a Way, to establish a House for his lineage, centuries after the Accords had abolished magical meddling with the elements. Those of the DeCadils who'd survived had been hunted down by the Council and dispatched. He'd barely escaped both the disaster and the Council by fleeing, and Lindala had insisted on going with him. To what end could he hope to bring them now? Then, he'd been young and foolish with hope. Now he could only hope to endure, like the metal he folded and pounded on the anvils. But what he would be forged into only time would determine.

Fyrvae made his way out the winding depths of the caverns, the red glow at the tunnel's end guiding him to the forges, their heat blasting him like the sun in the desert as he emerged, the sting of the mountain's chill and wind and fomenting storm swirling about him, held at bay by the fierce heat of the furnaces. The blast and smell of the hot metal and charcoal and smelting stopped him in his tracks for a moment. Fyrvae breathed deep then, and moved out into the open.

A Bolger swiped at him, grumbling, rattling his chains, the rankness of his body almost overpowering even with the pungent smell of the smithy about him. His ivory tusks clacked as he swore at Fyrvae listlessly.

Fyrvae did not deign to dodge. "Touch me and die." He stood his ground, well within reach of the vile creature, and stared him down. The Bolger moved back, grumbling to its guard mate in broken grunts with only the rudimentary semblance of a language. They could speak Common well enough if they chose, and just as obviously did not wish to. The other hooted in laughter at his fellow and the Bolger growled as he hunkered down, glaring at Fyrvae.

The second Bolger made crude gestures as Fyrvae strode past, headed toward the main furnaces which were his domain and responsibility and stayed stoked despite any weather, ready for his usage at the slightest notice. Yawning gap of a mouth, blackened at the edges and fire red inside, it consumed whole forests a log at a time when needed, and the Bolgers who stoked it snarled at him, but did his bidding even as they slunk back and forth, bodies dripping with sweat from the heat. These had already sweated the rankness out of their Bolger skins and smelled only of the furnace, and moved to obey when he beckoned. He reigned here, and they dared not forget it. His tongs could and had branded the disobedient. Better to face Fyrvae than Quendius, even at that. While the other forges worked on armor endlessly, he made weapons, fine weapons, and the craftsmanship he taught them would some day elevate them over their more brutal kin.

Did buyers come? He didn't know for a certainty. Quendius had not told him of an upcoming sale, but that meant nothing, and he knew that someone came, he could feel their presence on the slopes, steadily approaching the hidden fortress. His senses pinged with every step upon the stone and earth. Who else would come but buyers?

He buried his senses in the fires and the metal, and waited for rain.

Lindala curled her body about her daughter, and tried to keep the heat that Fyrvae had generated for them, but the earth and stone and even the river sipped at it, draining it away, till she felt even colder than before. Her daughter sat up, long hair swinging away from her face, and patted her mother's hand. She spoke little, as they all did, enslaved to the darkness of the caverns, but she hummed under her breath as she played small games with the twigs and stones about her. Lindala watched her, wondering what hues the sun would highlight in her hair, what colors lay in the depths of her eyes, seeing a mystery before her, a child growing slowly in the way of the Vaelinar race even though her entire life had been spent in the gloom of the caverns. They rarely spoke of her, or to her, as if that alone could shield the knowledge of her from Quendius. Lindala joined in her humming, her song one she used to keep the strength of the river in her thoughts. The swollen stream itself roared past them, a constant wind, its froth misting the air, adding to the chill. What would her daughter do when the baby swelled her belly? Would she welcome it? Would she press her face to her mother's stomach and listen to the gurgle of the unborn and feel the kicks of its movements?

If it lived. If she could stay strong enough to nurture it. Lindala sat, hunched over, her hands touching her daughter's, playing at the patterns of the sticks and stones, her mind plotting at getting food into the cavern depths. A chicken would be wonderful. It could eat the small bugs and lizards that skittered among the earthern cracks and walls, and an egg a day . . . even every two or three days, oh yes, that would be as if Godsent. She would have to coax the Bolger into stealing one for them, and she could do it, she thought. Winter crouched over them. If he brought her leather, even scraps, she could fashion protection for him. He had to feel pain, even though they'd been taught not to feel much at all. His tribe had been enslaved by the Bolger mercenaries who strengthened the will of Quendius. He was little better off than she, unshackled from the forge only long enough to bring wood in and stack it, and help bring mine carts up now and then from the caverns to work his muscles and remind him that there were worse places to be chained than the forge. Bolger enslaved Bolger even as Vaelinar enslaved Vaelinar, and those in the lands above turned their faces away from the atrocities. He might help them. Lindala determined that he *would* help them. She would find a way to reach him. She would have to convince Fyrvae to tolerate him even more than he did now. Kindness, like water dripping upon a stone, made pathways where none existed before.

Her daughter stopped humming, turning her face upward. She wrinkled her nose. "Stinkers," she said quietly. Her fingers tightened about a stone even as she smiled in anticipation.

Lindala smelled it, unworried. Then the stench blanketed them heavily, and she lurched to her feet. More than one. No more than one ever came down here! Heavy footpads and the sounds of boots echoed down to them, and her heart quickened in her chest like that of a frightened bird trying to wing away from danger. She pulled her daughter behind her as orange light flared into the shadow, and the heat of a torch seared across her vision and her skin. Encircled, they had no place to run except into the raging water itself, and that she would not do. Bolgers grunted and clashed tusks at her, but it was the figure hulking behind the torch who struck the greatest terror into her, yet she refused to turn her eyes from the glare.

A long silence, then, "You've done well."

Bolgers gnashed in contentment and quieted until it was just the one man and Lindala with her child hugging her legs from behind, little more substance to her than a shadow, who faced one another.

"What do you want of me?"

"I came just to check on your well-being. The rains have flooded the river. I am told it will be cresting. You should leave the caverns, or at least come to the upper levels, for your own safety." A pause. "And hers."

"The river doesn't threaten me."

"No?" Another long pause. Then the being shifted, signaling the Bolgers who dragged her child from behind her and held her between them. She let out a wailing cry, then fell silent, her lip caught between her teeth, jaw trembling. The man took a pair of silvery, gleaming objects from inside his cloak. "I had these made," he said to Lindala, turning them over and over in his hands, the oily light of the torch spilling down on the bracelets, "for you. I had a curse put into them . . . ah, yes, there are Vaelinars who work in such dark things, although rarely. I did not want you straying. After your bonding to the river, though, it seemed unnecessary, but I kept them. Now . . ." and he grabbed one of the child's hands from the Bolger and snapped the bracelet about her thin wrist, then the other.

Her daughter started to cry, trying to pull the shackles off, pain in every smothered noise she made. Her skin grew crimson and curled back in an open gash and Lindala reached for her, trying to stop her, trying to stop the damage. Her touch seemed to soothe, if only for a moment, and she pulled her daughter to her, feeling her quake in every past of her thin, fine frame. The air smelled of burning skin and blood.

"They will keep her safe. She won't wander far from here, with those branded into her skin. Accidents can happen, and we wouldn't want that. There are rings for the chains, but I can wait on those." He turned on one heel abruptly, and the Bolgers scattered before him, scrambling back up the passage, clicks of stone and dirt signaling their hasty retreat. "Congratulations on your child, Lindala. My pardon that it is late in being given. It seems I wasn't told. Together, however, we shall value her for what she is. Another Vaelinar slave."

He left in a haze of smoke and orange light, and Lindala gathered up her daughter, holding her close, trying to ease away the pain of the shackles, trying to stop the cutting and bleeding, and weeping her own river, to no avail. When she caught her breath, she listened for hope, for the floods to come.

The back gate to the furnace creaked as the great doors swung up, and Quendius filled the threshold as if bidden by thought to appear. Fyrvae squinted through the swirling heat of the forge at his master.

He wore ivory robes of soft curled and combed fur, hanging open over a bare torso, his leather pants cut to move supplely, the grain as soft as butter. The light gray irises of his eyes were spoked with obsidian streaks so that it was like looking into a dark star that had exploded into shards against a gray dawn sky. With his skin a soft, sooty charcoal, and his blue-black hair tied back, Quendius filled the doorway, the biggest Vaelinar Fyrvae had ever met in his life. Rumors said he had no Talent but that of strength. Fyrvae had never found any Talent in him except cruelty and shrewdness.

His square jawed face showed the barest approval at the forge stirring to life. "We've guests coming."

"I felt them, master." Fyrvae dropped in a half bow.

"I see you're getting the furnaces hot. Excellent. I want a sword finished. These guests are not invited, but they should be impressed with the caliber of the swords only you can make." Quendius stepped inside the forge, forcing Fyrvae to look up at him with a painful stretch of his neck and shoulders as he settled into a wide-legged stance. He wore the first of Fyrvae's specially commissioned swords on his hip, the only man who could have worn it that way, as most would have carried it in a back sheath. He, however, had the height and arm span to wear it as he did.

He did not wish just any sword, then, any cutting blade, but one of *them.* "A second sword, master, as agreed?" The making of a second imbued sword would free him from his indenture; that was the pact they had made when Quendius found him and offered shelter for the fugitives. Better perhaps that he'd stayed to face the judgment of the Council, though they were said to have little mercy for those who broke the Peace Accords. Even little mercy would be more than this man held.

"Agreements change," Quendius reminded him amiably, "as ours did when you tried to escape." The black shards in his eyes seemed to glint harshly, catching the reflected orange light of the banked fires. "Two swords for two Vaelinars, but now there is a third, is there not? I wonder if she could live in the daylight, away from the caverns. Away from yourself . . . and your wife. Best to stay in the shelter I've given you, and work your way to freedom."

Fyrvae felt rebellion rising in his chest and tried to quell it as cold realization leached the fire out of him. Quendius would never be through with him. Fyrvae and Lindala would always owe him, the pact would never be completed. They had sunk from indentured servants to slaves and now he knew they could sink even lower. Little choice left; looking up at the armorer, he contained his expression most carefully, unwilling to admit defeat. "You know more than I, then."

"So it seems. A second sword, and I want the best from you. You've been working on one . . ." Quendius' glance scoured the forge, and fell upon a nearly finished blade in a rack to the side. "Your craftsmanship shows. How much longer till that one is finished?"

"It's nearly done." His thoughts threatened to scatter impossibly far from him despite his need to focus. He had no life expectancy beyond that of the finished sword as a surety. He knew that. The Talent he poured into the metal and the fire, working it, took nearly every fiber of his being. Fyrvae considered the blade as well. He'd already made the hilt and pommel, which were waiting to be settled onto the blade's tang, the whole being a work of art, something he'd done to keep his mind occupied, something to keep him on the edge of sanity. He hadn't hidden it, for nothing could be hidden from Quendius. Still, it had never been meant to be one of his workings.

"Finish it, then. And then . . ." Quendius leaned over him, his presence more oppressive than even the heat of the furnaces. "Imbue it. *Finish it.*"

Fyrvae inclined his head to study the ground and did not move until the other had left, then he stood wearily, and took up his tongs and hammer.

The forge seemed lessened without Quendius hulking inside it, and even the Bolgers shuffled a bit. His leather apron, charred and weathered, hung on a peg, and he took it down for whatever protection it could afford, knowing that there was no protection on this earth, this Kerith, to be had from what Quendius asked of him.

Fyrvae bent over his work and added his silent prayer for rain to those being murmured in the caverns beyond and below. Born of the earth and tempered with fire, he knew his creation better than it knew itself. The time passed and he did not hear the rains open up, pelting the roof overhead, or smell the hot water steaming off the furnace-heated buildings, or sense the guard force gathered outside in the yard and given orders to round up those who drew near the fortress without permission. He knew only the mutterings of the Bolgers as they banked the fires, waiting to see if he would heat the blade again, readying to turn the grindstones if he directed them to, although he preferred to do that work himself. Rufus closed on him, doing small things he caught at the corner of his attention, stoking the fire, adding water to the cooling vats, watching him.

He did the grinding with Vaelinarran precision, ignoring the sparks as they flew up, scorching apron and hands and forearms, intent only upon bringing out the fine edge he knew waited in the sword, preparing it for its ultimate possession. He heated the blade for its final tempering, and sweat ran off his torso in rivulets under the leather apron as he hammered. The metals reverberated against each other, resisting and tempering, and he could feel the power rising to run through him, drumming in his veins, roaring through his muscles. As he examined the blade and saw no flaw in it, he put it in the salted bath to ensure an even heating. He would grant the demand made of him. Grant it, and more. They would be free or die trying.

Finally, he plunged it into the quenching tank, cooling it quickly and thoroughly, listening to it hiss as he did.

He fastened the hilt to the blade. He wet the blade and wiped it clean, marveling at the sheen of the alloy. Deadly, balanced, elegant, strong, two-edged. Fyrvae had made a weapon worthy of being wielded.

He laid it across his anvil and closed his eyes, sifting through the planes of elemental existence, drawing his power together, feeling the tide rise in him as it had built all day.

"You, Fyrvae, should have been a priest not a smith," Quendius had told him when he put the slaves' ring on him. An odd thing to say, then.

Now it frightened him that Quendius knew him better than he knew himself. It made him even more of a slave than the bonds of fear and consequence holding him, than the hostage held in the caverns below, than the fears of his childhood buried deep in his mind, even that of the lost heritage of his people.

He did not fear now. Now he was master of the elements and of the weapon in front of him, and he opened himself to the Talent, to the Calling. Around him, he could hear the Bolgers shuffle to the far corners of the forge, their chains rattling quietly, their guttural words muffled so as not to attract his attention.

That's right, you sorry sons of bitches. You know what I am doing. Fyrvae opened his eyes to feel them cowering in the corners, and looked at them, their bare scalps wrinkling with dismay, eyes squinting in hopeless fear. Their leathery cupped ears were pinned back, and the one nearest him managed words that he could understand.

"Master, pliss. We work hard. Do not hurt." The Bolger nearest him scraped the hard-beaten floor of the forge as he groveled toward Fyrvae, his thick hands curled in palm-upward submissiveness. He did not fool Fyrvae. If he turned his back, within reach of those chains, and seemed the least bit inattentive or weak, they would pull him down. He knew that, and they knew he knew it. The sharp reek of their fear began to fill the air with sourness, sweat that even the heat could not squeeze out of them, brought from the depths of their miserable bodies. One alone stared at him, his gaze steady yet respectful.

This was Rufus, as Fyrvae had named him, who faced him now, his forearm branded with the tong mark, old now, long healed, and although the enmity between them remained, it was partnered with a grudging respect. The Bolger watched him closely with everything he did. Fyrvae would be willing to swear that the Bolger learned from him, whatever he could, in that bony head of his. Not animal, not man, but shrewd enough to be dangerous. They held an uneasy partnership, he and Rufus did. Rufus learned from him, and he often found a grudging desire within himself to teach. To share the satisfaction of a hard day's work, to see the jewel of a blade brought forth from his efforts. Lindala knew Rufus and treated him kindly, something Fyrvae did not understand but did not stop, and Rufus repaid them with smuggled kindling wood from time to time, whenever his duties took him into the mines.

He took pity on Rufus and the other Bolgers, curs who were no less a slave than he was. He warned them. "First blood will not be yours," he told them. "Once it is loosed though, I can make no promises. It is a sword that *will* be blooded. Again and again. It will call for blood. Stay clear of it. Understand?"

They babbled back quickly. "Yes, master. Yiss. Yes." The Bolgers huddled farther back in the sooty shadows of their corners where their chains chimed softly as they continued to cower in fear.

They did not really understand. They did not know that he would pry forth a Demon and imprison it in the sword, just as he had in the first sword. In trying to fill that first blade with the very heart of the metal he worked, seeing it, seeing the fire he tamed and boosted to temper it, that first time, he'd worked with his Talents. Earth and fire, fire and earth . . . and he'd shaken loose a Demon, albeit minor, from the planes of its existence. Shaken it loose and poured it into the sword where Fyrvae then caged it. Just a tiny Demon, with a lust for the destruction a weapon naturally caused, and when Quendius handled it for the very first time, the sword had bonded to him. It struck unerringly quick and deep, as if it had eyes, paired with the skill of its wielder. Yes, a fine, fine weapon. *An unnatural weapon.*

Seeing what he could do, what use might be made of him, they'd tried to escape. That was when Quendius had made slaves of them instead of servants. When he'd had a Vaelinar ally bind Lindala to the river she had tamed for their pact, chained her to its underground waters until freed. To face the day, to be out of touch with the water, she would suffer terribly. Only Quendius held the key to that unbonding. As for Fyrvae, he was chained to Lindala. Quendius demanded a sword per soul that he harbored. Fyrvae would have offered the second sword up if he could have, but his Talents thinned, like a spark at the edge of a forge fire, barely glowing, threatening to go out altogether. Like a great working of magic that took a Godly toll, he could not summon what he needed to make another then.

Quendius could, and did, wait. Years. Fyrvae directed the making of many fine weapons while he collected the scattered bits of himself he'd nearly lost, and now, desperation fueled him. Ready or not, he'd run out of time.

Fyrvae looked upward, but he did not see the soot-stained roof of the building where smoke curled ever upward, and the blue-orange glow of flames danced against black reflection. He looked into existences not meant for his eyes to see, heard the discordant strains of beings never meant to be heard by mortal ears, touched and answered back and commanded and called Demons beyond the reaches. They snarled and fought him, whipping his soul in anger, scouring him with their power. They branded him from the inside out, and Fyrvae cried out in pain and anger of his own, whipping back at them. He lashed them as only a Vaelinar could, not born of their world, yet able to command it at great cost, and he willed himself to pay the price.

Once the Vaelinars had not been Lost, *Suldarran*, from their own world and Gods, but here on Kerith their greatness still could not be denied, and the lesser Gods and Goddesses of this place were laid bare to the Vaelinars who had the Talent and could harness it. He did. Having discovered it by accident, the Talent had doomed him to Quendius. Now he would return the favor.

Fyrvae threw aside unwanted lesser Demons, reaching for the greatest he could call. A roar of power and rage flooded his being, and he gathered it in, weaving its fiery lines as he wove the fires that forged his weapons, teeth clenched against the scorching anger. He rode the planes of his soul, soaring along scorching winds under a sun that would blind him if he looked with mortal eyes, and felt beings reach for him with a hunger to suck him dry except he did not allow their touch. Only one did he call. His hands gestured through the air, fingers threading the sigils of a calling despite its vast resistance.

A Godling Demon answered in murderous rage, lunging at him, no longer resisting, and his power erupted over them. The force catapulted Fyrvae back into his body, his arms upheld, trembling with the burden of his thoughts and workings, driven back onto his haunches. The Demon he called dove after him.

Something snapped in him as clear as a green branch breaking in two, and the pain shot through him. He buckled. In a flash, he knew that he had called one he could not handle, the answer to all his needs, and the solution that would kill him long before it got to Quendius. Fyrvae swayed as the Demon came at him, maw yawning crimson, otherworld rage bent on ripping open his throat, eager to take his heart and soul. He anchored himself with the only thread he could find, his love for Lindala, a ribbon of the riversoul she held, soothing, wet, and pure, against the fire of this Demon Godling that seared him. He grabbed for strength from her, wrapping it about him as if she could shield him from what he must be. The being took hold of him, and Fyrvae shoved back. He thrust the doubt, the pain, and the Demon off a heartbeat away from being shattered. Agony howled from his throat, followed by defiance. Around him, the Bolgers cried out raggedly, snarling in fear and excitement, hoping to bluff the thing they sensed unseen among them.

He grasped the sword, the double edge slicing open his palm, hot blood spurting upward and the Godling Demon swerved. Fyrvae grabbed up the weapon by its hilt, opening his fingers and letting his blood smear the length of the steel, where it ran into the channel he'd cut into it. The Demon entered the element shouting in greed and unwary need. Fyrvae thrust the sword into the furnace, blasting it a last time. The runes he'd marked on it suddenly shone, entrapping its captive. He waited till the last etching glowed, then took the blade and plunged it into the cold river-water. A last quenching of water. Now all the other quenchings would come from blood. It inhaled deeply and all went still.

An icy blast roared through the building. The forges all went out at once. Fyrvae staggered, going to one knee. The broken thing inside of him might be as solid as bone or as wispy as soul, he had no way of knowing, but the pain came back with a keen edge to it, no less an edge than what he'd sliced himself open with. He reached for a scrap of cloth in his apron and bound his hand, the cut deeper than he'd intended, the edge of the weapon as sharp as any he'd ever honed. Rufus bellowed out orders. Bolgers scurried, grunting, to replenish the fires, their lives dependent on keeping them lit. Fyrvae took a whetstone, sharpening the blade one last time, even as he walked to the great house. Rain poured down in buckets as he made his way through the storm, his eyesight blurring, reeling in exhaustion, his shoulders bowed, the cords and sinews of his body in tense relief against his wiry frame. Rain in torrents, blessed rain. Too late? He did not know.

Inside the great house, he made his way cautiously to the hall, bumping into things now and then when his body and will could not keep him on a straight path in the shadows, weariness claiming him. Fyrvae found the table he sought and laid the sword across it. It seemed to hiss even as he set it down. Quendius would know it immediately.

He backed off quietly as voices reached him, and footfalls. He was unwilling to be caught there yet was too exhausted to move faster. He found a corner behind a tapestry hung to dampen the draft of the hall, and lingered to catch his breath . . . and waited, leaning his fevered face against the cooler stones.

Fyrvae scrubbed at his eyes, tired and blurred by soot and heat, unable to get a clear view from his hidden niche in the dim light from the sconces in the room. Guards pushed two hooded men inside, their clothes dripping with the rain and smelling of wet horse as well. One wore a greatcoat, the other a fine cloak, and both had rough hoods over their heads, their hands tied behind them. If they were buyers, Quendius did not care for their coin to treat them in such a manner. Fyrvae watched as the guards tore the hoods away from their heads, revealing two Vaelinars, and he sucked his breath in, surprised. Words leaped to his tongue. *Run, fools!* But he bit his lips in silence as the Armorer strode in, stripping off his fine cloak of ivory fur and dropping it over a chair, immediately seeing the blade, a smile crossing his face as he touched a fingertip to it. He ran it down the shining blade with a murmur of appreciation. He looked up, then, at his captives.

Quendius gestured to the guards. "I'll greet my guests. You take what Bolgers you need and see to the care of the water gates. I want them opened, or we'll have every cavern flooded in a candlemark, and then see new fires are laid down in the forges."

The guards sketched obedience and left him facing the two strangers.

The dark shards in his eyes glittered like polished jet. He leaned one hip on the corner of the massive table, not quite standing, not quite sitting. "Uninvited as you are, what business have you here?"

The man he faced spoke as briskly as if he stripped off gloves and made himself at home, his tone matter-of-fact and otherwise unremarkable, a brilliant blue-green aquamarine glinting in his earlobe as he tilted his head slightly to gaze at Quendius. "I heard you manufactured and sold arms. I have need of such; many, in fact."

"Going to war?"

"If that's what it takes. The haven of Larandaril is corrupted by the masses of Kerith who crowd it. I intend to push them back and retake our lands, however it is necessary to do so."

Quendius looked the two of them over. The younger one shifted slightly but said nothing, watching his elder and the Armorer.

"You'd break old truces? The Accords?"

"Vaelinar blood made those truces, and they are being bent now, sorely, by the mongrels who trespass our borders with every breath they take."

Quendius smiled then. "Have you a name?"

"Gilgarran." The prisoner lifted and dropped a shoulder in muffled salute.

"Do you know mine, and if so, how?"

"You are Quendius, and it matters little how, for the man who gave me your name is dead. He is dead because having given me your name, nothing would have kept him from giving my name to others, and it seemed prudent to stop bad manners in its tracks." Gilgarran shifted. The laced hood of his cloak had slipped down when the other hood was jerked away, and waves of amber hair flowed to his shoulders, catching the glow of the muted light. A strand or two of silver showed among the amber, giving some hint of his age that his face did not show yet.

"My business is not known here, nor am I ready to have it known," Quendius told him simply. "No one comes here unless I invite them."

Gilgarran countered, "If you will not sell to me, then I propose an alliance. I'll fight for you, providing it's fighting you have in mind, taking back what should be Vaelinarran."

"An alliance?" Quendius stood, raising an eyebrow. "Bold words from an unarmed captive."

"All of our words thus far have been bold, hmmm." Gilgarran managed a humorless smile. "Truces, treaties, slaves, weapons, war, captives, alliances."

Quendius picked up the sword. In his hidden corner, Fyrvae felt something invisible tug at his chest again as he did, bringing fresh pain, and the blade glittered in the Armorer's hands. "It would be futile," Quendius noted, "to deny the work I do here. You can smell the works halfway down the mountain, if you've any senses at all. You can see where the timber's been cut to feed the furnaces, and the range mined for ore."

"But you're not ready to sell."

"No."

"My other offer, then. I bring alliance." Gilgarran kept his chin up, watching the Armorer's ash-gray countenance, even as Quendius weighed the two-edged sword carefully in his great hands.

"The trouble with alliances is that each party must offer something the other truly desires. Although I have some pity for the pristine valleys and dells of Larandaril, I don't really care what happens to any of the havens of my . . . kin." Quendius looked up from the weapon. "The only thing I want from you is silence." With a slight grunt of exertion, he swung, the sword taking Gilgarran's head off before he'd finished his sentence.

The second man dropped to his knees immediately, as the back swing of the blade narrowly topped over him and Fyrvae broke from his hiding place, running for the back hall corridor even before the first head stopped rolling, unable and unwilling to help the living man. Quendius staggered back with a curse, his wrists bowed as the sword came to unbidden life in his grip. He roared as he fought the blade which began to shriek for more blood, twisting and bucking in his hands.

Then Fyrvae burst out of the room and into the hidden back ways, the turmoil and screams fading in his ears as he raced for the mines and tunnels. He had loosed all he'd hoped to, and more. He prayed Quendius could not contain it, and it would turn on him as well.

Fyrvae had but one chance.

He could barely see in the caverns, stumbling in a broken sprint, his hands out, taking the brunt of wall and ceiling as he bumped and fell his way into them, his cut breaking open and the bandage sodden about him, and he nearly fell over Lindala when he finally reached their crevice.

"The raft! Get to the raft."

"The river is rising. You can hear it everywhere. It's cresting."

"I know, I know." He took her elbow, not to guide her, but to let her guide him. "They've opened the floodgates, there is nothing on the river to stop us but the water itself."

Lindala sucked her breath in, then tugged him after her, after stooping and picking up an ungainly bundle from their nest on the ground, their child wrapped in blankets rewoven from their ragged clothing. She hobbled as she ran, panting from her burden, and he slipped his hand to her braided belt to keep up with her. "We could have used another stick or two," she managed.

"No time!"

"I know. The rains came!" Her voice lifted a bit, unclouded by worry. They made their way to the banks of the underground river that raced through the caverns, usually silent and dark as a serpent but now bursting, its angry edges phosphorescent in the evernight of the mountains. Lindala put her burden in the center of the raft, tucking an edge of blanket carefully about the sleeping child, and bent with Fyrvae to launch the unsteady platform over the edge. He embraced them both, with a muttered word for warmth, the last of his fragile strength for now. The raft bucked over the edge suddenly, taking them with it, gasping and holding on for dear life. The rain-swollen river frothed about them, all encompassing. If the sword took Quendius down, all their bonds would be severed. If not, they would escape but perhaps into more suffering. Yet the price of freedom was one they'd sworn to each other they'd pay. All hope, all despair.

He embraced Lindala closely, whispering in her ear over the roar of the river. "Now pray for life."

The waters took them plunging downward.

Chapter Three

SEVRYN THREW HIMSELF to his knees as the howling blade passed over him. Something warm dribbled down the back of his neck, and he lunged forward, rolled, and came up, previously concealed long knife in hand, his bonds severed. A high keening raised the hair on his neck as Quendius struggled to retain his balance, sword in his grip. Sevryn threw a glance at Gilgarran's head rolling across the floor, and without another second wasted, scrambled to his feet and bolted out the nearest door, the view of surprise in his friend's eyes even as they dimmed overriding his own vision and that of the halls he raced through. His job now was to get out.

Outside, the rain fell in a dense, dark curtain. He plunged into it, boots sliding across mud, turned the corner, and headed across the grounds toward outbuildings. The immensity of the place loomed over him. He could, and would, take a wrong turn or two before finding his way out. Hooded, he had only noted that they had not gone underground while they were being brought in. That, at least, kept him from darting into the various cavern mouths gaping blackly at him. Skidding across the open space, he could hear the shouts behind him, and Quendius' growling commands.

No time to gather himself to find the way out. He whirled and took down the Bolger sprinting nearest him, leaped over the body, and cut through the pack of guards as they reeled back in grunting surprise. Three more slices and his way cleared. Sevryn wiped blood off his face, cold and thin in the rain. It wasn't his. He bolted at angles to his destination, zigzagging through the open. Galdarkan guards lunged out of an outbuilding, and he knew a prickle of fear. They would be much harder to take down than the Bolgers. Hounds, then hunters. And after them, Quendius . . . whatever he was, whatever it was he wielded.

The damp brought out the stink of the manure piles as he strong-armed himself over a log barricade. Pigs ran squealing from him, bristle-backs with raised hackles as he plowed through and jumped the other side of the corral. Mud and worse flew from his footfalls. At the far side, he turned and quickly let go two of his daggers. Two Galdarkans fell, one with crimson spurting from his neck, the other holding his leg and cursing him.

Sevryn scaled the side of the low barn and raced across the top. From its vantage, he could see the troops massing to bring him down, squad after squad filling the open yards between the buildings. His chances dropped with every man he saw emerge.

Damn Gilgarran. Why hadn't he let Sevryn speak? If he had, they'd all still be inside, talking, perhaps sitting with a goblet of brandy to warm them, with a round of bread and cheese in front of them, and Gilgarran still alive. Why hadn't he let Sevryn speak?

Sevryn jumped from the low barn to the taller building, catching at the eave and pulling himself up and over. Barely out of breath, he took the structure at a headlong run as arrows whistled after him. Bolgers swarmed the barn. He fought with boot and long knife, slashing and rolling their bodies off into the others coming up. Something heavy caught him in the back, bringing him to his knees. He went limp, overbalancing the attacker, and they both rolled and fell off the barn. He landed on top, removed his long knife from the Bolger's chest, and got to his feet as Galdarkan guards rounded the barn.

Sevryn lunged at them, scattering the archers before they could get their bows up and a shot off. He left his long knife in the back of one's knee, and pulled another as he headed toward the main yards again, thankful that in his arrogance Quendius hadn't had them searched nearly thoroughly enough.

Surprise his main element, he cut through one squad which was clearly astonished that he had doubled back into their midst. By the time they'd shouted they had him, they were all facedown in the mud, and he angled off again.

He found himself facing huge, solid wooden buildings that smelled of heat, smoke, charcoal, and steel. If Gilgarran had expected one forge, he'd underestimated by several, but now Sevryn understood his mentor's intense interest in the place. As he darted inside, he put a finger in his coat cuffs, loosening a thread, then dumped three small balls into his hand. They needed heat or fire to ignite, and what blasted at him would be more than sufficient. The great stone oven roared with the intake of fresh air as he threw the doors open wide, and Bolgers snapped and snarled at him from the corners. He grabbed a pair of tongs and placed a ball deep inside the oven. Grabbing a hank of keys off a tall hook far from the reach of those shackled, he tossed them at the nearest Bolger, saying only, "Run fast."

He planted the other two balls as well before the shouting of the guards drew near. Taking his own advice to heart, he raced across the compound.

Sevryn gave up the idea of finding a horse to get away. Unless he got his own trained mount, who was dead tired after days of travel anyway; he couldn't trust it to get through the troops without panicking and being brought down. He would be better on his own feet. He leaped through the pigpens again, heading for the main house. The gate he sought had to be on the other side.

An arrow struck. He felt it bury itself into his greatcoat and upper left arm. It stung, but the thick wool of his coat and the silk lining took the brunt of the blow. Worth its weight in gold, that silk lining was. He reeled anyway, letting them think the injury worse than it really was. Howls of triumph split the air behind him. Now he knew where they were.

Sevryn skidded to a halt in the mud, turning, unfastening his coat. Three more throwing daggers they'd failed to find when disarming him met his touch. Three tosses, four Galdarkans fell, one of the dead tripping the fourth who fell on his own sword with a guttural cry of pain.

Nearly out of blades now, Sevryn again angled away from the direction he truly wanted, leading them away, not giving them a chance to block him. Arrows struck the ground at his heels, *thunk*, *thunk*, *thunk!* He bowed his head and put all he had left into a sprint.

Out of the corner of his eye, he saw the gate. Still open, for what enemy did Quendius have in this hidden fortress?

Sevryn cut back, and went for it. He had but one purpose that Gilgarran had given him: to get out. Keep silent and remember the astiri, the Way. He burst through the gate, gasping, and into the mountain wilderness, and Quendius was blocking his path, sword in hand, keening like a devil wind in a high tempest. Galdarkans flanked either side of him.

"Almost clever enough!" Quendius laughed without humor. He brought his sword arm up, even as he beckoned his guard to close in. The weapon belled like a howling creature in his fist, blood ribboning down its steel and washing away in the pounding rain.

Sevryn dug inside of himself, soul deep, reaching for whatever Talents he had, and the shield that Gilgarran had insisted he learn to build. As the Galdarkans closed in on him, he found it. *"Don't kill me,"* he said, as he went down, a cut in his side, the greatcoat slicing open as the blade Quendius wielded went through it like a hot knife through butter.

The mountain spewed forth with a roar that deafened him. The explosion shook him to his core. A second time, and then a third, flames shooting upward to the leaden sky, the molten fury undaunted by rain and cloud. Billows of smoke and ash shot up, and his nostrils stung with the smell of the explosions and fire. Debris rained down on them, hot and fiery bits of wood, metal, and stone.

Quendius turned sharply. *"Velk,"* he spat and more, fury welling out of him, and Sevryn knew he was a dead man.

"Do not kill me," he got out in a hoarse whisper as the guard closed on him. Something clubbed the back of his head. Red flashes split the great black darkness crashing down on him, as he lost all control of his mortal body. This was why Gilgarran had not let him speak. His Talent, his *Voice.* His Voice persuaded, commanded, when he used it. Gilgarran wanted to be sure no one was prepared for it.

Too late, he understand Gilgarran's plan, as nothingness took him.

Chapter Four

HE WOKE, STIFF AND hurting, in a gutter full of the effluvia of the city, nighttime stained by the sputter of oil torches and lamps, streaking the air with a dirty orange, sooty smoke. Slowly, Sevryn rolled over. He lay, free and awake, in the armpit of some town, somewhere. His senses assailed him, after that first quavering breath that told him he was alive. He smelled worse than the gutter, as if he'd been on a week-long drunk, pissed himself, and fallen into the waste headfirst. He levered himself into a sitting position, peering at himself in the dim light of the back alley, counting limbs, then digits. Everything seemed to be intact, although he had no reason to think it would be, not with the last memory he had, and there was not a part of his body that did not hurt.

Having expected death, it could have been far worse.

Sevryn rubbed his hands together, feeling heavy calluses that he did not remember, and then scrubbing one hand over the back of his head. His hair felt like a rat's nest, nasty and matted and unkempt, but below it, he could probe and feel a sizable dent in his skull that awoke a piercing ache when he jabbed too hard. The injury did not seem all that recent, but the lancing throb through his head now made him groan and double over, vision blurring.

He clutched at his temples, jaw clenched against the waves of nausea racking him, and the sour taste rising in his mouth. After long moments, he began to pant and slowly the nausea subsided. When he could lift his head, Sevryn put a hand to his left shoulder. Stiff yes, but nothing fresh there either. Healed, then. Some time had passed. How much? And where had he been, other than some place doing manual labor, and where was he now?

He needed help. Help, money, shelter. Sevryn got to his feet, leaning heavily against the rough wooden side of a back alley building. He wouldn't be taken back. He'd die first, this time. The very timbers he clung to stank, his nostrils flaring as new odors assaulted him, but he held to it for support anyway, crawling along the side to where the crooked street opened up a bit and light splintered in. He looked down. His clothes were little more than rags and he could not honestly say if he knew them for his or not, clothes he'd owned or stolen. His boots fit poorly, the sole half gone on one, with the other sewn sloppily back to the upper and near to falling off again. Those hadn't been custom made, of that he could be certain, as his toes pinched uncomfortably and his heels chafed. He wore a cape that smelled of horse and might have begun as a saddle blanket. Sevryn ran his hand under it, holding it up to the illumination, examining it, then letting it drop into place. He tried to think, but the thoughts spun away from him like fallen leaves caught in a driving wind, swept away.

Sevryn pushed on through the alleys, reaching a better part of town, cleaner by the smell of it, although he carried his own cloud of misery with him. Propped on the corner of a building, with muted sounds of laughter and talk reaching him through the wooden boards, he tried to gather his thoughts again as his head ceased to throb.

Either Sevryn was leaning against a tavern, or his senses were no good at all. He could feel the warmth seeping through the cracks in the wood, hear the tones of congeniality within, smell the spilled ale on the floorboards and piss in the nearby gutter. Within a stride or two of aid, then, for Gilgarran had contacts all over the lands, but he hesitated. Where had he been . . . and for how long? He doubted he'd escaped soon after his capture. If Quendius had held him, had he broken? What had he revealed of his mentor, his training, what little he knew of Gilgarran's motives and movements? Had he been let go just to be followed? No, he could not risk exposing Gilgarran's network until he understood more of what had happened. He'd been kept alive for some purpose, and he was a liability until he knew why.

Yet, as he trembled in the cold of the night, his body thin, scabbed, and scarred, he stood on the edge of being alive. He hated to have come this far, only to lose the battle. He pondered his options. Go in and beg or . . .

"Hssst. Master, the game is on the move. He's been drugged as yer askt and he's a-comin' yer way." A ragged Dweller dodged out of the tavern alley ahead of him, and engaged in talk with a tall, lean shadow Sevryn hadn't spotted before then. With a quiet hiss of his own, he leaned back out of view, watching.

"It's as you promised?" the shadow grumbled.

"His pouch is near full. The innkeep stood him a few rounds, rich trader's son that he is. Yer marked him well, yer did."

"Good." A coin flipped through the air, metal catching the ambient light, shining as it spun to the eager fist snatching it out of the air. "Not a word of this."

"No, ser!" The Dweller lad dashed away, breath chugging through his sturdy frame, and the shadow scuffed his boots, readying his stance.

Sevryn studied the mouth of the alley and the thief. Kernan, from his height and bulk. Galdarkan were far taller, elves as tall but wiry, and definitely not a Bolger. He wondered about the mark and decided profit and nothing else motivated the attack, but the thief was wary enough he'd had the target drugged first. He could speculate on that, but it seemed obvious enough to him, and the sound of an inn door being thrown open wide, wood sides crashing against the frame broke his thoughts. The boom sounded like thunder, bringing an echo of fear within him that he squelched as well as he could with a bit of surprise, and then Sevryn could hear a wave of laughter from inside. A figure reeled across the broken street, stumbled in the gutter, and Sevryn could hear the rattle of a weapon harness and belt as the drunkard headed their way. The mark mumbled to himself, words Sevryn couldn't quite catch, and the man rounded the corner into their alleyway and began to fumble at his pants. An oddly stiff glint traced the leggings of his right pants leg, hidden by the darkness of night.

The cutpurse struck, knife hilt in his fist, a sharp blow behind the mark's ear. Shadows tumbled. The mark fell, not out but downed, and rolled in the dirt, grunting, trying to draw his sword and cursing at himself.

"Bloody hand. Bloody elves and bloody hand!" He shimmied away on his back, out of range of another blow, as the thief tackled him and the two rolled about.

Sevryn stepped in. He drew back his boot and kicked the thief in the back of the head as hard as he could. Bones snap-cracked and the thief went limp. The sole of his boot went its own way, as well, and a sudden draft shot through the remains of his footwear. Sevryn peeled the man off his intended victim, who looked up blearily, succumbing to the drink and drugs in his system, his mouth twisted about a curse.

He looked at the man's sword hand, skin black-purple and drawn tight over the structure of his bones, and Sevryn's eyes narrowed. He'd not seen a wound healed like that before, but he knew who the drugged man had to be, a tale repeated in many a tavern. He brushed the sword out of the trader's feeble hand as the man gave a howl of frustration.

"Train your bloody other sword hand, then, fool, you've a strong arm for a shield and another hand to hold a blade. Act like the man you were born to be." Sevryn leaned over, took the eating dagger from the other's waistband, a fine piece of weaponry in its own right, and used it to cut away its master's purse. The leather pouch jangled heavily in his palm.

The trader sagged back onto the street, eyelids drooping. Sevryn leaned still closer, enunciating his words closely, piercingly, to be remembered. "And it's this bloody Vaelinar who saved you."

The trader stared at him a moment, before his eyes rolled back into his skull and he lost all hearing.

He stalked a pace or two to the cutpurse's still form, and Sevryn looked the would-be thief over carefully. He should be sorry he'd killed him, but couldn't find the mercy within him. He pulled off the dead man's well-made boots. If not a fit, it was close enough. He'd have herb powder in them first, though, to sweeten the stink and kill off any bugs that came with them.

Sevryn tucked the boots under his arm and jogged away, quickly, to a safe distance before letting out a shout and hail that would attract attention. No sense letting the trader lie there as prey for someone else. He kept moving as the tavern door was flung open, amber light spilled out, and the street filled with curious onlookers.

He weighed the purse in his hand. Quite a bit if he was any judge, and if he were in a town with a traders' post, there had to be amenities somewhere as well—even if he must keep a low profile—baths, and an inn with door-latching rooms. Trotting through the back streets, he located a few places and kept circling, eventually pausing at the rear of a laundry. Inside, he could hear the women folding laundry that had been washed and dried during the day, and he could smell the bubbling cauldrons of hot soapy water, waiting for the next batch. He considered chancing a bath here for free in one of the said cauldrons but thought better of it. The water might scald him badly, and he had no wish to be found stealing a bath when he could pay for it. Clothes, however, were another matter.

Squeezing through the back gate, he made his way into the storeroom where piles of dry clothes waited to be picked up. He found what he needed—pants, shirt, greatcoat—and slipped back out while the women gossiped and pinched one another over a recent marriage, a coming baby, and someone's mean-tempered aunt, as if the lands had no greater concern. Perhaps they hadn't, as far as the laundry drudges were concerned.

He pried open his pouch. One gold crown, a handful of gold half crowns, and a wealth of silver ten pieces shone at him. He fished out a piece of ten, knowing it would pay for bath, barber, and silence. He hung the pouch around his neck, tucking it far inside his shirt, before making his way to the baths.

Inside, he found plenty of hot water, herbed soap, an excellent attendant who promptly fetched a good barber, burned his clothes without comment, brought more herbs to treat the head and boot lice, and managed to bring a trencher with hot stew and a cold beer, all of which were handled before the dawn's first light.

He canvassed the streets by daylight, fleeting as a shadow himself, still aching. By lane and sign, he realized he was in Brelin, a small backwater far from the mountains in which he and Gilgarran had come to ruin. The day warmed, the sun wan yet still strong despite the season. He paused as he came upon a fairer part of the city, and listened to the sound of children laughing.

No matter where he'd roamed, that sound seemed the same. It warmed him as the sunlight could not, and he paused to bask in it, letting it wash over him like the soothing waters of the bath he'd found late last eve. He could hear the slap, slap of a jumping rope and the stomp of shoed feet and boots in rhythm with the laughter, a few jeers, and the clap of hands now and then. Sevryn pushed closer, the corner of his mouth upturned as he listened.

He could hear them chanting now, the girls, underscored by the voice of a lad or two, as they danced and jumped to the skipping rope.

"Four forges dire
Earth, Wind, Water, and Fire,
You skip low
And I'll jump higher.
One for thunder
By lands torn asunder
Two for blood
By mountains over flood.
Three for soul
With no place to go . . ."

He bolted into their midst as his body went cold and grabbed the nearest girl by her elbow. Their chant stopped immediately, and they stared at him with big eyes. One or two darted away. He fought for breath, forcing it in and out of his icy chest.

"What is that you chant? Where did you hear it? Who taught it to you?"

The Kernan girl he'd captured stared at him, one eye brimming with an unshed tear, and scuffed her shoe upon the ground. "Why . . . you did, sir."

He dropped her arm, stepping back in shock. "I . . . what?"

"Don't you remember? You taught us . . ." She hung back, and then, as one, the remaining children turned and raced away from him, leaving nothing behind but the tangle of their dropped rope on the dusty street.

Sevryn put the palms of his hands to his eyes and let out a broken cry. He did not remember it, if he'd ever known it, but he forced it back into his skull now, and then stood, shaking. Something he'd known and could not have forgotten, he'd put into rhyme. Something he had never wanted to lose, and yet . . . had. He felt the need for another bath, healing, cleansing, and turned about, trembling so hard he could barely make his way.

He did not know what he'd known, once. But he could not forget it again.

He left the baths a second time a far cleaner and even more thoughtful man, the slender youth he'd been at Gilgarran's side grown to manhood and no longer able to pass as a callow lad. In idle talk overheard as he soaked, recuperating, another shock stabbed through him. It had been nearly eighteen years since they had made their fatal journey. He'd been lost and was just now being found. He would have mourned those lost years, but that he savored finding life again, and he'd brought with him a mystery that he needed to solve.

Chapter Five

721–723 AE

STAYING IN BACK ALLEYS suited him. He found cleaner, nicer streets to frequent, and swapped out clothes for when he traveled them, but many interesting things often dropped in alleys that couldn't be found in other parts of the city. For instance, that was how Sevryn had met Gilgarran.

Crouched behind a bakery sifting through troughs for burned crusts of bread and whatever else he could scrounge, cast aside by his parent, he'd been living on the streets for as long as he could remember. Quick-fingered but savvy, he stole only the worthless, avoiding guards and guardhouses. Sometimes he ran messages and gambling chits for meals or even a silver piece now and then, but he didn't earn much that way because he wouldn't join a street gang.

Not that a gang would have him if his lineage had been discovered, but his ears were barely pointed, and his stormy gray eyes showed none of the multijeweled qualities of most Vaelinars. Only his age could betray him, for he matured slowly, having inherited at least the potential for the long life span rumored of them. Some said they lived a full handful of centuries, others said they were near immortal. If the gangs were not so interested in themselves, they might have noticed that he stayed young, far younger than they, as they grew older. Stockier and shorter, too, than the high elves, he had spent most of his life successfully hiding from the scorn held for Vaelinars or half bloods among the true blood of Kerith. No one had a use for a half blood. Vaelinars, because the Talent for strange powers and magic rarely passed through, tainting their heritage, and the others because of their hatred for the invaders and sometime slavers. Never mind that the Vaelinars had brought new ways of doing things that were beneficial to all. They had also brought Godlike powers, and hatred, and war. Better to be dead than to be thought elven. Or, as the Kernan proverb went, "Better Death should knock on your door than a Vaelinar."

He found a place for himself as he finally grew into a young man's stature at the traders' stables whenever the caravans coming in had fork-horns pulling the carts. The immense bovines had their racks sawn off and capped, but that made them uneasy and difficult to handle. They could no longer defend themselves as they'd grown used to, and in an animal way, that drove them berserk from time to time. Though devoid of horns, their weight and hooves could be extremely dangerous and their ill temper kept the stable boys far from them, afraid of being crushed or trampled. He could move among them, talking, petting, soothing them into settling down to be groomed and harnessed, or unharnessed and corralled. It proved a steady and legitimate way of earning coin. Along the way, as he occasionally saved up to visit a tavern, he found his ability to soothe could keep him out of other troubles as well, avoiding recalcitrant drunks and bullies. Occasionally, though, when the seasons changed, fork-horns would be replaced on the trails by mules, and he would lose his income for a while, relegated to scrounging from the alleys to stretch out his meager savings. He thought to train his weapon skills, to be hired as a caravan guard when he was grown enough. Traders hired small, private armies of guards and kept them well.

It was on such a raw and hungry day between seasons and work that Gilgarran fell on him from an upper story window. Knocked to the ground, Sevryn lay flat under the man and only knew that trouble had hit him hard. He twisted out from under, immediately falling into his soothing voice to scramble away before his attacker's attackers fell on them both in pursuit. The gentleman wore fine clothes, and a mask, and good weapons, and everything spelled awful trouble.

"*I'm no one to bother with. I'm just going to walk away and everything will be fine,*" he started, as he clambered to his feet, spreading his hands wide in supplication.

"*Velk,*" spat the man. He rolled, knocking Sevryn's feet out from under him, and pounced, kneeing him and grabbing him by the ear. "Who are you to use a Voice on me?"

"N–nobody," Sevryn stammered as he panted for air. The knee on his chest kept him pinned, and then the gentleman pulled at him.

"Get up. Which way out, before we're chased."

His ear pinched painfully between fingers that felt as hard as steel, Sevryn carefully got to his feet and jabbed with his thumb.

"On, then, and don't think you can outrun me. Quickly!"

The grip on his ear released. Sevryn broke for freedom as if a pot of boiling oil had been tossed at him, and the master ran after, effortlessly, right on his heels. He dodged throughout the town, keeping to the shadows, desperate but not so heedless as to give his secrets away to anyone. Anyone that is, but the man trailing him. They crossed into the derelict section, on the town's far edge, where not even the desperate lived. Sevryn took him to his dodge hole, a cavern at the edge of an abandoned warehouse, deserted because of fire, with the timbers left creaking and swaying unreliably. It still stank of its ruination, a heavy, choking reek of devastation by flame.

Sevryn squatted on his heels in the corner of the lean-to, and looked at the gentleman who, at least, had to catch his breath. Behind Sevryn was a rotting half barrel which led to a tunnel through the precarious debris of the warehouse itself, an escape route for him that any sane person would think about a number of times before going after him if Sevryn made a break for it.

The gentleman caught his breath, narrowed eyes hard to see through the silken mask, but observing him. When he could speak evenly, which was before Sevryn could catch his own breath, that fact alone dismaying, he said again, "Who in the hell are you to use Voice on me?"

He thought of doing it again to calm the man down, but it didn't seem prudent. "No one. I'm a gutter brat. I don't know what you mean, but that's the way I talk to the caravan animals at the traders' stables. I can handle them, sometimes, when no one else can. I can soothe them. I get paid for it, when the stables are busy. When they're not, I mine the streets for whatever I can get."

"Calm them down, eh?" His visitor took his hands off his knees, and straightened, but he was too tall for the dodge hole, and had to bend a bit. "Do I look like an irate pack animal?"

Actually, he sounded rather like he could bellow like a fork-horn. Sevryn clamped his lips shut tight, holding that thought.

His visitor stayed wary, eyeing Sevryn. "Ever use it on a man?"

"Only sometimes. Drunks. No one who could remember me. I don't want any trouble."

"So you said." The other assessed him for a long moment. "Tell me your name."

That, he wouldn't do. "No one," he said evenly. "I'm just no one."

The man pulled off his mask. The startling, swift beauty of his blue-green eyes with their streaks highlighting the iris hit him, as did the planes of his face, and the points of his ears. He stared at the high-bred Vaelinar. "Tell me your name," the man repeated, staring into Sevryn's own, plain stormy gray eyes.

"I . . . I haven't got a proper one. No one admits to my birthing."

The Vaelinar took a deep breath. "One last chance, and if you've half the smarts you seem to have, you'll be telling me the truth. You know what I am. I don't recommend lying to me."

He bit the inside of his cheek, one hand moving behind him to touch the side of the rotting barrel, readying for another escape. "Sevryn," he said. "That's all to it. No House, no lineage."

"You've Vaelinar blood." Tension left the gentleman's body as he folded his mask neatly and tucked it an inner pocket of his cloak, seeming to have gotten what he wanted. "You know that, I presume."

It seemed futile to deny it, in the face of the other. He nodded.

"Who was your mother?"

"I barely remember. She was an herbalist. She made powders and fine soaps and scented candles, and she dumped me here. We didn't even live in the same town, and I can't remember where we came from anymore." He shrugged.

The other arched an eyebrow. "Kernan, then? Likely. Your father would be the one you don't know at all."

It didn't seem a question, but Sevryn answered it anyway. He nodded again.

"She brought you here and left you?"

Old feelings tightened his throat. He would look away if he could, but the eyes of the other drew him, like a moth to a sputtering candle flame, darting in and out of its influence and glamour. "She . . . she went after him, and never came back. There was a flood. South, where she went. Everyone said, such a shame. A shame." He wrenched his gaze away, his words strangled by memory.

"And she certainly had a name . . ."

"Mista. She read the weather, too. People would come from far away and bring her things. Leaves. Twigs with moss. Caterpillars. She would read the seasons ahead, and tell people when to plant, what to grow, when to shear." Sevryn put his chin up then. She had a worth. They had had a worth. He hadn't been turned out till her coin ran out, and her return was so long overdue, only the worst could be imagined. Lost. He'd lost her. Mista of the long sable hair fixed with many small jeweled combs, combs her lover, *he'd*, bought for her and which she'd sold one by one while they'd journeyed to look for *him*. Beautiful in Sevryn's memory with her sable hair and light blue eyes, smiling at him as she reached out to push aside his own unruly hair, reading his face just as she read the leaves and mosses of faraway places. His father had had gray eyes, like his own, she would murmur to him. Well, not like his own. His father had had Vaelinar eyes of many colors, rich and striking.

"Ah."

Sevryn cleared his throat roughly.

"Time passes differently for us than others," the Vaelinar commented. "He may have forgotten that."

Sevryn cleared his throat again and spat to one side, dismissing the father who'd left them.

"Well. This visit has surprised me in more ways than one." The other leaned a shoulder against a charred beam and the whole lean-to creaked ominously. He made a fist and rapped his knuckles against the wood. He looked to Sevryn again.

Sevryn felt himself color. "I . . . hmmm . . . have it rigged for noise. Just in case. It's lashed tightly, but it sways and moans."

"Good idea. It does seem a good deal more unsafe than it is. All right. Here is the thing. You've Vaelinar blood. Most of my kin would just as soon see you dead as would the others of Kerith for that, but I feel that blood is blood. I've my own ideas about the purity of our line and what our get have to offer. I've business to handle, but I'll be back for you." He looked about the bolt-hole. "You stay here?"

"Only if there's reason. I've lodging of a kind in town."

"Stay here on nights when the moon is full. Can you manage that? I don't know when I'll be back, but I will."

"But—"

"What? You have better prospects?"

Sevryn closed his mouth. He didn't like the idea of another winter when the traders' stables would be nearly shut down from the weather, and his life on the streets that much harder. Soon enough, the traders would notice that he did not age as they did, and he'd have to move on anyway. It had happened before and would again. "No."

"My name is Gilgarran. Use it, and I will know, and you'll be dead for your indiscretion."

"That is hardly incentive for me to stay to meet you."

The Vaelinar chuckled. "True, but it's only fair of me to warn you." He put his hand out. "Shake on an unlikely partnership."

"Partnership?"

"I need an apprentice and you need to find out who the hell you are." He waited, a touch of impatience dancing in his aquamarine eyes, lighter streaks accenting them with liveliness. The stud in his ear winked as though a star had been brought down from the skies.

Sevryn stirred. It was one of those moments when he knew the whole world, his part of it anyway, would change by what he did at that moment. Some people could move through life unaware of decisions that so affected them, but he could not. Something as minor as squashing a bug or as major as pledging a partnership could and would change his world. Of course, those moments were few and far between, but he recognized this one. He straightened, took his hand out from behind his back, wiped it on his trousers to clean it as best he could, before placing it in the other's hold.

They shook. The strength of the fingers he knew from a still throbbing ear, but this was tempered strength, and a warmth, and . . . a promise. He could feel it leap between them.

Gilgarran opened his hand then and stepped back. He fished inside his cloak, and coins jingled as he opened a purse. "I can't leave you with crowns or even half crowns, too many questions. Here are pieces of silver, and a few ten pieces. Use them wisely. The road for me may be long or short, and it may be a full turn of seasons before I'm back here. You'll make it through?"

Sevryn nodded as Gilgarran dropped the coins into his palm. "Yes, sir, I will."

And he did. Made it that long and longer before the elf returned, and took him as apprentice and showed him many things in the world he had never thought could be. There wasn't a moment he regretted the handshake or how it had changed him, only the after moments when he mourned having lost Gilgarran before either was ready to let go. Foster father, big brother, teacher. And he never thought to ask just what it was

Gilgarran had been doing when he'd leaped out of that third-story window to fall upon Sevryn.

Using all that he'd learned in his early years, sharpened and honed by what he'd been taught in his later years, Sevryn moved inconspicuously through the small trade road towns, earning a modest living doing little of anything and keeping out of the notice of whomever he could. A full twenty turns of all the seasons had gone by since that day at the forge—though he could only remember the last two—and he knew of no way to reclaim those lost years. In his life span, with the Vaelinar blood strong in him, two decades showed little except he had grown more toward maturity, but others who might have known him or Gilgarran were much older now if Kerith blooded. He did not seek to find that past or approach it. If he were being watched, he revealed nothing. If he were being trailed, he could not detect it, but if he were the hunter, he doubted he would be seen, so he took nothing for granted.

He eventually made his way to Calcort, the great hub of all the trader and craft guilds, the capital as it were of the far-flung cities of Kerith, where guildsmen reigned like kings of far far ancient times, and though he listened to the hubbub he learned little of what he truly wished to know. He kept his coin stocked by gambling at the taverns where luck did not seem to have abandoned him, although all else had. Even the alleyways seemed determined to keep their secrets from him.

Then one day he learned of a Vaelinarran entourage coming to Calcort and the lure, the need, of seeing and hearing those who had imprinted his blood and destiny hit him hard. He made plans.

Chapter Six

"I WOULD NEVER QUESTION your wisdom, but—"

"Yet you do." Lariel turned on her half brother, with a toss of her head that sent gold and silver highlights shimmering through her long platinum hair and her eyes of three colors, cobalt blue, sky blue, and silver lightning streaks, and watched him closely. Her face was all moon, sun, and sky, and its beauty gave him pause for a moment, bratty sister and bother that she had always been. The wall and door framed her, with the window at her shoulder, shuttered though it was, letting through glimmers of light to set motes dancing about her. She stood balanced, her lean and toned body, despite her formal gown, at the ready, her stance that of a swordswoman rather than a dancer.

Jeredon Eladar rocked back on one heel. No less formidable than his Warrior Queen sister, he deferred to her because she was what she was, ruler of Larandaril, and she had decided to make this trip to Calcort and meet with Thom Stonehand in spite of his own misgivings. Kernans and Galdarkans didn't have the answers she sought. If the Vaelinars did not know, no one did. If she had misgivings, she did not show them. A ruler had to believe in her decisions, once made. Lariel Anderieon stood under the high-arched ceiling of the best room the modest inn had to offer, far from the rooms of their holdings in Larandaril, and far from the best those lands could provide, and her eyes flashed as she waited for him to counter her.

"Vaelinars are liked no better here than in most of Kerith," he said mildly.

Her hand twitched in the silver-blue folds of her gown. Her mouth curved once or twice, then she answered, "What troubles us will trouble all of Kerith."

"You'll admit to them we are troubled, then? Vulnerable?" Jeredon pulled out a chair, turning it backward so he could sit leaning his arms on the ladder-back, and watched her as he straddled it.

Her mouth twitched, and she cleared her throat. "We have a concern about our fellows of Kerith. Our knowledge of the lands shows us that there are problems developing which can yet be turned away, but they need us to teach them how best to deal with it." Words meant not for him but composed for the mayor.

"Ah, the diplomat emerges." Jeredon flashed a grin.

She tossed her head again, angry, but not letting the emotion escape her lips as she marched a step closer to him. "You would do better?"

"If I were the younger instead of the elder, and king instead of half brother to the queen, I think I'd simply burn them out to protect our lands and let them fear us again instead of despising us as they do now. That might not solve our immediate problem, but it would give us the time and space to find out what is encroaching upon Larandaril."

The queen sat down wearily on the edge of her bed, and his sister emerged. "Burning them out might be exactly what we need to do. They can't even manage their own waste!"

"That is only part of the problem, and we know that."

"They press in on us, Jeredon. They lean on us, they crush us."

"They're drawn to what we offer, even as much as they hate us," he reminded her. "They need us, too. Some even still revere us. It's why they settle on our borders. We raised them up from mud and sticks—well, not all of them, but many—and they want more. The wars of the Magi left them in rubble, where they once knew more, and we showed them what could be achieved again."

"Well I know." A finger traced the air in resignation.

"Then why must I tell you this?"

"We brought our own wars," she reminded him.

"And we tithe to them, through the Accords. They all found a way to stick their hand out, aggrieved by us or not. And you think this Stonehand will welcome your proposal? That he will take the hundreds of families you wish to depose from our borders and ship them off here?"

Lariel brushed a hand through her silvery hair. Gold shimmered as she did so, gold in single strands, and gold rings on her fingers. "I don't know. I wish I had the Talent for that. It isn't mine to see tomorrow."

"Talent doesn't solve our lives for us, Sister. It merely enhances it." He quoted their teachers, chapter and verse.

Lariel picked up a bed pillow and threw it at him, with dead aim, and even he, with his quickness, couldn't dodge it. Laughing, he slipped sideways from his chair and feigned death as he hit the floorboards.

"Oh, get up, you oaf."

"No. I am dead. You'll have to send for the after-healers."

"After-healers!" She scoffed at him. "A myth even to us. If such a Talent existed, we would never die." She threw another pillow at him.

"Aderro," he pleaded. "Save me!"

Lariel broke into laughter. She got up from the bed, kneeled down beside him, her mouth arched as she bent down, preparing to give him the fabled kiss of life. Jeredon tried not to grin as her face neared his forehead. Instead, she doubled up her hand and punched him in the stomach, making him gasp for air. He rolled on the floor, flailing to breathe like a fish reeled in on a hook to land, and she sat down next to him, still laughing. His fault, he'd taught her how to fight like that. He rubbed his stomach's seized muscles and sucked for air.

At least he'd made her laugh. When he finally caught his breath, he jumped to his feet and gave her a hand up. They dusted each other off, waiting for the carriage to take them to the grand rooms of the mayor's office and the conference they had requested. "I suggest you refrain from that particular form of diplomacy until we gain what we want, Sister," he advised, as he straightened his tunic. She threw a wicked grin at him.

"At least, I vow I'm ready for anything." She put her shoulders back. Both dressed in Vaelinarran finery, including the weapons belts about her waist and his shoulder, and the gleaming blades sheathed in them. The citizens of Calcort might not wish to defer to their Vaelinar visitors, but they would most certainly respect them, if they had to swallow a sword blade to do so.

Sevryn leaned back against the building, a clay jug that smelled of beer between his feet. The jug was filled mostly with cider, with just enough beer in it to give off a faint odor, if anyone were to stumble over him as he sat waiting. Anticipation shivered through his veins as he counseled patience to himself. It wasn't as if he'd never seen Vaelinars in the last seasons; he'd been brushed by several times, kicked once, and cursed at as well, but he'd never stood toe to toe in good graces with one, and he missed the kinship. He wondered if they would recognize in him that which Gilgarran had so patiently nurtured. He could wait. He knew what he had to offer, and the day would come when the elves would stop, and look at him with consideration in their gaze instead of dismissal. Once he had counted himself as worthless; he knew far better now, even though Gilgarran's mission had failed. He would find himself a position from which he would eventually avenge his friend's death, but he could only do it one step at a time.

From his spot, he could see the mayor's courtyard and steps, opposite the columned building that was the traders' guild. Without seeming to notice it, sipping from his jug and singing a very soft drunken medley to himself about the winsome features of a barmaid, he sat, and the single guard who patrolled the alley passed by, saying to him, "When you're finished with that, move along," and he nodded back amiably, sprawled, apparently harmless.

Unless the guard were to pat him down and discover the five blades he had positioned about his body. Underarmed that day, Sevryn had decided not to weigh himself down too heavily in case he needed to sprint for it. As he pondered his options, he could hear the clopping of a high-stepping pair of carriage horses. The carriage pulled into the courtyard, and he could hear the scuffle of attendants running to meet it. Good horses had come with the Vaelinars. Before that, Kerith stock was mostly small and scrubby if sturdy ponies, but Vaelinarran steeds were horses out of ballads and poetry. Through the centuries, they'd been interbred selectively until all the horse stock greatly improved, even the stocky ponies. These had the looks of the tashya about them, the hot bloods. Footmen came out to hold the pair still. Without appearing to do so, Sevryn looked up under the brim of the old hat he wore, and watched the carriage rock as a man stepped down, then handed a woman out.

If her looks were not enough to identify her, her movement was. She moved with a contained grace, certifying that he watched the queen of the valley holding of Larandaril. Her older half brother Jeredon would be the man escorting her, and he was all the guard she had with her despite a small crowd of people, shifting and unhappy, staring and grumbling at the visit. He wondered why she'd come to Calcort and its Mayor Stonehand, but word would filter down to him soon enough. The walls to such meetings always had ears, sometimes too many, and the information would be garbled until sorted through for the nuggets of truth that mattered. He'd already had some word that the queen was unhappy with the settlements upon her borders, but he could not count that as anything more than gossip.

Sevryn lifted his jug to his mouth and sipped, obscuring his face should anyone feel his observation and look his way. He thought he'd escaped attention, but as they started up the steps, Lariel Anderieon halted and turned partially about, her gaze sweeping the area. She wore a flowing dress of dark, silvery blue that mimicked the colors of her silvery hair with its tones of gold in the silver strands of the fabric. She'd buckled her sword on for a quick cross draw, and he knew from that alone she would use it. Not only a queen of warriors, but a queen who could fight on her own. He'd heard that of her, and Gilgarran had always spoken well of her, despite her impetuosity. He shrank back a little against the building, slouched as if giving in to the drink in his jug and her gaze did not linger, but she turned to her brother and said something before taking the stairs and entering the Grand Hall. He would have been disappointed if she had not sensed something, however. The crowd watching continued to mill about until the mayor's guards spread through them and, like honey stirred into a hot drink, they swirled about and then slowly disappeared.

He should leave. The mayor's guard would be by again, to see if he'd left as he'd been told to do, and he'd seen what he'd come to see. The vision of both Jeredon and Lariel filled his soul for a moment until he realized he was like a starving man, and the vision but a sniff of the aroma of a banquet. He didn't want to leave. He decided to wait until rousted, or until the meeting ended and he could see them again, and perhaps tail them to wherever they stayed while in Calcort. He thought he might get close enough to utter a few soft words that would both save his life for encroaching upon them and catch their interest. He held his jug close to his chest, for it would be his first weapon in case of trouble and watched the clouds drift through the sky overhead as the day wore on.

He must have slipped into a bit of sleep, more lulled by the beer and cider than he thought, for he woke, drowsy, to the sound of something padding by very quietly. They startled each other, he and the intruder, his head jerking back in wakefulness at the other's closeness. The other bent down, hand pinching his neck, free hand dropping a half crown in his lap. Of shadow-dark material, the sleeved arm told him little except for indicating a certain wealth and eccentric taste in clothing, and a height from the reach and slenderness that indicated Galdarkan, Vaelinar, or mixed blood. No rings on the fingers but little scars from the handling of many blades, large and small, over time. He smelled of oil as well, weapon oil. Sevryn held himself very still as soft words drifted down to him.

"Go back to your tavern and drink well. A wise man would forget he saw me here."

Sevryn stared dumbfounded at the coin, burnished gold, trying to catch sight of his benefactor from the corner of his eye. Tall, eyes of hazel, hair of flowing sable, Vaelinar height and slender, almost out of his vision entirely. But not quite.

Sevryn's hand shot out to clutch the gold greedily and he mumbled something about food and drink and wenching. The hand on his neck relaxed, and with barely another sound, the man behind him scaled the wall up to the fourth-floor roof with an uncanny grace and a few well-placed hooks to aid him.

Sevryn waited for the sound of shifting roof tiles before he moved.

"A wiser man would have known better than to leave me behind him." Or to have tried to use suggestion on him, akin to but far clumsier than his own Voice. With an ironic twist to his mouth, Sevryn pocketed the half crown, striding into the courtyard where only a guard stayed by the front steps, and all appeared very quiet as even the carriage horses seemed to doze in the late afternoon sun. A moment touched him, and he knew beyond a doubt his future changed here, a moment he had not felt so keenly since that day he had shaken hands with Gilgarran. His vision darkened, then quickened, and lightning jolted through him, that swiftly, that intensely, that shivery and blinding, then gone. He hadn't felt it in decades, and had thought it burned out of him, hammered out of him, by those lost years. His hand clenched reflexively.

What should he do here? No hint of that, only that what he would do, ultimately, would change his life forever. No going back, whatever decision he made. Sevryn inhaled.

Gaining the courtyard, he spread his feet and planted himself. He pitched his voice and called with all of his Talent, carrying through wall and roof and stone and wood, aiming it like an arrow for its target, knowing that Vaelinarran ears would not fail to hear him. Not queen or armsman or assassin, though he could not help that. *"Jedael, Lariel. Navakke renti!" Take care, Lariel. The enemy hunts.*

He drew his blade, jug in his left hand as a clumsy shield, and waited for the effect of his cry.

Shouts erupted upstairs. Windows flew open, whistles pierced the afternoon. He could hear the crash of chairs and the clash of steel, one scream of pain, more yells and crashes. Then the assassin appeared on a second-story balcony and leaped, sword ready, with only Sevryn between him and freedom. His clothes of shadowsilk flowed about him as he landed, gathered himself, and lunged at Sevryn, eyes narrowed. No war lance could have hit him more surely.

Sevryn countered, but the other moved in with catlike quickness. He had the weight to put behind his hits, and drove the assassin back on his heels once. Shadowsilk rippled. The swordsman would have skewered him then, as Sevryn drove in, but the clay pot took the blow, shattering on his hand and protecting his rib cage. They exchanged another blow and parry before the front doors burst open, blades catching upon each other, ringing. The assassin gave Sevryn a look, stepped back, saluted him, and turned to sprint down the alley. Sevryn dropped his guard.

A poor move. The assassin turned in the middle of the alley, steel shining in his hand, and the thrown dagger hit home hard, punching Sevryn in the ribs and spinning him around and off his feet. He doubled over, curling down onto the street, his hand filling with blood as he clutched himself.

Guards engulfed him. He pointed down the alley, and boots thundered off. Two remained behind. He looked up to see Lariel, her hair in disarray, a bloodied sword in hand, and her brother with her as he knelt by Sevryn, unclenching Sevryn's fingers to move his hand away from the dagger carefully, then nodding to Lariel. "He'll be fine."

He did not feel it. Blurriness edged his vision of her.

"Was it you who spoke?" She looked down on them, both imperious and concerned.

"Aye, my queen."

She frowned, eyeing him. "Keep the dagger. Not many can say they met a Kobrir hand to hand and lived to tell about it."

Sevryn blinked. He looked down at the dagger in his side, point scraping painfully against a rib bone, as blood welled out, and saw the intricate K worked into the hilt. Legendary assassin, for whom the Accords had no significance or honor. He killed without discrimination or hesitation, and few lived to say they had been a target! "I . . . thank you." He felt a little faint, the sight of his own blood had always bothered him, and his thoughts spun a little.

"Get him up, Jeredon, and bring him back to the inn. I want to know how this street rat learned good Vaelinar. And how he managed to shout it up to us." She brushed her hand over his forehead, lifting off the old hat of disguise and pushing away a shock of hair, to see his eyes. She traced a fingertip about one high-tipped ear before stepping back to let Jeredon at him. Her face puzzled, she let her brother lift him up, both grunting, one with his added weight and blood seeping out his own leg wound, and he with the dagger twisting in his rib muscles. Jeredon put his shoulder under his arm, hoisting him, and walked him toward the waiting carriage. She hesitated as the mayor and his guard thundered out of the hall.

"You'll come with us, or we'll leave you to the mayor's kind ministrations."

An invitation. Was it? His thoughts muddled a bit, and he concentrated. Jeredon stood at the carriage, waiting. She stood next to her brother, waiting as well.

"I'll come with you." He knew the moment. It had already come and gone, and he'd already cast his fortune with it.

Jeredon boosted him into the carriage.

A step at a time, Sevryn moved into his future.

He only wished it was not with excruciating pain.

Chapter Seven

723 AE, Yellow Moon Month

"BOYS ARE STUPID, made of rotten wood," Nutmeg chanted softly to herself as she sat on the grassy bank, picking and braiding willow grass with its tiny snowdrop flowers as fast as she could, deliberately ignoring her brother who knelt at the river's edge to drink his fill of storm-cold water.

"Now, now, little bit," Garner Farbranch addressed his sister. "Rotten wood? That's a bit rough, don't you think?" He gestured at their orchards framing the land as far as they could see on either side of the river, boughs heavy with apples and nuts, the wind still lashing them to and fro with the sound of a frantic sea.

She twisted away so she wouldn't have to look at him, hands flashing with a nimble ease and quickness, her bow of a mouth curved in an intense study as she wove herself a willow-grass doll, amber curls tumbling heedlessly about her face, the sun bringing a blush to her cheeks and bits of cinnamon color to her warm brown eyes. She wore patched overalls, but a frilly blouse left no doubt as to her small but ultimate feminity.

He splashed a touch of brook water at her.

Her lips pouted. "Go 'way!" She moved her grass doll through the air. "Boys are squirmy 'cause they're all wormy!"

Garner hid a laugh behind a cough as he settled back on his heels to watch her. "All this because we won't let you climb the ladders?"

She flung an accusatory look at him. "I can do it! I can climb faster than any of you!"

"Without a doubt," Garner avowed firmly. "Faster than me, Hosmer, or Keldan. But Da doesn't know that, and he and Mom would skin us alive if they knew we were letting you climb. So you can't, understand? The wind is still up, and the ladders are twitchy and it's dangerous out there, so we can't let you shinny up. The branches would throw you across the orchard."

Nutmeg tossed her head. She danced her doll around in the air, claiming, "Boys are stinky 'cause . . . 'cause . . ." her childish voice faltered.

"Boys are smelly 'cause they're covered in swamp jelly," Garner teased back gently.

"Yeah!" Nutmeg crossed her arms. "I can help. I know I can."

He scooted over next to her, the youngest of them all, and the only girl, and put his arm around her. She was half his size—one of his best memories was the day she'd been born and had wrapped her tiny fist tightly about his finger.

Nutmeg sighed at her brother. He smelled of apples and leaves and the last of the storm wind, and she leaned into him.

"Sweetling, there's plenty of time for you to climb ladders. Really."

"But that's tomorrow, and today is now. It's not fair. I can't have a sister and now I can't go climbing." She wrapped her arms about herself tightly.

"And we're all sorry about all of that. Listen, Mom's going to need you tonight, when we're all tired and dirty and the cider presses are going, and she's in the kitchen 'cause we'll be *starving*. You know that, don't you?"

"But that . . . that . . . that's *work*."

Garner smiled wryly. "So is ladder climbing and harvesting if you do it enough. Trust me." He hugged her again, and stood. "And I'd better get back. or Da will have a switch waiting for me, and we don't want that!"

"Maybe you don't," Nutmeg pouted, "but I don't care!"

He tweaked her nose. "Course you do! I'm your favorite!" He dropped some apples for her to snack on and he sprinted off, the big canvas bag hanging from his shoulder flopping about his legs as he ran before she could pelt him in the back with her wicked aim.

"Favorite shmavorite!" she managed to yell after him. His wind-caught laugh came back to her, and Nutmeg smiled then, giggling at herself.

She sat back down with her willow-grass doll. "Sisters," she told the doll, "would be as nice as brothers. Some day."

Nutmeg lay back on the grass and watched the clouds till she yawned and decided a nap might be good. Her stomach growled faintly. First, an apple. Then a nap. She picked up the best-looking one, buffed it on her sleeve, and bit into it, abuses of power forgotten.

Tolby Farbranch emptied a canvas bag into the wagon bed, apples rolling about with a gentle thunder. "How is she doing, then?"

"Oh, she's bored. She wants to grow up."

Keldan, of the flashing blue eyes and jet-black hair, darted past his older brother. Hosmer had gray-gold hair, and Garner gray-brown hair like their dad's brindled salt-and-pepper hair. Their mother sat on the wagon's seat, watching them all with a smile. Keldan liked to tell them that he inherited all the hair worth anything in the Farbranch family though exactly where he'd inherited it from was something of a mystery. Lily had soft brunette hair that held some of the glimmer of her daughter's amber hair, and, though pale, she rode the board seat firmly. She held bone needles in her hands, placidly knitting a scarf that flowed across her lap in the colors of the autumn sea.

"I don't like her being by the flood banks," Garner said, in the august if changing voice of the nearly grown. "The Silverwing can be treacherous."

"She'll be safe there," Lily remarked. "She can swim even better than she can climb, and she can climb a caution."

Garner and Hosmer had ducked their heads to gather up empty bags and make their way back into the orchard, but their mother's voice rooted them to the ground and they traded looks.

"True," their father grunted, giving his wife a peck on the cheek as he climbed out of the wagon and swung to the ground. He looked at his unmoving sons. "What? Do you think a father doesn't know what his children are up to? Besides, Nutmeg was the youngest of all of you t' climb out of her cradle. I doubt she stopped, eh?"

"Well, then . . . why don't you let her harvest with us? We could use the extra hands."

"Because she'd scare me out of a year's growth, throwing herself up the rungs and over the treetops, and I need my height, such as it is, to stand up to those Kernan traders looking down their snooty noses at me," Tolby declared.

"I do believe," Lily said quietly, "they have far more to fear from you, my dear."

Tolby looked up at his wife, and then cracked an ear-to-ear grin. "I'd hoped they'd forgotten!" he shouted, and reached up to slap her on the knee. Lily's voice rang out in soft laughter, the first they'd heard from her in weeks, and it made all the boys jump with a laugh of their own.

Word was, Tolby had once had quite a temper, and it had been suggested that the Dweller would be better off out of the city and in the countryside, where he could knock heads with logs as thick as his rather than with his fellow citizens. His sons didn't know the truth of that, one way or the other, only that their father commanded a rough respect whenever they went to any of the towns. He was known for his honesty, hard work, and good products, whether it be fresh or dried apples or cider or, rarely, hard cider. Still, he held a flash in his eyes and his sons traded looks again, as they took up their harvesting bags. Short though Dwellers were in the scheme of things, often up to another's elbow or shoulder at best, their da could hold his own with any man. They had no doubt of that.

"I had a switch around here for slower pickers," Tolby commented, looking about, and the boys scattered like leaves on the wind, with peals of laughter. He took the last two bags for himself, and lingered by his wife's shoe. He curled his hand about her shod foot, and Lily smiled down at him. "How are you feeling?"

"I mend. I am doing well," she answered. "Poor Nutmeg hurts worse than I do, and she can't begin to understand." She brushed a wisp of gray-and-brown hair from his creased forehead. "No more children for us, Master Farbranch. At least, not for a while, and not without the help of the Gods."

He squeezed her shoe. "Should I complain? Three sturdy sons and a beautiful daughter? Lily, you've given me all I could ever have dreamed, and more." He blew a kiss up to her. "Now it's back to work for me, or those three will decide to see if they're big enough to threaten *me* with a switch for slacking off." He chuckled and sauntered off, whistling, slinging a bag over each shoulder. Lily's smile stayed on her face as she watched him go, and the sadness did not return to her expression for a very long while.

At midday, Hosmer trotted down to the small glen to check on Nutmeg, to find her curled up with one hand under her apple-kissed cheek, sound asleep. He reported his findings to his mother before returning to the harvesting where the wind threatened to do half their work for them, bruising tender fruits as it dashed them to the ground. The sound of the wind-driven sea rose in their ears till Keldan's sharp, easily diverted attention caught the shrieks.

He threw himself off the ladder. "Mom, Da, it's Nutmeg!" He pelted through the orchards toward the noise.

Ladders toppled as the Farbranch men bailed on their tasks, gaining ground on the youngest and passing him, Hosmer and Garner narrowly beating Tolby. Lily jumped down and managed a stilted run to catch Keldan by the shoulder. Without protest, he braced himself under her arm as a living crutch and they hurried after.

Nutmeg's shrieks came excitedly, as she staggered toward them from the river, holding in her arms an oddly shaped bundle as tall as she was, and staggering from its weight. "She's mine, she's mine!" cried Nutmeg. "I found a sister and she's mine!"

"Tree's blood," sputtered Garner as he skidded to a halt, then clapped a hand over his mouth for such profanity. Distracted as he was, Tolby managed a cuff to his ears as he strode past his son and planted himself in front of Nutmeg who chuffed and puffed to a halt, and hoisted her bundle in her arms.

"What is that?"

"It's a girl!" Nutmeg told him. She began to fall over under the weight, and her brothers dove to catch both the sodden rags and their sturdy sister. Nutmeg sat down on her rump as Garner drew the tattered blanket away from her burden.

"It . . . is a girl." He blinked.

"She was on a pile of sticks in the river and I catched her," Nutmeg declared. "It was all broken up and she could barely hang on, but I catched her, and now she's *mine.*"

Lily joined them, smoothed Nutmeg's tousled hair from her face in a quick check to make sure she was all right, then bent down to see what Nutmeg had rescued. Her hand touched cold skin. "She's alive," Lily said. "But only barely." She traced her fingers about the other's face, gently lifting the tangled hair from her eyes and mouth and shapely ears, then caught her slender wrist, where cruel bracelets bit into her skin, gashing them, and the pain of her touch made the child blink for a moment at her before succumbing again to the darkness. Lily caught her breath. "And she's a Vaelinar and a slave."

Chapter Eight

"THE QUESTION REMAINS, then, how are we going to deal with her? And the first of you who says throw her back sleeps at the cider press tonight." Lily's eyes flashed a bit as she looked around the room at Tolby, Garner, and Hosmer. Her word had already been made good by banishing Keldan to the boys' loft at the back of the house where, even if he had his ear to a knothole in the floor, he wouldn't hear much of anything as Hosmer and Garner knew from years of experience. After the river's find, though scarcely conscious, had swallowed a goblet of apple juice as if starving, and Lily had pulled one of her old, worn nightgowns onto her, the girls had been tucked into Nutmeg's attic room, where the warmth crept upward at night. Nutmeg had pulled her into bed and stretched out beside her, body curling protectively about the girl under the quilt Lily tucked in about them.

The older Farbranches retreated to the main room for evening chores and talk, and although they sat doing casual things, they all knew there was a great decision at hand.

Tolby rocked back in his chair, pipe in hand, and studied the best way of lighting it, turning it over and over in his hands. A harvesting season though it was, the night held the edge of Frost Month to come, and no one wanted to sleep on the drafty wooden floors of the press even under a pile of blankets, where the machinery and building creaked, groaned, and leaned with every push of the wind and earth.

Hosmer decided to stoke up the small hearth fire a bit, and Garner turned his attention to sewing a patch on his second-best pair of trousers. No one spoke as he quickly put the patch into place, then he inhaled.

"Throwing her back's an idea," he murmured, pulling the thread through. " 'Course, we'd have to toss Nutmeg in, too, 'cause I think they're attached."

Lily let out a soft chuckle in spite of herself, leaned over, and gently pinched Garner's round ear. "Who can blame her for wanting a sister with great louts like you around? She wants someone to play with who is interested in more than beating each other with sticks."

Garner grunted as he dodged only a little from his mother's hand, and neatly tucked the bone needle into the patch after tying off his knot and biting the thread apart. His hair fell over his brow in careless waves as he did so, and he brushed it back impatiently. His elbow jostled Hosmer casually as he did so, and his brother roused from looking into the small fire.

"I don't want trouble," Hosmer remarked.

"What trouble could there be?" Tolby asked.

"She's one of the invaders."

"Who came to Kerith centuries ago, bringing much with them, including horses and tools we use today."

"Slavers," spat out Hosmer.

"Some, and those days are gone as well. What would you have me do?"

"Sell her to Bregan Oxfort. He'd pay well for her, he always needs an elven escort for the trade Ways." Hosmer rubbed his nose in defiance, not meeting his mother's stare, but watching his father's face instead to see how his words were being taken.

Lily made a sputtering noise, but Tolby cupped his hand over her knee. "I asked," he said mildly. "Let them answer."

"She already wears a slave bracelet. We didn't do that to her, we'd just be passing the trouble along."

"And, of course," Garner offered, "it's not like anyone would want to know how we got a slave?" His lip curled at his brother.

"Oxfort wouldn't ask. He'd just drop coins in our hands, and even if he did ask, we've got that. It would prove the tale." Hosmer jerked a thumb at the hearth and remains of a bundle of sticks lashed together with poor rags and leather scraps, hardly sturdy enough to float a sparrow downstream, let alone a body, but it had, though little had survived to be caught on weeping willow roots downstream. "If anyone is going to ask questions, I'd rather they'd be asking them of the Merchant Prince than bringing them to our door. No one would dare step on his toes for long. He's Kernan kind, and powerful, with armies to protect his caravans."

"What could we possibly gain by passing her along like that?" Tolby's hand stayed on his wife's knee, but it squeezed a little.

"Gain?" Hosmer threw one hand up in the air, in appeal. "Oh, Da. We could sharecrop the orchards and move into town. We could buy that vineyard salon you wanted, and you could retire from keeping the groves, and just work on your brew and warehousing. And Mom . . . Mom could be near healers when she needed them, and have a small tailoring shop like she used to when you first courted her, and make fine gowns when she felt like it, and there would be lots of girls for Nutmeg to play with, and a real school, too."

"I see you've been thinking about this for a while," Lily responded mildly.

"I have! Ever since that last band of Bolgers came through and rousted us for hard cider year before last. I swear they've developed a taste for it over that swill they call booze, and they'll be back again soon enough, and there will come a time when Da can't handle them and with us not around—" He ground to a halt.

"I see. Why is it you might not be around?" Tolby drew a small glowing stick from the fire.

Hosmer looked at his father closely. "I can't stay in orchards my whole life, Da. It isn't in me. Sooner or later, I'm going to go and see what I want to do."

Tolby nodded slowly. He looked at Garner who merely shrugged. "I've no plans," he said lightly. "Yet." As wiry as the others were stocky, one had to look closely at his face to see the Tolby in him; his looks favored Lily more.

"The trouble with young bucks," the older Dweller remarked, as he let go of his wife's knee and actually lit his pipe and took a puff on it. "Is that they're ready to butt heads before they know what a full rack of antlers is, and what weight they'll be carrying. And before the old buck is ready to retire."

Hosmer cleared his throat. "What can we do?"

"Think of it this way: what if it were Nutmeg? What if we did have Bolgers attacking, and we'd put her on a raft and floated her downriver to safety? How would you want her finders to treat her, eh?" Tolby's thick brows lowered heavily. "I shouldn't even have to ask."

"I'd kill anyone who hurt her," his oldest son declared. "You know that!"

"There may be a day when we can't be here to help Nutmeg, and she has to depend on strangers. What then? We were all newcomers once."

"Dwellers belong here," Hosmer answered defensively. "We're some of the first kin! We've never invaded or taken slaves."

"People are people."

Garner shifted weight. "Not to them," he said, backing up his brother. " 'Course," and he retreated a little. "I've seen Galdarkans bully, too."

"If she is valuable as a slave, we would have had riders through here already. I can't say how long she's been on the river rider, but she wouldn't have lasted more than a few more days. She's near starved. From what I know of Vaelinars, they don't age as we do and their lives are as long as the great trees of the north. She could easily be as old as Mom and I put together, yet still be a child."

"She is about Nutmeg's age, physically. Her teeth are still young, with ridges, although she's lost one," Lily said. She pushed a hand in her apron pocket and brought out the band which had served as a bracelet, with a ring forged to it for fastening chains. "This one slipped off over her hand. The other Da cut away, and she'll have scars from that, always it looks. The metal did more than gash her, it branded her as if . . ." Lily stopped uneasily. "As if something evil branded or tattooed itself into her flesh." She held it out to Hosmer. "Do you wish to put it back on her?"

He stared at the loathsome thing, rearing back. He glared at the floor before muttering, "No."

"Then what do we do?"

Hosmer looked up, the fire bringing out the gold over the gray in his hair. His gaze flickered with the thoughts running through his head. "We keep her," he said firmly.

"What if someone comes searching for her? Or sends Bolger hounds after her?"

Garner snorted. "Put her and Nutmeg in the onion-and-garlic cellar. They'll never smell 'em there!"

"Baths for a week!" chuckled Hosmer. "But it would work."

Tolby let out a satisfied cloud of smoke, perfuming the air with its spicy apple blend of toback and his own herbs. "Good lads. Now, I won't say I haven't been thinking of going to the city, but those plans are off a ways."

"Till the statute runs out on his charges anyway," Lily added and stood, gathering up the hem of her dress, merriment crossing her face, and sprinting away as quickly.

"Bah," said Tolby. He blew a smoke ring in her direction. "Off to bed, then, plenty of work tomorrow. Those apples won't wait for us!

The boys dashed off from the main room, circling through the kitchen where they could be heard getting a pannier of bread and cheese before thundering up the back stairs to their loft.

"Funny. I don't remember mentioning food." Tolby cocked his head, listening to his sons storm the staircase.

"I don't think it needed to be." She leaned down, kissing his temple. "Thank you."

"No thanks needed. They're good lads, they'd have come to the right conclusion on their own."

"And what is it *you* think?" Her hand twisted in her apron.

"I think it's astonishing how quickly the Gods decided to give us another girl, my love."

"By the grace of the river." Lily looked up at the ceiling beams toward the other part of the house, where Nutmeg and the stranger slept.

"Rivergrace. Good name for a new Farbranch." Leaning out of his chair, he picked up the scraps of the raft and tossed it in the fireplace. The wood caught smokily, and the leather lashings flared up with a great stink as the fire began to consume the evidence.

Lily waved away the smell, coughing. "Tolby! Next time you've something smelly to burn, do it outside!" She dodged away from him.

He winked at her. "I've a bit to do before I sleep. I'll meet you in bed in a moment or two." Tolby stood and hugged her before making his way out the back door to see to the farm and other things. Lily caught a glimpse of him framed in the doorway by midnight sky and stars before he passed through.

She waited till the door closed and the sound of creaking stairs and such had quieted all over, then she went to the kitchen and down into the root cellars, lamp in hand. The area had been cut as a maze, purposely deceptive, against marauders and other dangers of living alone in the country. She'd only seen Ravers once in her life, but all knew the Demon wrath they held, and the malicious Bolgers were enough to put anyone in a stew. She stepped down twice more before reaching the dry and cool root cellar, where bags of onions and garlic lay nestled. She dug up a small box there, and opened it. Her dowry had come in this box. Nestled in a beautiful square of fabric was the ring Tolby had given her for his pledge. She could no longer wear it, years of farming increasing the size of her knuckles, so she kept it here, along with coins of their hard work, coins even Tolby did not know she saved. She pulled a remnant from her apron, spreading it out, and examining it carefully by the lamp's soft illumination.

Handwoven, crude, yet beautiful, it might have been a blanket once, but time had raveled it away till it could only serve as a neckerchief, and that had been its place when she took it from Rivergrace while she slept. Lily smoothed it out. Dark fabric rippled under her touch, and she could make out silvery threads running through it, and perhaps a rune or two which faded the moment she tried to focus on them. Magic ran in the weave of the material. She knew it. Magic that the Gods had taken from all of them, except the Vaelinars who did not bow to the Gods of Kerith and held their own powers. She should burn it, to protect them all, but she could not, as it was all Rivergrace had left of her beginnings. Someday her other daughter might want this. She folded it carefully, pressed it into the box, and buried it deeply in a corner under the edge of a rack.

Chapter Nine

NUTMEG WOKE TO FIND her bed shaking. Rubbing her eyes against the crust of heavy sleep, she blinked in the twilight, a gleam of splintery moonlight coming in through the tiny attic window, and saw the other lying on her stomach, her body shuddering. Nutmeg put her hand out, wondering, and touched her. The girl turned her face toward Nutmeg, cheeks dripping with tears, nearly soundless with her sorrow, her thin body quaking with need.

Nutmeg reached for her, her heart filling with ache. "Derro," she whispered greeting softly, the Dweller word for hello, how are you, good-bye, take care, all in one. "It's all right. I found you."

"Aderro," the girl echoed, her eyes opening wider in the moonlight, and she put a slender hand up to scrub the tears away.

"Derro," repeated Nutmeg firmly, correcting her.

The girl buried her face on Nutmeg's shoulder as they hugged, and her tears made a very damp spot on Nutmeg's nightgown. She didn't know what could be wrong, and she didn't want to wake any one and make the stranger more afraid than she already seemed to be. Nutmeg waited a moment, then said as she pulled back, "Are you hungry?"

Rivergrace stared at her, biting her lip, her eyes welling up.

"Hungry?" Nutmeg rubbed her stomach through her cottony night-gown and then brought her fingers to her mouth and made nibbling sounds and motions.

The other nodded wearily and then sighed, as if nothing could be done about it. Nutmeg clambered to her feet, and tugged the other out of bed with her. "Come on!" Then she brought her hand to her mouth, saying, "Ssssh."

Rivergrace nodded, her long hair all in a tangle about her face, and Lily's nightgown dragging in a pool about her feet, and followed Nutmeg down the loft stairs, one at a cautious time, as if she'd never seen wooden stairs before. Feeling a bit like a mouse, Nutmeg scurried the two of them through the main house and to the larder. She found a candle nub near the cooking hearth and lit it carefully, bringing a soft glow to the room. Grace hung back a little, and Nutmeg squeezed her hand reassuringly. Her newfound sister nodded slightly as she followed her lead.

"You can eat anything," Nutmeg declared, throwing the cupboard door open, and Grace reeled backward with a gasp, landing on her bottom on the floor, flinging both hands to her mouth.

She got to her feet, crying soft, wordless sounds, grabbing at Nutmeg and pulling her away, shutting the cabinet doors clumsily, hiccuping as they flew open again and she fought to shut the doors and find the latch for them, and pull Nutmeg out of harm's way all at the same time.

Nutmeg caught her flailing hands. "No, no. It's all right. It's all right," she repeated slowly. She held her quietly for a few moments, watching the girl shiver as rapidly as a tiny, captured bird with its wings fluttering, mouth open, eyes so wide that they looked as if they'd swallowed the moon. She waited a bit longer, till Grace squeezed her hands, then took a long, quavering breath.

Nutmeg let go of one hand only to unhook the cabinet door. She opened it carefully, stood on tiptoe, and took out a cloth napkin wrapped about a bit of soft cheese she knew had been left over. Then she reached back and found the box of smoked strips. Pushing the napkin into Grace's open hand, she balanced the box on her knee and managed to get it open and free three strips from it before the lid slipped back into place and she replaced it on the shelf.

Then she latched the larder doors and sat down, pulling on Grace's hand again. She fed the soft cheese to her in small bites, taking one for herself now and then, and they both enthusiastically devoured the smoked meat as well. Nutmeg took one of the many corked kegs of apple juice stacked against the larder and they shared that as well, pleasantly cool and definitely needed after the salty meat.

Grace sat back and uttered a tiny belch. Her eyelids fluttered and she covered her mouth. Nutmeg giggled. "Full," she said, and patted her stomach. She managed a delicate burp as well. Rivergrace did not giggle, but her mouth twitched a little. Then she stood, and pulled on Nutmeg, as if still afraid they might be caught stealing something to eat.

Once in the main room, Grace roamed about a bit, ducking her head and muttering a word now and then. Nutmeg followed, till Grace stood at the door. She opened it, and the night's air bathed both of them, billowing their nightgowns about them. Rivergrace shook again, then took a step out. Nutmeg wasn't sure what the girl wanted, but she had to visit the convenience Da had built for her and Mom, so she led her that way, and as she used the shed, it seemed to be what the other needed, too. Nutmeg made her wash after, as Mom taught her. Having a sister was work, she decided, sort of like being a mother, but she would do it right.

The wind through the orchard sounded like the sea, her da told her. Never having been to the sea, she didn't know; to her, it was the wind whipping through the branches and leaves. It sounded very loud that night. She looked up and pointed at the moon, saying the Dweller words for things she'd known her whole life and taken for granted. Rivergrace looked as if she'd never seen the moon before. But she listened to the noise of the river which also reached them, and dropped Nutmeg's hand. Nightgown balled in her fists to free her legs, she raced across the chilled ground, crying something, and Nutmeg could only race after.

At the river's edge, Grace stopped and swayed. She put a fist to her mouth, her nightgown flowing about her reed-slender body, and pointed back up the river. She threw a desperate look as Nutmeg caught up, panting.

"What is it?"

Grace pointed upriver.

"The river." Nutmeg lay down on her stomach and reached to the water, and patted it. "River. It's water. It's water in the River Silverwing."

Grace stared at her. She pointed upstream. Nutmeg jabbed a finger at her, and then swam her hand through the air, as if floating down that river. An expression flitted across Rivergrace's face and she nodded quickly, emphatically. She put her thumb to her chest, and made the same motions.

"I found you," Nutmeg said. "Floating down the river." She got to her knees.

Rivergrace inhaled sharply. Then she pointed at herself and held her hand in the air. One taller. One even taller than that. And she held out her hand beseechingly to Nutmeg.

Nutmeg chewed her lip uncertainly. She put her hand on Rivergrace's shoulder. The other took her hand and held it in the air, Lily's height, then Tolby's height, then cupped the top of her head.

"Ohhh."

Rivergrace stared keenly into her face. Slowly Nutmeg shook her head. She put up one finger. "Only you," she said, and then floated her hand down the river again. She pointed at Rivergrace and held up the single finger again.

Rivergrace covered her face with her hands, and began to weep again, nearly silently, as if she'd spent her whole life without speaking, and feared to make any noise. Nutmeg embraced her, thinking that being a slave must have been even worse than she could imagine. Afraid to eat. Afraid to cry no matter how bad things were that happened.

A sound clattered down the mere that neither the wind in the orchard nor the river in its bed didn't make. Nutmeg turned Rivergrace about, listening. Without any idea what it could be, a chill ran down her spine. Rivergrace rubbed her nose on her gown's sleeve, and listened as well. Her glance darted to Nutmeg in worry. Nutmeg beckoned.

Downriver, dark as it was, she found the cave in the bank she remembered, the one that river otters had abandoned for the coming winter. She dove into it, and pulled Rivergrace after, as hoofbeats and the jingle of leather and metal and the grunts of riders drew closer. In the mud they huddled and Nutmeg's first worry was what Mom would say in the morning when she saw the girls. Then she began to worry that the riders might find them.

The horses stopped at the river's edge. She could hear the splash as the animals milled around. She could smell the stink of the Bolgers riding them, and Rivergrace's hand dug into hers.

"Stinker," Rivergrace muttered softly, and Nutmeg understood her in faint surprise. She leaned into Nutmeg, as far away from the den's mouth as she could, but they were far bigger than otters and the hole held little room.

Nutmeg held her hand over her mouth, to keep the smell out, and to keep from coughing or breathing too hard. Her heart thundered in her chest, and she could feel Rivergrace's doing the same in her thin body. They ought to have run. Run and then climbed. Now they were trapped.

Nutmeg squeezed her eyes shut.

The Bolgers grunted and shouted among themselves, as if fighting. A heavy thud was followed by another, and then the sound of the creatures walking slowly along the riverbank. The reeds and brush that covered the banks crackled as something pawed through them, searching. The Bolger snuffled as if he could scent them over his own stench.

Maybe he could.

Nutmeg and Rivergrace huddled closer.

Grunting, the Bolger leaned down and looked in. For a long moment, the three stared at each other. The creature did not move, except to curl one lip back, and the moonlight gleamed off his ivory tusk. His arm hung down, relaxed, his knuckles brushing the soft, muddy ground. He flexed his hand, broken talons clicking on each other. His eyes fixed on them for what seemed forever, staring intently at Rivergrace. He looked as if waiting for Rivergrace to speak, but she shook against Nutmeg and not a sound came out of her but a smothered squeak. He'd been branded, a bunching of scarred skin. He rubbed his arm.

"Rufussss," he hissed quietly, so quietly that only the three of them could have heard him. "Owe." Then he grunted and stood back up, bellowing out something to the others and striding away. His bellows followed sharp slaps and grunts, but seemed to be obeyed.

Rivergrace and Nutmeg clung together, listening. With much jostling and splashing, the Bolgers forded the river and rode away. Nutmeg could think of no reason why the Bolger had not shared his discovery of them. When the sounds had faded completely away, they crept out and ran home. Nutmeg made her wash before they tumbled back into bed, in fresh nightgowns, although Nutmeg's other gown only came to Grace's knees, and she curled tightly against Nutmeg's plump body to stay warm, and they fell asleep. Both slept soundly through the sudden, drenching rain that hit and soaked the grounds, washing away the troubles of the day and early night, and stopped just before dawn.

In the morning, Lily found the discarded gowns, all muddied and damp. She waited for Nutmeg to crawl out of bed with a yawn, and raised the garments in her hand as she sat on the top step of the loft, for Nutmeg to comment upon.

"Rivergrace," Nutmeg said in wonder, "has never seen a convenience before. But now she knows just how it works."

Lily smiled. She put the gowns down. "Then, later today, you can show her how a laundry tub works."

They did not discuss the night further.

Chapter Ten

723 AE, Harvest Month

"LIKE A TWIG, she is. She'll break in the wind," grumbled Garner.

"Is not! She can do anything I can, and faster." Nutmeg wrinkled up her nose, glaring at her brother, even as he reached out and pulled one of the fancily plaited braids that Rivergrace had woven into his sister's hair. Grace wore the same crown of braids, hiding the points of her delicate ears, though nothing could hide the extreme slenderness of her body or the highlights of her brilliant eyes, colors of the most vivid blue-green with sparkles and streaks of golden sunlight through them.

"Not," echoed Rivergrace, putting her chin up, even as she settled into a position behind Nutmeg, glancing up at him through a defiant fringe of bangs that would never allow themselves to be braided no matter how Nutmeg tried, instead framing her forehead with chestnut curls that caught the red and golds of every sunbeam. The last of Harvest Month sunlight brought freckles out on her fair skin, dusting her nose.

Garner crossed his arms and tried to parody his father's sternness. "I can't let just anyone do this job. It has to be done well, if it's to be done at all."

"We can do it!" vowed Nutmeg, hand over her heart. Grace hesitated a moment, then signed her fingers over her chest as well, although he could read a touch of bewilderment on her face. She understood much more than she had those many days ago when first truly awakening, and he gave her credit for that.

"Please let us. Please!"

He waited for Rivergrace to say something else, but she merely looked up at him with pleading eyes. Garner looked down at her. "Well, Grace?"

She didn't say a word, but put her hand out and wrapped her fingers about the bail of the bucket he held, and gave him another long look with sorrowful eyes.

"She says please, too!" Nutmeg bounced impatiently.

"I haven't heard her say it."

Rivergrace pulled slightly on the bail. Nutmeg said accusingly to her brother, "You know she doesn't like to talk."

"I don't know any such thing because you won't let her get a word in edgewise. You do all the talking for everyone."

"Do not." Nutmeg huffed and stumbled for an insult, and gave up, crossing her arms across her chest and glaring at Garner.

Garner shook his head. "I can't let you two do my chores anyway. Da told me especially to get this done. He wants it done right, and those baby goats can knock you over, eat too much, not let the others in. Takes strong arms and good eyes to feed them right."

"We can do it, please," begged Nutmeg, her retreat to insulted silence forgotten.

Rivergrace tugged gently on the bucket handle. "Please," she said breathily, and then looked down as if she'd said too much. He let the bucket go into her hold. "All right," Garner told them, and handed Nutmeg the other three buckets of feed. "Just make sure you do a good job of it!"

"We will!"

"Will," Rivergrace echoed, and the two bounced off, buckets in hand, stopping only long enough to roll up the cuffs of their overalls, and nudge each other excitedly. Garner hid his grin till he went round the corner of the pens, and headed to the press where Hosmer stood, mopping his face, and taking a break from turning the great wheel of the machinery.

"Get the girls to feed the goats like Da wanted?"

"Of course," Garner said, taking up a ladle of water and pouring it over his brother's sweaty head. "Did you doubt I would?"

"You know Nutmeg and chores, and her stubborn streak."

Garner let his grin out. "Hos, you just have to know how to handle women." He dipped the ladle again and this time took a long drink as Tolby rounded the press with crates of new apples, putting them into the crushing bins. "I'll be sure to tell your mother you've become an expert," he said, as he passed by them. Garner sputtered the last of his drink out as Tolby's chuckle trailed behind him.

He went in through the kitchen back door and slid his arm about his wife's waist, hugging her roughly, as the breath rushed out of her and she fought for a laugh and to throw his arm off. He sat down at the table a moment. "Derro. What is it you're doing there?"

She held the bracelet up. "I took my ribbons from the fair and braided this for Rivergrace. It'll hide those awful scars for now, although I hope because she's young and young skin heals well, in a few years they'll hardly be noticeable."

He flicked it with a fingertip. "But those are your fair ribbons!"

Lily tossed her head. "I have a beau," she said, eyes sparkling, "who will buy me new ones next fair!"

"Do you now?" Tolby stole a kiss, and then sat back down. "I hope he has more money than I have!"

"No, but more hair!"

"Hey. Now, my love, that is not fair." Tolby chuckled to himself, as he swiped the palm of his hand over his thinning gray hair. "The hat wears it off, I swear, and I would be a foolish man to work without a hat against sun, wind, and rain."

"And you, my love, are anything but a foolish man."

"Sometimes, I wonder." Tolby pulled out his pipe and tapped it down, after examining the bowl and deciding half a smoke was better than none, and all he had time for anyway. The boys would be all right left alone for a while. "I thought I saw Bolger sign a few weeks ago, right after we found Grace, but the rains had come through and I couldn't be sure. Looked like a hunting party, I found signs of a kill or two, but I've seen nothing since, and yet . . ." He paused to strike his flint and set the toback alight. "I feel guilty. It's good to see nothing, but it doesn't sit right that no one has come looking for her. Not family, not owner."

"She's only a child."

"Less valuable, then? Perhaps." He clamped his teeth about the pipe stem. "Remember when the Bolgers came through two years ago, in the spring of '21?"

"How could I forget? They wanted every jug of hard cider you could unearth for them."

He blew out an aromatic cloud of smoke. "But that wasn't what they came for, Lily. They pulled all our hats off, and looked at our ears, before rummaging through the kitchen and larder and around the cider press, or had you forgotten?"

Lily dropped the ribbon bracelet onto the kitchen table, where it lay like a river of satiny colors, all bound together magically. She made a face.

"Filthy Bolger hands tugging at my hair to see my ears. I made you all bathe twice after they left. Yet, it seems I did forget, neh? Unpleasant memories." She tilted her face at Tolby. "They couldn't have been looking for her, then. She couldn't have survived two years on the river! Someone else would have found her long ago, and the journey . . . why, she'd have been to the great sea in weeks. Besides, they seemed to be looking for someone male."

"Oh, no, no. It's not Rivergrace I'm minded of. But Bolgers have come here before, looking for the elven, I'm thinking, and I don't know from where they would have come. Do you remember when I was but a young buck, and still courting you in town, and there were Bolger raids, and a bunch of us joined the guard and came riding out?"

"That's how you found these lands, wasn't it?"

"Aye, my love, it was. No one knew what the Bolger hounds were looking for then either and that was . . . could it have been? Twenty-some years ago. Tales told said they looked for a ship or boat on the river, but liars that they are, most of us dismissed that." Tolby sighed then, as if amazed at the passage of time. "We drove them back without a clue what it was that had set them off. The mountains are far away, and the other grovers out here, well, none of us use Bolger help. The critters have some intelligence, but they're sly and sneakers, and I won't use a whip or bully somethin' to get it to work with me. So they come and go, without any of us knowin' why or being any the wiser. At least they don't seem to have found their quarry." Tolby took two great puffs on his pipe after that bit of a speech. "I just wonder who they might have been looking for, and who would use such a band of creatures to hunt with."

"Are you sorry we took her in?" Lily looked at him solemnly, folding her hands in her lap, watching his face as well as listening to him closely.

"Never. I'm not one to say that the Gods take away and give back, I'm not so grand as to have a God's eye turned on me, you see, but if the Gods did take note, they'd not have found a better foster mother than you, my dear." Tolby smiled softly at her, holding his pipe.

"Are you thinking of looking for her people?"

"No," he answered flatly. "You and I both know, Lily, slave or parent, whoever had her took little care of her. If it had been the two of us, and our little ones, they'd have been cared for even if we had to open our veins to keep them fed. No one took care of the little one like that, no one, and they won't be getting her back from me!"

Lily stood, came round the table, and slid onto her husband's lap, looping her arms about his neck, and snuggled against him listening to the pulse pound fiercely in his indignation. "Thank you," she whispered to his jaw.

"Had to be said," Tolby muttered gruffly. "Remember the nights we'd find her sneaked back downstairs, feet in the larder cabinet, eating everything she could stuff into her mouth, half sick with it, and terrified when we caught her?"

Lily nodded against his chest. "How did you stop her?"

"I couldn't have her thinking she was stealing it, could I? Keldan noticed it, smart lad. 'Da,' he told me. 'She eats like a bird, a peck here and there. She's got to be still hungry, but I think it scares her.' So I watched, and he was right. She hardly ate at the meals, afraid of taking what she needed and wanted, so she'd steal back downstairs in the middle of the night and eat what she could lay her hands on. So I started waking in the middle of the night myself, quietly go upstairs, wake her, take her by the hand and lead her down, and fix her a small snack. I won't have a child who thinks they have to steal to eat. Then she knew she wasn't stealing, couldn't be stealing, and she settled right down then. And your tucking small snacks away in a napkin and giving it to her when you sent the girls up to bed, that helped, too. She is still a mite skittish, like one of those hot-blooded northern horses, but she's a smart lass. Just mistreated." He puffed angrily. "Mistreated horribly."

"No more," Lily breathed against her neck.

"Not if we have anything to do about it." He held her back. "She has a very long time before she needs t' worry. We Farbranches are a stout lot, and we'll be guarding her."

Chapter Eleven

SHE WOKE IN THE darkest of the night chasing dreams. For a moment, she lay in complete panic until she saw the thready gleam of moonlight filtering in through the window and knew she could breathe. Not rock and earth over her, but a roof, and a bed that cradled her. Rivergrace quieted, listening to the deep, soft sounds of Nutmeg next to her, and when her drumming heart had stilled a bit, she got up, carefully, quietly, easing out of the bed and down the creaky wooden stairs so as not to wake anyone. She had remembered the noisy spots and could get up and down them with the barest whisper of noise that even the sharp round ears of the others could not catch, although she trembled at each groan of the weathered wood. She could hear it, sharp as could be, the moaning of the wood, bent and carved into steps, lamenting its loss of life as a young, verdant tree.

Without lamp or candle, Rivergrace lifted the latch on the back door and went outside. The ground felt both damp and icy cold under her feet. Soon she would either not be able to make the trip at all or would have to find boots to wear. Grace hurried across the yard and into the grove, and down the lane to the river. The journey seemed both farther and nearer every time she made it. Definitely colder. She crouched on the bank, looking into the still, deep waters, drawing her gown about her like a tent as proof against the coming winter, hugging her arms about herself. She knew well now the difference between the sound of the wind in the trees and the Silverwing in its bed, both rushing on a journey through the valley.

The night frightened her. Not the darkness of it, but the unseen things that inhabited it. There were some she had seen, and many she could hear and smell, and she did not understand what they feared, but it seemed that all who walked the night were hunters of one sort or another. Did she hunt too? Maybe.

Rivergrace chafed her hands against her arms. Sometimes when she woke, she had no words. It was as if all of them fled her when she slept, running away, leaving her with no way to say or think anything. On such nights all she could do was to lie awake until they crept back slowly, one by one, with feelings and the ideas behind them. She didn't know why they left or where they went or what she could do to make them come back quicker, but she hated the trapped feeling of being unable to speak or even put words together in her head, to be remembered for shouting aloud later. It was as if it took all she could do to just *be.*

She stared into the river, watching the moonlight ripple across its current. Alert for the smell and sound of stinkers riding into the valley, she could stay a while but not too long, in case one of her family missed her.

Rivergrace stretched out her hand and leaned close to the water, and touched it. Icy cold thrilled through her fingertips. Something wiggled against it and swam off with a splash of a finned tail, into the dappled shadows of the reeds and deeper pools.

Can you help me, she thought after the fish. *I've lost something here, but I . . . I don't know what it is.* How impossible. How could she find the words to tell the fish what she'd lost if she'd never known them herself? But something. She knew she'd lost something on the river. Whenever she tried to ask Nutmeg about it, more and more haltingly as it escaped her grasp, Nutmeg would only hug her close and soothe her, on the edge of tears herself. She did not want to make Nutmeg cry anymore, so she stopped asking.

Whatever it was she'd lost, she was losing even the thought of it, the barest notion of it. The feeling of being on the raft, swirling downriver, was something she could only touch in dreams, and even those were becoming wispy and shredding away, like clouds on a windy Harvest day. Before that, beyond that lay something she could not describe. It was as though she had been cupped in great hands, the river flowing about her but not touching, time without meaning, herself breathing and living and growing as quietly as a stone on the ground ages, her thoughts as vast as the sky itself, and as slow as the mountains. She did not know what that meant, any more than she understood why she could barely sense her loss. In her nightmares, she remembered cold, and crashing dark, and screams and pain and then . . . nothing. Something had caught her up and saved her, and cocooned her from the river, then set her upon it once again, something to which a day meant nothing more than a breath, and to which years were only a sigh. So she would wander to the river and stand, knowing only an ache inside of her and with no idea why, her memories so thin she would lose them, too. She hugged her hands to her throat, feeling the sorrow well up in her unbearably.

Rivergrace sighed.

The cold of her feet turned to stinging burn and she stood, stamping them, biting her lips against the pain. She could not stay out any longer. She drifted back the way she'd come, pausing in the house long enough to get warm by the banked fire in the hearth, so that her chilliness would not make Nutmeg complain and toss in bed when she climbed back in.

She put her hand to her cheek. A frozen tear came away in her fingers. Why should she cry?

Quiet and wondering, Rivergrace crept back to her bed and snuggled under the warm quilts. Nutmeg stirred and threw a chubby arm over her.

"Aderro," whispered Rivergrace. The word caught in her throat. It was not one she'd been taught here, in this home. But she knew it anyway, with no idea of what it meant. She slipped into sleep as the warmth lulled her thoughts and words away.

Chapter Twelve

KELDAN PELTED INTO the house, his hair flying wildly, his face apple-red and sweating as he pounded into the kitchen. "Peddler on the road!" he managed to gasp out, seizing the water ladle and dashing his head with it.

"Saw her, did you?" Lily smiled.

"All the way from the new saplings, Mom. It'll be a short while afore she gets here."

"Good. Catch your breath and go fetch your father, then."

Keldan flashed a grin. "Oh, my heels passed him by already."

Nutmeg reached over and grabbed Grace's hand, her eyes on Lily. "Can we stay?"

Lily considered the two girls sitting at the table, working on darning and patches. Rivergrace uttered not a word, letting Nutmeg talk for her as she had these many weeks, although she grasped their language faster than Tolby and Lily had thought possible. *Just another way the Vaelinars seem superior.* She squelched that musing, and put her embroidery on the table. "I don't see why not. Mistress Greathouse doesn't come by all that often. Would be a shame to miss her, and with winter so close, it will be months before the road will even be open to her again." She stood, smoothed down her apron, and tucked a loose strand of hair behind her ear. "I've things to gather for her, so you two make sure we've apple cider and cookies or biscuits for her, while I work."

Nutmeg pulled Grace to her feet, heading to the larder and pantry, her voice drifting back, "Aye, Mom!" She towed the two of them to the stores, quickly checking the bakery shelves to see what the brothers had left. All seemed in order, so she took a freshly washed tablecloth and knotted it about the cookies and sweet biscuits. "This tells the boys they canna eat them, that they're for eating later, just in case."

Grace nodded. The Farbranch boys could clear a full table in minutes. She supposed such eating was normal for boys, although it still scared her a bit. Suppose she got grabbed up and eaten by mistake? She let go of Nutmeg's hand and checked the cider jugs herself, where they were snuggled away in what Tolby called the cold drawer. Almost in the cellar but still reachable from where she kneeled, the jugs got the chilling air from down below. It wouldn't keep meat, but it kept juice and cider very nicely. She nodded to Nutmeg as she painstakingly counted the large jugs. "Four," she said.

"Are you sure? Remember the hand fingers."

Numbers came slowly to her, much slower than words. Grace ran her hands over the jugs again, then blushed. "Seven," she corrected herself, and sighed.

"Good, that will be enough for company and dinner later. We won't have to haul any more up till tomorrow morning." She helped Rivergrace to her feet, and the two girls dusted each other off.

Grace asked quietly, "What is a . . . peddeler?"

"Peddler." Nutmeg bounced. "That's right, you don't know! She drives a wagon full of all sorts of things, plain and fancy, things you have never seen before, and things Mom needs in her kitchen and Da needs in the press and things that seem like magic."

Rivergrace looked at her doubtfully. "Really?"

"Really." Nutmeg made the solemn mark of an oath across her chin. She turned to dart back to the kitchen and stopped when Grace did not move. Her sister stood with one hand ringing her wrist and looking down at the floor.

"I do not think," she said slowly, "I should greet the peddler."

"Ma said it would be fine, and don't you think she knows best?" Nutmeg stood on one foot, watching. Grace had these moments, and she knew they were difficult times for her new sister, but her parents had told her that Grace must work things out for herself. They had grown fewer and fewer, but she stood impatiently. She shouldn't leave her alone if she were too scared to go see the wonders of Mistress Greathouse, but to miss the peddler? Nutmeg shifted to stand on the other foot, her gaze fixed on Rivergrace's face, waiting and trying not to fidget too much or force anything. Just when she thought she couldn't wait another moment, a smile dawned across Grace's face.

"I'll just be quiet," she offered.

"That'll do just fine!" Nutmeg grabbed her hand again and they raced to the front door, flung it open, and waited, eyes fixed on the road that wound by the river and through the orchards. It seemed forever and by the time the *clop-clopping* of the wagon ponies' hooves and the merry jingle of the bells on their harness reached the Farbranch house, both girls had sat down, their arms flung round their knees and their thoughts gone far away. Nutmeg jumped to her feet with a shout which drew soft laughter from Tolby and Lily seated behind them. Grace swiveled about, her eyes feasting on the sight behind her, where Lily had several bolts of her weavings set out on the big table for the peddler to examine. She couldn't imagine anything more wondrous in the wagon than what she beheld right there done by Lily's hands.

Nutmeg pulled her braid. "Come on!" She ran into the yard, beating her brother Keldan handily, while Hosmer and Garner leaned against the fence, trying to look grown up and unexcited at the visitor, although their eyes flashed in spite of themselves. Garner had a small pipe in imitation of his father and the puffs of smoke came faster and faster until he began choking and had to tap the bowl clean and stamp out the smoldering toback and put his pipe away. By then, Mistress Greathouse had driven her wagon smartly into the yard, snapping the buggy whip in her hand in greeting, her shaggy ponies bobbing their heads and coming to a halt, with a last jingle-jangle of bells and they stomped proudly, throwing their heads about and whickering.

"Derro, good Farbranches!" called out the small woman, a Dweller herself, wisps of dark brunette hair tangled about her face having escaped from the madly crimson scarf she wore. She stood and wrapped the reins about the brake as she set it, the canopy of the wagon behind her a colorful background, dyed blue as the midnight sky, and stenciled with glittering stars and moons and shooting comets. Grace held her breath a moment to look at it.

"Derro," shouted Nutmeg as she flung herself toward the woman, her brothers echoing the greeting.

Mistress Greathouse laughed as she took up Nutmeg and hugged her close, giving her a kiss on the forehead. "Missed me, then?"

"We thought perhaps we'd gotten too far out on the roads for a visit,"

Garner teased the peddler. He patted his vest pocket as he slipped his pipe into it and Hosmer stepped up, handing both the peddler and his sister out of the wagon with one great swoop.

Laughing, Greathouse reached up to pinch Hosmer's cheek. "You first, lad." The peddler searched the many pocketed overdress she wore, dusty from the road, yet colored like the rainbow, each pocket a scene of its own. She fetched out a small square package, wrapped in brown paper and tied in twine. She waved it through the air before passing it to Hosmer. "Gotten with much difficulty, and 'tis worn and such, but I doubt you'll mind that."

"What is it?" Keldan climbed up to the wagon's seat and tried to see from his higher perch, but Hosmer only put the package away quickly, saying nothing.

"Aw, c'mon. What'd you get?"

"Later," his brother murmured and turned away with a rub to a wheel pony's nose and went to fetch them a bucket of water.

Grace hung back as Nutmeg pulled and coaxed Mistress Greathouse inside. She ran her gaze over the wagon. Immense, it seemed, and as she peered inside, she could see crates and barrels and wagon posts hanging with all manner of goods and hardware. Not all the jingling and jangling came from the belled ponies, it seemed. She caught her breath at wonders she had no name for, as they peeked back at her from the dark interior. Had she come to gift all of the Farbranches? Where had all those unnameable objects come from? And why? She went into the house last, as quietly as she had promised, and stayed in the shadows slanting across the wooden floor as the Farbranches gathered close about the guest, laughing and jostling one another.

The mistress and Lily hugged one another, and Greathouse said, "I heard, Lily, and I'm so sorry," and the merriment left the weathered and lined face for a moment.

"Thank you, Robin, but I've been blessed many times over as it is." Lily hugged the woman back.

"Truer words were never said." Robin Greathouse released her gently. "Although I will say, the Meadowes are what delayed my trip. They had a gift to send to you, and wanted me to wait to deliver, and then word reached us."

"How sweet of them," beamed Lily. "You tell them their kind thoughts are like honey!"

"I will, indeed." Robin stripped off her driving gloves briskly. "Now, what have we here?" she added, getting right down to business. Tolby and Garner opened a satchel filled with finely carved pipes, and the peddler took stock, offering a price for the lot even as she examined each one, bickering back and forth with them. Rather than exchanging money, however, Tolby shot back a list of items he needed for harnesses and the press, Greathouse taking notes and tallying up the trade as she took a chair.

When they finished, Hosmer stepped up with a box of hats he had made, wide-brimmed all-weather hats of leather. Robin made a noise of interest, turning one over and over in her freckled, rein-calloused hands. "Excellent work. Looks to be waterproofed skillfully as well, Hos. Your workmanship is improving every time I come by."

He nodded, shoved his hands in his pockets, and waited.

"I owe you a half crown," she said, finally. "Fair enough?"

"Aye, Mistress, very," he said, his eyes lighting up.

"Good, we'll settle up when everything else is done." She packed the hat she was holding back into the box with a nod.

Saying, "Last, but certainly not least," she scooted her chair closer to the table before reaching over carefully and opening Lily's fabric to the sunlight. "Ahhhh." She breathed in appreciation as she waved her rough hand over it, wanting, but not daring, to touch. "What a fine, fine, beautiful cloth!

The sea of light blue opened up, with a faint shimmer of silver over it, and woven into it were flower buds like stars in the sky, scattered ever so rarely and exquisitely. Grace drew a step closer to look upon it, thinking she'd never seen a fabric so grand, and wondering that it had come from Lily's looms. Although she'd seen her Dweller mother working, this cloth had been done before she arrived, or very late at night, for she'd never seen its like.

"You've outdone yourself," Robin murmured. "This will make a stunning dress for some spring bride. I only wish you could cut and sew it, too, as you used to, years ago. It will be difficult to find a seamstress or tailor to do this justice."

"Now, now," said Lily, with a faint blush. "There are many more clever than I."

"Not with a gown, Madame Farbranch!" The peddler winked at her. "But who am I to argue? What have you in mind for this bolt?"

As Tolby sat back and reached for Grace and drew her on his knee, his arm around her waist with comforting warmth, the two women haggled price over the cloth goods till finished, both beaming in satisfaction. Nutmeg danced about the table, popping in and out, listening intently, jostling Garner and Keldan as she made her presence known. She helped her mother lay out two more bolts of cloth, neither so fine as the wedding cloth, but still quality goods from the look of them, one in a soft rose color and the other a deep ivory like that of clotted cream. Robin Greathouse shook her head in admiration. "If only there were six of you," she observed. "Or even two." Her eyes glanced over Nutmeg.

"I'm learning! I help a lot," Nutmeg shot back.

"I'm certain you do." Robin searched her pockets again and came up with a beribboned hair clasp, shiny and gay, catching Nutmeg as she whirled past and pressing it into her hand. "Help your mother wrap the bolts up and stow them in the wagon, will you?"

"You're not leaving," Lily said firmly, "without a meal and news, surely?"

"That would be unthinkable." Robin Greathouse flashed a smile, her face breaking into a dozen well-etched laugh lines. She waited until Hosmer, Garner, and Nutmeg were gone with their bundles, before leaning forward, the smile fading abruptly. She did not seem to notice Grace sitting quietly on Tolby's lap.

"I want you to take care. There's been a report of Ravers up north, heading this way."

Lily paled and sank back into her chair, holding onto the edge of the table tightly.

"Ravers?" Tolby repeated. "Ill news. You're certain it's not gossip?" Grace could feel his arm tighten about her.

"Would that it were. I don't like to carry such warnings, but it's as much a part of my job as knowing where the wells have dried up or Bolgers harry the roads. I'll know more when I return to town, and I'll send word back on the wing, but I doubt it will be any better news. They're raiding, as in the past, though 'tis been a while since they've bothered us, and 'twill be a fight needing to meet them. The Grand Mayor Hawthorne has put a bounty on 'em, but they take their dead with em, so no one's pocket is any fuller." Robin closed her mouth firmly and ceased talking as the grown boys chased Nutmeg through the door and their noisy presence filled the room. It was then, and only then, that she seemed to notice Rivergrace. Her hazel gaze fell upon her and stayed. "Who is this, then?"

Lily directed Nutmeg and Keldan to set the table and held an arm out for Grace. She kissed Grace's head, and slid over on her chair so that the two of them might share it. "This, Mistress Robin Greathouse, is our adopted daughter, Rivergrace."

"She's mine!" Nutmeg shouted over her shoulder from the pantry.

"Oh, really?" the peddler tossed back, smiling again. She waited till the food and dishes were set out, the cookies and fruit biscuits and great slices of cold ham, and the ever present apple cider before saying, "Let me have a look at you."

Rivergrace alone had not reached for food, although a tiny rumbling could be heard from her stomach. She sat, looking downward, trying her best not to meet the other's examination. Lily smoothed her dress out and said, "Go ahead. It's all right."

She looked up then, square into Mistress Greathouse's face. The other sat back, and blinked. Robin then glanced from Lily to Tolby and back again.

"It cannot be."

"It is," Lily answered simply. She deftly fixed a small plate for Grace and placed it in front of her.

Grace leaned back hesitantly against Lily and whispered, "What's wrong?"

Tolby bent over her, tucking in a napkin over her lap. "Not a thing, lass, not a thing is wrong. Eat up now. It's an early lunch but hearty enough for all that."

Robin reached across the corner of the table. "Give me your hand, child."

Grace stretched her fingers out, trembling. The peddler caught it with strong, workman's hands of her own, and drew her closer. Opening Grace's hand, she turned it palm up, and traced the lines with keen eyes and her forefinger. She also traced the scar that peeked from under the braided bracelet.

"Tolby. Lily. What are you doing? Where has she come from?" Grace pulled back, but the other only held her a bit more tightly, refusing to let go of her.

"She came from the river," Lily answered. She looked up from her plate with a set to her mouth and chin.

"I founded her," Nutmeg supplied and waved her fruited biscuit. "She would have drownded."

"She saved me," Grace echoed, barely audible.

Robin looked into her face. "Did you run away?"

"I don't know."

"Or won't say?"

Rivergrace's hand shook in the other's no matter how tightly held. "I c–can't remember . . . before."

"Shackle marks." The forefinger traced the scarring. "The Accords deny slavery by the Vaelinars among our peoples, but I've heard they still take a few of their own. The disgraced. They look aside when it happens. Did your family all wear chains, little one?"

Grace flinched and put her cheek to Lily's shoulder. "I don't remember."

A nod then. "This, you must remember." Mistress Greathouse looked intently in the small, slender hand she held. "You will need all of your strength, and all of the strength of those who love you, to face what lies in your future. It must be *won*, you must never go back, for the lives of many and many rest upon you. You are both far less and far greater than you seem, and all depends on how well you know yourself." The peddler curled Grace's fingers up, as if closing a book, and let go her hand.

Grace's face went pale as the moon.

Lily exhaled. "Mistress Greathouse—"

Robin waved a hand. "Forgive me for upsetting you, Lily. Sometimes things must be said." She pushed back her chair, and stood. "I've a long way to go, and other news to carry." She tightened the crimson scarf attempting to hold back her bounty of brunette hair that tumbled to her shoulders. "Garner, make sure one of your da's messenger birds is put in the wagon."

"Aye," he said, and left to do it.

Tolby stood and bowed, his expression grave. "You may think me a fool—" he began, and she interrupted him with a gesture.

"Never. The Gods give and take away as only they know fit. But I cannot think of a warmer, stronger house than this . . ." Robin's gaze fell upon Rivergrace again. "And she will need it."

"You've not heard of anyone seeking her?"

Briskly, Greathouse pulled on her driving gloves. "Not yet. If they should ask, I probably wouldn't hear them. Getting older, you know. I've a spot of hard hearing now and then."

"We're all getting older." Lily got to her feet then, and Rivergrace sagged in the suddenly too big chair. Lily moved to her guest and hugged her tightly. She must have whispered something fiercely in Robin's ear, for the other flushed a little, then nodded.

And then the peddler was outside, directing Garner, Hosmer, and Keldan to take the goods off her wagon they'd bartered for, and dispensing the coins earned for themselves and the household. The wagon ponies knew it was time to leave, and stomped a bit impatiently as if they yearned to trot freely upon the road. With a clatter and jangle and jingle, Mistress Greathouse set her wagon about, snapped her buggy whip, and drove back the way she'd come.

Garner dropped many coins into his mother's hand. Lily made a fist about it, and shoved her hand into her apron. The peddler had paid her more than agreed, as she often did, and those coins would go into the stash she kept secreted away, for a future she never discussed with Tolby. Garner then joined Keldan and Hosmer who trotted after the wagon, whooping and hollering an escort to the main road.

Tolby slipped his arm about Lily's shoulders. "It always puts the hair up on the back of my neck when she does that."

"A reading? She cannot help it. It doesn't happen often, but when it does, she is sworn for the truth."

"Aye, but it's eerie nonetheless. The last time she did it, she told me Hosmer was meant for saddle and blade. Look at him. A farmer through and through." Tolby shook his head.

"She told me I'd lose the child," Lily whispered. "So who knows?" She turned away. "I've dishes to do, and you've goods to put away."

Tolby gave a startled cluck, then grinned and headed to his outbuildings, whistling like a night wood owl at Garner and Hosmer to follow. Garner came trotting back from the road and caught up, but Hosmer lagged behind.

At the corner of the house, away from the sight of any eye, he came to a stop and pulled his parcel from his pocket. He did not undo it, but wiggled the paper down enough to see the dog-eared edge of a small handbook, and part of the worn letters on the leather cover: *A Guard's Training and Study Guide.* He let his breath out before tugging the brown paper back into place and secreting the book away again.

Chapter Thirteen

"WE'LL BE NEEDING a beacon fire," Hosmer announced the morning after the peddler had visited. All washed up for the day, his hair wet and slicked back, his face pink from the cold water, he tried to look grown up and solemn. The morning held the distinct chill of the winter coming fast, and the leaves of the forest abutting the orchards had begun to turn yellow and orange and red. He wiped his hands on a towel, eyeing his father at the wash rack. Soon, it would be too cold for them to wash up outdoors, and they'd have to be careful doing it inside, as Lily would fuss with every unnecessary slosh of water or dropped towel.

Tolby leaned a shoulder against the corner of the house frame, watching as Nutmeg and Rivergrace chased each other out of the convenience house and went to wash up as well. "What makes you think so?"

Hosmer's mouth worked. First one side and then the other, and then he looked down at his boots. Tolby waited.

Hosmer shifted his weight, then muttered, "Mistress Greathouse suggested precautions." He looked at the girls, his mouth twitched, and he fell into silence, holding Tolby's gaze intently.

Tolby nodded slowly. "I see." He looked out across the expanse of the back grounds, toward the orchards and wild groves, and the small rolling hills that surrounded them. So much land. Once he'd thought it could buffer his family from the evils of the world. Yet wilderness itself held a dangerous edge. Neighbors to stand with them in times of trouble or raids were far away. The corner of his own mouth twitched as if it ached to ask why the peddler would say anything to Hosmer instead of himself, but those words did not fall out. Instead, slowly, consideringly, he said, "Up there, I suppose," with a gesture of his hand.

Hosmer followed the jut of his thumb and nodded.

"Get to it, then, but don't be making a fuss about it. No sense to worry the lasses. Get your brothers to help you, but only after the other chores are done. Know what you're about making one?"

"Stone cairn, brush cleared all about, and so forth. Dried, hard wood for long burning, like a pyre. I helped Zamar Barrel do theirs last year."

"And you've been itching to have one for us, I imagine."

Hosmer put his chin up.

Tolby inclined his head. "I'll leave it up to you, then. Means a watch, or havin' a beacon won't be doing any good."

"We can do that."

"See to it, then." Tolby straightened up and sauntered into the kitchen, following the smell of a hot morning brew and bread, done with talking.

Nutmeg nudged Rivergrace in the leg. Grace looked up from the harness she was trying to thread into one of the new buckles they'd gotten from Mistress Greathouse, and wrinkled her nose. "What? It's wrong?" She held it out for Nutmeg to inspect, smelling of leather grease that they'd both worked into the harness so it would be supple enough to mend and work.

"They're up to something."

Grace wrinkled her nose. "Up a ladder?" she offered helpfully.

Nutmeg fell over in a peal of giggles. "No, no," she managed to gasp out. "No, they're doing something sneaky. For a few weeks now, and they think I don't notice."

"Oh. Always that."

"True. Brothers are sneaky." Nutmeg leaned against Rivergrace. "Maybe tonight we'll be sneaky, too."

"How?"

"I'll think of something," Nutmeg promised her, with a nod. Grinning to herself, her nimble fingers corrected Rivergrace's work and raced back to finish her own. "We'll show them."

Grace had tumbled into dark, gripping sleep filled with a voice she could not quite hear and the sound of the river in her ears when Nutmeg shook her awake. She roused with a gasp, but Nutmeg's hand was already over her mouth to catch the sound. Her sister leaned close over her. "Ready to catch the sneaky boys?"

It didn't feel right or safe, but if she said no, Nutmeg would go out alone and that would be even worse. Rivergrace nodded her head slowly. "Get dressed, then. It's cold out. Maybe even frost tonight."

Grace dressed in as much as she could get on, under the heavy warmth of the comforter, and then wiggled out to put on boots and coat. The hooded coat was tight across her back and not long enough in the arms, but that did not matter. It kept her warm as she tugged her shirt about to keep it from bunching. Nutmeg was perched at the top of the stairs, lip caught between her teeth, waiting impatiently. They scurried down as quietly as they could.

Outside, the moon hung low and thin against the sky. Despite its full face, its silvery- pale and translucent light barely seemed to reach the lands below. Rivergrace put a hand up to the stream of light, turning her fingers over in it from front to back to front again, then tried to cup it. Nutmeg tugged on her elbow.

"They've been going to the ridge. Too far to walk. We'll take Acorn."

Grace drew back. "The horse?"

Nutmeg snorted. "He's just a pony, and a fat old retired one at that. But he can carry the two of us, and he won't run or anything." Towing Grace with her, she went to the barn and grabbed a bridle, then headed out to the far pasture where the horses and ponies slept, one or another waking to graze quietly before going back to the herd and closing its eyes.

Acorn snuffled as Nutmeg caught him by his bristly mane and hauled the bridle onto his head. His hide gone all thick and wooly for the upcoming season, he looked like a round dustball with hooves sticking out the bottom. Nutmeg threw Grace aboard and then climbed on behind her, Nutmeg's arms around Grace to handle the reins. The pony let out a grunt and then trotted to the pasture gate where Nutmeg slid off, opened it, led the pony through, and latched the gate behind her before climbing back on. Grace's booted feet almost touched the ground as Acorn broke into a quick, shambling walk. She hung onto the mane with both fists, her head nodding with every jolting step. Nutmeg's teeth clicked behind her ear.

Sometime just before Grace's head was ready to fall off and her bottom seemed bruised beyond feeling, Nutmeg pulled Acorn to a halt. She pointed up the deep, dark hill in front of them. "Up there on the ridge," she whispered. "Dat's where they go."

"We follow?"

Nutmeg nodded. "Pony stays here, though." She jumped down, and put her arms out to catch Grace, who followed and landed unsteadily on legs both numb and aching. "I don't like horses," she stated.

"Pony," corrected Nutmeg stubbornly. She looped the reins around a bramble bush and tugged on them. "Tight enough to keep him here, but he can break free iffen he has to."

"Why?"

Nutmeg shrugged. "Da taught me that." She took Grace's hand in hers. "Time for sneakiness."

Crouching side by side, they crept up the hill to the ridge, vines tangling about their boots and tearing at their pants, brush snagging their sleeves. Nutmeg had to untangle Rivergrace's hair when a branch caught her up, yanking her back abruptly. She stood as still as she could bear while Nutmeg pulled, tugged, and jerked her hair free, as painfully as the branch had snagged it. She made no sound, but her eyes watered. Nutmeg made a small sound of sympathy before pulling the branch away, and they continued creeping up to the ridge. They made little noise despite the leaves and dried twigs underfoot, as a heavy dew had fallen and muffled their progress. It twinkled like tiny stars along the hillside, and as the night grew colder and colder, Rivergrace thought the stars might turn to frost before they got home to a warm bed again. She pulled up the hood of her coat, warming her ears, but her nose stayed chilled.

They emerged at the edge of the ridge. Grace saw keenly despite the night and pointed at something to their right that seemed very unhill-like. "What's that?" she whispered to Nutmeg.

"A pile of wood," Nutmeg answered in disappointment. "Maybe a bonfire, a big fire, to light." She sighed and chafed her hands together. "All those scratches for nuffin'."

"What's it for?"

"Signals, if we get in trouble and such. The other farmers might see it." Nutmeg put her palm over her nose a moment, muffling her whisper even more. "Supposed to have a volunteer cavalry round here. Hosmer always wants to join, but other than Bolgers, we don't get much trouble." She shrugged. "Least I know what they're doing."

"Not a surprise."

Nutmeg grasped both her hands, her warmth enveloping Grace. "Nuffin' exciting. Just lots of work. Stone and then wood, for burning a long time." She tugged on Grace gently. "Better get home."

Rivergrace moved to the ridge itself, hard rock cresting through the softness of the hill, and stood for a moment, flooded by the silvery moonlight. She could see the wide ribbon of the river down below, and the dark clumps of the trees before the ordered rows of the many orchards and fields, all cloaked by night yet visible if shaded. "We live down there."

"Yup." Nutmeg gathered her hood about her tousled hair. Her breath puffed out. "It's getting too cold. We need to go."

Grace nodded slowly, reluctant to tear her gaze away from the river, which seemed to call her even from so far below her. She let her breath out in a long sigh. She could not leave with the river in her eyes, so she turned about. The valley and wilderness on the other side of the hills ringing the Farbranch lands lay stretched out, with none of the orderliness of the orchards and fields. She thought she saw movement, and went to her knees, pulling Nutmeg over into a tumble at her feet.

"Grace!" Nutmeg rolled about, but Rivergrace kept her hand bunched in the other's coat.

"Riders," she said, low and urgent. "Down there, can you see them?" She pointed down below, and Nutmeg answered with a hiss, settling on her stomach and watching.

"Bolgers," she said. "And something else."

"They're headed toward the river road."

Nutmeg began to wriggle backward. "We've got to get home."

"Light the bonfire?"

Nutmeg shook her head. "I've got nuffin' on me to do that. And it's not built yet, not ready. We've gotta get Acorn." She slid past Rivergrace, down the hill, and Grace followed after. Halfway down, Nutmeg jumped to her feet. They could hear the pounding of hooves at the base of the ridge, loud pounding, and Nutmeg told her, "Forget being quiet, we gotta be fast!"

They ran and rolled through the brush and branches, loud enough that snoozing Acorn threw his head up with a snort and rolled his eyes about, wheeling around when they burst into the clearing. He tossed his head and stomped with a low whicker of menace until she clucked at him. Nutmeg grabbed the reins, throwing herself onto his withers first before reaching down to haul up Rivergrace. Acorn danced about skittishly, leaving Grace hopping about for a few minutes before she scrambled up. Holding onto each other and the woolly pony as tightly as they could, they urged him into a rugged trot toward the Farbranch home.

They thundered home, each step a jolt that made Grace feel as if her head would fall off, holding on for dear life. Heat rolled off the pony as he put his head down in answer to the tattoo Nutmeg drummed on his ribs, urging him for quicker. Branches snapped in their eyes. Grace's hood was torn back and flopped about her shoulders, the cold night wind suddenly in her face and ears and eyes.

They never knew what gave them away. Just that, suddenly, Acorn swerved across the broken trail, and a huge horse reared in front of them, blocking them. It was not a Bolger riding it. Grace looked up in fear and saw a . . . a thing . . . swathed in crimson wraps, with a thousand points of light for its face, and beetle-black wings at its back, and legs that were not flesh and blood but spiked cricket legs spurring the horse to cut them off. She had no idea what it was, but it gave off an evil aura that sucked the breath out of her. It pointed at her, sticklike wings thrashing with its eerie movement.

An angry buzzing surrounded them, then bramble crackled and popped, and the Bolgers rode out. Two more of the things led them. One swung about and leaned toward her. "Ssssstrange blood," it hissed. Points of light glinted inside the veiled cloth that wrapped its head. The night spilled across its garb, making it look like red-black blood.

Grace grabbed the right rein from Nutmeg's hold and pulled it, hard, wheeling the pony about and she kicked him as harshly, urgently, as she would ever think of striking an animal. Acorn squealed and bolted into a dead run, just under the outstretched arm of the nearest Bolger.

Nutmeg stuttered in fear, unable to get a word out. Grace leaned her face to the other's. "Get to the river!"

"The road is wide. They'll be catching us easier."

"Just get to the river." She had no plan, no thought but fear coursing through her veins and the need for the river.

Acorn found the nimbleness of his youth. He leaped fallen branches and skirted trees that sent the pursuers behind them off their course momentarily, and Nutmeg turned him to the river. At its edge, Grace jumped down and pulled Nutmeg with her. She tore the bridle off, slapping Acorn on his flanks. The pony let out a sharp grunt and took to his heels, tail flipping, as he disappeared into the gloom. She knotted her fist in the bridle. "Come with me." Without waiting for answer, she hauled Nutmeg behind her, and slipped into the cold, icy waters of the river. She remembered the other Bolger hunt, but this time, fear ran in her veins instead of blood. They were dead if those things and the Bolgers found them. She knew that. Dead as if black nothingness claimed them forever, forever cold, forever unable to touch the sunlight or the still river or warm flesh. Dead.

Nutmeg sputtered. "Grace! We'll die in here. We'll freeze."

Rivergrace shook her head. "No. Trust me." She wrapped part of the bridle about her wrist and tied the end off to a tree root hanging from the bank. "Do you trust me?"

Nutmeg tried to inhale and couldn't. She stared, the pale moon reflecting in her face, and shivered. Grace held her arms out and took her sister into them, and sank both of them into the water, rolling so that only part of their faces stayed above, and let the current carry them into an eddying cove. She breathed slow and still, feeling Nutmeg in her arms do the same. She let herself go to the river. Its waters warmed gently about them, till the chill left them. She drifted low into the water until only her nostrils were above it.

The river muffled the noise, but they could hear the search on the river road and bank. Nutmeg quivered in her hold. Grace tightened it, giving comfort. The river would hold them safe. She knew that. It would hide their warmth and their scent and whatever it was the others might use to track them, unless they could smell their very souls. If that were true, there was nothing could save them.

The waters rocked them gently. Grace could feel her heartbeat slow, quieter and quieter; her ears caught the noise of hoofbeats and shouts moving down the road, the anger and menace and sheer evil of the things after them. Nutmeg relaxed in her arms and only the leather ties of the anchoring bridle kept them from drifting gently out of the small cove into the river's main current and away.

They stayed even when it grew quiet. Then came a hubbub, a great shouting, and thundering of hooves, and fiery torches streaking the air, and Grace opened her eyes to watch it through the water, breathing with the same slow measure.

Hosmer led the force as they galloped by. Grace shook Nutmeg slightly and sat up in the waters, the icy air immediately sweeping over them. She hauled them back to the bank, hand over hand on the bridle, emerging from the river as if being birthed, a kind of lassitude coming over her.

Nutmeg erupted from the water behind her. She clawed up the muddy bank, yelling and screaming. Rivergrace followed quietly, water streaming down her, the warmth cascading away into a freezing chill, and her teeth began to chatter. The small cavalry wheeled about as Nutmeg bobbed up and down in the rutted lane, hollering and waving her arms. It was Tolby who got off his horse first, who grabbed the girls up.

"I'll be taking the belt to your hides later," he cried, and held them tightly, and it sounded as if he wept as he kissed their heads.

Hosmer stayed aboard his horse, one of the wagon horses, almost as shaggy as Acorn but blowing steam and pawing fiercely at the ground. "Sign up the road shows they were beating the brush, hunting for something. They gave up without a fight, though."

"Did you see them?" Garner asked as he got down, peeling off his coat, and throwing it over the two of them. Nutmeg stammered and stuttered out the tale of the Bolgers and the things with them.

Tolby choked and pulled the girls near. "Ravers," he managed, finally. "They rode off when we hit the road. Noise and bluster was all we had to throw at them, but it was enough, this time."

"Tree's blood," cursed Garner and Hosmer together.

"We'll have to get the beacon finished, and patrols up," Hosmer managed to add. The moonlight paled his face.

"Aye, no doubt of that." Tolby closed his arms tighter around his girls.

But Rivergrace went stiff in Tolby's hug, finding no comfort. It was not the blood of the trees that had been hunted.

It had been her blood.

Chapter Fourteen

IN THE BARNYARD Tolby dropped his hand on Hosmer's shoulder. His son turned about, and Tolby noticed for the first time that their gazes no longer met; he had to look up a bit to reach Hosmer's stare. His throat closed a bit at the realization.

"What is it, Da?"

"You'll be taking Banner. He's a cart horse, I know, but he's also the best rider we have, and if the militia takes you, you'll need y'r own. So Banner will be doing double duty. I trust you to not overwork him, eh?"

"I won't." An expression of joy passed over Hosmer's face, quickly replaced by one of solemn duty. "Thanks, Da."

"Think nothin' of it. And when you're gallivanting about, at the Barrels and Stonesend and such, you might be finding a pouch of good toback for me, right?" The small town and outpost held many luxuries the isolated farms and ranches did not.

"Right." Hosmer grinned, before turning away to finish his chores.

So it was that Hosmer joined the Silverwing Valley militia as soon as they got the beacon finished, riding with leathery old men of long experience and young boys filled with hot eagerness. Banner grew leaner and gained stamina with all the work, as did his rider, but neither complained. The duty seemed to make them thrive.

And it was then that Rivergrace learned the river had a name, the Silverwing, for its graceful flow down out of the mountain snows. They had always just referred to it as the river, as if there were only one, and there could be no other name for it. Brooklets and creeks and such abounded through the valley, but there was only one river. Knowing its name did not change her feelings for it. During the day when she and Nutmeg had free time, precious little now, for although Lily did not punish them openly, she saw to it they had many, many new tasks about the farm, Grace would go down to the river's banks and sit and watch the waters tumble past. Evening forays no longer seemed wise or possible.

The Farbranch holdings sat back from the river quite a bit, and Tolby told her why one morning when he whistled to fetch her up to take care of the goats. "It floods, lass, during rain and the melt off. Some years the Silverwing is treacherous and canna be trusted." He showed her the high water marks and silted areas where the river had crept out over the land from its bed. "I'm no fool, so I built back, even though it's a trial now and then." He chewed his pipe stem. "We've never been washed out." He opened the goat gate to let her through, and latched it behind her, leaving her wondering a bit over his words. It had never occurred to her that the river might be dangerous.

The first night of true, black frost brought a morning where the land held the chill, and she awoke to ground that crackled when she stepped upon it, and the wash water held a thin layer of ice. Grace snugged herself into her coat and visited the convenience as quickly as she could, and stood outside to wash up with Nutmeg who danced on first one leg and then the other, a dance that she assured Grace would drive away the cold.

Garner came down from the beacon ridge, both he and his mount looking red-nosed from the frost. He stayed in the saddle. "Where's Da?"

"Around somewhere. He needs to wash up," Nutmeg told her brother sagely. She eyed him. He had two bundles tied to the back of the saddle, one his bedding and the other unknown. "Wotcha got?"

"Nothing for you."

Nutmeg jostled Grace's elbow when she took a step back. Her brother's normal teasing manner had fled, replaced by a frown. She looked at Grace and shrugged, before grabbing the washrag and cleaning behind her ears vigorously. Then the two made their way to the warm house and breakfast while Garner's horse gave off a low chuff of unrest.

"Something's wrong," Nutmeg told her confidently.

Grace squeeze her sister's hand. "Enough trouble."

"I wouldn't hafta snoop if they'd just tell us," Nutmeg countered. They heard Tolby's hail from around the corner, and both turned as one to go back and see.

Grace laughed softly at that, but she froze solid in place as they emerged, and Garner opened up his bundle, throwing it upon the ground, and a grizzly hide fell free. It tumbled open, bloody and ragged-edged, a green pelt with the head still attached, dead eyes glaring at them.

"Blood and shit." Tolby stared at it. "Where did this come from?"

"I took it, Da. I skinned it this morning."

"You killed it?!"

Garner shook his head as he began to unsaddle his horse. "No. I heard the row last night. Fighting, something fierce. I rode down soon as the dawn cleared, thinking maybe the militia had run into trouble. This is what I found. More than this, but I'm gonna take this to Stonesend. Maybe even Calcort."

Grace drew Nutmeg to her side, unable to tear her gaze away from the gruesome pelt. Tolby frowned at them. Garner threw the saddle onto the fence post and then squatted by the skin. "See this?" he pointed to heavy scarring on each cheekbone. "Never seen that on a Bolger afore. There were two groups, and they fought. Don't know why, Bolgers don't fight among themselves, usually. Not like this. So we have our cider mill-raiding Bolgers and we have . . . these." Garner stabbed a finger at the pelt. "Raver pack with Bolger hounds, or some such."

"Keen eyes." Tolby looked at Garner. "Any Raver sign?"

"Part of one of the forearms, I think. Hard to tell. Carapaced, like a beetle or something, Da. I've got it in the other bundle. Never seen a Raver before, but this doesn't look like any wraith or haunt, like the tales."

"Best you get Hosmer and take it to Stonesend, then. They'll be needing to know. Don't tarry there, son. I could need you back here."

"I won't. We'll head out as soon as Hos has rested."

Tolby pointed at the ground. "And get that thing put away afore your mother sees it. She doesn't need the shock."

"Aye, sir."

He reached out and grabbed each girl by the ear, tugging them away from the wash stands. "You'll not be telling your mother either."

"N–no, sir," Nutmeg got out, squirming away from the tight pinch on her earlobe. "We won't."

Silent, Grace let her sister talk for her while her thoughts flew away on the wind. Strange blood. Hunters beyond the ridge. She tried not to feel afraid.

Lily bustled about the dining table with fluffy omelettes and fresh biscuits. She raised an eyebrow as Nutmeg only took one flaky biscuit and picked apart her eggs before eating. She watched closely as Grace set to her breakfast, Rivergrace noticed through the fringes of her soft auburn hair, and Lily turned away, satisfied as she ate most of her eggs and applesauce without noticing that Grace swept half of it into the napkin on her lap. The thought of what Garner had unfurled outside made her sick to her stomach. Nutmeg traded glances with her over the table, before looking down at her plate and picking over the food listlessly.

Tolby came in and pitched into the breakfast with his usual vigor and Lily stood back, a little smile playing across her mouth, her eyes sparkling with fondness at her husband. Both girls stood up to slip away, but Tolby cleared his throat, and stared them back into their seats. He put both his work-worn hands on the table. "I've made a decision."

Wiping her hands on her apron, Lily sat down. Decisions seldom came around the Farbranch household without both Tolby and Lily discussing it beforehand. She looked at him curiously.

"There'll be no fair for us this year. Roads are too chancy, and we've Grace to think of, as well. I know it'll disappoint you, but I think it be best."

"And that's that?" asked Lily faintly.

His mouth worked. "The boys will take the last of the goods to market and come home. We've missed a fair before."

"Only when the river washed out the bridge."

"And," he added gently, "the year Keldan was late in arriving."

She flushed a bit at that. "You think this best?"

He nodded. "I'm not out to spoil the fun, my love, you know that of me."

"I do. I can't say I'm happy about it, but we will abide. There'll be another fair."

"Two," burst out Nutmeg. "Spring and Harvest."

"We only go to Harvest," Tolby reminded her. "When we have goods to sell and buy."

Nutmeg's mouth knotted up but she didn't say anything else. Tolby rocked his chair back on two feet. " 'Course," he said to no one in particular, "when my daughters get a bit older, I can't see the harm in a Spring fair. Just for fun, you know."

Nutmeg leaped up and threw herself at her father, hugging him tightly. Then she yelled, "Chore time!" at Rivergrace, and Grace raced off after her, tugging her coat off the hooks by the back door.

Lily reached over and caught Tolby's hand. "I don't know why you're not liking the Spring fair," she said softly. "After all, that's where I met you for the first time, and picked you out of a great city full of suitors."

He grumbled as the back door banged shut. "And you think I'm wanting to take my girls there, so they can meet a husband someday, eh? Bah." He pushed his chair out and walked off, grumbling, and Lily did not dare let out a soft laugh till he had stomped out of the house as well.

And so they lived, more or less as they expected to, for a handful of years.

Chapter Fifteen

733 AE, Planting Month

"I MUST HAVE BEEN addled," Tolby muttered, shoving his hands deep in his pockets.

"We've promised them for years, and we can't hold them back any longer, dear." Lily touched her head to his shoulder as they picked their way along village streets, bustling with activity and feeling far too crowded for Tolby.

"They're too young, both of them."

"Not for beginning. They need to see the world, and who might be waiting for them, that's what the Spring fair is all about. Nutmeg is certainly ready," and Lily eyed her bosomy daughter walking along the lane in front of them, her skirts swirling with the rhythmic movement of her hips, her glossy hair tied back with a ribbon. "As for Grace, well, I don't know. Sometimes Grace still seems the child we pulled from the Silverwing and others . . . other times I think she is older than all of us."

Rivergrace moved alongside Nutmeg, her tall slender form bent as she leaned on her sister's shoulder, a dark, hooded robe hiding her youth and her body, her walk imitating the hesitant and crippled movement of a many-years-aged woman. Beneath the robes and hood, a wrapper headband held back her glossy chestnut hair and conveniently hid her ears as well, the fabric gaily beaded and spangled in a festive way. The brands had faded and moved to mid-forearm as she'd grown, but they'd never healed entirely, never gone away. She stood head and shoulders taller than Nutmeg now and seemed likely to get taller still, in the way of the Vaelinars. A light breeze whirled about them, swirling Nutmeg's long skirts and teasing at her hair, and the sun had chosen this day to shine brightly.

Their daughters' talk and chatter drifted back to Tolby and Lily and, as usual, Grace seemed content to let Nutmeg do most of the babbling. Her head turned back and forth though, absorbing in the sights of all those gathering for a Spring fair. It hurt him to see her guised, and yet they had all agreed that it would be best.

"Next year would have been better," Tolby stated.

"I think it's high time they met someone besides the Barrel boys," said Lily firmly.

"And what be wrong with the Barrels?"

"They're good honest people, and nothing is wrong," Lily answered, increasing her steps to keep the girls from getting so far ahead of them. "But I like a man with book learning, and the Barrels are as homegrown as they can get. There's more to the world, Tolby Farbranch, than grass and roots."

"I've got book learning."

"Of course you do. That's what I mean. They deserve a man as good as their father."

Tolby's rough cheeks reddened at that, and he looked as if he wanted to say another word, but then wisely took out his pipe and clamped his teeth shut on the stem. Lily hooked her arm through his and patted his hand, concealing a slight smile. As they moved down the paved walkways, a fine and brisk breeze snapped the many banners out and brought a waft of toback on the air, fine Dweller toback. He lifted his chin to it. She patted his arm, saying, "I want to visit the dress shop. Have a smoke and visit with the lads, why don't you?"

"You wouldn't mind?"

"Mind? And have you fussing about while I'm trying to look at weaves and cuts and patterns and mayhap try on a few hats?" Lily nudged him. "Go on."

"I suppose it's possible. The lads are horse-trading, looking for a new horse for Hosmer." He scratched his chin thoughtfully. "I'll give a whistle later." Tolby winked at her, his eyebrow canting rakishly.

She blushed. He'd often called for her that way when they first began courting. "I'll be waiting, then." She kicked aside the hem of her skirt, with a few swift strides to take the girls in hand, and walk briskly up the street toward her goal. He watched them go for a few moments, noting even Nutmeg now stood taller than Lily. How time flew and yet . . . and yet . . . the young girl he'd first loved followed Lily about like a shadow, never tarnishing, only adding to the fine woman she'd become. Smiling, he ducked into the toback parlor.

It smelled faintly of cherry-and-apple scented smoke, and a bit of rum, and he took up a rocking chair near the open door, settling comfortably into it. After patting a few pockets, he found his pouch and began to pack his pipe, listening to the talk about rain and some fungus on the grain crops unless they got a lot of sun soon, and the fine pelts from the cold winter trapping. More talk of Raver sightings to the far far northwest, and grumblings about the trade road taxes which, someone else pointed out quickly, helped maintain the local militias filled the air much as the smoke. He knew the Tanners, and Crofts, and Sweetbrooks, and the Barrels, but not all who sat within, most of them Dwellers, but a few Kernans also, and a tall fellow in the corner all wrapped in a gray cloak, his battered boots shoved out in front of him as though he'd gone to sleep in his easy chair. Tolby sat back after lighting his pipe, easy talk floating about him like the soft blue-gray clouds of smoke.

Nutmeg stood on one foot and then the other, watching her mother browse slowly through lengths of fabric as she ran her hands carefully over them, noting the warp and weft and dye as well as the thread count and content and all the many things that went into the yard goods. Although she appreciated such things normally, she had other things on her mind, Grace could tell, and she lagged back behind both as she could feel Nutmeg's patience simmering. Grateful she could finally stand tall and straighten her back, she found a corner where she was not likely to be seen, dark robes gathered about her. Underneath, Lily had let her dress for the festival and she gazed wistfully for a moment at the soft greens and blues of her skirt. Nutmeg cleared her throat and shot her a look. She wondered what bee buzzed in her sister's bonnet now. Grace glanced out the shop window. The town bustled with people and activities, with swap fairs and dancing, music, horse meets, all sorts of fascinating things. The wonder of it tiptoed through her being. Folk she had to look up to, instead of down at, slender folk, sturdy folk, folk with skin the color of soot, and gold, and tanned like old leather. Even a Bolger strode by without a word or stare, though she shrank back farther into the corner at that. Garner and Hosmer told her Bolgers were like any people, some good, some bad. They fought among themselves, tribal wars, and just as many were good folk as raiders, leastwise near the cities. She hardly knew what to make of it, the scene more colorful than the Autumn fair she'd been to, once. The window looked out on a world Rivergrace could barely imagine. Then she lowered her eyes quickly, lest someone passing by on the street could look into her face and see her most un-Dweller-like eyes.

Impatiently, Nutmeg shoved a bolt back onto its rack and then whirled about to tug on her mother's sleeve. "May we go get a fruit drink?"

"Why, of course. Don't wander too far though, all right, and . . ." Lily looked over at Grace briefly. "Mind your manners."

The corner of Grace's mouth twitched slightly. Mind Grace, she meant. Mind that no one notices the Stranger blood in her or calls her elven. Mind that she walked hunched over and shuffling, her pretty clothes smothered. She stifled a sigh as Lily dropped a few coins in Nutmeg's hand, and her sister swept by her like a wind in full storm fury, swirling Grace out of the shop in her wake.

Breathlessly, Nutmeg commanded, "Stay close and keep quiet!" as she pulled them both into an alley and ducked down the back street. She found a crack between mud-and-stone walls, and headed in sideways, still in firm control of Grace's arm. "This way." Wriggling carefully, she made her way between shops, then found a door in an unlikely spot, cracked it open, and crept in. In a storeroom full of barrels, kegs, crates, and bales smelling of toback, both went to their knees in the shadows till Nutmeg found the corner she wanted, and motioned Grace to look.

Through a spidery-thin crack, she could see the interior of the smoking parlor, its faint aroma wafting up her nose as she pressed her face to the wood. Nutmeg lay on her stomach so she could peer out the crack beneath Grace as they spied on the mysterious world of her father and his friends.

Tolby exchanged a few opinions about the breeding of sheep and goats and pigs, mildly expressed, but taken as authority. Yet he merely smiled and clamped his teeth tighter about his pipe stem when Croft, a hunched-over and rather unpleasant and seedy-looking fellow, asked for his recipe to making decent cider, and the room lapsed into momentary silence after Tolby's irritated grunt.

Honeyfoot, in the corner, pink-faced and gray-browed, his thin, snow-white hair in a frazzle about his head, made a cracking noise in his jaws, then grunted mildly before venturing a thought. "How about a tale or two? I've had enough of farm and ranch talk." He sat, not with pipe in hand, but a sack of candies which he popped into his mouth one at a time, sucking on their sweetness and crunching now and then with a contented smile on his round face.

"Grousing 'bout them tolls reminds me of the time Bregan Oxfort took on the Dark Ferryman at the River Nylara." Tanned and wiry, the miller Sweetbrook rolled a toback leaf on his leg, making a zigar for himself, with strong hands and arms that had turned many a mill rock when the river ran low. There'd always been Sweetbrooks at the mill and he was known as the young Sweetbrook and would be until his father passed. Then he would be old Sweetbrook and his son the younger. If he had a first name of his own, Tolby had never heard it. His dark hair was plaited back and clipped tightly at the nape of his neck, but his vest shone of gold-threaded cloth, and his trousers were piped in gold as well, showing his worth.

"Tell it, then." Tiym Panner stifled a yawn, his beringed fingers wrapped about a mug, his own outfit resplendent with a trader's wealth from his shoes (not boots) to the cap atop his head. "That's a tale I've not heard in a while."

"Well known it is, but still never to be understood," Sweetbrook countered. "Before the Strangers came, the Nylara, great river that she is, rushed through Ginton Valley bringing both blessing and curse, as any great river does. So it is with a Dweller's life. Sun can be too much and not enough, earth rock-hard or quicksand-soft, fire to burn us or protect us.

"The Nylara has a wide, stony bed, sharp and difficult to traverse, yet her broad waters must be crossed to tie together our peoples and provinces. At the flats of Ginton is the best place to cross her if it is to be attempted at all, and there are songs and stories of the tragedy of trying it. The clever Kernans tried to build a bridge cross't, to no avail. The arrogant Galdarkans said they could cross the Nylara wherever they pleased, but they could not find a better fording place. So the Nylara ran wild."

"Aye," mumbled Clem Barrel around a chaw of toback stuffed in his gums. "My granduncle drowned there."

A murmur of agreement ran around the room, and Sweetbrook waited for it to die out before going on. He laced his fingers behind his head as he sat back, his pipe dwindling in the smoking bowl balanced on his knee, smoke trailing up in a thin, silvery wisp. "Now the waters of Nylara defied all the attempts to build a bridge. Nothing could be done but rebuild ferry docks over and over onct they were flooded out, and begin again, and the ferries themselves were chancy to take but better than nothing. If not over the river, then it would be close to a month's travel to find a way to cross it, where she narrows steep and swift through the mountains, even then the weather oft closing it off. You can see why the Nylara was cursed many a time."

"Yet there is no doubt in anyone's mind that the Nylara is second only to the Andredia in th' beauty of her waters—fresh, clean, and good—even through those scorching lands which carry water rarely. She is far more needed and cherished than cursed, and we must live with the ways and will of her. Then the Strangers came."

Grace could not contain a tiny shiver that ran through her as the words passed through the walls and into her hearing, carried on scented toback smoke. Nutmeg slid a hand up and patted her wrist, as quiet as a mouse with only a tiny rustle of her clothes. The closeness of her sister helped diminish her worry a little, and then the warmth disappeared as Nutmeg crouched even closer to their peephole. She'd missed a few sentences, but Sweetbrook's gestures caught her eye and she bent nearer the crack.

"Disadvantages even to them, keeping their strength at bay in the north. The elves wanted a way clear to deal with all the lands as they would. It is said the Gods treat with the Vaelinars, even though they do not bow to them, and powers are given to the elves beyond our abilities. The Kernans might argue that, but the Gods have turned their faces from them for the sins of the Magi, so who is to say? It must be true, for they built a ferry across the Nylara that even the forces of the river cannot deter. It is a Dark Ferryman who handles the rudder, but flood and drought have never stayed him. We took the ferry cautious at first, then the traders saw their own advantage in using it, and it became commonplace, although the mysterious shadowy figure exacts a toll from each and every passenger before crossing. Only once was the Ferryman halted in his chore.

"Willard Oxfort is Merchant King. He has braved fire and flood, wind and ice, raiders and pestilence to bring us goods. If he has profited—and some say mightily—by his efforts, who can deny that time and again, he has risked all? Still, the Dark Ferryman chafed at him. The toll, he felt, was an extortion of the Vaelinars. What right had they to make a profit off the wild waters of the Nylara? And so he complains to his son, time and again, as they cross the Nylara on their many excursions. His son is a dutiful son and guards the trader convoy while learning his father's business.

"They came upon the southern shore of the Nylara, and out of the morning mists, the Dark Ferryman appeared, leaning on the rudder of his vessel. He beckoned for them to come aboard, and took the coins from Willard Oxfort with scarcely a notice, all bone and shadow covered with robes. Who can say within that cowled hood if eyes really watch or not? Yet he seems to know exactly what toll each passenger should pay." Sweetbrook paused, and a shiver went round the room from all those who'd encountered the spectral figure.

"On the other side, and waiting for three more crossings for his entire caravan to be boated, Willard grew angrier by the moment. Good profit wasted instead of turning to more investment, extortion paid to Strangers, who knows exactly what ran through the trader's mind? We only know that he complained loudly to his son and when the last caravan had been landed and the convoy started north again, Bregan reined his horse about, drawing his sword.

"Bregan had a reputation then as an outstanding swordsman. He more than guarded his father's and others' convoys, he was known as one of the best in all the provinces. Quick yet strong, with a keen eye and steady temper, his fame alone kept many a bandit away. Young then, he decided to rid his father of his tormentor, and he drew down on the Ferryman who stood and merely waited as if blind to the attack.

"On the first pass, he cut the coin purse from the black leather belt twisted about the Ferryman's figure. On the second pass, even as the Ferryman raised his staff to parry, he cut the specter in half, his sword passing through dark shadows that exploded in a burst of black fire and sparks with the very stink of hell itself. The fiery blast threw Bregan to the ground, and when he finally stood, nothing remained of the Ferryman."

A tobacco leaf could have fallen to the floor and been heard for the stillness in the smoking parlor. Sweetbrook looked around. He pulled his pipe up, relit it, and took a long, deep draft from it before laying it down again.

"His sword had melted away to nothing. His entire side, from foot to scalp, blackened and numb, Bregan staggered up. He picked up the coin purse and handed it to his father, the Dark Ferryman vanquished."

The tall figure in the corner unwound, standing straight, his cloak falling from his body in a cascade of silken folds, his very movement stopping the miller in mid-breath. His gaze raked the room, his angular face cast in the planes of Vaelinarran beauty, his pewter hair swept back into a long braid, his pointed ears plain as could be. "Tell the story properly or do not tell it at all," he suggested, drawing his cloak back about his shoulders gracefully. He pointed at Tolby. "I hear you know the truth of it." With that, the man swept out of the room, only the bang of the door at his heels to tell he'd even been there at all.

Tolby's eyebrows rose high enough to set up a ladder of wrinkles across his forehead as Sweetbrook traded looks with him. The miller nodded. "Tell it, then, if you know it," he said, his voice a little unsteady.

Tolby looked thoughtful before nodding back. "As there is more than one way to skin a stinkdog, there is more than one way to tell a tale, sometimes. This is one that takes place in our lifetime, and so the telling of it has wound round and round about, as slyly as the bed of the River Silverwing."

"True enough," muttered Honeyfoot, as he shifted his weight, candy bag rattling and crumpling in his hold. "More'n one way to hitch a wagon, I always say."

"And who would be knowin' more than you who canna get it right the first time?" came a shout from a corner Grace could not see, laughter following it and chasing away the tension she'd felt in the room.

Tolby grinned about his pipe stem, waiting till all grew hushed again. "As I have heard it, the elves did not bring the Ferryman out of their own desire to conquer the road north and south, as has often been said. Instead, it was the people of Ginton who went to them and asked for their help to somehow bless the ferries which crossed it daily and oft dashed to pieces on the rocky shores. Being a people close to the Gods, it had been thought that they could bring safety to the ferries and their operators. Instead, the Vaelinars brought their own magic to the river, their own ferry and their own ferryman. It did not happen in a day or a year or even a ten span of years. They studied the river long before they finally built a ferry to their satisfaction. They lost their own lives on the Nylara learning its flood and neap tides, so many bloods stain those docks. When it was done, they explained that they could not bless a mortal being, hence the Dark Ferryman existed to bring the boat safely back and forth. The toll they exacted would be used to maintain waiting docks at either side, and so forth. From traders they exacted more, because of the weight and wear and tear on the ferry. So the Dark Ferryman crosses the Nylara, come hell or high water.

" 'Tis true Oxfort chafed at the tolls like a pack animal with harness sores. He likes the Vaelinars not at all. On that day, he had his coins ready, although still he argued with the spectral figure over what he intended to pay. The shadow, saying but little, insisted on his exact toll. In disgust, Oxfort dropped the coins in his hand and loaded the first caravans and had them ferried over. The second and third load went the same, with Oxforts on the north shore awaiting the last of their convoy. It was then the Dark Ferryman stood adamantly, refusing to bring the rest of the caravans over.

"Oxfort turned crimson with fury. He shouted at the implacable figure, which finally put out its spectral hand and rained counterfeit coins from its fingers, brightly painted slugs, upon the ground. Oxfort had not seen fit to pay his toll honestly. Humiliated in front of his drivers and guards, he threw the last of his gold crowns at the Ferryman and rode off, not waiting to see if his convoy would be transported. It was, in the Ferryman's own good time.

"Meanwhile, Bregan stewed at the smear on his family's name. Never mind that it had been an impetuous act on his father's part, and who can blame him in a way, for having to give up hard-earned money to an unfeeling shadow. With a yell, he charged the Ferryman who parried with his staff, and a dire warning. 'Touch me not or the sins of the father will fall on the son,' it told him. Embarrassed at being foisted off like an inexperienced youth, Bregan growled and charged again. Yet a second time the Ferryman neatly parried the blade and nearly sent Bregan backward off the ass of his steed. The third time, Bregan did not fail.

"He paid dearly for his father's and his own vanity. The Ferryman vanished and did not return for a span of years, and only after much entreaty by the folk of Ginton, after mortal ferries could not stand up to the willful Nylara. As for whether this is true or not . . ." Tolby paused. "I can only say that I was one of the young guardsmen riding in hire of that convoy."

Grace let out her breath, but had no longer to marvel at the tale, for Nutmeg began to scramble backward out of the storage room corner, pulling and tugging on her skirt. They hastily made it back to the yardage shop and milliner's, praising the joys of a drink they had not had, leaving Rivergrace even thirstier than before. If Lily noticed the faint aroma of toback on them, she did not say so.

Chapter Sixteen

HOSMER HUNG ON the side of the corral, boots planted firmly and elbows hooked over the top rail, watching the horses and ponies milling about, their coats still shaggy and dense from the winter, their hooves freshly trimmed for the herding to market, their eyes rolling at the strangeness of many people about them. He wore the longcoat of the Silverwing militia, a homespun tailored coat, dyed the dark crimson of the tart winterberry, with a knotted kerchief about his left upper arm. Keldan jumped up to perch on the rail, laughing when a wild-eyed pony trotted past to nip at his boots, and Garner scaled the fence by his older brother.

"Thought we were going to eat first."

"Not yet." Hosmer stared intently across the pens.

"Know what you're looking for?"

"Pretty much. Short croup, good legs and hooves, large eye. Nothing fancy, just a good post road mount." Hosmer ticked off the features that would mean stamina and a good riding gait, agility and intelligence. Almost any horse he looked at in this corral would ride smoother than his wagon horse, no fault or virtue of either, one could not blame a horse for doing what it was bred to do. It wouldn't hurt to have one whose trot didn't feel like it would send his spine jolting through his skull either. Banner was a good horse, but he'd grown too old to do the kind of work Hosmer needed. He'd be retired back down to pulling the wagons and carts, or carrying Grace and Nutmeg around.

Garner drummed his fingers on the rail. He knew his brother could stand transfixed for an hour or two, just watching the beasts. He, on the other hand, would rather be down at the fairgrounds, strolling about and watching the pretty young ladies who were out strolling the booths, looking for handsome young men. Keldan twisted and squirmed about on his rail seat. Kel would rather be doing most anything involving dancing, running, juggling, *moving*. Garner put his hand on Hosmer's shoulder. "Why don't I take the lad exploring while you look over the stock?"

Hosmer's head jerked about, an irritated expression racing across his square face, and then he nodded. "A'right then. Go about, but mind you're a Farbranch."

Garner winked at him as he pulled Keldan down from the railing. "Could we be anything else?" With a cheery whistle, he sauntered away from the stock pens and the air redolent of manure and feed, beckoning Keldan toward the dance field and fair booths. As they closed on it, crossing the main street of the village, the faint sound of piping drew Keldan who stopped and threw his head back, rather like one of the colts they'd just seen in the horse pens. He raised his arms.

"Listen!"

"I hear it, and smell it, too." Far better smells than the ones they'd just left. Garner grinned and poked Keldan to stir him.

"Not that." Keldan turned slowly on one heel. "Listen," he said, and cocked his head to the wind. More like Lily in looks than any of them, even Nutmeg, he had a streak that none of the others had. Perhaps it had come from her side of the family, though Garner never thought of his mother that way, but Keldan looked as if he could run the hills and high mountains like a stag in autumn. He had this affinity for wild things. Garner had once seen him whistle down a hawk from the sky, the predator diving in and wheeling around before gliding to a low branch nearby where Keldan and the bird had eyed each other a moment before the hawk took to the air again. Tolby had had a free-roaming youth, but nothing in him ran like the blood in Keldan's veins.

Keldan turned one hand slowly. "Hear them?"

Garner shrugged. He heard a faint piping accompanied by the broken sound of rough singing and dancing in the field roped off for merrymaking, but he could almost swear that wasn't what Keldan heard. He watched his brother stand transfixed in the middle of the lane and took his arm to lead him off to the side, when he heard and saw it too.

A slow, deliberate thunder of hooves. Bullwhips snapping in the air over the pounding, and whistles light yet piercing, and even singing too.

Riders drove their mounts into the small town, dust clouds rising from shining hooves, a small herd of tall sleek elegant horses racing ahead of the riders. No shaggy plains horses or mountain ponies these, but satiny-skinned, nostrils-flared, slender-legged hot bloods. His pulse drummed to the running horses, and his gaze fixed on the lead rider. She was elegant, beautiful, her shining hair drawn back from her face as she snapped her whip about the heads of the free-running steeds in front of her. He thought his heart would stop entirely as she rode down on him.

"Vaelinars," breathed Keldan at his side. "With their tashya horses," he added, jostling Garner, and Garner found himself able to breathe at last. The Vaelinars swept past him, and the lead rider turned her head to look at them. He saw hair spun of wild honey streaked with silvery gold, and eyes of verdant green flecked with smoke and leaf green, and skin of translucent freshness offset by lips the color of deepest blood. She wore black smoke and silver, tight and silken about her curves. The jolt of her glance locked Garner's feet to the ground, and his heart fluttered for a moment with her mouth curving as if knowing his thoughts before her tall, iron-gray mount carried her past. She swung her arm about, cracking the whip again. Standing slightly in her stirrups, her whole body moved with a kind of languid, sensual grace, belying the strength it needed to handle such a whip, and with such a delicate precision. It popped over the pricked ears of high-flung heads, and the horses snorted in answer.

She was the most beautiful woman in the world.

Keldan tugged on him. "Who is she? Who is she?"

It took a moment for him to gather breath and thoughts enough to answer. He shook his head in wonder. "I don't know," Garner answered simply.

"That is Tressandre ild Fallyn," a voice said in Sevryn's ear. "There will be trouble before nightfall, Accords or no Accords. Watch yourself, Queen's Hand."

His eye caught by the spectacle of the riders moving swiftly past, Sevryn turned almost too late to catch a glimpse of the shadow who'd whispered in his ear, slipping out of view, but he caught sight of him from the corner of his eye—tall, storm-colored, with hair tied back in a long braid—and knew that Daravan had been murmuring advice to him. Daravan, little more than a hermit or a rumor in the matter of things, whispering advice into his ear. The spectacle and the knowledge troubled him even more than seeing Stronghold ild Fallyn ride in. At Lariel's court and on the streets, Sevryn kept to the quiet side of matters, looking like little more than the mixed blood he was, and without the startling eyes of the Vaelinars, the mark of elven blood that carried magic and power within it. He'd never known of another who held magic without the eyes, so even if he was seen with Lariel and Jeredon, another Vaelinar would dismiss his value.

He had, perhaps, after years with the Warrior Queen, developed an odd sensibility. Daravan was like his old mentor, nonaligned and apparently rootless, seemingly everywhere and nowhere at once, with motives as murky as his exact whereabouts. That Daravan was here, today, in advance of the ild Fallyn brooked no good, he decided. Even more unsettling was the knowledge that the elder Vaelinar knew who he was and what Sevryn did, for he traded on his aspect of being a gutter brat, a bastard of little or no use to anyone. And to think he'd merely stopped by to hear a bit of the local gossip, away from the larger cities, following the trade roads as if he were himself a vagabond peddler.

Life with Lariel and Jeredon had proved to be rich—rich with compassion, care, intrigue, and action. It held all the warmth of a family, and the brother and sister held him close in their confidence and trust. Though he still sometimes felt the sting of the Kobrir dagger in his side, and healers told him a splinter of the dagger might have worked its way into a rib bone, they'd gotten the poison out of him and mending had only been a matter of time. Neither sister nor brother had stinted in grilling him while they cared for him, and he kept his silence except when necessary, revealing no one, dead or alive. Still, they eked out a profile of him, and then Lariel had decided to put him to use, during which time he'd proved what he had not spilled during their interrogations. He was loyal, and loved them both to a fault, and would never betray their faith in him.

He'd never been happier. Or in more danger. Yet Sevryn could not regret the balancing of his life. He'd gladly give up safety for fulfillment, and had, over and over. Now, as he wandered the Spring fair, watching the Dwellers and Kernans bustling about, he listened for word of discontentment, of hatred, of fear, of despair. Since resettlement from the borders of her lands, she'd kept a keen eye out for the repercussions of that action. So far, there had been little, particularly with Ravers harrowing where settlements had once stood, death and bloodshed avoided by happenstance. Not that they would be thanked for sparing those they had moved. No, they could not expect that. Lariel had taught him that the Vaelinars' world was different from Kerith itself, and often they had to bridge that distance, or they would never understand the beings with whom they now shared an existence. He had never realized before that he straddled two worlds.

With a stifled sigh, he turned his eyes away from the vision of the ild Fallyn Stronghold riding in, and leaned a shoulder into a tavern doorway, as if gauging the crowds and brews available. With a practiced eye, he could tell who drank and why, the why being the importance of it. To celebrate or drown misery, to drink for joy or need, and a look about the room told him this was a town of happy if curious folk, with talk about the Vaelinars already brewing about the edges.

Why would Daravan mention the Accords? Vaelinars did not kill other Vaelinars not only because of the accords, but because of the sheer necessity of needing their own bloodlines to survive around them. The first centuries of bitterness and contention had settled long ago. What purpose would Daravan have in setting that into his thoughts now?

Having lingered too long in the tavern doorway to simply leave, his mind distracted, Sevryn entered and flipped a crown bit to the 'tender, taking a wooden mug of brew with him as he sauntered back outside and made his way down the small lane toward the fairing grounds. On this bright spring day, after a long and harsh winter, everything seemed to be in order. A handful of Bolgers pushed past him, one turning back to nod an apology, before the brutes headed toward the barns and stock pens. Sevryn lifted his mug in reflection to hide the grimace he could not contain whenever he encountered them. City-wise Bolgers, though rough and crude, more or less adapted to civilization, but in the wild, whatever veneer they had vanished quickly. Sneakers, he had little or no use for them at all, though he did treat with them for the sake of the Vaelinars. There is a balance, he'd had pounded into his head, for all beings.

Keeping himself to a saunter, he walked the edge of the streets, making a note of all he saw. Long, cold winter gone, yet these folk seemed to have prospered, which would be good news to carry home. He wondered yet again if what nagged at Lariel might be unfounded, but he knew better. Her senses were honed like the keenest of blades, and if she felt something ill taking root and prospering on its own, she would be right. His job would only be to confirm it so that it could be fought and uprooted for good. Turning his back on the small town—village, more than anything else with only its river and trade route importance elevating its status—he made note of the banners flying at the campgrounds on the open meadows, and his mouth dried.

Stronghold ild Fallyn he'd seen ride in. Its black flag, limned with silver with a bend in the form of a silver dagger, snapped defiantly in the wind. Across from it flew the banner of Stronghold Istlanthir, sworn enemy of the ild Fallyns, held apart from them only by the Accords, and Sevryn realized that Kever and Tranta had, no doubt, come to keep an eye on the Fallyns or perhaps to extract a long-awaited vengeance on Tressandre or Alton. On a slight hummock, over both, he could see the pavilion with the colors of the House Hith-aryn, and the emblem of its heir Bistane. His father Bistel was the oldest living Vaelinar on Kerith and still looked in his prime, silver-blue hair cropped close to his head, setting off dark blue eyes that blazed with intensity and lightning streaks of light blue. His son Bistane held the same eyes, if not the silvery hair. And neither was opposed lightly.

He groaned softly. All of them with blood hotter than that of the fine tashya horses tethered beside the accommodations or pacing inside the stockyard corrals. It would be too much to hope there would be no trouble. Almost with reluctance, he made his leisurely way to the fairgrounds, attracting little attention and observing as he went. At the outskirts, a clapboard booth attracted a handful of Bolgers, and he eyed it as he passed, without showing it had drawn his attention. A leathery, older Bolger squatted in the center, showing forge work for sale, spread out on a woven pony blanket, the aromas of both beasts hanging in the air. He had bits and buckles, latches and keys, all manner of ironwork save for weapons. Sevryn made a note on that, knowing that the weapons were undoubtedly available, too, but sold elsewhere and at other times. As he drew away, the smithy Bolger pushed up the sleeves of his shirt, exposing a forearm that had been branded long ago by carelessness or purpose, the scar bleached white with age, stark against his dark skin. It struck him for a long moment, and he decided it was only because of the need to remember the being. That Bolger would not be hard to find later.

He buried that thought in the back of his mind along with myriad other observations he would carry back to his employer. Ahead of him lay the true fair: sturdy tables, booths, and awnings, colorful as the newly blossoming flowers, and filled with folk celebrating the season. Even the haughty Galdarkans had come from the east, or a few of them had, their tall strong forms mingled in the crowd, with their bright overcoats of dark blue heralded with gold stars, remnants of the lost empire. Sevryn could see a few Vaelinars as well and some Kernans tall enough to be half-breeds like himself, but the lanes were abundant with the smaller and ebullient Dweller stock who thrived in these hills and valleys. Their excitement bubbled about them. Not bothering to contain a smile, Sevryn wound slowly through the throngs, enjoying the celebration.

He bought a cheese turnover, hot from the outdoor ovens, and tossed it from hand to hand to cool it enough for eating. The cheeses, both mellow and sharp, dripped from flaky pastry to his mouth as he nibbled contentedly. Someone jostled his shoulder. With quick hands, he saved the last of his morsel, gobbled it down, and turned to see who'd moved so closely by him, smelling of the faintest of riverlilies.

A hunched form brushed past, swathed in old, worn, dark robes with frayed hem and flanked by a curvaceous Dweller lass. A grandmother, no doubt, or village woman of some importance, leaning on the young girl as one would a cane. He glimpsed deep crimson boot leather, slender and sleek, the footwear at immediate odds with the hooded garb. It caught his attention. Sevryn sidled closer nonchalantly.

Tossing the last of his cheese turnover in the air and gulping it down, he sketched his way behind them, casually, turning away when they stopped at a booth, not wishing to be seen as much as he wished a clearer view. The back of his neck itched. He heard a muttering gripe about the Bolger booths at the outskirts of the fair, and registered that, even as he glanced down at the latest in halters and harnesses.

"Cursed Stinkers. They're fouler than the wallows at the butcher's yards."

"Mebbe so, but that's a good lot. Earning their keep by hard work, 'stead of banditing."

"Fah. Only good Bolger is a dead one, just like those slavin' elves."

He did not catch sight of the two men growling at each other. Instead, someone bumped the pair he followed, and the old woman spun about, catching her balance as she stood straight, her robes swinging open and he froze, stung by the revelation.

She looked like a caged bird, suddenly freed. The dark robe winged about her, caught in the spring breeze, swirling high and then cascading down to mask her again. But before it did, he caught sight of lustrous chestnut hair trailing over one shoulder, a slender hand clasped with that of the shorter girl, her face lit in surprise and delight at the laughter and endless talk of her companion. The sunlight brought out golden-red strands of hair tumbled among the darker auburns and brunettes as she caught her balance with unassuming charm. Her gown of simple weave matched that of the bubbly talker, gracing a willowy frame that ought never to have been hidden by drab and fraying robes, yet had been. She gathered herself quickly, even as the Dweller lass called her sister, and moved in to close her robes and pat her down, and they resumed their pairing of old woman and lass, shuttering away the vision from his sight.

Sevryn quickened his step, moved to catch up with her, see her closely . . . moved to see the shape of her ears, and color of her eyes. She could not be what he thought she might be, but she could be nothing else, he thought, as the Dweller led her away in a swirl of skirts. He couldn't let them go. By the fading sound of the shorter one's laugh, he followed them, deliberately letting crowds get between them, so that he could see the tall one more clearly. Then, as if sensing his very thoughts, she turned about and gazed in his direction, hood framing her face like a storm cloud of darkness.

A festive beaded cap cradled her head under that hood, hiding the curve of her ears, but it was her eyes that shocked him, a vivid blue-green reminiscent of southern seas lanced with gold streaks that might or might not be the sun dazzling him, her eyes glanced over him, lingering a moment, then moving on, before she dropped her head, pulling her hood forward and turning back to her sister's pull on her sleeve. The other's hands rushed to cover her, hiding her away again. Two views fate had granted him, and he was not likely to get another. He let his breath out, stepped back. People pushed between them, hiding what he sought, and Sevryn let them go. He had more questions now than answers.

"You look like a likely lad." A hand fell on his shoulder, spinning him around. Sevryn let his body flow with the motion even as he tensed for trouble.

Alton ild Fallyn blocked his way, body covered in the shimmering black-and-silver silks of his Stronghold, a masculine echo of his sister Tressandre. Thick wavy hair like honey streaked on amber fell to his shoulders in a loose tie, and his jade-green eyes held shards of steel gray in them as he appraised Sevryn from head to toe. A muscle ticked along his jawline. From that first moment of arrogant interest to the fleeting second of dismissal, Sevryn read the other's face. Looking for a Vaelinar and finding a half-breed or less, it seemed. Alton's shoulder twitched vaguely. Sevryn was used to that dismissive expression that followed as the ild Fallyn searched his eyes, and found him lacking. As Lariel's Hand, though Voice was more appropriate, few ever really saw him in her service and those who did, did not realize who it was they saw. His work for her as herald and liaison kept him quietly in the shadows and out of the way, and unknown. Alton had never recognized him in court, and wouldn't now, nor did he recognize Talent.

"Looking for someone?" He kept his voice light, allowing a bit of drunkenness to slur his words.

"Always, lad, always. We offer training for those who might benefit. Ride north and ask for Stronghold ild Fallyn."

"Training? In what?"

"Whatever you show the most Talent in. We have our ways, as you may know, of delving into your very self. Be it blade or plow, we will teach you. Find us if you're not afraid of work and learning." Alton dropped his hand, and backed away, his brilliant eyes looking for someone else before the last words had even fallen from his lips.

Stronghold ild Fallyn, one of the first to take slaves, one of the last to free them, and it was said in back alleys even today that they still gave hard apprenticeships, even to half-breeds whose eyes showed they carried a strain of magic in them, though it might be faint and tenuous. Alton's interest had faded the moment he'd seen his plain gray eyes. Sevryn let himself stagger sideways, carrying him out of Alton's way and even farther from his attention.

So the ild Fallyns had come recruiting. It wasn't for altruistic reasons.

As for the others, the probability seemed high they had come to keep an eye on them. Bistane's journey from Hith-aryn had been considerable; he may have had other business in the regions and lingered with the good weather, but that he was here today was no coincidence.

Sevryn let the current of the afternoon crowd carry him toward the music players and the dancing circle, a bare and level patch of ground pounded down by many feet over years past, festooned with beribboned poles and flower wreaths. He found a post to lean against, and do what he'd been sent to do, observe and gather. Wisps of clouds began to appear on the far horizon, but they stayed white and thready, no threat at all to the fine weather. He ignored the urge to find the girls again, for they were not his job, as far as he knew. Of course, he'd been wrong before. Sevryn lifted his mug to his lips and savored the barest sip of some good home brew.

Her fingers itched to slip through the ribbons and baubles at the booths they stopped at, but Grace stood back and let Nutmeg hold them up, rivers of shimmering colors in her hands, for them both to admire. Tolby had promised them each one pretty from the fair, but to choose one small item from all the bounties seemed an impossible task. A clasp for her hair? Or a bracelet for her ankle? The sellers even had clever rings for the toes, although the thought of that made her laugh quietly. How could she wear such a thing inside her boots? Nutmeg nudged her gently.

"Such silly things," she whispered to Nutmeg's ear.

"But beautiful, aye? Not for us, though. I hear to the south, where there is no snow for winter and the women walk about in bare feet, they wear rings and bells on their toes."

"No!"

Nutmeg nodded, stepping out again on finery row where pretty things of little practical use other than to dazzle the eye lay in trays in booths as far as they could see, or so it seemed. She looked at toys on strings that could bow and dance and wave their arms when the strings were jerked. Nutmeg lingered for a very long time at a tray of metal headbands gleaming with tiny gemstones, the wires twisting like tiaras and diadems, before wrinkling her nose. "If I got one of those," she declared to Rivergrace, "how could I know if a beau was staring at me or my jewels, hmmm?"

"Or something else entirely," Grace remarked dryly, and her sister gave her a little push even as she laughed and tossed her head.

"Can I help it if I have a bounty?"

"No, and it's certainly better than the days when you used to stuff apples in your bodice."

"I never!"

"Yes, you did!" Grace clapped a hand to her mouth to stifle her laugh which would have sounded clear and light over the peddlers' lane. Nutmeg threw her a look, her eyes frowning a bit, and then hugged her.

Muffled by the robes, Nutmeg said, "It isn't fair."

"It's better than having to stay home." Grace drew her back. "Now give me your shoulder, grandbabe, so I can walk." She let out a cackling sound, and nearly slipped off Nutmeg's shoulder as the other shook with outraged laughter as together they wobbled down the lane.

Chapter Seventeen

SEVRYN SAUNTERED BY the pavilions, listening to the light tones of voices carrying on the wind. They reminded him of sabers—nimble, curved, and with a deadly edge—as he drew nearer and heard contentious words despite the airiness of the tone. He put a shoulder to an aging tree and spoke softly to it, its bark gnarled and sloughing a bit, seeming to sink into its very being as he leaned upon it, letting its branches embrace him, its strength draw him in until he became of it, growing from it, as he listened to the Vaelinars talk among themselves.

Tranta ild Istlanthir worked on the hooves of his mount, the horse with a coat that glistened as if freshly forged bronze leaning back on him, nibbling at his shoulder as he pared down rough spots and cleaned gently but efficiently. Kever worked with the same dedication, but he held a whetstone, sharpening a set of blades strewn across the blanket in front of him, and the scent of oil lingered on the air. Tressandre sat a hillock away, her lithe form both revealed and hidden by the inky black and silver she wore, her eyes half slit in the sun as she soaked up the warm rays, leaning on one arm and seeming to watch Kever, but one could never be sure with Tress. Her attention was seldom focused on a single matter. Behind her, her encampment filled with workers, and Sevryn eyed them, identifying the Vaelinar strain, prominent, if not pure, in each. He noted as many musicians as stockmen in the group, and pondered that. Tressandre stirred a bit restlessly, drawing his and everyone else's attention.

She lifted a slender finger and gestured toward Kever. "Have you a favorite blade there?"

The corner of his mouth tightened and long moments passed before he responded, "Different blades for different matters." His hand never stopped stroking the whetstone upon the long sword he held. The Stronghold ild Istlanthir looks ran sharply in him, from the deep blue of his hair to the light green, streaked with dark green, of his eyes. Of all the Vaelinars on Kerith, the Istlanthir looked the most different, their coloring branding them as strangers even among Strangers. The ild Istlanthir, of all of the families, had never interbred with the races of Kerith. Or if they had, that distinctive blue hair had never been inherited. Kever stropped the blade one last time before testing it against his hand, nodding as crimson welled up from the slightest touch, and put the long sword aside.

"One might think," persuaded Tressandre, "you might be expecting trouble." Her pointing finger and hand settled languidly upon her bent knee.

"Expect or start?" Tranta countered, as he dropped his bronze gelding's hoof and straightened, patting the horse on his shoulder. He stared across the animal's withers at the ild Fallyns.

Tressandre leaned her head back, wild honey-colored hair falling from her shoulders and cascading in a tumble to just barely sweep the blanket she sat on. "One should always be prepared."

Someone snorted. Sevryn thought it might have been the horse, but it could have been the Istlanthir.

If Tressandre noted it, she did not deign to notice it. Her gaze stayed fixed on Kever, as he carefully selected a dagger to oil and sharpen, saying, "There is quite a difference between being cautious and being reckless."

"We cannot afford to be reckless, but neither can we resist judging our quarry, seeing its responses and reactions."

"You create pain wherever you walk."

"Pain is instructive. How a creature gives or takes it can tell us much. Not to mention . . . enjoyable." Tressandre's expression sharpened.

"The ild Fallyns are more than accomplished at dealing it out."

Her response came as a slight yawn, as if lulled by the sun's rays, and it fell into the silence between them. Noting little more than the jabs they always aimed at one another, Sevryn thought to melt away as quietly as he had drawn near, but then Bistane strode up, his charcoal hair tied back and his blue eyes ablaze with emotion. He stripped off riding leathers from his lean thighs as he spoke, his hands in a blur of impatient motion. "There are Bolgers strewn everywhere, some out in the open with the merchants, but whole groups of them in the shadows, at the stock pens or in back of the taverns or asleep in the alleys. I don't like it."

"This is rustic country. Bolgers are to be expected, and even tolerated," Tantra answered him mildly. "They have tribes throughout the area."

"This I know well, and there is a 'tribe' of lean, battle-hardened ones filtering among the softer country workers. I don't like it." Bistane folded his leathers to stow them away in his saddlebag, his gear neatly laid out by his tent.

"Battle-hardened," murmured Tressandre. "And who might they be fighting with, hmmmm?"

No one bothered to answer. Kever finished the care of the dagger in his hands while Tranta led his horse to the pasture fringing their campground and tethered it out to graze.

The daughter of ild Fallyn stood and stretched sensuously, her clothes falling into place smoothly about her body. "I think I shall stroll about and see what these people do for entertainment." A smile played across the curve of her lips before fading away. She crooked a finger to her musicians who gathered up their instrument cases hurriedly to follow. No one watched her leave, their heads steady as if each fought the instinct to do just that.

Bistane cradled one hand in the other and cracked his knuckles, then flexed his hand, before standing, his attention sweeping the campsites. Sevryn could feel the icy inspection and moved his senses a little closer to the warmth of the tree, still and silent though it was, knowing his own likeness was neither icy nor the warmth of a living person, either of which Bistane sought. He would not be able to evade the other's notice much longer, though, and began to seek a way out.

"Why on edge?"

"Why do you clean your blades, over and over?"

Kever grinned at Bistane, undaunted by piercing light blue eyes that watched him keenly. "I like to be prepared."

"As do I, kindred, as do I." Bistane chaffed his hands together.

"So what brought you here?"

Bistane smiled thinly. "You did, kindred, you and the ild Fallyn."

"Nothing more than that?"

"Nothing more that I would share with you, here and now. The very sprigs of grass might have ears . . ."

Sevryn spoke a word, sharp, yet near unheard by Vaelinarran ears.

Tantra's horse caught it and threw his head up with a bugle of alarm, his ears pricked forward, and stamped the new grass and soft dirt. Tender bits went flying, and his tether line snapped sharply in the wind as he jerked his head. When everyone turned to see what worried the beast, Sevryn stepped away from the shadow of the ancient tree and slipped off, back toward the fair and more innocent folk. He learned more by what they had not said rather than what they had. Events had drawn them here, all of them, events important enough that no Stronghold or House was willing to let a potential profit escape them. Yet, although sent here by instinct or by order, they did not know what it was they expected. Nerves could be used as bowstrings, were they so inclined. What he had felt, they had felt, from the east and north in their homes, and they'd come forth.

That was a worry in itself.

And, what had drawn Daravan here? What would have drawn Gilgarran? He had no inkling.

Sevryn came to a halt at the dancers' ring, listening to the musicians, one ear quirked toward the children playing in the soft grass while their elder siblings and parents danced, sometimes joining, but more often involved in games with their straw dolls and marbles and the like. He listened to their clear, high voices squabble and banter and chant childish magics, but he did not hear what he feared to: Four forges dire, earth, wind, water, and fire . . .

He had no more idea what that should mean to him now than he had years ago when he'd first heard it. Something he knew he had to remember, and had not trusted himself to retain, and so he had imprinted it into a child's game to be memorized. His breath eased out in a soft sigh, disappearing into the spring breeze that carried the beginning of another tune to him. It drew him toward it, as ild Fallyn musicians with the finesse only the Vaelinars held, joined in with the country players, and began to play the strands. The melancholy tune drew him closer, as he recognized it, and it caught at him.

A fine, strong voice began to sing.

"Over hills of drifting mist and
valleys cupped low with sun,
we wander yet, our souls in search
of the lost Trevilara.

Her name is forever burned
and yet stays buried,
carried on every wind and treasured breath.
Trevilara is lost and gone before us all,
A final hope, waiting for our death.
Oh, Trevilara, if I could but know you
If I could see and touch you through sorrow's rain,
My spirit would soar beyond the silences
Of all the stars, and my soul come home again."

Sevryn parted the last of the growing crowd to see the singer, and it was Bistane, his body curved in unconscious yearning as the last notes of the song melted away, followed by the final strains of the instruments, in a haunting refrain that echoed the singer. A soft murmur rippled through the listeners, and a few clapped. Bistane lowered his face then, as if noticing he'd drawn a crowd, and he stepped back, turning away from Tressandre's look of amusement, as she directed the players to quiet. She'd almost certainly baited Bistane into the singing by merely having the song begun, its anthem burned like the name Trevilara, into their very being. He did not feel it as they did, yet Sevryn cleared away an annoying catch in his throat. None of them remembered who or what Trevilara had been, save that it embodied all they had lost.

"Enough melancholy," Tress declared. She tossed her head, her lustrous hair cascading over her shoulders. "A dance!" She gestured to her servants who brought up their winds and strings again and merry notes filled the air, notes that made the feet want to strike and the body twirl.

She grabbed up Bistane's hand before he could pull away, and then the hand of a tall, Kernan lad who'd come close to stare at her, and with a laughter that rang joyously, swept them with her to the dancing ring. The villagers joined them, no strangers to dancing, the awe of Bistane's singing forgotten, and the circle swung ever wider.

Grace squeezed Nutmeg's hand. "Oh, listen! They're dancing again." Nothing in the booths could pull at her like the sound of the music did.

Nutmeg tugged her forward. "Come on, let's watch."

Her heart did a little squeeze. How could she watch without wanting to dance? But she followed her sister's impetuous movement through the last of the winding shopping lane and onto the beaten ground where sawdust had been sprinkled over the bent grass and spring flowers, and many feet had tapped the earth into a firm surface. Nutmeg's small shoes flew across the grounds and Grace after her, the music sinking into her body like a stone into the river, causing ripples of wondrous change. Forgetting her hobbled stance, she straightened as someone caught up her free hand, and she and Nutmeg melded into the marvelous circle.

Spring sunlight struck them. Grace tilted her head back inside her shadowy hood, seeking it as instinctively as a flower pushing up through the meadow. Warm flesh pressed her hands and her feet wove an easy pattern as they danced, and the circle swung ever wider. The melody grew louder and faster, carrying her with it. Laughter bubbled out of her, but she could not even hear her own voice, for they all laughed and sang a wordless song to the music sweeping them away. Faster, faster, intricacy of steps lost, she was little more than running sideways gracefully and in time, and then . . . oh, then, as Nutmeg clung to her right hand, she swore her feet left the ground. She no longer danced, but flew!

"Tressandre!" a male voice sliced warningly through the merriment.

Rivergrace did not see anyone, her vision a blur of faces and the colors of their clothes, and the circle of dancers rose higher, spinning faster, and she could feel the music running through all of them. It felt like the Silverwing at flood tide, crashing down from her mountain roots, dangerous and beautiful and irresistible. Her arms held tightly on both sides, as if her fellow dancers feared letting go and crashing to the ground, and they spun.

Wheels did not seem to turn as fast as they did. Her ears roared with the sense of it as joy and fear ruled her body equally, and she could barely hear Nutmeg's laughter as the frantic music thrilled through her. Sound and soul carried them. The Vaelinars woven throughout the circle raised their hands, seemingly to lift them up as they all swung around. What magic was this? Her cloak unfurled about her, threatening to fly away. She twirled through the air as though on a swing from the highest apple tree she could imagine . . .

"Tressandre!" the male voice bellowed in anger, and the circle faltered as his rage touched Rivergrace, and whatever Tressandre was must have felt it, too.

The music slowed, troubled. She saw the ground begin to rise toward her feet once more, and the blur of noise fell apart into jumbled sounds. Nutmeg let out a high, shivery noise more of terror than happiness and she murmured back a soothing sound she only hoped her sister could catch. The circle held together despite a high-pitched scream here and there, and she could see pale faces emerge, as well as those like hers flushed with the melody that charged the air. A sudden emptiness made her feel weak, uncertain that her legs could hold her if they ever touched ground again . . . They slowed and lowered, and slowed, and then—

Someone screamed sharply, the sound cut off abruptly. The music crashed to a jarring halt. Rivergrace let go in alarm, falling to the earth, stumbling to her feet. Villagers tumbled about each other like a pack of unruly puppies.

"Raiders, and to arms!"

She wove on her legs as if she'd been drunk, unsteady as a newborn calf or foal. She grabbed in midair for something to steady herself and found nothing. The crowd rose around her, wobbly, tumultuous, pushing and shoving.

A piercing shout rose above the noise. "*Ravers!*"

Men and Bolgers ran past, weapons in hand. Nutmeg tumbled on top of her. Grace grabbed her, pulling her around and behind her. The cloak muffled her movements, the hood falling back over her eyes as she looked for the trouble, seeing only people running in every direction. She saw no one she recognized, not Da, not Garner or Keldan. . . .

"Nutmeg! Grace! It's Ravers—run to the shops! RUN!"

From out of nowhere, she spotted Hosmer, looking about frantically, his short sword in one hand, and his stout applewood quarterstaff in the other. He did not see them, but she saw him and let out a whistle that began and then fell short from her lips gone suddenly dry. He heard it anyway. He twisted about, and waved his sword toward them, before dashing to the open road, his militia coat flapping about him, as disaster rode down on them.

He ran toward the Ravers instead of away. Her throat went dryer than her mouth. Nutmeg hauled on her arm. "Come on!"

She turned in the direction pulled, and a Bolger bumped them hard, grunting, a great two-handed sword in his hands. Nutmeg went sprawling. He picked Nutmeg up by the elbow to set her back on her feet with scarcely a look, his leathery face split in a grimace, his forger's apron still on, his homespun shirt rolled up over his scarred and branded arms. He pushed the girls away from the stampeding, fearful crowd and then headed after Hosmer.

She could see the shapes then, dark riders on lathered horses, and strange, loping runners beside them, so many she couldn't count them with one look. Ravers and Bolgers and the runners, dust boiling about them, shadows shrouding them. Nutmeg bolted toward the village behind then in a weaving run, but Grace found herself frozen in place, staring. The faceless, hooded things bearing down the road seemed bent on one thing, and one thing only.

She could hear the high-pitched, hissing cry, a keening that lanced through the air, like a whirlwind whistling high over all the other catastrophe. "Ssstrange blooood." It drained her will to hear it.

The forces collided in a thunder of grunts and steel strikes and the squeal of horses. Then, like branches parting in a high wind, the invaders divided, two thin groups splintering off as the main core wrestled with the defenders. She could not see Hosmer's square form among them, and feared to. She tore her eyes away from the sight, pivoting then on legs still feeling spindly and weak. With a deep breath, she forced herself to run after Nutmeg whose short legs still carried her swiftly across the fairgrounds, over the debris of fallen booths and scattered gaieties trampled beneath. Fleeing side by side, yet far behind the crowd, they gained the main street.

Bolgers charged from the side alley. Nutmeg veered away from the Stinkers. Grace could not tell if they were friend or foe as she chased after her sister. Her heart thudded in her chest, her head reeled. Something loomed in the corner of her eye and she darted to the side. A Bolger, riding low, charged past her, fist grasping at thin air, cursing. He leaned even lower from his saddle to grab up Nutmeg, thrashing and squealing as he hoisted her into the air and over the neck of his mount.

No breath to scream with. Her throat froze as the Bolger reined up, turned his mount and then pounded past Grace, his face grimacing in triumph. She clawed as him as he rode by, his boot catching her in the chest and shoving her aside. She went to her knees with a smothered sob.

She did not stay down. She would not! Grace leaped to her feet and stood in the dirt a moment before whirling around and running back to the trampled remains of the fair. Images ran through her mind, the swordsmith, his crude stand at the fair's edge. She found the booth at the edge of the chaos and fell to her knees again, searching with trembling hands. "Here, here, help me, help me, Gods. Help me find it!" She sifted through broken wood and torn cloth, frantically, hands shaking so hard that even if she found what she needed, she didn't know if she could hold it. Words bubbled from her lips like water from a spring, and then, oh, then, she grasped the cold hilt of a sword, crude and hidden, but there with a handful of others. She only needed one. Then, she got to her feet slowly and walked in the direction Nutmeg had been taken.

Sevryn felt the power Tressandre wove pulling at him, leeching strength from him. He leaned away from it, watching the circle of dancers in their unknowing joy, each who joined adding to the power of her enchantment, each feeding her as she danced with them, her head thrown back and her whole body aglow with a kind of fierceness. He could see Bistane rise up in anger and yell at her for entrancing all of them. If she heard, she ignored him. She pulled at all within her range, feeding off them to fuel the magic woven into the music, and Sevryn denied her his power. It took a moment or two of centering himself as Gilgarran had pounded into him many a time, and shrouding his efforts so that she would not even know she'd touched him. He was no fool. Tressandre did not make merry for its own sake. The ild Fallyn were searching for Talent, however they might find it, and she was filling herself with every remnant of it she sensed. He brushed his hand through his hair, stepping back from the spectacle when Bistane bellowed in rage a second time, and hells broke loose. Then, in a matter altogether different, or perhaps the same, the raiders hit, as if summoned by Tressandre's flaunting of power.

Sevryn drew his katana. Streaming people fled past him, lurching, their strength weakened by Tressandre's hold on them, unknowing, screaming, and yelling. He spotted Bistane throwing off Tressandre's hold, and bolting to his pavilion for armor and arms. They brushed past Sevryn as he stood assessing the panic, and he felt that moment on him, that tinge of his own power that said he stood at a crossroads, and the choice he would make now would forever change his life. It came upon him rarely now, so rarely that he knew it had all but been burned out of him in his lost years, although it had never been a gift he could summon when he willed. It crept upon him now, and he turned slowly in its hold, casting for that turn, that decision of fate that lay upon him.

He saw the girls. The tall one took up the Dweller lass, shielding her with her own body from the chaos jostling them in every direction, and he made his choice. He trailed after them as they worked their way through the shards of the fair booths, his attention on them and them alone. Buffeted by people running by in every direction, he lost them and then found them again. Sevryn tightened his hold on his katana as one man, a Galdarkan, caught his arm and tried to wrestle it from him. He lunged toward the man, giving in, and then twisting his arm away, and brought it back with an elbow to the other's throat. The Galdarkan dropped to his knees, wheezing and blinking in surprise. Sevryn strode on, with no time to see what became of the Galdarkan.

A sharp hiss broke his concentration. He ducked, even as he turned toward the sound, with an instinct that saved him. Steel sang by his ear so sharply he could feel his hair catch on its edge. He dropped to one knee and looked into the swathed face of a Raver on foot, black-carapaced armor shining in the light between torn, crimson wrappings. It swung again, but Sevryn was not there to meet the blade. With a roll, he moved to his feet, at the creature's flank.

It had no scent but that of strangeness. Its ragged cloak hung in wisps about its oddly jointed body. Sinewy or bone-thin, it moved in ways no man could move naturally, making it difficult to anticipate its actions. It hopped straight up, as Sevryn struck, his own blow slicing the air where the thing's knees had been.

Sevryn smiled grimly. He collected himself and they stared at one another a moment, taking one another's measure. He rolled his wrist, turning his katana as he moved in. The Raver reacted as he thought it might, twisting and bending in unnatural angles, but it mattered little for the thing avoided the katana and never saw the daggers Sevryn tossed with his left hand, one, two, three, right at the hooded face.

It went down, thrashing, with a screeching keening that pierced Sevryn's hearing, kicked and died. He retrieved his blades quickly, turned, looked about and found no sight of the girls. His heart sank.

The streets cleared, except for stragglers heading out to join the fighting. He could see Bolger bodies lying in the gutter where they'd cut each other down, foe and friend indistinguishable. He wondered at that a moment as he broke into a slow jog, searching, as other townspeople hesitated to fill the streets. Had the girls gained the security of a shop?

Another keening shriek sent him running past the storefronts, through a jagged alley, and he burst into a clearing, where a horse lay on the ground, panting, a Bolger crushed under it, and a Raver pacing around its quarry.

She stood, legs over her sister, short sword in hand, blood dripping from it and running down her wrist as she gripped it. His call to her dried in his throat as the Raver lunged at her with a chittering cry. She ducked away in a twist, imitating its own jerky movement. It brushed past her and he felt a rush of icy power lashing from it, whipping at the girl. She staggered with a sobbing noise, but held her ground over her charge.

Before he could move, the Raver lunged at her again. She tossed her head to one side, then fell onto her back, sword up, and plunged it into the thing as it leaped over her. With a shriek it fell, kicking. She rolled to one knee, throwing all of her body weight onto the sword and the Raver. Its carapace cracked, and black blood fountained upward. It thrashed with a last gurgle. So quick, this dance and its last movements, that he had only had time to raise his katana and take a step forward.

Sevryn watched her get to her feet. She threw back her hood and tore off her beaded cap, freeing her chestnut hair, revealing her ears with their delicate Vaelinarran points, and she flung her arms into the air with a shout of victory from a cracked and hoarse throat.

She looked at him. He had no words for what he saw on her face, innocence gone, replaced with a sharp wisdom and tragedy, then triumph. The wind caught up her crone's shroud, swinging it darkly about her body. She tossed it open defiantly, her chin up, the gaze of her amazing eyes pinned to him. A silvery light reigned upon her brow, a power for which he had no words, and which faded even as he watched. A sudden sharp wind caught the garment, tearing it away from the festival gown underneath, its brightness stained with crimson blood, black ocher, and dirt. He could not turn away from her eyes, no matter what the cost, and no matter that he had come too late to save her.

She put a hand down to her sister, drawing her to her feet. "It's over."

Sevryn lowered his katana. For him, it had just begun.

Part II

Chapter Eighteen

737 AE

A ROUGH-EDGED SPRING morning dawns on the western coast of what the Dwellers call the First Home on Kerith, where the Silverwing River tumbles out of the mountains and cuts its way through the hills and river valleys, its blue-gray waters chill and foaming with melting snow and ice. While the First Home is a huge, sprawling continent, the Silverwing is but one small river, although it reigns supreme on its journey through the western highlands. It slows through the high country orchards of the Dwellers, where apple trees sink deep roots into the rich soil and bask in the mountain air lanced with both winter cold and summer warmth, as if to bless the myriad valleys before cutting deep into stone and flowing south, ever south until it pours into the mighty inlet where fresh water meets salt. The day is one of rough edges because winter hangs over it mightily, giving way with great reluctance, and the ground remains frozen deep down, and the dewdrops scattered on the grasses everywhere still hold tiny shards of ice within them.

A young woman sits on a cutaway bank, a long-handled dipping cup lying on the grass beside her, her lustrous hair rippling down her back and glistening damply as if just washed and drying in the new sunlight, absorbing gold-and-chestnut rays into the strands of rich brunette. Surely she has not washed in the icy, rushing waters of the river below her, but the cup at her side would make one wonder, if there were anyone but her about to enjoy the rawness of this dawn. Her tunic is dappled with drops of water raining slowly off her hair, and her patched trousers are also damp from sitting near the spray of the river. The grasses about her are awakening with newly minted green, pushing up from the browned layers of deep winter.

Silver-winged alna, fishing birds famed for their habitat along the river, hop about the bank and daringly skim its frothy surface to bring up tiny blue gills. Rainbow-hued trout will not be swimming these rivers for weeks yet, but the little blue gills will feed the alna well enough. With sharp beak and talon, they shred and gobble down their feast, then chirp and whistle to one another. They seem intrigued and unafraid of the woman in their midst, as if used to her visits or calmed by her aura as she sits, her thoughts intent upon the currents. One or two bold birds gently pluck a strand of her hair for their nests and dash out of range of retribution, then fly across the river toward the wilderness. One of the silver-winged birds, a young one from the silver tipping ever so lightly its feathers of deepest blue, hops upon her arm and eyes his perch curiously. He feels confident enough of his safety to begin warbling, his young voice in cheerful tune with the roar of the river and the softer voice of the morning breeze.

The young woman's gaze flickers toward the bird ever so gently, and the corner of her mouth tilts up. She does not move as the bold alna hops along her arm and gains a higher perch upon her shoulder. The creature seems unaware of her knowledge of his venture. He preens himself, and then gently preens a tumble of curls nearby. Doing so, he leans upon her cheek, chirping quietly in great content. He stays, huddled against her cheek, not as if seeking warmth, for her flesh has not yet warmed to the sun, but as if seeking something else, something indefinable. She does not move, lest she disturb the bird, but finally her eyes blink, long lashes shutting away eyes of remarkable colors, and then opening again. He startles before settling back, caressing her face with his beak. After long moments in this communion, the alna flutters back to the ground. He casts a look at her, and then takes wing, the silver tip dark blue of his feathers reflected in the tumbling river below before he circles and begins a journey out of her sight.

Borne by the wind beneath his wings, the young alna circles westward and then south, carried along the western coast itself, and the broken shoreline where the Jewel of Tomarq Vaelinar reigns on cliffs, its fiery eye sweeping the ocean in regular searches. The beam sweeps over the alna uncaring, searching for ships upon the ocean marked by its talisman. Those unmarked will be seared by the sudden fire which leaps to life in its hard-jeweled vision, and the ocean waters seared of unheeding and unwanted invaders. If the alna had wit to know, the small sleek bird would see that the ever-present fire in the Jewel's eye has dimmed, and is dimming. It is a Way which is troubled. Heedless, the young alna circles over the square corners of the Vaelinar keep holding the stony cliffs above the greatest natural harbor of the western coast, a harbor that would take three days on horseback to cover. Thus the Jewel of Tomarq looks long and hard at those who would sail into its arms. The alna snaps insects from the air and drinks from the courtyard fountain of the hold before taking to the air once again and the mysterious wind current which it and it alone skims.

He sweeps down the western coast, searching, silver-tipped wings dipping. He crosses village and town, and a web of trade routes, then he turns inward and northward again. The sun sets in his eyes and then rises yet again. The current carries him over the Blackwind Mountains where even the snow falls dark and shadowy and fell things run the ridges. They sense him and pause, throwing their heads back to send howls shrieking up at him, a Way gone horribly wrong from the moment of their creation. The alna trembles a bit, wings shivering. Unaware of the force that holds him or the time that passes, for he is only a fisher among birds, he feels hunger but will not skim lower for food. That instinct alone undoubtedly saves his life. At the southern foot of the Blackwinds, he soars over the Two Sisters Bridge, a Way built centuries ago through this impassable spine of obsidian and granite and fell creatures, its columns of platinum and spiraling webs of cable the only light thing about it, carrying a road that dares only to edge the foot of the peaks. Perhaps fittingly, he skirts the stone walls of Stronghold ild Fallyn in the shadows. The Fallyn have built high, spiraling towers daring the mountains in their height, with gossamer bridges looping from one tower to another, gleaming as if bedewed spiderwebs, so like the Two Sisters that even the ignorant could tell who the builders of each must have been. Even the enclosing walls are so high that one would have to have a bird's wings to think of climbing them . . . and falling. The play of light on the dark webbing draws the young alna near. It confuses him as he swoops close, for it is nothing as he imagined, the spidery webs are obsidian cable, the towers are massive buildings thrust into the air. He has flown beyond his reckoning, for time beyond his counting, as if the wind's current has its own eerie placement in the scheme of things and he must feed to continue flying.

Laughing voices and the ring of steel lure him closer, as if he hungers for companionship of some kind. Courtyards with burgeoning gardens and stone-patterned walkways and benches abound among the towers and outer walls of the immediate stronghold. The flash and noise of a training yard catches his bright eye and he lands nearby. A woman swathed in shadows dances with a bit of lightning in her hands, her hair, colored like wild honey, swirling about her in a cloud of silk, and her opponent attempts to match her steps with steel lightning in his own hands, but he fails. Swords ring as they close and the woman falls back, laughing, her slender hands and arms moving in elegant patterns that drive the man back to the wall of the yard. His voice sings out in protest.

"Fight, you sluggard. How can I learn without an opponent?" Her laugh dances about her, but it holds an edge. Her free hand moves to her belt and unhooks a coiled whip. It cracks the air.

He jumps aside with an uneasy laugh. The shining silver in his hand moves with him, tracing his passage, and he points at her.

They close, the two, and the bird watches them with bright eyes, comprehending strife and combat in curiosity. He would flee, but the swirl of clothing and laughter and sheen of the blades mesmerizes him for a few moments, and he sits with his wings tucked about him, resting. Weariness bleeds away from him.

The blades clash, clang, parry each other off, and then curses fill the air as the two join harshly and throw each other off again. *SNAP!* The whip lashes out, and the man grimaces aside, bright crimson staining his cheekbone.

"Don't toy with me."

"Me? Do I look a fool to toy with you, Lady Tressandre? Now put that thing away, you've blooded me."

"I'll have you in the dirt under my boot. I heard you kept the Kobrir from Lariel. How ever did one as clumsy as you manage that? When the queen sends me an envoy, I want to know what he is made of, as well as why she sent him!"

"She did not send me, I am merely here asking for the hospitality of your hold after weary days on the road."

"Then if you won't stand on the merit of your queen, you had better prepare to stand on your own."

With a hiss, the black snake of a whip strikes through the skies over the alna with a *crack!* and he hops in sudden fear of it even as it coils about his blade and sends it flying from his hand. The wielder inhales sharply, drawing near, flicking the whip back with her slender wrist before popping it at her opponent, lunging with her sword at the same time. The man reaches out and grabs the whip, yanking, throwing the woman off-balance, and before she rights herself, he has a dagger point under her chin.

"Now," he says, "you will drop it."

She makes a sound of disappointment before leaning closer, and draws her full mouth over the bleeding cut on his face and kisses it with a murmur of passion. "Then I shall have to see that you are given the full hospitality of my keep before I send you home to Larandaril, with a message of my own."

Still frightened by the emotion and movement of the two, the alna flits away, then casts himself upward from the stronghold and over its holdings.

There he manages to snatch a small fish from the lake to the Fallyn's east. He eats warily on a flat rock, his beak and talons expertly shredding the flesh from the bone and gobbling it hungrily. When he takes to the air again, he circles a few times to gain his bearings and the current returns, seizing him and carrying him off again.

His pathway is anything but linear. Rather than a bird on the wing, his journey is more that of a hound picking up a scent and tracking it, losing it, searching for it and then picking it up again.

The rise and fall of the sun is but a glow in the bird's eyes and he seems to acknowledge no weariness or time, only hunger. Days pass. Only then do other winged beings even sense him, as he trespasses on their territory briefly, in and out, snatching what fish or mouse or insect he can. He sleeps once or twice, head tucked under his silver-tipped wing, high in a swaying treetop so different from the river flats and marshes where he normally sleeps, the wind that carries him tugging at him now and then. It either rocks him to rest or nags him to fly onward; the alna is unaware of the current's true nature or intents.

He fights it but once. As his path takes him over the great, damned sea gulf known as Crooks, for the many tortured turns and coves hammered out by massive tsunamis pounding on its southern shore, he grows skittish. The edges of the inlet reek where salt has burned freshwater land to a brown crisp, and the beaches and water sound with the faint cry of a thousand voices calling for help. From the edges of his predatory eyes, he can see the flickering of the pale shapes of ghosts past and present in the waves. It is a forsaken land and it frightens him to the core of his being, runs against his instincts. He would falter if it were not for the undeniable zephyr carrying him.

Beyond the tortured shores, he wheels inland, across the golden domes of the Magi, gone now except for the gleam of their once wealthy cities. His wingbeats grow ragged as he toils, until at last, he glides into the east. Never born or sculpted to be a hound, the bird lowers in a staggering flight to a pond, where he naps on the muddy bank, exhausted. When he awakens, he snaps up swarming gnats and a small frog or two that gathered to eat the insects as well, and revives. He launches again, his flight erratic, his youth and stamina spent.

Yet he finds what he has been seeking. It draws him, and he wheels about it, two figures on horseback in a hidden grove, both in mercenary gear, one of them wearing a back sword with an elaborate, silvery cage for the hilt. It draws him like the shining scales of a fish darting under water, and he can feel the ache in his chest, his craw, his wings, his talons at the sight of the two. The sword exists still, and is worn by one who has tamed it. Not by the immense man but by the smaller, near-skeletal companion riding with him.

The tall, dark one throws his head back with a growl as a shadow slips over him. At his movement, his companion stirs on his mount, moving something off his shoulder and then aiming upward. An arrow is loosed.

The alna lets out a shriek as it pierces him and drops away sharply, falling, falling, despite the wind which has borne him so far, tumbling earthward in the east.

"Leave it," the first man said to the hunter from atop his horse, who shouldered his longbow in protest, without a word, his face furrowed under a single, deep crease which might have begun as a scar before it became a deeply grooved frown. He kicked at a few more grassy mounds before giving up and remounting.

"I did not miss," he said flatly.

"You rarely do. You've lost the arrow, give it up."

"Birds do not tumble from the sky and disappear."

"This one did. Perhaps you merely nicked it, but you've beaten the bush long enough. I have more important quarry in mind." Quendius stood in his stirrups, stretching his long legs, his keen gaze fastened on the river valley below, his tashya mount moving only slightly as the rider shifted his weight to watch a company below unaware they were being viewed from the heights. His companion said little in return and moved even more sparingly, his lean face turning to watch the stir of Galdarkans far below their hillside grove. The area had once been known as the Shrine of the Sun and the Magi who'd lived there had intended to build a monument for all time. Little remained of it now but broken columns and a golden half dome sunk to the ground like a polished nugget, glowing all the more golden for the blackened earth beneath it. Around its fringes, an encampment had been thrown up.

"Do they search for lost magic, I wonder?" he murmured, to himself really, for his taciturn lieutenant seldom answered.

He did, this time. "No. There is none to be found anywhere, and they know that." Leaning back in the saddle, he fell into silence.

"A pact with the Gods broken soundly, then, to lose what they once held. Gods like that must have been strong once, and are now broken themselves." He paused, as if considering his spoken thoughts. Quendius sat back with a grunt. His mount moved also, restlessly, as if echoing the unspoken emotion from the rider.

Quendius laced the reins over the palm of his hand after long moments watching the Galdarkans down below. "They've bought too many weapons from me. I close one forge, they follow me to another. They do so quietly, purchasing in increments, but their purpose is indisputable. They are stockpiling."

The lean, quiet man twitched a finger. "You knew this two years past."

"I did. I've the time to make certain, however. We both do. They do not." Quendius gathered his reins and flashed a wide, unpleasant grin. "Their plans are no longer their own."

Chapter Nineteen

SHE FOUND HIM LYING on the marshy grasses where the river slowed a bit, danced in and out of her favorite cove before rushing again downstream. She often tarried there, to watch waters that swirled in, calmed, and gathered a quiet strength before rushing out again and rejoining the rapids downstream in the spring melt off. In summertime, this hollow would be even quieter, with fish tickling the bottom of its depths. It had saved her life at least twice, and now it seemed as if it had saved another life. The alna lay crumpled, a broken arrow shaft in his breast, his eyes half-open and breath labored, and he did not even stir when she picked him up. She stroked his feathers down and turned him carefully in her hands to see how bad the wound was. It seemed fresh and that would help, but birds bled out very quickly, and she hesitated to probe the site since it had clotted a bit.

Grace looked up. The skies threatened a drizzly rain to come and so she made him a shelter of sorts, and carefully removed what was left of the arrow, working the arrowhead back out of the flesh. At first she thought it Bolger-made, and set it aside while she cleaned and packed the wound, and trickled water into the bird's beak, singing softly while she did so. He flinched every time she touched him, but less so with the song swirling about him, and she could see the edges of the wound draw closed, fresh pink flesh forming. Her brands ached as she worked, her scars burning and the neat white marks flared an ugly purple as they hadn't in years. The creature rallied enough to tuck his feet under him and his head under his wing, to sleep or die quietly, although she hoped it would be sleep. She drizzled water over her arms and hands to wash off his blood and tiny feathers and debris, and to soothe her scars. Rivergrace traced them with her fingertip. The one on her left arm scarcely showed now but her right arm pulsed with pain where Tolby had cut away the shackle. She blew softly over her skin to take away the stinging.

A few days passed with her visiting every day, bringing crickets and garden worms and even a small fish, to find the alna brighter and cheerier each time until one day the bird actually fluffed up, startled by her appearance and wary despite the blue gill in her hand. His show of spirit brought a gentle laugh from her. He'd healed faster than she, for her arm still stung a bit, but she'd rolled her sleeves back and let the sun leech away the darkness that infected it. She laid the fish down on the nest, and the alna snatched it away, backing up to eat the offering greedily, and she knew it would live. So it did, even as the arrow wound left a bright patch of silvery feathers on his chest. The last time she visited, the alna burst from the nest in a flurry of whistles and flaps, taking wing as if she'd thrown him into the air. He circled about, and landed near her with a challenging warble. She laughed at his bright eyes. "Very well, then, I won't tame you," she told the defiant bird.

Something metal bright sparkled at the ground near her boot toe. She reached over and picked it up, finding the arrowhead she'd forgotten about. She turned it in her fingers several times. Blood had dried rusty brown on it, and mud and grass from the nest dirtied it a bit, but the fine, beaten silver of its workmanship shone undeniably through the grime. A true craftsman had made this arrowhead, shaped and honed it for swift death, and as she rubbed it clean carefully so as not to cut her fingers, she wondered that the alna had survived it, a true shot that had somehow not buried itself deeply. She worked the last of the arrow shaft from it, and palmed the object. She ought to throw it far away, or give it to one of her brothers, but she felt reluctance with any thought but that of saving it. It might make a nice clasp for a small shoulder bag, at that. Rivergrace put it in her gathering basket and gestured at the alna, who swooped up again, darting down at her boldly to steal a hair and winging away. She laughed despite the smarting of her scalp. Nutmeg always wore a kerchief and nagged at Grace to do the same, so she supposed she deserved having birds and twigs alike snatch at her, tangling and stealing.

She lingered along the riverbed only long enough to fill her basket with herbs for drying and hurried back home, a day full of chores still ahead of her. Hosmer had ridden out the day before for a militia tour, but

Keldan and Tolby and Garner would still demand a hearty lunch, and then she had baby goats waiting for her, and then she and Nutmeg had weaving to finish and then . . . well, there was always something. Smiling, Rivergrace hurried her steps. The early morning breeze tugged at her cloak despite the lacings tight across her chest, and tried to shiver up her trouser legs, worn and patched and too short, as always. She made her own trousers and skirts, but could not seem to keep pace with her long legs. The orchard filled with sound, as it warmed to the day, even with clouds gathering on the horizon. It would be a difficult day to stay inside. Plotting tasks that would keep her and Nutmeg busy but out in the spring until the rain finally began falling, a smile danced about her face.

Hosmer reined his horse to a halt in the clearing. The gelding tossed his head and let out a chuff of irritation, eager to be stretching his legs out a bit again. Frowning, Hosmer squared his shoulders before reaching back into his saddle pack, opening the flap, and pulling out his oilcloth map to puzzle over it. He had the meeting place right, and he was far from early or late, yet the dell lay empty. The fire ring had not been used in a while, for this was a run they did not often patrol, and it had not been used that morning either. His brow lowered in irritation, his first thought being that he would have to make the patrol alone. His next thought was that one or two might have been drawn away by problems elsewhere, for that was the way of life on farms and ranches, but not every last one of the four. The patrol, then, had been changed for some reason and he hadn't received notice. When he got back, he'd have to peg Nutmeg by the ear and find out if she'd forgotten to tell him a carrier bird had come in. Meanwhile, there was nothing for it but to do the patrol on his own, for it needed doing. Hosmer gathered up the reins.

The gelding picked his own way up the small hillside, agile and surefooted, a blend of mountain pony with a hint of the tashya hot blood in his dished face and high-carried tail. He'd cost Hosmer most of his hat sales coin. He snorted as they reached the ridge, tossing up his wide-blazed head. Hosmer dropped his hand low, guiding the horse along the narrow trail, marking the overgrowth of shrub and grasses as they worked their way through, the passage of hooves bruising foliage and sending an aromatic cloud over them. At the break, reaching a long, flat butte known as Ironhead, Hosmer sent the gelding into a lope, covering the ground in ever lengthening strides. At the butte's far side, a slope led down into a maze of small valleys and hills and Hosmer gave the horse free rein, leaning back in the saddle to help balance a bit. They crested a second small hill and a black flurry burst in front of them, shrieking and cawing, causing the horse to rear, Hosmer grabbing for the mane to keep his seat. The carrion eaters winged about him in a dark cloud, gained the air, and circled above him, his ears ringing with their shrill protest.

Hosmer settled the horse, his heart thumping in his chest. It struck him, somewhere in his throat, that a kill lay ahead. Not just any kill, from the number of skraw overhead. One of size to attract so many. He swallowed and tried to push the gelding into a walk forward, but the beast whinnied nervously and set his teeth against the bit, refusing. He put his boot heel to the gelding's flank with a grunt. The horse grunted back, lowered his head, and planted his hooves. He swung off then, dropping the reins to a ground tie. The horse undoubtedly had better sense than he. He strode down the crest, through chest-high bracken and tangleweed. The smell hit him first, the flat coppery smell of blood, and then the sound, for not all the skraws had taken flight, the sound of wet shredding and ripping and devouring. He could hear the flapping of wings as they hopped and jostled each other.

Another step and he looked down on blood glistening blackly on the beaten grasses and bracken, bodies broken and akimbo, horses and men, a feast for the skraw as they hopped upon the carnage. Hosmer put his fist to his mouth. They were hardly recognizable, but here lay two of the four missing militia. Lent Barrel and his brother Guthry, slaughtered, and only their longcoats with the embroidered breast flap pocket to tell him who they were, for the birds had been at their faces. Their eyes were gone, throats nothing more than glistening gashes to the sky.

Hosmer stumbled back and then made himself stop. He could not flee like some unthinking animal, no matter how horrible the sight. Tolby would shake him by the scruff of the neck for not knowing more of the scene than simply horrifying death. He swallowed hard.

He circled the area widely, then, picking up tracks. Hounds and horses, Bolger horses, from the pony size bare hoofprints. Picking his way closer, teeth clenched, shooing off the skraw, he found the spear under the body of one horse, and the arrowheads buried deep in Guthry's still intact chest. What was left of Lent did not tell Hosmer what killed him other than ambush. Perhaps the horse had fallen on him and then hounds had taken him, for he'd been ripped almost beyond recognition. Hosmer took a bracelet from his right arm, slipping it off torn flesh, slick with blood, and put it in his own pocket. That was all he could bring back to the Barrel family.

A branch snapped loudly. Hosmer straightened, wheeling about. It struck him that, fresh as their deaths were, he was in jeopardy. Leaping over the massacre, he ran back to his horse. The gelding rolled white-ringed eyes at the smell of blood on Hosmer's boots as he grabbed the reins and swung himself into the saddle. The horse bolted without urging, back the way they'd come. The skraws flew about in another agitated flurry, and did he hear under the gelding's grunts of efforts or did he hear the faint howl of a hound?

He angled across the hillsides, avoiding the butte, for he'd be easily seen riding upon its great, flat top, the bracken thrashing at his leather chaps and stinging the gelding. He could hear one howl joined by a second behind him, no longer so faint as it had been. The hunt was on.

He found a freshet of water trickling down, and took to it, the gelding snorting in protest at its icy spray from his pounding hooves, drenching Hosmer as well, and, hopefully, washing away scent as well as dryness and warmth. It went down valley a good long way before he had to pull the horse out of it and go cross-country again. The beacon lay foremost in his mind, then home to warn his family and gather up his brothers. Branches whipped his head and shoulders, a welt stinging across his cheekbone as he crouched close to the gelding's neck, urging him in their race with hands and feet. A gathering mist lowered over them as they came out of the valley and along the stony ridge, cloaking them and muffling thuds of striking hooves and the belling of hounds searching for a scent down below.

He slapped his horse's neck in a steady pounding rhythm, urging him on across broken ground that might kill both of them if the gelding stumbled and fell, but any slower and it would be certain death for them as well. He tried not to think what would happen once he reached the beacon, beyond lighting the bonfire. The gelding slowed to a steadier but ground-eating pace as they dropped back into the valley, crossing back and forth over a small brooklet. Hosmer barely guiding the horse as he let the animal pick out his own trail. The sun fled as clouds drew closer and befogged the rounded hillsides. He forced the horse to the heights once, to catch his bearing, and then looked behind them.

His heart nearly stopped. Raiders, a dozen strong or more, came pouring out of the mists over a crest two dells behind. He kicked the gelding downslope, but knew he'd been seen even as they knew they'd been seen. The beacon lay close but not close enough.

The pace slowed because it had to. The gelding's breath grew labored and foam dappled his body from effort. He flicked one ear back to listen to Hosmer and the chase behind them, the other ear pricked forward, hooves digging steadily into the ground, throwing back soft dirt to speckle both of them. Hosmer wiped his face to see better, surprised to find cold sweat running down his brow along with the debris, mud, and blood, stinging into the welt across his face. A long-ear bounded out of the grasses, both animals swerving, and the gelding went sliding. Hosmer lost the saddle and clung to the animal's hot neck as the horse regained his balance, throwing him back into place. He got his boots into the stirrups as the gelding lurched raggedly back into his pace, his breathing becoming ragged.

Hosmer hunched forward, holding the reins close and firm, rubbing the gelding's neck, coaxing him. He breathed with the horse, panting roughly, air burning lungs closed by fear. He had to make the beacon. The raiding party behind him could have only one destination down this last valley: his own home.

They burst free of the gloom and clinging mist, covered with a blanket of the heavy dew, rain that had yet to fall from the clouds. The gelding bucked over the last thick hedge before stumbling into the cleared ground around the beacon, a firebreak kept groomed by hand, hoe, and goat. A lean, scarred, dun-red form leaped suddenly from the underbrush, growling low and matching them stride for stride.

The hound snapped at the gelding's ankles. The horse let out a squeal of terror, and Hosmer pulled hard on the left rein, forcing it to wheel left, and the hound sprang past, its momentum carrying it away.

Hosmer drew his sword, fumbling a bit to get a firmer grip, his hand wet with foam and grime, but he clenched his hand about the hilt, dug a heel into the horse's side, and hauled hard to bring him around, charging the hound who'd turned.

A trailing hound but one so eager for fresh blood that he'd not yet bellowed out his find of the quarry to the packmaster and his pack, a hound so covered with gore from earlier kills that Hosmer could not rightly tell his true color, a hound with wide gleaming jaws and madness gleaming deep in his yellowish eyes. The creature hesitated a moment as if he might throw back his head to bell out his find until Hosmer let out a yell of challenge. The beast lowered his head, growling and frothing as Hosmer charged.

He hit on his swing. He could feel the brunt of the thrust into a body quite a bit heavier than he'd thought, and the hound tore the sword out of his hands when it lodged deep. With a furious snarl, the hound barreled into the horse, tumbling all of them heels over heads into sudden silence.

Hosmer hit hard. His left shoulder took his fall, even as he somersaulted onto his back and lay gasping for breath. The hound let out a shivery gurgling howl that did not quite escape the gash in his throat as Hosmer rolled over to get to his feet.

The gelding lay immobile, body entwined with that of the hound, and his neck at an odd angle. Heat stung Hosmer's eyes as he put a boot to the hound's body and pulled his sword free, then wiped it on the grasses. Without a look back, Hosmer staggered to the base of the beacon, fumbling at his longcoat pockets for flint. Hands shaking, it took four strikes to get the sparks flying into the dried grasses and oils under the beacon's roofing. It sputtered for a moment on the damp air clinging about the hilltop, and Hosmer could only watch numbly and pray for it to light. Then the tiny flames hit a pocket of sweet oil and burst upward with a loud *FOOOOM*, and the beacon caught. He wobbled back a step or two, his left arm hanging awkwardly. Hosmer looked down at it. He'd dislocated the shoulder.

With an unsteady step, he went to the edge of the firebreak and put his body to a green but sturdy sapling and bent and flexed himself until, with a rush of pain and then sudden relief, he got his limb into place. His fingertips tingled a moment as he flexed his arm gingerly. Then he lifted his head. A faraway howl drifted up from below.

Hosmer smiled grimly. He'd put his back to the fire . . . hell, he'd put himself into the fire before he'd let the hounds rip him apart and feast. Something shifted behind him.

He spun about and saw the gelding get to his feet with a heaving grunt and stand, head low. His jaw dropped. He went to his mount. The horse nuzzled his head on his arm, and whuffled wearily.

Hosmer rubbed his blaze. "Thought you were done for. We still might be." Taking the reins, he led the horse close to the beacon. The horse walked soundly, if sorely, holding his neck gingerly. Hosmer plucked a burning torch from the bonfire. "It's all downhill from here," he told the animal, and mounted up.

Chapter Twenty

THE WINDOWS OF HIS office held one of the most stunning views of Calcort that could be found, but, stubbornly, his chair faced the other direction. "Inspiration," he would tell visitors, "is always at my back," as if that were a truism rather than a rather nice sounding phrase. The truth was the light from behind proved advantageous for the many stacks of paperwork he constantly found before him.

Mayor Stonehand sat back at his desk, stifling an early morning yawn, and then rubbed one eye that absolutely refused to see clearly that day, little crusts at each corner, no matter how many times he rubbed it clean. He fetched up his seeing glasses, tiny rings of polished lenses, and perched them on his nose, details clearing almost immediately although . . . and he sighed heavily at this . . . it would not be long before he'd have to order a new pair of lenses. The Vaelinars charged dear for them, too. He squinted across the room at the map which sprawled over one entire wall. A sheer silken curtain hung over it, delicately painted, showing the Elven Ways like a delicate spiderweb over the far-flung free provinces of the First Home and western lands.

From the far beaches of the south, where the Net of Hilden kept all vermin from the precious grain warehouses of the Hilden Trade Guild to the road heading north and west, past the Lighthouse of Gitathiral on the treacherous, foggy coast, lit with a flame that ever-burned no matter what wind and rain and mist covered the cape, and still northerly until the vast, natural harbor of Tomarq where Grand Mayor Hawthorne kept his Council of all the free provinces and that great Jewel of Tomarq lay in its ever-moving cradle on the cliffs overhead, he examined the influence of the Vaelinars on his people. Stonehand rubbed his eyes again.

The curtain artist had vented all his artistry on the Dark Ferryman of the Nylara River, showing the phantom in a swirl of voluminous black robes on the banks of a surging, frothing tide. From there the Two Sisters Bridge, a suspension of girders and metal cables from one ridge to another hardly seemed miraculous, although the artist allowed himself another leap of imagination when the trade roads came to the Span of Seven, a vast, volcanic chasm and the seemingly bottomless crater lake at its feet. There were other Ways, three or four scattered and of much less importance to both the artist and the mayor, but the curtain left no doubt in the viewer's mind that the Vaelinars had stamped an indelible print on the lands they touched. None of the Ways shown duplicated themselves nor could be made by any hand native to Kerith. Not even when the Mageborn lived and the Gods still spoke to the Kernans.

He sighed again, as he smoothed down his vest and leaned forward to read the paperwork littering the desk before him. With hands moving swiftly, he searched through and organized the sheets into piles that had meaning only to him, save for the one that seemed composed of missives still unopened and wrapped in bulky coverings intended to protect them against wind, sun, and rain. He tapped his fingertips next to that pile, debating whether to delve into fresh problems or finish dealing with old. The door to his office opening solved his dilemma.

His aide came in, her face all puckered up as if she'd just eaten a fresh quinberry for breakfast, and indeed, she might have. She had the most curious notions about health and promoting it. He did not smell the tart fruit aroma, though, as she came near, a sheet of parchment rattling in her hand with irritation, and it might have been that same emotion that skewered her face up so.

He sat back and braced himself. He did not have long to wait.

"How could you? How could you allow that she-Demon to invite herself back here?" She brandished the parchment.

"Now, Perty." Two words no more slowed her than they could have dammed a swift-flowing river.

"After bringing the Kobrir assassin after her last time, and causing a ruckus in the city, and costing us crowns of expense, then forcibly relocating whole villages of good Kerith citizens—"

"Which worked out well," he reminded her mildly. "Everyone got more land and they are subsidized for a number of years, as well as tutored or apprenticed." Indeed, that land swap had worked out very well, for those of Kerith. He kept a place in the back of his mind, waiting for the other shoe to drop, often wondering what the Strangers had gained in the deal. He had yet to see an advantage to it for them, but that did not mean there hadn't been one.

"Not to mention her flagrant disregard for our own laws!" Perty sucked in a breath. He held his hand up.

"Enough." He waited to see if she would desist and she seemed to, holding her breath in, thin chest swelling with it. "When I leave office, Perty, you are welcome to campaign to succeed me, but in the meantime, I have made a decision which I consider paramount to the welfare of our province and I intend to stick to it." He raised his coal-black eyebrows, knowing how emphatic they were in contrast to the snow-white hair curling closely about his head. "I'm not going to ask if you agree, or even if you understand, for it is my opinion that if you did either, you'd not be standing here caterwauling at me."

Perty breathed. "That is correct," she returned.

"Good. Now I want you to authorize extra pay vouchers for the Town Guard to cover the additional security we'll be needing, without further delay." Stonehand returned his attention to his desktop, dismissing her without another word. She did not, however, move. Finally, he dragged his gaze back to her.

"Is there another problem?"

Her mouth still pursed with that tartness of an imaginary quinberry. "I should get a voucher for food stores and for game hunters. The Conference will be busy this year, with *her* attendance."

"Excellent thinking! Draw them up and bring them in."

Perty turned abruptly and walked stiffly out of the office. Stonehand watched the door as it closed firmly. Now then. Decisions. New business or old? He waved his palm over the stacks again, as if he could divine their importance by an invisible aura about them. Finally, he decided that the Demon he knew was better for the moment than the Demon he did not, and pulled a small stack of correspondence and other compositions closer. In a way, it was relevant to the voucher for the Town Guard, as this was a proposal to draw off some of the finer members of the surrounding militia from the countryside, disregarding their rustic nature, to recruit to the Town Guard. The move might be one to consider, for the current makeup of the Town Guard included the favored sons and daughters of a good many families who thought that said positions came with favor or should be the first step on a ladder to a great deal more. It would be nice, Stonehand thought, to have a guard whose only concern was *guarding*.

Taking up a sharpened charcoal, he made a note or two on that proposal and shifted it to the "Take Immediate Action" pile on his desk. It was the only one Perty was allowed to proceed upon, and every evening when he left, that pile was willed to her desk and her activities.

He had to admit that, although she had her prejudices, the woman proved time and time again to be a most capable bureaucrat. He could not blame her for her bigotry, Kerith was full of it, and he was not clean of it himself. As much as he hated Vaelinar politics and manipulating, he appreciated their intelligence, and well . . . their beauty. Lariel was as beautiful a creature as he could imagine in any of his dreams.

He reminded himself that she was also as deadly. One did not gaze upon a Warrior Queen without running the risk of being blinded.

He tapped another finger on his desk and tried not to think of indulging in the Dweller vice of smoking, although that temptation weighed heavily on his mind throughout the entire morning. The next scrip he drew close held another complaint he'd been considering, off and on, for several months, and that consideration had brought him no closer to a solution. He took his charcoal stick and scribbled in a note reading "Bounty? Pelts?" before setting it aside till the morrow. Sheet by sheet he worked his way through the pile, pausing only when Perty came in with her neatly inked voucher requests for him to sign, and reminded him that he had Council members to meet for lunch. It was not near time, of course, but his stomach had begun to rumble from its ample depths and she wanted to remind him that midmorning break would have to be foregone, for a Town Council luncheon was likely to be both tedious and overstuffing. He sighed heavily and rubbed his eye yet again as he signed the vouchers and dismissed her.

If he left the office now, he could walk leisurely to the meeting, gaining fresh air and vision, and exercise, taking his mind off his hunger and by the time he arrived, it would be time for the luncheon. That sounded like an excellent plan. He rose and gathered his coat and called out to Perty that he was leaving, and not to call a carriage. She glanced up from her desk as he passed by, her piles twice the size of his, and he could feel her stare at his back as he walked out of the office. He uttered an inaudible prayer that none of his daughters would grow up to be such an efficient and nearly intolerable person.

Lariel knelt by the font which carried the waters of the River Andredia into the inner courtyard and held forth a cup carved of that stone called chalcedony, said to reveal poisons within whatever liquid it held. The Vaelinars had the Talents and abilities to discern many things, but there were still elements of Kerith that had yet to reveal themselves, good and bad, and this was how she tested the river. She dipped the cup into the pooling waters that swirled in front of her and swished it around gently in the chamber. The creamy blue translucent vessel glistened with the dampness it held, and then took on a smoky aspect which wavered before clearing. She frowned and let the water dribble slowly back into the font with a sigh. Poison, but not strong enough to keep the cup smoky. Still, it detected a wrongness within, growing stronger with every year, and she had no weapon with which to fight it or that which corrupted it. Warrior Queen, they named her, and she had no foe to battle.

She stood slowly and then seated herself on the carved bench at the fountain's edge, setting the cup underneath it, to rest in waiting till its next trial. Her blood had made a pact to seal their Talents to this world, and in turn, that vow had blessed the river and all it touched and fed with its waters, a God-sworn promise. Had that been broken? And if so, by whom, and how? It might help if she told Jeredon and the others, but this had fallen upon her shoulders when she became head of the House, one of those unspoken legacies that she alone had been expected to be the guardian of. She would enlist their help when she had a plan, but until then, the suspicions remained hers and hers alone.

Lariel turned her face to look into the groves beyond the courtyard, tall trees with coin-shaped leaves that flashed both green and silver in the slight wind, their white-and-silvery trunks swaying. A bird soared overhead and came to a stop at one of the parapets where the messengers landed, and a slender hand immediately reached out to let it into the coops. Life went on. She could not be bitter that this had happened on her watch. Once she knew what she faced, she would gather her army.

Lariel composed herself and rose, crossing to the small gate of the courtyard, and spoke a word that only she knew to speak. The lock clicked open for her to pass, and she closed the gate behind her with another word. Standing on the other side, looking back, she could see nothing other than the gate itself and dancing shadow beyond. So the courtyard had been given to her, and so one day she would pass it on.

In the meantime, she had business to attend to. Dusting her hands, she broke into a brisk stride, crossing the entry yard and the side steps leading into the kitchen and main hall, calling out, "What word, if any, from Sevryn?"

Tiiva descended the inner staircase, her slippered feet making far less noise on the inner polished granite flooring than Lariel's booted ones, a slight smile on her face. "And how do you know we had any word at all?"

"I saw the bird come in, and it had better be from Sevryn." Lariel disliked Tiiva's mild teasing of her. "He's been on the roads far too long." Tiiva had put herself in charge of finding an appropriate consort for her, something she had no need or desire for, as of yet. Desire and passion, she had. Just not for commitment. One day she might have to put her seneschal in her place. In the meantime, she tilted her head up to watch Tiiva on the stairs. She carried a small scroll in one hand, her sweeping skirt gathered in the other so as not to trip her steps as she crossed to Lariel and bowed slightly. Her skin glowed a faint copper, and her burnished dark brunette hair with its streaks of copper accented a natural beauty which the sumptuous gown she wore could not rival, though it tried. She seemed amused as she handed the scroll to Lariel. A small pinfeather drifted from the object as she did, and wafted about before landing on the polished granite as Lariel peeled open the scroll. She inclined her eyes so that Lariel might have privacy while reading. Lariel had no doubt that a good deal could be, and was, seen from under those long lashes.

By the time you read this, m'lady Queen, I should be resting in the outer courtyard.

It was signed with an elaborate "S."

She must have frowned, for Tiiva added, "I hear he asked for ild Fallyn hospitality."

"I have no hold on his personal affairs nor would I wish to," Lariel reminded her aide. "He seems to be returning, at any rate."

Dismissed, Tiiva made a shallow curtsy, before almost turning about, and pausing. "I'll alert the staff to freshen his rooms. Oh, and we need to order a staghorn count. It's been a handful of years, and I believe you were worried about their restocking. If the herd needs to be thinned, now would be a good time to stock the larder."

"Do it, then." Lariel looked up from the scroll a second time, seeing a faint sheen over the small piece of paper that indicated something hidden for her eyes only had been writ as well, and her gaze met Tiiva's. "Ah. Would you care to ride out yourself, with a few to assist?"

"As you wish, Queen Lariel. I will admit that a day or so away from my duties would be most refreshing."

Lariel gestured. "Go, then. Take anyone you need but Jeredon."

The corner of Tiiva's mouth twitched ever so slightly before she inclined her head and left, taking the stairs with the same light, deliberate, gown-sweeping steps as she had descended them. Lariel gave her an ever-so-brief glance, weighing her reaction over Jeredon. She noted it as she made her way through the building toward the Rider's Gate, knowing that her aide seldom showed any emotion and wondering if it had been played out for her, however quickly, on purpose. Jeredon and Tiiva. Not a bad match, if one were to consider matches instead of other business at hand.

Lariel pushed impatiently through the Rider's Gate and found Sevryn seated on an upturned crate, harness and saddle in his arms, watching a stable lad trying to coax his horse into behaving. The hot-blooded animal, though covered with trail dust, did not look at all tired, and pranced from side to side, eyeing the lad suspiciously as if he might bite or kick the youth. Sevryn was being no help at all, using his Talent now and then to whisper a word of command only the horse could hear, keeping him in an alert state, ears flicking back and forth to listen and obey.

Lariel reached over Sevryn's shoulder and took a firm grip on his ear in a sound pinch. "Let the boy do his work," she suggested.

Sevryn froze and cleared his throat. After another pace or two back and forth, the beast began to quiet down and finally dropped his head and let himself be led away. The stable lad did so with a look of quiet triumph on his face. Sevryn waited till they had rounded the corner before shifting his body, removing his ear from her hold. "See that? No harm done. Stuffed him full of confidence."

"Like you, that beast of yours is often too full of himself."

"That's why we had him gelded," Sevryn responded lightly. "Trying to do the same to me?"

Lariel laughed. "Never."

"That is good to know." He hefted his saddle in his arms. "You look a bit overworked this morning, my queen. I suggest a cold glass of apple cider while I do my duties here and clean up, and then we can talk about my journey. I haven't much I can tell you, I fear." They entered the tack room in tandem, and he put his gear up on the pegs and barrels, then turned to her, half smiling. The bustle of stable workers continued beyond them, and the restless kick of a hoof against a wooden wall echoed.

The smile never reached his eyes. Disturbing eyes, storm-gray and yet one colored except for the pupil, eyes that were not of Vaelinar and held no hint whatsoever of the Talent he carried within his genes. Sevryn was that which no one had run across before, and that very feature which always disturbed her made him invaluable. No Vaelinar would even dare guess that he carried their magic in his veins. Decades of outbreeding on Kerith had proved otherwise. She saw the pink pucker of a new scar along the curve of his throat, and as his attention followed her gaze, he shifted uncomfortably and pulled the collar of his shirt up to cover it.

"Later, then," she agreed. "I'll meet you in the kitchens, since you look underfed as well."

She did not hear his answer as one of the stabled horses let out a long whinny, and the tack door closed on her heels as she left. Lariel took up a chair in the kitchen, ignoring the workday around her, and asked for a glass of cider as he'd suggested, dropping the scroll carelessly as she did, and the glass spilled when she reached for it, inundating the message. With a tsk of fuss, Laraiel wiped the scroll and table over quickly.

Faint words rose to the surface under the wipe of cider, the mild acid proofing the ink he'd used. *Ild Fallyn looks to the east. And there are spies in Larandaril. Lady Tressandre sends a request for an Honor Duel with the Warrior Queen.*

Lariel frowned heavily over that last. Duel! Who did Tressandre think she dealt with? No wonder Sevryn did not give words to that last request; once spoken, rumors would spread through the holdings like wildfire. Tressandre made it plain that she chafed under Lariel's rule in Larandaril. She would take the title from her, if given the opportunity. Well, that opportunity would not be extended! With a mutter, she crumpled the scroll and tossed it in the kitchen fire, watching it flare orange and then turn to blackened ashes as she drank her juice and pretended to warm herself a bit. The juice held no flavor at all as her thoughts mingled with the flame, dancing on the brick hearth. Sevryn had told her three things, one she had feared inevitable, one unthinkable, and the last a total shock to her. Of all places on Kerith she had deemed safe, her own Larandaril was the foremost. Now, it was not. That, too, had been inevitable, she supposed. She knew the moment she stepped outside her holding that the world could not be held secure. But this place, her home, her heart, always had been.

Till now.

She finished her juice and set it aside, leaning back in a rare moment of leisure and letting an expression of boredom and relaxation settle on her features, despite her racing mind. When Sevryn came in, she must have looked half asleep, basking in the warmth of the kitchen, for he laughed softly and said, "The kitten has been in the cream, it seems." He sat down, clothes changed, his hair wet and slicked back, the points of his ears plainly visible and the new scar neatly hidden away from view under a high collar. "Any way I can get a meal now?"

"Of course." Laraiel raised a finger, and the second cook nodded, grinning, bustling away to the larder and warmer pantry to throw together something for Sevryn. Lariel stood and got a wet cloth, leaning over Sevryn to wipe down the table, explaining, "I spilled my juice. Other than that, your advice was sound."

"Can't have a Warrior Queen looking peaked." He crossed his legs at his ankles. "Where is Jeredon?"

"Out training. How were the roads?"

"Muddy." Sevryn eyed his boots, which he'd scraped though they could hardly be called spotless, and tapped the top of them. "Should be a good planting year if it lightens up, otherwise rust will get to the crops."

She nodded. "So I have heard. You're coming with me to Calcort?"

He winced slightly, one hand going almost unconsciously to his rib cage and rubbing there. "If you need me, I will attend."

"I do. I need as many ears as I can have about me, for there is much to hear in the provinces these days. I intend on going to the Conference there. It's been a session or two since I've gone. Summer court in Calcort seems prudent."

He shrugged as if disinterested. "Rumors only, m'lady queen. Always rumors. It keeps the rest of us from being bored to death." He dropped his crossed feet squarely to the floor, sitting up and paying attention only when the second cook approached with a platter and crockery for eating.

Sevryn managed a crooked smile. "This business comes first, if you don't mind."

Lariel speared a bowl of berries from his platter, saying, "I don't mind at all."

They sat in silence, eating, Lariel wondering if he had anything further to tell her, and he no doubt wondering if he really had to return to Calcort, where the Kobrir assassin had gone after her and he'd stood in the way. She smiled faintly at the memory, at chance meetings, and fate. Using her fingers, she ate her berries, enjoying the burst of sweet yet tart flavor in her mouth, promising of lusher, riper flavor yet to come. They both ate, Sevryn heavily and she lightly, discussing things that seemed important but weren't really, trading insignificant information, his attention on devouring his meal and hers on wondering when and where they could speak freely.

Time, she realized, was no longer on her side. Even a river did not flow forever.

Keldan saw the blaze from the treetop in which he perched, smoke-colored against the looming rain moving in, and an orange glow flickering wildly off the storm's edge. He blinked and rubbed his eyes to be sure he saw what he did, then yelled down. "Da! Da! *Tolby.* The beacon's afire!" He flew out of the tree limbs in a mad scramble, letting the last branch whip him to the ground where he landed in a crouch and straightened. His father turned slowly, expression not comprehending, and Keldan grabbed him by his coat flaps to face the northern horizon.

"The beacon is burning!" When Tolby's eyes widened in realization, Keldan let go, saying, "I'll run and get Hos and Garner," legs bunched to dash away even as he spoke.

Tolby grabbed him by the scruff of his neck, stopping Keldan in his tracks. He looked toward the north with eyes gone dead. "Your brother already knows. He had militia patrol today." Then he let go and said, "Get Garner and your mother and the girls to the house. Now. And don't the two of you lads be gadding off. I want you here. Understand?"

Keldan stared into his da's face and nodded slowly. He'd seen his father angry before, but he'd never seen him frightened. Tolby let go with a little shake and pushed him off, and Keldan ran like he'd never run before, his shirttail flapping behind him. Tolby stared for a long moment at the beacon hill, the brilliant oranges of the flame stark against the edge of the storm clouds behind it, black and gray. It could be something as simple as a small party of Bolgers out looking for cider again, or it could be something unthinkable. He turned decisively, throwing his tools into the cart bed and startling the pony who flung his head high against the harness before swinging himself into the cart, leaving behind ladders and baskets. The pony let fly with his heels before lunging into the harness and rattling down the orchard lane with all the speed of his shaggy little body, cart jolting along after. Tolby reined him toward Beacon Hill.

Too late Hosmer realized that two kinds of hounds followed, the bellers, those that howled his trail back to the riders, and the stalkers. It had been a stalker that nearly took him down at the beacon and as his bone-tired mount tried to pick a way down the hill, the roar of the bonfire growing fainter and fainter, another leaped at them.

Pain ran from his foot to his waist as jaws clamped down and then ripped, the thrust of sudden weight bowing the horse to its knees and tearing Hosmer out of the saddle. He thrust the torch down, sweeping the flame past the hound's ear and across his body with a scream of rage. Hosmer let go the reins, falling free, and rolling away from both beast and horse. The gelding scrambled to his hooves, eyes wild, and kicked out, scoring the hound across the hindquarters as it swung about to turn on Hosmer.

He'd dropped the torch. It lay on the ground between them, orange flame sputtering a bit in the dampness of trampled grass and dirt. The hound yelped and snapped as it rolled from the kick, and the horse bucked away, but the hound swung about on Hosmer again, intent on its true and only quarry. The hot blood and flesh of the horse would fall to its jaws later, its glowing yellow eyes seemed to tell Hosmer, but he was its prey now. It dropped to a low crouch, growling with a deep bass tone, and crept after him.

Hosmer crawled on his back, elbows under him, one hand bent stiffly, trying to free his sword. The harness and belt twisted about him, and he couldn't grasp it. He stayed down only because it kept the beast off him for a few more moments, and because he was listening to the sounds about him. How many stalkers were near? How long did he have before he'd be swarmed, with no hope at all? He thrashed, longcoat and sword harness constricting him as he flailed. The hound snarled, legs bunching for a pounce. He got the hilt of his sword in hand, finally, cold metal filling his palm, and he coiled his fingers about it.

They both leaped at the same moment. Hosmer kicked, shoving his boot under the torch, flinging it upward, as he threw the rest of his body up. The torch flew into the hound's arcing body, flame spewing across the beast's sleek skin as it lunged after Hosmer. The hound swerved just a hair, enough that Hosmer could parry with his short sword, and he moved with the weight of the beast, letting it carry past him, slicing as they moved. The torch bounced to a stop across his boots, as the hound fell off the blade to the ground and rolled, snarling in pain and fury. It whirled about and charged.

He snatched up the torch and braced himself. Jaws stretched wide, huge enough to bring down a bull, and he stared down them. He wanted to slice, letting the hound's momentum carry him past again, but the beast wrenched himself in mid-leap, squaring himself off, and Hosmer found himself off-balance. Orange-yellow eyes glowed with a fierce intelligence, jaws gaping wide, ivory fangs gleaming. He struck with both hands, with nothing left to guard his throat as the hound met him face-to-face. Hot drool dropped onto his face and teeth sank into his throat as he fell back, hitting the ground hard, breath swooshing out of him, waiting for the jaws to close.

They never did.

The beast's weight pinned him down as the light in its eyes faded and its muscles went slack and jaws let loose. Hosmer gasped for breath, choking at the fetid smell of the hound, and managed to wiggle from underneath, aching in every joint. He did not know if the torch, sunk deep in the earlier gash, killed it, or if it was the sword plunged into its barrel-wide chest.

Nor did it matter. He tugged his sword loose and staggered back. His horse whickered and came near, nostrils still aflare with the smell of the hound. He dragged himself astride, struggling to get his sword back in its sheath as the horse moved away, quickly, as though the smell of blood and death could be outpaced.

Somewhere down the hill, each step jolting him in the saddle, Hosmer realized his right pants leg had gone all slick with wetness. He leaned over to look at himself, and saw blood dripping along the cuff and boot shank to the ground. His horse came to a stop as his weight shifted, throwing his head up nervously, nostrils wide both with the need to breathe and with the scent of blood on them both. Hosmer rubbed the palm of his hand over his face. He couldn't ask more of his horse who'd already given so much. He'd either make it home . . . or he wouldn't. He nudged the fingers of his hand downward, trying to see where the blood began, and found a long gash in the fabric, raw skin showing through, and sucked a sigh of pain. He could wrap it, but he couldn't tie it off.

He shrugged out of his longcoat, binding his leg as well as he could, the gash running from mid-thigh to mid-calf. He couldn't probe to see how deep it was, just bending slightly to tug his coat about it made his head spin and his ears pound with that loud deafness that came just before passing out. He had to stay on the horse or that which had torn the Barrels apart would catch him.

He lifted the reins again, and his horse began to pick his way along the slope he had avoided again, wheezing now and then as they traversed the long way down. The horse's legs trembled as they moved and Hosmer talked to him quietly, a running litany of encouragement and, well, memory. He talked to him of the orchards and the beehives they kept, sweet with honey, and the Silverwing in all its seasons. He talked of harvest and making cider, of breaking ground for new trees, of budding time and flowers. He reminded the horse of Nutmeg and quiet Rivergrace, of the love between his mother and father, and the strength the two of them gave all of them. He talked until his throat grew dry and hoarse and he could talk no longer, but continued in a broken whisper, guiding his mount downward step by step, feeling his leg bleed out and his mind grow weak. His thoughts faded, then, slowly, his words.

He woke suddenly, grabbing for mane and reins, about to slip from the saddle altogether, and found himself in the thick brush and groves at the base of the hills. His horse snorted as the bit jerked in his mouth, and Hosmer righted himself. He could hear the renewed howling behind him, far behind, but it wouldn't stay far behind long. He closed his eyes.

Da, forgive me, but I can't lead them to you . . .

He leaned over the weary horse's neck, his voice coming out in a faint croak. "Take me where they won't find my body," he managed, reining the horse away from the small track which would lead to the river road that led home. The horse took a reluctant step forward, then swerved abruptly, almost unseating Hosmer altogether. A figure emerged from the blur of his weariness.

"Well done, lad, but not done enough." A long hand reached up to snare the bridle, pulling the horse to a stop in his tracks, and Hosmer looked down into a remarkable face, elven, with eyes of gray and black and white lightning in them. The Stranger ran his free hand along the horse's head, a soothing stroke, and both of them relaxed at his touch. "A fine horse you have, but you're not asking enough of him. He is tashya bred. He has the bottom in him to take you home, and enough left to keep you ahead of the pack." The other continued to stroke Hosmer's mount. "You've not asked enough of yourself either. Go home, lad. It was ill luck that crossed our paths this day. The hunters are after me, but they found you and others. They're Ravers and they'll not stop till they've taken down all the quarry within reach of here. You must get home, and keep your family safe."

"I'll lead them after me," Hosmer husked in protest.

"No. They already have your home in their sights. Trust me on this. I cannot stop them, although I will delay them a bit." The Vaelinar let go of the bridle, placing the palm of his hand under the horse's jaw and murmuring a few soft words in his lilting language that Hosmer did not understand, but the horse seemed to draw in. He threw his head up with a proud whinny.

"Who are you?"

The other looked at him. He seemed to blend back into the shadows of the grove, unremarkable except for his height, and the storm-gray cloak over his shoulders, and the storm of his eyes, a hint of pewter hair tucked under the hood. "I don't give my name out," he answered slowly, "but I think you may have need of it someday, though your memory will be short till then. I am the one called Daravan. Now, go!" He slapped his hand on the horse's hindquarters sharply and the steed bounded away, Hosmer holding on with the last of his failing strength, headed home.

Chapter Twenty-One

GARNER SHINNIED UP to the top of the tree, inspecting leaves and such as he went, the emeraldbark towering above the apple trees, like the dignified sentinel it was. Its verdant branches ruffled little as Garner moved among them. Fringing the orchards, these emerald-barks served as more than windbreaks. Their tough bark endured the scourge of many an attack that might kill the orchards, but also, because of their native attraction, they held signs of any infestation first. As Tolby had often shown his sons, the health of the apple trees was dependent upon the health of the wild groves and countryside about them, life interwoven with life. Garner turned leaf after leaf over in his palm, seeing little sign other than the nibblings of caterpillars, expected and not worrisome on this scale. He settled in the uppermost branches a moment to look out. A gentle wind led the edge of a storm from the north, rain to be expected, even welcome, but Garner frowned. The wind carried another omen to him, this one unexpected and strange, and he tilted his face to it, listening.

The bell of hounds on a scent, their deep baying alerting those who'd loosed them. He wondered what they hunted, their howls not familiar, nothing like the hound packs in the valley that occasionally went out. The wailing, faint as it came to him, raised the hair on the back of his neck with its barely-heard lust for blood. Garner drew back a little on his high-top perch. He would not want to be the quarry in that hunt.

Fumbling about in the shoulder-slung pouch he wore, he found the sprayer and dowsed the upper leaves for precaution. A mixture of toback juice and herbs that Tolby and Lily had concocted years ago seemed to keep harmful insects from ravaging their trees. Finished, he stowed his gear, then shifted about on the branches and stood on a limber, swaying one, taking a last look about. That was when he saw Beacon Hill flare with orange, and then settle into a steady blue-orange glow, its smoke far different from the storm rolling slowly in from the north. Below, on the slopes, he saw a running figure.

Without question, Garner slid down the tree, skinning his hands, not feeling the pain, as he jumped the last span, hitting the ground in a deep-kneed crouch. Wishing, for once, he had a horse or pony instead of his own two feet, he set a course for the runner, grass and brush snagging at his trousered legs as he dashed headfirst toward the trouble. Bolgers could be as cowardly as slime dogs, and he figured to scout out which way they were coming in. He'd worked too hard to let them make off with another year's harvest and pressing. Tools jingled and jangled in his sack as he vaulted over fallen limbs and gnarled bushes, the beacon burning in his eyesight.

Then he realized the howling had stopped, and the only noise he heard was his own thrashing about. Garner dropped to a walk, and then stilled altogether, trying not to breathe hard, his senses pitched to the wild woods about him. Sweat dribbled down his rib cage and flank, plastering his shirt to his torso, and something he'd run through began a small, but persistent itch along his left hand. Nothing mattered but the eerie silence around him. Running after trouble was one thing, having trouble run after him quite another. If his da were around, he'd cuff him on the head for being so stupid.

He heard nothing other than his own breath rattling around in his lungs, and took a deep one, relaxing a mite. He'd gotten away with it, this time. Garner turned on one heel to scout for a tree fit for scaling and taking another look-see.

The thing leaped at him.

He caught a huge blur at the corner of his eye and went down, rolling, its weight carrying it past him, brushing him with a shell-like hardness that cut and scraped as it crossed over him. Garner grabbed a handful of soft dirt and mud as he got up, throwing it at the thing as he jumped back in retreat. It batted at the debris, standing up and bringing itself to its full height, with a rasp and a chitter, black stick wings humming in irritation. The Raver eyed him as he might a nicely grilled steak, and Garner pulled at the short sword in his sack, jangling among the pruners and trowels and sprayer. It came free in his hand as he jerked it, and the sprayer tumbled out as well, toppling at his feet. Garner kicked it aside.

Soft, torn crimson cloth so dark it looked black wrapped the thing. Inside the shroud, he could see tiny pinpoints of light. Could it even see? It sensed him, that he knew. But could it see?

Something inside the rags clacked. It jumped on stilted legs, vaulting him, and Garner turned with a gasp, jabbing at thin air. The Raver landed and made a noise of . . . what? Amusement? It towered over him, shadows weaving about it, as if it could draw the very storm's edge closer to it. He thought he smelled the char of burned wood on it as well. He wondered who had lit the beacon, no longer wondering why, and if that person had survived. He tried not to think that his brother had been among the patrollers.

All that mattered now was that he get past this thing, past and away, to warn the others just what it was they faced.

It jumped at him again, soundlessly, and Garner fell back, sword thrusting upward, trying to find a soft spot in the ragged body, finding only hard shell that turned back his blade again and again as it brought him down with hands that felt like razors. Much heavier than the stiltlike thing had looked, Garner could not throw it off. He parried with the sword, again and again, feeling it strike then miss, then slice again, hot warmth running over him.

He kicked up with both feet, knees doubled, at the center of it, squirming away. It rolled off with a harsh squeak, chittering, and then went silent as it scrambled back up, those eerily dancing lights inside its hood fastened on Garner as Garner stood, crouching slightly, muscles bunched. It waved its hands, rags shivering about it, and he could see pincerlike fingers running with crimson. Bright droplets fell to the ground. His face and chest stung.

His blood.

Garner bared his teeth. "Come on with it," he growled at the Raver. "Let's see what you're made of!"

Its wings lifted. Garner braced for another leaping charge, but the thing ducked and came straight at him instead.

It hit him hard enough that the sword went flying one way and he another, grappling with the Raver. He could feel something sink deep into his side. He gasped with the push of it; it was digging deep. Garner threw out his free hand, reaching for a branch, dirt, anything to fight with. He grasped something hard and round and brought it up, smashing it over the shrouded head.

The clay sprayer pot broke into a thousand pieces, dumping the concoction all over the two of them. It stung like fire in his wounds and eyes. Tears sprang up instantly, Garner coughing and choking. The Raver leaned in, the pincer in his side digging through his flesh, digging for the kill. Garner put the heel of his hand up under the thing's hood, catching a hard edge of bonelike jaw and pushed inexorably upward, struggling to breathe, the thing rasping and rattling at him, its pincerlike hand sinking into him. It seemed to go on forever.

Bumblebee let Tolby know first that they drew near something. The shaggy pony lifted his head, let out a long whinny of challenge, and jolted to a stiff-legged stop, the cart bouncing roughly behind him. A true son of Acorn he was, though he was a good deal bigger than his sire, a pony who would not let any horse back him down. Tolby glared into the scruff-edged woods along with the pony, seeing nothing but hearing something at the edge of his senses. The sharp crack of a branch. The quiet of the birds and varmints about, as if the area listened with him. A faint hint of a rank scent he could not quite make out. Something trespassed beyond them.

Whatever it was, he wasn't going to meet it sitting in the cart. He gritted his jaw in decision before knotting the reins around one hand, his breath escaping in a gruff curse. He threw the wheel brake into place and stood up. Bumblebee shuddered beneath his bushy winter coat and tossed his head with a chuff as Tolby wrapped the reins about the brake and jumped free of the cart. He grabbed his long-armed pruner as he did and made his way toward the thinning wild woods and heavy brush, even as he heard the shambling movement of something headed his way inexorably from off the Beacon plateau. Twigs snapped, then stopped, and something breathed heavily, pushing toward him. Tolby wrapped his hands about his pruner tightly as he set his heels.

The noise came to a halt. Whatever it was, it came to a rest just beyond his line of sight. Tolby growled softly to himself. He had been in enough fights in his life and wasn't particularly interested in starting any more, but he was still young enough and strong enough to *finish* one if he had to, and he was damned impatient with anything between him and that bonfire on the hill. There weren't enough Bolgers to stop him.

He heard broken wheezing, and then a horse pushed through the tree branches, staggering toward him, head down, reins loose, his rider slumped over his neck, barely in the saddle. Tolby's jaw dropped, and then the pruner pole, rattling. One of the greatest fears of his life stopped before him.

His heart thumped heavily in his chest with the jolt of it but he shook free of the moment. He leaped forward before the horse could stumble back into the undergrowth as it rolled a wild eye at him. Tolby grabbed a fistful of mane as it shied from him, nearly losing Hosmer altogether. The horse shuddered to a grateful stop as Tolby pulled the head to his chest, and muttered a gruff command, and rubbed his knuckles over the animal's forelock. The horse let out a low moan, and put his head down. Tolby reached for his son, trying to steady the thunderous pulse in his chest. Hosmer fell off the saddle and into his arms like a wet sack of grain, head lolling. But he breathed. Thank the Gods, he breathed.

Bow-legged with Hosmer's weight, Tolby got to the cart bed and laid him down as easily as he could. His son's head lolled to one side, and then an eye opened. "Da?"

"Don't say nothin'. You're almost home." He put the cart tailgate up, doubling Hosmer's legs a little to get him to fit. He was covered in blood and dirt, the longcoat wrapped about his leg slick with it, and the sight made Tolby's throat tight. He thought of loosening it, then realized why Hosmer had tied it so tightly, trying to stem the flow of blood. Home, to Lily with her poultices, was his only chance.

"Have. Have to. Tell you." Hosmer swallowed. Under the soot of smoke, and mud, and grass, and spilled blood, his skin had gone sheet white and pale. "The beacon—"

"Been lit. Not your worry."

"Da." Hosmer's face screwed into a terrible grimace as he fought for a breath. "Listen, will you?"

Tolby fumbled with the horse's reins, tying him to the cart bed. His voice came out gruffly, barely at all. "Spit it out, then."

"The Barrel boys, dead. In my pocket for the family. Bolgers. Hounds. Ravers tore 'em to bits. All dead but me. I lit the beacon. Get home. Run, Da. Nothing will stop them." Hosmer took another deep, shuddering breath. "Please," he breathed out, and then his eyes flickered. Tolby's blood ran cold at the sound of it. His son's body went slack, but his chest heaved again, and again. Tolby ran his hand over his son's face, brushing it clean.

He jumped in the cart, unwrapping the reins, and snapping lose ends at Bumblebee's haunches. "Move your ass!" he shouted, and Bumblebee bolted in surprise, then put his pony head down and ran as best he could, Tolby standing in the fore of the cart, yelling and whipping as they went.

Keldan searched the nearby orchards frantically, finding no sign of Garner or his gear. Finally, he slowed to a trot, his mouth gone dry. The need to get home surged through his mind. Rounding a small freshet of water trickling through the outer lines of the grove, he aimed for the ranch. Lily stood outside, waving her apron, laughing at Grace and Nutmeg's quest to corral a small but very agile young goat. Lily looked up and saw him. For a moment, the laughter and happiness at the goat chase lit up her expression, then she realized he'd run in, alone. She dropped her apron down.

"What is it? What's gone wrong?"

Keldan bent over, hands on his knees, drawing in huge gulps of breath. He pointed behind him, sentences short as he tried to get his wind. "Beacon's lit. Da says, trouble. Get you together. Hosmer on patrol. Can't find Garner."

Nutmeg put her hand to her brow, squinting up at the hills. She looked to her mom and let out a snort. "Bolgers again. I'd like to twist their whiskers."

"It's the wrong time of year to be raiding our harvest and mill. They come in the fall. It's almost summer." Lily brushed a strand of silvery hair from her brow as she frowned, and worry settled on her face. "We'll be hiding this time instead of taking a stand," she added, despite a stomp of a foot from Nutmeg.

Grace had caught the little goat, its soft ear in her grasp even as her gaze went far away, before seeming to come back. She rubbed the soft flap between her fingers, saying, "I hate the cellar."

"I've made the choice, and we'll stick to it, until Tolby gets here and decides otherwise. Better safe than sorry." Lily pointed at Keldan. "Get fresh water down there. I'll get the girls busy. Loose the goats, the chickens, the ponies. Everything stabled up goes free."

"They'll be scattered from here till sundown," Keldan protested.

"Then it's more work facing us later. I'll not give the Bolgers their meal in a pen! When you're done, find me inside. We've readying to do. No dillydallying now!" Lily slapped Keldan on his shoulder, pushing all of them into movement. He staggered off on legs still wobbly from his run, then threw his shoulders back and steadied himself.

Rivergrace rubbed the tiny, stubborn goat along the neck in farewell, and pushed it away. It bounded straight up on its spindly legs and dashed toward the pens with a defiant bleat. She made it to the pens first, dragging open the pole gate. She and Nutmeg dashed through, waving their arms and flapping their skirts, sending the goats out in a mad scamper, stiff-legged in surprise, their bleats filling the air. It would take days to round them back up, yet she could not bear the thought of the Bolgers spitting and roasting her babies. Nutmeg circled her and went to the coops, shooing out the rooster and the chickens in a flurry of feathers. She sneezed as she emerged, a basket of eggs in her hand, and took to her heels as the ponies stampeded past her, snorting and galloping as Keldan took a green stick to their haunches, driving them away from mangers of hay and into the open fields. With the barn and corral cleared, he disappeared in the direction of the well, clay jugs in his hands.

Grace gazed about the farmyard. She upended a few of the tidy stacks of crates and barrels, making it look as if they'd gone through the area in haste. She dusted her hands and followed Nutmeg in slowly, where Lily had already thrown open cupboards in the kitchen and removed a few small treasures . . . pots and lids, and a few dishes, and placed them in a crate to take down to the cellar. She added a sack of breads and cheeses, looking up. "Go through the rooms. Fill the traveling backpacks with a few items, sturdy wear, cloak, boots, and such. Leave the drawers and cabinets open. Stuff a blanket in the pack if you can, but don't take much. I want it stowed below when you're done."

Nutmeg nodded, and headed for the upstairs, Grace on her heels. They did as their mother had bidden, and Rivergrace found her reluctance growing as they went from room to room. She took the backpacks down to the root cellar carved out for hiding, darker, deeper, than the main cellar, with bags of stored onions and garlics, to hide their smell. She'd never been down here with the whole family before. It would be even more crowded, and she had to stoop slightly to go in and out as it was. Going out, she knew she couldn't go back in. Her throat tightened until she felt like a corked bottle, unable to breathe. Light-headed, she leaned against the tunnel wall for a moment. The darkness and closeness pressed around her. She would have run, if she could have, her heart thumping in her chest. Nutmeg nudged her from behind. "Come on, we're almost done."

When the nudge didn't work, Nutmeg just pushed her up the tunnel, grunting and mumbling, and giving Grace a shake. Lily gave neither of them a chance to speak, shoving their arms full of bolts of cloth and sacks of odds and ends she'd gathered, saying, "Stow them as best you can. That'll be all we can take down there, we need room for ourselves."

Grace bolted back down while she had the will to do so, emptying her armload as quickly as she could. Upstairs in the main house, she stood quiet and still for a long moment, willing her pulse to steady and her nerves to calm. Lily emerged from the kitchen and pantry area, her mouth half open to say something when a clatter arose in the yard, Keldan shouting and the noise of wheels on the road. They rushed to the door to see Tolby standing on the seat of the cart, whipping Bumblebee stoutly, driving him at a dead run into the farmyard. Grace felt her blood go cold.

Tolby sprang from the cart as Bumblebee came to a halt, put his shaggy head down, and wheezed. "It's Hos," he yelled to Keldan. "Help me get your brother down." Over his shoulder, he said to Lily, "It's bad. Go get the cleanest cloths and hottest water you can. And your staunching poultices. We'll carry him down to the cellar."

"Can't we take care of him up here first?" Lily wrung her apron with her hands, wiping them off, bracing herself.

Tolby shook his head. "Ravers, he told me. Ravers on the road, with hounds and others. Not a minute to waste. There isn't a tree or house worth the lives of any of you."

"Get him inside, then!" With a hand to her mouth as if to stifle a cry, Lily ran inside her home. Nutmeg reached for the harness on Bumblebee and Grace sprang to help, freeing the lathered-up and bone-tired pony. She and Nutmeg watched as the two men shouldered Hosmer's limp and bloodied form from the cart bed as carefully as they could, but his square, heavy frame almost overwhelmed them. He groaned as Tolby stumbled crossing the threshold. Small gobbets of blood dripped from the longcoat wrapped about his leg. Grace watched the crimson blood dribble down, transfixed, then a thought struck her. "I'll get the vinegar."

"Why?"

She looked at Nutmeg. "The blood, that's why. We can't leave a trail into the house."

Nutmeg shuddered. Turning to the tired pony, she grabbed a fist of his mane to lead him away from the cart and toward the back pasture. Grace fetched out the strong apple vinegar and began wiping down the floorboards, erasing all trace of Hosmer's being carried into the house, through the pantry, and down into the hidden cellar. She sprinkled the vinegar about in the farmyard, and kicked dust over the wet patches. Then she corked the bottle, handing it to Nutmeg. "Take that down with you. They might be needing it to dress his wounds."

"Take it yourself." Nutmeg scrubbed her hands on her apron, smelling of pony sweat.

"I'm not going. I can't." Rivergrace looked toward the river, and as if alerted by her gaze, a silver-winged alna rose on the horizon to circle lazily, belying the urgency of the moment.

"You have to."

"I can't. You don't understand, but it chokes me down there. It falls on me like a . . . a huge boulder, and I can't breathe, and I can't think . . . I'll climb the highest tree on the border I can find. They'll not look for me there."

"Hounds won't need to look. They'll smell your fear sweat, and there you'll be, treed and easy pickings. Get inside!" Nutmeg put her hands on her hips.

"No." Grace shook her head. "I can't go to a hole in the ground! I can't."

Nutmeg's eyes narrowed, then she bent over to grab up one of the water buckets on its side. "You just stand there like a bump on a log!" she shouted, before running off.

Stunned, Grace froze in place for a moment as Nutmeg's figure disappeared beyond the gate and shrubbery in a flurry that even her sharp gaze could not track. Her thoughts stumbled. She opened her mouth to yell after her sister, then she heard the faint calling of hounds on the wind, far away yet carried on storm-laden clouds. A chill wind swept around her. Not Nutmeg, no. She followed after her sister.

Jeredon came into the study, leather straps slung over his shoulder, his hands working as he braided the ends into something remotely resembling a lead rope, although it could have been almost any project that preoccupied his fancy. Sevryn looked up from his reading. Jeredon stopped and rocked back on one heel.

"I should have known," he remarked. "Feels like an angry nest of hornets round here." He plopped down into a chair, crossed his ankles, and kept braiding.

"It's not me, I swear." Sevryn signed through the air. Jeredon snorted.

"What news, then?"

"Little. Tressandre is as ever, as are all the ild Fallyns."

Jeredon took his attention from his braiding to run a keen eye over Sevryn. The corner of his mouth drew up. "I see she marked you."

"She tends to do that." Sevryn put a finger to his collar and shifted the material slightly, his fingertip tracing the new scar delicately as he did so, and a faint heat rising in his face.

"My only question would be if you like it as much as she does."

Sevryn only smiled then as he dropped his hand back to his book. "That would be telling. But no. I took it as an emissary, and she took it as a trial of my mettle. I could hardly run."

"Indeed." Jeredon's chin lowered as he began braiding again, fingers flying. His project took on, more and more, the aspect of a quiver strap, with an ivy pattern in the weaving itself. What had seemed haphazard to Sevryn at first became clearly the work of a master as Jeredon continued to labor. He put that realization at the back of his mind. Things were seldom what they seemed about the Vaelinars.

He returned to his book, a treatise which mentioned Gilgarran more than once, and tugged at the nostalgic edge of his state of mind. His mentor's training had been much like Jeredon's weaving, he thought, sinking into the text. He did not rouse himself until the click of Lariel's boots entering drew his attention. Closing the book on his finger, he looked up to see that Jeredon had fallen into a light doze and his sister stood over him with a look on her face that seemed to indicate she was torn between letting him sleep and waking him with a fright.

She felt his gaze on her and winked at him, still torn in consideration. Jeredon broke the moment himself, his right booted foot twitching slightly and then he awoke, with a lazy yawn, looking up into his sister's face. "No wonder I dreamed of a vantane's sharp gaze on me," he remarked.

Lariel smiled at being compared to a war falcon. She leaned one hip against the study table. "And you its prey?"

"Always. Although your amusements are not so sharp as those of the ild Fallyn."

Sevryn made a noise at that, and smiled innocently when both Lariel and Jeredon focused their attention on him. He put his book aside and stood. "I am at your service, as always, Queen Lariel."

"I need Talent, not good intentions."

He made a mocking little bow, in deference to his half blood. "I apologize again for my shortcomings. I can at least throw myself between you and a sharp object."

"There is that." She made a dismissive gesture with one hand. Jeredon looked from one to the other, his expression carefully neutral, but his eyes lit with curiosity. "I can only be thankful that, unlike the ild Fallyn Stronghold, I can speak securely within my own walls."

"Praise be," Sevryn answered, "and so may that continue, my queen." He straightened his tunic, picking at a bit of unseen lint as Lariel gazed hard into her brother's face.

Jeredon rattled his leatherwork in his hand. "Nothing on my mind is as important as the length of this quiver strap, at the moment. Anyone care to go hunting and bring in some fresh game for dinner? You should step away from your paperwork, Lariel, it's made you cranky."

She shook her head. "I've too much work to prepare."

Sevryn wrinkled his nose. "I spent time in the kitchens today, and Cook could definitely use a bit of game to inspire her. I'll go, Jeredon."

"You? You chase more than you bring down."

"I resent that."

"How can you resent the truth? Any more than one should revile the sun in the sky and the moons at night?"

"Show me a truth first, then I shall banter with you whether I resent it or not."

"Gentlemen," began Lariel firmly, but the two continued as if she had not said a word.

"You would not know a truth if I rubbed your half-Vaelinar nose in it."

"And you think there is no truth unless a Vaelinar birthed it first, and that, Jeredon, is more wrong than saying the ocean drowns the sun every night."

"Gentlemen!"

They stopped and looked at her. Lariel took a breath. "A hunt," she said, "sounds appealing. Or it did."

Jeredon beamed, while Sevryn looked aggrieved. "I shall not argue further," he answered. "But Jeredon is wrong."

"He frequently is. But, as his sister, only I am allowed to know that." Lariel linked her elbow to Sevryn. "You'll need a fresh horse. Yours is played out."

Jeredon grinned ear to ear. "I know just the animal." He trailed out of the study after them, to hear Sevryn pleading, "Please, my lady queen, do not ask me to ride a beast that Jeredon has picked out."

Her laughter rang back up the stairwell. "I'll ask no such thing. Just be wary of any mount I may assign you!"

Sevryn groaned.

Jeredon nocked his arrow. Keeping his eyes on a brace of field-fattened birds, he traced their line of flight before letting the string snap and arrow fly. Without watching to see if he hit or not, he turned back to Lariel.

"It was bound to happen sooner or later. You've commanded a loyalty, sister, that few have, but spies are inevitable."

"If I knew who it was, I'd cut their ears off and send them out in a box by courier." Lariel crossed her wrists as she sat her horse, and the tall gelding moved restively under her as if sensing her cross attitude.

"I'll get the bird," Sevryn offered. He put his horse into a lope, crossing the newly greened field even as Jeredon pulled another arrow from his shoulder quiver and put it to his bow.

"You will use this spy to your advantage."

"Of course," she answered shortly, her eyes on Sevryn. "And if there is one, there is likely another." She sighed heavily.

"The Accords have been in effect long enough to chafe at some of us. You know that."

"It's more than that, I think. Some of the Houses are gathering up the half-breeds that they've disdained for centuries. Crossing those with purebloods, building the strain back up again. Discarding those who do not measure up, indenturing those who do."

"Breeding back a Vaelinar line?"

"I think so. Or at least true-blooded enough to be finding Talent where they can. It could be a good thing, or it could be disaster. Talent built our Ways, but it did not lead us home."

"That doesn't mean it will never do so."

Sevryn approached, the game bird tied off and hung over the pommel of his saddle, and handed the arrow back to Jeredon. "Convinced her to lead our spies a merry chase?"

Lariel gave him an ill-disguised look of "How did you know?" while Jeredon barked a laugh.

"We can do no less." He shrugged at her mild irritation that he'd guessed her words while he was out of earshot.

"Spoken like Gilgarran, if he could be found." She twitched a rein in even more annoyance. "Years and years since I've heard from him. I've tired of waiting for him to come to me. I should put a bounty on his head."

Sevryn made a move, or perhaps it was his sudden stillness, that drew her attention, and she eyed his neutral expression. She and Jeredon traded glances then.

"Perhaps," Jeredon said quietly, "a direct question would be best."

"Perhaps." Lariel brushed a strand of hair from her brow. "Sevryn, what do you know of Gilgarran?"

Sevryn rubbed the back of his neck before meeting her eyes. "Gilgarran found me," he answered. "And is dead, these past nearly three decades."

She reeled back in her saddle, Jeredon stabbing an arm out to steady her. "All these years," she breathed, "and the answer in front of me all this time."

"I never knew you sought him. Even if I had known, I might not have said much, until necessary." Sevryn shrugged, without apology. "It's the way he trained me."

"None of us here can fault the way you were trained, and we should have recognized such discretion." Jeredon kept his grip on his sister. " 'Tis true, we never asked."

"I never had such a need of him before." Lariel took a breath, sounding shaken. "He would know why there are Vaelinar eyes looking to the east. What lies there but the ruins of the past? What do I need to fear?"

"Perhaps I should tell you how he died."

She nodded, color coming slowly back into her face, and Sevryn began to tell his tale, pausing only when Jeredon found a clear shot, and they brought down enough game to justify the hunt. His tale offered only a few answers, leaving far more questions. His words left her unresolved, for she had not only a spy to deal with, she had Tressandre's challenge.

Some prey, it seemed, would be more elusive than others.

Chapter Twenty-Two

GARNER STRUGGLED UPWARD from darkness. He felt sucked down in a black pool of water and fought for the surface. He swam upward, forcing himself toward the light, and broke through, arms thrashing. And went nowhere, a weight holding him down and leaden sky meeting his eyes.

With a grunt, he managed to roll out from under the dead weight of the thing squashing him. As he wrenched to one side, its pincers pulled free from his chest with a sucking sound and his back arched with the pain of it, a scream trying to tear from his throat but not getting out. He expected a gush of blood, but none came, just a seeping from a wound that closed even as he rolled to his side and tried to press it shut. Garner got to his knees. He looked at the Raver, dead and even more grotesque than before, sodden with Tolby's home brew, his sprayer smashed, his short sword sunk to the hilt in the fraying crimson rags of the thing's cloak. The shroud had slipped aside a bit, exposing a helmetlike head, and he twitched it back in place, not wanting to see more of the freakish thing than he had. He must have hit a vital spot, even as the thing had been digging for his. Thank the Gods and Goddesses for ribs. He got up on one foot but had to pause in a kneeling position, neither up nor down.

He stared at the corpse of the thing. He ought to search it and see if there was anything about it worth anything, but the thought of touching it again raised gooseflesh on him. Garner clenched his jaw and prodded it with his free hand. Something fell from the cloak with a thunk into the crushed grass and bracken. He fished it out.

It dangled on a wire chain. Garner tried to focus on it, but he could not tell if the chunk of metal was a seal or an amulet or just a twisted bit of jewelry. Whatever it was, it carried the same greasy feel to it that the Raver did. With a grimace of distaste he pocketed it, knowing that he wouldn't pick anything else off the body. Whatever secrets it had, it would keep. He was alive and would have to concentrate on staying that way, and from the black edges closing in on his vision, it would take all his effort.

It occurred to him that the beacon had probably been lit for good reason. An avalanche of thoughts followed that first one. Where there was one Raver, there were bound to be more, and that there could be trouble at home, and that home was where he needed to be. He labored to stand up, made it, and stood swaying. Then he put one foot ahead of the other. It was rather like walking home after a big night drinking with the militia volunteers, just as unsteady and his head throbbed just as much. He'd made it then. He'd make it now.

Rivergrace dashed over the uneven rough pasture after Nutmeg, yet even with her long stride she came no closer to spotting her sister anywhere. Nutmeg could never beat her in a footrace, but Grace had no idea which way the other girl had gone. She paused to listen, her blood pulsing through her ears, the sound of faraway baying growing stronger, but not a leaf crunch to tell her of Nutmeg's flight. Then, from the riverbanks, four or five alna took to the air, silver-tipped wings beating frantically as they gained height, and Grace veered toward the disturbance. Parting the reeds, she found Nutmeg struggling up the cove's bank, heavy bucket in her arms.

"What are you doing?"

Nutmeg spun around, water splashing. "This," she said, and swung the bucket at Grace, dousing her from head to toe in a wave of icy water. Nutmeg stood there grinning. "That's river water," she said emphatically. "So you come down to the cellar with me, and you sit down in the corner and close your eyes and you listen to the river sing. And, as long as you do that, you can bear it down there."

Grace blinked. Soaked, her long hair dripping about her, even her shoes squelched as she took a step in surprise. But, she could feel it. She could feel the arms of the Silverwing about her. Her mouth opened.

"And I've half a bucket left!" Nutmeg finished in triumph, hooking her arm through Grace's. "So come with me and no dillydallying."

Tolby met them at the front door. He looked from one to the other, then shook his head, no time for questions. He beckoned. "Garner?"

Both shook their heads in answer.

Tolby shifted unhappily, running his calloused hand over his thin hair. "There's no way around it. He'll make it back or hole up on his own. I have to trust that I did not raise stupid children. Get on with you now, your mother's worried and needs your help." With a cluck, he herded them into the kitchen and down the trapdoor into the main cellar, and then from the cramped passageway into the even deeper second cellar, where he dropped the heavy door into place overhead, and barred it.

Grace closed her eyes a moment, standing with her back and shoulders bent, and tried not to think of it. Nutmeg dropped her half a bucket of water as she went to her mother's side by Hosmer's still, pale figure. Lily reached out and stroked her daughter's hair. "I've done all I can. The bleeding is stopped. I've never seen such a tear as that, but he should mend all right if there's no infection."

Nutmeg tucked covers in around Hosmer, her motions an unconscious echo of her mother's own fussing. "He lit the beacon," she said.

"That he did." Tolby pulled out a small item from his vest pocket. "And brought this back for the Barrel family. Two sons died up there, the whole patrol ambushed. If they hadn't gone to light it out without him, we'd have lost him, too." His gaze went over Hosmer's silent form, and his lips closed tightly.

Unsaid but thought, *and we still might.*

Grace crossed her arms in front of her as if to shield herself from the thought.

Nutmeg sat down next to her, putting an arm about her shoulders, yet another echo of Lily Farbranch. "What do they want?"

Tolby sat down and pulled out his cold pipe, and put the stem in his mouth anyway, as if it would help to chew on it. "No knowing, yet. Let's hope we won't be knowing too much later either." He gazed up, at the dirt roof, broken only by the heavy drop door he'd barred into place, his eyes going dark with thought.

"I heard hounds," Grace offered.

"We used vinegar," Nutmeg added. "No blood trail down to the cellars."

"Good thinking," Lily said briskly. "Now, all we can do is wait." She began to attend to all the candles but the one near Hosmer, its light reflecting from its hood, pallid but seeming all the stronger as the others got pinched out one by one. Tolby drew her by him. Keldan sat at his brother's feet, leaned his head against the corner of the cot, and drifted off into sleep almost immediately.

Grace shut her eyes and felt the river's cold touch on her, through her clothes, soothing her skin. With her eyes closed, she could almost forget the closeness of the tiny cellar, the warmth of the forms crowded around her, the smell of the blood on Hosmer, and the heavy burlap bags of onions and garlic to the fore of the cave. High water or the slow stream of late summer, the Silverwing had always moved her. Now it seemed to envelop her in its care, as Nutmeg had said it would, sighing along her skin as it evaporated slowly, keeping her chill and still.

She did not dream, but felt her inner self drift away in a kind of haze, to murmured voices only slightly louder than the river itself, though it was no one she knew talking, nor words she could quite make out, all hushed, all muffled as if the weight of the earth itself was upon them. She felt small and insignificant beneath the words, as if she had never been meant to understand them nor could she do anything to stop their falling, any more than she could stop the rain, yet she thought that they might sweep her away, if only she could understand them. After long moments, their sounds became dull and pounding, thundering down on her. Puffs of dirt rained down from the dirt ceiling overhead in fits and spurts, and they fought to keep from coughing. Nutmeg's arm on her shoulder tightened.

"They're here." Her voice muffled, her fear all too clear.

Rivergrace closed her eyes again to fight her own fear that pushed her to get up and run, to bolt from their shelter into even greater danger. She balled her hand into a fist, her nails digging sharply into her palm until her fingers went numb. Thumps and bumps grew louder but not at the hidden trapdoor. Tolby clamped down harder on his pipe stem, the noise of his teeth clicking sharp in the quiet.

Grace could feel Nutmeg shivering next to her. She leaned hard against her sister to comfort her, but nothing stopped the attack overhead. Little bits of pebble and dust fell down periodically, then stopped. After what seemed forever and a day, the stomping grew fainter.

She opened her eyes, with a soft sigh, the knots unwinding from her neck and shoulder, but Tolby sitting in the dim candlelight across from her took the unlit pipe from his mouth. He seemed to be listening intently, his head cocked, then he said, softly, "Smoke."

Keldan stirred. "It would be stronger if they'd found the cellar chimney."

"Maybe." Tolby looked downward, and they all fell into silence again, while the smell of burning filtered in and around them. Greenwood smoke was different from dry wood smoke because of its very nature. Grace blinked as it began to fill the area, stinging her eyes and making them water. The urge to run pushed up in her throat, filling every pulsing thought. She'd be safe at the river, safe in the water. She had to get out.

Nutmeg gave her a little shake, as if hearing her labored breathing. Grace tried to take a deep, still breath and her whole body fought her as the reek of the smoke swirled about them. Not just wood burning. Their life. The stench of burning fruit and flesh began to rise in the cellar, and Grace and Nutmeg both hunched over, shoulder to shoulder, fists pressed to their mouths. Everything they knew from their first memories they could now taste in char in their mouths, in the stink of every breath. It was a burning she knew she could never forget.

Hosmer groaned. Lily put a hand out and rested it on her husband's knee. "They're going to smoke us out."

He shook his head. "Not intentionally, but . . . maybe. Hold on, long as you can. If the candle goes out, we'll have to go, ready or not."

Lily took her scissors from her apron and began to rend it into shreds. "Wrap your faces," she ordered each of them as she handed out long strips. Rivergrace hesitated as she took hers, then dipped it into the half bucket of water near her. She pulled the sash into place across her mouth and nose. The others followed suit. Lily laid the final sash gently across Hosmer's face and he became silent again, as if eased. Then they lapsed into quiet, gazing upward for signs of prowlers through the wreckage, for signs of anything.

She must have slept, smoke or no smoke, fear or no fear. She lost sense of time and shifted wearily in her corner of the cellar, careful not to jostle Nutmeg, aware only that the sash across her mouth and nose had dried. A small stump of candle still burned across the way. Lily rested her head on Tolby's shoulder. The smell of burning still hung strongly in the air. Heat wavered about them, a hot, heavy heat, and she thought of a chicken baking in one of Lily's clay pots. Panic began to crowd her again, pushing up from the pit of her stomach. She couldn't stay in there any longer, waiting to be roasted or crushed. She pulled the sash from her face. She gathered her feet under her and stood, her muscles cramped and stiff, moving to the trapdoor. Splinters scored her hand and broke her fingernails as she muscled the bar aside. Putting a shoulder to the trapdoor, Rivergrace strained to stand, and tried to raise it. It did not budge. She put her hands up, searching the bar, making sure she'd cleared it. Then, holding her breath, she pushed up, waiting for the trapdoor to give way, swinging up and outward.

It stayed firmly in its frame.

"Grace," said Lily softly.

She did not stop to listen. She pounded on it, her fists sore and bruised, her body aching to stand tall in the cramped space, the darkness smothering her, the smoke suffocating her. "I have to get out!"

"I've already tried," her father said tiredly. "It's blocked. We'll not be getting through till it's burned out above."

"Or we'll dig our way out through the air pipes," Keldan added. "When it's all done."

She kept pounding. Tolby got to his feet and put his arms around her in a fierce embrace.

"We'll die down here!"

"No, lass, we won't, and we're still alive. That's something to be said after a Raver raid."

She shuddered in his hug. "I have to get out!"

"We all do, and we will. Somehow." Tolby's eyes took on a fierce glint in the dying light of the candle. "We wait till it's a bit safer."

"I can't!" A scream began to rise in her throat, choked and stifled, fighting its way clear. Tolby held her tighter, muffling her voice against his shoulder.

Then, from above, came thuds and thumps and heavy scuffling. Dirt poured onto them from cracks about the framing. Rivergrace froze, Tolby putting his head back to listen, his own breath caught as his chest went still. Dull thunder reverberated throughout the cellar as the noise buffeted them from one end of the small, cramped cave to the other.

Searching. The raiders had to be searching. They would be plucked from their hiding hole like a roasted animal from its cooking pit. Rivergrace craned her neck, waiting for the breakthrough. Long moments passed in which she was certain her heart barely beat, her breath shallowly escaped, and then, Tolby inhaled and exhaled deeply. He let Rivergrace go with a little shake.

"We wait," he said.

She stumbled back to sit next to Nutmeg, and they held each other's hands. This time she did not sleep. She dared not, afraid it could be the death of her.

Hunting finished, Lariel urged her horse into an easy lope, ahead of Jeredon and Sevryn, the set of her posture revealing her tension to the two who followed. As the boundaries of the hold came into sight, she threw up her hand and they rode to a halt beside her.

"Sevryn, I am sending you to the healer today. No arguments, I want those wounds and scars of yours attended to."

Sevryn's mouth moved imperceptibly as he rested his rein hand lightly on his horse's neck, but he made no sound of disagreement. His very un-Vaelinarran eyes watched her.

She added, "Then, I am sending you back to Tressandre."

It was Jeredon who made a noise. Her gaze rested on him. "It serves no purpose," he said.

"It serves my purpose, for now. The Andredia is not recovering." She made a gesture through the air, a wave of frustration. "The river is dying, and with it, Larandaril, our pact, and many lives."

"You blame ild Fallyn?"

"I have no one to blame—yet. But if they look east, then I have to look east as well, and if we fail here, then ild Fallyn will rush to strike the deathblow, you know that. If they knew what I've been facing, they would already be harrying our gates. They covet this land, polluted and dying or not, and I don't want to hand it to them. I've combed the library, I've read the scries, I've done all that I can think to do."

"Every warrior has a power they must bow to, sooner or later," Sevryn remarked gently.

"I won't bow to this one." Lariel's chin went up and her horse stomped under her, feeling the fight in her. "Tressandre has sent me a challenge."

"What? She dares to?"

Lariel shrugged.

"Outside the Accords? You won't do it, Lariel." Jeredon's mouth set firmly.

"Of course not. She has to be answered."

"Let her stew. Answer her at the Conference."

"I haven't refused to go," he countered Jeredon mildly.

"You're a fool, then. The ild Fallyns bow to Larandaril very reluctantly."

"I serve where I can."

Jeredon muttered, and reined his horse half around.

"Don't leave, brother. You have to know this. I will offer her an alliance in her eyes on the east."

"And tip your hand?"

"Yes. She has to know that we know, it's the only way to garner her respect. I want you to search out Daravan."

"He keeps his own counsel, and tight at that."

"We came alone to a strange land and stayed alive by staying together, more or less. Except for him."

"As you wish." Jeredon inclined his head. "He trails trouble or perhaps it trails him."

"I know. I cannot leave a stone unturned, even if I unearth a viper." She put her heels to her mount then, hard, and the tashya horse threw its head up with a trumpet of challenge, bolting off. The two men traded looks, then leaned low in their saddles and went after her, all three charging to the holding in an all-out horse race, which Jeredon's mount won by the merest nose in a hail of stable yard dirt and a storm of shouts from the riders.

The smell of smoke grew a little fainter or perhaps it was that they had all gotten used to it, but the heat felt more and more stifling and sweat rippled down their bodies, turning their shirts and blouses black in the faint light of the cellar. Rivergrace plucked her blouse away from her body uncomfortably and moved to stretch her long legs out in front of her, accidentally jostling Keldan as she did so. He grunted as she breathed an apology.

"I feel like I'm bent in half," he whispered.

She nodded miserably. Before she could whisper back, a deep rumbling noise ripped through the cellar. Dirt erupted, splattering all of them. They jumped to their feet. Nutmeg let out a hoarse shriek and threw herself over Hosmer's still form to protect him. Wood, stone, and clay groaned and cracked as they were torn asunder. Tolby shoved Lily behind him and pulled out the short sword he'd girded at his waist. A sudden gust of air blew into the cellar, blowing the candle out. For a moment, they stood in inky blackness, the rending of their sanctuary filling their ears.

Then sunlight slanted in, through a ragged hole from where their air pipes had led.

"Tree's blood, you going to wait all day to come out?" Garner yelled down to them cheerfully.

Keldan wiggled through the tunnel first, his brother pulling him out with a painful grunt, and then they went out one by one, all but Tolby who stayed to guide Hosmer's still form through as carefully as he could from his end. At last, they all stood together surrounding Hosmer at the end of the farm and orchard, where the air pipes to the cellar had been pulled apart and out so Garner could free them.

Around them, the world was even more destroyed than Grace had imagined. Flames licked at the blackened stumps of the framework of the house, little left beyond that. The barn, the press, dark and glowing ghosts of themselves, orange and gray ash and blackened charcoal. Nothing remained but the stone foundation Tolby had laid in his youth, and heat from the fire had cracked the stones wide open. She turned her gaze quickly from the sight of a spit, and a carcass upon it, not wanting to think what it might have been.

Nutmeg cried out. "Oh, poor Bumblebee!"

Garner shook his head, leaning on Keldan. "They tried to get that old pony, but he was too shrewd and quick for them. That's what's left of Yellowbeard when he came back to defend his haystacks. A stringy meal they made of him." He nodded his head toward the spit in memory of the billy goat that had chased Rivergrace more times than she cared to remember, as ornery himself as the little goats that he sired were sweet.

"You were close enough to watch?" Tolby shaded his eyes, looking across the cloud-studded sky where the coming rainstorm had veered away from them, and sun peeked through momentarily, dazzling those who'd been in the cellar for what seemed nearly half the day.

"Not that close. I saw the hounds, but the smoke and such filled their nostrils and any scenting wanted from them, they couldn't do. They'd torn the house apart, Da, and fired everything by the time I got to the windbreaks. So I climbed up and watched, and hoped by Tree's blood you were all safe." He looked at Hosmer. "And most of you are, it seems."

"Bolgers?"

He shook his head slowly, wearily, and Keldan stepped closer to take more of his weight on his shoulders. "Ravers and Bolgers. You'd not have made a stand, none of us would. Outsmarting them was all we could hope for, and we've done it." He gusted a sigh. "A lot of rebuilding to do . . ."

"No." Tolby hiked up his belt. "I'm not a quitter, but it's time for a change. The city, I think, where Lily can do that weaving and tailoring she's so good at, and I can have a press closer to the drinkers who profess a fondness for my cider. Still . . ." He looked about. "It'll be a long walk. A night in the trees for all of us, and we'll start tomorrow."

And so they did.

Chapter Twenty-Three

SOMETIME BEFORE DAWN, when all seemed still except for the grumbling snore of her husband and the soft, deeper, yet quieter purrs of her children, Lily undid the ties Tolby had fastened about her and slid down the tree. By the dark of night, the wreckage of her life seemed pooled in shadow everywhere she looked. Not only the house and outbuildings, but the orchard itself had been torched, the green and fruiting trees burning reluctantly, it seemed, but still burning. Only here on the outskirts, among the emeraldbarks, had the trees withstood the fires. She'd seen the hills scorched black after wildfires and seen the greening return, after seasons, and so their own ranch and orchards might come back. The Farbranches were the ones who wouldn't recover from this.

She and Tolby had talked quietly long after the others had fallen asleep. Time to move on, they agreed. Time to let the children know a different life, and time for them to slow down a bit. And time, perhaps, to hide Rivergrace in the crowds of a city rather than in the open country. She never spoke of the attack during the fair a few years back, but Tolby knew something had happened to fill her with silence, uncharacteristic even for her. Nutmeg remembered being taken by a Bolger but little else, and Grace never said anything beyond washing her hands over and over for the next few days, although it had been one sister who found the other. None of them ever spoke of that time, until this eve, when Tolby told her he feared that the Ravers had marked the family and they might find peace hard to keep. The raiders were fierce and their ways unknown, unfathomed.

Lily found a sharpened poker and went to the part of the house she remembered. The main cellar had finally fallen in, the kitchen floor which was its roof burning through, and she moved carefully because everything still held a surprising heat. The stone stairs rocked under her light steps and she paused at every other one, fearful of being dumped downward all at once. It took her a few moments squinting in the bright moonlight to find her digging spot, and bring up the leather bag of coins she kept buried there. Her hands went over the pouch of Rivergrace's things. After hesitating a moment, Lily buried them again in the oilcloth sack she'd put them in so long ago. Perhaps it would be best to keep the past buried.

Feeling soiled and gritty, Lily retraced her steps through the broken foundation of the home she and Tolby had built together, and where they'd spent a loving life together. She looked round, her heart aching, yet knowing they could have lost much, much more. Hosmer's injury should heal cleanly and although more serious than Garner's, it was Garner's wound that worried at her. It looked like a shallow yet long flap of skin gouged aside, but it showed festering, and she knew his ribs had cracked as well from the blow. He'd said little even when they'd discovered that he was injured, more concerned about Hosmer, but a quiet, somber Garner was a Garner in pain. She knew both her sons well enough to know that Hosmer, hurt as he was, was healing quickly while Garner might be denying just how much attention he needed. She would have to find poultice makings along the road and insist he use them.

Bumblebee had come snuffling back, stiff-legged from the hard drive Tolby had given him, yet nudging at all of them as if worried about them more than himself. Rivergrace and Nutmeg had fussed over him, rubbing his legs and grooming him, he groaning and leaning on them both like a big, overgrown dog. She patted his shaggy, slumbering form now as she passed, and found the windbreak tree she and Tolby had shinnied up. For a few brief minutes that night, it had been almost as if they were young again, climbing trees as young lovers in a glorious spring and summer. She remembered one moonlit night when they had climbed to a tall tree outside their town, and picnicked, and Tolby had thrown twigs at passersby from the tavern down the lane who could not for the life of them figure out where the debris had come from. But the climb tonight had been a lot harder, with joints stiffer than she cared to think about.

She stood at the trunk, craning her head back and wondering if she could clamber up again without waking Tolby. Lily got to the first big fork in the tree's branches, when she could see torches on the road, flickering. They'd come back!

"Tolby! Tolby!"

Her voice, pitched low but urgent, stopped his snoring, and then he shook his grizzled head. "What?"

"Wake up! They've come back."

The tree trembled as he thrashed around in it before untangling himself from his own ties. "What are you doing way down there?"

"Never mind that. What are we all going to do?"

"Stay up in the trees, and hold our tongues. Get yourself back up here."

Lily began climbing again, slipping once or twice, and grateful when she got close enough that Tolby's strong hand could reach her and pull her back up to the fork where he perched. He hugged her tightly. "Don't go bolting away on me," he said.

"I wasn't. Should we wake the others?"

"Not till I get a better look. But they'll need to be awake, to keep quiet." Tolby gave her a last squeeze before edging away, and higher, to the willowy treetop which swayed under his weight. Rain had come in the faintest of patters, not putting the fires out, but making the stench even more foul, and the damp drops hissing where they touched the hottest spots. The sky had cleared then, and he peered across their ruined farmland. Tolby stayed for long moments as Lily held her breath. Finally, he called down, "I cannot tell what comes. Wake them, have them hold their silence."

Lily leaned across the fork of her tree, to the branch tethered there and tugged on it, lightly but insistently. The branch, bent over from the windbreak tree next to hers, shook about Nutmeg and Rivergrace, waking both of them. They, in turn, stirred Keldan and Garner. After hushed complaints, all were awake save Hosmer, who lay lashed to his tree with Keldan, and only moaned now and then in a deep dream, which Lily had lengthened with one of her "syrups." Tolby muttered down again, "I cannot see! They're moving slowly, searching. What fiends can see at night, even with torches?"

"No hounds, though," offered Keldan. He began to unstrap himself. "I'm going to run take a look."

"Stay here!"

"If they're as slow as you say, I'll be there and back before they've noticed." Keldan looked upward at them, waved, and dashed off before Tolby could stop him.

"He had better be, or he'll be dead," Garner said quietly. Lily made a sharp sound, and all of them went quiet, waiting.

Rivergrace watched the smoky orange torches draw closer, slowly, deliberately, bobbing in the night. Before she had been desperate to be outside, regardless of the enemy, now she wished for shelter again, and hugged the tree tightly, bark cutting into her clothes.

Keldan appeared again, like a will-o'-the-wisp out of the night. "Da! You've got to come."

"What is it?"

"It . . . you have to see it." Keldan gulped. "It's everyone," he said, as Tolby slid down and landed with a thump beside him. "It's everyone come to answer the beacon and help."

As the night shifted slowly away, the wagons and riders had filed into what was left of the Farbranch home and orchards, gathered in a circle, with the militia riding patrol, not too far away and not too near. Dawn came fitfully, and their time to leave grew close. Still and all, what do you say, Tolby reflected, to a man and good friend who'd lost two of his sons, even though he had a barnful of them still to his name? It made no difference he had more children. The loss of one always cut just as keenly. He pressed the bracelet that Hosmer had saved into Cavender Barrel's hand, saying only, "From what Hos said, I wouldn't send anyone looking that didn't have a strong stomach and heart. There's not much left after the Ravers to bury, Cavender. You have to be warned on that, ugly as it sounds."

His friend's shoulders bowed, as he fixed his eyes on the item, and closed his hands about it tightly, until his scarred knuckles showed white. "Thank ye, Tolby, and give me thanks to that boy of yers. They did their best. Are ye sure ye're not staying?"

"No, my mind's made up. I've had the life I wanted. Lily's been hankering to go back to the city a bit. I reckon it's time, while we're still young enough to start again."

"We'll be missing you. Good folks, and neighbors, and all."

"I know, Cav. We'll be missing you. But I'll be carting back and forth. If I buy the place I want, I'll still be needing apples." Tolby swung about, gesturing. "Anyone wants to salvage this, I'll deed it to them. The trees are strong, good sap in 'em, deep roots. I grafted good stock onto good stock. They'll come back."

"Aye, they will. We'll ask about. Maybe a young couple or two might pitch in together to work it."

"That's good talk." Tolby smiled grimly. He pressed Cavender's hands again, tightly. "We're so sorry, Lily and I."

His friend pressed back. "We'll have a good talk about it with the Gods themselves, we will, when it's our time. What are they thinking, taking the young, eh?" Barrel sighed heavily. He stepped off. "Looks like they're waiting on us."

Indeed, the small cart they'd put to rights, and a small wagon someone had lent them, were filled with their packs and supplies from the cellar, and the few things they could scrape out of the ruins and ashes. Bumblebee stood in the cart's yoke and tossed his shaggy head impatiently, while Hosmer's still tired tashya-blooded horse was tied behind. They'd been lent two mules for the wagon, and Hos lay in back, Garner sitting at his side, legs tucked under him. The girls rode on the front seat with Keldan driving, while Lily waited for him at the cart, still saying good-byes. They drove out to a dawn still hung with smoke on the air as the fires burned out in the new day, and their friends accompanied them to the road.

Lily never looked back. Rivergrace put a hand out in farewell to her river, and a cloud of alna rose, circling over them twice, before winging their way back across the water to the forest deeps.

Sevryn lay on the healer Frelar's cot, feeling her tough hands knead the knots and soreness out of his body, testing the flexibility of his joints and muscles, and then, finally, rubbing ointment into his new scars. The bruises would heal and the scars fade out, she told him, but he knew that, and it hurt no less this time than the last. He slowly relaxed under her hands.

"You have good Vaelinar blood in you," grunted Frelar, as she rubbed the ointment in a second time, just for the sting of it he thought. "These are new but nearly healed as it is. The scarring will be minimal or fade altogether."

"That would be about the only good Vaelinar blood has done me."

She slapped his left buttock. "Listen to you. Think the queen would talk to you at all if you weren't blooded? Queen Lariel is what and where she is because she knows the true worth of a person. She sees beyond blood and skin, as one of her station should."

"Vaelinars are born to such stations."

A strong hand found a knot just above his shoulder blade and knuckled into it sharply until it was all he could do to breathe. "Stations, even among the Vaelinars, are earned. Never forget that."

How could he ever? But he did not answer the healer, just let his breath go finally with a low moan, as she diligently searched out old and new tensions and plied her trade on them, muttering about pain and how some seemed to seek it out and others inflicted it. Her words receded into a dull roar in his ears as Sevryn gave himself to a kind of surrender.

He found memory in pain, sometimes. Shadows of what had been years ago, buried beyond his knowing until a sudden pain might reveal the shadow to him, a flash of light sharpened by senses on the edge. Often he saw his mother's face, the only time he could see her clearly anymore, her whip-thin body busily packing items for him, or doing laundry, or cooking, or talking to him about the way things in the world went. Often he sensed that her words had been Gilgarran's or perhaps Gilgarran merely echoed his mother's sentiment, but she had little regard for sentiment or Vaelinars in general, and in that way they had been similar. Neither had had any tolerance for Vaelinarran bonding or lack of it. As much as he'd loved her and missed her, he'd been cut by her abrupt dismissal of him when she'd left to journey on, and it wasn't her memory he sought.

Four forges dire . . .

Carved out of his pain, he knew those words only from the game of children and he heard them often now, whenever he traveled, accompanied by the slap of a skipping rope on packed dirt or street. He heard them endlessly, and had no more idea today what the rhyme meant than he had when he heard it that first time. Forges meant smithing, and smithing encompassed a world of possibilities, but from that time he could not remember, he had pieced together Gilgarran. They had encountered a forge which had brought about his mentor's death, and that death he could remember, although not all of it. What had he hidden inside the meaning of the elements instead? Why not forges to the east, south, north, and west? If it meant so much to him to ensure not forgetting them, why did he not encode a direction into the rhyme? What had he been thinking of, and what was he losing by not remembering? *Dire . . .*

Yes, he knew something dreadful, and it lay just beyond his grasp despite Gilgarran's training, and even though Vaelinars plotted in decades, he doubted time remained on his side.

Despite his thoughts, and the sharp knots Frelar kept finding throughout his body, he moved toward a warming sleep and nothingness. The only edge he found in his dream was that held in the hands and in the remarkable eyes of a young woman standing over the body of a Raver, pulling her Dweller sister to her, her eyes filled with a silvery defiant light that kept him at arm's length no matter how he wanted to hold her. Sevryn had not seen her since, and yet seen her nearly every night in his dreams. From that vision, he drifted unknowing.

Until the healer pinched his ear bruisingly and hissed, "Wake up. Think I've nothing better to do than listen to you snore? Lariel asks you to meet her, a candlemark or so after dinner."

"Then I will do so." Sevryn stretched. His skin, which had felt tight and drawn, now felt oiled and comfortable, the puckering of scars fading already. "Mistress Frelar, you work miracles, as always."

She snorted. He pressed a gem into her hand anyway, ducking out of reach before she could smack him for it, grabbing his clothes and making his way through the bathing area, tugging them on as he ran, laughing. He knew well that Lariel had paid for his tending, but surely Frelar would find value in the prettiness of the gem anyway, although she was not the type given to vanity. At the entrance to the baths, he sat down on a low boulder, its surface smoothed into a bench not by hands but by centuries of people so sitting upon it, and tugged his boots on. There was no backlash to Tressandre's challenge other than the refusal he was to carry to her, and he wondered at his summons. Had she changed her mind about sending him? Lariel kept her own counsel on many a thought that passed through her mind. Her brother had retreated into frowning silence, the matter chafing at Jeredon though he no more wanted her crown and responsibilities than he wanted his head turned backward on his body. Or so he'd often said to Sevryn.

Sevryn wandered about the light and airy keep of Larandaril, enjoying the mild spring day, checking on his gear and horses, the gardens, the gossip, the farms edging the castle. He enjoyed the day despite the notion always in mind that Lariel wished to send him back to the ild Fallyn Stronghold. A deep, dark fortress at the edge of cliffs and mountains, forboding and formidable, as far from here as could be imagined, that stronghold looked more like the birthing place of a Warrior Queen than did Larandaril. Biting words to that effect had sprung from the ild Fallyn Stronghold before.

"What infant springs from a soft and cushioning lap to the hardness of war? None. She smiles and the infantry falls to their knees in praise of her, but what battle, let alone war, has she ever won for us?"

Unseen, certainly unheard by most of the Vaelinars when he first joined Lariel's entourage, he had not argued the point although Lariel's exploits in battle were storied, little more than a girl-child at the time, a standard-bearer for her grandfather.

When his hostess had given him the challenge to carry, he had demurred. Tress' full mouth had curved in a snarl. "Oh, yes, I know the stories, and yes, I will duel her. Tales have her running the invaders off while barely able to stand in the stirrups herself and swing a sword. If one believes that."

"You bring armies trembling to their knees."

"Deservedly." Tressandre's eyes flashed whenever he told her that, and she pushed her wild honey-colored hair from her face where it had tumbled forward, and lifted it from her shoulders with a disdainful gesture. "She is the queen while I am the whip, the sting, the solace after. My Talent is named while hers goes unnamed. Did you know that, Sevryn? The head of a mighty House and yet they have never declared her Talent. Why, she might be as dry of it as any of you eyeless half-breeds."

If she ever read anything in his gaze, Tress did not show it. It pleased her to treat him as if he were blind, and all he could say in his defense was that he had eyes enough to see her terrible beauty. That pleased her even more, though she dismissed him as little more than a servant of her hated rival.

He dozed after the evening meal, lazing in the sanctuary of Larandaril, knowing that these days could be few when he did not have to worry about having his back to an enemy, knowing that when he awoke, he would have to think about meeting the wishes of his queen. It was a dreamless sleep, for which he thanked the Gods as he rose and stretched, moving effortlessly into the exercises of a swordsman. The inky cloak of night cooled off as he washed and dried and dressed lightly. Outside his rooms the night watch walked halls silently and every other sconce had been put out, so the hour had turned late while he slept. He judged that it was time for his appointment with Lariel.

The watch outside her doors eyed him, then moved aside at his nod. A tall Vaelinar with brown-and-gold-sparked eyes and thick brown hair braided back watched Sevryn step through the doors carved with runes and words he ought to be able to read, but could not yet. The archaic Vaelinar language still escaped him, and the detailing of this fine work made it that much more difficult. He traced the edge of it as he passed through, his touch a kind of tribute to a world still just out of his reach.

Soft perfume rose to greet his senses as he moved into the room. Lamplight mingled with muted candlelight, casting shadows within shadows. She turned her face upward, her skin as fair as a newly harvested pearl, and he paused. She would be beautiful to anyone but him, he who longed to see only one face, only one set of remarkable eyes. He stopped and bowed, his mouth twisted by the irony. She tapped a piece of paper. "Tressandre ild Fallyn sent word this evening."

"Then I don't need to return?"

"This isn't about me, and the messenger bird did not come for me. I thought it had, and I beg your forgiveness for opening and reading what wasn't mine to read." Lariel's gaze stayed on him evenly, a certain coldness to it.

"I hold no secret from you." He spread his hands.

"Don't mistake my anger, it's not directed at you, but at the House that thinks to drive a wedge between myself and those I trust." Lariel paused, and took a deep breath. She handed him the note.

Darling Sevryn, it read. He winced at the elaborate handwriting.

"Remember," murmured Lariel, "it's couched to be deceiving if intercepted."

His hand curled about the paper. "She lies."

"We both know that."

I have come upon intriguing information about the man who is undoubtedly your father. Come to me when you are free of demands put upon you, and learn the truth.

He felt the blood leave his face. "I swear, she does not buy me!" The paper crumpled in his fist.

Lariel waved off his words. "I know that."

"Then, why?"

"Wouldn't you want to know of your father? Your mother?"

"Perhaps."

"Sevryn."

"She calls my service to you a demand put upon me?" He looked from his hand to her face.

Lariel stood. “She hints that she wants you to put aside your post, and go to her.”

“I won’t.”

“What if I order you to?”

He stood, rocked in place.

Lariel’s expression stayed open, yet unrevealing. “She has a spy in my house. Perhaps I need a spy in hers.”

“Don’t ask me to do that.”

“I could never ask you to bathe yourself in the deception that an ild Fallyn does. You’ve done far too much for me, already. However, she expects you back, one way or the other.”

“And if she knows who my father is, what then?”

“It matters, and it does not matter. It doesn’t change who you are, or the loyalty you’ve earned from me.”

“You’d trust me in her folds?”

Her mouth quirked a little. “I trust you, although I’d rather you weren’t in her folds.”

“Then I’ll simply be your messenger, your envoy. I won’t stay.”

“Fair enough.” Lariel smiled faintly. “If she has even the slightest crumb of information, of truth for you, know that Jeredon and I will hunt down the rest of it for you, with you. We won’t let her leave you twisting in the wind, Sevryn.”

He let his breath out, and nodded.

“Just remember that, whatever you say face-to-face to Tressandre ild Fallyn, take care of the knife at your back.”

“Always.” He bowed, retreating from her apartment. He heard something crackle and spit into flame as it was tossed into the small, banked fire against the still damp spring air.

As he hurried down the stairs, brushing past Tiiva, whom he scarcely noticed except for the rustle of her gown as she moved aside to watch him, he wondered how Tressandre had known to bait him. He had indeed reached for something he should not have, for something that would never lie within his grasp, for a life that would never be that of a half-breed. His lineage might make a difference, and it might not. As for the ild Fallyn, they had little use for him, but he knew where he stood with them.

He did not wish to go back, save for one thing. The memory he needed lay hidden in pain and Tressandre alone had the key.

Chapter Twenty-Four

MISTRESS GREATHOUSE RODE out on the road to Stonesend, sitting on a high-striding pony with bells braided into its mane. Her mount whickered at Bumblebee as if greeting the tired cart pony with delight and encouragement. Rivergrace and Nutmeg leaned out of the wagon, waving at the peddler who waved a gem-studded riding whip at them and seemed to signal the end of their flight and the beginning of an adventure. She wore a braided crimson-and-gold scarf about her luxuriant tresses, but silver now highlighted the dark brunette, and there were lines about her laughing eyes and mouth.

"Derro, derro, and well met, even if it is under hard circumstances!" she called out. "You'll be driving to my house, where I've extra beds put up, and a healer waiting. Lily, you look done in. You make these strong young lasses help you settle everyone when we get in."

Lily let out a soft, short laugh, and Nutmeg elbowed Grace as she did, for it was the first time since they took the road that their mother had, her face perpetually creased in heavy worry for Hosmer and Garner, and her laughter much missed.

"We're in your debt," Tolby said, his voice a husk of itself, as well.

"Nonsense! You've come a long way, but there's rest ahead. Hurry along, now!" She waved her little quirt briskly, pivoted her showy mount, and led the way onto a well-used side lane off the main dirt road leading through groves of trees with green-gold leaves that even looked like coins, up to a small hill where her home perched grandly.

Nutmeg had often mused to Rivergrace about what Mistress Greathouse's home must look like, large and grand, she thought, for the peddler was undoubtedly the richest person they knew, and she grabbed Grace's hand now and squeezed in excitement. It was a cottage, or perhaps better described as three cottages built onto each other, each a little bigger and grander than the last, but no manor or mansion. A white picket fence surrounded the jumbled home, with an immense barn behind it and a second, open one below it with pole fencing about it.

"Two barns!" breathed Nutmeg.

"That's no barn, lass, that's her warehouse," Garner told her. "Must be like a treasure chest."

"Ooooh," both Rivergrace and Nutmeg breathed as one, staring at the building. Their awe seemed to carry to Hosmer who stirred and tried to lift his head. "Home yet?"

Garner put his hand on his brother's shoulder, wincing as he did, for it jarred his sore and torn rib cage as the wagon bounced over a summer rain's pothole. "Not yet. Soon. Just rest easy." Hosmer nodded and let his eyes close again. His face looked pale under his weathered Farbranch complexion, but it was better than the high flush which rode Garner's cheeks. Lily glanced over her shoulder at both, frowning, and clucked to the mules to hurry them up the lane.

Once there, Keldan and Tolby unharnessed the animals and put them away after caring for them gently in deference to their hard days, while Lily directed Rivergrace and Nutmeg about what to unload and what to shift aside so that Hosmer and his litter could be gotten out. Garner grimaced as Nutmeg tossed him a bale, and shrugged the weight aside.

"You'd better be telling Ma about that."

"Later. Once Hosmer is put to rights. I can wait."

Rivergrace put out her hand and touched his flank, and he shivered with the pain of it, though her touch had been light, and she pulled her fingers back quickly. "You can't wait much longer."

Nutmeg braced herself in the wagon bed, brushing her unruly hair back from her face, her hands ready to tug out a backpack. "You always healed faster'n anyone else. What's wrong?"

He tried to shrug, then pulled himself upright, one arm hugging his ribs. "Don't know, rightly. It hurts like a thorn or something caught in me. Might just be my rib, might not. I know Ma thinks it cracked."

"Maybe it had a stinger or a barb and it caught?"

Rivergrace watched Garner, feeling her face grow cool as if her blood had run to ice at the notion. "It could be some poison, deep in you."

"I'll see the healer soon as Hosmer is resting, all right?"

"Promise?" she asked faintly.

"Promise."

Mollified, Nutmeg went back to work, but Rivergrace stood there for a moment, staring at her hands as if expecting to see them covered in blood or some strange fluid, before scrubbing them on her skirts vigorously. She knew Garner watched her for a moment, but she could not help herself. Keldan's return stopped the question forming on Garner's lips, and they all turned their attention to getting Hosmer out of the wagon and into the back cottage where the healer awaited them.

The man was tall, much taller than a Dweller, whip-thin, with scars marking his tanned forearms with thin white steps up and down. He met them at the back cottage where the incense of healing herbs rose on the air, and indicated where to put the litter down. Garner came in on his own, hesitantly, and breathing shallowly. The healer bowed. "I am called Berlash." He touched Hosmer, then Garner. He frowned as his hand left Garner's wrist. "You will stay as well." Not a question, nor an order, but merely a statement of fact.

Garner eased into a chair by the door. The room filled quickly, but Berlash seemed unconcerned. Dressed in muslins dyed a serene blue, his silvery hair held back in a gleaming obsidian band, his feet clad in soft hide moccasins, his only concerns were the two injured.

Nutmeg craned her head back to look at him, then the healer knelt by her brother's side. "Kernan," she announced, as if making up her mind.

Berlash smiled. "Indeed, young Dweller. From the east and faraway Meranta, so I am different even from most Kernans. Have you heard of it?"

"Mama bought me hair ribbons from Meranta once. They had bells on them. I wore them until they wore out, so I saved the bells for new ribbons. I'll wear them on my wedding day."

He chuckled. Then he bent his attention to Hosmer, drawing aside the blanket and snipping away the bandages with small, slender shears. Hosmer woke as Berlash viewed the wound, his touch neat and quick and sure. Though Hosmer's eyes looked bleary, he said, "It's sore but not hot."

"There's been good work here, and some of the neatest stitches I've ever seen. I would say he should be up and walking with a crutch soon as he can, to make sure the muscles knit well and strongly. Just not to overdo and keep it clean. I'll give you an ointment to help continue the process. Bandage it lightly, let air get to it now."

Hosmer and Lily both nodded. Berlash stood, turning to Garner. "Lie down and let me see what ails you."

With a shrug, Garner did as bidden. He pulled his shirt up, wincing a little as Berlash cleaned his shears, then repeated the same quick, neat job of snipping away the bandage. Nor did his expression change much as he probed the wound carefully, although Lily and Tolby frowned as they watched.

"What did this?"

"A Raver. It came after me, tried to pincer its way to my heart, I think."

Berlash looked up at Lily. "You've been poulticing this, too?"

"Tried."

The healer nodded. "I've something a little stronger that will soothe. A Raver attack is something to survive, and he's doing quite well, but there's a poison in there, and I'll need to open him up, flush him a bit. I imagine good strong Dweller bones saved him, but he probably cracked a rib or two at that."

"Exactly what I thought," Lily said.

"It's not as deep as your other son's gash, but that was a clean wound from the beginning. This . . ." Berlash stood and began to search through jars and bowls on one of the chests. "The very being of a Raver is poison to us. If there's any shard of it left in him at all, it'll continue to fester. I think I'll ask you all to leave but you, ma'am, and we'll get to work."

Tolby took Keldan by the elbow and wagged an eyebrow at the girls. They filed out the doorway as asked, hearing Lily saying, "But it will heal, won't it?"

"Indeed, madam, and quite quickly once the venom's gone. You'll have your two hearty lads back in a few weeks."

Tolby let out a long sigh as they passed from earshot.

Mistress Greathouse set down her steaming mug, the fragrance of the tea filtering throughout the room. Tolby sat back, his booted feet up and crossed at the ankles, his cold pipe gripped in his teeth, one hand on Keldan's shoulder. Keldan had a plate of tarts across his lap and paid attention to sampling each, sweet fruit to savory meat tarts, arranging them in order of his appetite. Nutmeg sat at her mother's feet, resting her head on Lily's knee. Rivergrace curled up in a small armchair, her legs tucked under her, listening to the back rooms in case either Garner or Hosmer should call for them although the healer Berlash had remained with them. "It's a tragedy about the Barrel boys. Tearabouts, they were, but we all knew they'd outgrow that. They gave their lives trying to send out the call. For that, and for Hosmer's own efforts, they'll be long remembered." She folded her hands in her lap. "Now, we've all got to look to the future. You've come far these past few days." Her gaze fixed on Tolby.

"I'm not running away, Robin, " he answered firmly.

"That, we all know."

He squared his shoulders back. "We've been talking about moving back to a town for a while now. I've still a good name in the business and seems like the time to trade on that. I make a fine cider, hard cider, and a nice sparkling wine. I don't need to grow the apples and grapes myself, I know what I'm doing. Farming life is wearing on Lily a bit, and it's time to find a good life for the lasses as well."

Rivergrace and Nutmeg traded glances then, and Lily cleared her throat as if in warning.

Mistress Greathouse smiled and asked mildly, "What did you have in mind?"

"Startin' fresh like this, I figure to manage a press and such for someone, with an understanding I can buy up in time. I'm not too old to make an offer like that."

"Any man would be a fool not to entertain an offer from you, Tolby Farbranch. As a matter of fact, I've had three letters forwarded to me, in the hopes that you might be contacting me when word of the raid went about. The Meadowes are making sure there is help for the Barrels and you. Perhaps there will be good news in one of them. If not, I know of a placc, needing much work, that can be bought outright. We'll talk more when you've read your mail and thought about things." Picking up her mug and sipping and changing the conversation as deftly as if weaving delicate threads, she said, "And what about you, Lily?"

Lily drew back a little. "Some tailoring, I suppose, and weaving. Wherever Tolby goes, I had hopes I might find an opening."

"Some weaving?" The corner of Mistress Greathouse's mouth quirked. Then she beckoned to them and said, "Come with me!" After a soft call to Berlash that they would all be out of the cottage for a few moments, she led them out the back door and to the immense barn. A brace of the biggest dogs Rivergrace had ever seen sat by the warehouse's closed doors. The male, black and russet brown, padded over to the trader and leaned against her with such affection she had trouble staying on her feet. "This is Peace and that is his mate, Quiet. Aptly named, for I've had no trouble here at all since I bought them as pups and word got around. Excellent watchdogs although they cost me a fortune in meat." She laughed at herself as she scratched the dog's ear, then pushed him away. He sat back down next to the female and, bright brown eyes sparkling, growled at the Farbranch family as they trooped past in Mistress Greathouse's wake, everyone save Rivergrace. As she passed, trailing the others, both dogs sank to their bellies and whimpered softly. She hurried past quickly, not understanding, but the trader turned inside the warehouse, a glint of sunlight revealing the surprise on her face, and one eyebrow rose sharply before she reached for a lantern and shut the door at Grace's heels.

She scarcely needed a lamp. Bright beams of rainbow light struck from angled glass in the ceiling beams, sending dazzling rays with motes dancing in them like small gems throughout the warehouse interior. Tolby looked up and mused for a moment, as if taking in the practicality of such a thing in the midst of its beauty. "Ship prisms," she said. "Handy things, when there is sun. Like a mirror, they reflect sunbeams down and about."

He nodded.

She crossed through the aisles of crates and bales, many of them marked and tagged but their guide moving too quickly for them to take in the veiled and hidden treasures. Even at that, the warehouse seemed less than half full, but it was summer and she was on the road in the summer, selling her wares. "The family name is Greathouse, but not because we had one. From as long as we could remember, we were named Greathouse because we worked in one, while we built our peddling business. My mother did laundry and cleaned house while my dad took to the road. We've all come a long way, I'd say." She reached back for Lily's hand and took it, and steered her to the corner, where sheeted ladders took up much of the room. A twitch of their joined hands and the sheets came tumbling down, to reveal racks with bolts and lengths of cloth . . . a good many of them crafted by Lily herself over the last ten years.

"I could never," Mistress Greathouse said, "find a tailor or seamstress to do them justice. So I saved them until that day when you might find time for them. I think that day has come?"

Lily let out a long breath, then held very still, before slowly shaking her head. "I can't believe this, Robin."

The other held up her hand. "Hear me out first, then." She lowered the lantern and set it on a safe, barren spot on the floor. "I'm not getting any younger, as the saying goes, and I'm selling some of my holdings. I won't be giving up the road for a while yet, because I enjoy it far more than I like shopkeeping. It's risky, I know, but I meet fair folks and have the wind in my face, and it reminds me of the years my husband and I shared together, few as they were. I've such a shop in mind, Lily, that needs someone like you. It's a ladies' tailoring and millinery shop, and the woman who ran it for me has had to leave, to take care of her grandchildren. The apprentice there will stay, but she has no ambitions for owning the place or doing more than putting in her hours. She's a good seamstress, but she cannot design or weave. You show Adeena what to stitch and she'll do a fine job of it, but you know a shop in Calcort needs more than that."

"Calcort!" gasped Lily, and Nutmeg after her. Rivergrace listened, not quite understanding, except that Calcort was not a town, but a great, huge city.

"I know, I know, it's not what you had in mind. But I'd like you and Tolby to think about it. The press I mentioned is also in Calcort, near the old town gates, which is very countrified, with the shop in the refined quarter, a handful of streets to the east of it, on the border. I don't own the press, but I know the pair of gentlemen who do, and they're ripe for a good offer. As for myself," and she looked Lily square in the face. "I'd like nothing better than to pass my shop into capable, talented hands like yours."

"But the cost—"

"Bother the cost. Look around you. I've more money than I hope to spend, and so will my son and his children, after me. I won't let the shop go free, but a partnership, and I promise to be a silent one. Go to the city for me, and look it over? Before you say no?"

"And if we say yes," muttered Tolby, "there will be some explanations to be made."

"That, I know." She placed a gentle hand on Nutmeg's head, then tucked a long tress of Rivergrace's hair back into place. "Those explanations will have to be made no matter where you go, though, aye?"

"Tolby . . ." said Lily, and nothing more. Husband and wife gazed at each other silently, as though their thoughts were being spoken to each other, or perhaps it was only the memory of many discussions they had shared with each other over the years.

He shuffled a foot. "We've dealt with you over many a season, and you've never been anything but fair with us. It's not like me to accept sight unseen, but I'll make this deal with you. If there are problems, we'll handle it like the fair people we are. Agreed?" He put his hand out.

Mistress Greathouse beamed as she took it and shook firmly. "More than agreed. I'll get to the paperwork in the morning, then, and after a day or two of rest, I'll make sure you are all set to be on your way."

Keldan leaped in the air, scattering dust motes and fallen sheets, and Lily scolded him before taking him by the ear and making him hang the covers back over the racks as they had been, but he did not complain, even with his ear pinched apple-red.

Only Rivergrace held back. Explanations? Because of her, of course, needing to be veiled and hidden away. The last few days she had scarcely dared think it, but now it rose again, like a stubborn and unwanted weed, in her thoughts. *Had* the Ravers come seeking her? No way to know for sure, but it seemed a certainty that Tolby wanted the safety of town barriers and streets even though it would strangle him slowly, losing the freedom of the highlands he coveted so much. Wanted it enough to take a deal, unseen. She shifted her weight uneasily, as the burden of her thoughts pressed down upon her. It would be best if she left them now, before she brought any more trouble down on them.

She lifted her gaze to find Nutmeg watching her. Nutmeg shook her head slowly, denying whatever doubts she read in Grace's face. Grace shuttered away her thoughts before Nutmeg could read anything else.

Chapter Twenty-Five

HE MIGHT HAVE BEEN ordered and enticed to return to Tressandre ild Fallyn, but he was determined to take his own time getting there. As soon as he made his way through the maze of the boundary of Larandaril that kept it hidden and mostly safe, he turned his mount's head toward another of the Holds, the first Hold, that of the Ferstanthe.

It took him days to get there, several spent on a smuggler's cutter. Haste rode his thoughts much as he rode the waves and roads, and when he finally pulled up on a crest overlooking the Hold, he took his first deep breath in a very long time.

Ferstanthe stood near the site of the Vaelinar birthing into the world. A lush green had returned to the valley and hills, forested again although these trees had far to go to obtain the majesty and maturity of the ones blasted to smithereens upon their arrival. He'd seen the weavings, the paintings, heard the tales of land as far as the eye could see laid low by the forces which had brought them. Long ago, the timber and stumps had disintegrated into the soil, as was the way of all life, feeding the saplings which would follow them with rich compost. Still, the devastation left scars as far as he could see, gouges in the granite of hills farther away, and a difference in the green blanket covering all. It was new growth compared to what he'd just ridden through, and it showed in the lighter coloring. This part of the countryside was but a babe compared to the ancient forests and plains surrounding it.

The domes of the clustered buildings had grown from the last etching he'd seen of the great libraries. Azel d'Stanthe of Ferstanthe, always building, always collecting, always protecting the knowledge that he gathered. He reined slowly off the crest, taking a breather as he moved toward the holding, wondering what it is he sought and how he would ask for admittance. Only Vaelinars were allowed here, and Sevryn knew well that he was not Vaelinar enough. He only wondered how far they would let him approach before he would be denied another step.

He rode all the way into the holding, handed the reins of his mount over to one of the several stable lads who came running, and passed through the archway of the first great building before the magic which held it safe and inviolate began to reject him. It scarcely mattered then, for he was inside the welcoming lobby, stripping off his riding gloves, to see Azel pouring hot tea for another guest, and both looked up at him. Daravan lounged back in his chair, booted feet crossed at the ankles, his whole body swathed in that storm-gray cloak he habitually wore, and his eyebrow rose in mild surprise.

Azel d'Stanthe straightened. He wore robes of indigo with a light parchment stripe about his frame, which resembled that of a tall robust tree, and he moved with a deliberate, ponderous grace, big even for a Vaelinar, with broad shoulders and a bit of girth. The glasses he wore slipped down his nose as he appraised Sevryn, their faintly violet-colored lenses catching the late morning light filtering in through the many glassed windows.

"What brings you here?"

Daravan snorted faintly. "What do you think brings him here, Azel?"

"Perhaps I misstated myself. What Talent brings you this far?" d'Stanthe pushed his glasses firmly back into place with an index finger as he continued to watch Sevryn intently.

"As I have not the Eyes, I cannot have the Talent," Sevryn muttered. He shifted his weight from one leg to another, as if riding weary, and slapped some of the dust off himself with a glove blow to his leg. "I came in hopes of answers."

Daravan pulled his cup close to his chin and blew on it gently to cool it before bestowing an enigmatic smile on Sevryn. "Answers here come dearly, and often with a raft of new questions."

"All life and knowledge is like that."

Azel took a step closer, his robes rippling in rich colors about him, and Sevryn noticed that he wore cuffs about the wrists, to keep ink from staining the luxuriant sleeves. They'd both interrupted him working and while

Daravan had extracted courtesy from the librarian, he doubted he'd engender the same feeling. "By what right do you come here?"

"Come now. Would you make him quest? He's already done that by getting here." Daravan sat up in his chair.

Azel turned his attention on the tall, storm cloud complexioned Vaelinar with a muffled noise of irritation, to which Daravan said lightly, "Really. A puff toad being prodded at by a stink dog would look more hospitable."

"Hospitable, is it? If I were anything else, I would have tossed you out on your ass the moment you showed up. I still haven't forgiven you for stealing a copy of the Accords last time you were here."

Daravan only shrugged. "I needed to see if Bistane and his crew were following their private oaths' addendum to the Accords."

"You returned it in abominable condition."

"I ran into bad weather."

"There would have been no weather at all if the relic had stayed in the library vaults where it was supposed to have been housed!"

Daravan gave Azel a glance as the librarian drew himself up in outrage before looking to Sevryn. "Perhaps he is more the puff toad than the stink dog?"

Sevryn kept his face as neutral as he could, under the circumstances, and Daravan's eyes flashed a little in enjoyment. Sevryn was not sure the other was helping his situation much.

"What business have you here?" queried Azel again, impatiently.

"My own. I could tell you it is Queen Lariel's business, but that would not be the truth, at the moment. What I discover might well become her business, but I won't know it till I learn what I need to know, and so it is irrelevant until confirmed."

"See, Azel? He is no callow youth hoping to find the lyrics to the latest serenade making the rounds. He has serious inquiries for your library."

Before the librarian could answer, Sevryn said to Daravan, "Thank you, sir, but I'm not sure you're helping."

"It is hard to tell, isn't it?" Daravan sat back in his chair, picking up his cup and sipping his beverage with merriment fairly dancing in his eyes.

Sevryn looked steadily into Azel's face. "You can turn me away, and I fully expected not to get as far as your lobby, in any case. There are few about who have failed to remind me that I am less than Vaelinar. I can tell you only that what I'm looking for are the answers to questions first posed to me by Gilgarran, and I have hopes what I need to learn I can find here. If you will allow me." He gave d'Stanthe a bow that was only slightly ironic.

"And if I do not, I daresay you will be scaling my wall like some little street urchin and in my library anyway."

Sevryn's mouth fell half open in guilty amazement, for he had been thinking along that line, if he failed in diplomacy here.

"How did I guess? Gilgarran always did have a fondness for ragged orphans with quick hands and wits." Azel sighed. "All right, then. You can wait in the other room, clean up, rest, and when I'm done with my guest here, I'll be in to talk with you. Your search will be much easier if I have an idea what resources you're looking for. Mind you, nothing here can be removed—" he shot a glance at Daravan at that, who happened to be looking innocently downward at his cup of tea, "and I've taken precautions to see that reinforced. That way." He pointed down a side corridor, and Sevryn bowed to take his leave.

Halfway down the corridor, he heard a muffled sound from Daravan as if he'd had an ear boxed.

Shade dappled the smaller lobby, and the water bowl was tepid rather than warm, but he doubted it would be stocked just for him. Likely it was set up every morning in anticipation that someone might come. He washed as had been suggested, taking great care to use the small scrub brush on his fingers and nails, leaving the washbowl and cloths a great deal dirtier and himself a great deal cleaner.

There was bread, fresh from baking that morning, and a soft cheese, and fruit, so he helped himself while sitting at a window and watching the holding go about its business outside the library walls. It seemed quite a while before Azel d'Stanthe came to get him, although the sun's slant did not agree with him.

"Now, then," murmured Azel. "Tell me what you seek, if you can, so that I can guide you."

"Children's songs and rhymes, if you have a collection."

Azel hid his surprise quickly, only remarking, "To know a being inside and out, one must know his culture, even that which begins in infancy. Follow me." He moved quickly, in his element, as if the air from the library itself buoyed him, and Sevryn stretched his legs to keep apace. "Have you any more than that?"

"Unfortunately, no. I hoped I might find something I could recognize, if it had been recorded."

"Naturally. And not so far from Daravan's serenades, is it?"

Sevryn felt his face warm. "Perhaps not," he admitted. Nothing more would he say at this time, for if he had made up the skipping rhyme that he'd taught to the street children, he'd important information coded in it. However, he might have just taught them something feverishly that, once upon a time, he'd learned himself. The feeling that he needed to unravel that rhyme had begun to grow on him with a kind of urgency, even though he knew time passed for him almost as leisurely as it did for a Vaelinar. He feared to wait any longer to understand.

They made a few turns and then Azel halted, and spread his arms. "It is more of a collection than merely books. There are toys here, as well."

Sevryn looked down the chamber in dismay. Even with help, it might take him days to peruse the journals and scrolls here, and examine each toy, and he looked up to find Azel watching him with an almost benevolent expression. He said hesitantly, "It is a scrap of a song, a child's rhyme, a street chant."

"Ah. Very regional, those are. Not Vaelinar, I presume, and I would further guess that it is your own past you're in search of?"

Close enough. He nodded. "The streets of Calcort."

Azel spun on one heel. "This aisle, then, and perhaps the second, although that is more from the Dweller areas fringing on the trade routes of that town." He studied a high, arched window nearby. "You've the best half of a day, and then I'll send someone for you. If you need someone in the meantime, merely ring this." And he tapped a wall gong which vibrated boldly even at the slight tap. With a nod, he left Sevryn alone.

Halfway down the stack, it struck him with a single, sad piercing that he had not had much of a childhood, for he had little familiarity with anything he found on the shelves. The games and tales collected here he'd had only a passing exposure to, being far busier keeping himself alive and fed. Azel and his fellows had gathered their information by racial group, so he had to examine all, for he had no way of knowing whether his rhyme came from Dweller or Galdarkan, Kernan or even Bolger. "Fly, crow, fly, till you can't fly higher . . ." fixed in his mind and held on there as he handled the items, searching. Knowing that it came from rope skipping narrowed it down for him considerably and although the sun gleamed through the windows at a low angle when he finished, still he had finished.

He straightened, running his hand through his hair. He'd found nothing similar, both disappointing and disturbing, meaning that what he'd heard had been unique and very likely had come from himself as the originating source, a code meant for him and him alone, in case something happened. And that something had. He couldn't remember what he needed to know.

Sevryn did not need the gong to leave. Used to back ways and blind alleys and trained to remember, he retraced his steps easily. At the small lobby, he penned a thank you, promising to keep the vast library in his thoughts as he traveled and to forward contributions to it. Then he slipped out, much more quietly than he'd come in, but words from the front lobby caused him to pause in the shadowy corners.

Daravan sounded tight and a bit angry, countered by Azel's soft-toned but equally firm response.

"I cannot believe you have nothing but one slim tome on the assassin Kobrir."

"You came here as a last resort, having done your own searches, and I allow nothing to be added that is not fact, and proved. The Kobrir has always been hidden."

"Bah. You cannot tell me that a line of rumor does not breathe anywhere in those works." A chair made a noise as if Daravan had settled roughly onto it, in disgust.

"You and I both know there is, but not if I can help it. Nor, if I can help it, will anything be revised. The books will exist as written, as known and perceived. New works will be added as knowledge is expanded but not surplanting the old. That is my pledge. Knowledge and information for any who wish it, a foundation for building."

"Save me."

A soft groan as Azel sat down, as well. "I can't, Daravan. There is little known. You, of anyone, realize that." A rustle of paper, or perhaps sleeves. "Why the sudden interest?"

"It is not sudden, it is ongoing, but if you must know, the Kobrir are surprisingly active again. Whether it is one or a handful would even be helpful knowledge."

"Targets, other than Queen Lariel?"

"Bregan Oxfort, for one, although the fool never knew it."

"Hmmm. Any motivation?"

"None that I care to discuss now. You, old friend, are too vulnerable."

"Me? Here? I am surrounded by a fortress."

"Old paper burns far too quickly," Daravan commented, and his words fell on a sudden quiet.

Finally, someone cleared a throat. Cloaked in ever lengthening shadows, Sevryn couldn't be sure who until Azel spoke with that careful deliberation of his. "I have heard two names mentioned. Kosh and Kurtiss. Whether they are two people, or two manifestations of the same, I could not tell you."

"Rumor."

"Indeed. As is the rumor that they are not Vaelinar but Galdarkan. Or, perhaps even another race created by the Mageborn."

"What?"

From the noise, Sevryn knew that Daravan had leaped to his feet, perhaps overturning an ottoman or small table, and for a moment, the two rustled about, setting to right the furniture and spillage. Sevryn was grateful for that clatter, it had hidden his own sharp intake of breath. It grew quiet again.

"Only rumor?" repeated Daravan.

"So I have heard. It could be true. They are built more like us than most of Kerith, and the eyes are always veiled. I've not seen proof that Talent is used in the work, it's always been the blade and the poison, for all their agility and swiftness. It could be."

"I was blind," muttered Daravan. His voice still carried surprise in it, and Sevryn knew he had been stunned by something he had never considered.

"The world," Azel said mildly, "is full of possibilities."

"Bless you for reminding me." A bootstep. "As always, to repay your generosity, I'll be sending meat supplies your way, as well as any tokens of journals or writings I might find in my travels."

"Your company is always welcome, Daravan. Perhaps someday you might allow me an interview."

"Interview?" This time, no surprise, but a carefully neutral sound in the other's voice.

"You are obviously one of the old ones, of fullest power, yet there is no mention of you anywhere in the earliest recollections of our being lost."

"Am I not?"

"No."

"Perhaps you are mistaken."

"Perhaps. But if I'm not, maybe one day you will humor an aging librarian and allow a recording."

"One should always have a dream for the future, Azel. Always."

Sevryn stirred then, his senses sharpened by the underlying malice or wariness in Daravan's voice, as well as the obvious fact that the two were taking their leave of each other, and he wanted to be out the door long before either of them. He slipped out of the purple corners and into the dusk, his mind as curtained with thoughts as the day with the coming night.

Chapter Twenty-Six

"YOU CANNOT ARGUE with him, Da." Keldan leaned out over the wagon seat, reins firmly in hand.

"He is charging us for a traders' caravan, rot his phantom hide." Tolby crossed his arms over his chest, chin out, and glared at the Dark Ferryman who remained immovable, implacable, hand out for the toll. Behind its ebony looming figure, the Nylara roared in its deep-cut banks, still flush with meltdown from the winter snows, angry and dangerous in spring's floodtime. Even the reputation of the Ferryman made crossing dubious. He shifted his weight slightly. "I haven't the coin to spare for his mistakes."

"We're driving one of Mistress Greathouse's carts . . ." Keldan's voice drifted off as Garner jumped the cart's side and landed lightly on the ground beside Tolby. "Perhaps he thinks we're hauling freight for her."

Tolby ground his teeth.

Rivergrace leaned from behind Keldan, drinking in the sight of the great, fierce river, so different from and yet akin to her beloved Silverwing. So violently did it cascade past, that a fine spray misted them and she lifted her face to it, breathing in its scent. Water, everyone said, had no scent, but she could smell it. Or perhaps it was the earth it flowed over and carried within it, the brew of vegetation along its banks, the minerals of the rocks it tumbled at its bottom? She didn't know. She climbed down from the cart, even as Keldan snatched at her elbow and missed, and went to join Tolby. The misting grew heavier as she stepped nearer, but her father seemed immune to it as it sparkled along her cloak and exposed skin. For a moment she felt as if the river could tell her where it sprouted from, in the depths of faraway mountains and pristine snowfields as far as the eye could see, but then that moment slipped away and the river merely shouted in her ears of its relentless power and drive to the sea.

She shivered and put her hands in her sleeves to warm them a bit. Tolby and the phantom both seemed to notice her, then, for the first time.

"You should be in the cart," her father said, his voice gruff with irritation and a bit of—she wondered a bit—was it fear?

"I wanted to see," she answered softly, and looked at the Dark Ferryman. He towered even over her, his cloak floating on the breeze, but there was nothing to be seen inside his cowl, not even darkness upon shadow. A cold chill washed out of the bottomless pit of his being, swirling in shadow upon shadow. Looking into the aching emptiness made her dizzy and she put a hand on Tolby's shoulder to steady herself. The being rippled, and she knew she had gained his full attention, and she cowered in spite of herself.

Garner shouted from behind them. "We can camp here and cross by ourselves tomorrow."

"The river's at flood tide. I won't risk my family for a few half crowns."

"Da! That's our seed money," Garner protested, Lily's voice shadowing his own. "We'll go downstream and take our chances there. Or take Bregan Oxfort's route," he added, with a threat deep in his young voice.

"You'll do no such thing! He's a robbing beast, but I'll pay it." Tolby dug in his pants pocket, deep, where he had his small leather bag of coins stowed safely away, his shoulder shrugging out of Rivergrace's hold, sending her off-balance.

It was the phantom that caught her. His icy touch cut through her like a sharp blade and she gasped, and the pain ebbed almost immediately, but he kept his transparent ebon hand upon her wrist.

"Aderro," the Ferryman said to her, his voice hollow, yet the tone somehow warm.

Rivergrace blinked up into that cowl, searching for a face, a hint of one, a soul, too, perhaps, something stirring deeply in her mind. Not the joyous hail of her family, Derro!, but aderro, with an unfamiliar accent, the same word yet not. She stared at the Dark Ferryman, her thoughts as tumultuous as the Nylara thundering past them.

He said more to her, then, but she understood not a word of it, the language lilting and flowing, and when the phantom came to a halt, he paused, as if waiting for her to respond. "I don't . . . I don't understand," she managed, as Tolby reached out and gently took her wrist back from the Ferryman's hold.

"Leave her be," her father ordered. "Get back in the cart, Grace." He clenched his coin bag in his other hand.

"But . . ." she paused, unable to say what she felt, shivering in the chilled presence of the other. "I should know, shouldn't I?" She looked at Tolby. He raised his hand then to brush her hair back from her brow.

"Now is not the time. Let me settle with the Ferryman first, and then we'll talk."

"He knows me," Rivergrace said firmly, and the realization grounded her. She lifted her chin, frowning, to look back into the emptiness leaning over her. "I speak common," she said. "And we are not traders or haulers. This is all we have left after a raid. We can't pay the toll you ask." Talking to the Ferryman was like throwing small pebbles into the deepest, darkest pool of water in the Silverwing when the river was quiet at late summer, flood tide gone, rains waning, the water still and moving deeply. She and Nutmeg used to do it, just to see the ripples that would spread outward in serene circles. Once, they'd frightened a bottom-dwelling fish and it came leaping out, thrashing and splashing and like to scare a year's growth out of both of them. She waited now for a reaction from the Ferryman.

He flowed over and through her, before drawing back and coalescing in front of Tolby again. "Toll," he said, "one silver crown bit."

Tolby blinked rapidly. He undid the string to his little pouch and fetched the coin out, dropping it into the outstretched inky palm. The coin sank into sooty nothingness and disappeared. "Board," the phantom ordered, and turned his back on both of them.

Tolby tossed her onto the cart where Garner and Keldan caught her, and he jumped up to his seat beside Lily on the wagon. The fare was a pittance compared to what the Ferryman had asked before, and Tolby wanted to get across before the capricious being changed his mind a second time.

Both carriages jolted onto the rough wooden bed of the barge, and the Ferryman leaned into his rudder and cast off, unbothered by the force of the river or any other nature other than his own. Rivergrace hugged herself as she settled down next to Garner.

Nutmeg put her arms around Grace. "Mistress Greathouse dropped the apple right out of the tree. It's time, and past time, we tell you."

Grace leaned against her sister as she tried to fold her long legs and settle in between them and the bales of goods. "If you're going to tell me I'm not Dweller-born, I think I know." They held each other, laughing on the edge of tears, as the carts rocked roughly back and forth against the Nylara's swell, and the Ferryman fought to take them safely across. The laughter seemed to work against the forces of nature which tried to beat them back, for the river settled a little, and other than a constant bucking against the current, the ride was smoother than anyone anticipated.

Campfire light glowed over all of them, as the night air smelled of burning wood and supper and herbs steamed for drinking. Lily pressed a warm mug into her hands, and sat down next to Rivergrace, settling with a soft rustle of her skirts. "It's not that you have Vaelinar blood," she started. "We all know you do, and you know you do, surely, by now."

She hadn't thought of it, before the fair at Stonesend, but it had stared her in the face there, much as the Ferryman had stared into her face that morning. The only question would be, "How much, do you think?" Grace tilted her face to look up at Lily, for she sat on the ground, and her Dweller mother on a keg.

"We think . . ." Lily paused, wrapping her own slender fingers about her drink, the knuckles showing white. "We think full-blooded. You've the eyes, which we can't hope to hide in Calcort, and the height, the slenderness . . ."

"The beauty," finished Keldan. He cleared his throat and picked up another skewer of meat and turned his attention to that.

Family, she thought, and took a sip of her drink to savor that. Other family. "If you knew I was Vaelinar from the beginning, why . . ."

"Why didn't we return you?"

Nutmeg said petulantly, "You were mine. I found you. I pulled you from the river."

Grace nudged her booted foot with her own. "You're my only sister. That won't ever change. I want to understand what Mistress Greathouse meant."

Tolby knuckled his daughter's head with the bowl of his pipe. "Let your mother talk."

Reaching down, Lily lightly traced the marks on Grace's wrist. "These scars, faint now, were raw and fresh wounds then from the shackles that made them. It wasn't just a chafing or rubbing. They were gouged and branded, horrible to see even though they'd mostly healed by then. You were someone's slave, and there was no way we intended to give you back. You were barely alive when the Silverwing brought you to us. Wars were fought with the Strangers over their slavery, and it was ended, but some Vaelinars still manage it. And for one to enslave another, an even deeper crime. It would have meant your life, and possibly all of ours, to unknot the question of where you came from and how to return you."

Rivergrace took a long, slow breath. "I escaped."

"Somehow, yes. If there were others with you, they never made it. Your raft was little more than kindling and splinters and falling apart bit by bit even as Nutmeg pulled you out."

"The Bolgers came looking for me."

Tolby lit his pipe. "We don't know that. They always raided before, and there's little doubt they'll raid after we're long gone."

"And the Ravers?"

He shook his head again. "No more murderous around you than they are around any living thing of the First Home. We do not hear of Ravers for years upon years, and then they be back, raiding, then gone again. No sense to it. Fear, if you must, Grace, but fear your own. They're the ones who put shackles on you, and if you had family . . ." He paused. "You've a much longer life to live than we do, and time to find the answers."

"Time," she echoed. "And care."

"Yes." A puff of grayish smoke wreathed his head and faded away in the night air. "When you search, you must do it very carefully."

Hosmer slept by the fireside, but groaned a little as he tried to roll and couldn't, for Lily had bolstered his leg so that he couldn't do just that when he slept and twist or hurt it. She moved to his side to stroke his temple and quiet him. Rivergrace stared across the tiny sparks and motes of glowing ash that drifted upward and burned out. There would be a time when her Dweller family would leave her, like it or not, for her years would be different from theirs, and the thought settled about her uneasily, for she'd never really considered it before. Her drink grew cold long before she remembered to drink it down, as Nutmeg spoke up about the adventure facing them, and the others broke into noisy plans, noticing but forgiving her silence.

When she put her head down to sleep, it was with the faint roar of the Nylara still in her thoughts, underscored by the voice of the Ferryman who had spoken words to her she didn't understand.

Or had part of her remembered? And would that part whisper it to her in her dreams? And if not in tonight's dream, then when? She closed her eyes uneasily.

Sevryn stood in his saddle a moment, easing his legs and ass and thought that if Gilgarran could catch him now, he'd get a swift slap to the head for being saddlesore after so brief a time. Gone soft, he had, although the ride from the Stronghold to Larandaril, and then to the great library and then angling back toward ild Fallyn had scarcely been an easy one. Still. He chewed on his lip briefly. Gone soft.

The knowledge scarcely eased the pain.

Sevryn laughed at himself as he reined his horse down toward the river plain where the Nylara cut through like a hot knife through soft butter, and the Ferryman awaited his duties. Although the rolling hills gave way, the ride took longer than the vision promised, and the sun held a high throne by the time he made the ferry dock. No caravans or farmers waited; he pulled up alone and dismounted, waiting for the Ferryman to notice and appear. It gave him time to catch his breath and stretch his legs and ease the kinks, and he looked longingly at the northern mountains. Far beyond them, a good week's ride or more, lay the ridges which circled the ild Fallyn Stronghold, made passable only by the bridge which their House had made, a bridge which only Vaelinarran engineering coupled with Talent could have even attempted, the Work of a lifetime. It was the Work which had established ild Fallyn as its own Stronghold, its own dynasty, in a world which magic had left, and the Vaelinars regained their own, strand by twisting strand. A Work like that was not done by one individual but by several, working in concert, braiding their Talents and molding their world to fit their dream. It had destroyed a few. A few of the Ways had been horribly corrupted. Most had never come into being at all. He wondered at the strength of the Vaelinars who'd attempted a Way and if he could ever have dared.

The Ferryman approached, taller than Sevryn but not by much, but all the more impressive by the voluminous robes he wore, all of dark and shadow and magic. The Ferryman requested his toll and Sevryn paid it, wondering as many others before him where that coin actually went when it dropped into the Ferryman's palm. He led his horse onto the raft as it bucked the strong current of the Nylara and shifted underfoot in violent rolls. Sevryn wished he were farther north, closer to the road's end, crossing the wide and milder Greenbank River which bordered the ild Fallyn lands.

He would indeed have to toughen up, he thought, scratching his horse under the chin and calming him as the Ferryman pushed away to struggle with his will against that of the surging river. Tressandre regularly rode down from the north, driving her horses and goods for sales and fairs, to spy and to meddle, and to find new lovers. She never gave a care for the length of the road, nor had the journey ever seemed to drain her.

He could feel the power of the Ferryman and it made the hair on the back of his neck rise as the creature gained safe passage for them. The raft rose and fell, heaving back and forth, and his stomach lurched queasily. His horse put his head down, whickering uneasily, the whites of his eyes showing despite soft words from Sevryn. For a moment, it seemed as if the center of the river was a whirlpool and they swirled about wildly before coming about to safety.

They landed finally after long, inexorable moments in which the river fought to wash them off the raft, and spray drenched them, and the ropes which guided the raft across the river strained and came near to snapping but did not. Sevryn moved to lead his horse off the raft, more than a little unnerved. The horse jumped aside skittishly, and he took a firm hold on the reins.

The Ferryman stopped him from stepping onto the bank.

"Seek the Forges," he said, deep voice rolling out of the cavernous opening of his hood.

Sevryn rocked back on his bootheels. "What?"

Had he even heard it? His horse took a bolting leap off the raft, dragging him alongside, and Sevryn turned him round, and curbed him to a halt.

"Wait."

The Ferryman turned. "Crossing?" he asked.

"You just brought me here. What did you say to me? What Forges?"

The being did not elucidate. But he lifted his hand and pointed. "Go." The Ferryman boarded the raft and left.

Sevryn watched the Dark Ferryman disappear into the spray and white-water caps of the Nylara, and then he stepped back, still trying to soothe his unsettled horse. As he turned to the horse, hand stroking the curved neck, he saw they had landed on the far side of the Greenbank River, and the flesh rose and danced on his arms.

He spun about. The wide, shallow, and tranquil waters of the streambed faced him; gone was the mad and furious Nylara, and the Ferryman, and the docks. Everything gone but the verdant shores for which the Greenbank had been named.

The Ferryman had taken him the Way he'd wished, and left him with two burning questions. How had the creature done so, and how had he known about the Forges?

Chapter Twenty-Seven

HOSMER GOT TO HIS FEET and walked, slowly and gingerly, with Garner under his shoulder as a crutch, something that would never have been possible normally because Garner was taller, but with his own injury, he walked crouched over. So the two fit together like some odd puzzle. It worked well whenever their journey paused or stopped for the evening, with the exception of Garner's spirited rendition of "Two Frogs," a Dweller ditty that involved a good deal of hopping during the chorus, much to Hosmer's muttering. He had no choice but to join in the hopping if his "crutch" did, and the two of them would curse and hop about the campfire while Lily, Nutmeg, and Rivergrace melted into pools of laughter. The return of the two to health brought smiles to everyone else's faces despite the good-natured ribbing the two constantly aimed at each other.

Even Bumblebee would swish his thick tail and give pony snorts of humor and toss his head. The stiffness left his legs while in the Greathouse stable, and Rivergrace thought it was because one stable lad had taken a liking to the barrel-bellied pony and massaged and rubbed his legs down twice a day while they all rested and healed. Whatever it was the lad had done, Bumblebee hit the road with them looking like a new, or at least, much renewed equine and very proud of himself with ribbons woven in his thick mane. Tolby winked at Bumblebee. "Don't let that old man fool you," he commented to his sisters. "He can run a great deal faster than he lets on, particularly with a hungry Bolger or two on his tail!"

Lily cleaned her last pot and put it away carefully, nestling the lid next to it. She wiped her hands on her apron as she sat down by the fireside. "If we must talk of fooling, then we must decide on our story for Grace. It's time to deal with what Mistress Greathouse, and we have known all along we must come to dealing with this."

"Me," responded Rivergrace faintly.

"The story of you, aye."

"Best to stay as close to the truth as possible, when telling a lie." Tolby put his pipe away. "Less to get tripped up on, later, and, Tree knows, we all have our share of stubbed toes in life."

"You have to lie about me?"

"Perhaps. There are hard questions we've no answer to, and you could suffer because of that. We didn't take you in and love you to lose you.

"A truthful lie will be our best defense," concluded Tolby.

"That shall be our plan then," Lily responded softly, and she looked at Rivergrace. They all turned considering expressions on her at once, and Rivergrace shrank back a little to have her entire family staring at her. She knew, or thought she knew, herself, but she found herself waiting with her breath held.

Nutmeg said firmly, with a toss of her head that was like Bumblebee's. "I found her."

"And we kept her, for it was obvious she'd come from poor circumstances, thin and bruised and very quiet." Lily folded her hands on her lap.

"We cannot mention or let the scars on her wrists show." Hosmer's jaw tightened.

"The slavery quit long ago."

"Or so we were told, and then—" he gestured at Rivergrace. "We find her with shackles."

She rubbed the faint scars, grown up her wrists with age and barely visible if she wore long sleeves or bracelets. "Someone could . . . claim me?"

"Maybe. It would take a lot of nerve and power, but the Vaelinars have never been shy that way."

She sat back from the glow of the campfire, hoping the night would hide the shadows she felt across her face.

"We hope that the risk of claiming you is, in their minds, not worth it." Lily put a hand out, brushing the back of Rivergrace's head in apology for her words. "And, after all these years, they may have forgotten a child who escaped on the Silverwing River. Someone built that raft, meager as it was, and sent it on its way. That someone would be the person the slavers looked for, not you."

"You never found them."

Tolby shook his head. "Not a scrap of them. We looked for days, upstream and down, but you were the only one washed to our doorstep, and you barely made it, as it was. So . . . we tell the truthful lie that you were found, but not that you were a slave. A wasting child, left behind, and we took you in. Then there is the matter of your lineage, and that might weight the matter—why they didn't scour the countryside looking for you? Mixed blood."

"Though she has Vaelinar blood, she's never shown a scrap of their magic." Garner poked a stick into the campfire, stirring up ash and spark.

"I wouldn't say that," Keldan frowned. "She has a way with animals and the like."

Tolby grunted. "That's the Dweller upbringing. There's not a one of you who can't charm a seedling from the ground or a rabbit from the bush if you needed to. No magic in that."

Keldan rocked back. His thick, curly hair fell over his brow as he nodded. "Truth in that."

"What's the lie, then?" Garner crossed his arms about his chest, a protective movement over his rib cage that he'd begun doing, a habit that he scarcely noticed, since the attacks.

"We didn't find her on the river," Tolby told him. "We found her asleep in the barn, as if she'd been left there or crawled in for shelter."

"Why didn't we try to find her family?"

"Because," Tolby said, firmly. "She's half blood and no one accepts Vaelinar half bloods, and we could not leave her to that fate."

Rivergrace found her throat almost too dry to ask, but she managed it. "Is that true?"

"Half-blooded? We've no way of knowing, lass, and it couldn't matter less to those who love you. But in the city, you'll see and hear a different tale. Vaelinar true-blooded and blood-tainted, invaders like all the others, none of it liked by the Kerith-born. There are some who will say the only good Vaelinar is a dead one because of the strife and slavery they brought to our lands. Others will say that we never could have turned back the Raymy or survived after the wars of the Magi if they hadn't come. As for the Vaelinars, they hate any thinning of their heritage. There's no love from them for those with mixed blood, and that's what Mistress

Greathouse worried about. She knows the towns and great cities. It may be hard for you, Rivergrace." Tolby watched her face.

How could it be harder for her than for the Farbranches who'd lost everything they'd built? Walked away from years of their past? She'd been found, and saved, and loved. The ache to know what she might have been if they hadn't found her gnawed at her. Wretched and alone and despised. How could she be worthy of what they'd done, what they were doing, for her? "You shouldn't have come here. You shouldn't have brought me."

"It was time to move on," Tolby answered firmly. "Nutmeg and the boys have prospects to find that don't lie at the bottom of an apple barrel. As for you, perhaps more than anyone, you need to be out in the world. It's a knife's edge, my lass, and I know it, but you've got to begin walking it sooner or later, and now seems to be a good time, while you've still got us for family. We can help you keep your balance, keep you safe." His voice lost some of its country lilt as though even the city had its own way of talking, stern and solid, and she inhaled after a long moment.

"I understand. I'll be careful for all of us," she murmured as they all waited for an answer, of some sort.

It seemed to be the right answer, for they sighed almost together in a kind of relief.

The day dawned when the city towers of Calcort could be seen from the road, even as it wound through crofts and holdings, smaller warehouses and factories, and the very air smelled of its industry rather than the ripening shoots of the fields. Rivergrace and Nutmeg put their shoulders together, staring.

"It's immense," Grace breathed, faintly.

"It's huge." Nutmeg ran her hand through her thick, amber hair, flipping it back over her shoulder. "We'll get lost."

"A Farbranch? Lost? Never. We were born with the northern moon in our night eyes, and a map of the First Home in our hands," said Tolby.

"That does not explain our courting days when you came by late at night, exclaiming the new roadways turned you around and kept you from the right time," replied Lily.

"Well, um." Tolby cleared his throat gruffly. "I might have been delayed by a game or two of knuckles, trying to win you an engagement ring and such."

"That explains it." Lily shot him a glance of such sheer adoration that her husband turned red in the glow of it, and she chuckled.

"What happened to the ring, then, if he won one for you?"

"The ring? Oh," and Lily put up her unadorned hand, turning it back and forth. "We sold it to help buy the cider press. A future for a future. It seemed a fit bargain then, and still does." With a smile at Rivergrace, she tucked her hand back into her apron as the cart jostled her slender figure about.

"I'm old enough to remember that," added Garner. "A great hubbub when it was delivered, on a huge wagon barge pulled by eight great horses. Everyone turned out to help unload it and look it over, and we had dancing and building for days. I kept walking under the table and people would sneak me cookies." His voice grew silent, and a shadow crossed his face, as they all remembered that the press was nothing more than a charred ruin now, for all its greatness then.

Traffic on the road grew crowded, and Tolby guided the cart to the side, so that faster traffic could pass their slower-moving little carriage and greater wagon. Hoofs clomped loudly on the tightly-packed dirt, and riders wanting to get by quicker clucked their tongues and popped their riding whips in the air and occasionally on a hide. There were great, shaggy long-horned beasts that looked incredibly menacing, for all the yokes and harnesses upon them, as traders and their long caravans drew close, then went by them. There were many strolling on foot, or with hand barrels, carrying backpacks of tools and goods. Some were couriers, with overcoats embroided in the bright threads of important crests, and some riding were soldiers and guards, their mounts in fine fettle, and Hosmer's eyes gleamed in spite of himself.

Rooftops gleamed in the bright summer day. The canopy of blue sky was streaked by mere wisps of clouds here and there, moving like ghostly banners over the city of red clay roofs, and bright blue-glazed tiles on domes and eaves, and painted wood wherever the eyes could see. The city looked like a fallow field given over to wildflowers which bloomed all at once in a cacophony of color, a field that would last more than a day or even a season, in all its glory.

It did not, however, smell like a field of flowers. It smelled strongly of dung, and burning charcoal, and hot metal forges, and other scents that Grace could not name, and made even Bumblebee put his head up and whicker back in challenge as they approached huge gates through which everyone drove. Keldan wrinkled his nose, but Hosmer clapped him on the shoulder. "You're smelling the brewery," he said, with a wide grin. "It smells much better in a mug!"

His brothers laughing at him, Keldan fingered the reins tighter and gave a tight cluck to move smartly out after Tolby and the carriage cart, which headed north and west as soon as they passed the gates. Rivergrace craned her head back to look at them, massive, with copper shielding that had been pounded out in a pattern of circles and stars which dazzled her eye when she tried to follow the train of the etchings. They trotted and bumped and rattled across streets that were as much flat stone as hard-packed dirt. Tight narrow streets lined with buildings that leaned upon each other gave way to wider streets, with buildings no less close to each other but far greater and grander. Then, after many streets, the lane widened and wandered a bit, and the buildings here had room between them, if only so that they might fall down in piles of refuse that spilled out onto the roadways. Things skittered from them, even in broad daylight, that moved too fast for Grace to identify although she knew their ilk well enough.

Nutmeg pitched an apple core at one with unerring accuracy, and the rodent disappeared with a disagreeable squeal under a heap of garbage. She sniffed. The cart and wagon continued to rumble northward, through most of the far-flung city, with Grace and Nutmeg talking to each other about how people could live so close and where their gardens might be, until the narrow streets broke into wide, rutted lanes and houses became small farms and stockyards, and then even vineyards and orchards, with a stony ridge of sharp hills replacing the actual walls of the city, and it was toward this end, where finer houses and shops began again, that Tolby turned the cart and the wagon followed, down a broken-stone road where weeds dotted the gutters and the shops grew smaller and shakier. So odd to see how the finery of the city grew and shrank without warning, and although they were far from the rodent-filled garbage heaps near the gate, this quarter of the city was old and quiet and faded looking. It was outside the Northern Gate, Tolby pointed out, the gates massive wooden posts that swung across the curving lane, cutting off the quarter they drove into, which sprawled over low hills where the city had literally overflowed its ancient boundaries and nurseries and small farms nestled right up to the lanes.

He pulled up at a rundown establishment, a brewery and winery, whose warehouse doors were thrown wide open and two carts were being hurriedly loaded inside even as Tolby jumped down and strode in. They all followed, although Keldan kept a hand on Nutmeg's shoulders and Garner stayed at Rivergrace's side, for the men inside were Kernans, tall and rough-cheeked and a surly looking lot.

"What goes on here?" And Tolby raised his voice to be sure he could be heard over the din of the movers.

"Place is going. We've orders to strip it bare." A stoop-shouldered Kernan with cheeks shadowed blue-black with stubble patted his pocket, and parchment rustled there.

"The place is gone," Tolby told him. "Into my hands, lock, stock, and barrel from Mistress Greathouse. And," he turned on his heel, gesturing to the carts. "If I'm not mistaken, those are my barrels."

The stoop-shouldered man let out a curse and simply ran from the warehouse, without another look backward, leaving his crew dumbfounded, their hands full of crates and barrels, and their jaws hanging.

"Put everything back and I'll not have the guards on you," Tolby told them. "Following your orders, you were, even if the man giving them is a thief."

The Kernans did as suggested, grumbling a bit, and cheering up only when Tolby opened a keg of hard cider from their own wagon for them, and they left with a promise to look in now and then for odd labor. After the other carts had pulled out, Tolby closed the warehouse and they went to look at the housing and the press.

A strong wind might have blown down their new home, from the looks of the weathered and leaning wood. The well in the back had been boarded over and lay under a heap of composting leaves, and the small vineyard looked as if it had never seen rain or a pruning hand, although it stretched for a good bit off the street and into the free hills off the northern gate. Tolby scratched his head in dismay and looked at the ruins. "What have I done?"

Lily put her hands on her hips. "I've slept in a cellar and up a tree. The floor looks all right for tonight! Then, we'll see."

Chapter Twenty-Eight

A FOG CREPT UP the foot of the great oceanside cliff, buoyed by the heaviness of the sea and its spray below it, battling for a greater hold on the shore but soon to lose it to the blast of summer's sun and heat. Yet it lay frothy gray and white over the tumbled stone and sand and looked convincingly as if it might gain hold as it glided off the gray-blue waters and onto land. Tranta climbed out of the fog and mist, hand over hand, foothold by foothold, scaling pylons that had grown ancient, though he remembered the day they'd been placed in the rock. Although, admittedly, he'd been but knee-high then.

Tranta adjusted his ropes and reset himself, feeling the dampness of the fog trying to seep inside his clothes, but he did not mind the chill even though the wind pressed and keened by him. He'd inherited this task, but he'd begged for it long before that, and it had often been his before it became part of his legacy. Now he did it thoughtfully, lovingly, meditating as he climbed as effortlessly as others set out for a stroll. The sea cliff knew him, and welcomed him. The Jewel would be another matter altogether. Its fire could scald him as well as any intruders sailing along the coast, making for the great, widespread natural harbor far below him.

The Jewel of Tomarq should recognize him as from the bloodline which made it, but there were times when it had not, and those times had all come recently. The moment of acknowledgment each time had come closer and closer to the moment of immolation and annihilation for which it had been created. His jaw tightened as he scaled another rocky ledge and paused a moment, gathering both his breath and his resolve. The mists swirled down below as if another stirred them yet unsettled by his own passing and by the wind off the ocean which would soon sweep them away altogether. His dark blue hair had been slicked by the dampness to his head and down the back of his neck, and he thought to himself that he might have considered doing this another day.

Few were the days, however, that did not begin with heavy fog about the cliffs on which the Jewel was mounted, and Tranta berated himself for being a coward. As his brother had instructed him, he should remind the Jewel that it came from his blood, not that he belonged to it. Who was master here?

It did not take a genius to feel that, undoubtedly, the being with enough power to incinerate an invading fleet would be the master. Tranta wiped his face with the back of his hand and resumed climbing.

By the time he reached the uppermost edge, the mists had curled away and the wind which whipped about had nearly dried his hair. Sun blazed down from a sky so blue it looked like a brittle shard of agate, and he secured his climbing rope in his harness and stretched to loosen his muscles before stepping toward the metal-and-gem rigging known as the Jewel of Tomarq or the Shield of Tomarq. If those of Kerith had had their way, there would be a temple here, with priestesses and novitiates worshiping the Jewel as it deserved, he thought. His mouth twitched. A novitiate might actually be welcome, but his House had never let a temple be built. For one thing, the power of the Jewel was such that those living nearby would be at risk—as the Jewel itself would be. Constant vibrations would mean frequent retooling, danger to them all. Not to mention that it was not a Godly thing at all, but a highly tuned focus, magically formed yet chiseled by mortal hands and eyes.

Rock crunched under his light step as he approached, and scraggly brush that grew determinedly out of cracks tried to entangle his ankles, but all his thoughts were bent upon the Jewel. He could feel, as well as hear, its hum below the sun, feel its Eye searching for enemies upon the sea, and he spread his palms. His ears filled with its deep, heavy thrum, almost out of range of his hearing, keen as it was. He filled his mind with its existence, how it had been conceived and labored to be made, and his House which had brought it into being, and after many, many long moments of him standing there, wind and sun beating upon him, he could feel the regard of the Jewel turn partially from the ocean and upon him.

The razor's edge of its sensing swept over him. Now came the moment of his most extreme danger, and the urging for him to assert himself as its ultimate master pushed at him, shoved at him, and Tranta ignored it. Not master, perhaps, but . . . brother. He could never make a Jewel of this sort, although he could unmake it, and he could tend it. Heat shimmered over his body, the heat of a firebrand, of the sun, of ten suns, and then it passed. A sudden chill fell over him in its absence, and Tranta shivered.

He stepped into its aura and placed his hands upon the rigging, testing it, finding the gold-and-platinum-spun rope as solid as ever, resistant against wind and rain and salt and blasts of sand. He checked the arms and gears which turned the Jewel from side to side, slowly, ponderously, but the faceting of the Shield was such that it almost continuously faced the curve of the entire harbor, so that its minute shifting did not reduce its effectiveness. It was a marvel, he thought for the hundredth time during his legacy, a marvel of both magic and engineering. The oils which lubricated the gears lightly were fed by a great barrel which leaked slowly where needed. He checked the drum and found it still half full, not needing stocking for at least a hand's worth of decades.

Lastly, he stroked the gem itself, massive, as tall as a house and wide, although much thinner, dwarfing him. Only the cliff it resided upon seemed bigger, and that not by much. He took a tuning fork from his vest pocket, put it against the gem, and listened to the vibration it transmitted to the instrument. Nothing to be done. He pocketed the object thoughtfully. Weaker, ever weaker, but nothing to be done. He mulled it over. The vibrations were correct, but fading, as if a mere echo of the original tone which focused the Shield, and, like all echoes, must eventually still. Everything else worked impeccably and would unless disrupted purposefully, but the Jewel itself failed, and he had no way with which to stop it. It was time, he thought, to let the others know so that it might be dealt with. If it was his failure, he must bear it.

If it was not, Gods help them all. There might not be a remedy.

He stroked the gem one last time, carefully, reverently. "For all that," he murmured, "you are magnificent."

Pebbles crunched behind him. "Indeed," a hoarse voice agreed.

Tranta swung about.

A being stood at the cliff's edge, dressed in rags which had once been elegant clothes, the elaborate hilt of a back-sheathed sword sticking out above his shoulder. He wrapped a climbing rope about his other shoulder, and wore a harness similar to Tranta's. "Thank you for leading the way up." He moved forward with a broken gait, and something feral gleamed in his eyes, eyes that marked him as one of them. Tranta had never seen him before, and that in itself brooked deep suspicion.

"What do you want here?"

"Merely paying homage, like yourself." The figure halted, not far from him, but out of sword's reach.

"Leave and leave now before you are burned to ashes."

The man laughed sharply. "If you could have done so, you would have. The Shield does not turn her eye for you alone." His hands stayed at his sides.

Tranta's fingers flexed of their own volition. "Leave."

The man shook his head slowly. "I have business here, worshiping the great Shield, the Jewel of Tomarq." And he smiled humorlessly, his mouth strained in a lopsided gash.

Tranta reached for his throwing daggers, but he never touched them. The intruder lunged with a speed Tranta could never have predicted, great even for a Vaelinar, grasped him, and threw him aside. Rock crumbled as Tranta rolled, attempting to get to his feet, but his legs dangled over nothingness.

He clawed for a hold on the cliff's edge, even as sand, dirt, and pebbles began to give way under him. He saw the other take a great hammer from inside his ragged coat and heft it, swinging at the Jewel. It struck with a boom, a vibration of thunder that deafened Tranta as a handful of shards rained off the gem's faceted surface, and the voice of the hammer blew away the cliffside entirely, and he plummeted downward.

It struck his mind as he fell, that he had always feared the fire of the Jewel. It never occurred to him that he could fall from the cliff. He fought to arch his body into a dive.

Chapter Twenty-Nine

A STEP SOUNDED OUTSIDE the warehouse, a firm, solid boot step but barely heard over the noise of sweeping and hauling. Tolby quirked his head before throwing the door open to see who stood outside.

A broad-shouldered Kernan stood squinting in the bright sunlight, his rich garments and jewels bespeaking a comfortable wealth. He wore his brown hair braided along the skull, then falling freely to sweep his neck and shoulders; it smelled of scented oil and glistened in the bright summer sun. He might have looked like any trader in his prime, although far more fit than most, but the dark mahogany skin of his exposed right wrist and hand so different from his Kernan fair skin, as well as the sword belted on his right hip, betrayed his identity. A cleverly made metal cage embraced his right leg from ankle to hip over his well-cut pants. Tolby would have known him even for the years passed between them, although it took him but a moment. Tolby bowed. "Derro and g'day, Master Oxfort."

Bregan Oxfort gave a wry smile, acknowledging that trying to conceal who he was would be an utter waste of time. Age had given him a few fine lines about his pale blue eyes, but he was definitely his father's son still. He showed no recognition of Tolby in his own gaze, frank and direct though it was. He leaned slightly on a cane, more for effect than for weakness of his body, and pointed his chin to the building. "About time Mistress Greathouse thought to clean this up. Readying for a sale, is she?" And a light sparked deep in his trader's eyes as if ignited by his words, the only thing about the meeting which truly interested him.

"Sold and done." Tolby stuck his hand out. "I am Tolby Farbranch, Master Oxfort. Met you before, but I doubt you'd remember me. Good meeting you again."

"Farbranch, mmm?" Bregan shook his hand with little strength in his right one, although Tolby marked it as considerably better than the last time he'd shaken Bregan's hand. That had been years ago at his and Lily's wedding, at which the Oxforts made a brief appearance, as thanks for his service as a caravan guard. Bregan had been rolling in misery for his troubles then, that and in strong drink. He'd heard that Bregan had been roughly sobered up, but how, and why, the rumor wind had not said. The Oxforts had come with a present. They'd left a pot and lid for the wedding, to become one of Lily's treasures, and one of the few that survived the burnout. Oxfort cleared his throat as if bringing a thought to mind. "You've a reputation for good cider."

"Thank you, sir. I do, indeed, and hope it follows me here."

"Can't be the same apples, though. You're far from the Silverwing." Oxfort appraised him shrewdly. Tolby felt a faint flicker of surprise that the trader knew his old orchard far better than he thought.

"Just as fresh, though. Time for a new blending, for cider and hard cider, I think. I'll be getting shipments from my old valley, and stock from hereabouts. I guarantee you'll enjoy my product." And he winked with more confidence than he felt, and he could hear his brood rustle around behind him, the sound of all movement hushed, as they watched and listened.

"Good man! Good fortune to you getting fresh fruit with the stranglehold the Vaelinars have on the Ways. But if anyone can do it, you can."

"Only with the help of good trader caravans."

Oxfort's mouth twitched, and he gave a nod before turning stiffly on his weak side to go, then his sight fell on something inside, and he stopped. He frowned. "Who is that?" His mahogany hand clenched the knob of his cane till the knuckles nearly went white.

"Why, my family is back there workin', or they were." Tolby jerked his head toward the shadows. "Three strong sons and my two daughters."

Oxfort's hard stare came back to rest on Tolby's face, a darkness in his faintly blue orbs. "That is no daughter of yours."

A chill swept over him and Tolby drew himself up. "Adopted, she is. And we love her no less."

Oxfort opened his mouth as if to say something else, then closed it again, lips thinning. "Good day to your family as well, then. If your hard work here does not pay off, let Mistress Greathouse know I would be interested in buying out your paper. No sense keeping a good man anchored down to bad paper. I might be able to do something with these grounds."

"I will, sir, but I think we'll do."

The trader gave a perfunctory wave before stepping onto the street and taking up the reins of a finely bred horse and leading it away behind him.

Tolby felt the tension leak slowly from him, even as it galled him to think that Oxfort wanted to buy his mortgage out from under him. He'd remember that. Business is not personal, but the Oxforts had power. If they'd wanted this place, why didn't they move to buy it out sooner? Not a good enough bargain then, he supposed. Garner's hand fell on his shoulder and he suppressed a jump.

"Is that what we're to expect, Da?"

"From some."

"How can you hate a man without knowin' 'im first?"

"It's more simply done than understanding." Tolby patted his pockets down, looking for his pipe, then just stood there trying not to clench his fists.

"They're fools, then."

Keldan said quietly, "We'll just have to watch out for fools." Sawdust curls liberally sprinkled his thick, curly black hair, and dusted even his eyebrows. He looked more like his father and brothers with the gray-brown of the dirt spattering him.

Tolby turned about. "Is the place clean yet? Sounds awful quiet unless it's clean."

Immediately, the five stirred into action, the sound of sweeping, hammering, stacking filling the air. Hard work was better than thinking sometimes, Tolby muttered to himself, and reached for his saw. Dust motes swirled about in the air, and in them seemed to be a pattern as if foretelling the future, but he had no head for that. Leave that to Lily and Robin Greathouse, and they weren't about now. Lily had walked to the milliner's and tailoring shop to present her keys and letter, and she'd insisted on going alone the first day.

He wondered if she'd done it that way in case the store was in as bad shape as the winery and press. Thoughts like that were as useless as dusty cobwebs in his work area, so he brushed them out of his mind as he bent back to measuring and sawing. Despite the din of their work, he grew well aware when the shadows began to lengthen, and his heart gave a joyous extra beat when he heard her steps on the broken stone walkway outside. He did not lift his head from sawing, however, till she broke the light of the threshold, calling out, "Derro! I'm back, everyone!"

She wore a shiny key on a velvet ribbon hanging from her belt, the insignia of a storeowner, the key she'd kept in her purse until she could present herself and her papers at the shop. Summer heat flushed her face, and her hair was no longer as neatly swept up and knotted as when she'd left that morning, but her eyes sparkled.

He straightened slowly. "So. How was it?"

"It has so much possibility, Tolby! Good work space and chairs for the customers to sit, and a wonderful full-length mirror, and fine tables to lay out patterns for cutting and . . . well, just wonderful." She fanned her face as she ran out of words. "Of course, the assistant there has no imagination, and the manager who left is dreadfully old-fashioned . . . even Stonesend was more abreast of styles, so I have my work cut out for me." She laughed at that, pressing her hand to her mouth at the horrible pun, as her family gathered round her.

After she sent Nutmeg and Rivergrace off to see about dinner—they'd put a clay potted fowl to cooking before she'd left, and it ought to be ready by now—Tolby kissed her forehead. "That good?"

"Yes. Yes, I think it is."

"No trouble on the walk?"

"None. This neighborhood is in the fringe of a fine but disliked neighborhood of Vaelinars, it seems. Many avoid walking here."

"The shop?"

"In an area that used to be quite fashionable and still has a draw. People will come if they like the clothing, I think. We won't starve, at any rate."

"A good thing, that. Those three boys can't be filled with apples anymore, and they've holes in 'em, I wager."

"You'll see they're well fed." She kissed him back. "You've never failed us."

"Yet," he grumbled. "Yet."

"Ever." She hugged him tightly.

Tressandre looked up from her desk, and her eyebrows arched into an elegant look of faint surprise as he came through the doors held open by an ild Fallyn servant. "Back, then?"

"So it would seem. Perhaps your allure is irresistible." He kept his tone light, wary of her mood which he'd entered unsure of, and still had not a clue.

"I doubt that. I sent you with a . . . message. I presume you have an answer for me?"

He tried to read her face beyond the arched eyebrows and could see only her anticipation. A dark gnawing grew in the pit of his stomach. "First, a question, if you would allow me."

"Ah." She pushed back from the desk. "Then my missive reached you."

"It did."

"And you are interested?"

"Only if I can pay the price."

"Of course, there is one. It shames me," and Tressandre flicked a glance downward, but did not convey the emotion she confessed to as she looked back at him, "but nothing in this life is free, even for a countryman."

"What do you want?"

"I want to value you, as the queen does. I want you by my side, instead of hers, sharing in my trust. The Stronghold of ild Fallyn wants you."

"And all this because of my supposed father?"

"Perhaps." She tapped sharp fingernails on the desk, leaning back onto it. "Do you think of nothing else you can offer us?"

He could only think of the obvious. She wanted to get to Lariel through him, to know of her what Lariel did not display publicly, and that Sevryn would never do. "Leave my post and duties and join you, on the possibility that you might give me my paternal lineage? What if you are wrong? What if it is only a crumb in a trail of crumbs I could spend my life following?"

Her nails rapped impatiently.

He shook his head very slightly. "It is a handsome offer, to join the ild Fallyns, but one I cannot accept. Thank you, but no. My trials shall remain mine, though you have my gratitude for trying to help."

Tressandre stood. "You have an answer to my challenge, then?"

"Warrior Queen Lariel refuses to accept your challenge to a duel of honor."

Tressandre grabbed for a bell and rang it sharply. Its tones clanked into the sudden silence, and a servant appeared in answer to its summons.

"I will know what I wish to. You'll want to tell me before you leave." She paused, considering him, then gestured at the servant. "Take him downstairs to the blue chamber. I'll be down when ready."

The servant shifted abruptly and a chill of anticipation ran through Sevryn. Before he could move, an unseen weight descended on his neck, and he fell in agony, sliding into darkness.

He came to, fighting the restraints on his wrists and ankles, his body swaying between the heavy chains that held him strung aloft. The chamber, small and high-windowed, stood close and stark except for a few tables, stands, and blue-tapestried walls. Grooves in the floor led to a drain, and a rusty brown residue stained the otherwise blue rock. His clothes had been stripped away, and Tressandre, sitting cross-legged in a pose for meditation, raised her head to eye him, strands of sunlight highlighting her hair of deepest, darkest honey.

"Never believe that I am a creature of nothing more than desires," she told him.

Sevryn fought the mild panic coursing through his body like blood in his veins, fought the need to be free of the restraints and chains, fought the Voice trying to rise in his throat and ask her, no, *force* her to release him. He swallowed down the panic. "I would never belittle you like that." He told himself that she would be the key, her pain could be as nothing to what he must have gone through every day in all eighteen of his lost years, years his mind had locked away for good, experiences he had to remember, to understand, to have unlocked. Her pain would only release him. Or so hc prayed, as fear rose in him like bitter water.

She rose, her lithe body moving with tightly controlled grace. "Yet you left and came back." She picked something up from the stone table near her, and a glint of light streamed over the exquisitely slender blade. It gleamed steely sharp in her hand.

"I'm not so foolish as to think you sought ild Fallyn hospitality simply because you were roadworn, you who've been the Warrior Queen's right hand for many a year, most of them unseen though under our own noses. Your loyalty is legend, and I am even more keenly aware of that now. She had to know she sent you back to face my ire."

"I come and go as I will."

A soft laugh sounded at his words. She picked up a second, even sharper and more slender blade, a flaying knife, and pricked the ball of her thumb on it. Crimson ran down the steel quickly. "We both know better than that." She sucked the blood from her hand. Dropping the knives, she picked up a vial of crystalline glass, twisted and gilt, its clear structure colored by the liquid within it. She swirled it, eyeing the substance critically until satisfied by some quality within it before replacing it on the table. "Do you like pain, Sevryn?"

He answered carefully. "Sometimes."

"You seemed to enjoy it in bed with me not long ago."

"That would be one of the times." He turned his wrist imperceptibly in the chain, felt it chafe against his skin, holding him tightly. He had pegs to stand on, but they bit uncomfortably into the soles of his feet. Not that far off the floor, but it was far enough that his body relied on the chains and pegs suspending him, aches beginning in joints and ligaments that would soon begin to throb.

Tressandre smiled briefly. "Pain opens us up to many possibilities."

"Do you think so? I would think it merely . . . hurts."

She shook her head as she retrieved the second knife she'd dropped. So very slender and deadly looking. He admired its workmanship even as he feared it held in her hands. She approached him, the blade in her long, graceful fingers. She had to stretch to kiss his mouth, but she did so, her neck arched and hair tumbling back over her shoulders, her mouth hot as it sought his. He yielded to her, letting himself sink into the sensual heat of her kiss, tasting the sweetness of it and the last coppery vestige of the blood she'd licked from her skin. Then he kissed her back, savagely, in the way he knew she enjoyed. After a length of time, she moved back, settling on her heels.

She scratched the inside of his thigh as she did. He looked down, to see a long welt dripping blood slowly, drop by crimson drop to the stone floor, her knife blade wet in her hand. Before the soft sound of surprise escaped him, she'd gone to her knees and licked away the blood, and looked up at him. The fear that she'd sliced so close to his vitals fled to be quickly replaced by a desire for her mouth.

"Again. Do you like pain?"

His answer came with the unbidden yet undeniable stirring of himself, a low groan he let escape to please her. She chuckled at that, a deep and throaty sound of delight, and stroked him once.

"Why," he said, his own voice deepening, "take pain when you can have pleasure?" He looked downward at her. His Voice throbbed at the back of his throat, asking to be unleashed, demanding the chance to save him from whatever it was Tressandre had planned for him, and he swallowed it down roughly.

"Because pleasure is different to each and every one of us, but we all know pain." She laid her cheek against his leg as she spoke. "From the moment we are thrust into the world from the safety of our mothers' bodies into harshness, we know it. Pain is what binds us together. Who has not felt the pain of hunger, of loss, of rejection? The pain of fear, of cowardice, of coveting?" She rose from her kneeling position and leaned close to him, face-to-face, her eyes sparkling. "It is pain that sharpens the senses, hones them, makes them so very, very aware of the possibility of pleasure.

"You may want to know what I expect of you." Tressandre tossed her head, sending her hair cascading down her shoulders and back. She smiled at that.

"There is nothing to tell you." The words came out gravelly, dry, as his throat tightened.

She traced her knife slowly up the inside of his other leg, blood springing forth before the feeling of the slice, so clean, so sharp the blade. Then the fiery touch of the sensation hit him and he sucked in his breath. Tressandre bent to lick the wound, her tongue tasting him from knee to groin, and the mingled senses made him dizzy for a moment. He twisted his wrists in the shackles, wanting to bury his hands in her hair and hold her to him.

Tressandre murmured wordless sounds as she ministered to the wound, before straightening again. The knife flashed in her supple hand.

He felt another sharpness as she laid his torso open, curving down toward his loins. A shallow yet fiercely bleeding cut along a line of nerves that made him want to sing out, and only the savage biting of the inside of his cheek kept him quiet, the one torture overriding the other. Yet she could do worse, and he wondered when she would demand of him what she really wanted, and if he would tell her what she wanted. He did not believe he would, but the dread that he might not be able to help himself shivered its way into his bones.

She picked up the crystal vial as she carved another line across the flat of his belly. Looking downward through a fierce sweat that began to pour from his brow, he could see she had etched her initial over him. She unstopped the vial with her teeth and spit the cork to one side. Deliberately, she dribbled the liquid inside over the wounds.

"This is kedant. It's a venom, Sevryn. It's been diluted, but only a bit, for my purposes. It is rather like pouring salt on open wounds, only it has a more lasting quality."

His flesh hissed and burned as the drops ran into the bloody cut. Like a hot brand, it seared into the ragged edges of his body with a fire that ate throughout him, consuming him in agony even as it cauterized and tormented, and he let out a low moan, a keening, unable to hold it in. Tressandre laughed joyfully as if he'd presented her with a gift. "You will heal quickly, but the kedant seals itself in the scars, ever present. It takes a very, very long time to dissipate. Every time I . . . or anyone . . . touches you here." She put her palm over his thigh. "Or here." His stomach. "Or here." His flank. "You shall throb and burn and ache with the pain of it. It shall not heal fully for a very, very long time. Even for a half blood, a long time can stretch near forever."

She ran her bloodied fingers over his face, caressing him tenderly, outlining his features as if learning him by touch. "I am not waiting for you to talk." She smiled again, softly, her lips curving.

His breath stopped a moment. She had no purpose for what she was doing other than her own pleasure, and he could do nothing to appease that until she was finished. Sevryn fought to breathe again, roughly.

Quickly, she etched two more lacerations along his thighs, close enough to skirt his privates, tender skin there screaming in agony as she did, and blood seeped out between his clenched teeth from his lacerated mouth. She laid the knives down.

"Realize this. She sent you back knowing what may happen. If she had ever been as close to you as I have, she would know you're a resource that should not be squandered. I know what you are capable of, far better than she. She must be desperate." Tressandre wet her fingers again in his blood and licked each one clean, slowly, deliberately. Then she held her hands before her, turning them this way and that, as if inspecting them, before dropping them to rest on the tabletop as she leaned his way. "If not today, then soon you'll come to me. I have the only release from the kedant. And when you tell me what I need to know, we will be prepared, even if our Warrior Queen is not. Some of us have an appetite, a need, for blood and death that she seeks to avoid."

Tressandre stretched close, whispered to his ear. "And when I send you home to her, you will remember that. She would call her healer to you, but her healer won't be there. She is gone to Tomarq where Tranta ild Istlanthir has fallen from the cliff of the Jewel. He lives still, although he has little memory, I am told, and he may even walk again, but that is gossip only. When her healer returns, there will be no respite for you, until I wish to give it." She traced his shaft which had not softened, despite the roar of pain through his body and the pounding of his heart. "It is pain and only pain that keeps us truly open to pleasure."

Tressandre turned and left him then, to recover, more or less, or until she was ready to let him go. When she shut the door, he let loose his Voice in a scream of anger that no one else could hear through the carved stone of the chamber.

Chapter Thirty

THE SPARE FIGURE ENTERED the pavilion without fanfare, the guards parting to let him through without introduction, despite their bristling efficiency and alertness, although they looked him over. The sword sheathed at his back drew their hard glances, but they looked away quickly as if they could not bear to stare at it, and fear glimmered deep in their weary eyes. The man sitting at the far end of the pavilion, his head lowered over maps and charts flung across a table looked up without a word. The intruder bowed and then dropped to his knees, drawing the great war hammer from his belt and laying it across the floor at the booted feet of Quendius.

"It is not as forged. A good weapon but not great, though it holds a Demon inside it. I've failed you."

"And you know this because . . ."

"The Shield of Tomarq still stands."

"Did it take any damage at all?"

"A few powdery splinters fell from it, but it did not fracture or cease in its vigil of the ocean. I thought it faltered, though I cannot be sure." The kneeling man flexed his hands. "My senses are not what they were."

Nothing about him was as it had once been, even more so than the he could guess. Quendius gazed upon Narskap, his Vaelinar form little more than steel inside skin, so lean had he become, with great shoulders and arms from working at the forge, and more than a little madness in his eyes. Quendius was taller and bulkier than the other by far, but he respected him. "They are greater," the weaponmaster commented, not unkindly.

"It does not excuse the failure."

Quendius shifted in his campaign chair, the leather creaking as he did, the stormy nature of his eyes shifting as well with the thoughts in his mind. His sooty skin took on the aspect of shadows, playing back and forth across his body. He toed the hammer. "The power of Gods and Demons varies as much as the strengths of mortal flesh, it seems. I have a use for the hammer, as it is. Perhaps it is not meant that I should carry a weapon as demanding as the sword you carry. I have the first blade." He paused, thinking. "I can use this, however. Yes, I can. It will serve as bait."

The other raised his seamed face. "For whom?"

"Abayan Diort." And Quendius grinned broadly.

"Then, with your leave, I will go to my tower." Narskap looked upward. "Have it bolted from without, and I will bolt my door from within, as well."

The grin bled from his lord's dark face. "Is this necessary?"

"It is." The other's steely body vibrated, as if he went to great effort to control it, even bowed in rest at Quendius' feet. "You'll know when it's safe to unbolt the door." Without another word, Narskap got to his feet and made his way across the keep to a far tower, armored and isolated, and within a candlemark, the keep echoed with a howling that raised the hair upon the flesh, a howling of despair and madness, the keening of one who fought both himself and Gods and Demons. It might go on for days before it would cease and the door to the tower could be unbolted.

Quendius did not move from his seat until the howling began, and then he stood to pick up the great war hammer lying on the floor. It tingled in his grip, and it spoke to him in a low, guttural tone of the damned being captured within it, a minor God of little ability it seemed, and he ignored it. Its only use now would be to entrap Diort. He called for his scribe and set that in motion.

Chapter Thirty-One

ABAYAN DIORT SITS ON a throne of melted slag which was once a great relic used by the Magi of Kerith, under a canopy against the blazing sun that burns down inexorably upon the warlands. If one had eyes keener than a hawk, one could think he saw the various sigils of the Magi etched into the metal, each of a different discipline and pride with their own cadre of pledged followers and Galdarkan guards. Each is now dead and gone, only their guards left to hold their pledges, still at odds with each other as were the Mageborn who warred among themselves. Only the battle is different, confined to minor territory skirmishes and a hearty dislike of each clan. It keeps them scattered, at each other's throats, holds them a far distance from the greatness that could be theirs if they would but join together.

The throne is nearly all that is left of the Shrine of the Sun. A small, wadded-up piece of parchment is hidden in the palm of his fist. He has read it and will not look at it again. He surveys what is left of his kingdom, the seared and oft infertile warlands, but the plains are vast and, as the nomads that his people have become, it is survivable. Some clans even prosper. They inhabit the ruins of the past, rebuilding around it carefully so as not to disturb the reminders of what was and what happened. They are Galdarkans, inheritors of the Magi kingdom after they destroyed themselves and it, and even the Galdarkans could not hold onto the ruins. It ran through their fingers like fine-grained sand.

His fist closes ever more tightly about the hated letter. The sun beats even more gold into his copper hair, and his eyes of smoky jade seem to drink of the summer-blue sky overhead, deepening into a truer green, and when he gets to his feet, he towers over even the other tall Galdarkans standing to wait for him. As he frowns, the tattoo of leadership on his right cheekbone appears to flash more vividly, the ink ebony. He reaches to the messenger bird, a small, fine-boned falcon, resting on its perch. It makes an affectionate chirp as Abayan strokes its breast feathers. It nibbles its carved beak down his finger. Then both hands wrap about its throat and he strangles the bird and cracks its neck before throwing it down lifeless.

"Find me another falcon," he orders. "One with feathers not so ill-omened."

A woman behind him has risen quietly, in his shadow, her body of Vaelinarran slenderness, her beauty bespeaking that of those called elven on Kerith. She puts her hand on his shoulder, and leaves with the guards to fetch another messenger bird.

Left to himself except for two lieutenants under the canopy which scarcely holds back the sun at all, Abayan throws his head back and glares out at the warlands. "The Ways must be taken," he declares. "They strangle my country. They will either be mine, or destroyed. They are webs of deceit and the makers of them shall pay for enslaving our country." And he drops the message in his hand into a small fire of incense smoking at the rim of the Shrine of the Sun, and watches as it turns to light gray ash. "Destroyed or mine," he repeats.

Chapter Thirty-Two

"WE HAVE AN APPLE PRESS." Tolby took a rag out of his back pocket and wiped his brow and head with it, then dusted off his hands before shoving it back into his pocket with a grunt of satisfaction. "And a damned fine one, if I say so myself. We'll have a good line of hard cider stocked by while I get the crusher and press ready for the grapes. It'll be a fair amount of work for us, but I think we're up to it."

"Grapes won't be ready for picking till nearly first frost anyway, Da."

"Well, I know that. It's to our advantage. We'll have this old place in shape by then, I think. Time for me to teach you all a bit about wine making." He looked about the area in satisfaction. The immense warehouse had been transformed from a cavernous wreck to a building with equipment, barrels, and racks, all ready to store, process, and eventually ferment. "Tell you what, though. Today's the end of some hard work. I say a bit of a holiday is called for. Lasses, Lily said for you to come down to the shop if I was done with you before noon, and I am. Lads, come with me. I feel like a bit of a smoke and some tale-spinning. Time to reacquaint the city with the Farbranches." He scratched his chin at that.

"Let me come with you, Da." Nutmeg reached over and put her hand on her father's arm. "You know I love the old stories."

"Not today. Back home, the toback shop is a fit place for a woman to visit now and then, but I can't say how it would be here. Might be a bit rough for a female, and she unwelcome at that. Let me see how it looks, and later I'll sneak you in for a tale or two, a'right?"

Nutmeg wrinkled her nose at that, but nodded in agreement, even as she took off her apron and shook it. Motes of dust swirled about in the bright sunlight streaming through the wide-flung doors. Rivergrace hesitated as she took off her scarf and apron and shook them out. She had not yet been to the shop or walked the streets of Calcort.

"Best clean up," Tolby warned. "Lily wants the two of you more than presentable. And mind you stay away from that boarded-up well in back. 'Tis closed off for a reason. Likely, it dried up, but if not, it could be poisoned with disease. You use the pump off the side porch, even if it's slow, you hear?"

"We hear." Nutmeg touched Rivergrace's wrist at that, knowing how her sister was always drawn to water. Neither of them had been out to investigate the old well, sunken and disreputable looking, boarded up and choked over with dried caroweeds whose tiny yellow and wizened fruit attracted wee songbirds every morning and evening.

Rivergrace echoed a soft word in agreement and turned away as the boys buffeted one another, patting themselves down for their own hand-carved pipes.

Grace led the way back to the house which had been set to rights under Lily's hand, clean and shining as it could be, although Tolby had promised to rebuild walls and rooms as they went. She ducked into the small back room which the two of them shared and quickly washed down in the basin of water they'd left waiting, throwing the used water out in the garden, and drawing a fresh one for Nutmeg. She changed her blouse and bodice, then brushed her hair out on the back porch as she waited for her sister. Far across the yard, at the edge of the house grounds, she watched tiny city birds sit upon the boarded-up well, and chirp and fight with each other for the tiny swarm of gnats hanging about, their feathers flashing with brown and gold and bronze tones.

She rose and walked to the well and tried to peer down through the weeds crowding the boarded cover. She could feel the dampness below. She missed the Silverwing, the sound and feel of running water. Grace toed the tall, gnarled weeds growing about the mouth of the well, just beginning to think about something that she lost when Nutmeg's whistle pierced the air behind her. She whirled around to see Nutmeg waving her bodice about.

"Come lace me!"

"I had better. You can't go prancing about the streets any other way!" Laughing, she joined Nutmeg and promptly laced her firmly into her garment. She held a small note in her hands, the way to the shop marked in Lily's small, neat script.

"Think we look fit enough?"

The two eyed one another. One tall and slender, the other shorter and well-curved, both clean, dressed in sweeping skirts, blouses, and embroidered bodices, ribbons in their shining hair. The corners of Rivergrace's mouth turned up. "I think we look fit for a Spring fair."

"Good. Mom doesn't want us scaring off any customers!" Nutmeg tugged her blouse into a slightly more comfortable position. "Let's hurry. I'm starving, and I don't want to miss a lunch if she's putting one out." She handed the note to Rivergrace, took up her kerchief handbag, and they set out from the side yard.

A small crowd had gathered by the pressing house, and they paused. Tolby stopped in mid-gesture, and pointed at them to the curious Kernans and Dwellers, men and women, lads and lasses, surrounding him. "My two daughters, Nutmeg and Grace. Inside, you'll find my brawny sons hard at work. Or you best be finding them."

Surprised, they dropped in slight curtsies. Nutmeg said, unabashed, "What's going on, Da?"

"Neighbors," he responded. "Come to say their greetings." With that, he gestured back at the pressing house, inviting them in to see the work he'd done. Nutmeg watched them go with a grin.

"Da," she said.

Grace smiled. "It takes a good neighbor to find good neighbors, right?"

"Or curious ones. Did they look like kittens?"

"They," said Rivergrace firmly, "looked like city folk. And so do we, tardy ones!" She tugged on Nutmeg's sleeve to hurry her out to the streets.

By foot, it was much farther than it had seemed on the cart, getting from the corner where their property spread out to the more crowded lane of homes and shops. Their new property, at the northeastern corner of the sprawling city, actually lay beyond the city gates, along with other small estates. Steep cliffs to the north and along the lake to the east protected them as well as the city wall did, it seemed. Rivergrace hoped they would find the bakery which gave off such wonderful smells of hot bread in the middle of the night, borne on the summer air in a tantalizing aroma. The lane began to be peopled, and oh, such people. Anyone she could imagine filled the lanes. Maids walking about with baskets on their head, filled with that bread she smelled baking at night, calling for fresh loaves and buns. Lads running through, carrying messages and packages for delivery, shouting, "Make way! Give way!" They ran by without waiting to see if anybody did, sometimes knocking people off their feet, and curses would rain after them.

Some of the wooden signs hanging out on the street they could easily recognize. Shoes, harnessworkers, metalsmiths, jewelers. They paused before one that showed two hands reaching out for one another, the sign swinging back and forth in a gentle breeze, and they contemplated it. Nutmeg tilted her head one way and then the other before saying tentatively, "A healer."

The words had scarcely left her mouth before a delivery lad burst out of the door, slinging his leather satchel over his shoulder. "Make way," he said importantly. "I've documents to deliver! Contracts! Give way!" and he dashed off between the two of them before they could take a step to the side, his satchel banging Rivergrace in the side. Startled, she laughed at herself, and Nutmeg, too, for standing about with their mouths open, wondering.

They decided it might be dangerous to stand about that shop any longer and moved on quickly. There were candlemakers and soap shops and perfumeries, all richly scenting the air with their various aromas. There were paper sellers and ink sellers. They did not gawk at the Dwellers, Kernans, and Bolgers walking the streets, going about their business or hawking their wares, but they did watch the few Vaelinars who strode among them, far more visible than the two had ever seen them before, and . . . this intrigued Rivergrace, veiled. They wore hats or thin gauze masks that covered their faces and their eyes like a galaxy of jeweled colors from view, and they moved through the crowd with unknowable purpose.

They needed no delivery boy to shoulder people away. The citizenry simply stood aside, with narrowed expressions, giving them all the room they needed to pass in the crowded lanes. Words followed in their wake, gone seemingly unheard, a phrase of honor now and then, but more often a low, muttered curse.

A cobbler sitting outside upon his stool, brushes quickly buffeting and polishing a pair of boots, spat, "Bloody slavers," as a well-dressed gentleman passed him by without acknowledgment, but the words dashed upon Rivergrace like a spray of icy water caught in the scorn. He looked up, meeting her shock. "Beg pardon, m'lady, but truth is truth." His calloused hands went back to polishing the boots vigorously.

Nutmeg hooked Grace's elbow, marching firmly on, keeping her in step. Grace looked down at her sister's face, unable to read much past the slight heated color blushing her rounded cheeks.

At the corner, she gave Nutmeg the small map and notes from Lily for her to peruse. When Nutmeg looked up and pointed out the direction, she ventured, "Perhaps I should wear a veil . . ."

"Don't be silly. Hiding a thing often makes it seem more than it is. I think they wear those veils as a quiet way of shouting, 'Make way! It's a Vaelinar here, so give way!' "

Rivergrace laughed in spite of herself. "Do you think?"

"Do they clear themselves a path? Of course I think so! It gives me an idea, though," Nutmeg went on, as she steered them down the right path. "Decorated veils might become very fashionable. I wonder if Mom has paid them any attention?"

"Nothing escapes her eye. Nothing." Rivergrace mulled her words a bit. "Decorating them, though, might be something she's not thought about."

Nutmeg nodded vigorously as she led the two of them down the eastbound lane, twisting slightly toward the south as if the hills to the north set all of Calcort sliding downward a bit. The street here sang with vendors no less colorful than the other, and many of them sold wares Grace had never even known existed in the world, let alone wanted, and the two of them moved in slow wonder, taking it all in.

And then someone took Nutmeg's purse.

Tiiva came into Lariel's chamber quietly, ledger in her hands, and sat down without preamble, saying, "You've got to do something. He's skulking in the woods, hunting, and he's scaring the clothes off everyone."

"Everyone?"

"The game at least. They've practically fled the immediate area, as if knowing a predator was among them."

Lariel did not take her eyes off the arrow she was fletching, her nimble hands moving quickly and surely as she created the weapon. "He is not skulking, he's camping. And he'll come in when he pleases, as usual."

"At least send Jeredon out to him and make certain he is all right. The ild Fallyn will do what they can to pique you after your denial. Tressandre took him in and nearly as quickly threw him out."

She looked up at Tiiva then, whose neutral expression seemed as carefully wrought as the hunting arrow Lariel held in her hands and whose copper skin was as unlikely to show a blush as any Vaelinar's skin. "What others would call hurt, the ild Fallyn call foreplay." She set down the half-done shaft and capped the skin of glue.

"Don't you feel a bit of remorse? You sent him back to her."

"I," corrected Lariel firmly, "sent him as my envoy. If he's injured, then it's an injury to me, and he must come report it. If he does not, then there is no injury and I have no quarrel with the ild Fallyn. I cannot act without evidence that anything is otherwise. I won't be provoked, and he knows it."

"Still . . ."

Lariel sighed heavily. "All right, then. Take Jeredon and go out and tell him his queen commands him to return to the court so we can prepare for the Conference. Is that acceptable?"

A faint smile played about Tiiva's mouth. "Yes, my queen. It will have to do." She rose, and left with a quiet rustle of her elegant skirts, the ledger book balanced on the edge of Lariel's desk and quite forgotten.

Lariel glanced at it. She picked up her arrow and began fletching again, her mind on other thoughts as her fingers worked nimbly. She did not even notice that the edge of the arrowhead, not finally sharpened, was still keen enough to bring her blood out and stain its surface. His pride would never let him tell her if things had gone badly. They both knew she dared not take offense from the treatment he'd met. He wouldn't tell her. Never.

Nutmeg sprinted after the thief without thought, just as she would have gone after one of her brothers who'd dumped a pail over her, Rivergrace half a stride behind her. Neither bothered yelling for aid, as it would only take breath, and they needed that to chase the urchin down. He dashed through the throng of folk as if they were not even there, and the two of them plunged headlong after him, getting a few elbows and protests as they did, but the chase didn't seem to draw undue attention or surprise. Grace supposed those in the city must be used to thieves of all sizes.

Nutmeg kept on the young fellow's heels, with the help of Grace who could see head and shoulders above most, and called out twists and turns as the urchin dodged into alleys and down back lanes, twisting tightly into a shadowy quarter of the city. The uneven paving below their flying boots turned into hard-packed ground, and then the urchin doubled back suddenly, past Grace's reach and would have been gone but that Nutmeg threw herself in a diving tackle that brought both of them to earth with a gasping thud.

The boy rolled onto his back, laughing and choking for breath, and raised his hands in the air. "I give, I give. Dun be settin' the guard on me."

"Who needs the guard!" Nutmeg demanded as she promptly sat on the young man's chest and pegged him down by his ragged collar. "Now give me my purse back, and don't you be telling me you tossed it somewhere."

"Mercy, mercy, ye wouldna hurt a poor motherless boy, would you?"

"Your mother is probably waiting around the corner with a stick. My purse!"

He laughed again at that, dark brown eyes twinkling, even as he squinted his face up at her, expecting a blow or two. "Can't be city-born, you run too well. I'd say you were country bumpkins, but you know too much. So you caught me. Just finish me, and don't let anyone know, 'cause I got me rep, you know?"

"I don't want your rep, I just want my purse," Nutmeg told him emphatically.

Rivergrace leaned against a building, in the shadow, watching for anyone else coming in or out of the alley, although she heard no one, she thought there might be a pair or two of eyes spying. The urchin rolled an eye at her, not unlike Bumblebee when he thought he might be carrying too much weight for his own good, and looked back up at Nutmeg from under a fringe of curly brown hair.

"Must be a mighty full purse to be important enough to chase me into a back alley where anything could be waiting."

Nutmeg took a deep breath and shook the boy by his collar. "I have three brothers," she told him. "And I'm not past stripping you down like it was bathing day to get it off you."

"Now that's an offer I canna turn down." The boy grinned. He was still grinning when Rivergrace bent over him, letting the sun strike her face and her eyes. He paled then and tried to wiggle out from under Nutmeg.

"It would be wise," she remarked, "to give it back."

"Let me up, then."

Nutmeg let him sit up, but stayed sitting on his ankles. He reached inside his patched pants and pulled out the purse, hefting it as he did so. "Pretty light for all this fuss."

She grabbed it from his hand as Rivergrace straightened up, keeping her gaze steady on the urchin. "It's not what's in the purse, it's the bag itself. My grandma made it for my mom and she gave it to me."

He shrugged. "What if I needed it more than you?"

Nutmeg opened the purse and shelled out the three bright coins inside and dropped them in his lap before standing up. "Then take them."

He whisked them away with a sweep of his hand over them. Rivergrace blinked. She hadn't even seen him pocket them, but they were gone. "Ye're a real lady," the lad said. "But ye'll be losin' that purse again, sooner than soon." He rose, and dusted himself off. "Not city folk, and ye'll be marked in any crowd. So iffen ya dun want to be losin' that again quick, ye hold it like this." He took the purse from her and showed her how to carry it, tucked under her elbow and with her arm through the strap in a certain way. He corrected her a few times as she tried to wear it the same way. Finally, he patted her arm. "There. N' one'll be grabbin' it now, or light-fingerin' it open. It's not only secure, but, well, ye're holding it like one of us." He lowered his voice and looked about. "We dun be stealin' from ourselves, ye know."

"Ah."

Nutmeg wrinkled her nose and then echoed Rivergrace's noise of understanding. "Thank you. I think."

"No bother." He balanced on one foot as if about to dash off again, then paused. "Seein' as how ye were so generous, and 'tis a hot day, how about I buy you two lasses a winterberry ice? No hard feelin's an' all?"

They traded looks. He shrugged as if their hesitation hurt his feelings a bit, but he tried not to show it. "My older sis, she has a stand. Just about the corner or two. I'll be leadin' ye back to the market lane, not down another alley."

Grace nodded. "That would be nice of you."

"No beard hairs off my chin! She owes me." He flashed another grin before jogging off, leaving them to follow in his wake again, although at a considerably slower pace than before. After three sharp turns, they emerged from the shadowy backside of buildings into the sunny and bright street, the noise of the throng greeting them again. He did indeed have a sister selling cold juice, although she looked old enough to be his mother, with lines in her face, but she smiled, and dried two clean glasses on her much-patched apron and ladled out the winterberry drink when he asked her.

Nutmeg talked with her a bit while something else drew Rivergrace's attention. Behind the stand, in the open street with very little traffic across its span, a handful of children milled about, chanting and playing, their skip rope slapping the dirt in steady rhythm. She drifted over to watch and listen.

"Four forges dire
Earth, Wind, Water, and Fire,
You skip low
And I'll jumper higher.
One for thunder
By lands torn asunder
Two for blood
By mountains over flood.
Three for soul
With no place to go.
You skip low
And I'll skip higher
Four on air
With war to bear."

The chant made her shiver, but they hardly seemed to pay attention to the words as their feet and rope kept beat and soon they were onto another rhyme, something about boyfriends and kisses and soon a missus, without any notice that the sunshine had, for a moment, grown much colder, and the very air had seemed to have a voice that chanted with them.

Rivergrace turned away as Nutmeg called her impatiently and realized she had been called several times before. “We have to get on.”

Rivergrace finished her drink in a gulp and pressed the mug back into the seller’s hands. “Thank you,” she said, and hurried after her sister, waiting for the summer to warm her again.

Chapter Thirty-Three

"DERRO! AND THERE you are, at last. I was hoping your father would let you come today!" The shop door flung open even as Nutmeg and Grace stood on the street, admiring the trim double door, the wainscoted window, and the sign creaking on its hanger arm out over the street, carved with a hat and gown. It took their breath away, the place seemed so grand, and neither could find words to think that Lily owned it now. Their mother stood framed in the doorway, her trim Dweller figure seeming even smaller, but her smile and her energy more than filled it as she flung out her arms to bring them in.

"Look at you! Did your da not even give you time to wash up? Nutmeg, you look like you've been wrestling with your brothers again!" Lily removed a cloth from her belt and dusted them both down vigorously with snaps and flicks before tucking it back at her waistline and beaming at them. They had not seen the place yet and Nutmeg's mouth hung open as she caught a glimpse of the back wall lined with racks and wardrobes, not full of goods, to be sure, as Lily had not yet begun work or gotten clients as she wished, but oh, the possibilities. A chunky young woman, her hair pulled back into a drab bun, her face always creased with a worried frown that looked like it might be permanent, came from the second room, and curtsied to them.

"This is Adeena," Lily announced. "Adeena, my daughters. Nutmeg, with bright eyes that so aptly named her for the spice, and Rivergrace, with eyes like an ever-changing sea."

Adeena was of Kernan stock, so she stood taller than either Nutmeg or her mother, but Grace towered another head and near shoulders over that. If anything surprised the seamstress, it did not show in her face. Nothing showed other than that perpetual grimace of worry.

"G'day, and I hope the sun was fair but not too warm."

"It's a beautiful day out, but getting hot, and the nights about as short as they can be," Nutmeg told her. "Have you got your bolts in yet, Mom? And patterns? And have you tables and have you those great caged dolls for fitting?"

"We have," Lily told her, "everything that a high-toned shop has." She sat down on a padded stool. "What do you think?"

"I think it's wondrous," Grace murmured. She glanced about the two-room shop, with yet another small area behind curtains. There were perches for hats and gloves, as well as racks for clothing of all kinds. She touched the brim of a straw hat, decorated with a spray of flowers that looked so real their lack of scent disappointed her.

Nutmeg leaned over a table, covered with cloth, and a paper pattern browned and frayed at the edges from many uses. "Is this what you're making now?"

Lily chose her words. "It's something Adeena and I are discussing."

"This is not at all what we saw on the streets. Mind you, we came the way the common folk walk, so I have no idea what grand people might be wearing. But this seems . . ."

"Old-fashioned?" Lily offered.

"Something like that. And Grace and I had the most marvelous idea. The Vaelinars wear veils, sometimes even covering the eyes. We could make them like starry skies or fields of butterflies, sparkling, so much more than just gauze."

"Really?"

"Really. Some embroidery, a sparkle here and there. Imagine, Mom. So many people wearing so many things out there."

"The Vaelinars used to shop here," Adeena offered quietly. "Sometimes their custom is all anyone wants, sometimes they are shunned. It is difficult to know how tastes will run from year to year. Yet, Mistress Farbranch, they are monied and if you could get their trade back, it would more than help sustain the shop."

"And we need that, we certainly do." Lily eyed the old pattern a bit. "Still, we don't need to throw the baby out with the tub water. This has its uses, it's a basic pattern to base others upon. It follows the lines smoothly, with a flow to it. Let's keep this for reworking." She stood up briskly as Adeena leaned over to roll the pattern carefully and stow it away.

"And you, my young lasses, are already dirty, so I think I'll put you to cleaning the back workroom and fitting area! It'll be an adventure, there's much left back there. Ribbons and buttons and pins and more." Laughing, Lily led the way to their adventure.

They spent the rest of the afternoon having great fun making order out of chaos, binning buttons according to size and type and color, matching ribbons to each other's fancy before hanging them neatly from wooden arms that were fastened to the wall and could swing out "like herb drying arms," Nutmeg declared, sweeping and dusting and readying great racks which would hold far more bolts of cloth than they currently had in the shop, and when they were done, Lily had come in with cold mugs of flavored water, and they sat and looked at the results of their work. Then Nutmeg told her their tale of the urchin and her purse and had their mother laughing far more than scolding before the story was done.

Lily wiped her brow and took a deep breath. "No doubt that Tolby is your father," she remarked. "You tell a tale as well as he does, and if it weren't for that, my young lass, I would have punished you for taking such a chance! Chasing off into the city after a thief? Do you know what kind of trouble you could have gotten into?"

"I wasn't worried, with Rivergrace with me. After all, she faced down a Bolger renegade once!"

Grace had been drinking and choked slightly as she pulled her cup away and coughed. "I don't know what got into me then, Meg, and you can't hope that would ever happen again!"

Nutmeg put her chin up. "I know a thing or two about throwing my fists, and kicking, too, if it comes to that. It all worked out, anyway."

"So it seems."

Nutmeg had kept back the part about giving the lad the few coin pieces she'd had in that purse, and Rivergrace decided against reminding her of that. It seemed prudent not to.

Taking off her apron, Lily began to fold it neatly. "I'm sending the two of you back now. We'll have cold meat pies and salad for dinner, since it's still quite warm out, unless the men got into the fixings while we were gone. If not, we'll have to make do with stewed vegetables. I can't do it now, Nutmeg, but if the shop picks up, it could be we can offer your new friend some work. They have a great trash dump outside the gates, and we'll be needing someone to haul our scraps and such now and then. Think he could handle Bumblebee?"

"No, but Bumblebee will probably learn the way on the first drive, and he can just go along and make it look official."

That brought another chuckle from Lily. "No doubt! On your way now. Adeena's gone home already, but I want to look at the patterns without her worrying so. Times change, and she seems afraid of that. I understand why Mistress Greathouse did not offer to sell her the business. It would be too great a burden for her. Not that you should ever let her know such thoughts." She eyed the two of them and both nodded in agreement. She stood. "Away with you, then! See you before candlelight!"

In a tale told in the toback shops, after the sun has set, and weak lamps reflect the blue-cloud smokes of those passing time by, one sometimes speaks of the poor shopkeeper who is alone in her shop and looks up to find a stranger standing by her door. The tale-teller will speak of the fear which flickers briefly through her eyes as she puts her shoulders back and greets the stranger. The stranger is no mean being to overlook or be light with. He is tall and shrouded in black, hiding even his eyes and the back of his hands from sight, but he is well spoken when he finally speaks after long moments of listening as if to assure they are indeed truly alone.

"Good day, milady, if it is still day without, and it is, just barely."

"And good day to you," she answers evenly if warily.

"Do you tailor as well as seamstress here?"

"I have a husband and hardy boys," she remarks lightly. "I cannot help but tailor!"

"You are newly come to this quarter."

"Newly come to the city at that," she tells him, slipping a hand into her pocket where a pair of freshly sharpened scissors fall into her grasp. "How might I help you?"

"It is my thought we can help each other. I need some work done, and it appears—" the shade looks about the near-threadbare store, "you could use some work."

"That may be. What have you in mind, before I make promises I cannot keep," the seamstress tells him shrewdly.

"A hooded cloak, but more than that, and the fabric I will provide." And he proceeds to tell her exactly how he wants it cut and sewn, and how it should fall about the body and arms, and she is afraid although she does not let it show in her eyes. The cloak he describes is surely not for a man wishing to go about proudly in the daylight, showing himself off. No, it is made for the dark of the moons, and back alley shadows, and worse, she fears. When he finishes talking to her, he eyes her expression closely. "And no," he says, "it is not the sort of garment an ordinary man might wear. As to your making it for me, I think you are well qualified and I have no fear you will betray me in any way, for I saw your two fine daughters leaving here tonight and followed them far enough that I am certain what lane of the city they live upon and how to find them if I need to."

The seamstress draws herself up at that, eyes sparking as though she were a flint and had been struck. "I will take your job, m'lord, and not because you threaten me! But because you have told me what it is you wish, and I listened willingly, and that means a bargain is struck between us, one that I will honor, even if what you will do with the garment may have no honor in it. That, sir, is between yourself and your soul."

Surprise shows in every line of the man's phantom body although he is still covered head to toe, and then he nods. "Done, then."

She slips her hand out of her pocket, letting the scissors drop. "It matters not how well this garment is sewn, if the material is not of the same ilk."

"Oh, it will be." And he shrugs out from under his longcoat a bolt of fabric more smoke than cloth, more night sky than shadow, and lays it on the counter. "This is nightweave. As to where it came from, it speaks of the Elven Ways, and as to how I came by it, you are best not knowing. It should be enough, barely, to do the cloak I request. I will be back in two weeks' time to collect it. You shall fit me tonight, and I will leave a crown piece, with another when I collect it."

A gold crown is a fine payment for such a job, but the seamstress continues to hold her head high. "Two," she says, "upon leaving me the cloth, and another two upon delivery."

"Done again." And the man chuckles. "We have a bargain." And he shakes her hand as one man does to another, before she takes out her measuring string of knots and measures him quickly.

As the days pass, she stays in the shop late when others have gone and she fashions the hooded cloak as described, with long, loose flowing sleeves, and deep pockets, and a boot-sweeping hem. It is truly a magnificent thing when she is done.

It does not surprise her that, when she finishes the last stitch in the hem, and holds it up, comparing it to her knotted string of measurements, he enters the shop and is watching her as she turns.

He dons the garment. It is as though he is smoke and shadow and night and nothing more. She blinks, and shivers at what she has made, and tells herself that the work in itself is a thing of beauty, and she cannot begin to guess how it will be used. Instead of two crowns, he fetches five gold crowns from a coin pouch marked only with an embroidered K and places them on the counter, saying, "Well done, and thank you," and leaves in a mist of darkness that she can barely see.

She pockets the coins. And, in the corner of a wardrobe which she and she alone ever uses, the woman puts away the remnants of the night-weave, for she is a good and resourceful seamstress, and there may be a need for another such cloak, someday. She does not ever speak of the cloak she has made, for even a country Dweller recognizes one of the Kobrir when she meets one. With the coin, she can keep her family and shop together.

Such is the way of the world. For every day, a night; for every evil, a good.

Chapter Thirty-Four

JEREDON FOUND SEVRYN camped at the edge of the Andredia, asleep actually, back to a boulder water-rounded from days when the river used to rage over its banks regularly. He dismounted and dropped the reins to the ground. His horse flicked ears in surprise, then began to crop the summer-weary grass while Jeredon quietly approached his quarry.

Not a muscle twitched, but Sevryn arched one of his brows and remarked, "A bull in full charge would be quieter."

"Perhaps, but I didn't want to startle you into flight." Jeredon crouched by the night's fire and made sure it was cold, scattering ashes and unburned bits of wood about.

"I had that banked for tonight." Sevryn stretched langorously, like some great forest cat found napping, the movement slow and studied, careful.

"She requests your presence in civilized structures tonight." Jeredon scratched the edge of his long Vaelinarran nose. "Actually, she requested it last night and the night before that."

"But you could not find me. I heard you gallumphing through the woods like some young pup, looking."

"Eladars do not gallumph."

"You do." Sevryn got to his feet and shook out his ground blanket, wincing once as he did, and Jeredon quickly turned his attention to the river, as if he'd not been caught watching. What he saw on the river was hardly reassuring. He rose, went to the bank, and stooped down, fetching up a fish that had floated belly-up to the shore. He looked it over carefully, before tossing it into marsh reeds nearby.

"Seen a few of those?"

Sevryn nodded. "And worse."

"How much worse?"

"Enough that I've spent my days prowling about, looking, taking note. It's not just fish." He paused a long moment, his hands on his horse, tack waiting to be buckled in place before concluding. "Something in the land is bringing death to our shores."

"She won't be happy."

Sevryn finished cinching up quickly, deftly. "I think she knows already. I think she's afraid the rest of us will begin to know. It's the only reason I'm coming in now; she needs to know."

"She needs you."

"I was ill-used."

"I don't quarrel with that. Had I known what Tressandre planned, I would have dissuaded Lariel. Once done . . ." he shrugged. "As brilliant as Lariel is, her only fault is making up her mind too quickly and without counsel. She's headstrong that way. The ild Fallyn have always trespassed dangerously close to the edge. She hurt you."

"She tortured me."

Jeredon blanched but could find no immediate response. Then, reluctantly, he asked, "For what reason? Sheer ire?"

"To see if she could break me, to see if I might betray Lariel, having not gotten what she wanted any other way. To see if Lariel might respond because of me. And to answer any unsaid questions, I did not break, and I will not parade my injuries. I won't give either an excuse to duel."

Having run out of words, Jeredon snapped his mouth shut.

Sevryn said nothing more as he packed the rest of his gear quickly and strapped down the saddlebag. Jeredon swung up and watched Sevryn settle both legs into his stirrups a little gingerly, but again, he did not remark on that. Instead, he examined the river again, gaze sweeping the riverbanks, and saw what he had not noticed before. Marsh reeds, tough as could be, growing in the most foul of muds, going black and dying at the river's very edge. River birds, normally swooping about in the early morning, gone. He wondered if the night still sang with toad and frog croaking, and fox barks, and the quiet hoofbeats of velvethorns coming down to drink, their fawns at their side. What kind of disease had washed into the river?

"Good news that I found you," he finally remarked. "We're leaving for the Summer Conference, and she wants you with us."

"And bad news that I have seen death on the waters of the blessed and ever-pure Andredia." Sevryn turned his horse's head toward Larandaril and chirped, sending both mounts springing into movement.

The apples came in glorious bushels. The golden Sun Fairs and crispy Red Mornings and tart-sweet Puckers and small but flavorful Little Jewels, and from the tall mountain orchards, Snow Lots. The storage sheds spilled over with their fragrance and all the Farbranches breathed in deeply, happily, the familiar scent which layered over the rich city smells. These were early apples, most of them varieties they'd never grown themselves except for the brilliantly red Snow Lots, and Tolby examined each and every one carefully and cut samplings for all of them, so they could taste and help him decide on a mixing. The neighbor children crowded in, holding chubby hands out for culls, their eyes bright as Tolby tossed them out, one by precious one.

The girls worked at Lily's shop in the early morning hours till the heat began, then went home and napped for an hour as it seemed everyone in Calcort did, then worked for Tolby until late afternoon. They would return to Lily as the sun lowered and fine ladies began to walk the streets and shop for their goods again, so their day seemed doubly long.

Rivergrace could not sleep when the others did, no matter how the incessant heat beat down and made her feel drowsy and lethargic. She crept out of the tiny room she shared, knowing that the small furtive noises she made couldn't wake Nutmeg, and went outside to sit by the old well, listening to the occasional songbird who also braved the midday heat. Water moved below; she could hear its wet sounds, a slow and sure beat against the stone depths of the well. Over the past few weeks, a branch and tangle at a time, she'd cleared the boards and watered the shrubbery growing about the base, so the covered well stood free and the songbirds still had their bushes to perch upon and eat from. She sat down, tucking her knees under her chin, to listen to the water hidden in unseeable depths.

She thought of the Kernan women she'd seen last eve, from the far south, she'd been told, wearing soft flowing pants hemmed with bells that chimed gently as they walked, loose flowing blouses belted with a sash over their pants, their hair tied back with belled ribbons that gave off a different melody echoing the music from their strides. She wondered if she could convince Lily to make an outfit or two like that, freer and cooler than the long gowns and skirts that Calcort women seemed to favor. She missed wearing her worn-out and patched overalls, so baggy that the wind seemed to rush through them, keeping any day from being so unbearably hot.

The hills behind the small vineyard shone russet and gold with their midsummer grain crop, the ground itself almost a red clay. She watched the horizon for long moments until she realized that the brightness of the sun made her squint, and she looked away, rubbing at the corners of her eyes as Nutmeg would have her do, to keep lines away.

A tiny songbird ignored her hands and flitted past her elbow to wriggle through a warped board and disappear into the well. She could hear it flutter and chirp faintly, then it reappeared again, all wet, and fluffing itself up as it perched on a long, dry branch near her.

"Had a cool dip, did you?" she said to it. It flicked its tail at her and continued to preen its newly dampened feathers.

Grace reached out a finger, slowly, and it eyed her before giving her a preening peck, then hopping off a short distance to resume its contented grooming. She laughed at its saucy fearlessness of her as she leaned back.

It was not that she missed home. They all did. It was that, for the Farbranches, home is where the heart is. Lily had said that at least once a day since they set off, and it was clear their hearts were with each other. It was her difference that worried at her, like a loose thread being pulled that would lead to a ragged cuff, then a frayed sleeve, and soon no shirt at all as it all unwound.

Not that going back was an option. Word had come to them from Mistress Greathouse that anyone trying to resettle onto the holding suffered Bolger raids until driven off, and now the land lay abandoned. The goats had been recovered and another horse or two, but that was all that could be taken from the once bountiful ranch. Rivergrace reached out again and tickled a sleeping bird, head tucked under its wing, thinking of her silver-tipped alnas. It chirped drowsily at her before hopping away and making another sleeping nest for itself in the dust and tucking its head back in place.

Grace toed one of the warped boards, and it popped off its nails as if it had turned into a hop toad and come alive. She set the board aside, peering inward. The smell of moss and brackish water drifted up, but nothing noxious or evil. Reaching inside, she grasped a handful of stringy branches and pulled, uprooting a slime-darkened weed and hauling it out. Things had been dumped in, all jumbled, it looked like, to fill it up. Boards, bits of old furniture, cloth, and dirt, and weeds had grown through, trying to flourish without light and without much success. She tossed the slimy growth aside and looked down at the masses inside, choking the well. The desire to set it free coursed through her. She pulled another long, dank-looking weed out of it, and found herself humming a nameless tune, a song she did not know she had in her, something she could not remember, yet which came unbidden to her lips. She paused, sitting back, before tossing the debris on her small pile. If the songbird could weasel its way down for a drink and live . . . the water should be good.

Convincing Tolby, however, might be quite a feat in itself. She hauled the board back in place. Better to do the work and ask later, she thought. Below, something lapped in the water, as if her thoughts had echoed to the bottom of the well. She went to wash up and dry off, still humming as she handed a fresh towel to her sister when Nutmeg awoke grumbling, puffy-faced in the afternoon.

Lily looked up from cutting as the daylight slanted low through the high windows, and Nutmeg shifted, her hands applying the pattern deftly and keeping the material taut as Lily's shears snipped through it. "Grace, would you check all the lamps? I'll be here late tonight, I think."

Grace picked up the can of sweetly-scented oil and went through the workroom first, checking the lamps and sconces and refilling those which needed it, her natural height making it easy for her. She just entered the main shop where Adeena sat, doing work orders for the day, when the main door was flung open with such force its bells clanged loudly, and it bounced against the frame, shaking the whole building. Adeena bolted off her stool, sending it over with a clatter, adding to the noise, as Grace looked in astonishment at the urchin standing on the threshold, an ill-tied sash over his shoulder holding a pouch at his hip.

"Messenger!" the lad cried out, importantly and loudly.

Grace lowered the oilcan which she had raised in case she needed to bash someone over the head, and looked at the messenger. "Gone honest now, I see."

Her streetwise friend looked at her, and then warmth flooded his cheeks. He tapped his pouch. "I be messengering. I uff a packet for Missus Lily Farbranch."

"I'll take it for her, then," Grace answered mildly, putting her hand out, aware that both Lily and Nutmeg stood behind her, watching curiously.

"That's him," Nutmeg said. "Took my purse and I had to pin his ears back, as if he were Keldan."

The urchin grinned, peering behind Rivergrace. "Your lass is a fair runner, missus," he acknowledged. "Ran me down and made me give up my hard-earned pay, she did."

"Hard-earned!" Nutmeg gave a feminine snort.

"Turned me to thinkin' the error of my ways," he continued blithely, as if telling a toback shop tale. "Her scolding and then her kind gift had me thinking about what a miserable lot my life could be if I didn't change. So I did."

"Good. Then I'll expect nothing will be missing from here." Lily put her hand out to Adeena, righting her stool, and settling the shaken woman back in her place.

"Not a thing, ne'er. Dun steal from friends. Errr . . . or anyone." He cleared his throat before unlatching his pouch and drawing out his delivery, and shoving it Lily's way. He stood watching while Lily opened it. Nutmeg looked askance at him while trying to keep a focus on her mother. She nudged Grace. "Supposed to pay him, I think."

"No, lass. I been paid already. I'm suppose'ta wait for an answer, though." He shifted from one foot to another, his too big boots nearly falling off his feet as he did.

Rivergrace eyed him. "A pair of socks might be a fair exchange for the swiftness of the delivery, though. And for a promise to be a bit quieter in the future."

"Socks?" The urchin's face lit up. "Like, to keep my feet warm in the winter?"

"Aye, and to keep the boots fitting better, and the holes not so bothersome." Rivergrace went to a drawer in the long chest, and rummaged around till she found a plain, but new and very serviceable, pair of socks and gave them to the lad. He turned them over and over in his hands, caught in the glory of examining them.

Nutmeg would have read the packet over her mother's shoulder, but

Lily had turned neatly away, blocking her. She lifted her chin and nodded at the messenger urchin. "Tell the sender his commission is accepted, and I'll look forward to receiving the material."

"Aye, missus!" The lad saluted grandly before dashing out the still open door, and then back in again. "M'name's Walther, so's you dun forget!" And he was off again, his new socks stuffed willy-nilly in his pouch and flapping behind him as he ran.

"What is it?"

"An order for a man's dress suit. I have his measurements on string already, as he notes, so I should be able to tailor it properly. He only wants one fitting."

"Only one? For a dress suit?"

Lily closed up the communication and slipped it into her apron pocket. "Most men seem to dislike fussing with clothes. I doubt he's an exception. At least, I won't have to provide the cloth and thread. Walther will no doubt be banging back into the shop in a day or two." She smiled, and tweaked Nutmeg's nose. "Now if we can just get the trade of some fine ladies, things would be going nicely here."

"We're trying. I think Keldan's building a form for you, so you can put a gown in the front windows, for everyone to see."

"Is he now? And whose idea is that?"

"Grace's," said Nutmeg as Rivergrace murmured, "Meg's."

"I see." Lily stepped back into the workroom, calling back over her shoulder, "Good work, both of you."

Rivergrace began to finish the lamps in the room while Nutmeg hurried after, her face brimming with questions about to spill over into words. Adeena resettled with a sigh, pulling her ink cuffs up over her sleeves, and taking up her pen again. Grace stopped by the desk. "If he comes in again, he's a good lad," she told the assistant before passing into the storeroom to put the oilcan away and gather lighting sticks.

Nutmeg came to get her, a long, trailing gown in hand. "Put this on," she announced.

"Me? Whyever?"

"They're strolling the streets now, all the fine ladies. I want you to stand in the doorway and look, well, tall and well-dressed."

"Nutmeg!"

"I mean it. Till we get a form or two to put in the windows, we can do this. And you look . . . tall."

"They'll be looking at me."

"At the gown, anyway."

From the corner, Adeena said mildly, "It's a good idea. The wealthy shops actually send costumes and gowns to some of the richer families when the dance season starts. It's as well they know we sew for Kernan and Galdarkan as well as Dweller. As much of a stewpot as Calcort is, there are many whose businesses only serve those of their own kind, and Kernans are the vast majority here."

Nutmeg brought something out from behind her back as Rivergrace stood in unhappy hesitation. "And wear this." She held out an embroidered veil, its gauzy beauty sparkling in the late sunlight.

Rivergrace took it, her throat going a bit dry. Go and appear as what you are not, and hide what you are. How could Nutmeg ask that of her, and how could she refuse? She looked down and saw not an inkling of anything in her sister's face but eagerness. "Just . . . just a few moments, then."

"Call me! I'll help with your hair."

Nodding, Rivergrace stepped into the changing rooms, clutching the veil in one numb hand and the gown in the other. Nutmeg bounced in after, helping her tug the new gown about her, finally jumping onto a tall footstool to finish the outfitting. Whatever misgivings Grace had, they slowly tiptoed away as the soft folds of the dress fell into place about her body, transforming her bit by bit into a stranger.

Nutmeg balanced on the stool carefully, pulling the veil into place over hair that had been brushed and pulled into lustrous obedience. Rivergrace watched as the material dropped over her face, hiding yet revealing her features but not the color of her eyes, or the small dimple to the right curve of her mouth, or the slight pitch of her ears. Nutmeg made a small sound of awe.

"You'd never know it was you."

"Until I bumped into the doorway or tripped over my own feet." She sighed at the figure in the mirror.

"You wouldn't do that if you'd think about where you were going instead of other things."

"Or think at all." Rivergrace twitched an edge of the veil into place over her shoulder and pulled her sleeves down to cover her brand. Laundering had brought the freckles out on her fair skin and even tanned her a bit, but that scar had only gone white and stayed, determined to mark her. "You want me to stand where?"

"Just outside, at the window." Nutmeg hopped off the fitting stool, instantly becoming much shorter. She squeezed Grace's hand. "They'll all want to look like you!"

"Or find a use for those nasty old rotting fruits just lying around." She turned and followed Nutmeg through the shop, eliciting a soft cry from Lily and a gasp from Adeena as she went. The gown flowed about her ankles, never quite burdening her, yet never quite as free as it might have been. She supposed it could have been worse. Much, much worse. She stepped into the lowering sunlight, saying, "And what are you going to be doing?"

Nutmeg had hauled her stool with her, plunked it down, and took up another veil, an embroidery hoop and needle. "I am going to sit right here with you and work."

"Why can't I sit and work?"

"You have to look like a client. A very pleased client, too." Nutmeg wrinkled her nose up at Rivergrace, setting her nimble hands to work on the veil, putting in tiny bumblebees of gold thread against the darkest of blue netting.

She put her hip to the doorjamb and watched the walkers upon the streets, noting as Nutmeg already had, that the women of quality had begun to come out, strolling among the vendors and enjoying the cooler air and beginning of dusk.

Chapter Thirty-Five

MAYOR STONEHAND LOOKED at the two Vaelinars facing him with unreadable expressions, their riding clothes far grander than what most citizens would wear to a celebration, and he fought the desire to wring his hands in his dismay at their displeasure for his plans for the Warrior Queen. Fine livery draped their tashya horses, and he took note of every gem set, every silken fold of cloth, knowing his wife and daughter would grill him at dinner that evening, and that the cost of the dancing gowns they had ordered would soar at the retelling, for they would be no less well dressed than a Vaelinar's horse! His own dignity as mayor nagged at him. He had everything in readiness for Lariel, and they sat doubting him! "She can't enter by the East Gate. Dignitaries come in by the West Gate. We've security there, committees waiting to greet her, folk and vendors ready to line the streets for a look at her. It's always been done that way." He pled his case quietly and hoped his confidence would sway them.

"Which is precisely why we wish to come in without ceremony, by way of the East Gate, on the morrow."

Stonehand bowed in acknowledgment in the direction of Jeredon Eladar. A button on his vest bulged out, threatening to pop, yet another unruly event thrusting against his strived-for serenity and efficiency. "I understand, Highness, truly, but can you not talk her out of it? People are hoping to catch a glimpse of her, as her visits are so rare and her presence so well felt and beloved, Queen of the Andredia and Larandaril. All preparations have been made, and I assure you there will be no such incident as during our last meeting."

The half-breed Vaelinar riding with Jeredon moved imperceptibly in his saddle at that, his clothes equally distinguished, and his silence and deference the only thing which might indicate his status. Thom did not remember having seen the young man before, but as he was here now, he would be treated as Jeredon and the rest of the queen's entourage would be treated, with dignity, respect, and extreme caution.

"Let us hope not." Jeredon sat back in his saddle in a ripple of gold-threaded cloth which caught the last rays of the summer sun as it dipped toward sunset. "One does not dice with the Kobrir."

"May I make a suggestion?"

Jeredon quirked his head toward the other rider, faint surprise crossing his face to be quickly replaced by his customary neutral expression but not before Stonehand had caught it. "Do so."

"Let me scout the city first. Upon my report, she can decide which gate she wishes to use."

"A possibility. Mayor, your permission?"

There should be nothing untoward to fear. Stonehand inclined his head as he stealthily checked the security of his vest button. "Of course, granted."

"Do that, then. I'll expect you back by midnight."

The other nodded, guided his horse past the mayor and the gate guards of the eastern portal, and melted into the thin crowds.

Stonehand exhaled slowly. "An equitable solution," he offered.

"I hope you'll think so in a few hours. He is formerly a citizen of your streets, and he knows, as the saying goes, where the bodies are buried. If there's anything amiss in Calcort, he's likely to find it." Jeredon Eladar smiled thinly, and the mayor took a gulping deep breath, popping a button wildly, and it disappeared into the air as if from a slingshot. Trying not to laugh, Jeredon left Stonehand standing in total discomfiture and dismay, wringing his hands.

Sevryn stabled his horse quickly, admonishing the lad as he did so, noting that there would be a tip if the horse and livery stayed in the same good condition. The stabler and his lad promised and Sevryn had no doubt they'd stick to their word because he'd put his Voice into his instructions, and it would take a bit of willpower on their part to disobey. It could happen, but since most common thieves tended to be lazy, he doubted it. He stripped down as well, changing into his road clothes, and packing away the regalia gear that Lariel and Tiiva had insisted they all wear, with good sense, for it was the clothing that would be remembered more than the personage inside them. Sevryn doubted, as he hit the streets, if Mayor Stonehand could give any kind of description of him at all.

Lariel's head of security, one Navdon, had concurred that the surest way to flush out trouble in Calcort would be to send Sevryn through, with a free hand to look about, knowing that Stonehand would undoubtedly not agree after first being insulted and annoyed. Navdon, one of Bistane's bastard sons, had the same finely honed innate sense of trouble legendary to his father and his legitimate brother. He'd discussed options with Sevryn, finally coming upon this method of getting in and out, and it was to Navdon he'd report rather than Lariel who would be gathering together political intelligence on who was likely to be at the Summer Conference and who was likely to have spies there instead. Street and court intrigue were two different matters although both could be equally deadly.

He'd footed it about the quarters, ducking into taverns both renowned and of ill-repute, drinking little, listening a lot. The folk of Calcort seemed remarkably indifferent to the coming of the Warrior Queen, or any other Vaelinar for that matter, to the Summer Conference, worried more about heat and crops and the increase of Raver attacks up and down the coast. A few even pondered the brutish Bolgers clanning together again as if they were getting their spines up for another bout of wars. Darkness had just fallen when he reached the northwest quarter, with its spattering of once-fine neighborhoods and a few country manors of note, and it looked as if he'd have a very early evening, when he saw a shadow that ought not to be moving rippling at the back of an alleyway.

Sevryn put a hand up, catching the corner of a low eave and hoisted himself up silently. As noiselessly as he could manage, he merged into the skyline, crept closer, and looked downward across the rear end of the alley which slanted into another back way, smelling of night refuse and stale beer. It took a long moment to recognize one hunter in hiding and catching up with another, and he sucked his breath in very slowly and quietly.

Daravan. And on whose tail, he could not quite tell . . . yet.

That Daravan happened to be in Calcort at the time Lariel planned to be might be a worry, or it might not. That Sevryn had crossed his trail a second time in less than a moon's turning was. Daravan's patterns were as unknowable as any arcane mystery, yet either he trailed Sevryn, or some meddling God had put Sevryn on Daravan's trail. Either way boded ill.

He flattened himself to the roof even as the fiery wash of pain from his healing scars reacted to the touch, and with teeth biting his lip to keep him silent, he put his head down, watching and listening, and wishing for the Talent of Hearing, so that he could hear those below and muffle their sensing of himself. Alas, that was not his ability.

He watched the two. It struck him that Daravan was not stalking the first but quietly, after observing him, moving into position for a meet. That begged the question, then . . . who was the second man? He flattened himself farther, ignoring the flare of pain as if he were lying on sun-fired bricks, and crept closer.

Words, softly murmured, passed between the two. A hand on a wrist from Daravan. The other, shrouded from head to toe, pulling back. A noise of scorn. Then the second man moved into a moonbeam, shifting from shadow to light and into shadow again, but not before Sevryn saw him. Kobrir!

He tensed to leap, but the shifting of the man into shadow was the first step of his leaving, disappearing into the darkness of the back alleyway. He held up. What had they exchanged? Daravan moved away too, and Sevryn scuttled along the rooftop following him, as quietly and as quickly as he could. Daravan strode below, moving deftly behind the cluster of buildings, giving no sign he heard Sevryn up above. Sevryn swung down to the streets, falling into a light crowd lengths behind his quarry, while he debated with himself on following Daravan or catching up to him and seeing what story the man would spin for him.

Before he could decide, Daravan whistled at a crowded corner outside a run-down tavern, and within minutes, one of the streets lads appeared at his side, panting a bit with hurry. He slipped a package to the lad who stowed it in his pouch, straightened his sash, and rocked back on his heels, listening as Daravan gave him a coin piece. Then, threading the crowd as skillfully as a tailor with a needle, the lad barreled off.

Sevryn decided to go after him. Cutting the sash and lifting the pouch would be a great deal easier than getting the truth out of Daravan. He angled down the street after the messenger.

The street filled with the lithe bodies of Calcort women and their attendants, shopping and enjoying a bit of gossip, perusing wares, and filling the night air with their soft perfumes. He slipped through their parties as carefully as he could, trying to cause as little notice as possible, and watched the lad as he stopped at a fruit drink stand.

The messenger took a drink and made as if to drink it, but his attention roamed about. Hell's blast. He was searching for a tail.

Sevryn ducked back into the crowd and went around the block, picking up the messenger ahead rather than from behind. Tailing from the front took a bit more finesse but there was no way a still-wet-behind-the-ears boy could best him at street running. It had kept him alive for decades as he matured and grew more slowly than any other street urchin, and he'd had to step lively to stay alive. He slowed when the messenger did, and kept pace with him by watching him in the reflections of the nicer shops using glass windows or mirrors at their fronts. Then he began to drop back as the crowd thinned and the shops did as well, readying to cut the sash.

Suddenly, the boy looked up with wild eyes like an unbroken pony, mane of disheveled hair over his forehead. He looked straight at Sevryn. Then, with a squeal, he swerved right and darted away.

He'd been made. With a grunt, Sevryn sprinted after the urchin. They turned the corner back onto a more crowded street with far more fashionable shops, and the messenger lad kept to his heels, drawing away with the speed of the frightened and determined. Sevryn was losing him, and whatever Daravan had slipped to him, and the Kobrir had possibly given/sold/transferred to Daravan.

The lad barreled into a ladies' shop, the doorway filled with two young women, Sevryn right after him, colliding helplessly into soft figures, abdundant gowns, and fleshy curves, all falling into a heap. He grabbed for the messenger boy, catching him by the shirt and sash, as the lad tried to wriggle free.

A wisp of veil broke loose and fluttered past him as he pinned the boy down, and he turned his head to look into a pair of most remarkable eyes, eyes of the ever-changing sea and river, Vaelinarran eyes that struck him to the core. He waited for the lightning of prophecy to strike him, but it didn't; it had not since the last time he'd faced her, as if burned out, finally, having shown him the way to his destiny and flickering out. He let his breath out softly.

"Aderro."

He'd found her again.

Chapter Thirty-Six

THE LAD BEGAN TO KICK and wail, his voice rising in an ever louder shriek, his frayed shirt tearing as he attempted to wriggle out of Sevryn's hold. He doubted if she of the eyes could hear him, or anyone, over the caterwauling of the urchin, but from the pile of clothes and bodies in the dress shop doorway, a Dweller lass pulled free and caught the lad by the ear, pinching him till it turned beet red.

"Shut it," she warned, "or you'll lose the ear, and don't think I won't do it. Imagine how much easier it will be to beg with an ear gone."

The lad shut up immediately, with a sniffle and another roll of his eyes. The Dweller lass drew her legs under her, sitting up more comfortably. "Now," and she glanced to Sevryn. "What is going on?"

"I dun noffing," the lad spat out before Sevryn could say anything.

He got to his feet, helping the young lady with the remarkable eyes to hers. When last he'd seen her, she'd stood over a Raver's dead body and unless he was mistaken, the Dweller lass with a death grip on the urchin was the person she'd been defending. The hometown militia and crowds of farmers carrying crude weapons and rushing in had separated them, led her away, and he'd never caught up. He had spent days inquiring about her, but no one admitted to actually knowing her, and Sevryn had finally given up, recognizing a community stonewall when he saw one. Not a day went by that he did not think of her and her quiet, desperate beauty. She had grown a bit, though faint freckles still dusted her nose, and the remnants of a veil hid a cascade of lustrous, dark chestnut hair. She dusted herself off and started righting what had been a beautiful gown before the incident, checking seams and workmanship as she did.

She reached out and dusted him off gently as well, hesitantly, as though afraid to touch him, and he stood very quiet like a wild animal just gentled, just as afraid to move. Her palm brushed the scars across his torso and abdomen, the cloth between her touch and his skin all but nonexistent, for the feeling she brought to the surface. First, the fiery burn of the kedant, pulsing through him, a rage of heat that quickly turned to aching need, need that stopped the breath in his throat. Pain roared, searching for other pain, throbbing. He could not move as her touch quickened him, then sent a warmth coursing through his blood that had nothing to do with Tressandre's venom. He wanted to bring her close and taste her lips and murmur to her, and held himself very, very still, frightened of the intensity of his ache. Awareness of the cloth between them came back, the faint rub of fabric across his abdomen and chest, as she dusted the last blotch of dirt away. Then, she stepped back, and he realized the fiery scars crisscrossing his skin felt cool and soothed, as if her touch alone had bathed away the poison even while causing other emotions to spring to life.

She paled a bit, rubbing her arms as if in pain, and tugged her sleeves into place, but not before he caught a glimpse of an unusual marking about her left forearm, a tattoo or . . . was it perhaps a brand? It seemed new and raw, pulsing with pain, and he reached to touch her, to soothe her as she'd soothed him, but she moved a step back and it might have been across a ravine for the distance it put between them. "Why are you chasing Walther?"

He blinked, bringing himself back to the problem at hand. With a steadying breath, he found words. "He has something I want," Sevryn told the short one, his gaze still on his unexpected find, slender and nearly as tall as he, and steadfastly ignoring him.

"Do you, Walther?"

The lad stared at his too big and scuffed boots. "I," he announced, "have a deliv'ry. For Missus Lily."

"There. You chased him down for nothing. Perhaps someone else pinched your purse."

"It's not a few coins I'm interested in, even if he could manage such a thing off me." Sevryn leaned over the boy, with reddened ear still caught firmly between sturdy Dweller fingers. "I want the man who gave you the delivery job. Think you could find him again tonight?"

"Iffen I wanted to, but I dun't."

"I think you do. If I want him, you do."

A mature, firm voice interrupted. "If the delivery is for us, m'lord, then you're meddling in business you've no need to be. You may be of Vaelinarran blood, but this is Calcort, a free city of the provinces, in case you need to be reminded." The shopkeep emerged from a back room, a sharp pair of scissors glinting in her hand, not by accident or mistake, he thought. The corner of his mouth quirked at the thought she meant to intimidate him with it, but he bowed to the Dweller woman who had been incredibly beautiful once and had aged into a fine handsomeness, and now wore a shopkeep's key on a chain around her neck, with a tailor's apron about her waist.

"My pardon, mistress, if my business has spilled over into yours." He crooked a finger at the lad who managed another self-pitying sniffle, the little weasel. "I have a need to meet with the fine gentleman who gave this lad a message."

"S'not a message. 'Tis a deliv'ry like I told you." Walther fumbled at his pouch and got it open, the satchel reaching from hip to mid-thigh on him, and he pulled out several lengths of cloth, neatly folded and tied.

"Ah, yes," the seamstress breathed as she took them in, fingers stroking the goods with a kind of reverence. "I've been waiting for this. Perhaps you've been mistaken, m'lord."

Fabric? He'd chased down a miserable street beggar for yardage? Mistaken or just plain taken by Daravan? Sevryn hesitated only a heartbeat. He flipped a coin through the air which Walther caught in mid-spin, ear pinioned or not. "Tell him the seamstress has a question about his goods, and bring him back. It'll be worth coin to you."

"No trouble," the Dweller lass said sharply, looking at the seamstress and back to him. He saw the resemblance in the two, mother and daughter likely.

The woman at his elbow spoke softly, "Always trouble, with the Vaelinars. Is that not right?" She looked to him, eyes of river water, and lake water, and rain, with sun dappled off their depths.

"I've heard that bandied about. It's trouble I'm trying to avoid now." He stared down at the messenger. "Will you do it, lad?"

"Soon as she lufts go o' me."

The lass let him go, and he sprang up. Before the dust settled with another wisp of torn veil to the floor, the messenger boy was down the block and gone.

Sevryn entered the shop proper, choosing a stool away from the threshold and the view of the street to perch upon. "I beg pardon for the intrusion and damage. I'll settle for that when I'm done."

"You'll settle now." The shopkeep approached him warily, her hand open. "I'm closing now, but I hope to have enough of a business left to open on the morrow!"

"Quite." He put two gold crown pieces in her palm. "For now and, hmmm, future."

"There had better not be a future," the other Dweller said, with a toss of her head, as she jumped to her feet. "I've a da and three strong brothers, and we won't have trouble in here."

The one who held his thoughts put her hand on the other's shoulder. "Nutmeg. He looks honorable."

"Aye, sure he does, for a grown man chasing down a street boy." Nutmeg snorted and went to the door, righting the stool and cleaning up where everyone had sprawled on the threshold as she grabbed a broom and dustpan. With a saucy toss of her head, she kept a cinnamon-colored eye on him as she did so.

Sevryn rested his bootheel on one of the rails of the stool. "My pardon again. I am Sevryn Dardanon, in service of Queen Lariel. At your service, as well."

The shopkeep put her delivery on her counter and inclined her head gracefully. "I am Lily Farbranch, and these are my daughters Nutmeg and Rivergrace."

He caught his surprise before it showed, he thought, but Nutmeg put her chin up, dustpan in hand, and said, "She's adopted—I found her, and that's it."

"Of course." He found all three watching him, and leaned back a little on his stool as if uninterested. She would be half-blooded or less, then, to be let go so easily, and it was clear she'd family now that loved her. He understood now why he hadn't been able to ferret her out. Abandoned, perhaps, and taken in by those who loved her, and the townspeople about them just as determined to leave things as they were. Just as he'd been lost and finally found . . . family, was it? who accepted him. He pondered at thinking of Lariel and Jeredon as family. Would they allow it, if they knew? He realized they waited on him. He gestured, feigning disinterest. "A good tale to hear sometime, but I'm afraid my attention is held by the messenger boy's employer."

Tension filtered out of the room. Rivergrace took up a hoop of embroidery and blew the dust off it gently, the veil fluttering as she did so before handing it to Nutmeg. "Shall I go back to standing in the doorway?"

"With Walther soon to come bolting back? I think not. We shall have to teach him a bit about doors and doorways before he knocks ours through," Lily answered dryly.

"He is probably more used to windows," commented Sevryn. Forcibly, he turned his attention on the bit of corner window he could see through, watching the night-clad streets.

"He has a good heart," Rivergrace told him. "He only does what he has to."

Sevryn did not respond. If he turned to talk with her, she would command all his attention and then some, and he dared not be distracted with Daravan on the way. He did nod, finally, feeling her watching him, like a burning spot on the side of his neck. He listened while they talked among themselves, quietly, righting the shop to close up after a long day, while he tried to catch any sounds of Daravan's approach, as likely to be from the back as through the front. Sevryn knew if it were him, he would not come in through the front door.

The two sisters disappeared behind a curtained doorway where he heard much rustling of material and a smothered giggle or two, and while he imagined the changing of clothes over that lithe body, shadows shivered a bit somewhere near the back storeroom. He held both hands palm up and empty, and Daravan's smooth voice commented, "I shall have to instruct my messenger in the difference between a troublemaker and an annoyance."

"I should have thought I'd rate higher." Sevryn stood and bowed slightly in deference as the shadows parted and Daravan stepped into the lamplight.

"If you did, you'd be disposed of. Do you wish to cause me trouble?"

"No, sir, not I."

Daravan scratched the corner of his mouth as if to hide an expression. He leaned against the counter. "Then let me commend you for finding me in a city that is a stewpot of people."

"Sheer luck. I was looking for someone else and came across you. You were looking for someone else at the time, and I thought it prudent not to interrupt you."

Daravan said wryly, "You, eh? I thought I heard a rather large roof rat."

"If you'd heard one, sir, you'd have not stayed in the alley."

"Ah, but it was my duty to be there. Some weeks ago, I, hmmm, found a coin purse after a night of drinking and cards. I thought to return it." Daravan's hand moved, slowly, to push aside his cloak, and tap a black pouch. Gilt threads cleverly sewn upon the pouch glittered a nearly unseeable "K" as he did so. Sevryn recognized the symbol with a sudden, cold piercing of his senses. "M'lord denied having lost such a pouch, however, and I realized he was not the man I thought he was, although so close in likeness I wondered if he might not have a brother." Daravan looked into Sevryn's face intently. "I withdrew quickly before trying his patience."

"A wise move, after an honorable one. Returning a found purse is very admirable."

Daravan shrugged. "I have little need of money not my own." He opened his gloved fist and rained a small stream of crown bits, silver and gold, onto the counter. "Your meeting place is fortuitous, as it reminds me. I do, however, have need of a suitable outfit, for being among the royalty this summer, although such events can be wearying, making an appearance seems extremely necessary. Mistress Farbranch is a seamstress and tailor of marvelous ability. I heartily recommend her if anyone you know needs a good suit or gown."

"I saw her handiwork but a little while ago, and agree."

Daravan inclined his head. "She keeps her peace as well, and discretion is always commendable. As for our business?"

Sevryn waved a hand. "I had only hoped to greet you in a quiet place, what with the ceremonies planned over the next month or so, and I thank you for your time."

"Good, then. I'm certain we'll see each other later." He tapped a last gold crown on the counter, a sharp rap. "Good eve, Mistress Farbranch, and to your daughters. When you need a fitting, Walther knows how to reach me."

Muffled, from the back area, Lily called back, "Aye, m'lord, I'll send word," and Daravan had gone before she finished speaking.

Sevryn turned on his heel sharply, stopping only in the doorway. "Thank you. With your permission, might I return?"

Lily peeked out from her workshop. "For . . . ?"

"A garment or two of my own. I might know a lady who wishes a new gown as well, and those veils are quite charming."

Pleasure warmed her cheeks and crinkled the lines at the corner of her eyes. "Welcome, then, m'lord Dardanon."

"Good." He hesitated another moment, but neither Rivergrace nor Nutmeg appeared, although he could swear he saw the curtains move, parting slightly so that his leaving might be watched.

Or perhaps he only hoped that as he left.

Jeredon slapped his shoulder sharply. "A quick turn, I thought." His voice scolded.

"Complications. The Kobrir are in town, and we are warned that there may well be an assassination attempt. I doubt it matters what gate we use to enter, but the various events and dances planned, as well as the Conference itself, will have to be watched closely. It's been confirmed there is more than one Kobrir and two are about. Daravan has tabs on one, but he thinks Lariel is still the target."

Jeredon hissed a breath inward. "I send you out to find a ripe fruit thrower, a crowd heckler, and you come back with an assassin."

"It's my job, eh? And I'm good at it." Sevryn swung up on his horse, settling in. The healed scar on his flank drew a little, but nothing like the kedant-laced network over the rest of his torso, and he found a little peace in that. How had she done it, healed what no other healer could? He found Jeredon's gaze still on him, and reminded him, "Lariel is not one to be afraid, so it looks like you and I are going to have to be the ones using caution."

"True, that. Well. Let's see what kind of night's sleep we'll get after we tell her your bit of street gossip." He reined his horse around, and Sevryn followed.

Chapter Thirty-Seven

NARSKAP WORE THE WAR hammer at his lean hip, with the greatsword sheathed at his back, his lean face etched with the ravages of a struggle Quendius could not begin to fathom, though he had heard the howling of it for days. His aide looked as if he could not bear the presence of others except for the weaponmaker, and even that seemed difficult as he stayed in the far corner of the pavilion. A man of few words himself, Quendius sprawled at the rough wooden table, the edges of his tent stirring in the early dawn air and said, "Sit for a while. Rest."

"There is no rest when caught between petty Gods and Demons."

"I could kill you now."

Narskap's color went ashen. "It's a good offer, and one I will relish one day, but that would bring no peace. Pray you never die at the hands of one of these," and he gestured at the two weapons he wore, his hands trembling before he hooked his thumbs back into his belt to still the quaking, and stand stoically in the corner.

"Shall we inform our buyer of the hammer's possibilities and consequences, I wonder?"

"It is a failure. Whatever Diort wants of it, it will ultimately betray him."

"All to our good, then." Bored, Quendius carved at the tabletop with the tip of a very sharp dagger, working the wood into a design, painstakingly etching and smoothing away curls and sawdust as he amused himself. The soft but aged wood gave way easily to his steel, and he soon had an intricate floral-and-vine design started, before he realized that Narskap had not answered him further and that a hush had fallen over the camp. He laid his dagger down.

One of his lieutenants brushed inside. "The clans are drawing near."

"Good. Have they closed the circle yet?"

"No. It's my guess that they are doing what you predicted, and letting the others join us before they do so. They seem to have no inkling they, in turn, are being outflanked."

"Excellent. Keep watch."

The lieutenant saluted and left.

Quendius looked into the morning light as it brightened, the sooty nature of his skin darkening in contrast to the light. Never lighter than pale fine ash or darker than a grayish charcoal, he looked as if he perpetually resided in shadow.

"Soon," murmured Narskap, as if reading his thoughts on how close the others might be.

"Does it sense a blooding?" Quendius eyed the hilt of the greatsword visible over Narskap's shoulder, wondering how his aide knew of things he could not know. It was not a Talent or ability of his line.

"Yes. Or perhaps it merely reads my own anticipation. But it knows. It grows eager now."

"Good. I think our buyer will need a Demonstration."

"I stand at your service." Narskap looked down as if composing a thought, or an emotion, or perhaps even a defense against his inner self, then raised his chin.

Quendius ran a fingertip over the design he'd begun in the table. He'd been apprenticed as a decorative woodworker, long, long ago. He could almost remember what it was like to have a fondness for woods, their grains, their strength, their glow, their aroma, the works they lent themselves to. Almost. It seemed a life so far away that it could not have been his, however. He had the Vaelinarran eyes but not the abilities desired with them, and he'd been tossed aside like a dulled and broken tool, useless, until he found a use for himself. Like fires filled a forge, the drive to find himself had filled him, and he had been granted part of his desire. The road would be a long one, and the horizon pleased him. He picked the dagger back up and continued carving the design. Wandering leaves for the border, with new budded flowers amid dewdrops and thorns, he decided. Definitely thorns.

He had finished the border along the end of the table before he could hear his camp coming to life in brisk, precise movements and knew the buyers and their wagons had made the perimeter before the lieutenant officially announced them. He brushed the sawdust and curls off the surface, pleased with his skill.

"Bring them to me, of course, once you've offered them water for cleansing and wine for libation."

Another sketched salute and his man disappeared.

Within moments, the Galdarkan company stood in his pavilion and he rose to greet them, Narskap coming to life and striding quietly across the space to flank him. He knew Abayan Diort, although he'd always met with emissaries before, but the tall, mercenary Galdarkan looked unmistakable, particularly with the ranking tattoo he wore on his cheekbone. The officers' insignia started quietly, and then grew with each commission and Diort's looked as masterful and complicated as any he'd ever seen. Although the Galdarkans would never claim the title of emperor as their Magi lords once had, there could be no doubt of Abayan's rising as high as any could. He wore field gear, not to impress, but because he anticipated trouble on any road, and he wished to be prepared for it. He looked comfortable in the cavalry armor, and Quendius thought he could understand the Galdarkan about as well as anyone could, without wearing Diort's skin.

He put a hand up, palm out, and Abayan did the same. The mercenary then signaled the two men flanking him to stand down and faced him again. "Thank you for courtesies of the road."

"I couldn't do less. You've never come to buy from me in person before."

"You've not requested my presence before. My purser was always sufficient." Abayan stripped off his riding gloves, tucking them into his belt. His baldric held a good sword and two throwing knives, for Quendius had not stipulated disarming his buyer, a subtle point he hoped to make.

"There has always been a fiction between us, as to whom the buyer was. I see no point in continuing the pretense. I have at my disposal, besides the usual lot you order, a weapon that only you can use, and so it becomes necessary to deal with you personally."

The red-gold eyebrows of the Galdarkan rose up, and his dark jade eyes seemed to reflect a smoldering irritation. "A weapon fits any hand, within reason."

"Not this one." Quendius seated himself and leaned indolently back in his chair. "It is, if you will, God-ridden."

Abayan Diort quirked his head at that, something unreadable replacing the irritation in his eyes as he stared down at Quendius.

"Yes," answered Quendius to the unspoken question. "It can be, and has been, done."

"You ask for a leap of faith, even from a descendant of guardians from a time when magic ruled on Kerith. The Gods deny us. You have always said you spoke with Gods, now you bind Their Word to a weapon? To what end?"

"You ask to what end? To conquer. Is there any other destiny with war?"

"What of your Accords?"

Quendius dismissed both question and agreements with a wave of his hand.

"Let me see it."

Narskap stirred. "Never draw a weapon you do not plan to use."

Abayan Diort stared him down, or tried to. The thin, hardened Vaelinar remained unmoved, and it was Diort who gave way, flicking his glance back to Quendius.

"Oh, I intend a Demonstration. Tell your men to prepare for battle." Quendius pushed his chair back, standing again, with a sharp whistle that sent booted feet running past the tent. "We've been surrounded."

Abayan's hands went to his baldric with a curse, pulling his sword. Narskap leaped over the table, catching his arms before he could draw, and Quendius said coldly, "Too ready to be turned upon, I think." He circled and looked down upon both Narskap and Diort, the wiry Vaelinar's strength more than a match for the husky, well-muscled mercenary. "I said a Demonstration, not a thugging. When you rode in here, a circle closed about us, an enemy sure that we are unaware of their ambush." He smiled thinly. "They are about to find out what we are made of, once again." He let out a splitting whistle and strode out of the pavilion. Narskap released Diort to follow upon his heels, the mercenary scowling and muttering low words.

The lieutenant gave Quendius the reins to his war steed. Narskap gathered up his own mount; after a moment's hesitation, Diort followed. The low hills and rounded knolls about them boiled with the movement of Bolger clans closing in on the camp. Bold in movement, unafraid, sure that they had their prey outnumbered. Quendius pointed a chin toward them. "Even without what I offer you, we have them, and they don't know it yet. I will take no prisoners, but I will take as mercenary those who give themselves up. Ride after Narskap. I don't offer you the sword he carries, but the war hammer at his waist. You won't see him draw that, for it bonds to its carrier. The sword is his. The hammer can be yours."

"Stay behind Narskap if you wish to be safe. Join me, when you wish to fight." With that, Quendius pivoted his steed and rode up the slope with a yelping yell of challenge, and Bolgers charged to meet him, infantry on foot and cavalry atop tough little mountain horses the size of ponies, with archers staying up on the rounded knolls. A hail of arrows rained down, beating upon the shield walls, and the archers fell back. Narskap put his hand back to the hilt of the greatsword and drew it, with a high keening sound of stone upon steel as though the sheath sharpened it even as it relinquished it. It took a moment for Diort to realize the greatsword made the sound itself and that it vibrated within Narskap's hard hold upon it. He threw himself after the swordsman, his horse's ears pinned back at the high-pitched howling of the blade.

The Bolgers beat drums, their heavy vibrations echoing through the knolls like low thunder and voicing commands to their ragged army. He'd fought Bolgers before, small ragged units and unruly bands of raiders, although the years of Bolger warfare had faded into history behind them. Yet this group of clans seemed disciplined and eager. They wheeled to flank them, even as a contingent charged down the throat of the hillside at the weaponmaster's troops. The shield wall moved up and replaced itself. The greatsword's high yowl tore through the sound of the drums as if it was merely a backdrop to it, and Diort watched as Narskap bore down on the first wave of cavalry coming his way, blade glinting in his hand.

The clans bellowed a guttural word. "Blood, blood, BLOOD!" with each drumbeat. It was the sword which answered.

It seemed to jump out, for the throat, the chest, the thigh, the arm, crimson spurting each time it struck, flesh opening straight to the bone and beyond, with the howling of the death a panicked accompaniment. It swung in Narskap's hand of its own volition and speed, and every Bolger that fell under it, fell with first a look of shock, then of absolute horror as the blade drank of its victim. It never wearied in Narskap's grasp. Never faltered. Never missed a hit, though the Bolgers began to slew away from it, swerving about with sharp, barking cries. Blood ran down its channel in rivers, and never touched Narskap's forearm as the hilt itself seemed to be a maw of darkness that eagerly gulped every crimson drop.

Diort's horse shied from the bodies, horses and Bolgers, tumbling in

Narskap's wake, a wake that began to open wider and wider as the clansmen fought each other to get out of Narskap's path. As his horse jumped the dead, Abayan looked down into leathery brown faces going pale, mouths stretched in cries of agony and fear, eyes losing their light in abject horror. The sword took more than life and blood. As they reached the top of the knolls, Narskap pulled his war steed up by sheer force, turning about in a tight circle, greatsword in his hand.

It howled. Archers ran in terror. The lines of the Bolgers broke, each running for himself, the fight forgotten. Narskap tried to lower his arm, but could not, and he put heel to his horse and headed downward, into the thick of the clans punching and kicking their way in retreat, and the sword went after them, like a whip eager for the lashing, and Bolgers fell, screaming.

Diort did not follow. He cuffed his war-trained mount to a halt, bile in his throat. War maneuvers were one thing. A slaughter was another. Yet he couldn't deny to himself the impression of the sheer inability of a foe to stand before the blade. Not forgetting that Narskap rode and fought like a master, the sword itself had a mind and drive of its own. The Bolgers recognized it.

If this could be done by the Strangers, the God-speakers, then he had to give blessing none such had been loosed on them before. Did they know the difference between Gods and Demons on Kerith? He thought not. If a God rode that sword, it was a God of the greatest darkness, of the swallowing of souls. For this, if no other reason, he had to own the war hammer.

Quendius joined him after a few moments, directing his troops who outrode the fleeing Bolgers and were cutting off retreat.

"How much for the hammer?"

"The price I quoted you includes the hammer, along with the other armament."

Abayan tore his attention away from the fray below. He had been prepared to pay all that he could raise, and he didn't doubt that Quendius knew that. He considered the weaponmaker. Nothing between them would come freely, and both knew it.

Quendius remarked, "The additional price I ask is an intangible," in answer to the unspoken.

"I have no firstborn."

Quendius chuckled. "Alliance. I want alliance."

"Against . . ."

"Whomever our enemies may be or become."

"A broad term."

"The world," Quendius told him, "is broad."

"I see." He paused as Narskap finally, wearily, managed to sheathe the greatsword and rode up to the knoll top. Narskap said nothing. Blood splattered his trousers, his vest, his face, but not a drop stained his sword arm. Not a drop within reach of the blade had been passed by. It had drunk deeply of each and every offering.

"I would be a fool to turn you down," Abayan Diort told Quendius.

"The Gods did not birth either of us to be fools," Quendius returned. He held out his arm, and the two gripped each other's forearms strongly.

Narskap passed the war hammer over, and Abayan Diort took it. He could feel a deep vibration inside the wood, he could sense rather than hear its own voice, and he knew a greater fear than he had ever known in his life. He did not show it.

He would be a greater fool if he did.

Chapter Thirty-Eight

NUTMEG HIKED UP the hem of her skirt so she could run faster, skimming the edges of the crowd. "Hurry! I want to see them coming in the gates!"

A basket of flyers newly printed and hailing the opening of Tolby's hard work thumped at her hip as Rivergrace did her best to keep up. A few of the crisp papers took flight on their own from the basket, to drift among the pushing crowd of people eager to see the entrance of the Warrior Queen and her entourage. Nutmeg found a place near the front, where even in her proud Dweller shortness, she could see, and Rivergrace stayed at her heels. Both of them handed out flyers as they'd promised, and then a commotion at the gates made everyone's eyes turn, and a sigh of anticipation ran through the gathered crowd.

A horn sounded through the morning with a challenge and flourish. The entourage entered, not at a ceremonial walk, but a controlled gallop, a charge of arched necks, flying manes and tails, and hooves striking the hard-packed dirt road, as tashya horses in regalia, their riders splendid in dark, rich clothing, hooded vantanes on one wrist and white leather reins in the other hand, took the city. Behind them rode packmasters with braces of dogs, milling about with happy barks and brays, their brown and black and tan and chestnut coats shining with health and vigor. The hounds ignored the crowds, tongues lolling. Huntsmen rode after, resplendent in brocade and silk, eyes and hair flashing like jewels, Vaelinars with skins of cream and faint copper, a soft gray here and there, and sometimes a bronze given by birth and not sunning. Just as Rivergrace caught her breath, the honor guard trotted in, weapons sparkling in their sheaths like lightning called down from the skies, their horses snorting and sharp hooves striking small pebbles from the dirt. Behind them, at a more sedate place, rode Sevryn and a handful of others. Unlike the Vaelinars before, this handful observed the crowd, carefully, closely, gazes sweeping and then watching a personage or two with a penetrating stare before moving on. When his eyes found her, he reined his horse back a bit, pivoting it in a tight circle, so he might not ride past without acknowledging her. Aderro, he'd called her, Little One, a word she'd forgotten and not remembered till he had said it. Aderro.

He raised a soft-gloved hand in greeting.

A warmth rose in her cheeks, and she put a hand up to hide it. A flyer flew from her fingers of its own volition, straight at him, and he caught it, grinning, before wheeling his horse about and rejoining the honor guard. They swept past, as the queen and her brother came into view.

She wore cobalt blues, her gown accented with gilt ribbons brilliantly swirling about her, her hair held back from her brow by a simple diadem, her right hand upon a bannered lance carried in her stirrup. She looked incredibly young and enchanting, and Rivergrace felt a sting at the corner of her eye as she passed, a tear of awe. Her brother rode at her elbow, just a horse's stride behind, in dark greens and chestnuts, his horse's coat blazed in red gold, and he carried a great bow across his back, with sword in hand. Nutmeg made an inaudible sound of wonder. In a thunder of hooves, they galloped past, and Rivergrace managed to let her breath out.

Someone behind her grumbled, "Just what the city needs, more cursed elves."

"At least they bring their coin purses with them."

Nutmeg turned away before the last of the entourage on horseback and carriage came through, catching up flyers from the basket and thrusting them everywhere in the crowd, promising them fine summer wines and the greatest cider they had ever tasted. Rivergrace trailed after, people often refusing a paper, and one or two muttering, "Vaelinars street hawking? I doubt it." A woman shoved past, hissing, "Hide those eyes!" Rivergrace spun about in momentary confusion as the crowd began to disperse.

She stumbled on the hem of her skirt and righted herself, only to see a man strut off, smirking, and realized she'd been tripped. She clutched the handle of the basket until the woven reed and stem bit into the palm of her hand. Nutmeg, far ahead of her, had seen and heard nothing or she would have pitched herself into the fray, her small but determined defender. Rivergrace smiled at that, and shrugged off the scorn, hurrying after her sister. Dust curled from the side lanes as the heat of the day and many feet shuffling through it carried it aloft like soft, brown smoke.

Tolby stood in rolled-up sleeves, immersed in work, when they returned and waved his hand. "Run along, go. Your ma is waiting for you."

Excitedly, Nutmeg found a straw hat and tied the ribbon about her chin. "They were so handsome, all of them," she chattered. "Not even at the Spring fairs have I seen anything like it! And the queen. Did you see how she rode? I bet she could use that lance, too."

"Do you think they love her?"

"Of course they do!" Nutmeg fussed with her apron, and then twirled Grace about to tie hers. "Why wouldn't they?"

"People grumble on the street."

"Do they?" Nutmeg peered up at her from her elbow. "I never noticed." She tugged the apron tighter and retied it. "I think you're losing weight. Come on, we might have time to buy some sugared bread!"

Even long-legged Grace had small hope of staying even with Nutmeg when she was in pursuit of hot fried bread on a stick, dotted with crystallized sugar gems. Head above most of the crowds, she spotted Walther, messenger bag flopping about his baggy pants, with a piece of bread on a stick, melting away through the people. He saw her and gave a toothsome grin and wave.

Nutmeg offered her a sticky bit, which she nibbled at, but it did not strike her fancy as it did her sister's. They finished it off just before reaching the shop. Nothing untoward happened in the long hot afternoon although Rivergrace, busy sewing in the far back where she would be undisturbed, thought she could hear people coming in and out, an unusual bustle of interest. She listened in case Sevryn Dardanon might make another appearance, but heard no voices she recognized, and finally bent her attention to her stitching—small, neat, and quick. Lily came back to check on her twice, expression bemused and mind preoccupied. Grace finished up and set the jacket aside, laying it out neatly as Lily came in a last time, saying, "You can go home, Grace, I've nothing left for you, but Nutmeg is still working."

"That's fine. Can I go do laundry?" Nutmeg thought of laundry as punishment, but she enjoyed it, cleansing away the toil and worry of yesterdays as she did it. The day had plenty of sun left for drying, and the clothes would snap in the wind and billow about, smelling of the flower tinctures she put in the rinse water.

Lily hugged her. "Would you mind trying this chemise? I've a new client trying to replace it, and I'm working on the order, but it seems to me this wine stain should come out. I can please her with both."

She took it and nodded, running the fine garment through her hands. "I think I can get it clean." After a moment, with a slight tinge of worry, she added, "Don't let Nutmeg walk home alone late."

"Oh, I won't. She's likely to black someone's eye and have the Town Guard called on us if there's any trouble." They both laughed, and Lily added, "Send Keldan after the two of us, when the lamps are being lit."

"I will!"

She was up to her elbows in water, cold and soaped lightly, for she disliked soiling the water more than she had to, when the shout of angry voices reached her, echoing through the yard, Tolby's voice in a stern growl. She followed it to the storeroom.

"Mortgaged? Paperwork? Get out of here. I rebuilt every keg in here with my bare hands, me and my sons did. Everything of any good had been stripped out of here, sold or stolen before then."

"Nonetheless," said the barrel-waisted Kernan standing opposite Tolby, his thumbs tucked in his vest pockets, "the manager mortgaged what little property remained in this establishment, and now the monies are due. The monies or the kegs and vats."

Garner loomed at his father's shoulder. "A lot of good kegs would do a moneylender. Unless you've a mind to try the business?"

"True, but resale would settle the debt. I know you're trying to make a start here, Farbranch, but 'twill go badly with you if word gets around your credit is no good and you don't stand by your paper."

"It's not our paper!" Keldan started to bounce beside his father and brother, and both caught him by the elbow. He shook his thickly curled head as they pushed him behind them.

Tolby rolled his shoulders and gazed up at the roof. His tone calmed. "And if I pay this . . . debt . . . what happens then? Another one of you shows up next week with a new bundle of papers?"

The Kernan cleared his throat. "You don't know me, Master Tolby, but I'm not one for kicking a man when he's down. This clears it all."

"Your word on that?"

The Kernan nodded as he pulled his vest into place. "My word, sir, and if it's as good as the word of a Farbranch, we should both be pleased. May this be the last of your good money after bad," he said, offering his hand to Tolby. "The summer season is a thirsty one and you should begin to prosper." He waited.

Tolby wiped his hands clean. "Let's hope the summer stays hot and dry, and our customers thirsty." But he did not shake the proffered hand. "I suggest, m'lord, that you get off my property before I set my sons on you."

Purple veins blossomed in the other's expression. "Master Tolby, surely you don't deny the debt—"

"I do indeed. Come back when you've proper copies of these so-called papers or when you want a drink of good cider or never come back." Tolby folded his arms over his chest, chin out, looking up at the Kernan's face, but seeming to be a good deal taller.

The man turned abruptly with a blustery noise, and darted through the doorway.

"Wait'll Mom hears."

"She'll not hear this from any of you." Tolby swung about, his still angry eyes resting on all of them. "That understood?"

"Aye, Da, but what if you owe? This'll drag down all we've done. We'll have to quit."

Tolby's hand shot out, grabbing Keldan by the scruff of the neck. "I won't be hearin' words like that again from you, or any of my children. Understand?"

Keldan hung his head, nodding. Rivergrace retreated quickly back into the yard, the sun, and the need of clothes to be rinsed and hung out in the light and the air.

Unbidden, she thought of the tall man, the one who seemed to be of elven blood yet not, with still, gray eyes whose presence unsettled her even when he was no longer near. She threw herself into her chores, not wanting to think anymore.

Tolby came out to find her wet to the elbow once more, singing softly to herself as she worked. Stains and odors disappeared under the sure workings of her hands, water rinsing the garments until they seemed brand new. He sat down on a stump and tapped the bowl of his pipe. He didn't speak to her till a cloud of smoke wreathed his head, the aroma smelling of cherrysweet and apple spice. He clamped the stem in his teeth as she snapped the chemise in the air and laid it over the line to dry. The stain had come out, as she'd thought it would.

He spied the buckets sitting by the old well. "Grace. What are those buckets doing there?"

She spread her skirts, putting herself between the well and Tolby. She tried to think of what it was she could say.

"Well?"

"I use the well for wash water, Da. The birds and animals drink from it. I think it's clean. I dredged it out."

"You think." He did not stand, but his words came growled about the pipe stem. "Rivergrace, it's not something you can know."

"You taught me. Good water grows good things." She spread her hand at her little side garden, where flowers had begun to bloom, and herbs fringed the borders, a garden she used for the laundry only, for cleaning and scenting.

"Well was boarded for a reason."

"Yes, sir. Seasons come and go, and sometimes things change."

He stood. A puff of smoke obscured his expression briefly. "I'll get a well digger in here. They'll know why it was boarded, and if it's clean now. Meantime . . ."

"No more buckets?"

"No more. It's a fair walk to the other water, have Keldan draw for you. He needs the exercise."

"Aye, sir." She watched him walk away, shoulders bowed in thought. The clothes billowed at her elbow, fresh and pure-smelling in the sunlight.

Chapter Thirty-Nine

"BREGAN OXFORT WANTS an audience," Tiiva said, shuffling through papers scattered upon her lap desk, and she tilted her face up toward Lariel, waiting for a response.

"Private or in general conference?"

Tiiva frowned slightly as she reviewed the letter again, more closely, as if trying to decipher hidden meanings within the spare lines. "He doesn't state, although given his status, I should imagine he expects a private audience."

Lariel stood at a window, watching the streets below, her thoughts hidden as if she wore one of the veils affected by those outside their holdings. The glass showed its primitive workmanship, slightly warping the view, and aging with a faint amber tint, but most architecture in the Kerith lands still merely used shutters that swung to an open windowsill, to be closed at night. The glass attempted to reach a higher level of civilization. Below, she could see the flow of people upon the streets, the Vaelinar-blooded distinct by virtue of their slenderness and height, and the veils they wore, long flowing veils on the women, and eye-shielding kerchiefs on the men, bandannas over the head, knotted at the back of the head or neck. The fashion had begun decades ago, merely a fad she'd thought, but now it seemed decorum in the city. When had she missed this? Was it both a flaunting of the blood and a hiding of it? A hiding of the eyes which denoted who carried the magic within them and who did not?

Already weary of the thought of meetings, she realized Tiiva waited for an answer, and carefully meted out her reply, knowing she could not slight the merchant prince. "I don't care to treat with him privately, but I will give him time to tell me what is on his mind. Negotiations of any kind, however, will be done at the general Conference."

"Fair enough." Tiiva bent over paper, and her pen scratched faintly as she answered the trader's request. "That will fill your morning tomorrow, before luncheon, and in the afternoon, there are tradespeople, crafters, and the like hoping to see you."

"Of course."

"Ferstanthe sends greetings and will arrive on the morrow, as will ild Istlanthir."

"Is Tranta coming?"

"I'm told he's recovered somewhat, and yes, he will be here although he may tire quickly."

Lariel's attention flicked back to the window and its view. "He is lucky to be alive."

"No one knows it more than he. He doesn't remember the fall, but he dreams of falling, a dichotomy which he holds may give him more answers someday."

"What about Bistane?"

"Arriving this eve. And the ild Fallyn are here somewhere already, I'm told."

Lariel nodded. "All right, then." She drew herself up as if bracing herself. "Thank you, Tiiva, and you're dismissed."

She rose gracefully, lap desk in her hands as she gave a deep curtsy and left, a guardsman closing the door behind her. Lariel twitched a curtain from the window in irritation. A dried aromatic leaf drifted down from the hem as she did, and fell to the floor at her toes. Neither Jeredon nor Sevryn were about or could be found, and she didn't like that at all, though she knew she could hardly be out and about without drawing attention. She disliked Conferences and treaties with a passion. It was a dance without music or passion, a coldly stepped intricacy of intrigue and displomacy and deceit. Circumstances forced her to attend this summer, when she would rather have postponed it, but she no longer dared delay. Sevryn required seasoning as her Hand, and she now had the pressing need to track the welfare of the Andredia, and she had to find a way to look east as well, to see what attracted the ild Fallyn's attention.

She could not discount the old trick of looking in the opposite direction. To look to the west, however, would chill her blood. The Raymy lay to the west, across the seas and held at bay by the Jewel of Tomarq. They were shielded, were they not? Yet that very harbor's vulnerability was why the Conferences had usually been held in Calcort. Just in case, as it were.

The heavy rustle and sweep of skirts told her Tiiva returned, rather more quickly than expected. Lariel glanced over her shoulder.

"Trader Oxfort is without. He asks if you can see him now and spare both of you setting an appointment later?"

"Fine. Send him in, then." Neither dressed regally nor veiled as seemed to be the mandatory custom now, Lariel sat down at the small dark-red burnished table and waited. The young fox had undoubtedly planned to hit her early with his demands.

Bregan Oxfort came in, an afternoon sun hat in his right hand, the white straw brim curled slightly as if bent to the man's tension. By any standards, the trader was a handsome, striking man, even with the weakness in the one leg, braced by a metal support that showed Vaelinarran craftsmanship in all its clever forging. It enveloped his leg from ankle to mid-thigh, hinged and caged over the knee. He used a cane on the left side for strength and balance, but other than a slight limp, the weakness that had been there last time she'd talked with him seemed far less. She had no doubt the cane was as much an affectation and for attention as aid. Even the mahogany color of the tainted skin on his right side did not deter from his looks, but then, the hue appeared among the Vaelinars naturally from time to time. Ironic that among the Vaelinars he detested, he would have been accepted regardless of skin color. Her own father had had a huntsman of just such a rich mahogany tone. Oxfort bowed. "My lady queen."

"Trader Oxfort." With a smile, she inclined her head to his bow. "Not your queen, of course. Be seated and be welcome."

"Thank you for seeing me on such short notice. I promise I won't be long."

"No great petition to put aside the Ways?"

He smiled wryly. "Would you entertain such a petition if I produced it?"

"Did I any other time?"

"Of course not." Bregan rested his cane on the tabletop between them. "I do wish to discuss the Ways with you, however, in particular the Ferryman."

Unsurprised, Lariel tilted her head slightly, waiting.

"I am not asking that he be abolished. As I mature, I have developed an appreciation for his abilities. A ferry under his guidance has never failed upon a river known for taking many a boat, with its crew and cargo, to their deaths." Bregan flicked a finger in the air, a mild homage.

"I'm glad you see his value."

"Reluctantly, yes. However." The trader paused, as if counting his thoughts. "What I ask is not for myself. My family has made its fortune and continues to do so. What I ask for is a tiered fee system for traders. We have many young people out on the roads now as our provinces grow. Their profit margin is narrow, and ofttimes they have every spare coin they can raise sunk into their caravans. I ask that the medallions we place on our caravans, by which the Ferryman determines his toll, be modified to reflect this, rather than only the size of the caravan itself."

His request interested her, for its selflessness if no other reason. "And your guild would monitor these medallions and newborn traders?"

"Of a surety."

"We would have access to your records if necessary?"

"As always." Bregan smiled into her examining gaze.

Lariel pondered his words before responding. "The Ferryman is not of my House, as you know, so I will have to bring this before the Conference. However, it seems a fair request, and you can consider my recommendation to be given."

The trader smiled slowly. "That is all I can ask." He pulled his cane back toward him and stood, leaning on it slightly. "I promised it would be brief."

"For a trader, remarkably so." She winked at him, standing herself. "I'll send word to you as soon as it is discussed. It may not pass this season, but I will do what I can to see it's justly considered."

"My thanks, my lady queen." With a bow, he let himself out, his cane tapping on the flooring, his walk steadier to hear than it looked.

A dangerous man still, she thought. Any infirmity there seemed more postured now than real. She would have to remember that. He'd been one of the greatest swordsmen in the provinces till his accident. Jeredon and Sevryn told her he'd switched hands, and his prowess had returned, and a left-handed swordsman was even harder to face than a right-handed one. Yes, Bregan Oxfort was a good deal more dangerous than he seemed physically. She'd no doubt there'd been a slender but deadly blade sheathed within his cane, as well. Had he considered using it? She put that thought aside. He'd laid it between them as if surrendering a weapon without actually doing so. No, she was not his target. Yet.

Garner stood with Rivergrace and Nutmeg, watching the well digger and his assistant. The digger stood nearly as wide as he was tall, a bald-pated Dweller with massive forearms; the Bolger assistant in his shadow held a long pole over his shoulder that balanced two buckets. The digger scratched a bushy eyebrow of far more hair than the top of his head had surely ever held. "I have this well in my recollections," he stated slowly. "But let's be testin' the water first, to see if it's good. Been some problems about, though few and far between, thank th' Goddess of earthborn waters."

Garner's face twitched as if holding something back, and he squeezed the hand he had on Rivergrace's wrist. Nutmeg leaned over to look into the well's depths, sun gleaming bright coppery highlights off her abundant hair as the digger undid a small cage from his belt. The digger hefted it in the air for them to see. "This here's a tufted songbird. We use 'em in the mines for bad air. Their bodies are delicate, like, and they know first of everyone if something poison is sneaking into the air, fumes and th' like. In the well she goes."

The little songbird flittered on the perch of her reed cage, fluffing up her yellow-and-white feathers. Her song had merged with the wild birds about, and Grace hadn't heard it at first. She could hear her now, though, distinctive and musical.

"It won't kill her, will it?"

"My birdie? Nae, lass, I've had her for many a year, as th' life of songbirds go." His seamed face deepened in a smile for her.

"Good, Master Fancher," Garner told him. "Hurt the bird and Rivergrace will have both our hides."

The digger let out a rumbling chuckle. "As long as she sings, th' air down there is pure; rock basin of the well and stuff will not be leakin'." He went to his knees and tied a long rope tether to the cage and lowered it down, slowly, gently, the cage swinging at the tether's end. The songbird whistled and sang merrily, voice getting thinner and thinner and then echoing a bit, but never failing. He left her down there for long moments till, with a satisfied grunt, he began to haul the cage back up, never letting the tether sway too much so that the reed imprisonment would not bounce off the rock sides. Once out, he put a finger through the reed bars, scratched the little bird's chest, and set her home on the ground in a patch of shade.

"That's all there is to it?"

"Nae, nae, much more to it." He jabbed a thumb at the Bolger. "Put a bucket of biter fish down, Smik."

The Bolger set down his pole, unhooked a bucket, and brought out a container riddled with holes and did much the same as his boss had with the songbird, lowering the container down till it splashed into the deep water below.

"Now, we wait. Let the fish swim about a bit in their jar." He squatted down as did Smik, both of them listening as if they could actually hear the movement of tiny fish way below.

"If they live, then our well's good?"

"Probably. The proof of th' pudding, though, is if it's drinkable, isn't it?"

"Who do you have for that?" Garner looked extremely interested.

"I try it on my farm animals."

"Goats can eat or drink cursed near anything."

The digger laughed. "Ain't that the truth!" Fancher scratched his other bushy eyebrow. "I use another critter or two, watch its health."

"Ever been wrong?"

"Never, but there's allus a first time, eh?" He winked broadly at Garner. " 'Course, th' easy part about testing for bad water is, if th' client drinks it, he dies and there's nae one about t' complain, see?"

Nutmeg gasped, and Garner said, "Meggie, he's pulling your leg. Any well digger who brought up bad water would be hog-tied and put out in the desert to dry."

"So's to speak." The digger winked broadly at Garner again, and beckoned for his helper to haul up the fish. The container came up leaking everywhere, before it was set back in its own bucket of water, and they opened the lid to see tiny silver fish darting back and forth in apparent good health and excitement.

"Now I'll be drawin' a bucket to take back and test, and I'll be lookin' through my recollections about this particular well." The digger thumped Garner on the back. "Tell th' master Farbranch you'll be hearing from me in a day or two."

"Good." The three of them watched the stout man and his thin, leathery Bolger helper leave, as he carried his songbird with him, and her cheery melody trailed after.

"Makes you wonder why the well was boarded up," Nutmeg said.

"No telling yet." Garner steered them both about-face. "Work to do, here and in the shop."

Two noses wrinkled. "Worse than Da or Mom," they grumbled as their brother marched them off, Grace wondering just what the well digger had "in his recollections" to find.

At the shop, Grace had just finished sweeping out for Adeena who complained constantly about the dust heat-driven winds brought into the city every other day or so, when a small crowd strolled down the lane, pausing at the storefront. The veiled ones stopped to eye her.

"You're the one," the tallest said softly. "You're a seamstress here?" Every word made the thin veil flutter and billow, a prison of the most exotic kind, and she fought not to stare.

Rivergrace dipped a curtsy, trying not to stumble at the unaccustomed maneuver. "I work here, yes. Please come in, miladies."

They glided in, the glove-soft leather of their shoes making but a whisper as they moved, their finely woven dresses accenting their willowy frames. Rivergrace put her broom aside, embarrassed. "I'll bring Mistress Lily out for you." She stopped as a hand caught her sleeve.

"Wait a moment."

Caught, she halted in place.

"Do you model the gowns? I hear the seamstress is excellent, but a Dweller."

"I have modeled for her, yes. And she has forms, miladies."

A second Vaelinar said, in a faintly aggrieved voice, "With the Warrior Queen here this season, there will be more meetings, dances, and events than ever, and nearly every seamstress in the city is booked. I cannot abide an ill-fitting gown, and you—" Rivergrace could plainly see her veiled eyes assess her from head to toe, "look as if you would do."

Bells chimed a bit impatiently as the other gestured. "What my companion is trying to convey is the press of time, even for the most excellent of tailors and seamstresses."

"I see." Rivergrace tried not to stretch her arm uneasily as her sleeve was released. "I think, miladies, that Mistress Lily can put all your fears to ease."

"Will she work with fabric not her own?"

"She will, and has. Please let me get her." Rivergrace dipped another curtsy and dashed into the back workroom before being detained again. Lily had gotten to her feet, clearly having heard every word, and stood waiting for her. She said nothing but hugged Grace tightly before going out to greet the potential clients. They talked for long moments before she and Nutmeg could hear melodious laughs, and then promises for business, and Lily returned, her cheeks flushed. "We'll be busy," she announced firmly.

Nutmeg let out a cheer, but Rivergrace could only stare after the women with a vague feeling of unrest.

The well digger was waiting for them as dusk draped cooling shadows all about Calcort on their way home from the shop. He'd left his assistant and bird at home, and stood as he and Tolby shared a pipe in the yard. The well seemed to draw the moon down inside it, reflecting it back as a soft, wavering eye peering from far below as Grace looked into it when she sat by its edge.

"It's bad," Nutmeg blurted out, as she saw the digger.

"Nae, lass, nae. I was just relating it to Master Tolby here. Oddest case of a well closing in all my history, and I wondered how I'd forgotten it, but I had, till I went looking through my records." The digger waved his pipe at her. "Not a drop of bad water in it, far as I be knowin'. The priestess had us board it up."

Tolby and Lily had never been much for priests and priestesses, although here in Calcort every few lanes seemed to have a small building with one or two living there. The religion they'd raised all the children in had been one of hard work and love for one another and all things in their keeping. If there had been any shrine at all to the Gods, it had been the orchards themselves. Grace stared mildly at Fancher in vague confusion.

"Seems the guardian of Tylivar had a dream one night that the Goddess came to her and said the well should be closed till she had need of it again."

"This well?"

"Aye. Tylivar sent a vision of this particular well to th' priestess."

Tolby blew out a smoke ring. "And only this one? No others in the city? Any reasoning?"

"Aye, no, and none given. The way of Gods and Goddesses aren't for the likes of us to know since the Magi let them down, although I hear the veiled lot talks to 'em fine. What Vaelinars and our Gods tolerate in each other, I cannot begin t'say."

"That means we can't leave it open?" Grace looked at the well in dismay, hating the thought of boarding it away again, and plotting to keep the boards with gaps, so at least the little living things that depended on it could reach it still.

"Frankly," said Fancher. "That guardian has passed away long since, and was more than slightly addled when she did go. I doubt anyone around here gives a whoop about your well now. Leave it open. It tastes like sweet water and I've found nothing wrong with it. I'm thinkin' if the Goddess wants it closed again, she'll be tellin' you soon enough. Till then." He shrugged. "Good water is always a blessing."

A few puffs of smoke wafted between them while Tolby thought, before looking at Rivergrace's beseeching face, and saying, "I'll stand on your judgment, then, master, and well met." Tolby shook his hand, a coin passing between them, and the two walked off across the grounds, as Tolby showed him what he'd done to the ill-managed and all but abandoned place.

Nutmeg waited till they were out of earshot. "Think we dare?"

"It hasn't poisoned me. I've been dabbling in it for a few weeks now."

"But, Grace, you're—" Her sister stopped in mid-sentence, her face stricken, and she looked as if she'd just bit her tongue.

Rivergrace glanced at her before supplying the word. "Different?"

"I can't help it. You are."

"I know," she said miserably. "More than ever, I know."

Nutmeg plopped down on the ground beside her. She knocked a pebble into the well, and a *click-click-splash* followed. "I hate the idea of you being veiled all the time."

"But you wanted to make the veils."

"That's afore I found out everyone wears 'em or they get hated for not wearing them." Nutmeg leaned her head on Rivergrace's shoulder.

"It's not so bad. And, look, we had those ladies come in tonight, just because they heard I worked with Lily."

"Because they're different, too."

But, they weren't different in the way she was, Rivergrace thought. They had been full-blooded Vaelinars, with court and House connections, taller and more graceful than she could ever hope to be, with stunning eyes that spoke of the magic they carried within them. She wasn't one of them any more than she was a Dweller. "You think so?"

"I think," Nutmeg said confidently, "you're my sister, I found you, and no one is ever going to take that away from us."

That made her smile. They leaned on each other for a long while, sitting by the edge of the well and watching the moon and stars drift across its still waters while the heat of the day slowly faded away.

Chapter Forty

EARLY DAWN BRIGHTENED the sky with red, fiery streaks. *Red sky in the morning, sailor and farmer take warning*, he thought. Abayan Diort reined to a halt, standing in his stirrups, and raised his hand in a gesture for the troops to wait. Burning torches dotted the stone walls of the city before them, a fortress of rigid determination and solitude, a city where his entreaties had been turned aside again and again. The time for talk was over. He looked at the stone. Built centuries ago and well kept, he considered the death toll to get through it. By sheer numbers, they would eventually overwhelm. Warfare, Galdarkan against Galdarkan, was not what he wished, but they had given him little choice by not allying with him when he'd brought the offer.

The war hammer hung from his baldric, its weight on his hip. A yearning called from it to him, to be swung in his hands, to be freed, a call that, however faint, never left him, and one that he'd never yielded to before. Abayan swung down from his mount, approached the flat plain before the stone walls, and looked up. The wall had a stone foot to it, under the dirt, a foundation laid down by old roads and workings. Overhead, he could see archers readying their bows. He put his hand on the hammer and drew it. They waited, unsure of loosing their arrows, for he stood barely within their range and was no threat to them yet, not with a hammer, a melee weapon. They had anticipated a siege, and had not worried, for they'd stores and water aplenty behind their heavy walls. His entreaty of alliance they sneered at, and had for years, and the new one yesterday was nothing new to them. Abayan clenched his teeth. He'd come to the end of his vaunted patience.

The hammer hummed in his grip. If he listened, he might even hear a guttural snatch or two in its deep whisper as he tightened his fingers about it and found a comfortable hold. God-ridden, they'd said. No, it was a Demon and he feared he already knew Its name.

"At my command," he told his lieutenant. His aide nodded, cold eyes watching him.

Abayan spread his feet slightly, standing firmly on the rock base of the valley. He would put fear in their eyes and hearts, fear of what he would do to their bodies with his weapon, fear of the pounding hit of the massive hammer. In one fluid strike, he hefted the hammer over his head and then pounded its head on the ground in front of him to wake its power. *Rakka*. It hit with the ringing of stone on stone, belling deeply, tolling out its strength. He felt the ground tremble under him in answer, and the trembling grew to a shaking that rocked him back on his heels as the very earth roared to its foundations and back again. The ground began to split apart under the hammer's head. He stared down at it, watching the stone open, a crack that ran toward the city, widening, fracturing off, a spidery crack that grew broader and blacker in the blink of an eye. It hit the city walls, and there was a moment of nothingness.

Pressure beat against his ears, a sound he felt rather than heard. Then, with an echoing *rakka*, a harsh grunting, the stone of the walls began to fracture. A slow trickle of dust and gravel started it, and then the avalanche began as the walls came tumbling down, a roar of dirt and pebbles following it, and the city's defense collapsed, one stone after another answering the call of the war hammer in a hail of debris. Screams pierced the morning air, screams of surprise and agony, and wails of dismay. Rock rained upon the dead and dying as they slipped from walls caving away underfoot, and were buried under the debris—archers, defenders, and onlookers. Screams continued as dust plumed upward like smoke, and the very foundations of the city shifted.

He lifted the hammer from the ground and gave his signal to move in.

Infantry poured from the gaps now, staggering uncertainly, their war cries stuck in their throats, yet waving their weapons with weak energy as they charged his troops. Chasms in the ground slowed both sides as they wound their way through the destruction to meet each other.

The weapon growled low at him to be struck again, and he answered it, with stone to flesh, blooding it as the enemy ran shrieking away from him. Metal bit into flesh, hammered it, mauled and pulped it, and he waded through, swinging the war hammer from right to left and back again like a scythe through wheat. No one stood before him.

He took the city in less than a candlemark, its resistance shattered by the fall of its walls. The hammer fought him as he stowed it away, its hum a guttural threat in his ears. The weaponsmith who had made it had no idea what being he'd instilled within it, but Abayan knew. This was the Demon-God Mmenonrakka, the earthshaker. He had suspected it before and now knew it as deep in his bones as the earthshaker had struck into the rock and stone. He would have to consider carefully where he would loose it again.

Abayan Diort rode through the destruction of the city. Not a stone in the wall remained where it had been placed and mortared, and behind those sundered structures, other walls showed cracks and sliding. Chimneys had fallen to the streets. The very bedrock of the city gaped open, ranging from a dark abyss which opened the town like a broken eggshell to spidery fractures cobwebbing the outskirts. The people crept out from the rubble and pressed their foreheads to the ground in abject terror as he rode by. His people, and he had crushed their defenses to bring them to him. All the words he'd spoken throughout his years had not done it. A single strike of the war hammer had.

He had never seen anything like it, nor had anyone else living.

Bright sunlight slanted through the window shutter and woke Rivergrace early. Nutmeg lay at peace, still, one arm flung out, a smile curving her mouth, her rosy cheeks a little pale with slumber. Grace slid out of bed and dressed quietly, then went outside to do a batch or two of laundry and catch the fresh morning air that drifted in over the hilly countryside to the north, before the smells of the city to the south began to overcome it. These early morning hours were hers, no one else about, and she could watch the sky awaken, although today the streaks of sunrise had already faded. Keldan and Hosmer had built a new cap and bucket pulley for the well, and she cranked up buckets of water for her tubs. Barefoot, the water splashed about her as she drew it and filled the tubs, taking care as she began to scrub and beat the clothes. She sang as she washed, the song that ran through her mind at such times, wondering if there were words to her tune, and not caring if there were or not, because the expression lay in the singing. The sun dried her almost as soon as she grew damp as the water carried away the soil and stains from the clothing, and she took pride in leaving the water almost as clean as it had been drawn from the well. She poured her tubs out near the gardens after fastening the garments out on her lines to dry and snap in the morning breeze only to find herself being watched. She dropped in an immediate curtsy.

The two Vaelinars who watched her did not wear veils, although their garments spoke of wealth. She peered up at them cautiously from her curtsy and the one whose skin looked like light, burnished copper beckoned her to her feet. She'd seen such rich color of skin among the elven but rarely. Even more rare was the bronze of gold coins, so deep it looked like gilding. She'd seen a man pass by on the Calcort streets who looked like that, drawing gazes from everyone, and ignoring them. These two had not come to ignore her, it seemed. The copper lady said, "We could not help but overhear the singing. Imagine our surprise to find such as you doing laundry."

"My deepest apologies for awakening you. I meant no offense."

"Offense? One might as well be offended by the bakers and the carters who are up at this hour as well. No, my dear, one can't be offended by honest workers even if their day seems to start a bit early. We weren't awakened, but taking in a bit of exercise when we heard you. We wondered if you were the famed laundress who magics away impossible stains." This came from the dark-haired woman behind the first, a fan in her hand, fluttering now and then as if to emphasize a word. Her soft laughter took the edge off, although her interest in Rivergrace stayed sharp. Her eyes of deepest brown had green sparks in them, but her blood seemed most notable by her ears of sharp and swept-back points, her hair tucked behind them.

Her face grew warm at the notion that anyone would speak of her. "I could hardly be famous."

The fan fluttered. "Town gossip is not to be believed, but enjoyed. Might your mother be the new seamstress we've gotten word about? We hear an old shop has new life in it, and engaging designs, and good craftsmanship now."

Rivergrace rose stiffly from her curtsy, unable to hold it any longer. "I hope so if you're speaking of Lily Farbranch, new proprietor and keyholder of the Greathouse shop. I'll get her for you—"

"No need," said the copper-hued one sharply and held up a hand to halt her. "Rumors on the street will carry us to her shop later, in good time. I have other curiosities at the moment." She swept close to Rivergrace, eying her up and down as if memorizing her in detail. "What House or Holding is yours? What Lines?"

Grace froze in her tracks. "I–I—"

"Come now. Farbranch is a Dweller name, I believe, and you're one of the Suldarran, one of us. Give me your bloodlines." The copper-hued one leaned very near, her look intense.

Grace felt her heart begin to pound, as if threatened by her, and the dark-haired one put her fan to the crook of her companion's arm as she murmured a soft word Rivergrace could not understand to draw her back. She felt her damp sleeve pushed up her arm, her thin white scar clearly visible, and she pushed her sleeve down, flustered, muttering, "Farbranch is the only name I know."

"Don't be daft, your blood history is evident. Why pretend you are a rustic when you are obviously not? Half, perhaps, not full-blooded, there is something other about you, yet . . ."

Grace took a step back, found the well's crossbars at her hip, preventing farther retreat as the other unnerved her. She wanted them to go away, but held her tongue, not wanting to rouse the others or cause trouble. The power of the Vaelinars in Calcort seemed to be like their faces, often veiled but indisputably there.

"Your mother and father. Tell me who they are." The smooth voice held an edge like a sword's blade, her visitor full of quiet menace as she cornered Rivergrace.

"She may well not know," her companion offered.

"Unfortunate, but a possibility." A hand tipped with long, elegant nails raised, traced the air before her eyes and then, almost gently, lifted a strand of her hair away from her brow, smoothing it back. She looked upon Rivergrace with a cold assessment that burned a fire through her, sending her senses reeling away, and she clung to the well to stay on her feet. "I see some of the blood in her, but . . . you may well be right. Yet another by-blow. She has the eyes but not a touch of power in her."

She felt the words around her, on the air, hot and stifling, her limbs going weak in every joint, her body struggling just to breathe, all thought fleeing.

"You're certain? What about the laundry?"

The copper-hued woman swung about, backhanding her companion across the face in a vicious slap. "Never question me again. I know what I know. Do you think it takes Talent to wash away a stain? Velk!"

The dark-haired woman put her hands to her face, smothering a noise, and then pulled a veil from her purse and dropped it about her quickly, concealing and hiding both her injury and her fear.

The interrogator traced her fingers over Rivergrace's face again, paying no heed as she gave out a soft gasp and collapsed helplessly to lie at their feet. Darkness sharply defined by the edge of a hot sun began to claim her and she heard faintly, "I do not comprehend what Sevryn sees in her."

"Perhaps it is only what any man sees in a woman."

"Perhaps."

Soft steps moved away from her as Rivergrace lost her struggle to understand and shadow claimed her.

"Lily says you'll be at the shop late, so I'll send Keldan by at lamplighting to bring the two of you home. We'll not have you fainting again in the summer sun. 'Tis different here than at home—the old orchards—and I expect the two of you to show better sense than to let the heat get to you." Tolby had his head inside a deep vat, and leaned out only long enough to send them on their way. He finished with a wave that set them off, and his last words were muffled by the good, aged wood of the restored vat to which each of them dutifully replied, "Love you, Da," before going.

Embarrassed but grateful to be freed and away from fussing, Rivergrace wore her veil pulled back, letting the fresh morning air sweep across her face, with its scents that she had become used to. The neighborhoods had their own flavor, each of them, but she loved the bakery best. The smell of fresh baking bread cooled into faintness, the baking done, the racks and shelves of the bread sellers filled. Some of them had small shops within their thresholds, with tiny pastries and drinks to be had, although most simply bustled about delivering their goods to the various estates and inns around town. A new aroma of freshly squeezed fruits into juice wafted to them, as did other, more unpleasant odors of city living. A songbird swept past her ear with a startled chirp as they passed under a cobbler's overhang. Looking up, she saw a nest tucked into its crossbeams.

Nutmeg caught her elbow immediately as her head tilted up, up, and back, and Rivergrace shrugged her off as her sister fought to right her. "I'm just looking!" She pointed up at the eaves and nest.

"Oh."

She nudged her sister. "I'm not going to drop again, all right?"

"I fainted once," Nutmeg declared, still standing very close to her, as if she thought she could catch Grace.

"I remember. I wouldn't call it fainting. You'd had all that hard cider and then the Barrel boy tried to kiss you . . ."

"Hmmmpf," said Nutmeg. "Felt like a swoon to me."

"No doubt it did." She wasn't sure what a faint felt like, for she didn't remember much beyond hanging the laundry and then pausing by the well for a break, and then waking with Keldan hollering for Lily, and dumping half a bucket of water on her. The rest of the morning she'd as soon forget, with Lily worrying over her before leaving, and Tolby frowning and stomping around, muttering something about being useless when it came to female troubles.

She hooked Nutmeg by the elbow. "At least he wanted a kiss. As I recall, they all wanted kisses from you!"

Nutmeg's cheeks grew even rosier as she admitted that to be truth, and they laughed at each other, walking down the row.

Snatches of conversation reached them. ". . . and rain coming, in a day or two, blessed be."

"Aye, not a pelting, though, shouldna be this time of summer. It'll be a warm rain and what wouldn't I do for a cold shower from the north, just for a day! What do you hear about the dance . . ."

"The miller is talking about raising his prices again, curse his hide. I make little enough money as it is, and now the grain is nearly as dear as gold . . ."

"Blame the traders for their profits, and beyond them, blame the cursed elves. They have a stranglehold on everything . . ."

"Messenger! Coming through!"

The two of them turned about to see if it was Walther, but another lad ran by, taller, calf muscles bulging from the cuffs of his short pants as he raced past them.

Something caught the corner of her vision from that quick glance, but when she turned her head, nothing was there. She tripped in her tracks and caught herself by grabbing Nutmeg's shoulder. She could have sworn she'd seen a figure watching them intently among the growing crowd.

Had someone been there? Did one of Walther's crew dodge around behind them in the shadows, practicing stealthy arts which, she was certain, did not suffer because their leader now had a legitimate job as a messenger boy? Dropping her veil into place, she looked about carefully and caught no other sign of someone, yet felt a tickling at the back of her neck as if being studied.

"You're jumpy," complained Nutmeg as she caught her by the shoulder a second time.

"Am I?" She patted down her skirts and fell back into a stroll before pitching her voice slightly above a whisper. "I think we're being followed."

Nutmeg swiveled about. "No one there."

"I can see that."

Her sister bounced back into stride. "Maybe it was an admirer."

Grace found herself smiling down over that. "You think so?"

Nutmeg tossed her lustrous hair back over her shoulder with an extra bounce. "They are bound to notice us sooner or later! They will be knocking down the door to ask Da permission to dance with us."

"I can hardly wait."

"I know I can't! Once the gowns are measured and made, maybe we'll have some free time. I hear the whole rest of the summer and the harvest months are filled with dances and teas and festivals." With another toss of her head, Nutmeg led them down the lane which began to grow crowded with workers and vendors and a few early shoppers. Dwellers and Kernans mingled cheerfully, doing business, the Dwellers with the perpetual cheer and bluster she knew so well, and the Kernans with a morose, resigned air. It was their city, a trader hub, but they barely held the majority of the numbers anymore, swelled with Dwellers moving in from farms to ply their industry wherever they could. Nutmeg moved among them with a sway of her body, like dancing without a partner, and Rivergrace did her best to follow her agile sister. She did draw looks, although Grace couldn't tell if it was because of her audacious plowing through the crowd or her prettiness as Nutmeg led. Laughing softly in spite of herself, she followed after, much as if they were racing to the tallest tree by the orchards to see who could scale it fastest. She bumped into a body and came to an abrupt halt, staring upward.

A bare chest of soft, golden hue, cloaked in a hide of forkhorn, the fur combed and burnished met her examination. He smelled of woodsmoke and incense. The man folded his arms and glared down at her, dark amber eyes full of Galdarkan disdain. She bobbed in apology. He jabbed a thumb across the road. "Two sides. You walk over there."

Rivergrace glanced across the street to the unpaved side with its littered gutter. Nutmeg had retraced her steps and rejoined Grace who drew herself taller and looked the man in his hard eyes. "Like you, I will walk where I wish," she answered, and sailed past him, Nutmeg in her tow. Something wet splattered at her heels.

"Some men!" muttered Nutmeg who now hurried to keep up with Grace's long, agitated stride. "Imagine that."

She did. Only she imagined that it was her veil, and not her gender, that had evoked the Galdarkan's arrogance.

Lariel stepped inside the Conference room which would be grand in any of the provinces, noting that the table had been replaced since the last time she'd attended, or at least had been given a new top, for the scars from her sword were gone. More than a scar, as she recalled, the tabletop had split where her blade struck. She stood inside the doorway a moment, gathering her thoughts as to what she would and would not say later in the day. It wasn't that she'd come unprepared, it was that her decision to say certain things seemed subject to a tide of approval, much like a beleagured shoreline, sometimes inundated and sometimes laid out to dry under an unforgiving sun.

"Your Highness," murmured Bistane out of the shadows, emerging quickly enough that he startled her despite his greeting, but she did not jump. His dark blue eyes held a smile for her.

Instead, she hooked her toe about a chair leg and pulled the chair out a little, so she could settle onto it, and look up at him. "Bistane," she responded. "Are you early or am I later than I thought?"

"We are both unforgivably early." He seated himself opposite her. "I was, in fact, hoping to find you here. I know your habit of preparedness." The intensity of the color of his eyes softened the harsh contours of his face and short hair. A warrior through and through, the hands he folded on the tabletop showed scattered scars and calluses. "I wanted you to be aware of this before I presented it."

"Oh?" She arched an eyebrow. Like her, he often cut through words and preliminaries, blunt but effective.

"I will propose abandoning the Accords."

She might have expected that from others, but not Bistane. Various among them had rankled about it for decades, even centuries, but it kept them in check and balance. She did not bother to hide the faint surprise which bubbled to the surface. He'd expected it, or he would not have taken care to warn her.

"You will ask why, and I will not be able to give a full answer in chambers, but I'll speak now." He leaned forward, resting on his forearms. "Whatever good the Accords have done us, their usefulness is past. We need to ready for war again, and they cause too many of us to hesitate. The Accords were meant not only to keep us from killing each other as we consolidated our positions but to keep us here, on the western coast. Now we must grow or our own entropy will be our worst enemy. We are meant to stretch our influence and enrich the lives of the world around us, Lara. We need to give up the past and move forward."

"You propose conquering?"

"Far from it. We will be conquered if we're not ready."

"Bistane, if there is one thing I've had taught to me, and taught well, it is that one never picks up a weapon unless one intends to use it. If we arm for war, there will be war."

"It's coming." Bistane took his attention from her and gazed out the window at the far end of the room. "I'm no ild Fallyn, but I can feel it. You know it's in my blood. We Vantanes are war hawks, nothing less. I won't start a quarrel, but I'll be damned if I'll let one plow me under."

"And if you can't say that in front of the others, what will you say?"

He turned his eyes back to her and smiled thinly. "I will say we need to reclaim our bloodlines. Take in and train the children we once tossed aside. Become as teachers to a world which doesn't want to be a student but can hardly refuse us. Go forth, and illuminate. Open the gates that the Accords keep locked."

"That, at least, sounds altruistic." Impatiently, she tapped a nail on the highly varnished tabletop.

"Lara. I won't lie to you. I may evade the truth with Tressandre, but I won't lie to you. She's sensed it as well. The ild Fallyn are recruiting half bloods to see if they can breed back lost Talents. As for war, the Bolgers are gathering clans again."

"They hardly threaten us."

"True, but they make good mercenaries for those who can. How long do you think the Kernans and the Galdarkans will stay disorganized and scattered? The only things that kept these lands from being held by the Galdarkans were their own allegiances to the Magi, each to his own small fiefdom, and they held old scores and enmities in memory of them. If they had ever united then, we would be under their yoke now. There is a vast continent out there, and we have but a handhold on the western edge of it."

She let out a soft sigh, in spite of her intentions, and Bistane leaned back. "I have to fight you on this."

He nodded slowly. "I thought you might."

"Sometimes I think the Accords are all that keep us civilized. It is not just the agreement not to war on one another, except for Honor Duels, but the ban against creating new Ways. You know, and I know, that our hold on magic is not what it should be. There are monstrosities out there, Bistane, that we created, and we cannot undo. There may come a day when one of us decides to create that which will be an abomination to all life. The Accords bind us against that."

"It keeps us bound to one another," he agreed. "Perhaps I think we're beyond that, and you don't."

"If you're right and I'm not, there is no harm done. You know we can rise to fight if we need to. But if I'm right and you're not, all that we have could collapse. We won't have to worry about Kerith tearing us apart, we'll be at each other's throats again."

"Do we not learn?"

She looked at his face. "I'm afraid to bet my life on it. What of our vows?"

"We strike back once, twice, and it'll be over. If we're ready. There's where you and I will knock heads, my lady. If we're not, they can overrun those of us who hesitate, who take the higher course of passive resistance. Your concerns about the lands, the Gods, will be plowed under with the carrion and bones." He pushed his chair away and stood. "At least you know."

"I thank you for coming to me and telling me."

He gave a short bow before leaving her alone in the Conference room. She looked at her reflection in the highly polished tabletop. If she had not come, this subject could never have been brought up, for a vote would never have been taken without her presence. But since she did come to attend, Bistane had seized the opportunity.

War, she thought. The very premise of it would sweep away the smallish concerns she had about the Andredia, even though she knew, in the long run, the health of the river would be far more important to the world. Who would listen to her troubles if they would be spending days arguing about abandoning or reconfirming the Accords?

Damn Bistane. His words would overshadow hers to the extent she was not sure she would be heard at all.

She would have to plan anew.

Chapter Forty-One

SEVRYN STOOD WITH HIS back to the wall of her apartment, shrugging now and then uneasily, his customary stillness fled, as if he were at odds with himself. His fidgeting sent his clothes chafing against his body, kedant-laced scars burning and aching, close to intolerable. He focused his thoughts elsewhere. She did not often have to summon him, he usually appeared whenever she needed him, as if he knew. Or perhaps it was because he and Jeredon often shadowed each other, and her. Perhaps. His unrest nagged at her senses, at her Talent, and that bothered her. What should she be seeing that remained unfathomable to her? He brushed his dark, bronzed hair from his forehead, shifting weight, wincing ever so slightly, a sudden darkness in his gray eyes.

Laraiel turned her attention from him to her writing desk and the sheaf of papers upon it, finding it easier to talk to them than directly to him, and ignoring her brother who'd come in as well, and claimed the nearest chair. "Wear your emissary badge," she directed. "Those who overlook seeing it have only themselves to blame for being unaware that you're speaking to them on my behalf. I want you to work your way through the delegates, our people and the others, and I want you to talk, quietly, of the need for the Accords. Use your Voice, Sevryn, but do not get caught. Understand? I have a need for you to remain undetected as you've been, and this request is no exception to that."

"Understood. Anyone in particular?"

"Avoid Bistane and the ild Fallyns. Bistane brought this to me, so he will be especially sensitive. Stay a good distance from his earshot." She pondered a long moment. "I might suggest Azel d'Stanthe. He hates these things as much as I do, yet he's here this year, so he must have a reason. Perhaps I can help him achieve what he needs."

Jeredon flexed one ankle as he remarked, "The historian takes no side," from the otherwise quiet depths of his chair.

"Of course. But there is always a first time, and if nothing else, I would like to know what's on his mind. I don't wish to have any more surprises to deal with."

Sevryn gave a ghost of a smile. "Shall I meet with you before the first addresses?"

"Yes. I'd like a summary by then."

He sketched a bow and left her with her brother. She stood and fussed with her day gown, her mind far from dealing with lacings and buckles.

Jeredon sat back on his chair and looked up at her, the amber highlights of his green eyes sparkling with humor, even when his thoughts were somber. "The Accords debate rises again? And here I thought Bistane came acourting and to sing for you, and try to win you with a duel or two."

She smacked him lightly across the nose with the belt she'd been trying to fasten. He laughed even as he ducked away and caught the belt, wrenching it from her hands. "At least he warned you." He rubbed the smarting bridge of his nose, the one feature of his face that looked so like that of their shared father.

"That he did. He will expect a courtesy in return, I'm certain, and even with his warning, there isn't a lot I can do except figure out how to dissent gracefully."

"You believe they'll bring this to a vote this session?"

"Yes. I also believe it'll go as Bistane wants it to, even over my objections."

Jeredon whistled softly. He'd been coiling the belt in his hands as if to snap it back at her playfully, but stopped, his face gone serious. The Holdings never moved that quickly on any discussion, but he could tell she expected just that. "There's only one thing you can do now, then, before the afternoon session opens."

"What?"

"Go shopping."

"Shopping?" She raised both eyebrows in surprise.

"I realize there often isn't a feminine bone in your body, but this season means meetings, dances, fetes and you need a new gown."

She shut her mouth. "I can't believe you'd suggest such an empty-headed, self-indulgent, exercise in . . . in . . ."

"Useless vanity?"

"Yes. That, and, and . . ."

"Go shopping," he repeated firmly. "Daravan is in town and he won't step foot within these walls, not without setting off wards or being detected. If, however, you go where he can get to you . . ."

"Oh." She reached out and grabbed her belt back from him.

He did smile then, widely, and the amber gems in his green eyes lit up. "I'm not totally useless as a brother." He stood. "While you're out, I'm going to hug a few maids and kiss a few cooks and see what they're saying." He winked at her just before going out the door.

Lariel stood in indecision. She should tell him, before too much longer, her worries about the Andredia and the vows that Larandaril stood upon, because he was more than her brother, he was the heir after her, and if she failed in her mission, the brunt of that failure would fall upon him. She hesitated long enough that his footfalls went beyond earshot, and he was gone, and she was left alone with her thoughts.

She smiled wryly. *Some of us talk with Gods and others of us seem merely to talk to ourselves.*

Whatever he suggested, she needed to do something. With a quick hand, she plucked her hooded cloak and veil off a nearby hook and shrugged into them. Daravan had to know, if he didn't already, that the Accords were in jeopardy of being put aside. Shopping it was.

Alone seemed best, and she had little fear of walking Calcort, knowing that she could best any ordinary attacker. The unpredictability of her movement meant that the Kobrir would not be likely to be stalking her either, although the evenings would be deadly for her, until his target and intent could be revealed. All the attendees would be mingling and politicking; it would take no Kobrir genius to know when and where to strike at night. It might not be her this time. What would be the fortune in that? She drifted along the city lanes, with only a vague idea of where she wished to go in her thoughts. She expected little in the way of success today at all.

A small child of the streets angled toward her, countenance screwed in a bashful expression, one grubby hand out begging for crown bits while the other frisked her for valuables, till she swung about and caught the thief in the ankle with the pointed toe of her boot. The child's face screwed up further as if to burst into a loud wail, and she said quietly, softly, "Don't. I know what game it is you play."

The child hobbled off with a contained sniffle, and she watched it disappear into the thin morning crowd. She could not even tell if it was boy or girl. It would tell its compatriots of its findings and warn them about her. She'd have to be more wary. Lariel shouldn't have let anyone get so close.

Calcort showed its layers of civilization as she walked. She could see the core of the inner city, a primitive fortress by her standards, though it must have been substantial in its time, for it still stood despite the centuries although its walls and arches were greatly diminished. Beyond that, she could see where the people of Kerith had built up, influenced by both the Raymy and the Vaelinars, and then the vast, outer rings of Calcort which showed the Vaelinar apprenticeship and tutelage.

She walked the old quarter, where Vaelinar manors had ruled the hills for a very long time, until Calcort itself had become unfashionable, and the Vaelinars drifted away in search of more interesting places. The soft chiming of ankle bells reached her, a music among the growing din of street hawkers, and she followed the sounds.

"How does the stitching look?"

Nutmeg wrinkled her brow as she looked over. "Grace, no one does a stitch like you do. So tiny and precise. It's fine. It's more than fine, it's incredible."

"It's good enough that I can stop and take a break, then?"

Her sister good-naturedly swung her foot to poke her. "Why do you even ask? Besides, you're done, aren't you?"

"I am. I'll put it on the form to hang the wrinkles out a bit." Grace stood, shaking out the afternoon gown gently and then pulling it over the dummy form. She stepped back to inspect her work.

"I don't see how anyone could not be happy with that." Nutmeg smiled at the dress.

Rivergrace shrugged one shoulder. "I think it depends on the woman, don't you? She didn't seem at all excited about all the affairs. It seemed a chore." She dipped the form in Nutmeg's direction, drawling in a flat, unhappy tone, "Good afternoon, milord-stuffed-in-the-shirt. I look quite well today, but I'm really very, very bored."

Nutmeg jumped up and made a gentleman's bow. She growled back, "I hardly blame you. All this nonsense, m'lady-pain-in-the-neck. You look beautiful in spite of yourself, however."

"Don't, I though? This is a divine little dress made by the most quaint of shops in the northeast quarter. A trifle, really." Rivergrace twitched the sleeve and sniffed. "I did the shop a favor by bringing my trade there."

"One does what one can for the common folk. I myself dropped a half a silver crown bit in a beggar's tray just this morning. I thought the gesture might help this suffocating headache, but there you are." Nutmeg made a grimace.

"I pity you, sir. No doubt you spent all day waiting for the Warrior Queen to appear? That seems headache enough!"

"Quite, quite. I wasn't born to keep waiting—"

"Dear me," said a third, soft and gentle voice from the corner. "Do I really keep people waiting all that long?" The woman stepped forward, dropping her hood from her head, her cloak pooling about her shoulders, its hem swirling upon the floor, her gold-and-silver-flashed hair tumbling free as she did, a gleam in her cobalt eyes.

Rivergrace dropped the mannequin with a squeak, and she and Nutmeg bumped heads bending to pick it up before the newly crafted dress it bore could be damaged.

Nutmeg dropped to one knee as Grace righted the dummy, patting the dress back into conformation and settling it firmly, as her sister muttered to the floor. "Warrior Queen Lariel, I beg your pardon. We meant nothing!"

"Of course you didn't!" Queen Lariel smiled, her eyes lighting with warmth and a tiny crinkle at the corners. The blues came out, highlighted by silvery splinters looking like sunlight on bottomless waters, and Rivergrace stared, entranced. The Warrior Queen dropped her voice into a conspiratorial whisper. "They are boring, all of them, very. It's why I don't come very often in the summers."

Nutmeg rose, her hand to her mouth, speechless. Rivergrace cleared her throat. "May we help you in any way, Queen Lariel?"

"Lily sent me back here to be measured. It seems I need a gown or two. I hate the thought. It's hot, and even the rain, when it comes, will be hot." The Vaelinar beauty gave a sigh.

She paused, her voice lingering on the air, and she stepped forward, hand outstretched to a bolt of fabric in the corner, its slipcover knocked askew by the falling dummy. "How beautiful."

She pointed at one of Lily's creations, blue with silvery stars, a gossamer cloth almost too delicate to be thought wearable, and as Rivergrace looked at it, she knew it was perfect. Nutmeg breathed an oooh at the same time. She dashed forward to pull the bolt out for inspection, and began to hold the fabric up to Queen Lariel, words tumbling out like the Silverwing river at floodtide. "M'lady, I have this design if you'll notice. It will drape like this and then the overskirt goes this way, nearly nothing, forgive me, but your figure is perfect for it, and it will flow but without all the layers the other shops are sewing this year, no heavy petticoats, you see, and—"

"Take a breath, Meg," Rivergrace cautioned. Her sister plowed to a halt, cheeks bright red.

Lariel stood holding an end of the yardage up to her waist where Nutmeg had placed it and grabbed her hand to keep it there, her expression slightly bemused but still open and warm. "I see."

Nutmeg stepped back. "Do you?"

"I do. Have you a pattern for that, or is it all in your head?"

"I've been working on one."

Lariel leaned forward slightly. "Might you wait on it? I'd like, for once, not to look like all the other ladies."

Nutmeg's mouth hung slightly open.

"An exclusive," Rivergrace said. "Naturally."

"Oh! Oh, yes." Nutmeg closed her mouth firmly. She reached for a brand-new measuring string as Rivergrace took the bolt back to carefully wind the fabric away. She marked it as having been sold as she did, turning back to find Nutmeg measuring the Warrior Queen in a flurry of motion, up and down the small ladder she used, all her uncertainty gone as she talked to herself and knotted the string in its proper proportions. Lily entered the workroom just as Nutmeg finished up.

"Your Highness, forgive me."

"No matter, Mistress. Your daughters have taken excellent care of me." Lariel smiled as she settled onto a chair, her gaze passing over Rivergrace for a slight moment as she did. "I hope you have the time to meet my needs."

"So do I, Your Highness, so do I."

With understanding smiles, the queen and the seamstress drew close to each other and sketched out wardrobe needs for the summer season, most of the gowns with the understanding the design and fabric would be exclusive until Lariel had appeared at the fetes, and Nutmeg and Grace hung on every word as they talked.

* * *

Lariel finished her business and returned to the streets, the sun at its apex, the streets baking with heat. Street urchins swarmed about her and swung away, shrieking at each other to leave her alone, scampering off as if she'd earned a reputation for flaying children alive. Her victim of the morning had evidently retold the tale of the encounter a number of times, Lariel's brutality growing with each retelling.

A voice at her elbow murmured, "Harsh."

She would not let herself be startled. Instead, she murmured to the tall figure at her flank and slightly behind her, "I expected someone shorter."

"She feared to send anyone else after you. All the urchins are in dire terror. When I found out the quarry she'd gone after, I knew it had to be you. Even among the Vaelinars, you're exceptional. You scared the snot out of her."

"You are an enigma, Daravan. Protecting street gangs now?"

"Only the tiny ones." He chuckled.

"This feels inherently wrong, you protecting the little one and me battering her."

"Don't let it worry you, Lariel. She would gladly have taken your purse and your jewels if she thought she could have. I merely kept her from being beaten when she came back without money to pay for a bed for the night."

She could not suppress a shudder. "How do we let our young live like that?"

"They are not our young, m'lady. This is not our world."

"I was born here. It's all the world I have."

He grew silent as he kept pace with her, and she realized she could not hear his steps slightly behind her, nor his breathing, but only his words when he spoke. If she looked, would she even see this ghost of a man?

He spoke again, saying, "Consider this. She works for her living, as we all must. After this morning, I believe she has decided on a different vocation."

She let out a breathy sigh, and he chuckled again. "Now then. Knowing that the Kobrir is here, what are you doing strolling about?"

"Shopping. Jeredon tells me I need a new gown, and that I need to talk to you."

"My taste in fashion leaves much to be desired. Anything you wore would be poetry upon a woman."

It seemed this day would be one of continual astonishment. She found herself smiling in spite of worry. "I have word for you, and my brother-counselor feels you might have word for me."

He took her elbow, his hand both large and strong upon her. "May I suggest a cold drink in a small place, then?" as he steered her off the lane.

The small inn he took her to was not a tavern, in actuality, but a trading goods store, where the manager kept a small bistro for his more wealthy clients, a nook of a room curtained away from his business. Daravan palmed him a gold crown and waved him off after he brought a pitcher of chilled juice and clean goblets, and then Daravan seated Lariel and served her, a wry smile on his face.

"The Conference starts this afternoon?"

"Petitioning does. Everyone likely to be here is."

He nodded. She put back her shroud and sipped the juice cautiously, unfamiliar with the opaque, faintly green and slightly pulpy drink, and liking its taste. He watched her from the depths of his hooded cloak, his face unreadable, a veiling of his own.

"Bistane met with me this morning, a forewarning. He will ask cessation of the Accords. He thinks it will come to a successful vote before we adjourn." She watched him over the rim of her goblet.

"In such haste?"

"Yes."

He reached for his own goblet, pouring a small amount into it and drinking it slowly before responding, "What did he ask for in return?"

"Nothing, yet."

"You think you cannot muster enough opposition?"

Lariel felt her mouth work, without words, her thoughts in conflict. Finally, she merely shook her head in answer.

"It's not like you to go down in defeat."

"Sometimes it's inevitable, don't you think?"

"Sometimes." He put his hood back. Even for a Vaelinar, his features had been sharply chiseled, fine-boned, yet there was nothing feminine about the high cheekbones and prominent brow and straight nose. His gray eyes held many silvers, from light ash to dark charcoal, and his hair looked as if it might be liquid silver. It was said of Daravan that he was one of the first of the Lost, the Suldarran, although she had never had confirmation of that, and if he had been, he must have been awfully young at the time. Yet, if he were, looking at him was a reminder of what they had all looked like once, before Kerith had put its own stamp upon them, thinning out their bloodlines, molding them to fit their new world. "I sense you save yourself for other battles."

"Perhaps."

He nodded sharply, returning his cup to the table with a definitive click. "It might be best to let the Accords go, Lariel. The Bolgers are reforming old war clans. We know the raids have stepped up, but those have been the initiative of a few old bandits. What we face now, however, will not be. They've already met one battle and gone down, so they will be scattered for a season or two before they get their spines back."

"Who did they attack?"

"I'm told it was Quendius."

"You've been listening to tales."

His hand shot across the table and pinned her wrist. "Do you think I would bring idle gossip to you, of all people? The Kobrir worked for me, getting this information. I do not treat with them lightly, nor should you with me." He did not raise his voice, but his jaw clenched and his fingers closed like a vise about her. She wasn't the sort of queen whom it was death to touch, although she meted out her own punishment to the unwise, but she did not move now, except to contain the thrill of pain that ran through her arm. "Listen or regret it."

"I'm listening." That Daravan used the Kobrir chilled her more than almost anything he'd said, and she set her teeth to concentrate.

"Quendius is harder to pin down than the wind, but you must find a way to deal with him."

"Gilgarran . . ."

"Gilgarran died trying to infiltrate the weaponsmith. Don't make the same mistake twice. And know this as well." Daravan stood. "The war you face is on three fronts."

"Three?" The Raymy she had never ceased to fear, and now he told her of civil war coming to her throne. What third front must she battle?

"The Gods themselves will bend low enough to join."

All warmth left her limbs. She shivered. He stood and shrugged back into his cloak and hood. He dropped a notepaper upon the table, having plucked it from her purse without her knowing, her bill from the dress shop.

"I recommend this seamstress."

In a swirl of shadow like smoke and little more, Daravan left her sitting. The paper fluttered with his disappearance.

Chapter Forty-Two

LONG AFTER SHE'D LEFT, a faint aroma lingered on the air in the shop, a fragrance which Rivergrace could not identify except that it was slightly sweet yet dry, slightly exotic, and very airy, and distinctive of the Warrior Queen. She wrapped up the measuring string, with all the knots in it specially tied to designate what was being measured, her fingers tracing Nutmeg's work. Meg had flitted about Queen Lariel like a moth around a candle flame, not caring if her wings caught on fire, herself a spark of brightness as she worked. Grace smiled as she put away the carefully tagged string in a drawer on the long worktable. The joy of the work had swept Meg away. She wondered what it must be like to be caught up in a tide like that.

Even more, as she looked toward one of the mirrors in the room before draping it, she wondered how anyone could ever think she had more than a drop of elven blood in her. There were her eyes, distinctively Vaelinarran, and the curving tip of her ears, and that was all. Yes, she stood taller, but not as tall even as a Galdarkan, and she was slender, but many Kernans and Galdarkans had her willowy build. No, she was nothing like Queen Lariel whose presence was both fierce and commanding, and incredibly gentle. No one could ever mistake a movement of hers for the controlled grace and strength of the Warrior Queen. The realization filled her with sadness and a little relief. Relief, because the worry her family had had about bringing her to Calcort seemed unnecessary. She did not stand out, no, she blended in with the others of muddied blood, insignificant, with only her scars to set her apart. She was, after all had been said and done, no one remarkable.

Uneasily, she looked at her face one last time as she pulled the draping cover into place. A broken shard of herself stared back, without a shred of comfort in its eyes. It did not reveal who or what she might have been or might become.

Noisy chatter in the other rooms brought her out of her thoughts, as customers came in for final fittings and purchases, and new fittings, and Lily's shop flooded with warmth.

Sevryn kept his fingers wrapped about a slender cup of watered-down juice that he barely sipped as he circulated about the Petitioners' lobby. He'd not been in the lobby long, having spent most of the morning and early afternoon among the Vaelinars, and now he moved among those milling about, hoping to catch an ear or two themselves before the session opened. He'd almost gotten used to the agony of wearing clothes, the mere brush of fabric sending fiery jolts through his senses, although there were times when he thought the kedant would drive him insane. Tressandre had not yet made her appearance at the Conference, and he did not relish not knowing when she would.

Lariel had placed her hand on his arm when he'd presented himself before attending. "I won't act against Tressandre, but there are concessions I can offer in exchange for the information she promised you. Shall I do that?"

He had placed his hand over hers and squeezed in thanks, answering, "My mother abandoned me to search for him. If she found him, he didn't bring her back to get me. I asked myself, what kind of man is that, who would walk away from his family, and who would keep them from being reunited? No one I would want to know. On this, there is nothing you need do. I am content."

Now he strode through those of Kerith with open faces, rather than veiled by careful design or fashion, and he searched those expressions he could easily read. He saw the powerful and the power hungry, the observers and the gossipers, the idle and the hardworking. He saw no one from the streets as he'd known them, nor did he expect to, for although this was one of the days when the general population was welcomed to mingle with the Vaelinars, guttersnipes had not been invited. He saw Bregan Oxfort, leaning casually on a cane he really didn't need, talking with an attractive young woman, although his eyes roamed the crowd as well. She did not seem to notice as she leaned close to him, chest heaving indiscreetly, that his eyes were seldom upon her. It piqued Sevryn's attention. For whom did Oxfort search? Or was he merely assessing the lobbyists, as was a trader's wont?

He brushed by a group of women who were discussing a healer who seemed to have an affinity for erasing wrinkles although his fee was nothing less than extravagant. The speakers were Kernan, although a veiled one stood nearby, a quirk of amusement to her mouth as she overheard. The mayor stood in a corner, well buttressed by his entourage and nearly unapproachable, but Sevryn had no business with Stonehand. The man knew where he stood with the Vaelinars and the Accords. Grand Mayor Randall Hawthorne, if he came to the Conference later, would be the man to collar. When the news reached him, he would come. Till then, Sevryn could only speculate about the Grand Mayor Hawthorne's position.

When a trader's herald came in, Oxfort and the young guildsman spotted each other immediately and the herald made a beeline toward him. Bregan stepped back from the crowd, isolating himself so that the herald could approach him. Bregan put one hand on the young man's shoulder as the other leaned toward his ear quietly. What words were passed, Sevryn couldn't guess, for they were clearly out of earshot, but Bregan quickly turned his body about so that his expression couldn't be read as if he did not trust himself not to show it.

Sevryn eased his way closer. Nothing would be gotten from Oxfort as he lifted a cup to his lips and kept it there for a long moment, not drinking but hiding a coin bit dropped into the herald's palm for his trouble. The trader's herald turned heel and left, Sevryn right behind him, even as the young man tugged his tabard into place and neatly palmed the half crown tip Oxfort had given him, Sevryn moving so quietly that few even noticed him leave.

He caught up with the messenger in the alleyway outside the large building, taking his elbow, and, unleashing his Talent said quietly, without letting him turn about. "You have news you need to tell me."

The youth froze at his touch, head going back slightly in response to the Voice, and murmured, "I already told you all, milord. I swear."

"Tell me again, and then all is forgiven and forgotten."

"But–but . . . I just did . . ."

"The weather is hot, and you light-headed. I want to be sure you overlooked nothing. *Now give me the news.*"

He fought Sevryn for a few more moments, then his arm went limp as the slight youth in his hold began shaking.

The herald had been trained against this, and Sevryn could see no way to get what he wanted without breaking him completely. He gave up on the tactic, sorted through his thoughts, and decided that there would have to be another way. Sevryn said softly, "Well done. You have a future as a herald." He released the young trader who sagged against the side of the building and never saw him step away.

Retreating to the corner of the alleyway, he paused to set himself to follow. The herald wobbled away, staggering as if drunk or sun-struck. He trailed, unsure of his course of action, knowing that the herald would be unlikely to show up at the guild and tell his master word for word what he'd just told Bregan, and also knowing that his own lack of appearance at the hall might soon be noticed. Even as he weighed options, he saw a splinter of darkness sunder from a corner and angle after the still tottering herald.

Someone lying in wait or just an opportunist?

Sevryn hesitated as to his obligation. And, in that moment, the predator caught the unwary quarry and pinned him to the dust of the alleyway. Like a small bird fluttering under a hawk, the herald struggled briefly, then stopped as the other hissed to him, "You carry a message. I would know what it is. Before you think of silence, consider that I am Kobrir and your silence will be eternal."

Both herald and Sevryn froze at that. His shoulders to the back of the small buildings comprising the alleyways, Sevryn drew a little closer after taking a shallow breath.

It seemed as if the herald managed to draw a breath as well. Then he let it out in a thin, wailing sound that might have been a sob or might have been a cut windpipe. A glint of light in the hands of an otherwise all-darkened figure cut the air. Sevryn poised on the balls of his feet, considering his course of action, when the herald bleated out, "Word reached the guild just a few moments ago. The hanging sword has fallen. Traders need to be wary of levies."

"You told this to Bregan Oxfort?"

"I did."

"Anything else?"

"No, milord."

"Then we are done." Kobrir's hand shifted, and the herald's legs shook once, heels drumming into the ground, and then went terribly still. Sevryn pulled back, and broke into a swift walk as soon as he was clear of the alley, a tightness in his throat and anger knotting his stomach, his own chance to strike lost, and a life wasted, a life that he had put into the Kobrir's reach.

Mouth tasting of bitterness, he mulled over the message.

Lariel would need to know before the session opened. Oxfort's code, if it was even that, could not be easier to decipher. Gilgarran had oft referred to the Galdarkans, the last of the vast Magi Empire, as swords hanging over the scattered free-trade provinces. Speculation that the elite soldiers of the long lost Magi might consolidate one day had always been held, the surprise was only that it had been so long in coming. Rather like the debate over the Accords.

Do all things, he wondered, happen in a day?

He merged back into the petitioners' lobby, with a half smile he did not mean, and a nudge to a pretty young serving lady who offered a chilled blush wine that tasted far more palatable than the failure drying his throat. It would do for a bracer, and he decided to recommend it to both Jeredon and Lariel.

Chapter Forty-Three

PETITIONERS' DAY STRETCHED into Petitioners' Night revelry, and Sevryn found himself more and more rankled by his inaction. When had it become more important to spy rather than to act? He should have saved the herald, revealing himself, and losing the information if he had. Nothing Gilgarran would have muttered about the greater good would have soothed his regrets. Even the fine blush wine did little to help. He did not respect his decision. He determined not to make another like it. He would not keep a part of himself locked away, filled with similar choices and regrets. He would find a way to serve his queen and himself.

Sevryn stayed in a corner, venturing out now and then only to talk to a new petitioner or lobbyist entering the reception, doing more listening than talking, murmuring a few responses as needed before drifting back to being inconspicuous. Or so he thought. He looked up from his long-nurtured drink to see Azel d'Stanthe of Ferstanthe watching him, the tall and rangy historian-librarian considering him from across the room. It would be imprudent to pretend he hadn't noticed, so he crossed to Azel, and gave him a slight, sardonic toast.

"Evening, milord, or so I believe it is by the drunkenness attained by most of those about us."

"An astute observation, I would say. It's been a long while since I attended the Petitioners' Day, or even a Conference, but it seems little has changed." Azel held a goblet close to his vest, but it looked and smelled as if it held only fruited juice and that greatly watered down.

"I might wonder what brings you out for either."

"Even an old, buried stone should be unearthed and turned once in a while. They say fresh air does wonders." Azel chuckled briefly. "You wear your emissary badge."

"I can remove it, if you wish," responded Sevryn.

"Remove it rhetorically and come onto the balcony." Azel moved off nonchalantly with a nod, as if dismissing him, and Sevryn turned away.

After very long moments and an uncomfortable chat with a petitioner's daughter who had attended her father's business only in hopes of trawling for a husband of high status, Sevryn escaped to the balcony. The loveliness of the Kernan lass held no appeal under the circumstances, and he was afraid Azel might have given up on him. He found the librarian leaning on his elbows, looking into the last of a very grand sunset, clouds light and dark and streaked with oranges, ambers, and reds of the dying light.

"If you're going to ask me if I can serve two masters," Sevryn said, sliding into place next to him on the balcony, "I will have to tell you, regretfully, that I cannot. But I do remove the badge, and often, to have a life of my own."

"Plainly spoken."

"You have seen and recorded far more than I could ever hope to. Subterfuge seems a little disingenuous around you."

"Yet still wise, I think." Azel looked down toward the street. "I saw a darkness down there a few moments ago, seemingly of shadow, yet moving with a purpose that was not random. I'll be brief. I came to Calcort to do a little research, both to promote the project I will submit before the Houses and also because of your recent visit. Folk songs and rhymes are often an oral history, long after that history might have been banned or distorted." The librarian paused, and took a sip of his juice. "It is often useful and sometimes disturbing to note those who come to my collections, what they seek, and what they find."

"Perhaps a talk can put your mind to rest." Sevryn would have said more, but a roar of noise from the rooms at their back rose, like a tide of merriment and disagreement.

D'Stanthe waited until it muted. "Or set yours in motion," he returned. "We must find a better way to talk, and soon." Then, with a grace belying his slightly stooped bulk, he merged back into the meeting rooms and crowd, spotted only by his height as he walked away.

Azel's words raised possibilities Sevryn hadn't considered before. Who had been to the libraries, and why?

Hosmer's square form filled the doorway to the storeroom, his arms crossed over his chest, a sparkle in his eyes as he watched his sisters stowing away their tools and fabrics for the day. "From the looks of the fine lasses who come through the door, I should be here more often."

Nutmeg pushed him aside with a shove from her hip as she came through, bolts in her arms. "If you're going t' stand around, be helpful!"

Hosmer laughed as she tripped over a trailing edge, catching her by one arm and her bundle with his other arm. He placed her firmly on her feet and crossed the area to the back, where he and Keldan had built shelves and racks for incoming stock. "That helpful enough for you?"

Nutmeg gave a muffled snort. She flounced her skirts back into order as Rivergrace carefully ignored the sibling bickering she'd grown up with. It was good to see Hosmer hale and hearty and back solidly on both legs, able to laugh again. He would not talk about the militia or his lost companions and no one pressed him about it these days, glad only that the haunted expression had faded with the hard work needed to get Tolby's new enterprises whipped into shape.

On second thought . . . Grace turned to look back over her shoulder. "I think," she offered quietly, "that we should stand him at the doorway, to model some of those new men's outfits you've designed, Nutmeg. The women will be drawn like gnats to honey."

Nutmeg tilted her head and squinted at Hosmer. "Maaaaaybe," she drawled. "He does cut a fine figure."

Hosmer gave a rumbling chuckle. "Hard work I'll do. Standin' round like a strutting billy goat or rooster, no. Show me what you need hauled back here, so we can head home. I've been workin' hard, and I'm hungry."

The two led him to the back door pile, where carters dropped their barrels and bundles. He hefted two kegs, one on each shoulder. "No way to get the lads to haul them in for you?"

"We are lucky," Nutmeg muttered, "to get them inside the door. Carters around here just kick their deliveries off the tailgate and hope it lands somewhere close to your shop."

"Can you be using your wiles on them?"

"I've tried. Rivergrace is oblivious to it."

"Grace?" He swung about to face her, with another bale on each shoulder, pausing as he settled them into place.

"Me? Like they'd look at me. I'm like a winter yearling at the first of spring, all shaggy and long-legged and gawky. It's Nutmeg their jaws drop at, anyway."

Hosmer clucked at her. "I see we need to get Da to give you his famous talk."

Nutmeg pinked. "Gah, not that one!"

She stared at both of them. "Talk?"

"Aye, sis. The one about men and women and attraction and such not. He's good at it." Hosmer grinned as he bypassed her, one of the bales slowly coming undone as he carried it by, and she followed quickly to gather up its tying rope so that he would not trip on it. A small, folded piece of paper drifted down as well. She picked it up and slipped it into her pocket, hurrying to gather up the bale before the fine fabrics tumbled from its oilcloth covering. He set both into place where she pointed, the two of them barely out of the way as Nutmeg came puffing up with more freight in her arms, more than she could handle explode that in all directions as they scrambled to catch it. The shelf and all came tumbling down as bales, kegs, sturdy Dwellers, and off-balance Rivergrace crashed into them.

"Keldan built that shelf!" Hosmer sputtered from underneath the pile of goods as he plowed himself free. Nutmeg's petticoats were all that could be seen of her as Rivergrace rolled out from underneath. The hope to be gone from the shop before the last of the sunset had faded from the sky fled, as they cleared the goods and scurried around to find tools and nails for Hosmer so that he could put the shelf back "Properly," as he stated it firmly, and then restock it.

Finally Nutmeg patted the last package into place, retying the bale. "Oooh, her fabric is in," she said to Grace. "Milady Galraya has been looking for this one, so we can make her outfits, and in a hurry, too. She wanted to inspect it first."

"Send Walther out on a run tomorrow morning, then. That'll please him."

"So I shall." Nutmeg dusted herself off, and regathered her tresses, tying them back from her face and off her neck, to cool down a bit. "Race you back."

"See here." Hosmer grabbed her by the scruff of her neck. "This is no orchard. The streets are busy out there, and there's drinkers and cutpurses and such. You two stay with me as Da intended." He frowned, which made him look tolerably fierce if one ignored the dirt streak down his nose. His tunic hung loosely on him, but his injury had taken the fat and not the muscle off him. He wore his short sword sheathed and tied on his hip, as the city allowed, not easily drawn but still available if necessary.

Nutmeg gave him a look from under her bangs. "Let's go, then. I'm tired and hungry."

"As are we all," Rivergrace echoed. She pinched out all the lamps and sconces on the way, counting each to make sure she'd gotten all of them as she went out the door. Lily had drummed into them the dangers of a fire within closed walls and buildings such as these. Crowded city quarters were like tinder, just waiting for a wild spark. They dropped the latch into place and then the lock that only Lily had a key for. Hosmer dropped a pace behind them, as the night life of Calcort surged around them like an irresistible tide, carrying them down the lane. The night smelled of the hot summer dust and spilled ale, and the fragrance of flowers and oils on the women as they sauntered past.

"I think I shall wear my belled pants and blouse tomorrow night," Nutmeg declared.

"Will you?" Rivergrace thought the outfit rather daring, as thin and clinging as it was, with its tiny bells ringing from the cuffs and sleeves.

"Hot enough. Unless it rains." She peered at the visible sky. "What do you think, Hos? Thunderclouds?"

"Not yet but, aye, closing in. Tomorrow afternoon, I wager." Like all the Farbranches, he had a good weather eye. They could feel the heaviness of the water in the air, the pressure of the sky and wind. Rivergrace lifted her chin, knowing only that rain was very very near. Thunderstorms, she could not predict, but rain, yes, she felt it. Of course, it was the word on everyone's lips. They practically danced in the streets to pray for it, relief from the unrelenting summer heat.

Nutmeg hooked her arm through Rivergrace's. "They say," she began, "that the seaside great city never grows this hot, that wind off the water keeps it cool day and night, no matter how dire the summer."

"Really?" She tried to imagine an ocean. She'd been told it held salt, so much salt that fish which lived there were far different from fish in the rivers. And how would it appear? Would it be like looking along an endless lakeshore? Would there be trees at its edge? Silver-winged alna diving along its shallow curves? "It might be dreadfully cold in the winter, with rain-driven wind."

Nutmeg tilted her head. "Could be. I'd like to visit sometime, though."

"I would, as well."

"In the summer."

"Definitely."

Hosmer grunted from behind them. "If we hurried a bit, we might make it t' the table before the stew gets cold."

Rivergrace stretched her long legs, making Nutmeg scurry along to keep up. "I'm just worried about making it before Keldan eats it all." Indeed, cold stew on a simmering night didn't sound all that disagreeable. Point of fact, a light dinner suited her better, some fresh greens and maybe a few edible flowers and fruit, a meal her brothers often sneered at. A bit of meat and gravy would only add to the flavor a little. She knew that her meeting her needs would be a far cry from that of the others, though, and the last thing she wanted was to be hearing stomachs growling and other complaints all evening. The growing throng made walking difficult. Shoulders and swinging arms buffeted her more than once.

Singing voices rose on the night air. She leaned down to Nutmeg. "I don't quite understand why everyone is so high-strung tonight."

"Petitioners' Night. Actually, I think it goes on for several days, when we get to petition the Vaelinars for aid or redress from the first times."

"First time what?"

Nutmeg looked up at her. "From the first time they came here and everything changed. Sometimes they took land. Sometimes slaves. Sometimes lives."

That didn't quite explain the tipsy celebration which seemed to be growing ever louder as they walked through the lane of taverns and closed shops, the poorer section of the quarter before it opened back up into homes and manors and closer toward their brewery.

Hosmer said, from somewhere close behind her, "The veiled ones tend to repay in coin, with few questions or proof needed. Many see it as a way to get rich quick."

"Ah."

"Fools," remarked Nutmeg. "The Vaelinars never forget, and easy wealth never lasts long. When trade and craftsmanship is needed again, they're often blacklisted. For generations."

"Petitioners had better be certain of what they ask for, then."

"A good idea, lass, that they should be," Hosmer agreed.

Before any of them could comment further, a group of bakers' boys and lasses came toward them, singing and knocking their tankards together, their flour-dusted aprons still worn about their necks and waists, their sleeves still rolled up for kneading, their faces flushed with the heat of the night and the drink. The Kernans seemed merry in a determined way, and the Dwellers among them reeled about with impromptu jigs. They spilled over the walkways and most of the narrow street with merry shouts and a spinning dance or two, heedless of anyone else pacing around them. Nutmeg and Rivergrace moved one way, and Hosmer found himself jostled all the way across by the revelers.

A Kernan stopped, her hands on her hips as she stared at them, her skirt tucked up into her waistband to reveal her petticoats and shapely legs, and cried out, "What are you doin' with her?"

Rivergrace stopped so abruptly Meg bumped into her flank. "I . . . I . . ."

"Not you. You!" And she jabbed a thumb at Nutmeg. "She's a disgrace for a Dweller like you. No veil, walkin' th' streets like a common tart. Think you're gonna make yourself look all uppity trailin' around with an elven castoff, do you?"

"Now wait here," Nutmeg shot back. "That's drink talking, not you. So I'll forget what you said, and step around." She began to steer herself and Grace by.

"Not so fast." A burly lad stumped up behind, and soon the walkway filled with the entire group, nudging and shoving each other a bit to get closer to see what might be going on. It took a moment to recognize him, face lit up like a harvest apple with redness from his drinking, but it was Vevner from near their brewery. "Watch yer words, lass."

The girl tossed her head. "I've had it up to here with snotty folk who think they're better than us because they rub noses with the Strangers." She leaned forward, her pouting lips curling into a snarl. "I work hard for me money. I don't sleep wi' or kiss fancy arses for it."

Rivergrace sucked in her breath.

"I can show you cuts, bruises, needle pokes, and knotted muscles from the work we do," Nutmeg returned in the baker lass' face. "Not to mention, I have to *think* to do my job! No one's counting what you do the lesser, so I'd appreciate the same respect."

"Sewin' in a shop for fine ladies? You call that work? Hah!"

Hosmer snorted. "I recognize you, girlie. Always first to belly up for our samplin's, you are."

"At least my father dinna have t' buy me a job! Or me mother." She put her face into Nutmeg's.

"Oh, that's only half my job," Nutmeg added. "The other half is thumping ignorant bumpkins like you!" And she did, knotting up her fist and thumping the other on the head as if she held a hammer. The Kernan lass gave a surprised sigh and dropped as if poleaxed.

The fight still might not have started, except that someone reached round and groped at Grace while the others stood and stared at their unconscious friend. She jumped back with a squeal, flailing her arms about. "Get your hands off me!"

Hosmer put his head down and charged into the revelers with a snort like a maddened bull, sending them under his boots and flying out of his path. Anyone still on their feet clenched their hands, and the fray was on.

Chapter Forty-Four

RIVERGRACE THREW OUT the family rule of no kicking the second time she felt a boot swung into her shin. Stinging from ankle to knee, she kicked back. The resounding thud filled her with satisfaction. No knuckle-duster like her brothers or even her sister, she elbowed the body on her right as she dodged another free-swinging boot, grabbed it under the ankle shank, and pulled the owner off her feet and onto her rump. Nutmeg promptly ducked down and gave the girl a right to the jaw which would have done any of their brothers proud.

A tide of brawlers muscled her away from the others, driving her off the street and into the mouth of an alleyway. The rule about hair pulling promptly went the way of kicking as her ribbons were torn from her hair with a smarting yank on her scalp. A blow to the back of her knee brought her down, rolling, dust flying. Hard hands on her arms lifted her and set her back on her feet, with a low growl and a stink overwhelming her that sent her whirling about to see her rescuer, and no hope of finding him as the revelers surged around her. Dazed, with the stink of Bolger in her nostrils yet none seen, she shouldered her way back toward Nutmeg who stood with her arms curled and her hair wild about her face, knuckles bared.

Hosmer ducked a roundhouse swing with an irritated growl, sized up the fighter, and dropped him with one clip to his chin, then Rivergrace lost sight of him again as the crowd swelled around them. Vevner from their neighborhood bakery held him back, the two swinging fists with grunts of satisfaction as she lost them.

Grace backed up a step, doubling up her slender hand, and swinging away with her wiry strength, not decking anyone but still able to set them back on their heels with a whoof and a shocked look in their eyes. Her current target's head whipped back, and he fell into the arms of a chunky lad who promptly hauled both of them out of the milling crowd. He flashed a grin at her and she recognized Keldan's friend Curly, always first in line for apple culls in the morning. He put a thumb up as he dragged his pal away from the tide of fighters. Looking around, she ducked a fist swinging at her, came underneath, and kicked the swinger in the shin as hard as she could. An indignant howl followed. Nutmeg cheered her on, before the revelers turned rioters enveloped her, and muffled squeals, thumps, and yells filled the air. Grace waded in after, shoving and swinging a path to Nutmeg's side. She turned back to back and said, "I'm ready if you are!"

A bucket of water came out of nowhere, raining upon the brawlers, soaking them. Neither had a chance to celebrate as a strong arm wrapped around Nutmeg's and Grace's waists and pulled them about. "What, by Tree's blood, do you think you're doing?"

"Fighting!" Nutmeg struggled against Hosmer's hold, swimming through the air in an attempt to free herself.

"Not on my watch, you aren't! Da will have my scalp." Hosmer grunted as he held Nutmeg aloft and kept a firm grip on Rivergrace who found her hair being yanked from behind and let out an indignant squeal.

"We don't need a riot among our neighbors."

"You swung, too!"

"Tha's beside the point. I know when to stop swingin', as well." He hauled them both out of the streets and put their backs to a shop wall, and eyed the mass of brawling bodies in front of them who no longer seemed to know or care who they were whaling the tar out of. "Lads!" he bellowed. "Nothing finer than to watch a lass down in the mud wrestlin'. My money's on the redhead!"

Almost as primitive as the instinct to fight, the instinct to gamble boiled up. Another bucket of water appeared from nowhere, slung through the air and over the brawlers, with a cry, "A silver crown bit on the brunette in braids!" Curly bounced on his feet, bucket swinging in his hand, a wide grin splitting his face.

Hosmer released Grace but kept Nutmeg hefted in his arm, her feet flailing to reach ground, and waded through the crowd, sorting them into a motley sort of order by the sheer strength of his voice and presence. By the time the Town Guards trotted in with sharp whistles to announce their arrival, he had everything quieted down but two girls in the mud, with interested gamblers passing coin bits back and forth. The guard officer posted his two men who began to disperse the onlookers while he assessed Hosmer.

"You look a likely lad. Start this or finish this?"

Hosmer gave him an innocent grin. "I, sir, am merely observing."

The officer grunted as his men pulled up the wet-and-muddied wrestlers and packed them on their way, with the last of the others. "I'd be grateful for the one and fairly vexed for the other."

"Then, sir, it's clear I finished this."

His grin seemed to be infectious, for the officer responded with his own. "You've mettle to you. If you're interested in being a Town Guard, look me up. First Guard Gregan Fist, aye?"

"If I'm interested, you'll be the one I'll look for. Hosmer Farbranch." He set Nutmeg down, finally, where she gave an exasperated snort, and both men looked at her. Her cheeks took on the full red blush of a ripe, crisp apple and she decided to spend some time putting her apron and skirts into order. The two men shook forearms and Hosmer nudged his sisters down the walkway, saying, "If there's no dinner left, I'll have your hides for it."

Nutmeg tossed her head and said not a word, striding in front of him as fast as she could, and Grace had to stretch her own legs out to stay apace. From behind them, she identified the sound of Hosmer laughing to himself.

At the second rousing rendition of the traders singing "Free Roads," Sevryn made his apologies for an early evening and slipped out of the Petitioners' Reception, his head slightly buzzing despite his attempt to inhibit the free flow of wine and other, heavier spirits being poured his way. Azel's words buzzed in his head, far stronger than the liquor he'd had. Few heads turned as he left, and he slipped into the outer courtyard, feeling the hot, close summer air on him, speaking of weather moving in, clouds dappling the sky overhead. He leaned on a balustrade for a moment, accustoming his eyes to the dark, and then saw a man-sized shape move quietly out of view of the corner of his vision. Without turning his head, he narrowed his attention in that direction and saw nothing further, no branch waving in the courtyard garden he might have mistaken, no night bird winging low.

He took a few casual steps toward the far side of the courtyard, yawning as he did as if to clear a muddled head, never looking directly toward the corner but angling his way to a better view. As he walked, he unfastened his dress shirt to loosen his wrist daggers knowing that if the Kobrir were to strike, he'd likely not have a second chance. Anticipate the worst, accept the best.

He found a statue to lean upon, paved stones of the courtyard encircling it. The moments of waiting stretched out while he listened, stilled his own breathing, searching the night for what lay hidden within it.

A hand fell on his shoulder and he jumped, nerves unstrung. Jeredon laughed low. "Catch you sleeping on your feet, did I?"

"Too much wine," he muttered. "I think the Petitioners intend to float their pleas into the Conference."

"Better come with me, then. It all starts bright and early again tomorrow."

Away from the courtyard and inside the massive inn which housed Lariel, Jeredon quirked an eyebrow at him and said, "I interrupted your hunting. Any idea who or what?"

"No. And how did you know?"

"I heard you stalking. You may have our blood in you, but your feet seem to be all Kernan, loud and clumsy."

"I intended to be both seen and heard, and thought drunkenly harmless."

"You nearly succeeded, then."

"Ummmm. Would that I had. I have news for Lariel, and she's not likely to want any of it. The Kobrir was spotted below the balconies late this afternoon."

"And perhaps this evening, too, then?"

"Perhaps."

"That might actually cheer her up. At least that one fights with blades and not words." With a wry twist to his smile, Jeredon opened the doors to the apartments, and the two passed between guards who were not likely to be able to withstand any real threat, despite their vigilance.

Lariel put aside her reading and stood as they entered. She'd pushed her hair back from her face and knotted it at the back of her slender neck in a bun of spun gold and silver, and her expression seemed both tired and guarded. "I trust you've been seeding the fields I asked you to?"

"Yes, m'lady." He bowed to her, kedant-laced scars rippling in fiery protest as he did so. "I wish I could gauge reactions for you, but everyone seems to be perfecting their masks for this Conference. I do have news, which I need to pass on, though I haven't confirmed it yet."

"Rumors, then?"

He shook his head. "Doubtful." He waited to sit until she reclined once more, her shapely legs tucked under her, and he found himself thinking of the other, wondering how she'd look sitting before him. Sevryn inhaled. "First, the Kobrir is staking out the Petitioners. A clear sighting at least once, and perhaps later this evening. We're all on notice, then, that his being in the city is no coincidence."

"Not that we ever thought it was," Jeredon provided. He sat on the floor, his back against his sister's footstool.

"Secondly. A traders' herald came to Bregan and gave him an urgent message at the gathering. I followed him to see if I could coerce him to repeat it." Sevryn paused, a dry, unpalatable taste in his mouth. "I failed, but the Kobrir did not. The message was coded, although I think we'll all agree as to its meaning." He repeated the lad's dying words and waited.

"Diort." Jeredon shifted his lean body. "Finally making his move."

Lariel lifted a finger. "This is what you haven't confirmed yet?"

Sevryn nodded to her. She considered it. "Still, it seems likely. Word will come to us. And Kobrir again. Perhaps this was his assignment."

"Again, I saw him later, so it's doubtful. Assassination, not information is his true calling." Sevryn watched as Jeredon kicked his boots off. He yearned to be in his rooms, garments off, scars bared without the ache of cloth touching them, no matter how fine, how sheer, it brought agony. Wine had dulled him for a while, but now as he sobered, kedant coursed through his body freely again.

"Agreed. What else?"

"Azel was mingling with the Petitioners."

She arched an eyebrow. "Really?"

"I'd say he has brought something to the table this time. No idea what it is, but he is working the Petitioners, listening, weighing them."

"Our historian is notoriously neutral."

"Things change," Jeredon told her.

"It's true that he rarely attends a Conference. He sends others in his stead. Tomorrow," she instructed Sevryn, "see what's on his mind."

He inclined his head.

"Anything else?"

"Nothing I can give credence to—yet."

"All right, then." She reached forward, gathering up the papers on her desk. A seldom seen weariness blurred her delicate features. "Perhaps the morning will bring us better tidings."

Sevryn left, grateful for thc dismissal. Stepping into his room, he heard both his footfall and a crinkle of paper. Looking down, he found a folded note that had been slipped under his door.

By early light, at the Plaza of Traders, for breakfast.
Azel d'Stanthe of Ferstanthe

Sevryn smiled. He would have fresh tender bread and hot brewed defer for breakfast, the drink a Calcort delicacy, along with intriguing conversation. What more could he wish?

Chapter Forty-Five

THEY DISCOVERED DINNER had been held for them, although not because of their lateness. The house smelled promisingly of dinner, but everyone occupied the receiving room instead of sitting in the kitchen, eating. A visitor sat in Tolby and Lily's parlor, hands on his thick thighs, his vest buttoned tightly over his girth, but not an ounce of him was fat. A Dweller, obviously, who probably deserved the name of Barrel more than any of the Barrels Rivergrace had ever met, and a trader, too, by the mantle he wore and the richness of his appearance. She hesitated as she entered the parlor, for an air of menace lay about him just as the impending storm lay over Calcort. Nutmeg glanced at her in dismay and Hosmer shook his head. No, they couldn't possibly know about the street brawl already, although the three of them stood in dusty and muddy disarray, Tolby had barely looked at them and Lily's attention seemed equally distracted. She waved at them, saying, "Dinner is late."

Their visitor responded, "And my apologies for that, young 'uns. I have business which seemed important." He turned his thick neck and head back to Tolby. "I realize that this is not good news to be bringing you now, but my colleagues and I hope to work out reparation with you. Although, as you contend, the second papers are likely forgeries, we face going through two courts. Ours, for the payment of the loan on those second papers, would go through civil court. A speedier process in the case of debt repayment. The forgery cases would go through criminal court and by the time it reached a verdict, you could lose this brewery and vineyard through default on the civil judgment, even if you won. It would be like bringing buckets to the fire after the house has already burned down."

The words whirled about as Rivergrace grasped to comprehend why this man sat like a thundercloud deposited in their home. Her knees bent and she sat down, almost missing the chair.

Tolby tamped a pipe evidently long gone cold, and studied it. "Your advice, then, is to pay the debt and hope for reparation later when the forgery is proven?"

"It seems the wiser, though disagreeable, course. You are admitting nothing by paying, but you are saving your business. The former managers ran it into the ground, but it has potential yet." The visitor looked about him. "Which, I have noted, you've put a great deal of industry into already. This is the summer season. You should be getting contracts for supplying, and making some funds. My colleagues and I are prepared to send a little business your way, to help." He leaned forward, breathing a little heavier because of the press against his girth. "I asked to bring this to you, myself, because I am Dweller also, and I know the hard work and honor that runs in our veins. Robin—Mistress Greathouse—spoke of the difficulties you'd already overcome. She untangled much of this mess before appointing me as a factor to work with you. She has paid my fees and will stand you a loan, if necessary."

Keldan, standing quietly by Tolby's shoulder, shifted weight then as if in slight disagreement, but Tolby did not look at him. Garner sat quietly, listening, taking notes as either Tolby or Lily had no doubt instructed him. He looked slim as a reed compared to the other sturdy Dwellers filling the room, and his hands moved swiftly, surely, as he scribed. Lily cleared her throat yet still sounded a little hoarse as she offered, "My business can help as well, Tolby."

"Aye, I know that. It just crams my craw to pay a bad debt with good coin. I ran the fellow off, it should have gone no farther. Curse me for a half-witted goat, I know more of city scoundrels than that! And I've no wish t' borrow money. We paid for this, to have it clear and not beholdin'."

Lily tapped a packet on her lap. "Mistress Greathouse says that Simon carries good advice."

The trader shifted his weight, and the chair under his bulk creaked with him. "It seemed best to consult with her first. I hope you do not hold that against me. Once aware of your situation, she urged me to help you with all haste."

"Best not to make an enemy of Greathouse," Hosmer muttered under his breath, and only the three of them heard him.

Tolby scratched his chin. "Don't be misunderstandin' me, Trader Simon, but I cannot for the life of me wonder if this proposal of yours is gift—or graft. Once burned, twice shy."

The trader chuckled. "I would think considerably less of you if you didn't." He boosted himself to his feet. "Give it a day or two of consideration, Master Farbranch, then send a messenger to me. We haven't much longer than that, I fear, before my colleague holding the paper will start proceedings to collect, but I think a man ought to be given time to think out his course of action."

Tolby stood also and took Trader Simon's hand. "Only fair. I'll be in touch with you."

Simon bowed to Lily and made his way to the door, with Keldan leading the way. Lily rubbed a hand over her eyes before frowning in Nutmeg's direction. "You seem a trifle messier than I remember leaving you."

"A bit of street revelry," Hosmer said smoothly. "It swept us up for a little. Simon is right in that, Da," and he swung about to his father. "This is a good time to be selling brew and cider. We ought to be able to pay a few debts and still rake in enough to tide ourselves through till thaw next year."

"If we had enough to fulfill a decent-sized contract, which we haven't."

"Then," Garner said, shuffling papers on his lap and looking up, "we offer better than that. Not quantity but quality. Private stock, for only the most discerning drinker."

Tolby stared at Garner a long moment. Then he responded slowly, "My drink is good enough for that."

"It's the best, Da," offered Nutmeg. "You know that."

"This is no time to be humble." Garner stretched his legs out, meeting his father's long look.

"And, my dear, my shop is making money. I can help." Lily refolded the reference packet from Mistress Greathouse, slipping it into her apron.

"I still can't abide paying a debt that this land doesn't owe!"

"It's Greathouse who should be paying us." Keldan's surly words dropped like stones in a deep, quiet well, and the ripples spread out among them. "Well, it's true. She sold us a bundle of trouble, and how is it she didn't be knowing that?"

Tolby tugged on his vest a moment. Then he said grudgingly, "It's my fault. She told me this was a business she'd neglected, that's why th' price was within my reach. She doesna know if these loan papers are genuine or forgeries, if we borrowed or not. It's to her credit she sent Simon for aid. It's my fault for forgettin' the crooks who lie a-waitin' in cities, schemers and such. I should have gotten our papers together earlier, and found a clerk t' certify everything. I was too busy with my hands ta use my mind."

"There's no help for that, now. Pay now and sue. It should all work out in the end. Trader Simon offered us a fair chance. They could have served and taken our stock." Garner put away his ink and pen as he spoke, then got up and put his hand on his father's shoulder.

"And I," Hosmer told him, "may get placed in the Town Guard. Surely there's a coin or two in that."

He drew sharp looks from everyone in the room, and his chin went up in answer as Lily inhaled steeply.

"Not only a coin but a story I think you have yet to tell us." Garner traded looks with Hosmer over their father's head.

"There is not enough money," Tolby said mildly to Hosmer, "to be worth losing your place here. Still that leaves me with four strong children. It could be worse."

Keldan coughed. "Could we talk over dinner? I swear my stomach thinks my throat has been cut." He nudged Hosmer and Nutmeg toward the kitchen with its great plank table, and the aroma that had filled the room suddenly smelled savory again.

"Now that is an idea." Tolby stuffed his cold pipe into his pocket and led the way.

Garner and Hosmer both jostled Keldan as they seated themselves, with Hosmer saying, "I've seen a cut throat or two. Trust me, your stomach shouldn't worry."

Rivergrace felt a chill run through her at his words, which carried an edge despite his teasing grin.

Lily pinched Hosmer's ear, saying, "Stop that. I've good food on the table, if it is a bit colder than I intended, and this is no time for your militia stories."

She had them all quiet and tucking into their dinner in good order, and Nutmeg leaned over to Grace to whisper, "The Town Guard could use her, too," even as she picked up a fork and smiled innocently. Over her first bite, she said to Keldan, "Curly throws a mean punch. And Vevner is no slouch either."

"Aye? How so?"

They spent the rest of the evening swapping news and opinions.

Her mind filled with worry, Lily shook out the clothes to leave them for laundry as the house settled down to sleep, Tolby calling out sleepily for her. Rivergrace's and Nutmeg's garments told more of a tale than Hosmer had, but she decided not to ask questions. They were safe, and she could think of far greater troubles than a scuffle with those who had been drinking overmuch.

A slip of paper fell to the floor. She scooped it up without thinking, and replaced it in the packet of news from Robin Greathouse, to be read more carefully at the shop in the morning. She would have to hire two more seamstresses, but Adeena offered two cousins with good stitching who wanted work and that seemed the best possibility. She had clients and fabric beyond her wildest dreams, but it seemed that those with money parted with it slowly. Perhaps she could speak with Trader Simon about getting her clients to pay on delivery or at least promptly. The little shop was indeed making a profit although she turned that back into fabric purchases almost sooner than she pocketed it. She would not place that weight on Tolby's shoulders, though. She would deal with it, and help him besides. With a sigh, she let down her hair, brushing it out gently and trying not to notice the new graying strands before going to join her husband in bed.

He woke on fire, lying atop his bed, sheet twisted under him. His thighs, loins, and the flat of his belly ached even without a touch upon him, but he had been dreaming of eyes the color of many seas, and that alone soothed him enough to get any sleep at all. Sevryn rose and bathed quickly, standing at the bowl of water, watching the gray light slant through the window shutters. The only welt that did not burn was where she had accidentally touched him when they fell together, as though her hand had drawn out the poison. He looked down at his flank, at the scarring. He did not imagine it. Instead of the fiery red mark, part of the scar lay flat and white, healed cleanly. Who was she and what had she done to him?

Yet the need to be with her far exceeded his for answers. He wanted simply to stand with her.

The obligations he must fulfill, however, to Lariel and her blood outweighed his own. He had seen her and her brother put aside their personal lives time and again in just that manner. As had he. Trouble was, he'd never regretted it before.

Perhaps sometime during the next few days, Lariel might need an escort to a fitting.

Perhaps.

The first shards of daylight struck Sevryn as he made his way across town toward the guild quarter, where the small bistro Azel mentioned reigned. Clouds parted momentarily, even as they built upon one another in great towers, edged in obsidian. The rich scent of defer, shaved from its blocks, and then boiled in frothing milk and spices rode on the heavily clouded day. He found a table with seats to the wall, angled oddly yet near a door, and sat after satisfying himself that Azel had not already arrived. A serving girl flitted near and off again as he shook his head. He sat and listened to faraway rumbling, his ears feeling more than hearing thunder from the distance as the storm moved in.

Azel entered after a few moments, his bulk moving with that eerie Vaelinarran grace, searched the room, and then spied Sevryn in the corner. It was like watching a bear lumber through a forest without cracking a twig or bending a branch. He crooked a finger at the girl before seating himself. "The defer here is one of the few good reasons to visit Calcort."

"And others?"

Azel paused a very long time until the corner of his mouth twitched. "I'm thinking!"

Sevryn laughed with him.

The girl must have brought Azel other breakfasts before, because she brought not only two steaming mugs of defer but also a platter of breads and cheeses, and two hearty bowls of oat stew, a concoction of cooked oats, dried fruits, honey, and nuts. A small pitcher of butter-dotted cream came along with two spoons for the breakfast stew.

They ate in silence for moments, enjoying the fare, and avoiding the unpleasantness of the meeting Azel had called. He had nearly finished when Azel wiped his mouth and sat back in his chair, eyeing Sevryn. "I'm glad you came."

"So far, I'm glad as well." Sevryn drew his mug of defer close to his chest, dropping one hand below the tabletop, where he could draw his knives more easily as he listened. He watched the room and saw only a crowd of diners, scattered at the small tables throughout the room and spilling onto the street lane.

Azel cocked his head. "I'm sure Lariel will have your ears if I do not tell you why I'm here, so I'll save them for you." He tapped his heavy hand on the tabletop. "I'm going to propose three more libraries, at points throughout these provinces and the warlands to the east. It will take funding and sponsorship, and training of new copyists and scribes. While you may not see the political ramifications immediately, she will." He gazed out over the room a moment, at the citizens breakfasting quietly, and going back and forth. "I intend to make them open to all."

"Open?"

"Open," repeated Azel firmly. "Anyone who can read may come in and read our copies."

"Even the Vaelinar histories?"

"Especially the Vaelinar histories. It is time we leave behind ourselves as the Suldarran, the Lost, and move to join Kerith. It's our home. We have to accept that."

"Half your power is in the unknown, the mythology of being not of Kerith."

"Yes." Something glittered deep in Azel's eyes. "A false influence, don't you think? Knowledge is the truest power. And, there are other reasons which I will tell Lariel if she'll grant me an audience, alone. Important reasons."

"I'll tell her."

He nodded. "You drew me out, as well. I came to listen to folk stories and children's rhymes, and I heard something disturbing on the streets." He leaned forward, dropping into a melodious bass and sang quietly, "Four forges dire . . ."

Sevryn slapped his hand over Azel's, shutting the man off. Azel continued smiling mildly at him despite that. "How did you know?"

A silvery flash illuminated the interior of the room for a moment as weather broke overhead, the long awaited storm.

"I didn't. I came and listened, and that struck a chord in me. I don't know why or who sent you to ferret that out, but I heard what you may not, could not. You were not raised Vaelinar, that much is obvious in every movement you make, nothing faulting you, but it blinds you to nuances that we can see."

Thunder rumbled heavily. Chairs and tables pushed across the floor as occupants decided to leave, hurrying back to their proper places before rain pelted down and flooded the streets. The area grew crowded, even the corner, as diners milled about.

"It's vital you understand," Azel told him in a low voice. "The Elven Ways we've made lead to life, but—" Azel jerked as he stopped abruptly.

Sevryn was watching. He swore he was watching and yet he never saw the strike. Azel sucked his breath in sharply, with a guttural sound of pain, people moving about their table, bumping, even as lightning overhead struck and thunder crackled immediately upon its heels, shaking the whole building. The historian keeled over facefirst.

Sevryn leaped to his feet. He shoved away those closest just to get across the table, rolling Azel over. A dagger impaled his side, and Sevryn pulled it loose, the handle branded with an elaborate K. He pocketed it as he yelled for a healer and the guards. Azel breathed, heavily, painfully. His life bubbled on his lips as he tried to say something more to Sevryn, but he couldn't catch it. He held the man in his arms.

"Keep breathing," he told d'Stanthe. "Just keep breathing. It'll get better. I promise," with no way of knowing if he could keep that promise.

Chapter Forty-Six

HE FELL INTO AN icy void of absolute darkness. The first assault he had not even felt, the second thrust he did, as the steel buried itself deeply into him. Surprised, he sucked in a breath, knowing it would be one of his last. He had more to say! More he had to say . . .

Azel felt himself losing all that he had known. The sensation of having hands, feet, a body, passed beyond him. Strong arms picked him up, warm arms against the sudden chill. A voice pierced his plummeting fall. Blood roared through his ears in a deafening flood as it carried death through him in an inexorable tide, but he heard the Voice.

It commanded him. It refused to let him let go.

He struggled against the compulsion and could not resist it. Weakening second by second, he answered it. He breathed.

He found a silvery strand trailing after him and clung to it, all that kept him from the final fall, obeying the order given him. As he pulled it into himself, it looped before him, toward a future he thought his life had abandoned. It might have been a rope, but Azel thought of it as luminous ink, written against the dark of nothingness. It was a sentence, a record, that he had yet to finish, its strand of thought and soul leaping out just ahead of him. Keep breathing. Live. Somehow.

Chapter Forty-Seven

RAIN POURED DOWN amid the grumbling of thunder, washing away the grit of summer, but not cooling, each drop as hot as the season that bore it. Roofs shed the water in cascades. Lily hurried under the onslaught, her oil-slicked, wide-brimmed hat protecting her from most of it, but her shoes quickly becoming damp in spite of trying to jump and hop puddles. Having worked the orchard for most of her adult years, her good shoes were in an inside pocket of her cape, and these old shoes had seen many a splash and far worse. Everyone still on foot bustled by in a hurry, skirting eaves and gutters and puddling holes as well as they could. A carriage sat on the side street nearby, its driver and horses wet as if standing for a while. She unlocked her shop quickly. Adeena materialized almost on her heels with a smile as she shook out her wet kerchief and placed it on a hook to dry.

"My cousins will be here soon, Mistress Farbranch. They're bringing samplers with them."

"Good, good, but I've your word on them already. I'm sure they'll work out." Lily kicked her shoes off and toed them under a table, dropping her good, dry ones on the floor. She'd barely stepped into them when the two veiled ones stepped through the door, sprinkling rain off them like a fine mist, looking as if the downpour had merely kissed them with wetness. Or, perhaps they'd been sitting in the parked carriage, out of the weather. The taller one, in a rustle of fine silks, put her veil back. "I was in the quarter breakfasting and decided to stop by and see if you've received my yard goods yet."

"Oh, yes! Late yesterday. We were going to send a messenger lad out this morn." Lily pointed the way to the back storeroom. "My daughters remembered that you wished to inspect it first."

Galraya smiled wryly. "Not often, but occasionally, I am shorted on my orders. It is thought that I have coin the way the sky has rain, and can afford to pay for goods not delivered." She glanced upward to the sound on the roof. "Would that it were so." She glided soundlessly after Lily, her companion staying in the outer room, browsing and murmuring to Adeena.

One shoe on, the other half on and stubbornly folding under her foot, Lily manufactured a coolness she did not feel, as she found the latest stock. She stepped back as Lady Galraya identified the bale as hers, and gave her a questioning look as if she wished to be left alone.

Adeena questioned her from the other room, saving Lily the quandary of asking if that was her wish. She dropped a half curtsy. "If you don't mind, I'll go see what's needed?"

"Of course."

Adeena fretted the moment she crossed the threshold. Drawing Lily aside, so the second woman could not hear them talking, she stared at the rear door where the deliveries were made and said, "The carter came by. He has a delivery for us but says he won't make it because you are behind on payments."

"I'm what?"

Adeena flushed heavily. "Not to him, Mistress, but to the textile warehouse."

"A few days, perhaps, at the most." Lily frowned. "It's none of his business. He delivers their goods; he has no say with their accounts."

"It's their way." Adeena wrung her hands. "They put pressure on for the warehouses."

"And no doubt wag their tongues." Lily felt the muscles along the back of her shoulders knot, and she hadn't even started on the day's work yet. "I'll take care of it, no need to worry." There was no way she'd have a Trader Simon in her doorway, trying to collect money they could ill afford to owe. Not after she'd told Tolby she could pull her own weight and help with his load as well! After her shift, she'd march down and settle a thing or two with the warehouse. She patted Adeena. "No worrying!"

"Mistress Farbranch?"

Lily turned and returned to the soft query from the storeroom. Lady Galraya smoothed her expression out carefully. "It appears the bale has been opened, against my explicit instructions."

"Actually, m'lady, as my daughters related, the carter was a little rough with the cargo and it had come partially untied. As you can see from the cords," and Lily picked up what was left of them, for Galraya had slashed through with what must have been an exceedingly sharp knife, and showed the different knots to the veiled one. "Nutmeg retied it as she put it away. It wasn't opened by us. Is everything else all right?"

"No one else has been through my things?"

"No, m'lady. Are you missing goods?"

"No. Not quite." Galraya turned her gaze to the shelves, and ran her hand over other bales. "All my yardage came in the one piece?"

"Yes, m'lady."

Galraya made a noise of unhappiness, then straightened. "Very well, then. It's all there, ready for your tailoring."

"Very good. We have your deposit?"

"Not yet, but, now is as good a time as any." Smiling thinly, the woman opened a sleeve pocket and retrieved a fine-grained leather purse. She shook out an ample sum. "Send a receipt by messenger, will you? Along with a fitting date."

"Of course."

The veiled one swept by her, a blush deepening her coppery skin, and she left without a word to her companion who dropped a blouse into Adeena's hands and scurried to catch up as she went out the door.

There was no mistaking the oddness of it all, but Lily had no answer, and no time for contemplating one. She shrugged it off as she signaled Adeena her intent to go in and begin working. The door had barely closed before it opened again, with a fluttering of noise and nervous laughter, and greetings from Adeena.

She turned at the workroom door, and saw two women, one young and one almost old enough to be the first one's mother, come in. They shook off shawls and dipped curtsies nervously in her direction.

"Mistress Farbranch! May I present Shyna and Goodie? Not only on time, but even early." Adeena's normally serious expression beamed as she drew the two to Lily.

The younger one, plump and with laugh lines about her eyes and a dimple in one cheek, bobbed again, and pulled a roll from her purse, thrusting it at Lily. "My sampler, Mistress."

The taller, older one whose face carried a perpetual worried look like Adeena's held herself back after a half smiling nod.

Goodie nibbled on a fingertip as Lily took the rolled-up cloth and opened it. Neat stitching of all kinds presented themselves in a small workpiece that gave her name and lineage, and embroidery decorated it with fanciful flowers and birds, the sampler a reflection of the girl even better than a mirror. Lily found herself smiling at it. "This is wonderful. I'm sure you'll work out fine, Goodie."

The dimple flashed broadly as Lily handed her back the piece, and she bobbed again. Adeena took her by the elbow so that Shyna could approach with her samplers.

These were several layers done, and she thumbed through them. The work, again, was very good, and she knew she could use both women without reservation. But something about Shyna's demeanor bothered her a bit. She hid her reluctance and handed the samplers back, saying, "Excellent workmanship. I'd be pleased to hire both of you."

Adeena stepped forward. "Shyna requires an early afternoon, Mistress Farbranch. Off a mark before suppertime, if that's all right with you. Goodie can stay until regular marks."

An odd request, but losing a candlemark of work time was hardly extraordinary. Adeena stared at her brightly as if trying to communicate something beyond words. Lily continued to smile. "That would be fine. I do pay by the candlemark, so if either of you wish certain hours, just arrange them with Adeena so that I can schedule your tasks." She smoothed her apron down. "Please settle them in, and get them started? I have a pattern to lay out and cut."

Relief ran through Adeena as she turned her relatives aside and began to show them the layout of the shop, work rooms, fitting rooms, and storerooms as Lily retreated, certain that Shyna's story would be filling her ears in a short time.

She seated herself at her desk and found the glasses that had come with the shop and helped to enlarge the stitching. The lenses were scratched with use and she supposed that they were little better than no help at all, but such things were expensive and she was embarrassed that she needed to use them. She unfolded Robin Greathouse's packet which included a small, sealed note to her as well as a letter of introduction to the trader and collector Simon and a small note to Tolby giving her advice on the situation. Robin wrote in her neat but elaborate script that the Farbranch holdings had been occupied but now lay fallow, as the raids continued and the lands were dangerous. Lily frowned at that. She had striven for many days to replace her memories of blackened, smoldering remains with the home she'd help build and had seen flourish. Perhaps it would again. Seasons, she thought. Sometimes seasons had to come and go.

A second folded note fell out, unsealed. She opened it curiously, for its paper stock seemed quite different from the other sheets. And, indeed, it did not belong with the others. The handwriting was stiff, stark, and marched boldly across the paper. Galdarkan, unless she was mistaken, although it was neither signed nor carried any identification. She had gotten used to Galdarkan script when helping Tolby to fill harvest orders. The written language was a common one, but there were peculiarities from one province to another, and one race to another, despite that. She stared at the flowing words inked blackly on the paper.

War brings together the swords we need. Do your job and hold back reaction as long as you can. I will send for you upon the unleashing of our plans.

Lily dropped the sheet into her lap in shock. Had this belonged to Robin and she included it by mistake? Or to Trader Simon? She could not question it lightly. Greathouse involved in the trade of warfare? No, she could not think it. But if not belonging to Robin, if slipped unaware into her letters, it belonged to someone who might be quite upset at the letter going where it wasn't intended.

Lily gathered it up, folded it back into place, and stuck it into a small, hidden drawer in the desk. As dangerous as it was to have it at all, it seemed to her far more dangerous to try to find out where it had come from, and for whom it was meant. When matters settled with Tolby, she would show it to him. Not before. Even the best of Dwellers could only carry so many burdens at a time.

"Will he make it?"

"You did," Lariel returned quietly, as she tiptoed from the nursing room and joined both Sevryn and Jeredon. "He wasn't meant to, but he might. He's far more muscle than he looks, and the upward thrust into his rib cage was deflected by that, as well as by a bone that he'd broken when young and that healed at a bit of an angle."

"The blade is poisoned."

"We thought it might have been. You have it, then?"

Sevryn nodded as he produced it. He laid it carefully on the table between them.

"That's something I'd hoped never to handle again." Jeredon tapped the ornate K carved into the haft of the dagger.

"We knew he had a target in the city besides myself. I can only hope that Azel was the only one." Lariel tilted her head toward Sevryn. "How could you not see him?"

Sevryn shook his head. "I don't know. I absolutely don't know. The lightning flashed, the thunder broke right overhead, the whole building rattled as if it would come down, I blinked . . . and it was done. I saw nothing. Not the first strike or the second." He sighed. "How could I have missed it?"

"The Kobrir is legendary for his swiftness."

Sevryn made a noise of disgust. "Preparation, not luck. Agility, perhaps, and timing. The storm opened with violence, people milled about in surprise. I saw it, but I saw nothing out of the ordinary until too late." He paced across the floor. "When is the turning point expected?"

Lariel lifted a shoulder and dropped it in a graceful shrug. "I can't tell you, nor can the healer. How he's holding on now, we can't begin to understand, but he is. A man of iron will."

"He had matters he wished to discuss with you, and what we talked about, he did not finish."

"But he did say something?"

"A little. He said you'd understand the implication more than I, and Gilgarran would box my ears for not understanding the intrigue. Azel wanted to build a few more libraries throughout the regions. Train and hire staff for them."

Lariel took a chair and pulled it close to her brother. "Not unreasonable. He won't have an easy time of it, but if he can raise the funding, the Conference would probably back him. I don't see the problem with it."

"He wants to have them open to everyone who can read and make use of them. All records would be available."

Jeredon glanced at Lariel. Her eyes of blues and gold and silvery streaks held an unreadable depth within them as she thought. She took an exceedingly long time to tuck a stray curl of hair behind her ear, and the silence lengthened.

Sevryn broke it by adding, “He said it was time to accept your position as being part of Kerith.”

“A radical thought that has some backers, but not without dissent. We don’t wish our histories laid open. That could be difficult,” she conceded. “Although I don’t think it would make him a target for assassination. Was that the last he spoke?”

“No. He told me he has some things which he could only discuss with you privately. I think he was waiting for the time.”

“I’ve always been available for Azel.”

Jeredon moved. “Sister, he knew the Kobrir was stalking. Perhaps he was waiting for a safer, more opportune time, not wanting to expose either of you unnecessarily.”

“Perhaps.” She sighed. “His recovery, if he makes one, will be extended. We may never know, or we may know too late. He did not mention Diort to you, so that isn’t what was on his mind.”

“It could be he meant that for you. He did say that, by quiet observance of who came to his library and what they researched, one could learn much. I don’t see any link between the traders’ message and d’Ferstanthe, myself, and I wasn’t given the time to find one.”

“More questions and precious little answers.”

Sevryn held himself quiet, waiting for her to ask yet again if there was anything else, for if she did, he would tell her about the child’s game. But if she did not, he would keep that close to him as long as he could, until he found his answers. The thought nagged at him that he dare not wait as Azel did and lose time altogether.

Lariel rubbed one eye wearily. “What do we do now?”

“We,” said Jeredon firmly, “watch your back day and night.”

She let loose a pungent curse. Sevryn did not move. Finally, she sighed and said, “I have a fitting this afternoon, and the Conference opens this evening.”

“A shop filled with lissome women? I doubt either of us will find that a hardship!” Jeredon stifled a groan as she stood swiftly and moved past him to the corridor, managing to plant a firm step on the middle of his booted foot as she did so. He limped after her in exaggerated pain, crying out, “M’lady, how can I guard you if you leave me behind in your wake?”

Sevryn followed as Lariel laughed and dropped back to let Jeredon flank her. After his failure of the morning, he knew that it might very well not help her at all to have either of them with her. *He hadn’t seen the strike.*

He did not want to consider what it would mean to lose her as well. The Kobrir liked the rib shot, to the heart, with poison to ensure the hit. He'd have to persuade Lariel to wear a warrior's corset under her gowns. It might not be so difficult to get her to acquiesce. Knowing her, she might even wear it brazenly *over* her dresses, as a reminder of what sort of Vaelinar queen she was, in times when many doubted her ability to carry out her title.

He shouldn't have worried about presenting that to her, he realized as they entered the small tailoring shop, carrying the knapsack with two well-armored corsets in it, as functional as they were decorative. Their weight alone told him that. Jeredon sent him a hunter's whistle as he took his sister in first, letting him know that all was clear. He checked behind as he stepped in, and the sight of her, the willowy one with the cool river eyes, was like a blow to his stomach, sending the breath from him.

Sevryn bowed. "Afternoon, aderro."

Rivergrace swung around from a sewing dummy as she fitted it with a dress and pins, her long hair cascading about her shoulders in dark chestnut waves, highlighted with reds and golds even without the sunlight to bring them forth. Her gaze lit as it fell upon his face, eyes of gray-blue and green-blue and pure deep-sea blue. "Greetings, my lord. Do you accompany Queen Lariel or are you here on another's behalf?"

"We," said Jeredon dryly, "are but dust specks in the wake of her brilliance." He winked at Nutmeg as she put her hand over her mouth to keep from laughing.

Lariel said to Nutmeg, "Have you brothers?"

"Three."

"Then you know what torture I suffer."

"Oh, indeed! Although," she eyed Jeredon. "I think we can even the tally. You, sir, must hold the silvered glass for me, so I can fit her from all angles. You are now at my mercy. And mind you, don't drop it or let it shake!" Nutmeg gave a menacing frown.

Sevryn put his knapsack into Rivergrace's slender hands as Jeredon let out a mock groan and Lariel chuckled. They touched, briefly, and he felt again that soothing, cooling wash of sensation from her. Could she be a healer and not know it? She had the eyes, after all . . . but no. It felt like nothing he had ever felt from any healer. Something else, something profoundly different. It stirred him even as it took the kedant fever from him, replacing it with a heat altogether different. Did she feel it, too? He thought she must as she looked up at him, a slight confusion on her face, quickly hidden as she turned aside to put the knapsack on the counter and open it, taking out the battle gear.

"What is this?"

"Those," Lariel told her, "are my new accessories. I hate to do this to the lines of such a beautiful gown, but I'll be wearing them under, or over, however you think it best. But wear them I will."

Nutmeg blinked. "Both at once?" She tapped the mail corset and the chain.

Jeredon coughed as Lariel said, "Well, no . . . not at once. That might be a little excessive."

"Then I don't see a problem!" Nutmeg trotted off to fetch her little ladder and the silvered glass, and the soft murmurs of Lily questioning Nutmeg in the back delayed her return only briefly. She came back out with her ladder over her shoulder and set it up, even as she pressed the silvered glass into Jeredon's grip.

"These are armor." Rivergrace stroked a finger over the tastefully bejeweled corsets.

"Yes, aderro, they are. Our queen thinks it wise not to let people think she's gone soft albeit she does have the loveliest of curves." Sevryn ignored the sharp look sent his way, although the corner of his mouth twitched a little.

"What does that mean, 'aderro'?"

"You don't know? It comes from the Dweller greeting, derro . . . the little people. We use it to mean 'little one.' It's an endearment," Jeredon answered in Sevryn's place, as he inspected the silvered glass in his hands, turning it about to examine the workmanship.

"I see," said Rivergrace faintly.

The collar of Sevryn's shift seemed a little tight and overly warm. He rolled his shoulders to ease it.

"You there," Nutmeg said smartly. "Pay attention. I need the glass here," and she pointed, "to look at the fit of the gown there." And she dropped the half-finished garment over Lariel's head, the two of them tugging it into place. The supple fabric fell into exquisite lines, and Lariel gasped at the glimpse of herself in the corner of the mirror facing her.

"Now. Before I finish the torso, I can gusset it ever so slightly to allow for the armor underneath. If we do that, it will be hidden, although . . . I can leave this seam open here and here, and bring the neckline down here," Nutmeg frowned in thought as she spoke, "plunging, as it were, but revealing the corset. Or, we can leave the lines as designed, and simply strap the corset over, and I would eliminate this drape here, at the waistline, since you will be cinched in. Your choice, Highness."

"I vote for the plunge."

Lariel rolled her eyes at Jeredon. She caught sight of Rivergrace standing quietly at Nutmeg's side. "What do you think?"

"I think," said Rivergrace softly, "that you will be magnificent no matter how it is done, and that a gown is the least of your problems." She clasped her hand over her mouth at that.

"I beg your pardon?" Lariel swung about to face her.

Rivergrace paused, as if groping for words, although she sank back a little as if she'd said too much.

"It's all right," Sevryn told her.

She looked at him, then back to Lariel. "It's only that. How can I say it? I sense a river about you. Deep and strong, with all the currents a free-flowing river has within it, Spring flood and late fall ebbing, pools and torrents, a blessing and a caution. You are far more than a dancing gown, m'lady." And she dropped into a curtsy at that, head down, as though afraid even as thunder and rain ceased and all became silent for a long, uncomfortable moment.

Chapter Forty-Eight

"ADERRO," SAID JEREDON, with a snort. "Little one, indeed. Your lass is a bloody prophet."

"No. No, I don't think so." Sevryn watched the rain pelt past the apartment windows as they waited for Lariel to ready herself for her appearance. Every drop added to the heaviness of the moisture, a veritable steam, rising from the city. "She hardly knew what she said till it came out. And she is *not* my lass."

"I'll argue that one later. She hasn't been raised among us, she's even more clumsy than you, and I'll agree she surprised herself even more than she surprised Lariel, but that is the way of prophets, isn't it?"

"Nutmeg calls her sister."

"Nutmeg? The saucy one who tweaked my nose when I didn't get the glass in place in time?"

"Aye, that one."

Jeredon grinned. "Came up to my chin on that little stepladder of hers."

"And you nearly wore that ladder, except I think she fancied your parting pinch."

"Someone had to cheer up Lariel."

Their Warrior Queen had laughed at the sparring between Jeredon and the small but feisty bundle of Dweller, but Sevryn doubted the humor would carry far under the circumstances. "Mmmm. She's going to stride into that meeting room looking for a fight."

"I'll have to appeal to her diplomatic side."

"She does have one, doesn't she?"

Jeredon shrugged at Sevryn. "She tells me she does." Putting his foot up on the seat of a chair, he leaned over with a soft cloth and buffed his boot. "So why isn't this Rivergrace your lass?"

"I've barely seen her."

"Makes no difference."

"What, no difference?"

Jeredon stropped the leather briskly. "None. Do you know nothing about us? Have you not heard Bistane sing "Lost Trevilara"? We are fated, Sevryn, to have soul mates or no real love at all."

"Rubbish." Although he could believe it with Tressandre. There was lust but no love in that one's veins.

"Amusing to hear my brother has a poetic streak," Lariel added as she swept into the room, fastening a bracelet that was more bracer than delicate linkage. She wore one of the Dweller shop's cunning belled trouser-and-shirt sets, her corset fastened over it, accenting the span of her trim waist. "I trust the two of you are washed, outfitted, and weaponed accordingly?" The weapons were to be cunningly hidden, as weapons were outlawed at the Conference. Nearly everyone would be wearing them, despite that, but discreetly, particularly as word got out about the attack on Azel d'Stanthe.

Sevryn bowed. "We are. At least, I washed," he added smugly. With a supple twist, he avoided the snap of Jeredon's buffing rag.

"The best I could hope for. All right, then. We are doomed to candlemarks of boring lectures and diplomacy."

"In that case," Jeredon told her dryly, "I suggest you lead the way and shield us as best you can."

Lariel reached out and tweaked his nose before doing just that.

Saying flatly, "Ow," Jeredon caught up with her. "I think it's still bruised by sturdy Dweller fingers." He rubbed his countenance ruefully.

"Serves you right. Even a peasant can hold a silvered glass straight."

"I shall count it among my many deficiencies."

Sevryn paced behind them, watching, as they stepped into corridors he could not count as safe. No place would be considered safe until they returned to Larandaril and even that small kingdom might be open to treachery as the ild Fallyn suggested.

Times had begun to turn, as Gilgarran and Daravan had warned him they would. And turning quickly.

* * *

Tranta met Lariel first inside the great hallway, a gray pallor still underlying the faint blue of his skin, and his hair had been braided over the shaved spot where his scalp had been gashed, then stitched. He leaned on a cane though not heavily. Jeredon chose to defuse his sister's emotion as she embraced one of her dearest friends.

"Going for that twin look with Bregan Oxfort, are you?" He toed the cane, not totally out from under Tranta but enough that Tranta straightened with a chuckle to right himself immediately.

"Unfair!" Tranta protested. "I was saving the juicy gossip that he was to be my dance partner until later!" He hugged Jeredon anyway, directing a low inquiry toward Lariel. "Is it true that Azel lies on his deathbed?"

"True, and yet we hope to cheat his Return."

"If anyone can, you can." He released Jeredon, absentmindedly striking him in the shin sharply with the cane as he did so. Jeredon winced, and Tranta winked toward him.

"So how is it you fell from a cliff face you've been climbing since you were knee-high to your mother?" Jeredon leaned on him, pleased to see that Tranta returned the wince.

Quietly, Tranta answered, "I did not fall, I was pushed."

"What? I was told you had no recollection." Lariel's chin went up.

"I hadn't. It's come back, faintly, in the last handful of days or so. I asked Tiiva for an audience with you, but she told me your ear was being bent in so many different ways, it would be a wonder if you had one left."

Lariel frowned as she drew Tranta close to her. "My apologies, dear cousin."

"None needed. What is said here, hopefully, will not be overheard." Tranta paused thoughtfully. "There is more."

Jeredon propelled them into a nearby corner, saying loudly, "Compare trousers, then, damn it all. I need a drink," and he stomped off. Sevryn eased his body into place between them and the growing crowd.

Lariel leaned close to Tranta to hear him speak as Sevryn buffered them.

"The Jewel of Tomarq falters."

"Ill news. How badly? Your House is strong?"

"As far as I know, we remain strong, but as to how badly, I can't predict at this point, Lariel. It weakens, then regains itself. I'm researching everything I have at hand to learn how to charge it, but I've not found much yet. The making of a Way is kept secret, you know that."

Regret flickered through her eyes. "I do."

"As for who met or followed me up on that cliff, I can't say either. Only that someone was there who intended I wouldn't live through the encounter."

"I'll mark your words." Lara leaned forward and kissed his forehead with a merry laugh she did not feel. Tranta broke away with a grin and a wave, to limp himself across the meeting room hall, belying the somber news he'd given her.

"At least we know it wasn't the Kobrir," Sevryn murmured as he rejoined her.

"What? Why do you say that?"

"He favors poison as insurance. He would have used that despite the fall."

She found a breath and took it, long and deep. "I don't know if you've given me good news on that, or worse news." She caught someone's eye across the way, and with a wave, moved toward them, Sevryn a step or two behind her as he would stay until sent away or the Conference ended.

As the attendees arrived and the room filled with Vaelinars in all their glory, their grace, their skin a rainbow of color, their flashing eyes and luxuriant hair, he felt a gaze tickle over him, a heat running down the back of his neck. Sevryn turned slightly and saw Tressandre ild Fallyn watching him from across the room. She pivoted away as if unnoticing, her dark honey hair glinting in the sunlight and lamplight, a jeweled riding crop hanging from her belt, her body wrapped in black and silver. Her beauty hit him hard until, after a long moment, breathing became natural again.

"Don't you think, Sevryn? Sevryn?"

He faced Jeredon. "I often think."

"Not on this occasion, it seems. Her Highness wants you to make rounds, and hand her guarding off to me for a while."

He sketched a bow and retreated, almost backing into Bistane who also watched someone across the room, but the figure in his regard was Lariel. Nor did he notice that several women watched him watching her, talking to themselves as they did, their eyes narrowed in envy.

Sevryn decided a drink would do him some good. He paused at the small tavern area, then decided the drink would still do him good.

"I'll have a light blush," the woman in front of him told the tender.

"I'll wager you've never blushed in your life, Tressandre," he said.

She waited till she had drink in hand before turning round to him, so close they nearly touched. He'd already poured himself a hard cider and the goblet in his fist fought to stay chilled.

"And would you care if I had?" She smiled at him over the rim of her drink.

"I don't believe so."

She leaned closer, and her free hand traced up his thigh, across the kedant-laced welt, and it responded instantly, burning, stirring him, and words left him. "Interesting. Your eyes darken when you lie."

He found a few. "Perhaps they darken when I finally tell the truth."

Tressandre considered him. She withdrew her hand, leaving him pressing against her, his voice deepening as desire swept him. He wanted to be in her hands again until his body freed itself from the constraints he and she put upon him, until the fire burned away. It had nothing to do with tenderness or passion. It went beyond and was far darker than that.

"Perhaps," she answered. "I shall remember that."

He did not stay for all of her answer, swiveling on his heels before she finished, knowing that if she looked at him now, it would be daggers at his back. No one left Tressandre before she was finished with them. But he had to move, or he would be enslaved at her side the entire evening, unable to order himself away. He gathered his willpower and kept moving, legs nearly numb, the cider shaking in his hand. He raised it finally and took a gulp, and the crisp, clear sweetness swept over his taste buds and woke his mouth up, and the rest of his senses began to follow. It was the kedant, nothing more. He sent his thoughts back to a simple tailoring shop and the one who worked there, and a cleansing coolness swept over him.

It brought a semblance of sensibility back, and left him wanting, but it was not for Tressandre.

A voice boomed over the crowd. "Seating time, kindred! The Conference opens."

He watched as the Vaelinars flowed toward the speaking hall, where it was rumored there were alcoves where whispered words from the other end of the building could be overheard, and he did not doubt that. He stayed in the back, on his feet, Lariel and her brother never out of his sight, and Tressandre never within it.

Lily stood and stretched, cramped muscles at the back of her neck and shoulders telling her that she'd been hunched over her sewing too long.

What had been a joy was now her livelihood, and one she pushed herself very hard at. Adeena looked up from her panel.

"It's later than I thought. The sky is still very gray."

"I thought you sent Shyna home."

"True, I have. I forgot." Adeena rubbed her eyebrow.

"Are you going to tell me why she has short hours?"

"She drinks, Mistress. If you keep her longer, she'll bring the drink here, and her work will suffer for it. Let her go, and she will eventually stumble her way home, happy, and be back at work the next morning as expected." Adeena sighed. "It's a way of living with her and her needs."

"I've no quibble with her work, as long as she is sober here."

"Good. I worried about bringing her in." Adeena threw her a grateful look.

"I could use more hours from her, but I'll accept your judgment. And half a loaf is better than none." Lily drew herself up. "I'm addled." She grabbed her cape from its hook. "I'm off to settle that warehouse and carter!" With a wave, she was gone, leaving Adeena alone with Goodie who sat at the far table, stitching a gown panel pulled across a frame to make it easier and quicker to work on. She heard the bell at the front door tinkle a second time and wondered what her employer had forgotten. She rose to her feet.

"Is anyone about—oh! There you are. I've heard such things about your shop!"

Adeena looked at the excitable Kernan, her hands fluttering about. "Thom, dear man, said I could order a new dress and there's no time for you to come to the mayoral manor, so I came to you, aren't you pleased, and I absolutely adore the fabrics you have to work with!"

The Dweller husband and Kernan wife couple were neither usual nor unusual in matches, although certainly an odd one. He rotund and short, and she willowy and tall, he quiet, though forceful, and this one bobbing up and down like a butterfly trying to ride out a steep wind every time Adeena had seen them though she'd certainly never thought she'd see either one up close.

"Mistress Farbranch is out on a business appointment," she offered. "Perhaps I can assist you?"

"Of course. She oversees all the work."

"Definitely, madam."

"What a joy of a shop!" Before Adeena could assist or contain her,

Madam Stonehand darted throughout the building and workrooms, crying out at the sight of the gowns and dresses being worked up, some laid out on the tables and others pinned upon forms. She stopped long enough to grab Adeena's elbow.

"That one. I simply must have that one."

She pointed at the gown Nutmeg had nearly finished for the Warrior Queen Lariel.

"I'm so sorry, madam, but that's been commissioned."

"Oh! Of course, of course it has. And the fabric, exquisite, although not my color. I prefer greens. However," and the mayor's wife dropped her voice into a conspiratorial whisper. "Surely you can tailor another gown?"

They needed the coin. Adeena knew that from the raft of bills that came in, and from the pinched look on Lily's face. The magnificent gown was not to be copied, but how would its wearer know? A different fabric . . .

"Let me suggest some beautiful fine *shattan* we just received, and in a soft jade that would be most flattering to madam's eyes and coloring . . ."

"Perfect!" cried the woman, clapping her hands together.

And the deal was done before Lily returned, and Adeena had gone back to her own panels, pleased at bringing in a nice sum to the shop's coffers. She hadn't the backbone to run the place by herself, but she knew how to be a good support to Lily Farbranch, and by all the Gods, she would!

Chapter Forty-Nine

"WE ARE MET TO CONSIDER Petitions set forth to the Four Kingdoms and to share our welfare and concerns with one another." Bistel Vantane stood at the front of the assembly, shoulders slightly bowed but his wiry frame otherwise straight, his silvery-white hair cropped close to his skull, his eyes of dark, blazing blue watching his audience with piercing keenness. Only close enough to be struck by him could one see the rings of lighter blue around each iris, a distance few cared to approach with Bistel. Bistane was an echo of his father's physical presence and only slightly less feared. Like the vantane, the Vaelinar falcons brought to Kerith, Bistel gauged those he watched for weakness. He let his gavel fall on the podium at his elbow. It rang with agonizing sharpness.

"The Petitions have been gathered, and we shall weigh their merits. First, I will digress. Azel d'Stanthe of Ferstanthe had hoped to appear in a few days, when our own concerns will be presented, before misfortune struck him down. Queen Lariel Anderieon has asked to speak on his behalf."

A murmur shot through the room. Rumors had sharpened the ears of everyone, and Lariel rose with slight trepidation and made her way to the podium. Acoustics of the room made it possible to be heard quite well from the front, and she paused to take a breath.

"First, I will address the rumors. Yes, he has been struck by an assassin. As of this moment, he survives. We can't predict beyond this moment. He has the best care we can give, but he will have no visitors. I'm sure you all understand why. When his condition changes, you'll all be apprised as soon as possible." Lariel stopped speaking to let the reaction sweep the others, listening to murmurs and protests and a few shouted questions at her, which she did not intend to answer even if she could. When the assembly quieted again, she continued. "Azel hoped to present as well as attend this year. Because he deserves a voice, I'll give to you now, for your consideration in future days, what he proposes." Lariel looked over them, saw them listening, a mix of expressions on faces familiar and unfamiliar. "He wished more libraries built, and the funds not only to construct them but to train new scribes and copyists and historians to maintain them. Libraries not only on this coast but to the east. Three, in all, across the continent." She lifted a hand and placed it on the podium more to steady her voice than to steady her body. She eyed Sanfer, Azel's nephew and only heir, who looked as shocked as anyone, before moving her gaze onward. The burly man carried the d'Stanthe looks and, she hoped, ambitions. "Moreover, he wished to have the libraries open to all on Kerith who wish to use them."

That brought outbursts. She knew it would. She waited for the furor to die down a bit, then raised her own voice. "A proposal set forth to you by the House d'Ferstanthe. Consideration, arguments, and judgment to be given, as customary." She left the front then, returning to her place by Jeredon.

"That went well," he said dryly to her ear. "You're still standing."

"Thank you," she replied, then took her seat. "I wondered. Sanfer, from his reaction, knew nothing about any of this."

"Azel didn't expect to need an heir just yet."

"No. I imagine he didn't. I think we've all been forewarned."

Jeredon put his hand on her arm and squeezed gently.

Bistel dropped the gavel head again, gaining instant and absolute quiet. "Now we begin the Petitions. Foremost is that of Bregan Oxfort, trader, of the lineage Oxfort . . ."

Lariel sat back and let Bistel's crisp words dissolve into a drone. The elder Vantane had no love for the Oxforts but agreed to present their petition in her stead, as Lariel presented Azel's wishes and hopes. She'd had no desire to hold the podium any longer than necessary. Jeredon on one side, the wall and Sevryn on the other, and Bistel's own severe overseeing kept those around her from leaning over with inquiries and comments. She should listen well, she knew. The foreknowledge that this assembly would be exceptional danced along her nerves.

Abayan Diort knelt on one knee by the great-stone-and-earthen dam and put his palm to the thick wall of the structure. At his right shoulder, the still blue waters of the lake held by the dam lay, a great eye staring back at a sky of its own color. At his left shoulder, the river tamed by the dam and its fertile valley, its far-flung city of Inthera, fanned out below. He remembered his days as a child when this valley had been flooded out, ravaged with ferocious regularity by the river. He remembered the laborers going off to work on the dam, many losing their lives, but it had been built. Rakka growled at him, the war hammer in a new harness across his back, as he sifted through his memories.

A messenger rode up the steep hill, and Abayan rose to greet him.

"What word?" He did not fail to notice bandages bundled the left hand of his soldier, and fresh blood stained the linen. He wondered if the city had barbarically cut off the left thumb of a messenger who brought terms that would not be accepted.

His soldier saw his glance and covered the bandage with his good hand. "They reject any terms you bring them."

Abayan stared down at Inthera again. "Why do they not see?"

"Commander, I spoke as you bade me."

He had warned them of consequences if they refused his terms. He told them to send their children, their revered out of the valley. He saw no movement below despite his words. "I know you did. They're stubborn and blind." His countrymen believed that the downfall of the Galdarkans sprang from the Magi themselves, each Mage fiercely independent and jealous of any other's power, each holding elemental magic in a unique way, and each commanding his own small kingdom with Galdarkan guards. His own name, Abayan, came from the Mage Abas that his family had served. The battles of the Magi had also turned the Galdarkans upon one another until the end. Once released, they retreated to their own holdings, fiercely independent. That separation played into the hands of any enemy. Already divided, they could be conquered one by one. He allowed himself a single sigh of regret.

"Give the order to stand down, and remind the troops to stay on the high ground as I instructed them."

"Yes, sir." His man reined away, hissing through his teeth as his horse broke into a rough trot, jarring his maimed hand.

Diort waited several long, crawling moments for word to spread through his troops, his hard look ever on Inthera, staring to see if any one at all below took him his threat seriously. A few moved to nearby hillsides, but whether they did so because word reached them or because they were shepherds preparing to go out and round up grazing flocks, he had no way of knowing. The wagonloads he hoped to see, he did not.

After a time, he raised his hand to give a signal. His cavalry turned as one, facing downhill, readying themselves to go in. Horses stomped and champed at their bits, and spurs rang as they moved restlessly.

Abayan reached back for his war hammer and the weapon leaped into his hand, wood vibrating with a low buzz only he could hear. A guttural whisper for his ears only. He flexed his fingers tightly about it as he brought it forth. No need for a practice strike. Rakka knew stone and earth. He swung it overhead, and waited another long moment.

Nothing hopeful moved below. With a murmur of regret, he tensed his shoulders and swung the war hammer into the dam's wall. It struck with a *BOOM!* like a crack of thunder, and he jumped back, off the wall and onto the high hill, and then even farther in case the crag of the hill should give away. Logic told him that he would need to hit once, twice, or even three more times to affect it. Instinct told him that Rakka had shattered the heart of the dam and he would die if he stayed to strike again. The earth spoke, groaning, echoing the Demon's name as it shuddered, *rakka*. A ripple moved across the lake, then another, then a singular wave rose, racing away from the dam, cresting across the sky-blue water.

His heart beat harshly. Once, twice. Then it skipped a beat as the war hammer rattled in his grip, wanting to be loosed again. He struck a second time, but the power of the first had faded considerably as it thudded into the dirt. The Demon was not limitless, it tired, and he could feel the fatigue in his anger. He wrapped his hand about the weapon tightly, lowering the head slowly to the ground and leaning upon it.

The stone began to crackle as ice does breaking upon a spring warmed pond. Puffs of dirt shot up as it fractured, and then the hillside started to rumble, dirt and stone boiled up and began a slide downward, carrying brush, grass, trees with it, a river of ground on the move. The earth-and-granite walls of the dam shuddered, holding a moment, then spidery cracks ate up its sides and began to split open. The stone walls of the dam broke in a series of loud jolts, pounding his ears with pain, and scores of the troopers around him covered their heads as the percussions sounded.

Then the water roared forth, freed, spurting out over the moving dirt and rock, blue water gray with froth and then brown with soil, cascading down into the valley. He watched the waves, wondering vaguely if they would turn crimson when they hit the city.

The butte crumbled as the water hit it. One of his troopers fell, and the horse slid downhill. It scrambled to its feet to run. A swift, light, long-limbed horse, it put its head down and stretched its body out in a panicked gallop. He knew how fast it must be going, ahead of the landslide, ahead of the raging water, and yet it lost the race, swallowed up and gulped down, swept away like nothing.

Inthera did not last much longer.

He looked back to see what, if any of the lake remained, its body pouring forth in a thunderous tumult through the broken dam. When that slowed to almost ceasing, he faced his troops again. With a wave, he signaled them to move in on the ruins of the city.

"You know the drill. No survivors unless they surrender totally."

He heard the echo of his order being yelled down the hillside, and his army moved. He stayed where he stood, Rakka talking to him, wanting one more strike into the stone and earth of its desire, and he refusing it. Well pleased with the pounding of the earth beneath it, now it wanted flesh and blood, the taste of life and souls. His head thudded with the effort as he withstood its demands. His muscles tensed into knots of pain as he stood and looked at the leveled Inthera, its fabled beauty floating off in tiny spots of rubble on muddied waters.

Far beyond, where those he thought might have been shepherds roamed, he saw the release of birds on the wind. *So,* he thought ironically. *The traders believed me and went to high ground and now send word of my conquest.* He considered sending archers down and then decided against it. The birds would have flown too far at any rate, and what would it hurt him to have fear and truth of his threats sent ahead of him? Perhaps it might save another Inthera.

He had tried logic to construct a nation, and it refused him. Now he would ply fear.

Chapter Fifty

QUENDIUS DANGLED THE LIMP bird in his hand, dropping it as soon as he tore the scroll from its leg. He read it quickly, his skin darkening with his temper as Narskap watched. When he lifted his eyes, they went to Narskap in his darkest obsidian stare.

"Bad news."

"I want to know how you mistook the hammer."

"Tell me what happened."

"This! This!" and Quendius shook the missive violently in the air. "First, he brings down a walled city that battering rams and catapults could barely scratch. Now, he hammers apart a dam, turning the escarpment it sat upon to powder and flooding Inthera."

Narskap tilted his head in thought. "Perhaps the nature and strength of the Demon escaped me. Perhaps it bonds with its true user. Perhaps only Diort can control it, as only I can control and focus the sword."

"Perhaps?" The cords on Quendius' neck stood out in barely muted fury.

"Can you number a God? Can you trap and compress one into what you wish?"

"He has power I would never have given him, if I had known."

"It is part of a God's being to be part of the great unknown."

Quendius crumpled the letter, dropping it to the ground with the bird's body. "Now tell me what I should do about it."

"I would stay his ally. I would become as close to him as a brother, a lover. I would have his troops know my voice as well as his."

"And then?"

"And then take him out."

Chapter Fifty-One

NUTMEG STRETCHED UP to pat down a seam across her brother's shoulder, before stepping back and looking at Hosmer critically. Finally, reluctantly, she said, "It'll do."

"Do?" he echoed, turning about in appeal to his mother and Rivergrace. "Do I look good or not?"

Lily smoothed a wing of hair back from her face, catching it up in the knot at the nape of her neck from which it had escaped. "To me, you look quite handsome."

He tugged at the Town Guard's tabard. "It doesn't make me look short?"

"You are short."

He scowled at Rivergrace. "Not by my family!"

"No, but in a place like Calcort." She spread her hands without further words.

"Can't argue with the truth." He turned to his mother and tugged the tabard one last time before casting a look at Lily. "Do you mind?"

"It seems terribly sudden. They snatched you up like prime steak on a table in a room full of starvin' people," Nutmeg said.

"There's need and opportunity. It was handed to me, and I was told I couldn't wait long if I wanted it, so I took them almost as fast as they took me. Da told me t' trust my instincts."

Nutmeg tossed her head.

Hosmer made a stubborn noise, adding, "Still, it's what I want to do."

"Then go and do it," his mother responded. "We've strong backs and many hands still here at home. You've already proven yourself, but I think it's something that runs in you, or it doesn't. You can't make a tashya horse out of a mountain pony like Bumblebee, but neither can you make a mountain pony want to race like the wind. It's either in the blood or it's not."

He clasped Lily's hands. "I hope Da thinks the same."

"We're two different people, my lad, but we're of the same mind on many, many things. That's how we fell in love and stayed that way. You should be remembering that as you grow older." With a faint smile, she tilted her head back to kiss him on the forehead. Hosmer was, indeed, the tallest of any Farbranch yet born. "When do you report?"

"In the morn. I won't be wearing my fine clothes then, of course. It's training for me, and I hear they're tough on the new lads." He grinned then. "Wait till I show them what a Farbranch can do!"

"Wait, indeed!" Lily stepped back, beaming.

He cocked an eyebrow at Nutmeg. "I don't think I'll be hearin' any complaining if I bring home a handsome friend or two for dinner now and then, will I? Since Vevner and Curly didn't seem to catch your eye."

Nutmeg scurried off, but not before her rosy cheeks went apple red as she ducked her head. Rivergrace stayed a moment longer to watch the man she'd grown up with as her brother, and he took his tabard off to hand it to her fold as she did.

"You're thinking, Grace."

"I know. It seems like yesterday you were taller and faster than me."

"I'm still faster." He winked. If he did not get the laugh he wanted, he did get a bright smile. He reached out and gave her a tight hug. "It's all right," he said to her, his voice muffled by her shoulder and hair. "I've recovered and the past is awful to remember, but this is still something I've always wanted to do. Da is the protector in this family, I've got to go out and find my own to protect."

"Is that what it is? It's not the need for blood?"

"I saw plenty of blood spilled on Beacon Hill. No, that's not what it is. It's because I don't care to see any more, ever, particularly from those I love." He let her go with a light shake. "A'right?"

"All right, then." She folded his tabard over and left him alone with Lily while she went to put it in his bureau.

She gazed at her son fondly. "Well said."

"Meant every word of it."

"I'll say no more then, except good luck. I already know you'll do us proud. I'll leave lunch fixin's for you in the pantry, I may already be gone by the time you're up."

"And I'm up at dawn!" he said mockingly. "Mom, you work too hard."

"It's the party season. When that's come and gone, hopefully I'll have paid all the debts and put aside a sum for the slow months."

"Da will have the brewery righted in another month, I think."

"He works harder than I do."

"Then I know where I get it from." He bent over to lace his boots before heading back to the cider press.

"Tolby was never one to quit, even if he knew he should." Lily folded her hands in her lap as she sat, her brow creased a touch as she remembered. "If he had been, he would never have won me. I had another courter or two, but he came along and would not give up."

"Do you think you'll ever go home?"

"Maybe. I know your da wasn't ready to give up there, but we hadn't much choice, had we? As for here . . ." Her hands rubbed each other lightly, soothingly. "I used to think this was where I'd want to be, but I think now that I'd rather plant a sapling and see it grow into a wondrous, blossoming tree than deal with a vain young lady wanting to be pretty for a dance. One lasts for a lifetime and gives throughout. The other seems to be interested only in taking." She gathered herself then, and stood. "I've work to do, and so have you, before the night is dark enough for sleep. Off with you!"

Grace paused in the doorway, knowing she'd heard words between her mother and brother she perhaps hadn't been meant to have heard. Hard work had caused the joy to fade from Lily's eyes as she laid out patterns and cut cleverly against the fabric, coaxing garments out of plain cloth, but her time for weaving her own materials had to be shunted aside. And that was one thing Rivergrace remembered keenly about her growing up . . . Lily in the candlelit corner, her loom and spindle moving like a finely tuned instrument in her mother's hands, the fabric flowing forth like a river of many hues and textures. Lily had wished for a shop and gotten it, and seemed to have found out that her wish and its fulfillment hadn't been quite the same.

She wouldn't ask to go home, but sometimes the River Silverwing cut its way through heart as it would carve through soft dirt banks in spring meltdown. She missed it keenly, in all its facets.

Nutmeg touched her, and she jumped.

"Come on," her sister urged. "We can get a few more candlemarks' work in tonight, while it's a little cooler."

"All right. Let me get my veils." Grace went to their room and pulled down the prettiest set Nutmeg had designed, stars and moons spinning across its blue gauze in silvery-gold tones. She placed them over her head and face carefully, hands patting them into place, thinking that never had she thought she would have to be concealed so that she could walk city streets. Yet even the Vaelinars looked through her as if she did not exist. How could she be so much of one, and yet nothing of it in the eyes of others?

She joined Nutmeg, her thoughts in silent knots. It mattered little that Hosmer's threat of bringing fellow recruits to dinner now and then set off a litany from Nutmeg of qualities that would and would not interest her in a lad. She didn't seem to notice that Grace answered rarely, if at all.

Adeena had the door flung open, and the shop lights sparkled against a cloud-dulled evening. Nutmeg bustled in, but Rivergrace paused on the threshold. She turned her head, listening. A booted step sounded behind her, yet when she turned, she could not see anyone there.

"Derro?" she called softly.

No answer from the street or the nearby alleyway. Had she even heard anything over the murmur of her own thoughts?

"How many more days of Petitions?"

"Are we guessing or do we want an authority?"

Lariel lifted her head from a pillow and glared at her brother across the room.

"An authority," he ventured. "Well, I overheard Bistane telling Tranta three more. And Bistel has taken leave, putting the representation in Bistane's hands."

"The coward." Lariel groaned, dropping her head back down, pulling the pillow from under it and placing it over her face.

"Oh, faint of heart one!"

"It's not my heart, but my ass and my head. Both hurt exceedingly from sitting and listening to the arguing."

"Which is why you rarely attend these Conferences, but your presence is needed. Most of these Petitions came in only because you're here, and your attention is needed for them to pass or be tabled."

From under the pillow, a muffled protest. "They can pass laws without me."

"Not many."

"Allow me a little more self-pity, if you please." Lariel reached up and hugged her pillow closer about her head.

Jeredon sat back. He considered the nearby bookshelf which held his fletching and carving supplies. He could finish an old project or start a new one, he supposed, until Sevryn returned. Or he could sit and doze until his sister threw her cushion at him for snoring.

A soft knock interrupted all possibilities. Tiiva did not wait for an answer but looked in, saying, "Pardon, Highnesses. Azel d'Stanthe appears to be neither losing nor gaining ground."

"Which is a victory in itself," Jeredon replied. The pillow-crowned queen did not stir.

Tiiva closed the door gently but firmly behind her. "Also, I have obtained some word from the trading guilds. I think," she added tentatively, "there is a rather large grain of salt to be taken with this. Messenger birds carried in news. Abayan Diort has forced an alliance with the city of Inthera."

"Forced? Word has it he was born there."

"They hold no allegiance to him," Lariel muttered, her voice barely audible.

"I think the guild is painting the news in their favor, in fact, inviting a certain panic, to make markets spike, unless I miss my guess."

"How so?" Jeredon watched Tiiva, immaculately coiffed and dressed, her gown falling in fold after fold of the richest material, yet never hiding her lithe figure or attributes. He'd often speculated that it would take the entire guild of traders to keep her clothed.

"Tales are being told that Diort brought down a flood on them, cracking the valley dam wide open, and forcing them to their knees. From the storm that just swept through here, and others customarily in the summer, I think it's more likely that Inthera drowned on its own and caved to his repeated requests for alliance to receive aid. We've all seen high summer flooding before as storms sail in from the south. Dams have given way before and no doubt shall again."

"Discount all of the news but the alliance then."

"It seems prudent to do so. Such manipulations are far below us."

Tiiva curtsied, deeply, toward the couch and reclining Lariel before waving farewell at Jeredon.

He had his head turned to the door, watching the last of her curvaceous figure retreat when the cushion was flung at him, catching him soundly across his ear.

"Damn Oxfort. We passed that petition of his, and now the guild is driving up prices in a panic, while their toll fees are dropping."

"Such is business." He fired the pillow back at her, catching her squarely in the jaw. "At least you can rest easy tonight knowing that Azel seems somewhat anchored."

"I'd feel more at ease if I knew what he wanted to tell me that he felt he could not pass to Sevryn first."

"Something so Vaelinar he felt it best not to discuss openly."

"Don't be an idiot, Jeredon. I know that. It was also something he did not wish to send by any messenger, as we keepers often do." She sat up with a sigh. "I'm turning in. Go find yourself a bed."

And she threw the pillow back at him in a helpful way.

He called after her, "Hopefully, I will find a bed with more curves and less lumps!"

His answer came in the form of a snort from the other room.

She waited until quite sure he'd either gone or fallen asleep, before donning a rain cape and vaulting over the balcony railing to drop down lightly into the street. Rainfall began again, in tiny, misting drops this time, without the fullness or the heat of the day's storm. With only a slight hesitation, she moved in under the cover of the balcony and waited.

"M'lady. It seems you knew I'd be watching out here." The deep male voice sounded faintly aggrieved.

"Daravan, you are everywhere. I knew if I went walking anywhere in Calcort tonight, I'd be bound to trip over you sooner or later."

"That you should wander at all is an ill omen. Don't think that Kobrir's job is done, with Azel dying."

"I would never be that hopeful."

"What news, then?"

She fell in with him as they moved through the night, Daravan weaving an unseen path for them. She immediately thought of him as a Dark Ferryman in his own element of nightfall. "Azel abides. Neither better nor worse, which is on its own a triumph." She skipped a small puddle, and his arm shot out to grab her around the waist and pull her to him. Her breath left her a moment as she looked up and could see only his eyes briefly, before he turned away and put her back down on her feet.

"Pardon, m'lady."

"No pardon needed for trying to help me, but I do pardon you for thinking me clumsy."

He chuckled at that. "No other news?"

"Only what you've probably heard on the street, some outlandish trader guild stories about Diort conquering Inthera. I've no doubt he's brought Inthera in, but doubt he single-handledly flooded them to do so."

"Wild tales flood like Petitioners' wine this time of year. That Inthera has fallen to Abayan's . . . charms . . . seems likely, however."

"I agree. I will have to put eyes in that direction although it seems the ild Fallyn have already been looking eastward."

"The ild Fallyn look everywhere, including under their own beds. But do they see?"

She did not answer immediately. He took her by the hand, his own larger and more calloused than hers; though hers handled weapons as capably as his, she felt herself thinking of her father's hands, guiding her, a very long time ago. His touch stirred her and she pulled her cape's hood up to shadow her face as the mist increased to a drizzle. A man did not often possess enough strength to impress her, and not all of Daravan's lay in his body. An enigma among all the Vaelinars, she knew as little of him as any of them did.

"Azel told Sevryn he wanted to build new libraries, across the continent, and throw them open to any who wished. Our lives would be bared."

"He's expressed similar ideas before."

"But never put them before the Conference. He has never been a man without sound foundations."

"He's survived. He'll soon tell you why."

She stared into the night, putting her chin up to the soft rain, and watching the clouds in their sullen march through the evening. "It fills me with uneasiness, as if Time stands against me, and I have no blade with which to cut It down."

"If you're uneasy, then I shall be also." Daravan let go of her hand. "Make sure Sevryn stands by you. I'm going east, to look at matters for myself. Give me a man, if you wish, and I'll see him placed within Abayan's troops."

"He'd have to be Galdarkan. There are none with Vaelinar blood within them. That's one cross we've not made since we came here."

"If you haven't any at your call, I do."

"Good. Thank you, Daravan."

He gave a half bow. "Unlike the others, Warrior Queen Lariel, I know what trials you passed to gain your title, and to prove yourself worthy to keep Larandaril. I know what you sacrificed, what you compromise, and what you gain by your vows. We should all bow before you."

He was gone before she could protest, and she bit back her words, for he could not possibly hear them unless she shouted, and what she wanted to say she would not have anyone else hear but Daravan. Not even her brother Jeredon.

No one else could know her heart and bear it.

The rain stopped pattering, and she took it as an omen to return swiftly to her balcony, climbing a nearby column to swing onto it and back to her room, making a note that she should be moved at least another story higher for security.

She leaned over the balcony to look back.

Yet another figure moved below.

A face tilted up, a glimmer of moonlight breaking through the clouds to illuminate it. Sevryn saluted her.

She would have to stop being so damn predictable.

Chapter Fifty-Two

"YOU'VE DONE WELL, recruit."

"Aye, sir, thank you. It comes from good teaching." Not all of it from the city, a good deal of it from Tolby, but Hosmer believed in giving credit where it was due, and what he'd said had been no lie although it made his drill captain pull his lips into a thin smile. If further truth be told, if all recruits were trained as he'd been, the city would be in poor shape for guards. He'd had days of training, not weeks or months. He'd have to put the word out to the militia that they were needed and would be welcomed by Calcort. The only muscles in his body that ached were those in his face, from being kept straight. Tree's blood be praised that Garner had not been allowed to follow him in, for Garner would have been mocking them in his way and Hosmer would never have kept his somber pose.

The Silverwing militia would never believe him that a ranked man had been the recruit class drill man, as well. A captain? Had he no better use to the Town Guard than that? But Hosmer would not question it. He would prove himself worthy, and better.

He held the folded bundle of his tabard under one arm, like the other recruits, as the drill captain returned to his post in the center of the guardhouse quad.

"New recruits, I salute you. Wear your tabards in loyalty and with honor." His blade flashed out, nearly missing cropping Hosmer's left ear, as the captain saluted them. Whickering straightened as if totally unaware of his near mishap and gazed down at them.

Hosmer bit his cheek as he donned his uniform. It fell into place about him, a little looser than it had been days ago when he tried it on for the first time, so perhaps the workout had been a bit more strenuous than he'd given it credit for. Still, nothing that he or, for that matter, even Rivergrace and Nutmeg could not have handled. Shinnying trees, hauling harvest carts, and chasing young goats about had kept them all in fairly good shape.

He turned to Buttennoff, whom they all liked to call Butterknife for his skill with daggers, saying, "Come to dinner tonight to celebrate?"

Buttennoff studied him, light Kernan blue eyes indecisive. "You have sisters?"

"I do, but pay them no mind. Their personalities are horrible, and they're going to treat you rudely no matter what you do."

His friend had no family in the city, having come from the southern capital, and would be alone this evening. Buttennoff relaxed visibly, his good-natured handsome face breaking into a smile. "I will do, then. Pick me up at the barracks after duty?"

"See you." He trotted off after his patrol sergeant to get his assignment. The new recruits usually worked on foot as horses and their upkeep were expensive in the city, and the back ways and alleys were often more suitably roamed by foot patrol anyway. He'd gotten his own quarter on assignment, and couldn't decide if it was terribly good sense or awfully bad judgment on the captain's part. Good sense, because he should know his own ground well, and bad in that, if there were any corruption to be had, it would be gotten through that same familiarity. Perhaps the captain hadn't even given the matter thought at all. He seemed to have the Mayor's Ball more on his mind these days.

Captain Whickering fussed more about that gala than any of the clients that bothered his mother, and hell knew she had her hands full of finicky women. He could only give praise that it wasn't in his shift for guard duty.

Hosmer would do his best, and if that pulled up the rest of the guards' standards by their bootstraps, so much the better.

Afternoon made little difference to the heat, as it lingered in the paving stones of the walkways and on the storefronts and columns, so that as the sun lowered, its assault did not diminish, nor would nightfall make it much cooler. Shyna pushed her hair from her face as she stepped from Lily Farbranch's shop, frowning. Her lips felt chapped as she licked them, and her throat dry as sand, and she made her way across the rutted street quickly, only the prospect of something wet and strong perking her up. The need for a drink ached inside her, a deep gnawing ache, something she'd expressed to Adeena often though her cousin had never understood. Oh, it would hurt tomorrow morning, too, after she'd drunk and woken up, but it wasn't the same. The pain from having a finger squished in a window shutter was different from having a needle stick, wasn't it? No one doubted the difference there!

She shrugged in her light cotton gown, damp under her arms and against the back of her neck, sticky with summer heat. She'd find a cool corner, mayhap, before the tavern filled, and sip her discomfort away. Then to home, a snuggle with the old man and a bit of supper, and bed. It wasn't a grand life, but she'd come to expect little, and as long as her old man didn't mind her drinking and kept a roof over their heads, things could have been worse. She ducked her head against the summer heat and hurried along the alleys to the small tavern she liked best, The One-Legged Frog, and slipped inside.

It wasn't that they knew her at the Frog, which they did, or that they let her run a tab, which they didn't, but that the tiny lodging stayed relatively free of the choking toback smoke the Dwellers loved to chuff in and out, as most of the customers here were of good Kernan stock. Dwellers had overrun Calcort since she'd been a girl, taking jobs and good housing, and though she couldn't deny they were a hard-working lot (unlike the aristocratic Vaelinars who never seemed to do anything of worth but always had coin), she felt crowded by them. Not a word could she say, though, not with Thom Stonehand their hearty mayor. As popular as he was short, not much grousing about him would be tolerated. No, the best she could hope for her lot was to be allowed to sit in her cups in the evenings and a bit of work during the day to help pay their way. Someday, she and her mister planned to move outside the gates and grow a sunflower farm with little to do but watch the tall yellow flowers reach to the sun, go to seed and be harvested while they sat in rockers on their porch.

"What'll it be, Shyna? Jug of the same? We've got some decent hard cider if you want a change."

"Dweller mill?"

"Aye, a new one."

Shyna muttered as she pulled up a chair and sat, and shook her head a vigorous no. "Give me my jug," she ordered, as she made herself comfortable, leaning back into the dim corner, feeling some of the sun's glow on her face fade.

"Will do."

By the time the small place filled to the brim, she'd been through her allowance of two jugs and sat morosely looking at the dry bottom of the second, preparing herself to go home while still in a delightfully rosy, if melancholy, haze. Someone jostled her arm, and she nearly dropped the clay jug, which would not have gone well, for the tavern cleaned and refilled the jugs from their cellar of kegs, and she frowned.

"Sorry, lass. Well, if it isn't a sewing maid from our shop!" a voice sounded softly by her ear, a voice that lilted of the elven and Shyna frowned deeper.

"What a pout! Don't tell us that fussbudget of a Dweller works you to the bone. Let us buy you a drink or two, a well-earned tip for good work," a second added, as two lithe forms slipped into chairs at her side. Shyna would have protested, but the jugs came out of nowhere and sat frothing on the tabletop before she could and truth be told, she *did* deserve a bonus for all her hard work. She picked up a jug. "To your health, m'ladies," she toasted, and sipped the foamy brew delicately, so as not to lose a drop.

The tavern being dim and the jugs overfull, she found it difficult to recognize the two veiled ones near her, although the one with a bit of copper skin showing beneath her gauze looked familiar. Gods knew that Lily Farbranch and her daughters drew the elven to their wares, as though good Kernan coin wasn't good enough. She set her jug down. "I thank you," she said formally, despite her thoughts, and a soft burp ruined her attempt at manners.

If they noticed, they gave no sign. Instead, they launched into idle gossip about fashion and gowns for the summer dances, smiling as Shyna loosened her tongue a bit and talked about that cape and this dress and such, proud of her work. Somewhere deep into another jug, the copper-skinned one leaned forward, saying, "That sounds beautiful. If only I could see it, I might order another one for myself. Alas, the shop is closed, we passed it on the way here."

"I," began Shyna, interrupted by a slight hiccup, "can get in."

"Surely not. You've a key?"

"Keys!" Shyna fluttered her hand about loosely. "Locks 'r nothing for those who know 'em. Want a look? I'll give you one!" She lurched to her feet.

With a sway and an occasional reel, she led the elven women down the lane back to the shop which did indeed seem very quiet and dark and closed for the night. Shyna squinted up and down the street. Very late, it was. She hadn't noticed. Her old man would be more than miffed at her. The free drink was fine, it was that she hadn't brought any home to share with him! She put her hand on the shopkeeper's lock and brought out a stout pin. With a twist and a few pokes, she had the lock open and dangling, and the three of them pushed their way inside, giggling.

The taller one, with dark brunette hair, pushed her veil away as she lit a sconce, and took Shyna by the hand. "Show me, show me!" she called gaily, but the copper one seemed more interested in shelves and drawers and the like to Shyna's confusion, as the first led her away. They pawed through the finished clothes and veils, twitching them back into place so no one would be the wiser, when the second whistled sharply from the workroom after many wooden bangs, slides, and shufflings.

"I have it," she said.

Shyna blinked. "What's that?"

"Nothing, lass, nothing. Galraya says we should go." The unveiled one patted her hand. "What fun we've had." She pushed two tens of silver into Shyna's hand. "Take a jug or two home on us, and lock up tight."

Befuddled, Shyna watched the two gathered up at the threshold, the copper-skinned one muttering as if unhappy, "The message was here all right, but they'll not know what it means. It must have dropped out of the goods. Tiiva must be told as soon as possible."

"Sssssh. Have you got it?"

"No, I left it, no one will be the wiser. Get the lock for her, she's so drunk she's fumbling it!" And the copper one fled into the night.

Shyna frowned, losing the words from her thoughts almost as soon as they were spoken, as her new friend closed the shop for her and put the shopkeep's lock back into place. She clenched her hand tightly about her coins. The unveiled one pulled her covering into place and touched Shyna's forehead gently.

"Go, drink, and forget."

Forget? Why in the hell did the elven think she was drinking? Shyna giggled and staggered off, in search of home or another jug, uncaring which she found first.

Shyna came in late as Adeena finished wrapping deliveries and marking them for the impatient women who sent messengers daily, fussing about the Mayor's Ball. Her cousin pushed her hair from her face and undid the top button on her blouse, and swayed a little on one heel.

"Oh, Shyna. You promised!"

"What?"

"You've been drinking."

"Just a snort or two."

"And you're late." Adeena tied the wrapping carefully about the jade-green gown and put it aside. "In fact," and she eyed her cousin, "you haven't even been home! Those are the clothes you wore yesterday."

Shyna waved at her as if shooing away an annoying gnat. "Quit nagging at me, Adeena. You've done it all your life and has it helped?"

"Not one whit. I should send you packing."

"I've done my work!" Shyna narrowed her eyes in her thin face.

"That you have, and it's been good work." She sighed. "What am I going to do with you?"

"Put me to work by the doorway and let the sun sober me up." Shyna put her hand out. "You know I try."

"Not enough. Mistress Farbranch has been most agreeable, and your time is your own, no questions asked. Think how long you waited for work before this."

Shyna looked away. "I can't always help it."

"You can't ever help it, and it's going to be the death of you. Of your hopes, if nothing else." Adeena took a deep breath. "Go sit at the farther worktable, then. You can trade with my spot. I'll move your panels over."

Shyna wove her unsteady way across the shop, banging first one hip, then a knee despite her slimness, as she walked. She sat down where told and waited for Adeena to bring her the day's job. She frowned a bit, looking about the shop as if bewildered, then closed her eyes to nap until Adeena was ready for her.

Adeena flew about the shop, thanking her shrine Goddess that Lily was out doing a fitting at a lady's home, and would not be back for a little bit, her daughters delivering two of the first-done gowns, and that no one would be the wiser as Goodie stayed in the back room, cutting out the simpler patterns. Like a true apprentice, Goodie had taken to Lily's way of laying out the designs quickly, and had a talent with the scissor blades. She did not look up as Adeena flitted in and out, back and forth, pushing delivery bundles quickly to one side, to set up the sewing frames.

They were both quite immersed and had done a good bit when Nutmeg breezed in.

She pulled off a woven straw hat, saying, "Oooh, good, you've got more gowns bundled up."

"Are you taking them yourselves?"

"No, I'll let Walther take these. The others we delivered because it seems Milady Fallbrook has discovered she's with child since we took her measurements, and she needed a few adjustments here and there."

Rivergrace slipped in from the back door, where Bumblebee stood tied in the shade with a fresh bucket of water at his disposal, the traces from the cart loosened. He swished his tail in contentment. He did not often get out and enjoyed having the girls back at the reins, it seemed.

Nutmeg put her pins in her sleeve as she talked. "We're back for the day."

"And not a moment too soon. We've three more dresses to finish for tomorrow night." Rivergrace pulled up the hem of her skirt as she leaned over the table, putting her frame into order so she could begin stitching neatly but in a great hurry. They worked with little word except to exchange advice or praise now and then, intent upon finishing the works of art for women who had ordered them. Lily came in and quietly joined them, little daggers of silver flashing in their fingers, dipping in and out of exquisite fabric, and none of them stopped till the lamps burned brightly outside, except for Shyna who left at her customary time.

In the morning, Rivergrace reached the shop before Nutmeg who stopped to buy her favorite treat of sugar-dipped fried bread. They had slipped out by quiet agreement, letting their mother sleep in a little. Hosmer strode out on their heels, grumbling, for he'd been assigned evening duty at the gala as well. It would be a long day for him, with a break in the afternoon. "I get to butler for the royalty and the wealthy," he muttered.

"Maybe they'll tip you."

"The Town Guard doesn't accept tips!"

The three of them shut the door behind them as gently as they could to leave Lily in peace.

She found Walther sitting, huddled up against the door, his messenger bag in his lap. Already, the sun beat down with its heat and the rain lingered only in the humidity steaming out of the ground. He looked asleep, but he bolted to his feet as she drew near. His customary brash expression was nowhere in place.

"Walther? What's wrong?"

"Got a job for me?"

"We will, in a candlemark or two. Several deliveries, but you can't be folding or mashing the bundles up. Maids won't have time to take the wrinkles out for tonight."

He nodded. The prospect of a job or two did not smooth away the lines etched in his face, however. He looked about skittishly. Rivergrace put her hand on his shoulder. "Come in."

She had Nutmeg's keys for the back, as only the shop owner held keys for the business door, and Walther trotted round about at her heels, unusually quiet. Once inside, she pulled up a stool. "What is it?"

He looked as if he could still bolt, shifting his weight from one foot to another. "That Warrior Queen is a friend of yours, nuh?"

"Queen Lariel is a good customer."

"She nice?"

Rivergrace gazed at him, with no idea at all what he was about. "She seems nice," she said, quietly.

"That big dance is tonight?"

"Aye, it's why we're working so hard on the gowns. Walther . . ."

He shrugged off his precious messenger bag and unbuckled it. "I ain't supposed t'do this, but I can't read much. Still. I know the people who sent it and the people supposed t'get it, and I know it's 'bout her." He fetched out a piece of paper, not sealed, but cleverly tied in string. "It can't be good."

Rivergrace took it hesitantly. "You think so?"

He ducked his chin down.

She looked at the knot. She could retie it the same way, her slender fingers clever with knots. She opened it deftly before Nutmeg could burst in and make Walther's betrayal even worse. She scanned the single line, written in an even and brisk hand.

Queen Lariel must be Returned.

She swallowed tightly, a prickle of fear running across the back of her neck.

She folded and retied it swiftly, handing it back to Walther. "What made you suspicious?"

"I was chosed, see, 'cause of my old contacts, for the delivery. I dun trust those who sent me, and th' ones I'm going to are even wurse. I know who 'tis about 'cause they said her name and spat in the dirt when they did. So I wanted ta warn you."

The only thing she could do would be to tell Hosmer that the Warrior Queen might be in danger, uncertain even of what the note boded. But she took Walther's instinctive reaction to heart. "I will tell my brother. Without mentioning you."

Worry fled him in a long exhalation. "I'll be back, for bundles."

"Do that." She watched as he darted out the door.

When Nutmeg came in, almost on Walther's heels, she did so shadowed by the Kernan guard Hosmer had brought home twice now for dinner. He bowed after guiding her through the door.

"Have a pleasant day, m'lady Farbranch."

"And you." Nutmeg held back her little jump until he passed from her view. Then she jumped and did a skip across the room toward the worktables.

"Hmmm. Sugar bread or the guard. Shall I guess why you really went astray this morning?"

Nutmeg tossed her head toward Rivergrace. "He's fun and handsome."

"I noticed."

"Not that it's anything serious." Nutmeg took her hat off and put it on its hook. "Grace, how can you not look at someone and feel different about them?"

"I am already different enough," she said softly. "Be content that you're happy. We all take joy in your smiles, Meg."

Nutmeg looked obstinate as if she would quibble with that, but then the front door unlocked and everyone else flooded in, the room filling with chatter and bustle and the rustle of sweeping dresses as they gathered them together for finishing touches.

The sun marched across the sky. Drivers and maids came and went, Adeena filling the last of the orders until only the most elaborate gowns remained, waiting to be delivered. Rivergrace moved between them, a river of fabric both sensuous and commanding, colorful and serene, a river as diverse and incredible as the people for whom they were intended. She wanted to run her fingers through them, but handled them only as needed to finish. Each one presented a picture of beauty that they would become when worn. Yet, hidden behind that beauty was the menace of Walther's morning note. She had to find a way to reach Sevryn or the queen's brother, or even the queen herself. She looked up to see Lily's gaze on her.

"What do you think?"

"They're magical and, yet, I think of all the work we put into them." She held her hand above the dresses, stroking them in her imagination.

"I think the two of you worked the wonders." Lily put a hand to the back of her neck and rubbed tired muscles there, even as the front door flung open with a loud *bang!* And Mistress Stonehand flew in, half wrapped bundle in her arms.

"Disaster! Calamity! I ordered jade and what do I have delivered? Blue!" And she tugged on a bit as it fell out of the package in her arms.

"Blue?" Nutmeg and Rivergrace immediately traded looks. That fabric was the distinctive weave chosen for Lariel's unique dress. Adeena put her hand to her mouth, choking off her dismay.

"We'll take care of this immediately," Lily said soothingly, taking the garment from the mayor's wife. "You'll have your dress, beautiful and proper, in time."

"See that I do!" And Mistress Stonehand swept out with as much fuss and unhappiness as she'd entered.

As soon as the door shut, Lily swung about. "What happened?"

Adeena sat with her hand over her mouth, and closed her eyes. She shook her head. "I did it."

"Did what?"

"Made her dress of jade. I . . . copied the veiled one's gown."

"Oh, no! Adeena, you didn't!" Nutmeg jumped off her little ladder from the dress form she'd been working on.

"I did. She offered a goodly sum of money, I knew we needed it. And now, I've sent it off to Queen Lariel by mistake. She's got the mayor's wife's gown."

"I never saw you sewing it."

"I did it early, early mornings and late evenings when you left for supper, before you came back. It was for the shop!"

"Our reputation rested on the queen's purchase, Adeena, and our promise that it would be unique." Lily caught her lower lip in thought.

Adeena rocked back and forth in dismay. "I'm so sorry."

"The best course is truth," Rivergrace offered.

"And trading! We'll swap the gowns," Nutmeg told her mother. "We've time."

"I'll go. I'll take Walther. He'll run the dress to the mayor's wife."

"You'll never get in." Lily fanned herself, with a look of defeat on her worn face.

"Oh, yes, we will! Hosmer's on guard duty."

"Nutmeg, I forbid it. You can't bring shame on him as well."

"He won't let us in," Nutmeg said firmly. "But he'll at least let us stand by while the proper authority gets asked. No one else would do that. And then, surely, she won't turn us away."

"No," agreed Rivergrace. "We won't be turned away." Even if it meant threatening the Warrior Queen herself.

Chapter Fifty-Three

"I'M NOT CARING IF you're my sisters, I can't let you through. And no following me over to the Great Hall either, 'cause I won't be letting you inside. Not even just to watch." Hosmer stared down at Nutmeg sternly, then up at Rivergrace.

"You have to, you just have to."

He waved a hand. "Look, I understand the problem. But I'm on duty, and you've no passes."

Nutmeg put her hands on her hips. "Where's Butterknife? He'd let me by."

"No, he wouldn't. You can stand out here for a candlemark if you like, and maybe catch her eye when she comes out, if she comes out this way, but that's all you can do." He started to say more, but a strutting Kernan came out of the inn, the doodads and gemgaws on his uniform reflecting blindingly in the sun.

"Guard Farbranch! Move this riffraff along. You're on duty, recruit."

"Aye, Captain Whickering, moving them." Hosmer shut his teeth till Whickering retreated into the coolness of the inn, and cleared his throat tightly. "Looks like you'll not be staying right here. Find a place off to the side. As for Walther, make him drive the cart round th' corner. He canna be blocking all the fancy carriages that will be pulling up soon." He eyed the boy and pony. Bumblebee eyed him back before letting out a pony-snort along with a flick of his thick tail. He shook a finger at the creature. "I'll be gettin' respect!"

Rivergrace considered. "Have you a paper and a stick?"

Hosmer shook his head. Walther stood up in the cart. "*Ay* do," he said proudly. He rummaged about in his messenger satchel before coming up with the charcoal writing stick and a fist-sized scrap of paper. " 'Tis me job." He handed them over to Rivergrace.

"Walther! How grand. Are you readin' yet?" Nutmeg praised him.

"Na much yet, but I'm learning my scribbles. Can 'most spell my name."

Rivergrace motioned for Hosmer to turn about so she could use his broad shoulder for a desk. Finally, after thinking up and rejecting several things, she wrote: *What danger is Returning to a Vaelinar?* and signed her name. She folded it, and steered Hosmer around. "Give this to Queen Lariel herself or Sevryn. He's the one with gray eyes."

"It had better be good, or they'll have my head."

From what she'd written, they might have it anyway. "Send them out to me if there's a commotion."

"You can bet on that, my lass." He did a military about-face and went inside the large, very grand inn with its many stories and brightly tiled roofing, angling sharply to avoid running back into the ostentatious captain.

They prepared for a long wait, but Hosmer came back out as if slingshot. He beckoned furiously at his sisters. "*Now.*" The color had drained from his rosy Dweller complexion.

Walther said, unperturbed, "I'll pull th' cart over and sit a while," even as Hosmer hustled them inside.

Thick walls kept most of the summer heat from seeping in, and the windowless halls stood in pooling shadows. Tiled floor made their shoes click as Hosmer quick-trotted them upstairs, and both were out of breath as they reached the third floor. Sevryn emerged from a shaded corner, his brows knotted and his gray eyes darkened in worry. "Whatever did you say?"

Nutmeg glanced toward Rivergrace. "I'm guessing it wasn't that we have her gown."

"No. It wasn't." She passed through the doors Sevryn opened to them.

Lariel stood in the center of the second apartment room thrown open to them, a simple wrap about her, alone except for Jeredon although the nearby table lay covered with cosmetic trays and hair-styling accessories which they had apparently interrupted. The silvery blue-and-gold jeweled corset lay there as well, waiting to be donned. Jeredon, bow in hand, guarded the third-story window.

"What is this you ask me, and why?" she demanded as Nutmeg and Rivergrace dipped into low curtsies.

"I beg all pardon," Rivergrace answered softly, looking down at the fine carpet at the queen's slippered feet. Sevryn took her by the elbow, pulling her up, and she lifted her gaze to see the Warrior Queen making an impatient gesture.

She tapped the fist-sized scrap of paper. "Do you know what you're referring to?"

"I'm at a disadvantage, being neither Vaelinar nor . . . un-Vaelinar," Rivergrace told her, trying to find a calmness she did not feel. Sevryn's hand on her arm squeezed a little as if to comfort her. "First, m'lady Highness, we have a mix-up at the dress shop. We have your proper gown out in our cart, and we need to take back the one that was delivered in error, with all apologies."

"And the second, most urgent mission is an explanation of this." Lariel stood rigidly. Her thin summer wrap might have been of impregnable armor from her stance.

She couched her words carefully. "A messenger boy was asked to make a delivery. He knew only that it concerned you, from those who had a dislike of you to those whose jobs involve unpleasantries. He wanted me to warn you. He couldn't read it himself, so he gave it to me. Forgive him, Queen Lariel, he knows it was a betrayal of his job, but he's good at heart."

Lariel's foot tapped the carpet.

"It read: Queen Lariel must be Returned. No signature or seal, and I have no idea what is meant by Returning, but it sounds ill-intentioned."

Jeredon's breath leaked out in an angry hiss.

"Return, aderro," Sevryn murmured, "often refers to death among us. We are the Suldarran, the Lost, and only death can return us to our true home."

"The writer asks for assassination," Lariel said.

"Oh, my." Nutmeg sat down abruptly on a nearby footstool "And I was worried about my sewing."

"It's nothing new."

"It is," Jeredon told Lariel, "when couched in Vaelinar terms such as those."

Lariel stared at him, before tapping Nutmeg on her shoulder. "Go get my proper gown, then. I presume this one is to be returned?" She poked a finger at the large bundle still wrapped.

"It is, m'lady Highness."

"Be about your business, then. I wish to speak with Rivergrace while you do."

Arms full, Nutmeg scurried to get the package and join Hosmer, who awaited her in the hallway.

"Does he know who sent it?"

"I don't think he'll name them, or the ones to whom he delivered it. He can only betray so much."

"It won't matter," Sevryn told Lariel. "We'll find only common Calcorts that way. The sender will have veiled him or herself quite effectively."

"True."

"Cancel your appearance."

She looked over her shoulder at Jeredon, a wry expression on her face. "Oh, you do hate dressing up, don't you?"

His mouth curled in a brief snarl.

"Highness."

Her eyes softened as Sevryn caught her attention.

"What are your wishes?"

"We go. We take all caution. Our hope that Azel d'Stanthe might be the only prey for the Kobrir is wasted, but we can't let them know that, or that we'll be intimidated. And, if at all possible, we enjoy ourselves. Tonight is the highlight of the summer." Her eyes of cobalt blue with glints of gold and silver rested on Rivergrace thoughtfully. "And you and your sister shall come with us."

"Lariel."

"Why not, Jeredon? This is a celebration, after all, and any defense I have planned will be well-hidden by their presence."

"We've no clothes grand enough, or manners, or . . ." protested Rivergrace, glad for once that Nutmeg had abandoned her, for she'd have gotten a stout elbow in the ribs for her remark.

"Feh! Anyone who could steal a ticket will be here tonight, and the others who couldn't will be dancing in the quad outside. As for clothes," and Lariel circled her slowly. "I have something that will do quite well. I would have worn it tonight, myself, but I fell in love with your mother's weaving. Sevryn, get Tiiva and see if you can't find something that will fit our shorter guest."

Sevryn let go of Grace with a certain reluctance, and it wasn't till then that she realized how comforting his hand on her arm had been. When Nutmeg puffed back upstairs, the proper package lying across her wrists, her little mouth curved in a breathless O as Lariel commanded her attendance at the gala. She did not, however, protest in any way.

The two of them had put Lariel to rights when Sevryn appeared, carrying a bar with a dress displayed upon it, his hand at arm's length as if unsure of the whole matter of women and dance gowns. "She says this may do," and he laid it across the back of a chair. He paused, his gaze sweeping over Lariel, and he bowed. "My queen, you look astonishingly beautiful."

"Thank you."

Jeredon sniffed. "She'll need a dart to the head to deflate it before she sleeps tonight."

Nutmeg and Rivergrace fastened the last clever clasp on the armored bodice. "A gown should only magnify the beauty that is already there. Too many women forget that," Nutmeg told them matter-of-factly, as she pulled a strand of Lariel's hair into place. "There." She stood back, a smile of satisfaction breaking out on her face as she breathed out at the sight before her.

The blue fabric hung in clinging, shimmering waves from Lariel's slender form, its faint pattern of golden stars and moons and silvery lightnings an echo of her eyes and hair. The armor only cinched her waist that much tighter the cloth, flaring slightly over her hips, a tier of silvery chains with golden bells ringing about it. Rivergrace thought she'd never seen anyone so magnificent.

After a moment, Jeredon coughed. "And, to think, she can put a sword blade through your heart just as quickly."

"Indeed." Sevryn's shoulder twitched.

Lariel's face flushed prettily at the reaction. "Now, you two."

"That is our signal to retreat," Jeredon said to Sevryn, and left the room towing him after. Faint sounds of scuffing followed but the door closed firmly.

Grace turned to her sister as she stepped into her garment. Nutmeg's borrowed dress of soft golden-yellow with belled sleeves and a gathered skirt brought out the sunny highlights of her hair and she squealed in delight as she twirled about in it. The hem swept the floor a little too generously, but the length couldn't be helped. "I shall just have to step higher and stand taller," Nutmeg declared. "I wish Mom could see me!"

"She knows, doesn't she?"

"I sent Walther in all haste to the mayor's, and then he's to return the cart to her."

"I'll see she's told. Not to worry." Lariel's voice faded as she leaned into a solid, ornate wardrobe, its doors flung open, practically engulfing the queen entirely as she searched through it. Garments murmured and rustled as she moved items back and forth. She emerged in triumph. "This one."

Neither silver nor sea-green, the fabric cascaded from her hands in a length of soothing color. Long sleeves flowed into lacy cuffs, ivory foam off an ocean's shore. The waist was dropped, and the skirt only slightly flared, so that it would pool about the ankles and feet. Rivergrace blinked to see something so grand handed to her as Lariel held it forth. "Try this on." One hand held out, she ducked her head back inside, with more rattles of searching. "My cup is missing. I can't think where I saw it, I know Tiiva packed it." The wardrobe muffled her words.

Nutmeg climbed onto a chair, taking the gown and gathering it carefully in her hands, as Rivergrace stripped down to her smallclothes and then stood under Nutmeg's arms as she dropped it down over her and then laced the back up quickly.

"Ahhh." Queen Lariel smiled as she emerged from the armoire, her mouth moving in soft curves of pleasure, watching.

Rivergrace turned to look in the silvered glass that hung inside the wardrobe door. She did not recognize herself at all, a tall, willowy figure embraced by a gown that spoke of seas and rivers and their mysterious ways.

"Grace!" Nutmeg put both hands over her mouth.

"What?" She spun about in alarm.

"You look . . . you look . . ."

"I know," Lariel said to Nutmeg. "She does, doesn't she?"

"What?"

"You don't look at all like my sister," Nutmeg answered solemnly. "Although I'm sure I'll recognize you the first time you trip over your hem."

Rivergrace put her foot out and hooked her slippered toes about the rung of the chair Nutmeg stood upon, pushing it sharply.

Nutmeg hopped down, laughing.

Jeredon and Sevryn returned warily to find the three of them putting cosmetics and perfume on each other, brushing the last strands of each other's hair into a feminine order that made no sense at all to the men, but in relief it seemed they were at least ready to leave for the gala. Lariel put a hand up to Jeredon, frowning slightly. "Send word to Tiiva to find my drinking cup, my tankard, if she can? I know we brought it, I just seem to have misplaced it."

"I will." He stepped out long enough to crook a finger, bringing a guard running, and then came back in and stood to wait, back to the wall. Sevryn seemed to find the window shutters fascinating, examining them and their view minutely as the women fussed with the last of their preparations. Nutmeg clapped her hands as she led her sister out, her cheerful dress sweeping the floor as she glided through the door.

Jeredon hung back to accompany Lara last as they left the suites. "Why," he asked her quietly, his eyes on the backs of the two guests.

"Because," Lara told him, "my best defense is in their underestimating me, as they have done before. Will I look formidable with young maids on my arms? I think not. And, because, sometimes it does a soul good to look through the eyes of childlike wonder." She smiled as Nutmeg did a little hop-skip and swung about, her gown billowing around her, before she began her trip down the staircases, her voice gaily ringing through the hallway. "Wait until Hosmer and everyone else sees me in this!"

Lily let Adeena and Goodie out, weariness in every fiber of her being, and closed the door on their heels. She could drive Bumblebee back and that was a blessing in itself, for she wasn't all that sure she felt like walking. The past handful of days had been more difficult than harvesting before a driving storm was due to hit, far harder than anything she'd anticipated. Perhaps, she thought, she was growing just a bit older than she'd given herself credit for. She cleaned up the last scraps, wondering if she would have the time or energy to think of quilting for the winter weather that would come, surely, in a season although the heat baking through the shop now made that seem improbable.

The carters and warehouses had all been paid, and the girls as well, and she even had a small coin or two set aside to give to Nutmeg and Rivergrace, besides what she and Tolby needed. Yet, for all their work, and blisters and sore backs and cramping necks, she could not see her way through another season. Perhaps she'd worked too hard at it. It had been like trying to learn swimming in high flood tide and forgetting that a wade and a short soak in a summer-heated cove could be very pleasant.

She opened her secret drawer and took out the sheet of paper that did not help with her worries. Should she mention it to Robin Greathouse at all, or burn it and forget it? A brisk but singular knock at the back door interrupted the last of the closing. She paused, shoving her hands and letter in her apron, then made the decision to answer it. She did not see the paper go astray yet again, as if it had a mind of its own, and drift under the worktable instead of settling in her apron pocket.

Daravan inclined his head in gratitude in the doorway. "Mistress Farbranch. I thank you for granting me access at such a late hour."

"It's not that late," she said, and opened it wider for him. He slipped through quietly.

"Late enough that the front door is shut, and if one hopes to go to the festivities tonight, he might be out of luck. Have you my suit for me?"

"I do. Walther has tried several times to deliver it."

"I've not been in the city. Unexpectedly, but profitably."

"No more time to waste, then! Let me fetch it for you, m'lord." Lily found a spring to her step as she went after it.

Daravan ran an eye about the shop, and then noticed something out of place. He leaned down and picked up a piece of paper nearly wedged under the foot of the desk. He opened it, scanned it, then snapped it shut quickly, placing it inside his vest. He'd returned to lounging against the counter when Lily came out and put his outfit in his arms.

He pressed a gold crown bit in her palm. "Many thanks, Mistress Farbranch."

She looked flustered. "You've paid already, and handsomely."

"And you asked far too little for your efforts." He smiled. "I shall look respectable and perhaps even handsome among my peers." With a sketchy bow, he slipped back out the door before she could give a proper protest, or the coin back.

Fortune, Daravan thought, often laughed at him. He'd gone east for intelligence and come home empty-handed to find it sitting on the floor of a tailor's shop, among fallen threads and fabric scraps.

Chapter Fifty-Four

THEY MOUNTED A GRAND carriage, Jeredon sitting with the driver, and Sevryn sitting with Nutmeg across from Rivergrace and Lariel. The conveyance had a leather top folded down, and carved ebony posts that held lamps, and pulls on the door that looked as if they might be gold. Grace glanced at her folded hands. There were tiny nicks from needle pricks and newly healing blisters from handling the fabric shears, and the delicate lace hanging exquisitely from her wrists seemed to emphasize hands which did not go with the gown. A worker's hands. She made a note to herself to take care not to snag the garment with her rough fingers, or scuff the fine-grained leather seats of the carriage by touching them.

Hosmer closed the door on them with a wry grin and a tweak of his sister's ear, saying, "I'll be along when the inn is emptied, but I'll be stationed on the front steps again!"

Nutmeg leaned out of the door, yelling back, "I'll save you some pastries!" as the carriage horses trotted away before Sevryn hauled her inside, muttering something about manners befitting the Warrior Queen. Unfazed, Nutmeg smoothed her skirts over her knees, and cocked her head at her companions.

"What do we do?"

"Dance, eat, drink. Not too much drink, I hope." Lariel had been looking over the carriage door at the streets where a steady stream of people seemed to also be making their way to the Great Hall on foot.

"I mean when someone tries to kill you."

"Hopefully," and she smiled faintly as Sevryn smothered a noise. "No one will, but if they do, stay out of the way and let my men handle it."

"There's only two of them!"

Lariel kept smiling at Nutmeg. "There are others, mingled throughout the crowd, and there are those who work for the safety of all the Vaelinars attending this Conference who may come to my aid. It'll be fine, and you shouldn't worry."

"It's just that I'm a little short to be a good shield."

Sevryn put his hand over his mouth and swiveled his head to the side, steadfastly finding something outside the carriage to fasten his attention upon. Rivergrace examined his profile, finding it handsome enough as Lariel reached out and touched Nutmeg's knee.

"You were not invited to shield me, but to have a good time and to share it with me. Those who have me marked will be bolder and more careless if they think I'm unaware. And, though I hate to ruin your anticipation, it could happen any time, even more likely not tonight."

"Why do you think so?" Grace asked, prying her attention from Sevryn who seemed totally unaware of her.

"The size of the crowd within and without will make it difficult to move quickly and unknown. I can almost guarantee my assassin will be a man known as the Kobrir." Lariel leaned forward then, as a shout came from outside, and she waved at the growing throng.

Nutmeg nibbled on her lip briefly, then ventured, "It sounds as if you're used to it."

"In a way. We're a very competitive people, and some of us have positions that are very unpopular with others. Our Accords were written for a reason. *Nor shall any of the Suldarran take arms against one another, or harbor any who would do so, in war or private offense, under penalty of their own life and the reputation of their House,*" she quoted.

"We don't fight anymore," Nutmeg told her. "Not since the Magi."

"I know. You're a very commendable people."

"Thank you," accepted Nutmeg gravely, and she settled back into the carriage, becoming uncharacteristically silent, although she watched the parade avidly, for—with traffic growing and other carriages before and after—they had indeed fallen into a parade.

The carriage slowed, the horses pulled from a high-stepping trot into a sedate walk, their necks bowed with impatience, their strides collected and elegant. Jeredon leaned down. "We'll be parked shortly." He wore green and gold, setting off his dark-brown hair which the sun had streaked with its touch, just as it had tanned his skin, and amber flecks marked his dark green eyes. He had the lines at the corner of his mouth that those with frequent, self-mocking smiles often carried, but his expression now seemed very somber.

Sevryn, on the other hand, wore dark blue which looked quietly elegant on him, neither setting off his features nor dimming them. Grace would not have said blue was his color, but she doubted he intended to display himself as the other Vaelinars seemed inclined to do, his dark bronzed hair tied back, and his eyes of light, stormy gray watching the crowds intently, never still, always searching. The aura of power the others carried seemed muted about him, and she considered the idea that, although he did not have the eyes of the Vaelinars, power might yet run in his body, though very deep and still, in the way of rivers.

She turned her face to find Lariel watching her. "Your brother doesn't resemble you," she said, caught.

"No, he doesn't. He is my younger brother, my father's son, but not from my mother. He has the Eladar looks, I think." She paused briefly. "Just as you don't look much like Nutmeg."

"There's a story in that, Your Highness."

"One I would hear one day." The carriage bumped to a stop and rocked as Jeredon jumped down and tugged at the door.

"Miladies," he said, as he handed Nutmeg out and reached for Rivergrace. "Follow the queen in. We'll be right behind all of you."

Nutmeg took Rivergrace's hand and Grace felt her sister tremble a little in unusual shyness. She gripped back.

Columns that seemed to reach nearly sky-high held the copper domed roof of the Great Hall. She tried to look up at it and found herself leaning so far back that Sevryn caught her. The quad in front of the hall filled with people and small booths as if a Spring fair had sprung up since the morning, and dance music tinkled faintly to her, two celebrations here, one inside and one without. A byway had been left for the coaches, but they were surrounded by dancers and gaiety, and the horses tossed their heads and pranced as if showing off.

A wall of noise went up as Lariel descended from the carriage. Rivergrace held her breath to listen, hearing cries of welcome and hatred mingled, sending a shocked surprise through her.

"Warrior Queen! Go home and stay there!"

"Most beautiful of the Strangers! Queen Lariel!"

A waving hand and bounding form jostled through the crowd. "Queen Lariel, a blessing here! Look upon us!"

Others shoved close to the carriage. "Hssst. War-bringer!"

Jeredon and Sevryn propelled them into the building quickly, the shouts fading behind them, but never ceasing.

"They don't know, Lariel," Jeredon said to her.

The corner of her mouth twitched. "They never do." She pulled her corset into a slightly more comfortable position at her waist. "I'm ready."

With a nod, he took them to the herald at a pair of immense double doors pulled back, with music swelling beyond them, and hammered gold-and-bronze tiles on the walls, alternating with lilies of lapis lazuli on white jade and green jade stems, and banners hanging down that were woven of the finest embroidered brocade. Vases of flowers filled the hall, and cut glasses sent the illumination from the many sconces shimmering about the walls. Rivergrace could not imagine any place on Kerith more grand. The lamps burned scented oil, the overhead windows let the sun blaze down in slanted glory, and the dancers swirled in colors that dazzled the eye. Rivergrace thought she heard a trumpet as the herald shouted out Lariel's name to the celebrants in the massive room. Heads turned as he did.

She could hear the whispers. "She wears armor."

"Nonsense, it's decorative."

"I tell you, that's an armored corset."

"With barb-tongued women waiting for her entry, I don't blame her," the bored man said, turning away from his companion and seeking another pretty face.

Nutmeg reached out to squeeze Rivergrace's hand. "They're calling us shop girls," she whispered, reporting from her side of the hall.

"But we are."

"Yes, but . . . never mind. We are!" And Nutmeg put her chin up.

Rivergrace squeezed back. "Hosmer would never forgive us if we started another brawl."

That brought a grin to Nutmeg's curving mouth. They followed in the Warrior Queen's wake, aware of stares that assailed Lariel and slid away only to end up on them. At the end of the long hallway, Grace managed a deep breath.

Three side halls adjoined the ballroom, each of those draped with banners and pennants and garlands of flowers, and holding a covey of attendees, two for the food and drink they served, and a third for a quieter place to stand and talk or sit and rest a while. Lariel headed to the third. If aware of the path that gave way to her, she did not show it, nor did she simply plow her way across the center of the room, but along the edge until she reached her destination. As she entered the room, a man's voice rose in song.

"At summer's last bloom, at winter's fall, at sword blade ever turning,
The war came to an end on the banks of Ashenbrook.
Through fields of death the river ran, its waters laced with blood,
Bearing a fallen king upon its tide, carried onto his Returning.
Spring has come and gone in time, with grasses ever greening
Still the Ashenbrook flows through killing fields,
Its dark and bitter waters running through banks of clay and bone.
Only men can sing of memory, of war and its darkest gleaning."

Bistane Vantane turned and bowed deeply to her. He wore white leather, supple pants upon a body even more supple, vest cut tightly over a shirt of the most gossamer blue, its sleeves flowing amply to end in tight and bejeweled cuffs. Rivergrace recognized the Vaelinar who had sung at the Spring fair years ago, and although she felt changed, he seemed unmarked by the time. His companion she also knew, from his calling at her father's brewery, Trader Bregan Oxfort. He wore silks of dark brown, quiet, somber colors, although every finger on Oxfort's hand held a sparkling ring, and heavy bracelets hung like chains from his sleeves. "Listen to that," Bregan remarked. "Women have been flocking about us for a candlemark begging for a song, and nothing. The Warrior Queen arrives and Bistane opens up like a songbird on midsummer's night."

"Surely songbirds give off sweeter melodies," Lariel murmured.

"I hope m'lady will favor me with a dance later," Bistane said to Lariel.

"Why wait? The night is young." She put her hand out to him and he caught it up with a grin that wiped the somberness from him entirely, and he spun her out onto the floor. Oxfort continued talking with his companions as if nothing had occurred.

"And I thought that was going to be awkward," muttered Jeredon as he sprawled upon a chair.

"Are you asking for trouble?" Sevryn remarked to him.

"Almost anything would be better than this. On edge and bored, two things I dislike being."

Nutmeg perched on a footstool near Jeredon. "Don't you care for dances?"

"I," he said to her, "much prefer hunting and riding and camping under the stars. Even more so, walking the forest and groves and . . . how can I say it? . . . listening to them."

"I understand."

"Do you?" He took his eyes from Bistane dancing close to Lariel and looked at her.

"It's a different voice, but it speaks all the same. I like going to the tall trees, the great red-barked ones near the seacoast, where it's damp and the soil is nearly black with richness. I've been there twice, and it's put roots in my soul. They tower higher than any building."

"I know the ones you speak of. They are old, you know."

"I know. We Dwellers know such things."

"Tell me what else you comprehend, then," and Jeredon put an elbow on his knee, and the self-mocking smile that had played on his features evolved into one of keen interest. Nutmeg leaned forward earnestly, a rare serious look on her face, talking and gesturing.

Sevryn said at Rivergrace's ear, startling her into a tiny jump, "Would you care to dance?"

She caught herself. "Should we?"

"We were commanded to enjoy ourselves, as I recall. A queen takes commands seriously." He held his arm out to her.

"I don't . . . I haven't danced very much . . ."

His mouth stayed very close to her ear, warm breath tickling her. "The music is changing as we speak. Listen. This is a country fair song, if I recall."

"It is!"

"Fated, then. Shall we dance, m'lady?" Without waiting for an answer, he put his other hand to her waist and swung her about onto the dance floor as the music picked up and launched into a lively air. He gave her a little shake, erasing the reluctance in her, and she gave in to the music. Lively steps, and kicks to each side, and twirls and then a promenade, and then a dip, a twirl, and all over again. Fiddles and pipes and drums awakened her, and Sevryn guided her with strength until they both laughed breathlessly, weaving among the others on the floor. Many of the Vaelinars had stepped aside, not knowing the dance, watching, and joining as they picked it up, but Bistane and Lariel reigned in the middle of the dance floor, in swirls of blue-and-white leather, a flash of color as Sevryn spun her by them. Some of the attendees carried small pets on their wrists or shoulders, bright-winged or soft-furred, with collars or leashes of strung gems on gold-and-silver braids, the pets holding on tightly as their owners danced away.

The music ebbed in a slow dance, then, and he pulled her to him, both catching their breaths as he showed her how to sway and step in time with him. He said nothing, but she felt his cheek pressed to her temple, and Rivergrace lost whatever words she wished to say. Behind the tempo of the music, she learned the beat of his heart and the flow of his breathing. The dance seemed to last forever, then suddenly the sound ended.

He broke away from her. "I need to see a smile," he cautioned her. "Lest the queen think we're not following orders."

"That should never happen," and she found a smile though still a little breathless.

"Excellent." He listened as the musicians struck up again, a full band this time, with horn and more strings and even bells. "Ah. Now this one is a little more difficult, but it's easy if you remember the steps in a box. Like this . . ." And he put both hands on her waist to guide her.

After a few missteps, she caught the pattern. She saw other women holding their skirts up in one hand, with the other placed on their partners' shoulders, and did the same. Freeing her ankles made following Sevryn much easier, and they fell into an even more intricate configuration on the dance floor among the others.

A swath of black silk tapped on Sevryn's shoulder. He stopped, pulling Rivergrace with him from the stream of couples to face the elegant Vaelinar woman. A diadem of cut obsidian bound her dark gold hair from her forehead and then freed it to tumble down her shoulders and back. The severe colors did not hide her, but allowed her to spring forth from the shadows, like the dawning of the sun itself, and her eyes of verdant green flecked with smoke and leaf green ruled a face of sharp planes. Her beauty looked as if it could cut.

"Tressandre." Sevryn bowed slightly.

"I claim a dance." Her gaze passed over Rivergrace, dismissing her. Rivergrace tried to contain a shiver.

"Would that it were possible, but I am escorting at the queen's orders. Perhaps another time."

"We will always have another time." Tressandre ild Fallyn curved her lips as she smiled, but no warmth entered her eyes. She traced her hand languidly over Sevryn's shoulder and then down his flank, as if reminding both of them she knew what lay beneath the civilized cover of clothing. Dropping her palm to the butt of the riding crop at her hip, she sauntered off without another look back. Sevryn watched her go, his jaw tight.

The music went on and then stopped, and then gathered again before he moved, taking Rivergrace's wrist and holding her lightly for a slow but sprightly dance. He said nothing for an even longer time. When they finished, he told her, "I think we need a cooling drink," and led her to the hall filled with tables groaning under the refreshments.

She put her hand out to halt him, to tell him that he need not squire her around, but she missed his wrist, stroking her fingers across his rigid torso instead, and he let his breath out in a hiss.

"How do you do that?"

"Do what?"

"Quench fire."

"I'm afraid I don't understand—"

"Never mind. Here, a pastry or two, and some light wine with juice?" He gathered a drink and treats for her without waiting for her answer and pressed them into her hands, before serving himself.

She bit into the small, flaky object, and the goodness of the crust hid a sweet-and-nut concoction that pleased her tongue as she ate. She hoped that Nutmeg would be able to smuggle a few of them out to Hosmer, for he loved sugary things. The wine soothed her thirst, and she gulped a second draft, bringing Sevryn's mouth to her ear again, saying, "Not too fast, aderro, that can be very intoxicating. If you thirst, I'll draw you some water."

Embarrassment warmed her. She began to stammer an apology when a tall Vaelinar with a cane limped their way and clasped Sevryn's shoulder.

"Introduce me, Dardanon, for I do not know this young lady," as he looked upon them both.

"Rivergrace Farbranch, guest of Queen Lariel, may I present Tranta ild Istlanthir, famed cliff climber and cliff diver of the Kingdom of Tomarq." Sevryn lifted his glass to the other.

Tranta took her hand, pastry and all, bowing deeply over it. She could not help staring at him, with pale blue skin and dark blue-green hair, towering over Sevryn and herself. He straightened. "Remind me to commend Lariel for inviting exquisite guests."

Sevryn shifted weight. "I understand Tressandre is looking for a dance partner."

Tranta brandished his walking stick. "I thank the Gods that I am unable to fulfill her needs." He did not take his eyes off Rivergrace. The three of them might have been the only people in a hall growing ever more crowded as dancers came in search of drink for parched throats. "I feel I should know you, m'lady Farbranch. The name, however, does not speak to me of our people."

"I'm Dweller."

Tranta laughed heartily. He balanced himself on his cane as he caught his breath to respond. "Did no one ever tell you that humor is one of the more tantalizing qualities, m'lady?"

"Tranta," began Sevryn, but the other waved him off, telling him, "Tiiva is looking for Lariel. It seems the queen sent her for something, and she's found it."

"Then Tiiva will find her, I'm certain." He put his arm out to Rivergrace. "Though perhaps we should help."

"Of a certainty, you should, Sevryn, but why the young lady? I can dance a bit, after a fashion, if the music is slow and you allow me to lean on you a bit." He gazed down at Rivergrace, his eyes sparkling with mirth.

"Perhaps you weren't hit on the head hard enough," Sevryn told him.

"Only death could keep me from the company of such a lovely person." He also offered Rivergrace an arm. She stood in hesitation between the two. A tension spun out between the three of them, like a spider setting its anchoring strand in a web. She turned as someone called Lariel's name, entering the area with a rustle of fabric and a click of heels upon the tiled flooring before sweeping into a deep curtsy.

The herald's call echoed her entry. "Presenting Seneschal Tiiva Pantoreth."

The woman rose without seeming ever to have been bent in subordination, and held out a cup. "Found, m'lady queen."

Lariel beamed. "And in good time. I won't keep you further, Tiiva, I know you've kin waiting and dances promised."

"Indeed." A faint smile played over the other's face.

"My apologies for sending you questing about like a servant."

"None needed. What would you have done without it?"

"Depended upon my avandara here."

Her escort made a movement of surprise, looking down at Rivergrace, and then his mouth went tight as if holding back words. Lariel touched Bistane as if to soothe him, but he did not voice his thoughts.

That seemed to disconcert the elegant woman more than anything else that had been said, but she merely curtsied again silently and left after giving Nutmeg and Rivergrace a curious sidelong glance. Nutmeg returned it, nudging Rivergrace as the seneschal left the dancing floor.

It did not slip past Lariel. "Something untoward?"

"She reminds me of a shop customer, Lady Galraya."

"It would be the skin. Copper is one of our warmer and more rare tones. Galraya is her sister-cousin." Lariel took up the cup, a tankard of blown glass, painted with gilt and blue, meant to be fastened upon a belt or girdle. A slender stemmed flute, it hung more as a decoration than a drinking vessel, with stonework gleaming within. She tapped it and it rang with a clear, hanging note, the tenor changed by the stones inlaid at the bottom.

Rivergrace had never seen anything quite like it. "Why are there gems inside the cup?"

"For my protection. They will turn color if the drink is poisoned. I shall drink more freely than I dance in tonight's crowd, I think." Unconcerned, Lara twisted a wayward strand of hair shaken down by dancing back into place. "In fact, a libation sounds good. Bistane?"

"A drink might do us both good."

The air in the room seemed to thicken, flowing about Grace like the Silverwing, dimming sound and light, drawing her into a current which would carry her away to an unknown destination as her gaze stayed upon Lariel.

She heard the Warrior Queen's voice, light and clear, answering something asked of her, as she moved toward the tables and ordered a drink, Bistane with his arm about her waist as she did. She handed over her goblet to the veiled server across the tables and waited as the androgynous waiter filled it with sparkling water before retreating into anonymity behind the casks and kegs. Lariel curved her arm to move the glass to her lips after a quick glance within, and returning her attention to Bistane. The fluid within moved sluggishly as if muddied.

Time slowed and pooled as the summer waters swirling into her beloved cove on the Silverwing, although Rivergrace saw Lariel with a crystal clarity in the midst of it. Her slender fingers lifted the glass and it sparked Grace's eyes with the cut brilliance of faceted quartz yet it held a dark and bloodied heart within it, a flawed shard that made her shiver in repulsion. Without thought, she flung her arm out to dash it from her lips, crying, "Don't drink that!"

"What?" Lariel turned in confusion toward her, the glass continuing its slow journey to her mouth.

"You can't!" She flailed, knocking the goblet from Lariel's hand, the beautiful object arcing away. Bistane caught it neatly in the air, barely letting a drop spill. He swung about and grabbed a tiny furry creature sitting upon the shoulder of the Vaelinar behind him. It squeaked in startled protest and Bistane dribbled a bit of the drink into its mouth.

The little thing blinked with wide eyes even as its owner shouted in dismay, then it coughed and gagged and spewed, and died shuddering in Bistane's hand.

"Poison."

Chapter Fifty-Five

RIVERGRACE GAVE A SOFT CRY and moved toward Lariel. Sevryn moved with her, but not toward the queen. His target was the last person who'd touched her, the veiled Vaelinar servant beyond. He hurdled the table, drawing his blade from his left sleeve as he did, and the servant bolted.

He heard Bistane's flat declaration of "Poison" as he lunged over the table, rolled, and came up running after his prey.

The Vaelinar ran as if its life depended upon it, shedding bits of clothing as he/she skirted the crowd, Sevryn close behind. The ripped veil floated on the air before descending on a bust of a former mayor of Calcort in an alcove. The servant's gown came off next, thrown into the dancers and causing a crash of bodies as they tangled in it. Sevryn leaped over thrashing arms and legs and curses.

His target now ran, swift and lean and clothed in black, out of the Great Hall, bowling over guards as he descended into the quad, into the depth of night, and a mass of people.

"Kobrir!"

His shout rang over the celebrating commoners, but the figure neither slowed nor veered. With unerring direction, the assassin cut through the booths and eateries, and into a ring of dancers, who with a shout, closed him off.

Sevryn burst into the circle, and onlookers tightened about both of them, a wall of curious and unmoving flesh.

"Fight! Fight!"

Kobrir dropped into a stance. Under his Vaelinar veils, he wore a mask of thin gauze, dark as a moonless sky, hiding his face. The only thing light about him were the knives in his hands, catching a glint of the orange gleam of firelight and torchlight.

They circled one another, and then closed in a dance of another kind, quiet, skilled, deadly.

Narskap looked into the night, thinning into a morning fog. He disliked the east. He did not care for the long travel to journey there, or the feelings evoked by the warlands crossed to get there, or the Galdarkans who populated it. Quendius seemed to love or hate nothing and showed little feeling as Narskap rose from the waning campfire and looked into a very early dawn.

"We move east," he said, "to Diort. But," and he pointed westward. "Someone advances on our heels."

"Scouts say nothing."

"There are scouts who haven't returned. Likely, will not. Get your troops up and on their feet, for the western enemy does not sleep."

"The sword thirsts." Quendius rose, his sooty skin nearly invisible in the night.

"Ever. And it knows where to drink." Narskap went to the horse lines to draw his steed out and began to saddle it. As he mounted, Quendius swung aboard his own, using the tying ropes for a bridle. His sharp whistles of command pierced the air, sounding like the hunting cry of a falcon on the soon-to-be morning air. Without voice, he quieted his troops with a wave of his arm, signaling them to ready for an assault.

The ambushing enemy charged from the hill as they readied. Narskap spotted a banner of the ild Fallyn and one of House Hith-aryn, but the banner little mattered there, for Bistel himself led the chargers, his head bare, steel-blue hair cropped nearly to the skull and the light blue streaks of his eyes blazing within darker blue depths. Narskap unsheathed the sword, felt it quicken in his hand, heard it keen in his ears, and he began to mow down any within reach.

A stroke to the right, and a Vaelinar fell, head all but severed from his neck, blood spurting. The sword leaped a second time to the font and stayed a moment, quivering, drinking, and when Narskap rode on, little blood stained the grass beneath the still twitching form.

Sevryn slashed to his right, the knives clashing as the Kobrir parried, and the ring of watchers grew heavier about them. He drew his left hand knife quickly, feinting to the left, looking for a gap in the assassin's defense. He found none, as he knew he would not. The only surprise was that the Kobrir evaded pursuit and faced him now. He wondered where the Town Guard was. And Jeredon. He had no time to shout for either. Kobrir struck with the quickness of a deadly snake.

Troops snaked about Narskap, drawing back as he swung the sword, its wailing cutting the air even as its steel did. They fell back, not in a maddened panic like the Bolgers, but they knew—oh, yes—they knew that the sword took not only life from them. He carved a pathway for himself, intent upon the banner Hith-aryn and the elder Bistel, eldest of all the Vaelinars on Kerith, rumored to have been born in fighting gear.

He would take Bistel down. Eating the soul of Bistel would make the sword invincible, and both the blade and its carrier knew it. Narskap kneed his horse hard, lunging uphill through bodies and archers and cavalry, his eyes intent on his goal. Dawn would bring death, and worse.

Steel gashed the air near his ear, so near he felt it pass before he heard the whistle. Sevryn ducked out of instinct, but too late; the knife had already gone by him. He felt a drop of warmness trickle down his neck. He thought he'd been missed but perhaps not. His ear might ache later. If he still had an ear.

He crouched low and swung to his left, catching the Kobrir off guard and off balance, and jabbed knee-high. He felt his weapon sink into flesh and sinew, heard the surprised grunt of pain as he did. The knife twisted from his hold as the Kobrir pulled away, and Sevryn found himself with but one blade. He tossed it from his left to his right hand even as he spun out of the other's reach. He could hear the crowd's reaction, the buffeting as they drew tighter around them, with shouts of encouragement and warning. They had no idea what they observed other than two knifemen in deadly combat.

Horses crashed before him. They thrashed with maddened whinnies and his own mount shied away. Narskap cursed and turned his horse about in a tight circle, then drove him back uphill to the Vaelinar war chief who cleaved his way downhill. They would meet, inevitably. He heard Quendius' sharp whistles and looked, saw the troops straggling yet mustering behind the weaponmaster. The tide had been turned and now the ild Fallyn and the Hith-aryn began to back away, to gain the room to swing about in retreat.

Quendius gave the whistle which meant to gather hostages of the higher ranked. Ransom would not be gathered, but they would spill the guts of all they knew before another evening fell. Narskap's shoulder cramped and his arm wearied, but he held his greatsword aloft, and swung it once, urging his horse after Bistel Vantane.

Their eyes locked. Across a handful of horses falling and surging, their riders clashing, their gazes focused on one another.

Then, Bistel pivoted his war mount around and rode into the night, out of reach.

Narskap and his sword howled for the loss of their quarry.

The Kobrir did not miss a second time. Sevryn felt the knife go all the way to the hilt in his thigh. Pain flashed back to the roots of his teeth. He clenched them against a cry as he stumbled down, and rolled to avoid a third strike. But the Kobrir did not stay. With a dead run at the crowd, he vaulted over their heads and disappeared, a dark shard among night shadows. Sevryn ground his jaw together and wrapped his hand about the knife hilt, knowing better than to pull it, in case the blade were all that kept him from bleeding out. He was on his back cursing when Jeredon got to him.

Jeredon helped him onto his good leg, eyeing the knife. "Should have missed everything vital, but we'll get a healer in before we pull it. Kobrir?"

"Yes, and gone, but I took his knee out, I think. He'll be hurting. Lariel?"

"Safe. Bistane has her."

The Dweller guard Hosmer shoved his way through to get to them, and put his shoulder under Sevryn's arm for a crutch. The two of them set him on the Great Hall steps. Hos put a finger to Sevryn's ear. "Nicked you, m'lord."

"Still got the point?"

"Aye."

"Not that close, then."

He'd almost had the Kobrir, but not close enough at all.

Chapter Fifty-Six

TIIVA CURTSIED LOW to the floor, her dress in a burst of creamy satin about her, her skin glowing warmly in the candlelight of the isolated alcove. Jewels gleamed at her wrists and dangled from her earlobes. Torchlight guttered low, and draperies and bunting muted their speech to near whispers. "You were difficult to find this time, m'lady queen."

"I would think," Bistane said dryly, "you could locate her by the screams." Cloth in hand, he attempted in vain to blot away stains and vomit from his leather vest and fine shirt. Bloody cloths lay strewn about the alcove, and Sevryn leaned his shoulder to the wall as was his wont, but this time it seemed a pose to mask pain.

"One would." Tiiva agreed. Her glance flicked to Sevryn, and the tie of cloth about his thigh. "The healer found you?"

"He did. An annoying flesh wound to the meat of the thigh, a clean cut. I'm nearly sound again."

"Good. The unfortunate news is that it's the height of the gala."

Lariel wrinkled her nose slightly. "Likely they think it's just part of the entertainment. Thank you, Tiiva. On your way out, please corner Mayor Stonehand, accept his apologies, and convey mine for the upset?"

"Of course. And I will impede his progress in this direction."

"Most perceptive of you. You're invaluable." Lariel watched her leave, and then reached down into the plunge of her gown and armored corset to remove a small vial secreted there. The blown-glass vial shimmered as the water of the Andredia roiled within, and she took it up to cup in her hands, as though communing with it. "This," she murmured, "is my charge and my strength." She held it briefly before Rivergrace stirred to place her hand over both the vial and Lara, her face paling.

"This water," she said with pain, "is also bad."

Lariel shrank back and Jeredon's attention snapped about. "What did you say?"

"The water. Inside the vial. It's not the same as the other, but . . . it has been fouled."

"That water," he said sharply, "is from the sacred Andredia and was freshly drawn before we came to the Conference."

Rivergrace bowed her shoulders as she looked wordlessly to the tiled floor. Sevryn moved over protectively with a limp and a firm step. Lariel rubbed her fingers over her brow. "Leave her be, Jeredon."

"First the poison and now this. She was right on that one, but she can't possibly know what she's saying about the Andredia. She has no idea of the blasphemy of our trust and pledge she suggests."

"She knows," Lariel told him sadly. "I don't know how she does, but she does. The corruption plaguing Larandaril has washed into the river. Or it comes from the river, and washes into the land. It's been decades. I had hoped," and Lariel turned her face away from all of them, "I had hoped I was wrong. We moved all those settlements to forestall this, and yet it goes on, and worsens. I've searched all that I know and found nothing. It's the reason I came to the Conference, in hopes of insight."

The expression on Jeredon's face closed. "You were going to tell me when? That it might spring from the Andredia itself?"

"When I had to." Lariel stood. "This is my trust and burden, and I would not have told you or anyone till I had no other choice. But as for you," and she took Rivergrace's chin in her hand, forcing her to look up. "How do you know what you know?"

Far away, a gong sounded the candlemark of late evening, four marks short of dawn. Rivergrace hardly had any idea of how the night had slipped by her, except that she had been with Sevryn for all of it, and now she felt trapped, his eyes and the eyes of everyone else upon her. She didn't know how she'd felt what she felt, nor said what she'd said, but that hardly mattered now. What was done was done, as Tolby would say.

"I can't say."

Bistane gestured impatiently. "Let me handle this, m'lady. Silence rewards none of us."

"I can't answer what I don't know." Forced, she looked into Lariel's eyes, purest of cobalt with sparks of gold and blades of silver glittering in annoyance. She had no idea why alarm had lanced through her, sharp as a blade and compelling. Only that it had.

"But you know more than you're saying."

Nutmeg protested, "She saved you!"

"Indeed she did. The question is how."

Bistane pressed closer. "She has our blood and eyes, although there is clearly something else about her. I sense no power, even with the eyes."

"She's my sister," Nutmeg said firmly.

"I came to them on the river," Grace added faintly. She put her hand up to shield her face from Lariel's piercing gaze, and her sleeve slid down her arm, lace tumbling away to display her skin. Sevryn grabbed her wrist as Nutmeg let out a smothered cry of dismay, and held her bared arm out, saying, "Scars. Made by shackles, unless I miss my guess."

"And you know shackles well." Lariel released Rivergrace's chin. "Those are more than rub marks. Those came from a branding." Her eyes glimmered in sympathy.

"A slave. What did she promise for her freedom?" Bistane paced once, turned about angrily and put his hand on Lariel's shoulder.

"These are faded." Sevryn did not release Rivergrace, his fingers strong and hot on her chilled skin.

She would not look at him or anyone but Nutmeg. She sat very still, as the silver-winged alna do, when watching the river for sign of fish below the water, hunting and wishing not to be noticed, but she had been noticed and she was the hunted. Her heart beat in her throat. Did they know where she'd come from? Would they send her back to slavery? What, if anything, could she trust from these people who looked like her, but to whom she did not belong except perhaps in chains.

"Plans to assassinate a queen may marinate for decades."

"Do you think so?" Sevryn stared into Bistane's face. "Sounds as if you've experience there."

"What are you suggesting?"

"Nothing more than what you've already suggested." Sevryn turned Rivergrace's arm in his hold, and slid his hand down to take hers. "You sang of Ashenbrook. It was, as I recall learning, an ambush that took place there."

Bistane made a growling noise, and fell into silence, his body between Sevryn's and Lariel's.

"I found her," Nutmeg claimed stoutly.

"Meg, don't."

Nutmeg flounced to her feet. "She came down the river on a pile of broken sticks, and I pulled her out, and we kept her safe, and she grew up with me. That's all there is to know. You can ask my da or mom or my brothers. She's never done a Vaelinar thing in her life, but look like one of you, and she's got a good Dweller soul in her. You're not taking her."

"We have no plans for her," said Lariel quietly.

"Yet," muttered Bistane.

"Still, I would like to know how my goblet showed no sign of poison, and without scent or taste, you knew it, and you knew of my vial."

"I can't tell you. I felt it. The glass was so beautiful, sparkling like a precious jewel, and in its heart, something muddy and bloodied and sullen."

"You saw it?

"I saw it."

Bistane's hand cut the air. "Impossible. The poison was as clear as the drink. You couldn't have seen this venom."

"I know, Bistane." Lariel turned her head and kissed the back of his hand that rested on her shoulder. "Don't make me send you away just yet. Be quiet for me?"

His jaw clenched angrily, but he held back a retort.

"What about the kingdom vial? From my River Andredia?"

"I saw it."

"Again? Was it the same?"

"No. I can't tell you . . . it's like looking at pain, hurting, bottled up." Rivergrace made a helpless gesture, unable to put it into words.

"You saw it? You felt it?"

"Both."

"The poisons differ."

"How can you see a poison that no one else can?"

"She does," said Sevryn flatly. "Leave her be."

A shadow stirred from the draperies at the corner, Daravan materializing from nothingness. Sevryn spat out, "God's blood, Daravan. How long have you been there?"

"Since the Kobrir fled and you gathered in here. I considered going after him, but the crowd was too thick. He could have taken hostages, and that would have proved disastrous. I have a suggestion." The tall Vaelinar folded his arms over his chest. He wore dark silvery-gray-and-blue, jacket over billowing shirt, and lean swordsman's pants tucked into his boots, and both girls recognized their mother's handiwork.

"He speaks while I cannot?"

"The difference, Bistane, is that I can rarely get advice from our elder," Lariel said in faint amusement. "We're all listening, Lord Daravan."

"She doesn't know what she knows. You need another talespinner to talk of her finding. Go rattle her door and bring the parents here."

Lariel turned to Bistane. "Find the commander of the watch and tell him to bring the Farbranches to us. Her brother Hosmer may still be on duty, as well. Go gently, but swiftly."

Bistane Vantane bowed sharply and left. His bootheels rang out a staccato of irritation as he stalked away.

Sevryn said to all, but his gaze leveled on Daravan. "I will say this only to those assembled here, and no further. That assassin was not the Kobrir."

"What?"

"We speak of poison." Sevryn tapped his leg. "My wound is clean. The healer had little damage to deal with. The Kobrir leaves nothing to chance, his blades are notoriously marked with venom. Always. Whoever that was, he was an imposter. A good one, and a damned good fighter, but not a legendary assassin. Whoever hired him either thought they hired the Kobrir or wanted us to think they hired the Kobrir. Either way, I would not let them know we suspect otherwise."

"Well, then. I was just beginning to think this lad was intolerably busy." Daravan smiled thinly as Jeredon crossed his arms over his chest.

Daravan said, "One other thing." He approached Lariel and spoke, his voice pitched to her alone, and her eyes widened as he did. She questioned, "How can this be true?"

"I only know that it is."

Jeredon had quieted when Daravan started talking and now moved into the light toward his sister. "What?"

"Can this be repeated?"

Daravan gave her a sharp nod.

"There was another battle to the east. Word is unclear, but it looks as if Diort had forces moving to join him and they were cut off. Bistel led and ild Fallyn accompanied him. He must have grown wings after he left here, like the war falcon he is. We have no word on which side they rode, nor what other forces are involved. Confirmation is awaited." She put her shoulders back. "It is time," she added, "for me to prepare for war."

Daravan's eyebrow flew up.

"You would not have told me if you'd known," she acknowledged of his surprise. "I've had other signs and suggestions, and I've stayed my hand, but no longer. It takes time to ready. I may have already waited far too long."

"You're not even certain of the enemy."

"I think," she answered slowly, "that they hope for just that confusion." Then, to Nutmeg and Rivergrace, she added, "I will not hear word of this beyond this room, or you'll find yourselves in more trouble than Nutmeg can talk you out of."

Lariel sat down, drawing a small table to her side. "Show me what you know," she told Daravan, "while I still have your presence and you still have my ear." They began talking softly and swiftly as the lamps burned lower and lower.

Tolby Farbranch, awakened from a deep and sound sleep, sprang from his bed with fists knotted and swinging. He cleared the room of Town Guards while still in his nightshirt and drew his arm back to take out the lad coming in the bedroom door when he recognized Hosmer.

He pulled his punch back. "What be happening?"

"You're wanted. Needed."

The commotion had awakened Lily and she sat up in bed, with the covers pulled up to her neck. "Grace and Nutmeg! Have they come home?"

"Everyone's all right, Mom. But you've been sent for. I can't tell you any more. Hurry up and dress, we've a coach waiting outside." Hosmer bent over to help his guard mates off the floor, further conversation overridden by groans and grunts of the downed getting back to their feet, holding bruised jaws and brows.

Tolby wasted no time jamming his nightshirt into a pair of trousers and his feet into his well-worn and most comfortable boots. Lily waited until the door closed behind her son before dressing herself, with quick, neat movements, and twisting her hair into some semblance of order.

Hosmer sat on a horse cart, reins in hand.

"You're certain the girls are all right?"

"They're fine, last I saw them. Warrior Queen Lariel sent for you."

Lily laced her fingers together. Compliments would have waited till dawn, only trouble came in the middle of the night, and she pressed her lips together in worry. Tolby's shoulder bumped close to hers and stayed in support although the two did not exchange words until Hosmer drove to the Great Hall itself, got down, and put his hand up to Lily.

"Here?"

"Here is where I was told to bring you. I was on duty at the front doors." Hosmer's expression changed quickly as if he wished to say something else, and did not. Lily took his hand to step down, worried now about what he was not saying even more than what he had said.

Crews moved slowly about the quad, bent over brooms and barrels, whisking and clearing away the last of the outside celebration, as the night faded into its last, deepest hours. A drunken shout here and there sounded far away from the circle of light cast by the lampposts at the hall. Tolby jumped down with a grunt. He ran a hand through his thinning, grizzled hair.

A Vaelinar noble awaited them inside the grand entryway. He looked irritated, and that did not help Lily's fluttering pulse any. Something unspeakable had stained his pristine white leathers, although she had a sinking feeling that was not what irritated him. She took a deep breath to compose herself and followed after as he waved. "Come with me. Be quick about it. Do not linger to ask or answer questions."

Within, the music played on for couples twirling slowly about the ballroom, and heads turned curiously as they came through. She had to nearly run to stay close to the Vaelinar noble whose every passing stride seemed to lengthen in irritation. They passed through two arches, and by guards, and then into a room designated as the Sun Alcove, although Lily thought it could encompass most of her new house. Her daughters sat within.

She dropped, kneeling at Queen Lariel's feet, certain only that trouble had awakened them from a deep, worry-free sleep. The finery all wore did not hide the steel they could be made of, nor the reputations of the veiled ones from years and years ago.

"Master and Mistress Farbranch. Thank you for coming to me." She leaned forward and said, "Please rise. And please put yourself at ease. No one is on trial here."

"Yet."

She shot Bistane a look of pure annoyance before looking kindly on Lily. "It seemed necessary to talk with you."

"They're good lasses," Tolby said. "Whatever has been done, was done with good intentions."

"We saved her from poison!" Nutmeg blurted out. She swallowed. "Rivergrace did, anyway."

"For which we are exceedingly grateful," Jeredon told him. "Still, the curiosity of a Vaelinar blooded one raised by Dwellers struck us. How did you find her?"

Tolby took his cold pipe out of his pants pocket and clamped his teeth on the stem. "I'll let my wife tell you that tale, but I demand respect for her from all of you." He glared about the alcove and leaned back against the wall.

"Agreed," said Lariel smoothly. "I need to deal with another matter first. Bistane. I think you may have news from home which you'll need to deal with. You may leave us now."

"Of what do you speak?"

"I speak of your moving to abandon the Accords, and of the army your father has led to the east."

He did not respond or hesitate, merely turned abruptly and did as she told him, the draperies ruffling at his exit. Daravan inhaled with a sharp hiss.

"Is that true?"

"The Accords? Yes. More than true, it seems to have been prophetic." She watched him go before she crooked a finger at Lily. "Please sit and tell me."

Lily eased herself in between Rivergrace and Nutmeg. "There isn't much to tell, Your Highness. It was spring and flood tide, and we were working our orchards, tending to the blossoms and trimming of dead wood and such, and Meg here played by the river. She found Grace on a bit of a raft barely more than kindling wood and a handful of it at that, and pulled her ashore. We've a bit of a cove there, and the water turns back on itself," she added as Jeredon made a tiny mutter of disbelief. "Grace was as big as Meg, but half-starved—"

"More than half," put in Tolby. "I'm still not seein' how a parent can let their child go like that." He hushed at Lily's next words.

"We don't know what happened or why. Only that the Silverwing carried her down to us, and she was nearly dead from it."

"Did she remember anything?"

Lily shook her head. "Little but sadness and loss."

"And the scars?"

"Fresh," Lily said to Sevryn. "We could tell she'd been in chains. Or worse. The gashes, the burning." She twisted her hands together. "We made a decision to keep her secret, to keep her safe, she but a weakling child."

"Her speech?"

"Seldom. It seemed as though she knew little of any kind of speech at all."

Rivergrace lifted a few fingers. "I remember a little when I hear Vaelinar now. It seems both familiar and very far away. I remember being cold and the sound of water in my ears, and not being able to see, and Stinkers that came and went." She paused to draw a shallow breath. "I remember the earth pressing down on us. On me. No. On us." She came to a halting stop, and Sevryn squeezed his hand about hers, his own thoughts tumbling back to dark times.

Jeredon shifted his folded legs, nodding to Lily. "Did anyone come after her? Were any warrants put out for runaway slaves or the like?"

"No. Of course, we lived out in the hills and valleys, and might not have known right away, but word travels. We had Bolger raids and those were nothing new, before and after her coming."

"And then the Raver raids began," Tolby said, bitterness edging his voice. "Burned us out."

Sevryn took a deep breath. "Bolger mercenaries with Ravers, aye?"

"Yes. The lands have been plagued with them this last handful of years. My son Hosmer lost most of his militia to the last one that drove us away."

"We haven't been able to find out what drives them, but they have gotten bold." The corner of Sevryn's mouth worked, but he fell silent then as if more words failed him.

"I kept," Lily said hesitantly, "a few of her things." She did not return the gaze of her daughters, but looked at Lariel steadfastly.

"What sort of things?"

"She had little in the way of clothing that survived the river, but there was a scarf or blanket scrap, handwoven, of beautiful thread. I put it away, thinking that someday I might, she might . . . she might want it, and I could give it to her." Lily swallowed. "It's still buried at the old house, in the root cellar. I didn't bring it with us. I should have. It had runes worked through it. I . . . I feared it might harm more than help her. We saw little love or care in her, m'lady. She had been worn to a shadow."

"It should be retrieved. It might tell us much."

"Or," stated Jeredon, "nothing."

"When death comes after me, I demand to know who made me the target. I would know who I can trust."

Rivergrace stirred as if unaware she moved, but she pointed around the alcove. First to Sevryn, then to Jeredon, then after a long hesitation to Daravan. "Find trust and honor in these," she said, and grew quiet again.

Sevryn felt Daravan's eyes on him yet could not still his thoughts. He'd escaped as had she. Dare he ask her to go back to that? Would it break her if she did? Or had she already been broken, to be used as a tool? She'd taken down a Raver and yet seemingly had no memory of it that she allowed. What else had she buried deep within her?

Lariel leaned intently toward Rivergrace. "Not a prophet, I think. She is my avandara."

It was the second time that night Grace had heard Lara say that word.

"Improbable," Daravan responded. "We no longer carry that Talent in our lines, Highness."

"We did once. Truth-seekers, verifiers. I think it may have returned." Lariel made a restless movement. "Thinking that is better than thinking she was used as part of a conspiracy. Which would you have?"

Rivergrace stood in her flowing gown. "I want to know what I am, where I came from. I'm going back."

"Not alone. Not to Raver-burned ground. I'll come with you." Sevryn pulled himself straight.

Tolby removed his cold pipe and jabbed it in the air. "I'll take her back. She deserves that much from me."

"No." Lariel spoke firmly but quietly. She eyed all of them, but her regard fell on Sevryn and stayed. "It's not what you say, but what you don't."

"I know the mountains from which the Silverwing flows."

"As do we. The Silverwing flows from one crest of the mountains, and the Andredia from the western slopes. You ask to leave my side at a time when I've great need of you. Why?"

"Because, m'lady queen, her broken memories echo my own."

Silence fell and stayed. Would she trust him without further explanation, or dare he use his Voice, not upon Lariel—for that would break every vow he'd made to himself and to her—but to her, to whisper to her his fears, his hope that Rivergrace might lead him to answers of his own. She saved him the decision.

"So be it."

"Grace isn't going anywhere without me," declared Nutmeg.

"I imagine not." Lariel managed a smile. "Sevryn will accompany you. Leave as soon as is possible and return the quicker."

"A day's rest and we'll be off." He took Rivergrace's hand and pressed it into her father's. "I'll call for you the next morrow. You can ride, I take it?"

"Yes."

"All right, then, I'll bring a mount for you. Nutmeg?"

"I'll be taking my own pony."

"Master Tolby?"

"I expect I can manage a horse." Tolby gathered his family about him, tucking his pipe into his pants pocket. "We'll see you at dawn tomorrow."

Daravan watched them leave, and the two of them stood alone, before commenting, "Is that well done?"

"I don't know." Lariel picked up the hem of her skirt and stood. "That's the damn trouble with life, isn't it? You don't know until too late."

Chapter Fifty-Seven

HE BOUGHT A HORSE from the guard, a half-tashya breed, a nice little mare with a red-brown coat and dark ebony socks, mane, and tail. She had a good eye to her, long legs, and the tashya speed and intelligence without being so fiery that an inexperienced rider couldn't control her. The guard officer who sold her patted her on the neck with a tear in the corner of his eye in farewell, saying, "Take care of Black Ribbon." Sevryn promised he would.

He also found a mountain pony with some tashya blood in him, stout and longer-legged but fast enough to keep up with the other horses. The temptation to buy a second pony crossed him, but he doubted Nutmeg would ride it. He procured one of the long-necked pack goats from the queen's own herd stabled in Calcort at the traders' guild. It stood nearly as tall as Rivergrace's mare, stubborn and able to carry a good weight in packs. It rolled an eye at him, and he tried to make friends with it by giving it a honey cake. It gobbled the cake down quickly enough and glared at him with suspicion when he didn't produce any more.

He brought the string with him to the Farbranch holding in the northeast quarter. Walther had popped up to give him instructions for a good tip, as well as a message from Daravan. As the boy bounded off, he had read and pocketed it. Now it lay scalding in his pocket like a heated rock refusing to be ignored.

The Farbranches awaited him, Nutmeg already up and mounted on a fat, burly little chocolate-brown gelding who arched his neck and whinnied a challenge at him as he rode up. Tolby handed Rivergrace up, her long legs clad in farmers' pants, her hair knotted up under a broadbrim hat. She beamed down at her mare. "Who is this?"

"That, I'm told, is Ribbon. Tolby's on Neatfoot and the goat is Daisy. He doesn't answer to Daisy, and I can't say as I blame him."

Tolby took Lily in his arms for a resounding kiss before mounting his horse. He pointed a thumb at Garner and Keldan who jostled each other to grab his boot foot to shake him good-bye. "You watch the business like the sons I taught you to be!"

"No worries, Da." Garner smiled solemnly at him. Tolby looked up and down the lane as if hoping to see Hosmer, but his watch had been that morning, and he did not appear. Lily stood blushing in the street and waved at them for as long as they could see each other, framed by both their grown boys. The girls turned about often to look back, until the lane curved enough that they were carried out of sight. The goat trotted along behind reluctantly until it let out a bleat of farewell and resigned itself to keeping pace as they moved outside the western city gates.

"How long a trip?" Sevryn ask of Tolby.

"A good two to three weeks," Tolby answered. "Depends on summer rain, and whatnot. Mounts should be faster than wagon and cart, so it mightn't be quite that long." He gave Sevryn a sidelong look. By whatnot, Sevryn gathered he meant road bandits and other hazards best not discussed in front of the others. He had no intention of leaving the main roads until he had to, so the whatnot should be down to a minimum, as any bandit was more of a coward and opportunist than anything else.

By the third day, Sevryn was impressed with his company. Both Rivergrace and Nutmeg rode well and tirelessly, which he hadn't expected. Bumblebee, the stout Dweller pony, had a lot of bottom to him, keeping up well although he whuffed and grumbled in the late afternoon when staked out to graze and rest. Older yet determined to keep up, Bumblebee had a good, smooth gait and Nutmeg never let him stumble. The two riders bathed and rubbed and anointed his legs with a smelly salve that they swore kept the stiffness away, and by added advantage, kept almost any flying bug away from the camp as well. What insect wasn't deterred by the odor of the salve undoubtedly was cut down by the pungent toback that Tolby put in his pipe and puffed away at each evening.

The girls seemed immune to the smoke as well, although Nutmeg wrinkled her nose the first night, noting, "Mom doesna let you smoke that at home."

"A man has to take his little pleasures when he can." Tolby winked at her. As the pipe seemed well broken in and used, Sevryn figured it was the toback and not the pipe that seldom got smoked at home.

Third night, he took the early watch, sitting on a hillock before the sun set, a small freshet bubbling away by the camp, Tolby telling a story of some kind to his daughters, his voice barely drifting up to Sevryn. Sevryn pulled Daravan's note from his pocket, the note that had remained so hot, he wondered it hadn't set him on fire.

~ *You'll be followed.* ~

That was it. Nothing more, not a jot of explanation, yet it had raised the hair on the back of his neck like a hound on a scent trail both hot and feared, and he hadn't calmed down yet. He did not think he could let this fall into Tolby's "whatnot" category.

Not, I'll be following. Not, Be wary of pursuers. Just . . . this.

Sevryn refolded the note and returned it to his pocket, musing. He didn't think that Daravan stooped to manipulating him in an attempt to keep him on his toes. If Kobrir or Vaelinar, Daravan would have told him, so it struck him that Daravan knew as little of the being on their trail as he did, only that they were likely to have one. He mulled that over. Neither friend nor foe. He would have to watch and wait and see if it revealed itself. He hadn't seen it coming out of Calcort or the low farmlands surrounding the city, when a tail would have been most visible, so it had guile enough to not be seen.

He put his back to a stump, set his heels in, and surveyed his watch. Tolby's voice fell off and silence came from below, until a basso snoring drifted up, and Sevryn grinned in spite of himself. The snoring would keep him awake until his watch ended, when Tolby would stroll up and relieve him. He could hear the whicker and stamp of one of the horses as it moved about on the tie-line.

Something splashed downstream in the small brook, a night fisher perhaps. He listened to the deepening dusk.

Another splash. If a night fisher, it seemed a trifle big to be making enough noise for Sevryn to hear it so clearly upstream. He tensed but heard no other untoward sound, even as he thought he would go investigate if he did. The noise never sounded again, as if knowing his thoughts.

As the moon's quarter face hung high in the sky, the snoring stopped and Tolby eventually made his way up to the hillock. He had a cup in his hand, which he offered to Sevryn, a Dweller brew of leaves with a faint hint of peppermint and a tart-sweet kick to it.

"The lasses sleep well." Tolby hunkered down next to him as he drank.

"Good. Do you expect any trouble at the old place?"

"I've heard no one has been able to settle out there yet. 'Tis good land no one wants to leave fallow, so, aye, I expect trouble."

"Bolgers don't usually ride with Ravers."

"But they have been, aye? I expect that one of us with the knowing of which clans are which could make sense of it, but there are few of us who take note of Bolger doings."

"Rivergrace calls them Stinkers."

Tolby nodded. "She has a fear of them. That and closed-in places. The first she can handle, the second, it's tough on her."

"This cellar we're headed to . . ."

"Cracked open like an egg. No worry there. We may have a bit of digging to do, to find my wife's cubbyhole, but that's about it. She told me where it is; it's the debris that'll slow us down getting to it."

"Good." Sevryn got to his feet and stretched his legs, handing the cup of brew back to Tolby. "I'm going downstream for a look-see. If I find any trouble, I'll whistle, sharply."

Tolby peered up at him, one thick eyebrow crooked. "Expect any?"

"Don't know. Seems wise to check around a bit."

"I'll be listening, then."

Sevryn moved as quietly off the hillock as he could, pausing by the banked campfire, letting the horses and goat smell him and know he was moving about, before making his way into the brush and following the stream. Each step came slowly and deliberately, moving with or around the underbrush rather than against it, to lessen the noise. He came upon a small clearing and found flattened stones on the ground, with the bone and skin remains of fish on them. He touched the stone and found them with a little warmth still to them, heated by the sun and then used if not to cook the fish thoroughly, at least somewhat. The diner, however, had since moved on. Sevryn cast about the clearing and found fresh horse sign as well although darkness muddled the hoofprints. He had missed horse and rider go by as he talked with Tolby, he guessed.

Either he'd been heard coming downstream or the diner believed in not staying in one place any longer than necessary.

Sevryn stared downstream, listening, and heard nothing other than the occasional skitter of a rodent through the tangled grasses by the brook.

Horses needed to rest and graze a considerable part of each day. If the diner did indeed follow them, moving from spot to spot to keep from discovery, his mount would not recover easily.

Sevryn quietly returned to camp, determined to push a little harder, hoping to gain a day or so advantage. He rolled into his blanket and dropped into a dreamless sleep. Gray dawn woke him, that and the nudge of a boot toe from Tolby as he returned to get another candlemark of sleep or so before breaking camp. On one knee, he could see the amber tousled head of Nutmeg still burrowed in sleep, but the blanket Rivergrace used was neatly folded, tied, and ready to be stowed. He went to the edge of the brook and found her there, lying on her side on the bank, one hand trailing idly through summer-slowed water, her eyes narrowed in thought and half sleep. He watched her for long moments. A frog croaked as the sun began to warm and he hopped away from the grasses and marshes near her. Her booted foot twitched slightly, enchantment broken.

"M'lady Rivergrace," he said, so as not to startle her further.

She sat up and dried her fingers on her farmers' pants. "Sleep well?"

He offered his hand to help her up. "It's fortunate," he said, "to be on watch when Tolby snores, and to sleep when he is awake."

She giggled at that, a sound of unforced and unexpected pleasure. "He can be loud, but I miss it when he doesn't. It's rather like knowing something fiercely protective is in the room next to you." She rose easily to her feet, barely tugging on his hand. "I'll start a breakfast."

"Not much of one today. Just rolls and fruit, no fire. I want to be away."

"I'll get Nutmeg up, then. She can sleep till the sun is high, if you let her."

"Not the lazy type?"

"Oh, no! Not at all. But sometimes she spins about so much, she winds down for a while."

"All that chattering."

She showed a dimple when she grinned, and he hadn't seen that before; it enchanted him. He would like to see her flash a true and genuine smile often. She slipped past him, a whisper of wind through the reeds and grasses, toward the camp.

Nutmeg stood yawning when they arrived, running a brush over Bumblebee's thick coat and shaking horsehair into the wind. "I swear I could build another pony out of all this."

"I take it he hasn't lost his winter coat yet."

Nutmeg crooked an eyebrow at Sevryn. "His winter coat would hang to the ground if we let it. He looks like a furry boulder rolling over the snow and frost."

He said to Rivergrace, "I think she's pulling my leg."

She slapped the pony on his rump, a cloud of dust and hair flying up. "No. Da says he's not all pony, he's a cross with one of those great cows of the north whose hair you can weave."

Bumblebee snorted as if knowing an insult when he heard one and flicked his tail at Grace as she dodged away.

Sevryn got his horse ready, rubbing the gelding's soft nose, calling it by its tashya name, Aymaran. The dark-gray horse, so dark that he would be called black save for his powdery-gray nose, snuffled back at him. As the horse aged, his coat would lighten to a charcoal or even snowy gray, but he was young yet. Part of Lariel's herd, he could not lay a claim to the beast, but he held a clear affection for him. He saddled up Black Ribbon and Aymaran, and Tolby rose with a creak of his knees, and took to readying Neatfoot.

They ate their rolls and fruit quickly, clearing the grounds as they did, munching with one hand and kicking apart the last of the fire to cool it. Then, before the sun began to truly rise in the sky and the dawn burned away, they were off. Tolby took the head of the trail, and Sevryn the rear. He let Aymaran drop his head and graze a bit, watching behind them and seeing nothing. If they were still being followed, he could not detect it.

Over the days that followed, they wound into rougher country, sometimes dismounting and walking the horses to take the weight off them and stretch their own legs. Bumblebee lost some of his coat and weight, and chuffed when they pulled up his tie-line in the mornings, grass hanging from his lips as he was interrupted in his morning graze. The others kept their flesh and looked fit, Black Ribbon gleaming like a ripened cherry under Rivergrace's grooming.

He found himself watching Rivergrace whenever he could. Despite her broadbrim hat, her freckles blossomed, and her dimple deepened. The sun lit a gold fire in her deep chestnut hair, and brought out light yellow streaks in Nutmeg's thick curls. Tolby's tales never repeated themselves about the fire at night, his repertoire a bottomless well, and Nutmeg never ran out of things to say about everything else. He grew used to the smell of the horse ointment and even Tolby's stinky toback, although the snoring still rattled his teeth at night. Sevryn found himself growing fond of all of them, and could not imagine a day when he could not look upon Rivergrace.

They crossed the Nylara without incident, although Rivergrace seemed leery of the huge Ferryman as if expecting something more than merely a hand stuck out for the few bits of coin he demanded of them.

He was leaning back in his saddle, half drowsing in the hot sun, watching the graceful sway of Rivergrace on Ribbon walking ahead of him, when he heard the loud crack of a limb snapping behind them. He bolted upright, and pivoted Aymaran, the horse throwing his ears up alertly. Tolby reined his horse about immediately, waving the girls on ahead of him. Sevryn gestured at him to stay and dismounted, running back through the trees and high grass, as light afoot as he could manage, bringing his dagger to his hand as he did. He found a trail breast-high pushed through the undergrowth, angling along theirs, but the horse that had made it, and the rider, were unseen. He bent by the tracks. Crudely shod. Mountain pony perhaps.

Sevryn straightened up and circled the sign, finding nothing clear. The rider had taken his mount back the way he had come, leaving no new trail. He would have to run a good long way to catch up, and he had no wish to leave the others alone that long, in case the rider circled around.

It convinced him of two things. They were being followed, and the follower seemed to have no wish to catch them, merely to trail them. It meant the danger lay at journey's end. He went back to Tolby, saying, "He follows only. For now."

Tolby considered that. "When we near, we can pick up a lad or two, if we need numbers."

"Good." He caught Aymaran's reins and swung up into the saddle.

For a handful of days and more, he'd forgotten himself and the task at hand, but whatever trailed them obviously had not.

Chapter Fifty-Eight

LARIEL ENTERED THE ROOM where Azel lay, his body taut from convulsions from the venom still being flushed from his body, a healer on either side, one working with his face etched in painful concentration while the woman on the other side bathed sweat away from one face, then another. She'd seen this scene at least once a day for weeks now, but the purging took less and less time, and Azel's agony lessened. She could not begin to guess if he were getting better or if his big frame was simply giving up, bit by bit. Sevryn's recovery had never been this grueling. She wondered if it was because Azel was full-blooded and Sevryn not, although they were usually much quicker to heal and harder to kill. Perhaps the venom the Kobrir used was now being brewed exclusively for use against Vaelinars. All these questions and more she would ask, later, after the crisis passed.

She sat carefully on the corner of the bed, trying not to disturb anyone, and put her hand on Azel's ankle, covered by a lightweight spread. "*Avana*, old friend. You look better to me. I pray that I'm right. I would never ask you to stay, in such pain, just for me. Yet, there is work here for you to finish, and if your soul wills it, you should stay. Don't Return, Azel. Stay if you can, and grow strong." Then she lapsed into silence. After long moments, the contracted muscles under her touch relaxed a bit, and both healers breathed a little easier. Neither of them said anything to her, even when she stood to leave. They had nothing they could say.

She wove through the small hallways and courtyards hiding the place where they'd taken Azel. Veils and a light, hooded cloak disguised her steps a lane or two away from the inn, where she dropped the hood back, tearing the veils off to breathe. Heat stifled the day and streets, the sun at its zenith, and Calcort shimmered in mirage waves under it, baking. Even here, behind thick walls and where windows were mere slits for light, the oppression crept in.

After changing in her rooms, she took a light meal and then went to the Conference halls. Bistane stepped out of a doorway and took her by the elbow.

"Talk to me. You must, sooner or later."

"Formal or here and now?"

"Here and now."

"You press our friendship."

"From where I stand, there is no longer one."

"Then perhaps you should become more illuminated."

"Lariel!" His grip tightened as if he thought to shake her. She did not look down at his hand, for if she did, he would be forced to let go of her, and she wanted to read the emotions in his hold that his face and words would not give her.

"I listen."

"Whatever is being said of my father, I know he rode out in defense of the kingdoms."

"Word from this battlefield is strangely muddled. I'd like to believe you, Bistane, but he rode with ild Fallyn. Old enemies, in a common cause? Unlikely, and you know that. Did they battle one another? Tressandre is keeping her own counsel, and your father hasn't returned yet for his accounting."

The hand on her arm quavered a bit. "He lives, that I know. As for the ild Fallyn, yes, odd allies, but we've both been watching Abayan Diort and not liking what we see."

"Diort's troops were not involved in this."

"No. Someone else hit them and hit them hard when they rode in to keep two armies from merging. My father sent to me. He stays behind to find out, and he will appear at the Conference when he has evidence."

"No coincidence you told me you wanted the Accords abolished."

Bistane stood closer to her. "You yourself put them in abeyance with the others."

"Because now I arm for war."

"And because you do, we should stand together! Lariel, you were loved because no one feared that you would carry out your title."

"Then they were fools to think of me and love in the same breath." She watched his face.

"Not foolish at all. Now they fear you."

"And I don't know this?"

"I have never overlooked you, Lariel Anderieon." His hand stayed steady on her arm, closing a bit in warmth.

"We are not allies, Bistane. Not yet."

"Nor are we enemies." He let go of her then, withdrawing from her space. "And I would have so much more with you, you know that." With his hair now cropped short and his eyes of blazing color, he looked more than ever like his father's son. Bistel had alliances but few closely held friends, known for his difficulty since their first appearance on Kerith. A mere youth then, Bistel still held the edge of a Vaelinar in his prime, though surely that prime was finished, and he was looking death in the face. Did that make him more or less reckless now? And did Bistane follow inevitably in his father's footsteps?

"I have a committee waiting," she told him, and pushed by. He let her go, though she thought she heard a sigh follow after.

Jeredon cornered her after the committee broke up, a luncheon tray in his hand, and a stormy look on his face. He let the tray crash upon a table, food bouncing up and over as he did, goblets rattling and their contents frothing up.

"I take it you found my reports on the armory order." She took a salad that looked fresh enough and picked a nut from the leaves to crunch.

"We can't quarter an army the size you want equipped."

"Of course not. We place our orders with an armorer, he will not be able to fulfill it, we shall settle for a lesser amount which we both can afford, and yet word goes out about our projected strength." She found another nut to chew in relish.

He stopped in mid-pace and gesture. "A foil?"

"A wise one, don't you think?" She seated herself to devour the salad in earnest. "Because more armorers have been operating more-or-less quietly out of watch of the Accords, we're not likely to find a single weaponsmith who can equip us as it is. It will not hurt, I think, to exaggerate our strength."

"What if we find one who can meet our order?"

"Then, my brother, we make allies who can foot the bill and fill the barracks."

"I'm against this."

She stopped eating. "That, Jeredon, is why I am Warrior Queen and you are not Warrior King. Not our circumstance of birth, but our resolve."

"It's not resolve. You're cursedly headstrong."

"How can you say that to me?"

He leaned both hands on the table's edge, his body shadowing her. "Because I have to. Because you have the title does not mean that it is right and meet in your lifetime to execute it!"

"Jeredon, sit down."

His jaw tightened.

"Please. Sit down."

He threw himself into a chair, legs sprawling, arms over his chest.

"Tranta did not fall from the cliff of Tomarq, he was thrown. The Shield weakens, and he can't find the Way to recharge it. We know that the Ravers have gotten stronger and bolder. Are they preparing for the Raymy to come back? If all our eyes and blades are turned to the east, what happens to our back from the west? Our coast has always been vulnerable and even more so now." She paused. "I know more than I'm prepared to say in this place, but you're more than my brother. You're my heir and my closest friend, and the voice of my father in my ear."

"And yet you haven't been talking to me."

"I needed truth instead of rumor." She turned her head away, looking across the room, away from its tapestried walls and bannered ceiling. "It comes in shreds, and I weave it together fitfully. Gods are stirring. We've been tolerated on Kerith, but now we may have come to our moment of judgment by Them. We're still Strangers, invaders." She looked back to him. "We've no Way home and no Way to the future."

"This used to be the Panner stead," Tolby mourned, looking down at char and broken stone.

Sevryn had squatted, digging through the ruin with a stick, looking at the green shoots coming up from the burned ground. "It's been a month or so, I'd say." He poked at the grasses and weeds.

"I'd no news on this. I've hopes they live and are hopping mad about it, and building elsewhere."

"Mistress Greathouse would have written, or Honeyfoot," Nutmeg told her father.

"Aye, so I'm thinking. Likely, anyway. Then again, the Panners kept to themselves. Like their family name, they oft took to the mountains, sifting the streams for metals and gems."

Sevryn stood, tossing his stick away. "Did they have any luck?"

"Some. Enough that they did not farm or ranch like most others roundabout here. Not rich, no. Just getting by, but th' Panners had a nose for stream mining." Tolby fetched out his pipe, and pointed the stem across the landscape. "Barrels are thataway. I imagine they've a lad or two who will ride with us to th' old place."

"Can we make it by nightfall?"

"It'll be close, but I think so. If the weather holds."

Rivergrace looked up. Clouds mounted on the horizon, and she could feel water growing heavy in the air. The hot, unbearable summer of Calcort had been left behind and now they were in the high country, where the edge of the fall months could be felt approaching. The mare shifted under her, ears moving forward and back, and she pawed at the ground.

"All right, then." Sevryn swung up as did Tolby, and he led the way out of the burned-out yard.

The weather did not hold. The skies opened up and poured, and they hung tarps from tree branches and huddled under them, trying to keep their stores as dry as possible. Daisy stood out in the open, his short tail bobbing in irritation, but refusing to come in out of the rain once his pack had been unloaded from him. Soon the camp stank of wet goat. When night came, it came without a moon, and Sevryn sat alone in darkness that had only the sprinkling of stars to guide him. He listened for that which trailed them and did not hear it, but instead Rivergrace's soft steps to the rocks he sat upon.

"He watches you as much as you watch him," Nutmeg said, shaking her pot to dry it.

"I don't watch him."

"And the sun doesna shine!" She looked up at the night sky, still dripping with rain. "You know what I mean."

"I don't know what to think."

"Grace, for all you're taller than I am, and raised with me, I know you're younger inside. It's the elven blood. But you're still a woman grown, and it's not wrong to be watching him."

"It's not that." Rivergrace packed up her share of the dinner things.

"Then what is it?"

"Something I can't explain. When I can name it, I'll tell you."

Nutmeg nodded slowly. "All right, then. It wouldn't hurt to go say good night."

Tolby had run out of his toback and so walked down the river a bit to settle himself, still upset over the Panner steading. It wasn't the Silverwing, not yet, but a tiny offspring of it, and it lay under the rainy skies like an afterthought, a puddle drawn thinly out upon the land. The Panners could never have plied their luck in it, Rivergrace thought, as she walked up to where Sevryn sat. What she might say to him, she really hadn't the slightest idea. It was much easier when music played and they had dancing to hide their thoughts.

She found a rock that seemed almost dry and perched upon it. "I came to say good night."

"And yet you found a seat to do so. Have you a long good night in mind?"

"I haven't anything in mind."

"Sometimes that's best." He shook his cloak out and laid it over her lap. She knotted her fingers in its comforting weave.

"You seem to know who you are."

"Do I now?"

She nodded slowly.

"Maybe that's because I've been thinking on it a bit longer than you have."

"You serve Queen Lariel and Jeredon. They hold you in high regard."

"I think that's because they're not quite sure what else to do with me. I didn't come from a Dweller family but from the streets. My mother was a woman named Mista, a Kernan, and when I was old enough to run well, she brought me to the town and turned me loose, saying it was time I looked after myself." Not quite the truth but close enough. Few would ever have that absolute truth from him. How could they bear it if he could not?

"She left you?"

"She did. I learned quick enough to hide my ears, which are not as pointed as they might be, but pointed enough, and I hadn't the eyes, so that kept me from being beaten about. I ran the streets." He looked at the stars, seeming to see something else. "I didn't age like the others, and so I realized I would have to move on, and did, from quarter to quarter and then town to town, hiding my blood."

"No one wanted you."

"No." He shifted from one hip to another.

"They want you now."

"I found a mentor who didn't believe that blood and ability was thinned by mixing."

"What happened to him?"

"He was killed," Sevryn said flatly.

"Is that what you meant when you said your memories were as broken as mine?"

He did not speak for such a long time, she grew nervous. "I'm sorry for prying."

"You're not prying. I'm trying to decide what to tell you." His hand came out as if to hold hers, then dropped back to his knee. Instead, he peeled back his sleeve, and then took her hand, putting her fingers on his wrist. A thin white scar met her touch, wrapped about his skin. She traced it before drawing her hand away. "I know about shackles. I was held for at least eighteen years. We had gone, my mentor and I, to a smithing operation in the mountains, hidden smugglers. We were caught. He died. I did not."

Before she could murmur sympathy, he added, "I don't remember those years. Not that they are vague or trouble my dreams, but that there is nothing. And I need to. I need to know where I was and what happened."

"Why?"

She sensed him looking upon her face, felt the warmth of his regard sweep her. "Why do you go back for a piece of a blanket?"

"I want to know who I am."

"As do I. Those missing years are as much a part of what I've become as the years I do remember. Perhaps even more important."

The force in his voice wrapped around her, and she shrugged into the cloak he'd placed over her. "I don't have a story like that."

"But you do. You came from somewhere, Grace. You rode downstream on a river, on a raft someone knotted together for you, and placed you on in hopes you'd find freedom, like an old tale."

"Maybe I did it for myself!"

"Likely you did not. And although Tolby is angered by parents he thinks did you no good, do you think he's right?"

"I don't know. Sometimes I feel like the Silverwing is my only parent."

"But it's not. Is there nothing? Not a voice or a song, or a touch, or a fear . . ."

She answered slowly, reluctantly, but feeling she must. "Aderro. I knew that word when you called me by it, but not why."

"And Stinkers?"

She shivered. "Yes."

"You called them that."

"Because they do. Their bodies reek of themselves and—" She looked away, into her thoughts.

"What else?"

"Smoke. Sometimes that smell you get around the farriers when the horses are being shod. The hot metal. The water barrels the shoes are plunged into." Rivergrace felt a moment of panic, as if the earth rose to close around her, and she fought to breathe through it.

He slipped his arm about her shoulders. "Don't fret. It's all right, and you're free."

She turned her face about quickly, finding they were nose to nose, and she thought . . . she wanted . . . to see what his kiss felt like, and she leaned toward him, brushing her mouth across his tentatively. He went as still as the rocks they sat upon, and she felt the warmth of his lips, and the sweet taste of the dried fruit they'd had from dinner still honied upon them, and then he drew her close and kissed her back, long and hot and soundly until she went breathless.

"That, aderro, is how a man kisses a woman," he whispered to her temple as he let her go.

"I like it," she answered when she found words again.

He must have smiled. The fear of her memories that had been trembling in the air about her fled, chased away. From below, she could hear Tolby clear his throat in a low, rumbling cough.

"I think," he nudged her, "that good night has been said."

"Oh!" She jumped up, dropping the cloak over his head as she fled downhill, and he laughed, the sound muffled by the garment.

She did not look at them as she returned to the campfire, but got her bedroll out and promptly dropped into it and lay as if sound asleep, thinking, till her heart stopped racing and she thought sleep might finally find her. Despite all he'd been through, Sevryn knew who he was. Troubled that she did not, clouded dreams took her away, dreams that she did not remember.

Chapter Fifty-Nine

DARAVAN RELEASED HIS MOUNT at the banks of the Nylara to approach the Ferryman on foot. The being sensed him, and turned, voluminous robes hiding the phantom save for an echo of eyes burning deep within an unseen skull. He spoke a word, and the being bowed deeply. Catching his horse under the chin and drawing him close, because the animal went skittish at being so near the phantom, he spoke two more words and stepped into the wake of the Ferryman as the being led the way to the barge. When he got off on the other bank, he was far, far from the Nylara, and another river churned at his back where black rocks tumbled like melted glass along the banks.

He mounted the horse and headed into the heart of the warlands, in search of warriors.

Chapter Sixty

THE SMELL OF SMOKE and burning still hung over the buildings, although most of them stood, and the window shutters were tied down as though expecting a winter storm. Tolby waved his hand over the area. "Barrels lived here," he said. "Run out like the Panners."

"Looks like they packed and left in a hurry. Whatever tried to burn them out didn't succeed. I think, Tolby, that your friends turned them back, and then left before another try."

"That could be it, Da," Nutmeg called from Bumblebee's back. The little pony, still round and furry, had toned up. He frisked about for a moment, showing his mettle, as their day's march had been short and he thought them done.

"I hope so. There's no beacon alight on th' hills, though." He took a long breath through his teeth before pointing. "We'll be headin' that way, then, in the shadow of the Burning Mountains, and along the Silverwing."

"We know the way." Nutmeg tossed her head.

"Th' lad doesna, does he? You two could find your way in the dark."

Sevryn made a sign against the words, averting them with a street superstition he hadn't felt in many a year. Tolby's fireside tales must have sunk in under his skin. He urged his horse next to Tolby's mount while the girls surged ahead, hauling the always reluctant goat with them, a branch with dried berries hanging from its lips. It munched as it lumbered. "Now is when we watch," he said. "Our follower hangs behind us determinedly. He should strike soon."

"I've kept my knife sharpened. Don't be worrying about th' lasses. They've good heads on their shoulders, and their brothers never coddled them. Rivergrace can throw a punch that will put you in the dust if she's a mind to."

He knew that. The image of her with sword in hand over a Raver body, pulling Nutmeg to her, would be forever branded in his mind. But Tolby had not seen that and did not know the strength of his children. Sevryn prayed he would never have to find out.

Leaning low from his saddle as they moved away, he read signs in the dirt, but much of it had been muddled by many hooves and feet and other tracks going back and forth. Bolgers again, he thought, and he did not see the odd footed track of a Raver running, though he'd only been shown that once or twice. Still, it was not a track easy to forget. Clawed and bladed, stiff and long-strided, nothing else made a track like it that he'd ever seen. Ravers were neither human nor wraiths, but something unnamed in his knowledge of living beings. They rode often, so not seeing the sign meant nothing, and from the yard being mucked-up as the Barrels had packed and moved out, he could have missed much. Carts and wagons had pulled out ladened and in haste from the wheel ruts and the castoffs still lying by the side of the country road, rummaged through and broken.

He beckoned to Tolby. "Take them on. How far?"

"We'd be reachin' it just before noon."

"I won't be too far behind."

Tolby pulled his floppy hat into place and growled at the goat to get it moving. The beast responded with a bleat and broke into a trot, ears flopping about its head and both girls muffled laughs at the similarities between the two, following after them.

Sevryn followed on foot, Aymaran coming after, stopping now and then to pull at a fresh green shoot coming up, his hoofbeats slow and deliberate while Sevryn looked at the land the way Gilgarran and Jeredon had taught him. Gilgarran had instilled a military sense in him, while Jeredon was a consummate hunter, and he used their expertise as he studied the area. The lay of the farmland and the hillocks surrounding it, the country lane which was little more than a horse trail past it and along the river, the jagged range of mountains which began to loom on the horizon, all these things gave him a likely pattern of approach for the raiders. He brushed along the edge of fields, vegetables overripe and going to seed, attracting mice and birds in droves and swarms of stinging gnats. Whoever had hit the farm had done so hard enough that none of the family came back to attempt a harvest. Dwellers were not the sort to give up on their labors, so he was not surprised when he came upon a corpse at the jagged mouth of a pass out of the hills. The attackers had driven the Dwellers off, by fear if not by brute force, and one of them had not survived the raid.

It had been chased here and downed, its hollow carcass lying picked bare by carrion eaters. He toed the skeletal remains. Bleached by the sun, its glossy black carapace looked more like lead, its rags of cloak strewn about it, torn away by that which had eaten at it. He stared down at the bared Raver, reminiscent of an immense insect with razor pinchers and clawed, serrated hind feet. They did not leave their own. The raiding party must have retreated in disarray. He kicked at the thing to better examine it and hunkered down as it rolled aside. He slipped his skinning knife out of his boot sheath to saw off a bit of the hand pincer, the thing as hard as plate armor. It resembled nothing human. He poked and prodded, shifting the casing aside for better examination, and when he stood, he thought he had deciphered part of their mystery.

If insect, their eggs could lie dormant underground or in caves for years, even decades before hatching, until some current of time or rain or sun brought them forth. That would explain the waves of Ravers that came and went without their Raymy masters invading as well. Like the leafcroppers that came in droves that could blot the very sun from the sky once a generation, the Ravers could emerge and devour anything in their paths. The leafcroppers could be fought with fire and potions, the Ravers were another matter altogether. They attacked without provocation, ruthless in their drives. And had the provinces even seen a major wave of them arise? What could happen when they did?

He'd found an answer that raised a hundred more questions. Aymaran nudged his shoulder as he gathered the horse to him, knowing he could not let the Farbranches get ahead of him, and they were no longer in sight. He put his heel to the horse's flank and the tashya bounded away in response, hooves drumming over the fields, mane flying like a banner.

The sun slanted down as he caught up with them, and the Silverwing roared into life, its blue-silver water frothing at steep banks as they rode alongside it. The country lane eroded into a wavering trail thatched with weed and brush, a spring and summer's growth overwhelming it. The goat kept snatching at whatever it could find to eat, chewing as it trotted, straggles hanging from its lips to be spat out when something more interesting sprang up to be eaten. Tolby slapped his hand on its rump and it skittered away from them, snapping its rope free from Nutmeg's hands.

With a yelp, she lay low over Bumblebee and set him after the recalcitrant Daisy. They thundered onto the Farbranch holdings in hot pursuit of the goat who bleated with every jump it made.

Orchards stretched as far as he could see, like spokes on a great wheel, the center of which lay in charred crumbles. Rivergrace let out a cry as they rode onto their lands, and brought her mare to a halt. She slid down, and stood, holding onto the saddle as if her knees had gone suddenly weak, and when she looked up at Sevryn, tears streaked her face.

Without a word, she let go and walked to the river to lie down on her stomach, hands outstretched to the water. Tolby let the goat bound away and dismounted next to Sevryn. "We'll let her be for a bit, and then go for a dig."

Sevryn nodded. Nutmeg joined her father and the two walked about the ruins of their home, talking in subdued tones that was not at all like either Dweller he'd come to know. His gaze remained on Rivergrace, her chestnut hair tumbled over her shoulders and back, her straw hat fallen to the side, her body like that of an unaware child, lost in wonder, and if she still cried, he couldn't hear it over the roar of the river.

Silver-winged alnas rose from the wild groves on the far side of the river, and a handful of them swept overhead. They wheeled over the water and Rivergrace, dipping down to skim the surface, snatching fish up with their claws and swooping back to the forest. One hunter wheeled and landed not far from her, where it ripped and shredded its meal apart, now and then cocking a bright eye to peer at her. Still with a hand in the water, she turned on her side to face it.

It continued eating undeterred, then hopped toward her unafraid. With a dip of its head, it rubbed its curved beak over her outstretched fingers, then took to the air, landing nearby.

"Do you tame the very birds from the sky?"

Rivergrace sat up, wiping her hands on her pant legs. "No, no. That one was injured. I found it and helped it heal. See the rough white diamond on its chest? That's from the scarring." With the back of her hand, she cleaned her face of tears and river mist. "It seems to remember me."

"It's only been a season or two."

"Who knows how long birds live, and what thoughts they hold in their head?" She stood up and walked to him.

"Our vantanes live for decades and they know their handlers, although I admit I rarely see affection in them."

"You keep them hooded and tied. How could you?" She straightened her shoulders, as if she had been the wounded one who'd been healed. "I'll get my trowels."

Ribbon had been greedily cropping grass and rolled an eye at her as she came up, but let her get into her saddlebag after shying away once, and then coming back to her soft chirp of encouragement. Rivergrace ruffled the mare's forelock. "Naughty, greedy one."

"We can let them pasture the rest of the day and return in the morning. I'm sure they'd relish that."

Rivergrace brushed her soft hair from her face, tucking it behind her ears, and handed him one of her trowels.

Tolby paced around the ruins of their home, and jumped down into the exposed cellars. A soft cloud of soot and dirt puffed up at the thump of his boots, setting everyone to coughing. He brought a rag from his pocket and scrubbed at his face before blowing his nose. "It'll be in a corner, down in the flooring," he instructed. "Remember your mother's canny talent for hidin' things."

Nutmeg tossed her head. "I never found a naming day present, ever."

"Aye, and I know how hard you looked!" Tolby began to poke about with a long stick he'd sharpened, as they all descended into the pits.

They found a pickle barrel, still lidded up with its contents in brine, and a crate full of jugged cider, and little else in the upper cellar. The lower cellar had to be crawled into, only half-open to the day. Nutmeg burrowed in like a squirrel, but Rivergrace took long moments before following, her face as pale as the moon. Tolby pushed his stick down to them as the cellar had partially caved in and it held no room for anyone else. The alna soared above, darting back and forth, finding a current in the rising hot air and riding it leisurely.

Nutmeg pushed out a crackled leather pouch with a grunt. "What's this, Da?"

"Likely that's your mother's stash." He reached down to hand both of them out.

Sevryn took a clean corner of his shirt and wiped a swath of dirt off Rivergrace's nose as Tolby hefted the pouch onto a stump of what used to be a front porch pillar. He unwound the rawhide string fastening it and opened the widemouthed container.

"There, Grace. See what's in it."

She scrubbed her palms on her pants legs again, although none of her was too clean at the moment, before reaching hesitantly in. Then she drew out an oilskin-wrapped parcel and began to peel away its layers as Nutmeg chanted, "What do you see, what do you see?"

"Nothing yet." Her voice, muted. Her breathing barely coursing through her slender form. Sevryn stood at her elbow, unable to do anything more than offer his presence. Then the last layer shifted aside at her touch, and she drew forth a shimmering yet begrimed remnant of fabric into the light. A scarf, a blanket, knotted at one end still, soft chestnut hairs entangled in it as it dangled from her fingers. It had the look of a scrap that someone hand wove and knotted to extend it, and in that weaving, thread danced in runes and symbols, and he could read the Vaelinar in it. He caught her hand before she weakened.

"I don't know this. How can I not know it? Tell me what it says." Her eyes beseeched him.

He took a breath to answer her when the silence shattered. The alna sprang into the air with a sharp cry, wings bating in a frantic need to gain height. The goat sprang sideways across the yard with a frightened bleat, and echoing it, calls hooted down from the hillsides.

Sevryn grabbed up Rivergrace and threw her atop Black Ribbon. "Get to horse!"

Tolby and Nutmeg ran. He whistled sharply for Aymaran, and mounted with a running leap from the broken, burned planks of the front porch, pulling his bow free and grabbing for arrows. Better with knives and swords, he'd rather keep the attackers from ever getting to melee to test his skill, and nocked his arrow rapidly.

They poured out of the groves at the foot of the hillside, Bolgers riding with brigands, whooping as they charged. Sevryn aimed at the lead pony, bringing it down in a tumble of falling horseflesh and Bolger, even as he nocked a second arrow. Tolby gathered up the girls behind him. He wrapped a slingshot about his wrist, aiming with uncanny accuracy, sending stones stinging into their midst.

From behind, a hoarse Bolger cry made Sevryn wheel about. He raised his bow to draw down, but the Bolger circled him, whipping his shaggy mount on a dead run toward the attackers. Confused, Sevryn held his shot. Had they been encircled or not?

Tolby dipped his hand into what had been an empty toback sack and now seemed filled with sharp river stones, and let fire with a wrist sling. He winked at Sevryn before reloading the sling, as Sevryn took aim again and let his arrow fly, choosing a bandit as target. The man slipped his saddle with a guttural cry, crashing to the ground.

An apple tree branch whipped another horseless, as the very orchard seemed to join the battle, hindering those plunging through it. But it was the Bolger who'd come out of nowhere who swung the blow that broke their cowardly backs, taking down a huge, hulking fellow in the lead. The two of them clashed, the one with sword in hand, the other brandishing a knife and staff, their ponies wheeling about each other. The sworded Bolger parried blows, then drove his sword in low and deep, and the hulking brute collapsed with a cursing scream, somersaulting backward off his pony.

At his fall, the remaining attackers scattered, wheeling about and retreating the way they'd come, sharp whistles drawing the slackers with them.

The Bolger who'd struck the blow trotted his pony down to them and stopped a good pace away as Sevryn lowered his bow cautiously.

He gestured with his sword, and bowed toward Rivergrace.

"Rufus," he said. He wiped his blade clean, and then gestured toward the back trail, and to Sevryn. "I follow."

"Why?"

The leathery Bolger sheathed his weapon. Nearing the end of his prime, old and weathered, he eyed Sevryn and nodded to Rivergrace. "Keep safe." He thumped his chest. "You remember?"

Sevryn stared at him, and then, slowly, shook his head.

"You will." With that, he kicked his pony and rode back downriver, and out of sight.

Rivergrace sat with her hands knotted tightly about her prize, struck wordless. Sevryn rode back to the stump, leaned out of his saddle to snatch up the leather bag and stow it inside his shirt. "We can't stay."

"We'll camp downriver beyond the Barrel steading. I know a sheltered spot." Tolby grabbed at the goat's headstall, catching Daisy by surprise, and led the way past them.

Sevryn paused as they moved out, looking back toward the Burning Mountains. He knew them. Knew their harsh, unyielding ridges, mountains that severed that part of the country with three ranges. The Bolger who named himself Rufus stirred his mind. He'd worn a smithy's rough, scarred leather vest, and he had burn scars up and down his forearms, and the weapon he wielded had been crudely if effectively made. Sevryn had looked upon him with a faint jolt of recognition, without knowing how or why, yet not enough to admit to it. Another forge slave, gone free, and plying his trade among the towns. What interest would such a being have in Rivergrace?

If he followed the Silverwing back to the granite that birthed it, would he find the mystery from which she'd sprung?

The Burning Mountains had taken Gilgarran to his death. He remembered not the how of it, but only that it had happened. If he dared follow the Silverwing, would he find himself as well? It was not his choice to be made. A queen awaited them.

Chapter Sixty-One

LARIEL RAN HER HANDS over the fragment in her lap, saying, "Don't blame Sevryn for not being able to read this. I can't either."

"Nothing?"

The queen stroked each thread, each knot, before looking up to meet Rivergrace's eyes. "I would almost say that this is a remnant from the before times, except that it cannot be. What we have from then is closeted, kept very close, and protected. It's a runic message, rather than our written language, and much of this is couched in expressions we've lost, when we lost our Gods and those who served our Gods for us."

"I will never know, then."

"Not true. There's someone I think who would like to look at it, if he's well enough." Lariel nodded to Jeredon and her brother jumped to his feet.

"I'll see if he's up to visitors. Come over if I don't return."

Rivergrace stood alone in Lariel's chambers, shadowed only by Sevryn, her Dweller family returned to their new home and catching up with days of hard work put aside. Lariel considered her carefully, the new sprinkling of freckles over her translucent skin, and bluish circles beneath her Vaelinar eyes that spoke of strain, before turning her attention to Sevryn.

"Now. The news you hold for me?"

"The countryside near the Farbranch holding showed a lot of raider activity. We found a number of places burned out or abandoned along the way, even stouthearted families that Tolby swore would have stayed until driven into the ground. The provinces are going to have to send guards there or lose the bounty, the farms, from these outlying areas."

"By whose hand?"

"Bolger and Raver, and occasionally local bandits." He paused, choosing his words. "I came across a Raver carcass."

"Rare, even when we can kill them."

"They are not human, m'lady Highness. I would judge them to be most like an insect, carapaced, so therefore self-armored, pincer blades for hands." He took the piece out and placed it on the nearby table where it lay like a deadly shard, its ebony color bleached by death and sun.

"I've heard rumor of such. Anything else?"

"If they are insects, you have to consider the fact they may lay eggs in numbers and those eggs may hatch randomly or they may hatch in waves, and if they do . . . we could be facing an inundation of warriors the likes of which we've never really faced. They will devour anything in their path."

Lariel's mouth tightened. "That, I haven't heard considered." She brushed her hand over her face with a faint curse. "Of course. Waves. Sequential hatching. How could we have been so blind? Yes, that could explain much, brought over by the Raymy and left behind to seed our lands. Once ravaged, we'd be at the mercy of the Raymy, and we know there's no such strain in them. This needs to be discussed, but I thank you, Sevryn, for confirming what a few of us have feared but obviously not feared enough." She folded the scrap in her lap and pressed it into Rivergrace's hands, closed the other's trembling fingers over it. "One thing at a time. Let's go see what Azel d'Stanthe can make of this."

Two healers stood outside the isolated room, talking quietly, their hands weaving the air in animated discussion, which they slowed only enough to wave them inside. The woman murmured, "Not too long, he's not as strong as he thinks he is."

Even so, he sat up in bed, propped by pillows not only at his head but under his shoulders and arms, in conversation with Jeredon when they entered. Sevryn blurted, "You didn't tell me this!"

"Oh, we only decided he was going to survive when he started complaining night and day."

Sevryn clasped Azel's hands tightly in his before stepping back. The librarian gave his attention to Lariel slowly. "Forgive me, Lariel, for not standing for you."

"Old bear." Lariel sat on the corner of the bed, as she had for many days, and put her hand on his ankle. "When you get out of here, the first thing I'll fear is you chasing me about the courtyard!"

His eyes twinkled. "Perhaps, but I'm just a historian. What would I do if I caught you?"

"I'll give you time to research it, first."

He laughed, which disintegrated into a deep cough, but that, too, evaporated. Jeredon passed him a mug from the tray nearby to wet his throat. He drank before saying, "I hear you have something for me. The poison gone, I'm now dying of boredom."

"Rivergrace has something for you, then. May I present m'lady, who has our blood in her and has been raised by the Dweller Farbranch family." Lariel gestured at Rivergrace who hung back at the closed door of the sickroom, as if she might bolt back across the threshold any moment.

"Come close," Azel said to her. "I don't bite."

She made a slight, fluttering movement like a startled bird, then caught her breath to say, "I don't know. You look hungry to me."

"Hear that?" He looked to Lariel and Sevryn, then back to Grace. "I envy you your upbringing, milady. No one has a sense for good food and good humor like a Dweller does." He patted a space on the bed near his hip, his gesture weak but determined. "Sit here and show me what it is you're carrying about."

She started to press it into his hands, but he demurred, saying, "Spread it across my lap. My hands still shake too much to hold it still, but the bed seems quiet enough." She smoothed it as he instructed, the small piece of blanket seeming even smaller across his large frame.

Jeredon stood watch at the window as the others gathered close. Azel studied it seemingly for eternity, his concentration broken only by an occasional wheeze from his chest. Finally, it seemed he drew a breath deep enough to speak.

"This," he told them, "is why you have historians."

Sevryn jerked his head impatiently. "Jeredon, shall I throttle him or will you?"

"Either will do. I think we can even get a commission from the healers outside. I hear he's become an extremely irascible patient." Jeredon leaned his hip against the windowsill, dislodging a flake of paint.

Azel's chuckle rumbled in his throat, and he tapped a finger on the relic. "I doubt anyone has seen anything like this in centuries."

"But what is it?"

"It is a Summoning, m'lady Lariel. It's been rewoven from a wedding shroud, delineating the Talents of the two partners. This one," and he outlined a rune at the corner which flared a little as he touched it, "signs Fire. This, Water with Sky . . . that would likely mean an affinity with weather," he added.

"Do we know who?"

He shook his head. "The names are part of what has been torn or ravaged away."

Rivergrace felt her chest tighten. A mother, a father, found only to be lost again, torn away by the erosion of time. "Any . . . anything else?"

Sevryn moved to put his hand on her shoulder.

"You mentioned a Summoning," Lariel reminded him. "What is meant by that?"

"There is an enchantment threaded throughout this piece. Their Talents have been given up, their birthrights, to protect against further enslavement and the loss of their souls, to be poured into a Vessel, Summoned to hold that part of themselves. You've brought me history sprung to life, a working, a Way few would even think of creating. I've read a theological discussion on this once or twice but never seen it attempted before."

"Azel."

"Hmmm? Oh." He looked up at Lariel. "Whatever wore or carried this may not actually exist but only be the Vessel which was Summoned, if you understand me. You found it where?"

"On me," Rivergrace said faintly. "I wore it."

Chapter Sixty-Two

SHE RAN FROM HIM. From all of them, but from him first, shaking off his hand and staggering across the room to fling the doors open. He bolted after her, but the two healers closed on him, thinking Azel had collapsed. By the time he disentangled himself, she'd disappeared and he'd no hope of catching her.

He found her where he thought he might, at the Farbranch brewery and press, the yard filled with wagons carrying kegs and barrels of drink out on contracts, and the Farbranches with rosy faces and sweat staining them pointed wordlessly to their inner yard. Nutmeg trailed him for a step or two, and told him, "She found that and opened it, and made sure the water was sweet. You'll always find her near water."

Dwellers, thought Sevryn as he outpaced her and she went back to Tolby at his call. Signs of Grace's Talent all about them, and they had no inkling of it, for what Dweller didn't have a feel for growing and nourishing things? They had never thought it odd or gifted in her. He paused in the wide, dusty inner yard of the brewery. A small garden took up a quarter of the area near an open shed barn, and Rivergrace perched near it. She sat on the edge of a well, one foot dangling over it, head bowed.

He dropped beside her. "Don't send me away."

She spoke looking downward, her voice echoing faintly against the water pooled below. "I have to. I'm nothing. I thought I'd find a mother, a father, instead I find . . . what . . . creators? I'm a shell existing only to be emptied someday. There is nothing to offer you, Sevryn."

"I won't let you believe that." He started to hold her hand, but she moved away, rejecting his touch. "I won't tell you how many, but I've kissed enough women that I know when I kissed someone real, someone living, someone who kissed me back as sweetly and truly as I've ever been kissed."

"Still water is a mirror," she answered. "Only that and nothing more."

"What you've been given is a beginning. You're Vaelinar, that bit of weaving tells you that, a Vaelinar with a strong affinity for water. You knew that, deep down, even if no one around you recognized it. We'll build on that."

"We?" She tilted her face toward him.

"We," he told her firmly.

"How?"

"If I have my way, we'll go back up the Silverwing, as far into the mountains as we can to see where your journey started."

"You serve the queen, and she needs you."

"You need me more."

She waved her hand helplessly. "What if I return, to the beginning, and . . . and all it does is unmake me. What if what I face is being emptied of all I am?"

"I won't let that happen."

"Can you fight Gods, Sevryn?"

"Sometimes I think that is all I've spent my lifetime doing." He brushed his mouth against her cheek. "I'll find a way for Lariel to let me go."

"I don't know if I can do this."

"Come, lass! Were you raised by Tolby and Lily Farbranch or not? There's no lack of spine in your family!"

"No," she murmured, "there isn't. Just remember, that vessels don't always choose what they carry, and they often shatter."

He left her in reverie by the well.

Daravan cloaked himself as he always did upon the roads, and when the sentries stopped him at the camp, they knew him but not as himself. He spat upon the ground. "Take me to Quendius."

The younger one, still round of face, Kernan, told him, "Disarm yourself," and his partner, lean, wiry, missing an ear and scarred, grunted a laugh.

"Try it," Daravan answered. He balanced his weight alertly on the balls of his feet. The veteran poked an elbow into the youth's rib. "This one allus carries."

"We were told—"

"The smith knows this one."

The young one shifted uneasily, then gave over to the other's authority. "You take him in, then."

"That I'll do. I'll bring back a pail of beer for us as well."

Daravan moved between them in the direction of the canopied, double tent he knew Quendius favored in the field, not waiting for his escort or the quarrel between them to be settled. He had word he wished to deliver, and wished weigh the effect. He brushed past the curtain netting at the doorway, with the wizened sentry at his back calling out, "Halt!" as he entered. The man stumbled in at his heels.

Quendius sat, elbows on a campaign table, playing at a game of pegs and falcons. He made his move, the chair opposite empty, and looked around.

"The Warrior Queen seeks to buy arms and armor," Daravan announced.

"If you hope to earn a few golds by telling me that, you're late."

"Did your informant also tell you Abayan Diort has offered to meet her needs?"

Quendius dropped his peg. An anger ran through him that darkened his ash-gray skin to a soot color, and his eyes went entirely black. "You've proof of this?"

"Copies of letters. May I sit?" Daravan glanced at the empty chair.

Quendius waved at him. He jabbed a finger at the sentry. "Next time anyone comes in here without detainment, you'll hang for it."

Bowing and gasping apologies, the sentry made a hasty retreat. Quendius remained leaning on his elbows.

"What else have you for me?"

"That is not enough?" Daravan felt the chair creak under him as he took it, the leather sling giving to his frame.

"Should it be? I'm not where I am because I settle for the first crumbs offered me."

"These aren't crumbs."

"Perhaps they are. Perhaps I know more of Diort than you do."

Daravan picked up an eagle and moved it swiftly. "And perhaps Diort thinks you don't look too closely at him, feeling that confidence. He has a war hammer that can take down a mountain."

"He also has allies."

"As long as they are useful. He's Galdarkan back to the ages of the Magi. The queen is Vaelinar. You are Vaelinar. In part."

Quendius bared his teeth in a smile. "What proof of this have you?"

"That he seeks to play one against the other? None but his actions. He's like you, Quendius. He's canny and shrewd and has the loyalty of his men to the teeth. He won't be caught easily."

"You offer to catch him?"

"Not I. That's your business. I merely deliver news." Daravan reached inside his cloak pocket and took out a packet of letters, throwing them over to Quendius.

"Tell Queen Lariel I will meet with her to sell her what she needs."

"Tell her yourself, and I'll deliver it."

Quendius made a noise, then yelled for his scribe. The little man came in, hair fluffed about his head and bedroll wrapped about his waist, his satchel banging against his rib cage. He threw himself on the ground and began to write what Quendius dictated to him, dried it, handed it over for a seal, then tied it and left it on the table in front of the weaponsmith.

"That's all."

The scribe skittered out of the pavilion, reminding Daravan of a mouse scampering to stay just ahead of a fox.

The tied letter stayed on the table between the two men. Neither reached for it.

"Name your price for the delivery."

"You have a sword—"

Quendius put his head back and roared with laughter. Daravan waited for the humor to ebb. "A sword for a letter? Perhaps I'll put one through your ribs and deliver it myself," he said when he'd caught his breath.

"You should know me better than that. I want a look at it."

"Any sword?"

Daravan did not answer. Quendius stirred after a very long moment, then yelled, "Get Narskap."

The spare man entered the pavilion. The lamplight played unkindly with him, making his face look even more skeletal than daylight did. He folded his arms over his chest and waited for Quendius to tell him why he'd been sent for.

"Show him the sword."

"No."

Quendius thumped a heavy hand on the tabletop. Game pieces jumped from the peg board. "Hand it over, then."

Narskap did not make a move. A cord in his neck twitched a little, and Daravan thought he could hear a hum just out of the range of normal hearing, drawn across the edge of his nerves rather than heard.

Quendius said to Daravan, "The sword is never drawn without blooding."

"A barbaric rite. Who made it for you? A Bolger?"

"A fine Vaelinar craftsman made that sword. Give him a look at it in the sheath."

"Why?"

"Because he has brought me information, and this is the payment he wants. And because I told you to."

Wiry arms flexed and untied the back sheath, swung it about, and laid the greatsword flat in front of him, across both forge-scarred hands, Narskap unmoving under its weight. Daravan stared at it. The hilt and guard gleamed in exquisite workmanship, no doubt of that, and from what he could see of the blade, it, too, was of incomparable caliber. He wanted to reach out for it, hold his hand near its aura, but feigned indifference instead. "A pretty, long knife."

"There is nothing pretty about this blade." Narskap swung it about and secured it.

He would learn nothing more, he knew, other than the accounting one or two frightened men from Bistel's small army had survived to give him. Did it leap out for blood like a hound? Did it swallow souls like the very heart of hell? Likely not. But whatever it could do, Quendius stayed cautious of it, only one man was allowed to wield it, and Narskap looked as if the burden would be the death of him.

Standing, Daravan reached for the letter. "Consider it delivered. You will know if there is an answer."

"Good." Quendius steepled his hands as he watched him leave, and Daravan had the unnerving feeling that the back of his neck seemed very vulnerable as he did so. Between those knobs of bone, swords could strike for a swift beheading.

He melted into the night, relieved only when he'd retrieved his horse and put the camp out of range.

Chapter Sixty-Three

Dry Month—Summer's End

"HOW CAN YOU ASK THIS OF ME?"

"Because it needs to be done. Lariel, one day you're going to make her your avandara, and the next throw her away like an old rag? Explain it to me."

Lariel put her hand on a stack of papers in front of her, her slender fingers curling about a writing instrument she'd just freshly sharpened for use. She wet her mouth to answer, looked away, and then looked back. "If she is what Azel believes, then she is not a person, Sevryn. She is a Way unto herself and likely an unstable one at that, her powers unknown, her makers unknown. Her effect could be one of total chaos. I need you with me, and Larandaril needs you. I can't afford to let you go again on a chase to find a past that in all probability doesn't exist for her."

"Because you want to go to war."

"Because we may *have* to go to war."

"Have you an enemy? A front? An incursion which must be answered?"

"Not yet."

"And you may never! What Abayan Diort is doing, he has a right to do. Galdarkans are his people, and if he wishes to unite them—"

She slapped her other hand down. "Don't you ever dare tell me that one being has the right to subject a people to his will by bringing them to their knees in battle! No one has that right. If these people wanted him to rule them, they'd have gone to him long ago."

"It's a civil war, Lariel, and you've no right in it. They'll unite just to turn on you, then. We're the strangers here. You know that. There's no winning a war when you step in between clans, tribes, who have lived for centuries fighting one another and the only thing they'll fight even more fiercely is an outsider."

"You speak of the Galdarkans as if they were Bolgers."

"War is our most primitive state. It brings us all down to our lowest levels, even though you may see the greatest acts of courage and self-sacrifice within it. That can't be reason enough to encourage it!"

Her fingers tapped. "Don't lecture me on what runs in my very lifeblood."

"Because it doesn't run in mine? Or because my blood is thinner than yours, weakened, tainted?" Sevryn rocked back on his heels.

"I never said those words."

"I'd like to see you deny that you've thought them."

Her hands twitched from tapping to shuffling papers between them, trying to restore order to a pile already impeccably stacked, a never-ending resource of dialogues and recordings from the daily meetings. Somewhere in the Great Halls must reside a legion of scribes and copyists. She took a deep breath. "You yourself brought me confirmation that we may need to face the Ravers in swarms."

"If we wait until they build an army as well, then we've already lost. It's not a war we face there, but an infestation, and we need to root it out before they raise themselves up. There won't be a front, uniforms, officers. They'll raid and their groups will grow, but you won't be able to fight them with rules of strategy and engagement."

"Bistel wasn't fighting Ravers. He speaks of inhuman weapons, of God-touched fighters who cannot be stopped without great sacrifice!" She shoved her paperwork aside. It went flying across the desk and into the air, drifting down like autumn leaves, covering the room in parchment.

He said quietly, "You brook criticism from me that you'd never accept from anyone else."

"Jeredon, perhaps." She leaned back in her chair to survey the mess. "Tell me again why you must leave me for Rivergrace, in the face of all I'm worrying about."

He bent over, picking up the sheets as he spoke. "I don't think I've ever lied to the two of you . . ."

"Omitting the truth isn't lying."

"No." He put some on the table and continued to gather. "I lost those years in slavery."

"Tell me what Jeredon and I don't know."

"I never faked not having the recall, but I ran across something I kept from you. I left a message for myself. When I escaped, I had a mind or enough of a mind to know I had to do that, that I had to lay clues to what I'd learned, what Gilgarran had gone to learn, so that it could never be forgotten in case I was caught again and perhaps to be understood by another if I didn't survive."

She sat forward intently. "And you've found it?"

"It's not that easy, m'lady queen. I wish it were. I've been years trying to decipher it, and I still don't have the answer." On one knee, still gathering the fallen paperwork, he recited:

"Four forges dire
Earth, Wind, Water, and Fire,
You skip low
And I'll jump higher.
One for thunder
By lands torn asunder
Two for blood
By mountains over flood.
Three for soul
With no place to go.
You skip low
And I'll skip higher
Four on air
With war to bear."

She frowned at him. "Where have you heard that?"

He could feel his face warm as he feared her mocking the verses. "I know it's a child's rope game, commonly played in the streets. It resounded in me, and I pulled the players aside when I first heard it, thinking I'd found the key, the answer to my lost years."

"And?"

"And they told me I taught it to them. In rags, a wastrel on the streets, but a man who stopped to play with them, and taught it to them by rote.

They stared at me as if I were a madman for not knowing what I'd done." He gestured helplessly. "Outsmarted myself, it seems. I devised such a cleverness that I can't unknot it. I've nothing beyond that, nothing I can tell you, and it haunts me. I learned something when Gilgarran died, that I dared never forget, and it's lost to me."

She shook her head. "Not entirely a child's game. Four forges dire of earth, wind, water, and fire comes from our very first days here, a warning. It's an old prophecy, Sevryn, very old. Like Trevilara, it's ingrained in us so deeply that it wasn't quite forgotten, although the sense of it, the need to remember it, has been. It's also not widely known. It's been passed from leader to leader, and kept, quietly. I don't know how you heard it, unless Gilgarran passed it to you without your knowing it."

"Yet you would equip an army from such a forge."

"I can't very well send men out facing death without equipment, without armor, without weapons. I won't go to battle without a plan and without hope of winning. Prophecies are always couched in riddles, Sevryn, and they seldom say what they actually mean. It's often been interpreted that a forge is meant as an event or one of our own Houses, since the elements are strongly entwined in the wording. We likely won't know till all is said and done, and what Bistel deigns to tell me only reinforces that."

He rose to his feet. "And so there is no answer?"

"Not known by me. Perhaps Azel or one of the apprentices he keeps hidden away behind his dusty shelves might keep interpretations you'll find useful. He's very weakened after yesterday, though, and he has never been able to remember what it was he wanted me to know. He remembers last year and ten years from yesterday as sharp as a nail, but the day the Kobrir hit him, he can't recall anything. The good news was that he was able to see you and Rivergrace. The bad news is that he's not what he was, and he may never be."

The hope he'd felt springing forth grew cold. She took the last of the gathered papers from his numbing hand with a murmured word he did not catch. "I can't afford to lose your counsel or your guardianship. Your request is refused."

"M'lady queen."

"No. No further appeal." She turned her face away from him, as she picked up her quill and prepared to make notes on the stack of papers, now crumpled and in disorder, on the desk.

Sevryn swallowed back a final retort and bowed instead, returning to a silent watch on her door, and window, and rooms, his face lined with thoughts he could no longer share with his queen.

Morning shimmered off the small, rounded foothills that looked like weather-eroded barrows of the dead . . . and well they might have been, as Narskap trailed Quendius across the warlands of the east. They had been riding for day upon day, and this new day promised no better, his eyes and mouth dried by a mild yet persistent wind. Quendius pulled his horse up and waited for Narskap to draw even. "Get me a direction."

His skin crawled with loathing, but he kicked a leg over his mount's rump and jumped to the ground, dirt and dried grasses scattering as he did. His horse stomped as he looped the reins loosely. He did not wish to do this, but it had been his idea, and he had little choice in the matter. Abayan Diort kept his army hidden and quartered in this Gods-forsaken land. He alone had a chance of finding Diort without escort, and Quendius had made his wishes plain.

He drew his sword. It quivered in his hold, as if surprised by being pulled and awakened when it sensed no death, and gave a howl meant for his ears alone, of joy, of blooding, of souls being rendered unto it. He dropped the blade on the ground and walked away. Walked until he could no longer hear its keening fury as the only storm against his hearing. Then he turned, and listened, felt, for another bond, faint yet present. Forger of the war hammer, although it had partnered with Diort, he still had a tentative hold on the weapon. It murmured to him, its voice a low, rumbling growl, nothing like the screaming howl of the sword, but he heard it still. Hearing it now, he turned slowly, face to the warlands and barrowlike hills, until he knew where it lay and rested, murmuring invectives against earth and stone moved by man's hand.

"There," Narskap spoke, and pointed. He strode briskly, no, ran, back to his sword and swept it up, sheathing it before its noise could drive him mad or deaf. Quendius turned his horse in the indicated direction with a kick and moved on. Narskap leaned against his mount a moment, beads of sweat dotting his face and evaporating almost before they formed, his hands shaking. To draw the sword without blooding it was insanity, pressing on him, driving him into the ground. But what would he have struck out here? The mounts? Quendius? He would have doomed himself further. He would wait and hope that a swift velvethorn might be flushed by their passing, bounding away in front of them, prey that he could cut down and perhaps they could spit and roast later, over the campfire.

The sword scolded him from its back sheath, its voice an angry hornets' nest in his ears as he swung up onto his horse and rode after Quendius.

Much later, with the sun low on the horizon and at their backs, melting into the end of day, he could smell the campfires and the acrid vapor of the middens before they crested a butte and looked down upon the plains where Abayan had settled his army. Tents encircled blackened fire rings, and outlying pastures by the river were pole-fenced for horses. Spread far, as the land here seemed meager and burned by the summer sun, the army did not seem as large, but he knew looks could be deceiving. Quendius stood in the stirrups, stretching his legs a bit, before saying, "They'll have seen us as well, but won't attack until they've seen who we are. Two of us won't be thought a threat." He reined down off the butte.

Narskap let his mount pick his own way down, loose stone and grass shivering from its hooves as they did, and before they reached the more level plains, two horsemen flanked them. No questions were asked or answers offered as they were escorted to the main tent where Abayan Diort stood, awaiting them.

They dismounted but did not hand off the horses' reins to his men. Abayan considered their faces a moment, then signaled his men to leave them.

"You've come a long way."

"You do not," remarked Quendius, "seem pleased to see me."

"I'm not displeased, but it occurs to me that I shall have to kill the man who betrayed my position. Or . . ." Diort's voice trailed off.

"Or woman? Fear not, it wasn't the lovely Tiiva who gave you away. She was too busy trying to have the queen poisoned."

"Unsuccessfully, I presume, or I would have heard."

Quendius inclined his head. "You don't seem distressed that it didn't succeed."

"Dissension was the primary goal. Lariel's death would only have been an unexpected bonus." Diort waved a hand toward his tent. "Come in, cool down, have a drink. It seems you know a good many of my secrets."

"Only one or two, as good allies should. We've no time to rest. There is urgency to our visit here."

"And, I presume, an explanation as to how you found me?" The gold of Abayan's skin seemed to mingle and glow with the last of the lowering sun as he watched their faces carefully.

"Narskap came to me. As the maker of your weapon, he has a tenuous bond to it. Nothing like the one you share with the hammer, but enough of one that he found you by it."

"Did he now?" Abayan singled his gaze to rest on Narskap, appraising.

"He does. And because of that, and the sword he wields for me, he came to me and told me of a flaw in the weapons, of a flaw that might be most fatal for you. I listened and decided the best course would be to seek you out, and remedy that flaw."

"Tell me the flaw."

Quendius gestured at Narskap to speak. He cleared his dry throat but the first word or so husked out. "My workmanship," he started, and then began again, "I have erred. The power imbued is not locked within the weapons as it should be."

"I have a healthy respect for my hammer," said Diort. "Are you telling me the Demon can break loose?"

"Even so."

Mmenonrakka loosed upon Kerith would be disaster. Gods and Demons existed upon their own planes, with their own balances, and here was further proof of what Diort had feared from the beginning. Narskap had meddled with those he should never have, and now look what he might face. Diort shifted weight. "What proof have you?"

"Do you doubt him? He talks with Gods and Demons, as no one on this earth has since the Mageborn died. I came to offer my craftsman to repair your weapon, not be reviled by your doubt."

"It is only." And Diort closed his mouth then on his retort, not finishing his statement.

Quendius made as if to turn away, pulled his horse's head down, and gathered the stirrup foot.

"Wait."

The hot, dry wind off the steppes grew in intensity, swirling about them, snapping Abayan's banner on the poles about the pavilion. They waited.

"What is it you need to do?"

"Bring him the hammer."

"It is always on me." Diort shouldered aside his cloak, pulling the war hammer from his baldric. He hesitated in handing it to Narskap.

"I need it a moment," Narskap told them. "Then you will hold it until I've built a forge fire hot enough to repair it."

Long moments passed, Diort's fingers growing white-knuckled as he clenched the haft. Then, he passed it to Narskap.

Narskap took it up, and mounted his horse. Abayan Diort threw his head back as if knowing he'd been taken.

"Now," said Quendius quietly but firmly. "You will accompany us."

"To what end?"

"Not yours. Not yet. You will be my guest while we decide your future. Leave your men quartered here." Quendius took stock of the encampment. "It would be a shame to let all this training go to waste."

"And when will I know what it is you suspect of me?"

"Soon," Quendius told him as he mounted up. "Order your horse made ready and pack clothes for winter."

"They will tear you down if I signal them."

"Not with Narskap holding the sword."

"He is one man against many archers."

Quendius smiled thinly. "The very last thing you want to make him do is drop the sword. He is the only barrier that contains it. None of us would survive if he fell while blooding it." He gathered his reins. "We need to discuss our plans, Abayan Diort, and consolidate our alliance. You may find this a more pleasant imprisonment than you expect."

Diort let his breath out in a gust of disgust at himself, and called orders to harness his mount.

Days of summer passed, heat bleeding into the cruelest month, the Dry month, and through it. Even a hot rain, thought Hosmer, as he sweated into his Town Guard tabard, would be welcome. No ice or snow could be brought down from the mountains to chill drinks, as none existed, and no root cellar could be dug deep enough to cool. Yet, with the instinct of his lifetime as a farmer, he could tell that Yellow Moon month, the season of harvest, with its nights holding the edge of fall and winter in it, loomed in the future. His da talked about the apples that would be coming in soon, a fresh new crop, brimming with crisp flavor and juices, and leaves that would drop not from the heat and lack of moisture but simply because it was the time of year for decaying as the days turned to winter and the quiet, muffled beginning of renewal.

The city didn't seem to notice or anticipate it. Its cycles were bounded on craftsmanship and work and other sensibilities he didn't understand. Rise early, work hard, drink hard, fall into bed. That seemed to be the only cycle here. For all that, he enjoyed working the streets more than the Conference, where the Vaelinars drifted in every morning, argued with one another long and loud, their voices ringing sharply, their elegant faces in permanent scowls of disagreement, the very air about them smelling as if lightning had just struck nearby. He watched waves of copyists and scribes rushing about, their hands filled with paper and stained with ink, their hair in disarray as if they pulled it in consternation even as they struggled to keep up with the flood of words and treaties.

He watched Sevryn Dardanon as he paced the Warrior Queen in her journeys to and from the Conference. The man noticed him as few did, always nodding. Hosmer knew he'd been by the brewery and press a few times to visit his sisters, but he'd been on duty and so had no idea what passed between them. He and Garner speculated that Sevryn had an interest in Rivergrace, but she'd become withdrawn and stayed that way, working quietly at the shop and at home, talking little and listening much as if she were trying to take in everything about them and impress it deeply within herself, so as never to forget. What could she be forgetting about her own family?

He shifted weight from one boot to another, bringing his mind to the milling crowd outside the hall. He'd begun to know them all by face and attitude. Some were petitioners still hoping to get their needs listened to, and waited for an opening in Last Cause Petitioners' Day. Others shifted about in the morning and the evening to shout and curse at the Vaelinars as they gathered, bellowing about war and slavery and thievery. Their protests seemed to fall on deaf, if pointed, ears. Frustration boiled as the sun did. His sharp eyes caught a silvery-haired Kernan woman as she reached into a sack at her side, filling her hand with an overripe fruit. He left the steps with a bound and reached her side.

"Don't be throwing that," he told her. "Not today and not tomorrow." His grip closed about her wrist, forcing her to drop it into the dust of the courtyard. Her lip curled at him, her mouth age-wrinkled with missing teeth, and her eyes shrewd.

"They'll take you, laddy-boy. Put a glamour on you and fill your eyes with magics and sweep you away."

"Fools, then. The only glamour I'll be following is the one of a pretty girl." He released her hand. "I'll bet you had the boys traipsing around after you, not so long ago."

That caught her off stride and then she cackled. "Oh, I did, I did!" She winked at him.

"That doesna surprise me at all. I can still see it in you. Now get in out of the sun before the heat does you in, aye?"

She poked a bony finger into his ribs. "I'll go, but you tell them for us. Tell them they can't be taking our children off on wild hunts for nothing!"

"I will."

He watched her leave, a sway to her hobbled walk, her head in the air, before he returned to his place on the hall steps. She took a handful and more with her, all complaining about the elven yet agreeing that it would do no good to bake their heads any more in the heat. As his wide-brimmed hat soon provided the only shade and he watched the crowd from under it, they all began to drift away. They would be back, he knew, in the evening hours after supper and a cup or two of courage and bitterness, to shout at the hall and its inhabitants again. At least he didn't have to stand boot-deep in rotting vegetables and fruit that day.

Buttennoff came by perhaps a candlemark later, judging from the slow ascent of the sun, with a knotted cloth napkin, and a mug in his hand. Hailing Hosmer, he passed the bundles over. "Your mother sent you lunch."

"From the shop? How kind of her."

Buttennoff grunted. They both knew he'd been at the brewery to talk to Nutmeg and had taken the lunch from there, as Lily spent every daylight hour at the shop. "How are my sisters today?"

"The tall one stays quiet, but Meg talked my ear off before I walked her to work."

"Good thing you had an extra ear to keep your hat from falling down to your neck."

His friend grunted again, watching as Hosmer unwrapped his cold meat and cheese to eat. "Think she'd come to Summersend with me?"

"She likes to dance. Ask her."

"All she talks about is that Jeredon, the queen's brother. It's like a mote stuck in her eye." Buttennoff leaned unhappily against a pillar.

Whenever Hosmer had been about, she'd filled the air talking about Butterknife, but he wasn't about to tell his friend that. Women were women and Buttennoff had to learn the hard way about them, just as he would be doing if he had time off duty to do any studying. He crunched a roll of crusty bread, soft and flavorful in the center. He tossed the last of the crust down into the courtyard in scraps for birds scattered about to dive down and steal.

"She likes dancing," he repeated stubbornly. "How could she not want to go to Summersend?"

"True." Buttennoff scrubbed at his chin, then straightened alertly. "What's this?" He jabbed his thumb at the Bolger making his way across the courtyard toward them, leather vest open over his chest, a scarred veteran of a Bolger, large leather sack tied to his belt and hanging over one lean hip.

"Dunno," Hosmer told him, because he didn't, and had no idea. He planted his feet in the Bolger's way. "Halt."

The Bolger halted. Looked him up and down as if taking his measure, and that made the hairs on the back of Hosmer's neck bristle a little. "Inside."

"Not today. Last Cause Petitioners' is on the morrow, anyway."

"And no Bolgers for that," Buttennoff added. "Just people."

The Bolger gave him a dismissive glance. He put his hand out to Hosmer. "Inside."

"Can't do. You've no business in there."

The Bolger thumped his chest. "Rufus. Tell Sevryn man here."

"Hey, now. We're not your servants." Buttennoff swelled up, but Hosmer put his hand out to the guardsman. "Why not, I'll do it. Wait here with him?"

"The queen will have your head for it."

"I'll just have a look-see. I won't interrupt anything." He nodded to the Bolger. "I'll be back."

The Bolger inclined his head, spread his feet wide, and settled into a firmly planted stance on the stairs. Hosmer left the two of them staring into each other's eyes, the Bolger seeming a little amused.

Deep in the inner recesses of the hall, where the wings held the smaller meeting rooms, he found the queen's audiences with its guard in the hallway, and by luck or fortune, Sevryn was talking quietly with one of them when he turned the corner. Hosmer hailed him with a wave.

"By the morrow," Sevryn said to him. "The sun's only been up a few candlemarks and you're already red with its glow. I'll have an ointment sent for that."

"We Dwellers favor a rosy complexion, m'lord Dardanon. Have you time to give me?"

"Always. Nothing wrong? The lasses all right?" Sevryn joined him quickly, brows lowered.

"They're fine. I've someone looking for you, not sure if you want him sent away or what."

"Queen Lariel's not taking any visitors today."

"Not the queen, sir, you. A Bolger who names himself Rufus."

Sevryn's open expression immediately smoothed. "Bring him around to the alley courtyard, know the one? It's shaded this time of day, and quiet. I'll be there in a moment."

Hosmer bowed and went back downstairs to escort the Bolger where he'd been directed. The long lines of the hall slanted over the small yard, where carriages and coaches sometimes unloaded, but no one lingered about now, with everyone inside and already working. Rufus trotted by him with a lope that suggested he ran as much as he rode, the sack thumping at his hip.

Sevryn slipped out without a word, taking the servants' corridors and going out the small side door to where Hosmer and Rufus waited. He looked little different than he had the last time they'd met, although perhaps a bit more weathered by the sun. Sevryn waved Hosmer to stand down. Whatever Rufus wanted, he didn't fear an attack.

"Well met," he said.

"You remember."

"You helped in a fight. I wouldn't forget that."

"You keep her safe?"

"Her family keeps her safe," he answered the Bolger, his throat tightening a little at the thought of Rivergrace.

"Good. I watch her, little." And he held his hand off the ground, as though he would pet a toddler's head, and Sevryn blinked back his surprise at that.

"What is this all about?" demanded Hosmer.

Rufus jerked his head. "I promise Sevryn man remember." His hands went to his weapons belt.

Hosmer had his short sword out and at his chin before he could move any further. Rufus froze in place, breath growling in his chest.

"Hosmer," Sevryn said. "Stand down. Any attack would have come by surprise."

Hosmer drew his sword away slowly, carefully. Rufus kept his hands on his belt until Sevryn gave him a nod. Then, quickly, with hands misshapen by smithing and by age, he undid the laces on his large sack, to give it over to Sevryn.

"What's this?" He opened the sack to look inside, and saw the top of a large, widemouthed jar. It took both hands to lift it out, the sack sloughing away like an old, used skin and falling to the ground. Balancing the bottom on one thigh, he opened the jar to see a thing immersed in scented oil, hair matted to its skull. It rolled as his hands shook, revolving slowly, turning until the thing's face bobbed upward, aquamarine gem encrusted in a bloodied earlobe.

He looked at Gilgarran's severed head, the eyes dulled but open and staring back.

Chapter Sixty-Four

THE WORLD CRASHED DOWN on Sevryn. He fell to his knees under its weight, Gilgarran staring at him, memories cascading down in an avalanche of pain and horror, of betrayal and survival. He heard a low, keening moan in his ears, felt his throat constrict. His hands convulsed about the jar. He knew everything.

Then he knew nothing.

He woke with his forehead on a scarred, splintered wooden table smelling of beer, ale, and garlic. Sevryn rolled onto his cheekbone and stared out of one eye. His dim view of the surroundings threatened to swim about in a sickening, dizzy manner, and he shuddered. A sodden cloth fell from the back of his neck as he did so, and he heard Hosmer saying, "Sunstroke. Nasty thing. It's dark and quiet in here, and you should be drinkin'. Weak beer or water."

A clay jug scraped the table by his hand. Sevryn sat up with a groan. Another sodden cloth fell from his head to his lap. He left it lying there as he wrapped his hands about the jug and stared into it to make sure nothing looked back before hefting it to drink. It went down his throat, and he choked before he remembered to swallow. Hosmer thumped his shoulder.

"Where am I?"

"I think this one is called Th' Lying Wife. Not sure, one tavern looks th' same as another to me. It was closest."

"Rufus?"

"The Bolger took his sack and left."

"What happened?"

"I was going to ask you that one, m'lord." Hosmer looked kindly at him. "Drink some more. I thought you were going t' die on that spot."

"I think maybe I did." Sevryn took another deep swill, and the water flowed into him, not cold by any means but wet and alive. Eighteen years of shackles, years of the most menial servitude and fear and loathing, working the mines, training men he neither knew nor respected how to fight, how to kill. Moments he could see crystal clear surged through his mind, pushing, shoving their way through, one after another. He swallowed hard. "Who knows I'm here?"

"No one. Seemed t' be no one else's business."

"Thanks for that."

"He had a head in that jar. Severed from its neck."

"I know. It came from a man who took me off the streets, treated me like his son, and taught me what I needed to know."

"I can put word out for the Bolger. We'll bring him in for the murder."

Sevryn said, "No. He didn't do it."

"You know who did, then?"

"Someone beyond the reach of the Calcort Town Guard." He put his hand out and clasped Hosmer's wrist on the table. "Thank you anyway."

"It'll be the Warrior Queen's business then, I'm guessing."

He nodded slowly. If he told her. There were many things he no longer told her. He would have to leave her side.

He got to his feet. Hosmer jumped to catch him as he swayed. "Maybe another mark or two in here, m'lord."

"No. No, I've lost far too much time already." He leaned on the compact, sturdy Dweller, reckoning what to do and how. "Do you know the healer's college, the small inn on Green Lantern Way?"

"I think so. A good place for you the rest of this day."

"It seems wise. Are you going back on watch?"

"I traded my shift. I'll go back after dinner hour, work late."

Sevryn hesitated before asking, "Could you bring Lady Rivergrace to see me?"

The muscles under his arm bunched a bit as if deciding and not favorably, then Hosmer shrugged. "I will. But you treat her fairly, m'lord, or I will find you wherever you are."

"I understand." And he did.

* * *

Hesitantly, Rivergrace stepped into the inner halls of the building. She lifted both hands to her veils, pulling them off her face and letting them tumble from the back of her head. She looked up quickly as Sevryn appeared on a threshold.

"This is where the queen's friend Azel healed."

"He's here yet, but sitting in a small patio now. I thought you might like to visit."

She frowned. "Hosmer said you were ill."

"I was. Am. A revelation," he answered, "not unlike the one that sent you running from here." He took her hand and drew her close.

"I won't answer any more questions."

"You won't be asked any, not like that anyway."

"Then why am I here?"

He looked into her eyes of river-blue, and sea-green-blue, and stormy ocean-gray-blue. "Because I needed you with me. Forgive me for that." He walked her with him then, and she didn't answer, but at least she didn't push him away as she had been.

Azel d'Stanthe looked up, and a broad smile spread over his face. He held both great hands out in welcome. "Sevryn! Rivergrace! Come, seat yourselves, tell me what is going on in the great world."

She sat on a wide, low foot ottoman, and Sevryn perched on a nearby stool after moving a few books first. "I apologize—" she began in her low, quiet voice, but he harrumphed loudly and waved her words aside.

"I'm the one, charging like a wild creature through all your perceptions. How are you faring?"

"I am settled into the role of seamstress, with some little talent," and she gave a wistful smile. She held up her fingers, one or two pricked from needles and still healing.

"You are flesh and blood, then." He chuckled.

"So it seems."

"I find that a relief."

"So do I!" She gave a fleeting but genuine smile.

Azel looked at Sevryn quizzically. "You?"

"The Conference is nearly over and I'll return with Queen Lariel. She has much to digest and decide upon."

"Do I hear true rumors?"

"That she is indeed a Warrior Queen. Yes."

"Hmmmm." Azel said nothing further on that, but Sevryn was sure he would, if not that day, then another. The historian sat straighter in his chair. He'd gained a bit of weight back, and he looked far stronger than Sevryn had a right to expect. "What brings you here?"

"I brought her hoping you'd tell a story."

"Me? A talespinner?"

"A true story. I want you to tell her of the Four Kingdoms, and of the Ways."

"Oh, lad. Well. I will have to shorten it down a bit, not only out of pity for the two of you but because," and he coughed then, and finally managed, "because I am short of breath as well." He poured himself a drink from a nearby pitcher, making a face as he swallowed a long draft from it. "Why do things good for you always taste as if they can't possibly be?"

That brought another flashing smile to Rivergrace's face, and Sevryn felt a spike of envy through him, that Azel could make her smile and he could not. If the afternoon went as he hoped, as he planned, she would like him even less.

Gesturing with one large hand, the other resting on his knee, Azel drew in the air. "In the beginning, we came without warning to ourselves or anyone else. In the years that followed as we regained what little history we could, we fought with each other and with this new world. There are far more to these years than I could possibly tell you, and there are those who would stop me from giving you that history. But my library is free," and he leaned forward with an intense light in his eyes. "Free as it should be as long as I have a say in it. Come visit me at Ferstanthe and learn all that you care to learn."

"Someday," she answered him softly.

"Good." He took another drink, stalling a cough. Sevryn watched his face, fearing that the drink might drug him into slumber, but Azel merely cleared his throat before speaking again. "Mine is the smallest of the kingdoms Sevryn mentioned. It isn't really one, except that we were established by a Stronghold and a House, and we're maintained free and independent. The sole purpose of Ferstanthe is to collect and preserve knowledge so that it can be known by any who have a need, any of Vaelinar blood, that is. I train scribes from all walks of life there, Kernan, Dweller, Galdarkan, even a Bolger once, most of whom go on to work for traders or other guilds and have little interest in Vaelinar ways, and they don't see our true library, our Books of All Truth." He traced a line through the air.

"Ferstanthe rests against a forest of trees, and along a great, lazy lake which grows reeds by the thousands. We use both the trees and reeds for paper and writing quills and such. Ink comes from the ores and other minerals around us. Vegetable inks are easier to make, but they fade rapidly." He paused and quickly added, "but I bore you with that. Imagine then immense trees, trees that were seedlings when we Vaelinar Strangers first came to Kerith, in 312. They yet grow, towering over buildings of marble and granite, domed buildings that are immense once you're inside but look as nothing against the trees. You can hear the ocean's roar in their branches when the wind blows and when it snows, it dapples their branches but cannot possibly cover them, for they are majestic among the hillsides. Among their trunks grow groves of smaller trees, vastly inferior, and it is those we log, for they grow quickly and flourish while our gentle giants take their time in everything.

"That is the kingdom whose guardianship I hold."

Azel looked at her, then at Sevryn. "It is different from the other kingdoms," he stated, "in that it is not founded on a Way. It is founded on the need to communicate, from the past to the future. Without wishing to distress you, you must understand how and why the others came to be."

A slight tremor ran through Rivergrace's body. She laced her fingers upon her lap. "The Ferryman is a Way."

"Yes. A phantasm, a being that does not exist yet does, whose sole purpose is a passage that neither earth nor water can block. Have you seen him?"

"Several times." Her voice was barely audible.

"You are not like him," Azel said to her.

"We don't know what I am."

"True, but he was created to be imposing, unknowable, a foreboding mystery. Let me tell you of another Way, the vast tree of life on the plain Hith-aryn, its roots woven like a great net below the plains, holding water within it, keep both the wind and flood of erosion from them. Most of the tree grows below the surface, you see, and it is this tree which keeps the northwestern plains green, unlike those of the warlands. The aryn has young saplings sprinkled across the plains as far as the eye can see and rolling hills move, and the grounds are fertile because of its creation. You'd like to see that, I think. The House of Hith-aryn, of Bistel and Bistane Vantane established itself with the making of this Way. There is nothing of death in the aryn, although it does bow to nature as we all do. It loses boughs and grows new ones, ever-green in its stand upon its kingdom."

They all paused as Azel coughed a bit, and blew his nose and had to gain his breath back.

"Look then to the ocean, overshadowing all the lands in its size. Tomarq is a fortress, as you know, built upon a Way that is meant to shield the coast. Two houses created it, Drebukar with its Talent of Earth that mined the jewel from its depths and Istlanthir of Fire, that cut and shaped it and brings the power through it that burns any it looks upon and perceives as enemy. Istlanthir is a House of fairly pure bloodline and retains its distinctive skin of light blue and hair of sea green or silvery blue to this day. The Jewel, or Shield, of Tomarq sits on a great sea cliff over the vast natural harbor of Hawthorne, with the Istlanthir fortress just below. It is tended regularly and with great caution, for it is an Eye which kills if it looks upon you as an intruder."

"Still, it is a wonder, this beautiful red-and-gold jewel. Immense, child, you can hardly imagine. As big as a house. It sits in a golden cradle which moves from side to side so that its eye views the ocean from north to south in a sweep which varies, so that one can never be sure which way the Eye looks. When filled with power, it glows like a beacon fire over the sea cliff and can be seen for provinces away."

Rivergrace stirred. "I met Lord Tranta. He'd been injured. Did the Eye look upon him?"

"No, lass. If it had, he would be nothing more than a puff of gray ash on the wind. He fell from the cliff to the ocean below, and is lucky to be alive," Sevryn answered for Azel who took the pause to drink once more, and to gather his breath before speaking again, saying to her in his deepest tone. "Tomarq is but a Shield. What would our lands be without its Sword?"

"Queen Lariel?"

"Our Warrior Queen, no other." Azel nodded at Rivergrace. "Because Larandaril is the Sword, her Way came from a pact with the Gods themselves through the River Andredia, and I know very little of it. The making of all Ways are closely kept secrets within the families who made that magic, but their intent and purposes are usually well known. Larandaril is shrouded. The river is sacred and to be kept that way, in penance perhaps for the life of a warrior and sword. The kingdom itself is a river valley, blessed in peace and orchards, in groves gentle and small brooklets running through dales and down soft hillocks. It is a place which I've visited only once or twice in my lifetime and where I think I would go for my last days, if I knew when my last days were upon me, for it must be as close to heaven as we can imagine . . ." Azel's voice drifted off, and his eyes misted. He reached for a clean handkerchief to blot them. His complexion grayed a little and he began coughing again. Rivergrace put her hand on his knee in concern as his shoulders and chest heaved.

"We should go."

Azel looked as though he would protest, but nodded his head wearily. He said, his words now hoarse and thin, "I hope you have seen some of the Ways through my eyes, child, and been comforted."

She stood, bent over him, and kissed the top of his head. She walked out of the patio ahead of Sevryn, stopping only when they were a corner and hallway beyond.

"He doesn't know the Andredia is poisoned."

"No. Lariel hasn't told him."

"I don't know if that's a kindness or cruel."

"For now, I think, a kindness. Grace . . . come with me."

"Where?"

"Up the Silverwing. I was given a gift or a curse, I don't know which, but I've memories now that I'd lost, and somehow they're braided with you, with a past you lost, too, and we need to go back."

She touched her wrist at the branding scar. "Why?"

"We've answers there."

"Any answer I find out now will probably unbind me, unmake me. I exist from day to day as though walking on a very thin and unsecured plank across a raging river. One misstep, and I'll be swept away, I know it."

"Listen to me."

"I can't." She turned her face from him, and it wrenched at him.

"I hold love for you."

"Oh, don't. Don't do this to me! Love someone who exists, who has a chance at living a life."

He reached for her chin, to tilt her eyes up to meet his, and she shivered at his touch. "It only hurts because you are living a life, Grace. Trust in me. Come with me. I have to find the forge, the mines, the slavers who marked you, and marked me."

"No. I can't."

"You can. You will."

She wrenched from his grasp. He did then what he'd planned and hit her, catching her limp body before she touched the ground.

Chapter Sixty-Five

"WHAT ARE YOU crafting?"

Narskap paused, his roughened hands in midair over a camp table, glittering shards below his palms reflecting the torch- and lantern light. "A conceit," he answered. "Nothing more."

Quendius folded his legs and sat down. He watched as Narskap tapped one way, then another, as if cutting a fine jewel although he wasn't, removing a small flake from the shard he shaped. The smith picked it up to ponder, a needle-sharp fleck that glistened as though dipped in freshly shed blood before dropping it to the side. It reminded Quendius of a thought that touched him often. "I wonder what color Gods bleed."

"In Their own form or if They take mortal flesh?"

"Either."

"It's unlikely we could wound One, either way." Narskap answered him as if he, too, had considered the thought. He put aside the item he'd been working on and examined another closely.

"I'll have a guest in the pavilion next eve. Do not come visiting."

Narskap nodded.

"We'll return to home base after this next mission." The direction they'd been moving in was obvious, but he thought he would confirm that to Narskap. Narskap was the weapon he wielded, a buffer between himself and that which he ached to hold but could not. Like any weapon, he needed to be oiled and sharpened and treated with respectful care.

"Good. I must meditate."

"Our hostage grows restless."

"A hostage now rather than an ally?"

Quendius wrinkled his nose. "However Diort prefers to refer to himself is immaterial. As long as I have suspicions that he intended us to be pinned between himself and Bistel's forces, he is not a free man. I need him, at any rate, to front us when we move to sell to Larandaril. He prowls his confines as though a hungry man, anxious to have his war hammer at his side once more."

"I felt no life in it when I took it from him." Narskap shrugged. "It is bonded to him. Our sword is uncontrollable, perhaps his hammer merely goes dormant. It is not for me to understand the Demons within them."

Quendius thought to himself that if Narskap did, he would be a dead man. Quendius could not afford him to have more power.

His smith stirred his project with one finger, selecting another piece to work upon, asking, "The queen has responded to your offer?"

"Yes. She's decamped from Calcort and is moving to the rendezvous we agreed upon at the border. She'll be within our hands." Quendius stretched and rose to his feet like a great, supple, charcoal-colored feline. "I'll leave you to your hobby."

"Thank you, my lord." Narskap spared him a brief glance before going back to his intent study of what he chiseled and shaped ever so precisely.

Quendius dropped one last look at the table before leaving. If he were to venture a guess, it would be that Narskap shaped arrowheads. He would force an answer from Narskap when he was ready, when he had a need to know what his smith was doing.

Chapter Sixty-Six

SOMETHING POUNDED ON HIM in his deepest sleep, and Hosmer tried to raise eyelids that felt grainy and glued impossibly together. The pounding on his shoulder continued with a rhythm that jarred his teeth in his clenched jaw. This was why he preferred to sleep at home rather than the barracks. He burrowed deeper into his cot.

"Wake up. Tree's blood, Hosmer, wake up!"

He put his hand out blindly to stop the jolting. "Mmmpf." It sounded as if he *was* home.

Insistently, Garner turned from pounding to shaking. "Up!"

"A'right, a'right." He pried one eye open. His disheveled brother looked down at him, lean face, intense eyes.

"You awake?"

"Almost."

"You smell like a spoiled root cellar."

"You woke me to tell me this?" Hosmer rolled over and pulled his blanket over his head to blot out the daylight. Garner snatched the blanket back as he did.

"No, I didn't. What happened?"

Grunting, Hosmer sat up to glare at his brother. He narrowed one eye down into what he thought was an effective stare, as it seemed to work on unruly crowds in Calcort streets. His brother curled a lip back at him. "They rioted at the Great Hall. Unloaded bushels of rotten food at us, threw their empty mugs, brawling, you name it. Last Cause Petition was canceled, and the Vaelinars pulled out in a hurry, in the middle of the night. We formed a wall to keep them safe. I think my new tabard is ruined."

"Ah, so that's it, then. The queen is gone? I'm glad I decided to talk with you before worrying Da and Mom. I knew Bistane was gone. He didn't show up for his usual hand of cards. I make good coin off him; he's not as good at keeping a smooth expression as he thinks he is. So Rivergrace went with her?"

Hosmer scrubbed his face with his hand. He did stink, and he had tried to bathe before he fell into his blankets early that morning. His mother would give him a hiding of sharp words and looks. He tried to grasp the sense of what Garner said. "Grace? No. Queen Lariel went with her brother. What's this about Grace?"

"She's been gone a day and night and day. Looks like time to worry them, after all." Garner vacated his cot.

"Wait. No, wait. She never came back with Sevryn?"

"Should she have?"

"I took her to meet him. He asked for her." Hosmer got up and started pulling clothes on. Clean clothes, but his skin seemed sticky and the process took a bit of doing.

"Hmmm. Maybe I shouldn't worry them yet."

"Garner, you're making my head ache."

"There's feelings between the two of them, brother. For all she's been quiet lately, I know there is. Nutmeg would shout it from the rooftops, but our Grace is still, deep water."

"You think he took her?"

"I don't know." Garner wrinkled his nose at Hosmer. "Wash up a bit, and we'll find Tolby. Better he be told, and do the thinking."

"They'll come after me."

"I'm sure they will. I would. We're almost to the Nylara, though, and I doubt they'll catch up with us." Sevryn leaned out of his saddle to pat Black Ribbon on her cherry neck. The mare had shown her versatility, pulling the small, one-person horse cart as easily as she carried a rider in the saddle. Rivergrace stared at him, her chin high, tied hands in front of her, her body bouncing about in the cart despite Ribbon's smooth trot.

"I would like to stop. I need to pee."

"Of course, m'lady." He reined off the small dirt road, into a clearing with suitable brush and soft grass, yellowed by the summer but still providing forage for both horses. "I could do with a stretch myself."

After he dismounted and settled the animals, he reached for her, saying, "I'd like to untie you."

"I'd like to be untied."

She wouldn't quite look him in the face, staring at a spot about a hand high off his head. He'd used his Voice on her first to keep her mild and quiet, but he was loath to do that anymore, to force her to his will any more than he already had. Rivergrace quiet and obedient was not the woman who held his thoughts. What truth would be in it if he forced her to say she loved him? None.

He undid her knots quickly. She jumped out of the cart even faster, on him with both fists swinging. He ducked the first one, but she came with a roundhouse to his right and caught him soundly. She knocked him to his duff and drew her booted foot back for a kick, and hesitated as he sat there, hand to his jaw.

"Go ahead. I deserve it."

"Get up. I won't kick a body while he's down."

He stayed where he was.

"Get up!"

"No."

"Coward."

"Hardly. I'll have your whole family and Queen Lariel on my tail in another day or two. Do you think I risk that lightly?"

She stared down at him, the stormy gray-blue of her eyes lit, the serene sea-blues of her eyes disquieted. "Why do you risk it at all? Treating me like some common baggage you can pick up from any whorehouse in Calcort—"

"Whoa, whoa, m'lady! While a kiss from you would be sweeter than any pastry, that's not why I have you."

"No?"

Bless her but she looked a little disappointed. He stayed on his rear, however, as she kept her fists clenched and ready, and her weight neatly balanced. "No."

The silence drew out between them, broken only by the sound of the two horses cropping at the last of the grass, and the warble of a nearby songbird hidden in the brush. She lowered her hands.

"You know the Silverwing like you know the lines in your hands, Grace. Is it clean?"

She opened her mouth, and then closed it, the curve of her lips troubled. Finally, she shook her head slightly. "There is something," she said reluctantly. "Almost there but not quite."

"A beginning of the taint."

"I don't know."

"You know. You just won't admit it to yourself."

She wrenched her gaze from him and looked to the distant mountains, ranges that braced the Silverwing on one side and Larandaril with the Andredia on the other. "Are we going there, then?"

"I think we must." He couldn't tell her yet what he feared the most, nor would he until he could match what he recalled with what he found at the forge above the Silverwing. If it was the place of his memories. He needed her strength as well as his to get through what he thought they might face.

She smoothed her skirt down but it didn't hide the tremor of her hands which stopped when she took a deep breath. "You intend to go into the mountain itself."

"The trip isn't worth it unless we do, and time isn't on our side. It would help if you rode, and I could leave the cart behind. It would help, Rivergrace, if you came wholeheartedly with me."

She found a loose thread on the cuff of her sleeve and picked at it pensively. "If I pull this, it could break cleanly and stop the unstitching. Or it could unravel entirely, and I lose the hem, unsewn. Which am I, Sevryn? Will I break cleanly or come unmade?"

"I pray, aderro, that you are made of sterner stuff than thread, and nothing happens to you that I can't guard you from."

Turning her back to him, he thought he heard her reply softly, "And I pray that I don't already know the answer."

He began to unhitch the cart.

They paused at the riverbank of the Nylara, its expanse dark and muddied for summer's end, but its current no less treacherous. She watched as the Dark Ferryman rode his barge across, unseen hands inside the voluminous robes moving on the rudder as ropes pulled themselves to haul it across. A few clouds wisped across the sky, and she wished they would hide the sun even if briefly as its heat drained her very will to move. Ribbon shifted under her, nostrils widening at the river, and she let her wade into it and then back up onto the sandy bank where the ferry landed. Aymaran tossed his head and tried to look above such antics, but when the mare flicked her wet tail at him, he didn't seem to mind the splatter of water.

"Even from here, it's a good two weeks," she commented.

Sevryn dismounted to let Aymaran drink, the horse pulling at the water with soft lips and eyeing his rider to see if he could drink his fill. Sevryn would not let him, they had no time to care for a foundering horse, so he kept a firm hand under the horse's chin. "I want you to pay the Ferryman."

Grace looked at the phantom drawing near. Gooseflesh rose unbidden on her arms and neck at its closeness. She told herself it had never attacked anyone, then she remembered Bregan Oxfort with brace and cane, forever altered. True, Oxfort had attacked it first, and yet, her pulse quickened. Sevryn took her hand, uncurling her fingers, and dropped silver bits into her palm. "Tell him you want to cross, and name the Silverwing, and hold its image in your mind, that part of the river you know best, and keep holding that image when you pay him, and as we ride over on the barge. Don't let it waver."

He thought to distract her, and she began to demur.

Sevryn closed her hand in his. "Trust me?"

"You've thumped me and kidnapped me, but I don't recall you've ever lied to me. Of course I trust you." She could feel the corner of her mouth twitch.

He kissed that corner of her mouth. "Then do as I ask."

The barge ground to a halt on the sandbar and the ropes snapped in place roughly, with the Ferryman gliding eerily off it and putting his ghostly hand out. They took their horses by the bridle, and Rivergrace looked into the cowled face of the phantom, seeing little in the emptiness but a dance of light which could be anything, and told him what Sevryn had instructed her. She bore it only because of her vision of the Silverwing, clasped tightly in her mind like a talisman.

After a moment, the ferryman named a fee, and she dropped her coins into his embrace. He clenched his hand about it, as he intoned to her a word or two of Vaelinar that she did not recognize. He waited a moment before turning away and beckoning them to board the ferry.

She held her vision of her home, even with her alna riding a wind current above it, the bright blue Silverwing tipped with white froth in its high tide days, swiftly flowing past her life, the river curled into the cove where she and Nutmeg bathed, played, and had hidden from raiders. The ferry bumped and heaved under her feet as she stood with closed eyes, imagining the place which had been part of the heart and soul of her existence, braided with the Farbranch stead and family. After an interminable time, with the ropes and barge creaking and the horses moving uncertainly, and Sevryn's even breathing near her ear, the heat of his body standing protectively behind her, she could imagine the familiar roar of the Silverwing, and the ferry came to a halt.

"Docked," the Dark Ferryman said in Common.

She opened her eyes and gasped.

"Hurry," urged Sevryn, nudging her gently, and she led Ribbon off the wooden flatboat onto the banks of her beloved river. She knew every rock, every cut of the current into its bed, the apple groves on one side and the wild groves on the other, and it surrounded her. As soon as they had all disembarked, the Ferryman cast off, disappearing into a mist off the water that she had not felt on her face when they crossed.

She swung on him breathlessly. "How did you know?"

"I didn't. It happened to me once, by accident. It seemed fortuitous to try it on purpose."

"I didn't do that."

"No, he did. Whether he does it because you know your destination so firmly or whether he does it because he wants to, I can't fathom. But it does leave me with an intriguing question or two, which I'll have to answer some other time." He gave her a leg up and patted her foot comfortingly. "It shortens our journey by a good bit." He started to shift away, but she didn't want to lose the feel of him close to her.

"Don't go."

He froze in place.

"Why does hearing your voice and feeling your touch make me even happier than being near the Silverwing again?"

"I don't know," he answered. "But it makes my heart leap to hear you say it."

"I've nothing to give you," she told him. "I don't know how long I have."

"Then," and he drew nearer, his body pressing against her knee, "we have to do with every day that's given us, don't we?"

"Do?"

"Treasure. Love. Remember." He moved his hand to her waist. He brought his other hand to her waist, and lifted her down off Ribbon's back, holding her against him, sliding her down and letting her feet touch the ground at the very last moment. Ribbon turned her head, the mare snorting in equine confusion as if to say, *down, up, down again, make up your mind.*

She buried her hands in his hair like molten bronze, silken and waving through her fingers, and brought her lips to his, and promised herself that she would remember every moment as if it could be her last.

Chapter Sixty-Seven

AFTERWARD, IN THE GLOW of his body and hers, she put her head on his shoulder to listen to the beat of his heart slow and grow contented, his hand on the back of her head massaging her gently. Cloak spread wide and rumpled under them smelled faintly of horse and goat, and bruised sweet grasses. An alna soared overhead, giving its keening cry, and wind whisked through the grove, branches rubbing and sounding. "He spoke to me," she murmured."

"He? Who? The bird?"

"The Ferryman. He speaks in your language, and I never understand him."

"What did he say?" His fingers tickled her neck.

"Nevinaya . . ." She stumbled, before grasping the second word, "Nevinaya aliora."

He took a deep breath, she felt his chest expand and rise under her face. "Remember the soul," he said. "If you recalled that aright."

"I don't know. What does he mean?"

"I've no way of knowing."

A kind of sadness washed through her. Her eyes filled, and she could feel her cheek and his skin dampen.

"What is it?" His fingers kneaded her soothingly.

"I never told them, my family," she said. "About the blanket. About me."

"Ah." The kneading stopped, and his large hand slipped up to her hair, combing it. "You may never have to."

"And if I do?"

She felt him kiss the top of her head. "If I teach you anything, may it be to accept from others what you so freely give them. Unlike a river, love flows both ways."

"I'm going after her," announced Nutmeg when Garner and Hosmer finished talking, a project that had taken some time, some jostling, a few shin kicks and glares between the brothers before all had been spilled out in front of the rest of them.

Lily wiped her hands carefully on her apron, taking her time, each fingertip meticulously dried, before she met her daughter's eyes. "All right, then."

"I will talk sense into her."

To hide her smile at that, Lily turned to Tolby, asking, "Who else?"

"Hosmer is not mine to say yea or nay, his work is with the Town Guard now. I'd be loath to let Keldan go, I need his strong shoulders."

Garner gave a lopsided smile. "Sounds as if that leaves me, Da."

"It does. Also, you're th' eldest."

"I can go alone!"

"No, you can't."

"Can so."

"You'll be needing me."

"Will not."

"Meg, Garner, stop it." Lily rose, took off her apron, and put it on a hook near the stove. "The object is to find her, not keep her away with the bickering. We have no idea what's on her mind. She could love this fellow, or it might have nothing to do with him."

"I think," Tolby said dryly about the stem of his pipe, "that it probably has a great deal to do with him."

"I think," Lily disagreed mildly, "that it might have everything to do with that blanket." Her words splashed into the middle of their conversation like a large stone into a formerly quiet pond, and she watched the ripples of comprehension hit each of them.

"She barely mentioned it."

"She's hardly talked at all for a while. We've not heard one word of what the queen might have told her about it."

"So," Garner said lightly, "we don't know if we should haul her back or not?"

"Bring her back, bring them both back. I'll not have her start a new life in less than honorable fashion," Tolby told him.

"A pitchfork wedding! Excellent."

Hosmer kicked Garner in the shin under the table. He jerked, the smile on his face unwavering. "Do we know where to look?"

"Larandaril?"

"He's the queen's man, he might have taken her there."

"I vote home," Keldan said, although he'd been sitting with his mouth shut firmly, a scowl on his face.

"D'you think so?"

Hosmer reached up to scratch his eyebrow in irritation. A dried fleck of tomato flew off at he did so. "Gah. I'm going to have to soak head to toe again. I'm flaking."

"I cleaned your tabard already," Lily murmured. "Most of the stains came out, I believe, although it's not really very well made."

"Thank you, Mom." He cleared his throat. "I agree with Keldan. Last I talked with Sevryn, he seemed keen on heading to the Burning Mountains, and the head of the Silverwing." He neatly skirted how he'd spent that last conversation or what he'd heard him mumble as he'd hauled the stricken man to The Lying Wife.

"If we're wrong, we can cut through the pass and into Larandaril on the other side, Da," Garner said. "Weather will hold nicely."

"Aye, otherwise I'd brook no talk of heading that way. Those mountains are treacherous past Yellow Moon month."

"You can't possibly think of being gone that long?" Lily's serene expression finally turned grave.

Tolby took his pipe from his mouth. "Either find her soon or let her go. We'll put word out to Mistress Greathouse and the others we know, that if they're met on the roads, that they're welcome to come back. That's all we can do."

"If we go to Larandaril, the queen may send word from us."

"A'right, then. 'Tis settled."

Garner clapped Keldan roughly on the shoulder as he stood. "Be sure you sharpen the pitchfork. Just in case." And he gave a roguish wink. This time it was Lily who kicked him sharply in the ankle, and he let out a howl and hopped about.

They made good time without the cart. He usually woke in the mornings to find Rivergrace cleaning a fish or two, saying that the alna had dropped them for her. He never doubted it, for there were always two or three winging along with them, particularly the one with the rough white diamond on its chest. They gave cry when anything came near the camp as they rested, and even at night voiced high hoots when a predator prowled, so he took to sleeping with Grace and letting the birds keep a night watch.

He marveled at her. Shy in coming to him at first, now she filled his nights with fire bringing joy, her hands exploring every fiber of his being. The kedant lying dormant in him surrendered to her touch, filling him with a yearning that ached until explosion and then ebbing away for good, its constant pain gone. Other fire filled him in its stead, a purer flame that he shared with her, and when he woke every morning, it was with a prayer of thankfulness for the contentment and fulfillment she gave him, and he tried to return to her.

He told himself he did. Her dimpled smile flashed often and stayed, and only once or twice a day did he catch her looking toward the Burning Mountains with a faraway and lost expression in her eyes. He thought he'd known what he asked of her, and had been willing to risk it, and now he knew he'd misjudged himself. He'd denied to himself days ago that she could be nothing more than a spell-wrought holder for another, and now he told himself again that it couldn't be true. He told Grace that in every way he could find, with every tender moment and touch they shared, pouring into her an awareness of herself and the life she led. She couldn't be destined to leave him. He wouldn't let her believe it.

Nights grew a touch cooler as they gained the foothills and began to climb into the mountains. Dry month waned into its last hold on summer, mellowing. Rivergrace had woven herself a brim of straw that kept some of the sun from her face, and he laughed at it, and she had pouted a bit until he counted her freckles with small kisses. Always faint, even the sun barely brought them out, he had to be nearly nose to nose with her to see them against her translucent skin, but she would fuss until he stopped her. The alna finally stopped flying with them as they crested the pass leading up to the mountain, and he began to take a night watch from moon high till dawn, tracing the journey from memory so long ago. The Silverwing dipped in and out of view, as rivers born among the cracks and rills of mountains will do, and the horses worked harder and harder to find patches of grass for grazing. He'd brought grain and began to dole it out carefully. Aymaran would greedily huff up every trace, but Ribbon ate delicately, her long-lashed eyes closing now and then as she savored every mouthful.

They toiled up the broken landscape, worn thin by sun and little rain, the mountain on the edge of its life cycle, where even a little rain would be welcome. As pebbles clicked away from the horses' hooves, tiny ground dogs ran across the dirt to hide somewhere more secure, and small lizards slithered toward safer shelter in the cracks. He let Aymaran pick his way up, and the surefooted mount did so confidently, Black Ribbon with her nose to his tail. They wound round the Burning Mountain, and as they did, the Silverwing and the valley where the Farbranches and the Barrels had once prospered fell far from sight.

He felt it the moment they happened upon the hidden trail, his awareness of it filling him, and he stopped Aymaran. "We're near."

"I know," she told him. "I can feel the under mountain." She put a heel to her mare's flank, riding around him. He hurried to keep up.

They rode in through piles of felled wood, old timber, bleached gray by the years and rotting. If they'd once been gates, he could not tell it now. Their gazes swept the clearing. A bowl carved into the utmost top of the mountain, its appearance was neither natural nor unnatural as it lay empty. He remembered dense shrub and brush although few trees, above the timberline as it was. Now, nothing.

"Old burn," he said. "Already overgrown, and most of the char gone. If anything stood here, no one would know unless they'd been here before." Voice soured with disappointment, he jumped from his saddle, searching the ground in long strides, kicking at clods of brush and bramble, hoping to dislodge something. He threw his hands up. "There's nothing here!" His voice echoed and broke. "There were barracks and a hall and two forges, and stables, outbuildings. Gilgarran and I came here, and they cut him down, and took me as a slave for nearly eighteen years, and there's not a sign of any of it. Torn down and burned, not even a hearthstone left." He loped over the grounds, coursing like a hunting dog for a scent or hoping to scare prey into breaking cover. He ran faster, breath harsh in his throat.

"Who needs to believe? Queen Lariel . . . or yourself?"

Sevryn stopped. She studied him from atop her cherry mare, her face calm but concerned, and met his look evenly. He touched his chest. "I know. She needs to believe." He kicked at the ground again, sending gray-and-dun dirt flying.

She slid off to join him. "Are we in the right spot?"

He sank into a crouch. "If you ask, so will she." He ran a hand over his hair, pulling it back roughly from his brow. "What I saw here years ago, Rivergrace, will cut her down, but she doesn't believe that, and there's no evidence left. They want her in a war, they're baiting her, and then they'll cut her down because if they try again to assassinate her, she'll be a martyr, a cornerstone of the Vaelinar resistance, and they might lose everything they've planned. He has a sword that devours whatever it slices, Demon-ridden, God-ridden, I couldn't say, but it will hew down legions facing it. I can't let her walk into that. She doesn't believe Bistel's reports on it, but she would believe *me*."

"What can I look for?"

"Anything. A hammer, tongs . . ." He muttered to himself as he wandered. "They had bellows here as big as two houses, and nothing remains. They must have razed it before burning and moving on."

She took the lower circle on the hill. His voice stayed in earshot though she lost sight of him over the crest, him saying, "He built like a cursed nomad, no foundations, *nothing* . . ." until she lost track of even that.

The mountain peak stared at her, rugged and craggy, with as many crevices and boulders to its features as a nightmare. Even a heavy blanket of snow would not be able to smooth over its countenance, she thought, as she wended her way slowly toward it. A maw of darkness opened toward her, growing larger as she neared it, and she realized it wasn't a shadow cast by a boulder above or to the side, but a cut into the stone, a cave mouth, and she stopped. She could sense water behind it, running below in caverns. She turned her head away from it, tearing herself from the call of it, not wanting to enter. Her heart pounded at the thought. Her boots scuffed over a worn path leading down into it and back the way she'd come, a path she hadn't even realized she'd followed, a depression in the pebbled dirt.

With a sigh, she ducked her head and went inside, the sun at her back to light her way. Once inside, she froze in her tracks, and her breath shuddered in her chest. The sound of the underground river grew louder in her ears, competing with the thunderous drum of her heartbeat. Only the river kept her from bolting her way back, out of the tunnel, out of the dark that threatened to crush her. Her sight wavered.

Oily torches burned fitfully in different anchorings along the way. Carts rumbled up and down the railings, as Stinkers lumbered behind them, pushing. Now and then a slender figure would ride the cart, being brought up from the depths, pickax over a shoulder. She would sit on the cold bank of the river and watch them, and they would never see her. She stayed in nooks and crannies as she'd been taught, and watched a world of shadows go by.

A Stinker fell before her once, dragged by the cart's weight as it rolled back into the cavern, and when he'd stirred with a groan to open his eyes, he'd seen her. She crept out of her hiding spot and gave him a drink of clean water scooped out of the freshets off the main riverbed and tunnels, and then a crust of hard bread from her breakfast. He'd gobbled everything down as if starving and she thought that he was even hungrier than she.

He'd visit now and then after that. She would give him leavings carefully gleaned from her meals, and he would bring her things from outside the caverns. A butterfly, once. A tiny mouse another time. A handful of wildflowers, wilting as soon as picked but still wondrous in her small fist. He came to her once with a frightful burn, a branding, and she'd made ointment from the cold water and mud to put on it to draw out the heat and then, the next day when he came, she'd cleaned it carefully and put a scrap of bandage around it. She'd cried for his pain because he could not.

One day he began bringing her extra sticks for firewood when the caverns grew icy cold and her teeth chattered so she couldn't talk to him easily. At first, she hadn't been sure if it was always the same Stinker, but after he'd been branded, she could tell by the scar on his arm. He wore chains like she did, but he smelled of the wood burning and the hot metals melting and the coppery smell of blood for some reason, and he was not at all like her mother and father.

He played sticks with her when he had a bit of time, and brought small objects to her mother as well, and she looked forward to the brief visits. She had until that day when other Stinkers came to hold her when the shackles were put on.

She felt herself thinning, growing cold, shredding apart like a wisp of a cloud in a high, wind-driven sky. This was where she was made. In such a place, she'd be undone. She thought she felt it beginning.

"Grace?"

Sevryn found her. He wrapped his arms about her chilled body. "Aderro. What are you doing, standing here in the old mine? I thought I'd lost you."

She pointed down into the caverns. "Here. Here is where I started." She began to weep.

Chapter Sixty-Eight

SEVRYN GUIDED HER TO the sunlight, chafing his hands up and down her lightly, worried at the chill emanating from her body. Her shivering came from more than cold, and it was far from cold even this high up this time of day. He wondered if she'd stared her last moment in the face and run from it. He pulled her close to warm her and keep her.

Aymaran trumpeted across the clearing in sudden alarm, throwing his head up. A shower of dirt and gravel rained down from above on the peak and the smell of Bolger enveloped them, that heavy musky sweat. He threw Grace to his left arm as he pulled his katana free. The debris clouded their vision, but the target could be plainly smelled.

The Bolger jumped to the ground in front of them, landing in a crouch and leather vest flapping open as he rose to thump his chest. "Remember," he said. "Rufusss."

He wasn't likely to forget and opened his mouth to tell the Bolger that, but she stopped him with a small cry.

Rivergrace shrugged out of his hold and stumbled forward, catching herself. She put her hand out toward the Bolger and touched his arm, tracing her fingers over the crude branding, a clumped scar, on his forearm. "You brought me flowers and a butterfly."

Sevryn watched and listened to her, realizing that she had pulled recollection out of the caverns.

His green-brown face split into a grin. "This high," he managed, and held his rugged hand just so high off the ground. "You hide in mines. Give me food. Little bites, like you."

She said, "What happened to my mother? My father? I had a family, didn't I?"

His face fell back into its somber expression, twisted by the Bolger tusks which all of them had, though his had been filed down. "You escape. On river, heavy rains." He swung his arm toward the mines. "You gone." He jabbed a thumb at Sevryn. "We capture him. Many years, bad. I wear chains. He wear chains. He run. Big man angry. Tear place apart. I lead hunt. Find you, still this high. I puzzle, but it you. I leave you free. No more chains. Big man burn this place." Rufus threw his head back and stared about the mountain and clearing. "I learn smithing. I earn freedom."

Sevryn said to her softly but pitched clearly for her to hear, and Rufus seemed unaware of his speaking as he did so, "He hasn't a sense of time. He tells the truth, but not in a way we can count on."

She let her breath out in a long sigh. The truth in pieces, a hand-stitched quilt of memories whose journey she could not follow. Yet. She caught Sevryn's hand and held it tightly.

"Do you remember the sword?"

Rufus tore his eyes from her and looked to Sevryn. He gave a nod. "Hungry. Big man call Cerat."

"*Cerat,*" Sevryn repeated. "Drinker, in Vaelinar. Only it means more than that, rather like the night drinks the day, or death drinks life."

"A fell name."

"Yes." Sevryn drew himself up as he made a decision. "We'll go down the mountain and through the lower pass to Larandaril. Come with us, Rufus."

"Watch her?"

"Yes."

"I go."

"We can't go yet." Rivergrace inhaled slowly, holding onto Sevryn's forearm, taking both strength and warmth from him. "I have to see the river."

"Aderro . . ."

"We came for this. I came for this. I can't let it go." She shifted, removing her still-cold hand from his, and retraced her steps into the caverns. Rufus grunted. They had little choice but to follow.

Inside, the Bolger lit torches, old ones, but still so soaked in crude oil that they flared sullenly, and smoky orange halos flared out from them.

Rivergrace walked ahead, her steps so quick and sure, he would have bet she didn't need the torches to see. They kicked through old campsites, evidence of occupation of the most menial kind, remnants of poor attempts to survive. The sound of the underground water grew louder, although it dripped from cave walls everywhere. She headed toward a main canal with a malevolent odor permeating the close air of the caves. They heard her when she stopped because she began to sing in soft, unsure and halting words and melody.

He would not let her end in a place like this. Her destiny to cleanse the water or not, he wouldn't stand by and see her disintegrate to clean up refuse Quendius had left behind. He put his hand on her shoulder to drag her back, to swing her up in his arms and carry her out if need be. Touching her brought him into her line of power. He felt his own senses snap to awareness of her. He knew Vaelinar power, he used it, had had it around him most of the last few decades, freely, unhidden, unfettered, unconstrained, and even in Tressandre's case, unwanted. The touch of her power shocked him. It was and was not Vaelinar. It thrilled through his body and took from him, coaxing, draining, exhilarating, and frightening. Most of all, he could not refuse it. Benevolent but determined, it *would* cleanse this water.

Rivergrace waved her hand. "Move the stones, Rufus."

The Bolger jumped into the black, sluggish pool. He found the sluice and began to turn it or tear it out. Water rose behind it, dammed, runoff from the vats in the forges and the mining operations. He could smell the minerals and oils floating in it. The dam held it back, but not successfully, and kept fresh water from diluting it. She leaned over, combing her hands through the river, always singing and he could not resist her music. Sevryn closed his eyes to feel the golden lines and silver lines in him being spun out and taken. He felt thinner and thinner as they were until he fell to his knees.

"There." Her voice, tired but triumphant, snapped his eyes open. She sat next to him, leaning on him, her body so insubstantial he hadn't felt her weight. As transparent as a ghost, he saw and felt her come back. On the cave flooring, piles of slag and goo glistened in the torchlight, beginning to dry and harden where her hands had combed it from the waters and thrown it aside. Rufus bent his shoulders against the rising current, holding the rotten wood dam in place, and she said, "Get out now. It'll sweep through."

Sevryn gave him a hand up, and wood splintered wetly, and the sluice and dam came apart, water foaming up iridescently in the cavern depths, and swept by them.

They helped each other back out. Sevryn looked at the piles as they passed them, seeing the black and copper and even blood-red rivulets turning into solid heaps of refuse. *That she had done this.*

He knew then that she was meant for the Andredia, that they could lose her yet, and he didn't know how to tell her or how to lead her onward. He put his head down and kissed her forehead, hiding his anguish in the daylight as they emerged.

Chapter Sixty-Nine

"NO WORD FROM SEVRYN?" Lariel stripped off riding gloves as she asked, each tug on the soft leather punctuating her words, her forehead pinched as she did.

"None." Jeredon, already dismounted, gave the reins over on his gray gelding to the horse boy, a wizened, silver-haired elder who always cackled when called by his title.

"Daravan, I could expect this from. We don't hear from or about him for decades, but Sevryn I thought more of. If he's not dead, I might kill him for this." She swung her leg over, jumping down lightly from her tashya mount.

"We don't know what he's doing."

"No. We just know that we're two days from meeting with the weaponsmith and armorer, and that he's nowhere about. He has Gilgarran's stubborn lack of regard for protocol." She reached back and pulled a long hairpin, and her silver-and-gold hair tumbled down to her shoulders and back, freed.

"He's already given you an opinion on that meeting, I believe."

"You disapprove as well."

"I've always found that if you draw a sword, you'd best be prepared and able to use it, for you'll be forced into using it. You know that far better than I. You won the title of warrior."

She gave her reins over to the horse boy who bowed before leading them away to the tether lines. "Jeredon, our home is being destroyed. Slowly, agonizingly, and the Andredia with it. I don't know if they've opened some fell Way into my kingdom or if they're poisoning the waters. I don't even know yet who *they* are. But I won't stand idle. I will destroy them before their work is done."

"You're meeting with Abayan Diort who raises armies in the east." He paced her easily, shortening his long strides to do so, as they crossed the camp toward the pavilion tent of the Captain of Arms, Osten ild Drebukar.

"He isn't the one attacking us. Yet. He's too busy consolidating himself in his homelands, and between us lie the barren stretches of the warlands. You don't bring an army across that lightly, there is no way to live off that land. The logistics alone keep him away from us for the time being." Lariel paused outside the captain's quarters. "It's the man partnered with him that I want to size up, this Quendius."

"And I agree with her," Osten boomed, exiting his pavilion, extending his hands to Lariel. The youngest scion of House Drebukar, his older brothers tied to Istlanthir for the holding of Tomarq, he'd come to Lariel as Captain of Arms, welding their houses together in politics and support. Tall, broad, dark-haired, and green-and-caramel-eyed, his shoulders and arms impressively muscled from years of swinging a sword and lance, he had had little work to do in Larandaril, going back and forth between the two kingdoms, training personal guards mostly. Now, his eyes gleamed with the knowledge that his skills might finally be of use. He rubbed the scar which divided one side of his face from the other, a reminder of an errant blow which had marred his handsome features but not split his skull as intended. It was said to have been a training accident struck by Garran ild Fallyn in defense of his sister, but with that House, one never knew. "Quendius has eluded most of our efforts to find out who he is, what he can do, and where he bases himself, but it seems he's been selling weapons for some time, in defiance of the Accords."

"Which have been laid aside."

"But which, when followed stringently, greatly limited arms manufacture and sales." Osten held the insect netting aside for Lariel as she ducked her head to enter his pavilion.

"It doesn't seem to have deterred either him or Diort."

"No. It will be interesting to see how this partnership of theirs functions, eh? Quendius is a mix of our blood, and Diort's purebred Galdarkan guardianship must boil in him for treating with the weaponsmith." Osten pulled out a campaign chair for his queen and seated Lariel with a flourish.

"I think you thrive on this."

He seated himself, still smiling broadly at Lariel. He adjusted his tabard divided into halves of both Tomarq and Larandaril. "It is your presence I thrive on."

She gave a feminine snort, and he winked at Jeredon. "I hear I have a rival! Bistane hardly left your side during the Conference."

She flicked her fingers at him.

"Enough teasing," Jeredon muttered. "We enter the site day after tomorrow at high sun, and what do we expect?"

"We expect them to already be camped and waiting, with wagons and crates of the goods they intend to supply. I'll be posting the men tomorrow as we move into the area, and the day of, I'll inspect the cargo. Tiiva will be there for an accounting, and we'll dicker on the prices."

Lady Tiiva had already retired for the evening. Despite her affinity for hunting jaunts, her delicate constitution did not lend itself well to trips of this sort, it seemed, and they'd made a forced march to keep this appointment. Lariel had found only a few days of peace at home after fleeing the Conference, when this meet had been set up. He tapped a broad finger on the fold-up table beside Lariel. "Jeredon will be making his way through their entourage, seeing the quality of the weapons on his men, and the maker."

"You think they will sell us inferior goods?"

"I think they may well try. Not inferior, per se, this Quendius seems to be adept at what he does, but not up to the quality of their own arms. We'll make our deal and depart."

"Giving us what?"

"Enough arms and armor for a start, and enough intelligence to deter any surprises. The best offense, m'lady, has always been a good defense as you've been well versed to know."

Jeredon crossed his booted ankles as he stretched out in his chair. "I think we ought to just wipe them out, then and there. Save us trouble later."

Osten shook his head slowly, his thick dark hair waving about his head like a mane. "They could be allies later. I expect we'll be fencing with them now and then, but my gut tells me they're not the enemy we need to brace for."

"No insult to your gut, Osten, but none of the younger among us have really been in warfare. What does Bistel's gut tell him? That's what we need to know."

"Other than giving us stories of a living skeleton wielding a bloodthirsty sword, Bistel has been remarkably quiet," Osten answered Jeredon.

"He's Bistel Vantane, of Hith-aryn. We should never discount what he tells us."

Lara said quietly, "That's enough. I won't go through this argument with either of you again. There will be a war, a great war, and we must be prepared to see it through."

"You can't know that. And, if you insist on pressing it, your words become a self-fulfilling prophecy."

Her mouth tightened and thinned. "I'll send you from my side, Jeredon, if need be. No arguments."

Osten cleared his throat in the awkward silence. Lariel stood. "I'll leave you two to discuss how big a detail we take in with us and how to scout through their camp discreetly. Curse Sevryn's hide. This is his business."

The two men stared at each other after she'd gone.

"Do you think she's wrong?" asked Jeredon, finally.

"I think," Osten answered deliberately, "that none of us know what magic Lariel works, but it runs in her blood just as yours and mine does in ours, and she holds her title justifiably. I look forward to interesting times."

Jeredon grunted before venturing, "I don't suppose you brought some good, hard liquor with you? It doesn't even have to be good, frankly."

Shouting jolted her awake from a deep and thankfully dreamless sleep. Lariel sat up in her cot as the tumult surrounded her small tent. She did not use a pavilion as Osten did, preferring to keep her presence in any camp relatively unmarked, but it seemed the commotion raged about her. She grabbed her sheathed sword and strode outside, blinking in the flaring light of torches.

Guards immediately surrounded her. "Assassins on the grounds, m'lady."

She looked through a wall of muscular flesh, trying to spot Jeredon. She finally saw him at the torchlit edge of camp, arrow fitted to his bow, ready to sight on whatever target presented itself. Osten's booming voice shouted orders that cut through the noise and quieted it, so she refrained as he took charge. She turned slowly inside the circle of guards, but the nightfall revealed nothing to her beyond the illumination. A three-quarter moon hung silvery in the sky, and she would have preferred to see by that alone. The torches made her feel more vulnerable.

"What happened?"

"One of the watch is down, garroted. Body still warm and twitching."

"Who found him?"

"Your brother, on the way to the latrines. He wasn't supposed to be found till morning, if at all."

Or he was supposed to have been found quickly, she thought, lying on the path to the latrines was hardly out of the way. She continued her examination of the outskirts of the camp, fires out for the night, the scattered groves they had camped between, the Andredia lying not far away.

She paused, a fierce burning at the back of her neck. Lara pivoted nonchalantly as if still searching in vain, but her gaze fell on a small stand of trees just beyond the tether lines and far from the latrine trenches. A shadow separated itself from other shadows, swathed in black, and she felt his eyes meet with hers. A black-gloved hand saluted her, and then the Kobrir was gone, swallowed up by the element that favored him most.

Lara took a deep breath. "Stand down," she said. It would be worse than useless to send anyone after him, for the camp would empty and she would be even more exposed, perhaps a desired result. "Whoever it was is gone." She pushed her way through the guards, calling out, "Osten! Tell everyone to stand down!"

He had begun to bellow out her wishes when a new riot started by the horse-lines. The grunts and thuds of fists hitting flesh and the sound of scuffling carried. This was hardly the Kobrir's style and why would he double back? she thought, and headed that way, guards thundering on her heels. A higher-pitched voice cried out, "We know her! M'lady queen! Rivergrace is missing!"

A short, determined form separated from the fray, flinging herself on Lariel, knocking both of them to the dirt. Osten lunged at them, whipping out his blade to lie across the throat of her attacker. Nutmeg blinked in amazement at the sword slicing between them.

"Hold!" sputtered Lariel, fighting for breath under the sturdy Dweller.

"I suggest you don't move, lass, because I'm not withdrawing," Osten rumbled at his hostage, his damaged face scowling downward.

Nutmeg, atop Lariel, froze.

"Withdraw," Lariel told her captain as she began to wiggle free.

The blade removed with great reluctance and Osten held it loose, not sheathing it. Jeredon brought up a second Dweller hooked by the elbow, tall and slight comparatively for Dweller stock, who commented wryly to his coconspirator, "Nutmeg. You can't tackle a queen."

"I didn't mean to! I was throwing myself on her mercy!"

"And knocking both of us on our duffs." Lariel straightened her nightdress and dusted herself off.

"I take it you know these two." Osten began to sheathe his greatsword, sliding it in very slowly.

"This is Nutmeg Farbranch and this, I suspect, is another of her many brothers."

Garner bowed as well as he could, one arm still tightly hooked with Jeredon's. "Garner Farbranch, m'lady Lariel."

"Neither of them is tall enough to have garroted Frink, so I'll post a walking guard and advise you in the morning." Osten saluted her.

"Do that." Lariel knew they would not have another encounter tonight, but her men needed to know of the concern and measures they would take.

"You have a man down?" Garner, whose resemblance to Nutmeg was not easily visible particularly in his sardonic expression, nudged his prone sister with a toe, adding, "You can get up now."

"Yes. His body was found just before your appearance."

"That would explain our welcome." Garner eyed Jeredon, sizing him up. To his sister, he mouthed, "Impressive."

Nutmeg blushed. Flustered, she worked on setting her blouse and traveling skirt to rights, as Garner continued, "We thought someone had crossed our trail a few times, but never caught sight of him. He's quiet and clever, but even so flushed a bird now and then."

"You're lucky you didn't see him. It likely would have been the last you looked upon." Jeredon slung his bow over his shoulder. "That does not, however, explain why you're here, skulking in the middle of the night."

"We were NOT skulking." Nutmeg's stomach growled loudly in emphasis.

Lariel laughed. "And that explains what they're doing here in the middle of the night. Come on, I'll have a table set, you can talk, we'll listen, and you'll tell me why Rivergrace is missing."

* * *

Talk waited a short bit till Garner and Nutmeg had plenty of food in front of them and Jeredon, sent out to take care of their horse and pony, returned to listen to the tale, for Nutmeg seemed loath to say anything without his being there. Nutmeg ate as if starved, while Garner watched her with a twinkle in his eyes, letting his sister grab the first of the foods laid out for them, and waiting till she'd gobbled some down before fixing his own plate. Jeredon watched, too, his face twitching slightly.

She looked up to see the two men eyeing her. "Oh," she retorted to their silent appraisal. "It's fine for you to not go hungry. You'll eat raw fish." She shuddered.

"Raw fish became a necessity when you dropped the flints into the river."

"That wasn't my fault. You said there was a snake creeping up on me!"

"You did jump."

"And the flints jumped with me!" She blotted the corners of her mouth delicately with a napkin and sat back. Jeredon watched with a kind of fascination.

"Farbranches," Lariel intervened calmly. "I think we need to know what this is about Rivergrace and why you're so far afield seeking her."

"She's disappeared."

"When?"

"The day before the riots, as close as we can reckon. Sevryn asked our brother Hosmer to bring her to him, and she never came back."

Jeredon swapped a look with Lariel. "Where," he asked quietly, "was she supposed to meet him?"

"A hospice, a hospital. Something like that."

"They went back to see Azel again." Lariel grasped on the first thing that made any sense at all.

"He never mentioned it."

"Azel wouldn't. He treats visits to him for information with utmost confidentiality. He's a librarian, a historian. He would do that." Lariel added to Jeredon, "Send a bird to him, see if he'll confirm it. I am a bit surprised, though. I didn't think Rivergrace would ever go back after what he told her."

Nutmeg leaned over to pinch a piece of fruit off Garner's plate since hers was now empty. "That's the fellow who read her blanket?"

"Yes. The . . . mmm . . . fellow."

"She wouldn't talk about him, other than to say he'd nearly died, and he seemed a gentle man. He said her scrap was part of a betrothal blanket or wedding blanket, and most of it was torn away. She cried about it and wouldn't talk to us. We let her think about it. Sometimes you have to let Rivergrace be alone." Nutmeg licked her fingers of the juicy fruit matter-of-factly.

Lariel looked at the two Dwellers, pondering her choice of words. Jeredon, out of their view as their attention fixed on her face, shook his head slightly. She agreed silently with her brother. Rivergrace's revelation to her family was her decision to make, and it seemed she had decided not to tell them of her true self. Lariel would leave it that way unless there came a time when she had no choice but to tell them of their adopted daughter's destiny. "You came after them with no idea where they might have gone?"

"We thought of two places, our home on the Silverwing, and your kingdom, Highness," Garner said as he slapped away Nutmeg's hand hovering to steal a piece of nut bread from his plate. "We saw some tracks toward the Nylara, but nothing beyond that, and turned for here. It's a long ride, and your borders are sealed. We couldn't pierce Larandaril."

"It is that. No one treads upon the kingdom without a badge for passage or unless it's opened to them. However, I can't send you home just yet either. We've not seen or heard from Sevryn ourselves, but I can't spare anyone for a search party now. I've a diplomatic meeting high sun after tomorrow. You'll accompany us, stay quiet, and watch closely. These men are neither friends nor enemies, but I need your silence about them, lest you reveal something you shouldn't. After the meet, Jeredon will take a handful of men and supplies, and we'll go looking. Agreed?"

"Very generous of you, Highness," Garner told her and bowed over his plate.

"Speaking of generous." Nutmeg looked at them hopefully. "Is there any more nut bread about?"

Chapter Seventy

SEVRYN DASHED COLD WATER on his face, washing away grit and the odor of woodsmoke, and bringing him alert. He stayed crouched by the river, looking at the range of Blackwinds rising just to the north of him. The Blackwinds joined to the Burning Mountains and then arched to the high Heaven's Teeth to the northeast, but it was the Blackwinds which drew his intense scrutiny. They crowned Larandaril and he was in those lands, and thought of what they'd often said of the queen . . . that she knew whenever anyone stepped into her kingdom. He knew she did not, but he wished it were true now.

Rufus had told him of wagons and coaches moving through the trader passes along the edge of the Blackwind, headed to the northern tip of Larandaril, and so they had come here, but for what reason, he wasn't sure. He did not quite trust Rufus who never explained why he'd been watching smugglers or why he wanted Sevryn to know about them, for that matter, but in his halting manner, he'd informed Sevryn. Caravans taking that route ran a risk of crossing the Blackwind runners as well as bandits, villagers displaced by Lariel when she moved towns off the borders years ago hoping to forestall the contamination of her lands. Neither would be pleasant encounters. Those risks might be run if snow had cut off other passes or wildfire by lightning strikes closed the lower routes, but he couldn't see a reason to take the Blackwind road in these days. More likely these were smugglers who'd chosen to come down out of the same range he wished to head into. He debated his options.

Rufus gave a hissing whistle behind him. The Bolger could move quietly if he wished, very quietly, and knew to stay downwind. Moving to the riverbank, he jabbed a hand toward the sky to the west. Narrowing his eyes, Sevryn saw what the other did: a faint hawk on the wind, circling to get its bearings as if just taking to the air or being released. Jeredon fancied red-tails for messengers. Could he be hunting nearby? Sevryn argued with himself whether he wished to meet with Jeredon yet or not. If smugglers were moving along the far border of Larandaril, he ought to know what they might be carrying when he did ride on to meet with the queen. She'd be furious with him as it was. He nodded to Rufus that he'd seen the bird. Another took wing right after it, and he knew then it was Jeredon. He always sent two messages out. The only question now was where the hawks headed. North or northeast? Could be any of four or five holdings. If he was with them, at the queen's side where he belonged, he'd know where they were sent, and why.

No, this matter of belonging had changed for him. Rivergrace did not divide his loyalties, she fulfilled them.

He'd taken his own path, and would walk it.

He wiped his hands on his trousers. "I think we'll head up into the Blackwinds a bit. I want to see what that caravan is all about."

Rufus grunted noncommittally. He washed himself, a brief splash in the water before they trudged back to mount up. Rivergrace had already bathed, from head to toe it seemed, her chestnut hair glistening wetly on her shoulders. She smiled brightly and he felt taller. He knew the feeling couldn't stay, but he treasured the moments he had.

Treasuring moments with biting insects, however, was not what he had in mind. Grass ants found their way inside his shirt and began biting as he lay on his stomach and he responded by clamping down on the inside of his cheek to stifle his anger, but it wasn't the ants which infuriated him. He looked down from his perch at the encampment, his throat closing and his mouth going sour. He couldn't mistake the tall, heavily muscled figure of charcoal gray moving among the wagons, bellowing though he could not hear the words, cuffing those who did not move fast enough. He should take the bastard out now, but he needed to know why Quendius camped at Larandaril's edge. Bold as brass, he strode across the foothills of the Blackwinds, his camp aimed toward the borders of the kingdom, without trespassing, but menacing. The sun lowered on the horizon and soon would be dipping into dusk, and he'd get close then. In the meantime, he slid his hand inside his shirt, viciously pinching and crushing whatever ants he could reach and scratching away the others.

He concentrated on balance and clean thought, fighting back the rage that fountained inside him. Gilgarran would have his ears for losing control. *The ild Fallyns,* he'd coached, *are sadistic with a purpose. The pain and anger they wreak brings loss of control and discipline, all to their advantage. That they enjoy it is merely a bonus to them. Remember that.* Only one of his many lessons about control. Nothing was to be gained by that, by the rage, except giving Quendius an advantage the murdering son of a bitch didn't need. Quendius moved in constant anger and domination but everything he did was calculated. Besides, he enjoyed it as well, and that fact roiled in Sevryn's newly regained memories.

He watched as two men struggled with a long, willowy post and then got it set into the ground, a banner unfurling into the wind. The bronze eagle of Abayan Diort over the sun of Galdarkan Guardians rode the air under a flag of treaty, and Sevryn drew back. Now he understood why they were there, and why Jeredon had been close by.

They were readying to meet with Lariel.

Did she know who Diort carried for a partner?

Worse, would she care?

He crawled backward till he could safely stand, then he swatted himself free of ants, cursing freely, until his rage thinned enough that he dared to return and face Rivergrace. As he passed Rufus, he grabbed the Bolger by the flap of his vest.

"You knew."

Rufus widened his stance for balance. He bobbed his head once.

"Next time, I'll kill you first, then kill him."

The Bolger's leathery face split in that wide ear-to-ear, hideous grin. "You can try." He grunted and shrugged out of Sevryn's hold.

Rivergrace stood by Black Ribbon, scratching her chin and singing a made-up song about sun and river and fishing birds as she waited. She stopped when she saw the anger on Sevryn's face. "What is it?"

"We ride," he said, "in hopes of catching the queen before she does something incredibly stupid."

She did not ask what he thought stupid, but only, "Have we a chance of catching her?"

"If we ride the night. Stay close, let Ribbon pick her way. We'll ride hard till the sun sets, then we've no choice but to slow. But I won't be stopping till I find them." He pulled Aymaran about, hard, with a jerk on the reins that made the horse whinny in pain, a sound Sevryn ignored.

Rufus mounted his hardened wiry mountain pony and waited for Rivergrace. He took up the rear, not using reins but his knees to guide the pony, his hands cradling a short bow, and his flint-dark eyes alert.

Rivergrace hugged one slender arm about herself, skin still damp from her washing, with the faint taint of the Andredia clinging to her, as they rode. Worse than the Silverwing in its foulness though not as strong . . . she could not begin to explain to Sevryn what she felt in it, what she feared in it. Dipping her hands into it, her being had dissolved away, into the river, and she reeled herself back only with great effort, losing herself, with no way to help it or herself. She would not touch the Andredia again, that sacred river, unless forced. She could not. She would follow Sevryn all the days that she had left and pray they were many, even for one of Vaelinar blood, but never would she draw water from the Andredia again.

The moon hung high above them as night came, not yet full but so bright and silvery she could see her shadow on the ground as they rode. Ribbon chuffed and tried to snatch clumps of grass whenever they slowed, grumbling that she hungered and her smooth gait roughened as she tired. Grace rubbed the mare's neck in sympathy, fighting to keep her eyes open despite the occasional jolt as the horse's body shifted suddenly. She must have fallen asleep anyway, jerked back to her senses as Sevryn's horse shouldered into them, and he swept an arm about her waist, lifting her effortlessly onto Aymaran in front of him. She sat sideways against him, his arm still about her, and he murmured to her, warm breath tickling her face, "Lean against me and sleep, aderro."

She did, with his voice echoing in her dreams. They dissolved into a comforting nothingness.

"Derro, derro!"

Hands pulled, yanking her about roughly as they dragged her down. She fought to stay with Sevryn but he let her go. She thrashed as they captured her, arms about her neck squeezing, choking . . . hugging the life out of her.

"Sister, derro!"

A face salty wet with tears meshed against hers, crying happily, and Rivergrace surrendered to it, throwing her arm about her captor, saying only, "Let me breathe!" Nutmeg responded by adjusting her arms about Grace's ribs and squeezing even harder.

She could hear Garner's dry voice saying, "I tell you what. Got a deck? I'll cut you the cards for her," with Sevryn quietly declining.

"Surely she's more valuable than that. I'll trade you a fine tashya horse for her."

"Jeredon!" Nutmeg let go of her long enough to pinch someone from the aggrieved yelp and then a hearty laugh.

Rivergrace found her own feet to stand on, gathering her balance and wits, surrounded by bodies.

"A welcome I hadn't counted on."

Jeredon thumped Sevryn's shoulder. "Not for you. You'd best practice ducking, for when my sister comes for you, you'll need it."

Sevryn beckoned at Garner. "Get that deck, and I'll cut you to see who talks with Queen Lariel."

"I won't gamble with those odds."

Lariel strode across the field, dressed in rich blue-and-green hunting attire, and the storm in her eyes could be plainly seen. "Clear the camp," she ordered, drawing her sword. "You gambled with my trust and my offer of service. Now let us see if you can fight your way back!" Ice encased every word.

Jeredon took Rivergrace by one elbow and Nutmeg by the other, hauling them out of the way as Sevryn took a stumbling step in disbelief, putting his hand to his sword hilt but not pulling it. She bore down on him and swung, sword whistling sharply through the air as it barely missed him, and the follow-through took her about in a clean circle. He drew then.

"What are they doing?"

"I believe they're sword fighting," Jeredon answered Rivergrace. "We'd best give them a wide area to settle it." He reinforced that by pulling them a bit farther away with him, Garner at his heels. Troops surrounding them fell into a respectful quiet, no offhand bets on who might win and who might fall, as if sensing the queen's deadly mood. A tall, hulking Vaelinar with an immense scar dividing his face nearly in two crossed his arms and leveled his gaze on them to watch. He looked as if he had the strength to break it up if he wished, but he made not a move other than observing.

Sevryn did not answer her blows with strikes of his own, but countered and parried. The swords clanged and belled with every hit and when they did not, when the blades hissed through the air, Rivergrace cringed, not knowing what force or flesh would halt them. She taxed him. Rivergrace could see that clearly, that Lariel knew swordwork and had the strength to wield hers quickly, cleanly, and deadly.

The queen wove her anger into a dance of blue and green, gold and silver glints of lightning. Sevryn held her off, his blows getting sluggish, his steps less sure. She saw the strain on his face, and held her breath for him, knowing if she made a noise or a move, he would know it, and any lessening of his concentration could be fatal.

Rivergrace had no doubt that Queen Lariel would strike a killing blow if she found the opening. Jeredon's hand tightened on her with a bruising grip, every muscle in his body rigid with tension. He thought so, too. She did not want to look but could not tear her eyes away.

"You . . . leave . . . my . . . service . . . when I tell you to!" Lariel slashed diagonally, catching his sleeve as he dodged, sucking in his gut and jerking his head back, and a sound of pain escaped him. "You would leave for a moment that cannot last? Her destiny is death!"

He struck back then, driving in on her before she could recover from the blow, their swords locking crosswise, his hand pinioning hers at the hilt, finding strength in his fury. "How dare you take away from what we have! How dare you tell me when I can and cannot love!"

They strained at one another, and Lariel gave way when Nutmeg uttered a gasp. She dropped her sword to take one deep, heaving breath and then sheathed her weapon. She looked at Grace and then to Nutmeg. "I am sorry," she said.

"What do you mean? What does she mean?" Nutmeg said, and pulled Grace about to face her.

"It's nothing." She could feel the day's heat pounding down on her, her pulse still thundering from watching Sevryn dance on the edge of his death, and her senses reeled.

"Don't tell me that!"

Rivergrace looked down at her sister, her rescuer, her pillar of strength and practicality. She put her hand to Nutmeg's rosy cheek. "Someone has told a bad fortune for me. But we don't believe in fortune-tellers, do we?"

"Never," Nutmeg said stoutly. "Never if it takes us apart." She held onto Rivergrace tightly. Grace looked into the other's spice brown eyes and tried to forgive herself for lying to her sister.

Above them, a flaming arrow arched into a too-blue sky.

"My appointment waits," said Lariel. She strode her to horse, Osten holding the bridle for her to mount. "Do you attend me, Sevryn?"

"I always have, but you cannot meet with Quendius and Abayan Diort. That road leads to disaster. I left you because I found one of the answers to the Four Forges. I've been up to where Gilgarran met his death at the hands of a weaponsmith, m'lady queen, and where I lost many years. Bistel does not tell tales. Quendius forged a weapon there, a weapon that—" He paused, realizing what Azel d'Stanthe must have been about to tell him before the Kobrir struck his blow at their ill-fated meeting. How could he not know what Azel's next words should have been? Every world has its balance, and if there are Ways to life, then the opposite would be as true. "A weapon, Lariel, that is a Way unto itself, a Way leading to death and beyond."

"We don't construct such a thing."

"He has."

"He's a half-breed, and no one has ever reported a power within him."

"He wouldn't be the first half-breed overlooked," he told her quietly.

Her hands twitched on her reins. She beckoned to all of them. "We make the appointment. We look. Listen. Learn." She wheeled her horse to the crest of the foothill leading to the Blackwinds and stood alone, the wind at her back, waiting for them.

Jeredon tossed Rivergrace and Nutmeg aboard their horses, while Sevryn stood, head lowered, to suck in air deeply. He came to her, and put his chin on her knee, Aymaran trailing at his back with a puzzled whicker as he stayed afoot.

"Whatever happens, know that I love you."

She wiped the sweat from his face with her fingertips, then brushed his hair from his brow. "As I love you."

"Then that is all that matters." He kissed her hand before swinging about and mounting his horse.

The Vaelinar woman with copper skin and the great man with the scar joined them at the hill's edge, Garner bringing up the rear, eight in all, and they rode up northward till they saw the banner unfurled and rippling in the air. Rivergrace felt the noblewoman with the brilliant green eyes look upon her, and uneasiness built. It was not the same one who'd come to the shop, and yet . . . she could not name the fear that prickled at the back of her neck each time the copper Vaelinar's gaze swept her.

Nutmeg rode Bumblebee. He bumped Rivergrace's boot with his nose and teeth as if seeking her attention, and she laughed in spite of herself, leaning over to scratch his forelock.

Jeredon paced Nutmeg on the other side. "That one is like a great dog," he said.

"He is a pony whose heart makes him so stout."

"Indeed? I would have thought that came from his stomach." Jeredon dodged away from Nutmeg, put his heels to his sleek tashya horse, and dashed forward to join his sister.

Nutmeg knotted her fingers in Bumblebee's mane. "No one," she told him, "thinks their horse is better than you."

He snorted and whisked his heavy tail in agreement, as they slowed to a trot, approaching a circle of tents and wagons, with heavy wooden crates piled on the ground, men working at opening them with heavy iron crowbars. She could smell the dark iron on the air as they entered.

"Queen Lariel. You are prompt."

"I have much pressing business." She dismounted as Abayan Diort came forward to hold her horse for her, his Galdarkan height just above hers, his bronzed body gleaming in the sunlight. "Tiiva, get a count."

The copper Vaelinar slid off to unsling a satchel from her saddle, taking out a bound book and writing instruments, and began to walk among the crates. Jeredon and Sevryn stayed at the edge of the camp, their attention alert, taking in all they saw about them.

Rivergrace suddenly thought that Rufus was not among them. She swiveled about in her saddle, looking back, and realized he had not been in the queen's camp. Had he faded off during the night?

Sevryn caught her eye, his eyebrow quirking. She thumped her chest as Rufus often did. He lifted a shoulder and dropped it in a shrug. He had no idea either.

"Taking a count before we've even talked offers?" Quendius rose from a great leather campaign chair, gold-braided leathers strapping it together, giving it a look of more than just a folding chair. A rich tawny fur upholstered it, with stripes of ebony upon it, the like of which Rivergrace had never seen. Behind its back, barely seen, a tall, thin man stood, as sparely dressed as he was fleshed.

"She can work while we talk." Lariel gripped the forearm of Quendius with her own, a warrior's shake. "You seem able to meet my needs."

The weaponmaker towered even over the hulking Vaelinar captain of the scarred face. His skin of ash gray set off eyes of the same color, flecked with shards of black, like splinters of darkness growing in his appraisal as he looked at her, then swept a perfunctory gaze over them, dismissing all save Tiiva. He watched her for a moment then looked to Lariel. "I am able to meet many needs," he said, sinking back into his chair.

"Not observing the Accords?"

"M'lady, if everyone observed the Accords, only the lawless would have weapons, and we'd be under their bootheels. Besides, I understand they've been set aside."

"You've enough gear here to conquer a nation of lawless."

Quendius smiled, and his eyes stayed cold, the black splinters growing darker. "Whatever it takes."

Lara tapped her sword belt. "Shall we talk quantity and pricing, then?"

Rivergrace began to ignore them as their voices dropped into a drone, counting the army, breaking it into infantry, archers, cavalry, and their various needs, none of which she could grasp save that Abayan Diort, his handsome face tattooed with rings and bars and insignias brought out men dressed and armed in gear, as if to show Lariel just what they were selling for each. Perhaps they were.

She could feel Nutmeg shift her weight back and forth, forth and back, in a tiny, unconscious dance of impatience beside her. Sevryn and Jeredon split into different directions, traversing the camp. Quendius saw them, and said nothing, but the mercenary Diort's attention was riveted on them. Tiiva moved from crate to crate, Lariel's Captain of Arms assisting her as they inspected the goods within, her pen moving quickly as she made notations. Garner had stayed with the horses, and she could hear him whispering gently to them, a nonstop stream of soothing noises. An eerie sense of timelessness dropped upon Rivergrace's shoulders.

Lariel stood. "Negotiations seem completed. I'll have a look at the goods myself, and we will send contracts and payment to you when we're done scribing them, if we decide to deal." She crooked a finger at Jeredon and Sevryn who'd regrouped, and Rivergrace looked at his face, smooth and expressionless, and he did not look back at her.

"It's as I advised," Sevryn told her.

She frowned.

Quendius rose behind Lariel. With him came the thin man, nearly as tall as he, a sword at his back. They passed Rivergrace by a step and she could hear a high-pitched whine emanating from the blade, and a cold shiver lanced through her. This was the thing Sevryn had feared, had warned of. *Cerat*, Rufus named it. Souldrinker.

The weaponmaker nodded to Abayan Diort who put his back to the pavilion. "We should deal now."

"I like to think upon contracts as weighty as this," she said to him, over her shoulder. Tiiva moved away from a wooden box of weapons, her hand still on her papers.

Lariel leaned over the nearest crate, lifting a lance, saying, "It seems porous and not well tempered. Is this the best you can smith?" She looked up at Quendius.

He beckoned his hand to his shadow. "No. This is. Narskap."

Cerat sprang free from its sheath, leaping into the thin man's hands, arching toward Lariel. She cried out, then, a warning leaping to her lips. "Remember the soul!"

She saw Sevryn move after his queen. Heard him say, in a Voice unlike any she'd ever heard him use before, "*Strike me.*" He arched toward Lariel.

Cerat shuddered in its wielder's hands, then curved away from its intended path, and came down on Sevryn with a screeching like that of metal grinding metal.

Rivergrace screamed. She felt her throat tear with her agony as Sevryn dropped, twitching, his death cry one of purest pain and fear. The sword twisted in him, drinking of all that he had been and ever would be.

From under a wagon, a brown-and-green leathery form erupted, charging at the swordsman, face contorted in a growl. Rufus tackled him. Cerat pulled sluggishly from its drinking, falling to the crimson-splattered dust as it tore away from its wielder's hold. She saw all this as everyone erupted into motion about her. The great Captain of Arms shoved Lariel against a wagon, arming himself, and Jeredon unslung his bow with a shout.

Rivergrace put her hand out and took up the howling sword. It shook violently in her hand, and she laced one over the other to hold it. It tried to jump from her, and she clenched it tightly. She could feel Sevryn in it, being swallowed, disappearing mote by mote, and she sobbed as he left her. She pulled the sword up. Its hunger lanced through her, white hot with rage and lust and need. It burned and she could hear someone screaming and screaming, high thin voice over that of the sword's howl, and the agony of her throat told her that she was the one screaming.

It would drink. It would kill and feed. She existed only to take it where it could.

The metal seared her hands. Rivergrace put the point in the dirt at her feet, driving it into the ground, giving it only dust to swallow. Pain pierced her shoulder, and she lifted her face to look into that of the swordsman, the bones in his face so sharp in relief, it was like looking into a skull.

Rivergrace spat at him like a cat. His hands clawed at the back of hers, and then he collapsed with a surprised sound as Nutmeg hefted and broke the massive campaign chair over his head. Abayan shoved her aside, grabbing the prone man and dragging him off. Osten ild Drebukar let out a roar, and the hillside below thundered with Lariel's cavalry, waiting for trouble and heeding his call. A trumpet sounded. Quendius shouted orders. In moments the smugglers had fled, routed, the wagons cut loose and hoofbeats stirring up a cloud of dust that hid their retreat, cavalry on their heels hoping to catch stragglers.

Osten pulled Lariel to her feet.

He knocked the lid off an unopened crate with his heavy boot. Naught lay inside but straw.

"They showed you enough to bait you," he said.

"That doesn't matter." Lariel moved over to Sevryn's body, and she looked across at Rivergrace. "How can you hold such a thing?"

"How can I not," she answered bitterly. "It is the last of my love." And she walked away, dragging Cerat in the dirt behind her.

Chapter Seventy-One

THEY PREPARED A PYRE, dashed with the sweetest of oils, in order to give Rufus a burial as the greatest of Bolger clansmen would receive, for defending Grace and knocking the sword from its wielder, but they could not find his body when they went back to get it. She searched and searched, and finally stopped, defeated. Quendius had left none of his dead behind.

She watched Jeredon wash and tend to Sevryn's body, the tiny nearby brook a tributary to the great Andredia, but she would not approach, her own body numb and cold as ice despite the sun beating down as Lariel and Jeredon took their leave of him. "He comes back with us," Lariel told her. "We are his House, and his family, and he'll be buried with honor in our lands." Jeredon wrapped the lifeless form gently and lashed it over Aymaran's saddle to be taken back to Larandaril. The tashya stallion fussed and stamped his hooves, shying away once or twice from the smell of the dead before he finally allowed Jeredon to burden him. She made no sound at all except her own hoarse breathing through her ragged throat as he did so. The coppery smell of hot blood faded but a little. Over it, she could smell the corruption of the brook trickling down to the Andredia. She could taste the wrongness as well as death in the air. It hurt her every fiber to inhale.

Lariel sent her army downhill with the Lady Tiiva, Osten ild Drebukar leading Aymaran to Larandaril, and finally laid her eyes of cobalt blue and gold and silver on her gently. "Come home with us."

Rivergrace shook her head.

"Where will you go now?"

She dragged the tip of the sword up and pointed northward, into the Blackwinds. "The Andredia."

Lara's face paled even as she straightened her body. "Rivergrace, I can't ask any more of you than you've already given."

"You don't ask it of me! I was meant for this. Sevryn knew it. He tried to tell me, and there is no reason now for me to try to stay."

"Grace." Nutmeg put her hand on her arm. "There's every reason for you to stay. Sevryn meant you to live."

Rivergrace looked down at Nutmeg, seeing her merry face streaked with blood and dirt, and a garish bruise across her jaw, her brown eyes clouded with worry. "I can cleanse the river," she told Nutmeg. "It starts up there, and works its way down here, and all that is pure about the river is poisoned. He had forges in the mountains, Meg, pulling Demons from their most fiery hells and branding them into the steel. He used the river to tame them, quench them, make them so that he could bind them. He used Silverwing and then the sacred Andredia, and it calls to me. I was meant for this."

Nutmeg rubbed her arm. "You've always answered the river's calls. Well, if you're going, so am I."

"You don't understand."

"No. You've not told me everything, but this I know. We're family, and that means all the sorrow, all the joy, woven together. You need us, and we're here."

Garner seconded his sister.

"I can't take anyone with me. The sword. I don't know how long I can hold the sword back." Her arm shook a little and she let it fall point first, to lean upon again.

"You won't strike any of us," Nutmeg said confidently.

Lariel inclined her head in thought a moment. When she lifted it, she said, "The Andredia is my trust. The Way is imprinted in me, though I've never been there. You won't get there without me, and, Gods help me, I will drop you, Rivergrace, before you murder those you love."

Rivergrace looked into her eyes for a long time, then murmured, "Thank you."

Jeredon stirred. "Lariel . . ."

She shook her head at him. "No, like Rivergrace, this is what was meant for me. Our House made this pact, and you know it stands violated now. It was a long time ago, and we didn't know it. It happened on my watch, and I saw the signs, and I didn't know what they meant. I can only pray it's not too late. In the morning, I'll know the trail there."

He stood, standing over his sister, and put his hand on her head, ruffling her gold-and-silver hair. "Then we all go."

"You're the heir. You have to return."

"I'll return when it's all done and finished, and not before, and we won't be needing an heir." He looked at the smoke staining the slope as the pyre burned, and the smoke trailed downhill from them, but they could still smell the death in it. "In the morning."

"He sleeps. Finally." Quendius sat on the cold ground beside Diort.

"Put him out of his misery."

"There will come a day when he will craft another sword for me."

"Is that how you use us all? Till there is nothing left?

"Is that not how flesh and bone and soul are meant to be used? Molded to a destiny?"

He would argue with that, but he could not as it rather fit his own philosophy from time to time. Instead, he asked, "Why did you decide to kill Lariel Anderieon?"

"She came not to buy but to divide us. Did you not watch her actions? Did you not see her toting up our strengths and our weaknesses? And just think what a great sword Cerat would have been with her soul imbuing it."

"Lost to us instead."

"We will have it back. Even now, he works to return it to me. He is bonded to it, and it calls to him, if he doesn't die of the agony of his loss first. He will be a relentless hound upon its trail. Never underestimate Narskap."

"Then what? What of my hammer?

Quendius did not answer him immediately, then replied with a question of his own. "Tell me, Abayan, what was the last great war fought in these lands?"

Diort had been fingering the scars and tattoos on his cheek and stopped to turn his eye upon Quendius. "You know as well as I do."

"Remind me." Quendius crossed his ankles and returned the stare.

"The battles of the Magi that created the warlands."

"Who won?"

"None of the Magi. The Gods came down to crush them for their powers, for the destruction brought upon the land and the people. They left the land scarred, so we'd never forget. Some say the Raymy wars were greater, or the Bolger wars, but the Gods did not cut us off because of those battles. No. The Magi created hell even as they created magic."

"And if I start such a war, do you think the Gods will notice me?"

"Is that what you want, Quendius? The Gods to notice you? Why not pray at a shrine?"

"You mistake my ambition, Diort. I don't want to be a tickle upon Their senses or a whispered plea in Their ear. I want Their full and undivided attention, and I will get it by defeating Them or becoming One of Them myself. I'll have nothing less, or destroy what's left of Their precious lands trying." He smiled wryly. "I began with the Andredia."

"To what end?"

"They will deal with me, or Return me," Quendius told him.

Unsure if he dealt with a man of brilliance or insanity, Diort changed the subject. "I did not bring Bistel Hith-aryn after you."

"No, I don't think you did. You're pardoned, Abayan. Your war hammer lies in the packs off the spotted gelding." Quendius waved him off. "Go get it, and sleep on plans of vengeance."

Diort moved away, leaving Quendius staring down the mountainside, pondering the improbable. One of Lariel's entourage had retrieved the sword, a sword that no one but Narskap could wield, not even himself.

How?

And why.

In the night, Rivergrace woke once, to hear Jeredon and Lariel arguing, their voices pitched low, Jeredon pleading and Lariel insistent. She didn't listen to their words, for it overrode the voice in her head, in her dreams, that was the only voice she wished to hear. She knew that soon enough, she would forget the exact sound of it. She rolled onto her side on the ground, finding it hard and unyielding and quiet. After a time the voices subsided, and she found sleep again, but without dreams, and she woke in the morning with tears dried on her face. Jeredon had fashioned a sheath and strap of sorts and left it next to her and the sword. She sheathed the sword and shouldered it, the weight heavy, the presence like a fiery brand eating through her.

"The Blackwinds," said Lariel, and her face was pale in the early morning light, her hair pulled back and bound, and one hand bandaged slightly. It looked as if she had cut her left hand, for crimson stained the wrappings and when Rivergrace looked closer, she realized the little finger was gone entirely. Lariel caught her glance. Her mouth tightened, and she moved her hand upon the reins so that her bandaging couldn't be seen well. "The Blackwinds run from here to the northeast. From the west, the high, jagged range known as Heaven's Teeth meets and cuts through it to the east. My eyes are open now to the Way and the Andredia flows from here, up this mountain. By good fortune or by his twisted planning, we're only a few days, at most, from the wellspring. If Sevryn was right, Quendius may well know where the river begins. We may encounter stragglers from Quendius' troops, but the worst thing we can meet are the Blackwind runners."

"Not all Ways created were successful. The runners were bred to be shepherds on the borders of our kingdoms, sentinels, bred from the hunting dogs we brought with us, and the Bolger fighting dog known as the Ukalla. What evolved is a large, fierce creature that will fight savagely to the death anyone not bonded to it. They ravage the high country, eating bear, deer, whatever they can find. Few exist, but we don't want to meet one. If we do, leave it to myself or Jeredon. We're the only ones who can form a bond."

"What about Rivergrace?" Nutmeg's head swung about, ponytail bouncing.

"I'm not Vaelinar in the way they are."

"More importantly, we don't want to leave anyone behind." Lariel tapped her tashya mount which sprang away with a leap in the cool morning. The season had begun to turn almost without notice, summer gone, autumn creeping in.

They picked their way out of the foothills and straight up into the mountains, so different than the ones above the Silverwing. These were formed of hard, yet porous black rock, and pushed out of the ground violently, often in tilted stacks, as if the hillside itself had risen up and then fallen down. Lariel threaded them through it, finding dirt and grass among the rock. Rivergrace leaned from her saddle once to touch it, finding it abrasive and cruel. She wondered what made rock like that, and shoved it out of the earth itself. Black Ribbon kept her ears back, still on short rations and unhappy.

When they finally camped in late afternoon, there was little enough room on the trail for any to lie down. Nutmeg pulled Rivergrace to her, pillowing her head in her lap. She lay there reluctantly, the sword against her body from ankle to hip to rib cage, while her sister combed her hair until she wearily dropped into sleep.

She awoke in thin daylight to see Lariel standing a few feet away on the trail. She held a string in her hand and a thing dangled from it, as she turned from side to side, casting with it. At the last turn, the thing on the string swung forward as if pointing up the mountain, and Lariel let out her breath softly, then reeled the object in. Before she pocketed it, Rivergrace realized it was the queen's missing finger. She swallowed tightly, as horror rose burning in her throat, and she turned her face away quickly before Lariel could know she'd been watching.

Lariel called softly to all of them, bringing them awake, and gestured up the side of the mountain, saying, "This way today."

Garner looked longingly down the other side, where the black rock hardly pierced the landscape, and green grass and brush grew, with groves fringing it. "Not that way?"

"No." She spared him a fleeting smile. "Perhaps on the way down."

"There's fish in that river down there," he added.

"We'll need a good meal going home."

He nodded and went to round up his mount and Bumblebee just over the ridge. He came running back, shouting, even as Jeredon emptied part of a waterskin over his head to bathe. "On our asses. Troops!"

Jeredon threw the waterskin at his sister and half ran, half slid back down the trail with Garner. He came back alone.

"Where's Garner?"

"Garner has my bow and quiver. He's holding the pass for us. Up, up, get your horses."

"How many?"

"A handful or so. He's a good shot, already downed one. He'll buy us time before he follows."

They mounted and rode, horses clambering across the broken escarpment, hooves sending rock and pebbles tumbling. The sounds of curses and shouting followed them. Nutmeg looked back once fretfully, and then leaned low over Bumblebee's neck, and snapped the rein end over his haunches. "Faster there, sooner back," she shouted to Rivergrace.

The rock grew hard enough and close enough that they finally had to dismount to lead the horses. Even nimble Bumblebee had to scramble to pick his way through, and Nutmeg wished wistfully for Daisy the goat. As the bare trail split, winding about a plateau and then up to one of the craggy peaks, Lariel halted them. She put her hand in her pocket, turned away and dangled her finger from its string to find their way. Jeredon's face grayed as she did, and Rivergrace drew him back, saying, "Give her this."

He glanced down at her before nodding reluctantly.

To their relief, she pointed off across the plateau, giving them rest and an easy path for most of the day. Nutmeg looked back again and again as she crossed it, the horses plodding wearily, with no sight of Garner. She stifled a sniffle and rubbed her nose on her sleeve.

"He's not dead," Rivergrace said to her.

"I never said he was!"

Rivergrace pulled her ponytail. "But I know he isn't."

"How do you know?"

She paused. "I just do." How could she tell Meg that Cerat, the sword, murmured when it looked for souls nearby, lost and wandering, for the gathering. It was best not to know how she knew.

When they reached the plateau's edge and faced a great, double-sided crag, a deer's trail ran along its side and upward, cutting through a steep pass. Jeredon eyed it.

"We could try coming up the back side."

"With no way of knowing if that's a sheer drop off or if it goes through."

He scratched his head, hazel-green eyes showing his unease. "It's a closed pass, Lariel."

"I know."

"All right, then. I'll take the lead." He dismounted, looping the reins over his left arm, right arm ready to pull the sword on his left hip. Sweeping a look over the mountain pressing down on them from above and towering along the sides, he stepped into the pass she'd chosen.

Nutmeg followed after, coaxing Bumblebee who put his ears flat against his skull, not liking to be away from his trailmate Ribbon. Nutmeg drummed her heels against his still substantial girth to get him to mind. He kicked once, a little half buck, and squealed as she did.

The pass echoed with it. And then a low, deep, vast *BOOM* sounded, with a growling *rakka* thundering down to them. The growling sounded again, *rrrrrakka*. Rock and dirt began to shimmy down, and the mountain seemed to shiver. Jeredon threw his head back. He swung about, grabbing Bumblebee's bridle and slapped him on the rump. The little pony bolted past.

Lariel followed and Rivergrace's mare lunged behind them, whinnying in sudden fear. The pass resounded and stone moaned and then it began to move, a river of dry dirt and rock, heading at Jeredon. He turned to run with no place to go but the way they'd come, as the slide came down on him.

Nutmeg screamed. Dirt flew up and an immense cloud hung over them. Their eyes and noses ran and when it cleared, the mountain had stopped falling and they saw no sign of Jeredon.

Nutmeg leaped from Bumblebee and flew back over the fallen stone, her short body jumping fearlessly over dirt and rock that shifted when she landed, still moving. She screamed when she came to a snapped tree jutting out of the slide, and began to dig. They saw Jeredon emerge, or at least his torso. Lariel began to walk over the loose slide to help, and it rumbled under her feet.

"Go on," he shouted to her. "Go on!" He coughed for a moment, then clawed at the debris with Nutmeg, clearing his chest down to his hips. He touched one leg as Meg pulled rocks away from him. "I can't feel it."

Brother and sister stared at one another. Lariel said, "I'll come back for you."

"I know you will."

Nutmeg wiped her face with her begrimed hand. "I'm not leaving him, too. I'll dig him out."

Rivergrace felt as though the small part of her heart still left broke into pieces. "Meg."

Nutmeg smiled at her. "I know. But this is Dweller work. Stout bodies, hard heads. Now go on."

She swallowed a dry lump in her throat, and turned Ribbon away, up the path Lariel had chosen. She rode alone and in silence for a span of moments then Lariel's mount came after and neither spoke for a good while.

They circled the crag. Lara took out her guide and consulted it without even bothering to hide it from Rivergrace, her severed finger swinging loosely from the string and then pointing up a left fork. Far below them lay the lands of Larandaril, green and stretching as far as the eye could see, heavy with groves and a brilliantly blue river forking through it. A pall of darkness lay over the river when Grace looked at it, but she knew that Lariel did not see it that way.

"Will we reach it before nightfall?"

"I think so. My . . . guide . . . pulls very strongly now." She pocketed her little finger again. "How do you know if they live or not?"

"Cerat." Rivergrace touched the sword blade. "It hungers for souls."

"I can almost hear a noise. It's like having a bee hanging over your head."

"Louder, to me, but yes, it does that, too."

"Cerat," repeated Lariel. "Deathdrinker."

"Souldrinker. Rufus told us the name."

Lariel opened her mouth as if to ask another question, but a quavering howl hung faintly on the mountain air. Rivergrace took her hand from the sword. "That's not Cerat."

Lariel tilted her head, her eyes intent as she listened. Then she looked to Rivergrace, and she saw fear in the Warrior Queen's eyes. "I'll meet it at the cave, the last passage I can open. From there on . . ."

"I'll find the Way."

The howling grew closer, climbing the scale, a piercing cry of hunger and anger, and Cerat faintly mimicked it at her back. Lariel drew her sword. "Dismount."

She kicked off Ribbon and without another word of explanation, Lariel cut her horse down and then Ribbon. Both horses fell to their knees and then their sides, throats opened in a bloody red gash, bleeding their life out on the dirt. Rivergrace put her hand to her mouth.

"Run. After me. That won't buy us much time."

They clambered up the steep side of the cliff, finding that deer's trail to be more of a goat's path and then it opened up to a dark maw yawning into the peak, with a singular white marble column blocking its way. They clung to each other, catching their breath, hearing the noise of the Blackwind runner behind them, savaging the horses.

Lariel put her knife to her wrist. "Listen to me," she said, and she began to talk, quickly, breathlessly, as her blood started to flow down her knife and onto the column, and the mountain opened with a deep moan, and musty air spilled out.

Rivergrace listened, then drew Cerat and went on.

The earth breathed around her. Not as she breathed, not steady movement in and out of air, but a long, steady, quiet moan of rock and dirt and water pushing against one another in its very deepest recesses. She felt it more than heard it and its heaviness; its pressure weighed on her. She could hardly breathe with its weight. Her hearing was muffled. Her throat began to close and her heart to pound, and she could feel the panic welling up in her, the crazed need to claw her way out. Out, out!

Rivergrace stopped dead in her tracks. Both hands wrapped about the sword's hilt; she leaned on it as if it were the only thing that could keep her upright and on both feet. Its metal body vibrated to her touch. It sang softly to her, a soft ululation for the day, for the air, for the hunting of prey which would spew blood when struck, hot and full of life and color. Rich crimson and sharp-edged bone-shard white, the pink of muscle. Even the death of a soul held colors that this underground imprisoning did not, and it urged her to go find them. It would lead her from the stillness of the caverns and take her out into the air and freedom, if she would only let it.

She laced her fingers tighter about the hilt until her knuckles shone like small moons in the twilight, wrapping her will even harder about it than her flesh, denying it. She would lead it, not it her. When she swung it, it would be because she had made the choice. Cerat growled at her unhappily. The vibration within its metal form grew stronger until her bones ached to hold it, her whole body abuzz with its throbbing. Her teeth rattled until she clenched her jaw tight. The fight to remain in control drove her panic down. She took a step.

Sun slanted inward at her back from the wide cavern mouth, a beam as pointed as the weapon she carried. Its finger jabbed inward and she followed it, afraid of what she would do when the light could no longer reach her path. She had the oiled torch stuck in her waistband, and flint and steel to strike it, but could she put aside the sword long enough to do it? Would Cerat leap out of her control if she took her hands and will from it?

She took one trembling hand from the hilt and wiped her forehead with the back of her hand. Heat pooled in the caverns, though she could feel a coolish breeze from somewhere deep ahead. Her side ached. She could feel blood trickle sluggishly down her skin, smell its coppery scent, and that made Cerat hungrier. It had its shrewd side, though. It knew better than to ask her for her own blood. Not that it didn't want it, but slyly, it knew that it would have it in sweet time, as if it were death itself and would have all things sooner or later.

Rivergrace pushed herself forward. The cooler air coming toward her was far from sweet. It carried a tang upon it, a rankness akin to that of carrion ripening in the sun. It stained the back of her throat as she breathed and made her choke with it. Something foul and unspeakable waited for her.

Aderro.

No, she cried back to Sevryn. *Don't call me, you're lost and gone, and all I can do is hope with every step that I move closer to you.*

Her footfall echoed in the tunnel. *Aderro.*

You could have found another way to save Lariel. To show her what the sword could do and what Quendius was capable of. You could have! Instead of leaving me . . .

Her body began to block the thinning sunbeam from the cave mouth. It flickered like a guttering candle going out, throwing darker shadows in front of her as the cave floor began to slope downward and grow uncertain with broken ground and rock crumbling under her steps.

"You've can't have her. She's my sister. I pulled her from the river and found her! She's mine!" Nutmeg's spice and fire in every word echoed inside her memory.

You belonged to her because she found you.

"No," Rivergrace said firmly to the earth and stone. "Because we loved each other."

What does love mean?

It's like a river, a river that fills you to overflowing, cleanses you, feeds you, cradles you . . . can sometimes even sweep you away in a devastating flood, but a river you would never want to be without. And it flows both ways, like a miracle.

She shook herself from memory. The mountain leaned on her, corrupt and besmirched. "Come out and fight!"

Rivergrace pulled a tangle of hair from her eyes. She wanted something to attack her. To rush on her from the dank, foul unknown in front of her, to pounce on her so that she could cleave it away. With each pass of the sword, she would carve it and let the rage warm her blood, boiling away the fear. Anything would be better than this chilling fear, this uncertainty that beat at her. She called up anger inside of her. The curses at her Vaelinar blood. The raiders who burned her home down and destroyed the Farbranch life. The slag mines that boiled over into her rivers and polluted them, killing all that every drop of water might reach and touch slowly, bit by bit. She would bring it down, the thing that did this, *now*.

If only she could find it.

She stumbled over a rock and crashed to one knee. She bit her tongue as she landed. Sharp pain jolted her bones and lanced through her mouth. She knelt long enough to gather herself. She wanted to hew away at the stone that tripped and hurt her. She shifted Cerat in her hold.

"Show yourself! Come out and meet me"

Her voice echoed harshly, beating off the sides of the cavern. Things skittered and flew past her, wings flailing, bats with their high-pitched screams and blind eyes. She ducked and covered her head, their clawed feet and wingtips scratching at her hair and arms. Then, suddenly, gone.

Did it listen for her? Did it wait below? Demon, demi-God, or perhaps an ancient Vaelinar sitting on a throne of stone? How patient it must be, letting her carry the battle to it, unworried about her existence at all.

The day shifted. The sunbeam slanting thinly through the cave mouth vanished, and she was left entirely in the dark, without even a bat's high scream to echo around her and show her the walls, the ceiling that grew lower and lower with every movement she made.

She knelt and put Cerat on the pebbled cave floor to slip the torch from her belt. She struck it, three times, flint to steel, before the sparks ignited the torch. It burned fitfully as she took it up in one hand and the sword in the other. The sword twisted, leaping in toward her leg and nearly bit her sharply. She deflected it just in time.

So that was how it was to be. She gripped it tightly in her sweating palm.

The torch lent sight but also bedazzled her a bit with its orange glow. She lowered it and held it in front of her as the cave floor twisted and turned upon itself. The closeness began to choke her again. A stone snake had swallowed her, crushing her in its coils. She would die here. Others might have died before her . . .

"My blood stained these stones once, and will again. When it does, you must fly, Rivergrace. The rest of the journey is up to you to finish."

"Queen Lariel . . ."

"My blood," she repeated. "The blood of my family sealed this pact, and we failed in our trust. I'll spill my life to renew it, but only you can cleanse the river. Now run!"

Lariel took her dagger and opened up her arm, and the Demon dog that guarded the way lunged at her, to hunker down at her feet and lap up each steaming crimson drop. "Run!" It would be bound unless she ran out of blood first.

Grace had, but only a few steps. Behind the massive boulder that fronted the cavern mouth and there she knelt, taking out her own small knife and putting it to her wrist, letting blood run down and pool until she grew faint before tearing her sleeve hem and tightening a cloth bandage about the wound. It would smell her blood and come to it. Come, she prayed, and be filled before the queen runs dry and falls to her sacrifice that opened the path.

The sword twisted in her hand again. She tripped, her shoulder going roughly into a jagged curve in the cave, and the torch falling from her hand as she did. Her curse rang out, echoed, and then she realized the orange glow of the torch fell. And fell. And fell as an ever smaller orb of fire. Then it went out in a shower of tiny sparks as it hit bottom.

Shaking, Rivergrace took firm hold of Cerat again. Now blinded, she used it as a cane, tapping. The hole in front of her seemed endless but she finally found a small way around the rim of it. Sand showered away from each step, but she did not fall as the torch did.

How to find her way?

Aderro. Listen to yourself. Follow your love of the water.

Fresh or salted, clean or foul, it did call to her. She took a deep breath riddled with the corruption of the air, and closed her eyes, and imagined where the water might lie, where the wellspring of the Andredia came up from the rock and down from the mountain, and from which all its waters began. She took each step carefully, knowing that the river might draw her to it as the crow might fly, yet she walked on earth and rock, and treacherous at that. Each halting step she took cautiously so that she would live to take the next.

The cavern walls grew lower and the passage narrower. She could feel it, even through her shut eyes, as it closed in upon her. Her heartbeat echoed through the stone. She thought of her alna, her silver-tipped free flier, and how its heart had beat frantically in the cage of her hands when she'd held it for healing. Her footfalls drummed on the stone.

Then her eyes flew open, and she saw, dimly, a faint glow ahead. And she heard the echo although she made no movement.

She was no longer alone.

Chapter Seventy-Two

CERAT THRUMMED IN accompaniment to the steps as they drew near. Rivergrace could feel it stir in her hands. It wanted to leap out, but she held it close to her even though the smell of her blood made it whine with an irritating buzz that sawed along her nerves. So near to the wellspring now that its corruption left a stain upon her with every breath, like a slimed coating upon her tongue and throat, she paused.

"It is written there is a dome," Lariel had told her. "Of natural rock, perhaps quartz or agate, cut so finely that it is translucent and the sun can beat down upon it, and shine through, as though the Gods made a window to look upon the Andredia. When you see light at the tunnel's end, you'll know you have found it."

And she saw light. Faint as a wavering breath, a turquoise blue upon the black of no light at all, awaiting her.

Between her and it, a shadow loomed, piercing the blue halo. Pebbles crunched under its boots as it drew near her, and she it.

"Give me the sword."

Like a wind hissing through the tunnels, words carried to her. Cerat answered in her hand, tip going up, pointing at the speaker, carrying her toward him.

Cyclone wings of shadow wrapped about him. He stood in a maelstrom of dark and storm, and she saw a blade gleam in his hand, a throwing dagger, his face obscured by the slow-turning shades enveloping him. He wrapped himself in oblivion.

"You will die here."

Then she'd be that much closer to Sevryn. The sound of water bubbling up could be heard clearly under his words, over them, through them. "We both may," she told him.

"Give me the sword, and all is forgotten."

Forgotten? That was all she had, her memories. They filled her up. Created to be a vessel, she held so much more than her creators had ever intended. She overflowed with all her yesterdays, so that nothing should ever be forgotten.

"No," Rivergrace answered flatly. She charged at him, giving Cerat its wish and will.

The being darted aside. She fell underneath the dome, seeing an agate-blue sky overhead as she rolled, and kicked out, and caught the attacker in the knee. He fell, swathed in black and shadow, even his face, tumbling head forward and coming back up on his feet. He swung, cuffing her in the side of the head, and she reeled back, biting her lip. Her vision blurred, then steadied.

"The sword," said the Kobrir a third time.

"No." Anger welled up in her, fused her, and she welcomed it. She twirled the blade about, then straightened her wrist, and put her other hand upon it, for its weight made it a two-handed sword for her. She fought for her balance and waited for him. "Come and get it, if you dare."

With a hiss of anger, the Kobrir jumped, but not at her. He jumped at the cave wall to the side, and rebounded, somersaulting in the air above her. It happened so quickly that she readied for him out of instinct rather than planning. Perhaps it was Cerat, eager.

Perhaps it was that silvery fire that raged in her.

Perhaps it was the Kobrir's destiny.

She dropped a shoulder and went to her right knee, jabbing her arms to the left, elbows straight and braced. He leaped on her with a scream as the blade impaled him, ran through him raggedly, and Cerat sucked at his soul. She couldn't hold him. He fell off the sword when she dropped it down, and lay in a rapidly growing pool of blood bathing him and the blade.

He looked up at her in sheer amazement. His clothing lay in blood-sodden wings about him, its life ebbing as his did. Cerat jerked, straining to reach the crimson puddle. She would not let it.

"Narskap . . . did not . . . tell me . . . this." The Kobrir threw his hand up in one last convulsion of life, arched his back, and died.

Rivergrace looked down at her chest, where the Kobrir's silver thorn blossomed as it pierced her, below her left breast, and she did not feel the pain till the next breath. She would pull it free, but now her life pulsed in her ears, beats of time, and she knew she hadn't much left.

She stepped into the blue twilight. She had come down one passage, but another lay before her, blasted into the mountain crudely, hacked into the heart of this sacred place. Rails led out, an overturned cart rusting away on its side. A well of stone and mortar stood around the wellspring, damming it from where it flowed up and over a streambed, forcing it down another. She saw the great blackened wall where wood piles had burned, and bellows heaved to bring air, and two anvils stood anchored into the cave, stained with the rust of blood as well as metals beaten upon them. The Andredia ran sluggishly into vats and manmade bowls to cool and temper the steel, and the water smelled of the souls sacrificed therein to call down the Gods in this sacred place, before it slowed down an unnatural riverbed, carrying its poisoning with it. This must have been a forge long before the other, and fouler, and darker.

Her soul quailed at the enormity of it. She ached to cleanse it and hardly knew where to begin, or if she would live long enough to complete the task. She hesitated.

As if sensing her weakness and testing it, under the agate sky, a thing erupted from the stone. It unwound with a hiss, and unfurled its wings of marble-veined quartz. Eyes of fire opened to stare down at her. A drake of stone, of quartz and marble and mica-limned granite, hunched over her, alive yet not alive, with blue agate tracings upon its figure, and it blocked her way to the wellspring.

She was not enough. Even with Sevryn here by her side, and Lariel, and Jeredon, and Garner and Nutmeg, she doubted they could take this stone dragon down. Born of tales from the toback shops, it rumbled a growl, the sound a tumbling of rock over dirt and stone, that came boiling out with white steam that stank of the tainted river. Meshed of earth and water and fire, this impossible creature snaked its neck back and forth, sharp-paned head with hooked beak of a mouth opened to show teeth of hardened gemstone. It lifted a taloned foot, and flailed its long tail about it, end spiked with granite-laced quartz. Rivergrace stepped back.

Her thoughts spun away. How had the Kobrir gotten past this? How had those who mined and smithed here not awakened it? Or had the pain of the Andredia created it, too late to save itself. Four forges dire; earth, water, air, and fire . . .

It coiled and followed her movement. Its wings lifted and moved, and a wind rushed from them that pushed at her, tearing at the ragged ends of her journey-worn clothing before whistling away through the caverns. She put her face into it, blinking into a gritty veil of sand that stung her eyes. Pounding her sword upon the stone drake would be no more useful than slamming Cerat against the anvil.

Breath lanced through her with fiery, aching pain, the dagger buried deeply in her, a silvery thorn she dared not pluck away. No time to think. Only remember.

She turned on one heel, slowly, to face the wellspring and the dam that plagued it. The drake's head rose as it gathered itself to strike. The water called to her and she answered back. She began to sing, in a thin, halting voice, the song she sang to the Silverwing and to the well she'd opened in Calcort, and to every drop of water she'd ever touched. A song that came to her anchored in her past, almost regained, never quite understood. She wrapped both hands about Cerat, the sword with her love's soul entrapped in it, and whispered to him to lend her strength from within the steel. She had but one strike, possibly two. No more.

She wheeled about and hammered the blade down on the rock wall about the Andredia, putting her back to the dragon. Steel clanged and belled upon stone. The cavern reverberated with it, and the drake let out a screech that made her ears bleed, and still she sang. Rock gave. The wall cupping the font cracked away, and the Andredia trickled down, moistening the gravel at her feet. Hot breath and steam scalded the back of her neck, her shoulders, her hair singed away. She struck again, crying in agony. Cerat tolled its blow as if a massive instrument, ringing, and it held the note as she felt the river answer. It geysered up, freed, erupting in cold spray and foam, flooding. Her voice broke. Cerat splintered. As it gave way, she did too, half turning, collapsing, her eyes on the thing made of crystal and gold and granite and jade and copper and all else the earth could hold, the fire in its eyes extinguished. The drake collapsed upon itself, returned to unmoving stone.

She felt herself unravel, unmade, the vessel shattered. Her life whirlpooled in the waters of the Andredia as it rushed around her. Rivergrace fell to her hands and knees in the cascading spray. With every drop that touched her, she melted, washed away.

* * *

As she spins into nothingness, scenes flit before her eyes. From small hands that hid food and gave crumbs and strings of meat to Rufus when he came down to visit, to being thrown on a raft in high flood, to watching her mother and father swept away from her, to the raft tossing and turning and being caught up in the hand of a Goddess. Called to the sword Cerat by its maker as well as the Demon intended to be called, the Goddess struggles to deny the summons. She anchors herself in the small, half-starved body of a girl child who welcomes her in fear and loneliness and mourning and love aching to be shared. The Goddess is summoned, both into the child and into the sword, sundered, corrupted by the Demon that shares the sword, its element of riverwater befouled, Her very existence tenuous and yet . . . caged in mortal flesh, a hold that She cannot deny and must use. The other mortals are torn away, the raft is but a small pause in a moment of infinity, and She spins it away, trying to win her battle against Her enslavement.

Rivergrace tilted her face upward, seeing a reflection in the mists above her, a face looking kindly down at her, as her flesh melted into the debris of the font, her existence washing away into the sacred waters of the Andredia. Nearly twenty years the Goddess had held her in her palm, trying to stay the power of the sword which slowly sucked Her being into it save for that which She pushed into the child. The day came when the two of them as one could not hold the raft from its journey any longer and it rushed downstream in spring's flood tide bearing her into the mortal world. Now her cage, the sword Cerat, had been broken on the very font that the Goddess gave life to, and received life from, freeing her trapped essence.

A vessel for two mortals and one immortal and now all were freed, and the purpose finished. Gently but undeniably, the Goddess reclaimed Herself from the child who had grown to a woman. Rivergrace put her hand up. She had been so much more than a vessel. Sevryn had told her truly. She held all that she had been meant for, and much, much more, beyond Vaelinars and Gods, she held herself and a love for those around her. Fulfilled, she relinquished herself as Rivergrace in surrender, and her song fell quiet.

The river roared about the cavern, then subsided into its natural bed, flowing down through the mountain as it had been meant to do, its color deepened by the agate dome overhead, the forge battered and washed away by the power of the water unleashed, and the hand of a Goddess. It swept away all in its path inexorably, carrying the debris down the mountain, cascading out into the air and daylight, falling in veils to the riverbeds below awaiting it and filling them with life.

A form washes ashore.

A splintery shard is grasped in her hand. The blood is washed from her clothing and her body, and the wounds upon her flesh are healed, thin white lines marking their path upon her. She does not breathe till a misty aura surrounds her, and a Voice that cannot be heard by ordinary ears whispers, "The pact with House Arsmyth holds, and this I give to you alone. A life for a life, a memory for those I took from you. Remember love. Arise with your true name, Vahlinora, and seek that which you loved most." The aura fades as a rainbow does in the rain, fleeting and visible for only a moment and then the wonder is gone.

She takes a deep breath and coughs. She breathes again. The sword in her hand, what is left of it, falls into ruins. It releases a wraith which gazes down at her, touches her forehead and murmurs, "Aderro," before it flees upon the air. Her third breath is a sob as she gathers herself, rising, riverwater falling off her in droplets to the parched ground.

She feels heat in her body, substance to her flesh, pain remembered as a dim ache. A bird flashes overhead on wing, and she looks up. It could be the same day, or another, or a new day two decades from the one she remembers last.

She has been told to search, and so she does, tracing her steps haltingly down the mountain.

Lariel sat, bowed over her weapons and armor. The sun slanted down on her, bringing the gold out fiercely in her hair, her face translucent and pale. Her shirt rode indecently high on her ribs, the hem torn away to wrap her left forearm from elbow to wrist. She looked up the mountain, her gaze fixed, waiting. She sat watch by the pool of blood Grace had left, to help sate the Demon dog.

Unheard, Rivergrace came up the trail from below. She stood a long moment, looking at the queen, at last understanding a little bit about why Lariel wore the title she did.

"I'm not there," she said.

Lariel swung about, crying, "Grace!"

"The Andredia is freed." Her chestnut hair stirred on her shoulders as the sun and a gentle wind dried it. She swayed with it. Lariel put her arm out to catch her by the shoulder.

"And you?"

Rivergrace smiled. "I have memories."

Lariel hesitated with her mouth curved half-open, as if holding back. A curl of smoke reached them, smelling of roasting meat and bitter herbs. "I built a pyre," she told Grace. "I didn't want the Demon eating our horses."

"Good." She couldn't bear the thought of seeing Black Ribbon's ravaged body. She reached up and held Lariel's hand on her shoulder, a half embrace. "At least the walk is downhill."

The moon rose early in the daytime sky as it sometimes does, golden as a crown piece although not quite full, and they walked the rest of the day and all of the night under its glow. They spoke sparingly, their path taking them down the mountain trail, the water pouring from the mountain pacing them. The river filled slowly as the hungry land drank it down and they watched it first grow damp, then trickle, then become a freshet, a brook. By the dawn, when they reached the bottom of the mountain, it had gone ahead of them, and they walked by a river that would join the others, its current carrying it into Larandaril.

Garner had found Jeredon and Nutmeg before they did. The smell of woodsmoke and food reached them with tantalizing goodness, along with voices and laughter on the air. They were all wrapped in bandages, and leaning upon one another, but they were none of them mangled, not as Grace had feared.

Nutmeg saw them first. She rose to her feet and ran, catapulting herself at Rivergrace, crying, "You did it!" She spun Rivergrace in a dance about her, hands tight upon her as if she would never let go. "The river runs from here, Jeredon tells us, into the high hills and then back down into the kingdom. You did it!"

Lariel went to her knees beside Jeredon and they held each other tightly for a long moment without words. He, alone, had not gotten to his feet. Then, holding him by the shoulders, she pulled back for an intense look.

"I will walk again," he told her. "Someday. Meanwhile, we may have to find a smith to make me a chariot."

"That will be the second thing I order, then," his queen sister answered.

"And the first?"

"You know the first."

"Would I ask if I did?"

"I have a war to prepare for, but this time, they must carry it to me, for I will not rush headlong to it."

He gave a sigh, then a nod, and they hugged again.

Nonplussed, Garner kept turning the spit upon which he roasted a few rabbits until Rivergrace leaned over to knuckle his hair. "Kiss the cook," he responded, grinning, and she planted a kiss on his tousled head.

Nutmeg pulled the packs to her, rifling through them, saying, "Grace, you're hardly clothed. You'll sunburn and freckle like you always do."

She looked down at herself, faintly surprised that she was indeed, still blood and flesh, and took the clothes Nutmeg handed to her, her thoughts still somewhat absent and far away.

On the morning wind, a horse neighed. It rang down the mountain, a faint trumpeting challenge, and they all paused to listen, their heads turning in its direction. Rivergrace took a tentative step that way.

"It can't be," Lariel said.

"Sssssh," her brother hushed her, his keen hunter's gaze sweeping toward the wilderness. "It can't be. We sent him to Larandaril carrying the body . . ." He listened, his eyes glistening.

She dropped the garments Nutmeg had pushed into her hands and walked to the rough trail, each step coming faster and faster until she broke into a run. Her heart beat in her throat with every step as a horse came into her view, hurtling itself heedlessly down the mountain pathway, Aymaran's mane and tail bannered on the wind, and he bore a pale rider on his back.

She raced toward it as it raced toward her, and her heart leaped as he called to her, his voice full and mortal and bearing love.

"Aderro!"

Kerith Timeline

A Recollection of Some Curious Events

300—Magi create Galdarkan guards.

223—The Raymy are defeated and retreat across the ocean, leaving Ravers stranded behind.

90—Magi wars. Most magic users die and magic fades from Kerith.

0—Collapse of the Empire.

90 AE (After Empire)—Creation of City States through trader guilds.

112—Galdarkan Rebellion, the collapse of which sends the survivors into the barrens as nomads.

312—Vaelinars invade Kerith, starting a hundred years of slavery, strife, impressments.

423—Accords signed, principally between the Houses and Strongholds of the Vaelinars for their own civil wars, but are extended to the City States.

501—Bolger clans unite, begin warfare.

511—Vaelinars step in to help defeat Bolger clans, but then retire to a deep seclusion, as their numbers are hard hit. Kanako defeats the Bolger tribes, but his lineage dies with him.

700—Vahlinora is born.

703—Gilgarran dies.

721—Bolgers emboldened, and Raver raids begin anew.

723—Nutmeg Farbranch pulls a waif from the Silverwing River waters.

723—A major assassination attempt in Calcort signals new animoisites toward the Vaelinars.

733—Ravers and Bolgers join together in raiding groups with new aggressions.

737—Accords Conference in Calcort brings riots, and the Accords are contested.

737—Abayan Diort begins forcible unification of the Galdarkans.

Glossary

aderro: (Vaelinar corruption of the Dweller greeting Derro) an endearment meaning little one
alna: (Dweller) a fishing bird
astiri: (Vaelinar) true path
avandara: (Vaelinar) verifier, truth-finder
Aymar: (Vaelinar) elemental God of the wind and air
Banh: (Vaelinar) elemental God of earth
Calcort: a major trading city
Cerat: (Vaelinar) deathdrinker
Daran: (Vaelinar) the God of Dark, God of the Three
defer: (Kernan) a hot drink with spices and milk
Dhuriel: (Vaelinar) elemental God of Fire
emeraldbark: (Dweller) a long-lived, tall, insect- and fire-resistant evergreen
forkhorn: (Kernan) a beast of burden with wide, heavy horns
Hawthorne: capital of the free provinces
kedant: (Kernan) a potent poison from the kedant viper
Lina: (Vaelinar) elemental Goddess of water
Nar: (Vaelinar) God of the Three, the God of War
Nevinaya aliora: (Vaelinar) You must remember the soul
Nylara: (Kernan) a treacherous, vital river
quinberry: a tart yet sweet berry fruit
Rakka: (Kernan) elemental Demon, he who follows in the wake of the earth mover doing damage
skraw: (Kernan) a carrion eating bird

staghorns: elklike creatures
stinkdog: a beslimed unpleasant porcine critter
Stonesend: a Dweller trading village
tashya: (Vaelinar) a warm-blooded breed of horse
teah: (Kernan) a hot drink brewed from leaves
ukalla: (Bolgish) a large hunting dog
Vae: (Vaelinar) Goddess of Light, God of the Three
vantane: (Vaelinar) war falcon
velvethorns: a lithe deerlike creature
winterberry: a cherrylike fruit

Personae

Abayan Diort—mercenary Galdarkan captain and leader
Adeena—a Kernan seamstress
Alton ild Fallyn—a son of ild Fallyn Stronghold
Azel d'Stanthe—the scholar of the shrouded Vaelinar domain, Ferstanthe, holder of lores
Berlash—a healer for Greathouse
Bistane—warrior poet
Bistel—patriarch of House Vantane
Bregan Oxfort—Kernan trader, powerful son of a powerful family
Cavender Barrel—Barrel family patriarch
Croft—a weasel of a Dweller
Daravan—a rogue Vaelinar, unlisted in their original rolls
Frelar—a female healer at Larandaril
Garner Farbranch—oldest Farbranch son
Gilgarran—a Vaelinar ranger
Guthry Barrel—of the Silverwing militia (D)
Honeyfoot—general supplies merchant
Hosmer Farbranch—middle Farbranch son
Jeredon Eladar—older half brother to Lariel Anderieon
Keldan Farbranch—youngest of the Farbranch boys
Kever ild Istlanthir—a son of House Istlanthir
Kobrir—known assassins, Kurtiss and Kosh
Lariel Anderieon—Warrior Queen
Lent Barrel—of the Silverwing militia (D)
Lily Farbranch—wife of Tolby Farbranch, a seamstress

Mistress Robin Greathouse—a Dweller trader
Nutmeg Farbranch—daughter of Tolby and Lily
Osten ild Drebukar—the youngest scion of House Drebukar
Perty—Mayor Stonehand's assistant
Quendius—a Vaelinar half-breed weaponsmith and armorer
Randall Hawthorne—Grand Mayor of the free and western provinces
Rivergrace—an escaped slave of Vaelinar heritage
Rufus—a Bolger forge slave
Sevryn Dardanon—a Vaelinar half-breed of the streets
Sweetbrook—Dweller miller
Thom Stonehand—Dweller mayor of Calcort
Tiiva Pantoreth—last direct blood heir of House Pantoreth
Tiym Panner—wealthy Dweller trader
Tolby Farbranch—Dweller rancher and former caravan guard
Tranta Istlanthir—Vaelinar caretaker of Tomarq
Tressandre ild Fallyn—heir to Stronghold ild Fallyn
Willard Oxfort—a Kernan trader of great wealth and power